TENDERNESS

The Changeling
The Wave Theory of Angels
Unexploded
All the Beloved Ghosts

TENDERNESS

Alison MacLeod

PENGUIN

an imprint of Penguin Canada, a division of Penguin Random House Canada Limited

Canada • USA • UK • Ireland • Australia • New Zealand • India • South Africa • China

Published in Penguin paperback by Penguin Canada, 2021
Simultaneously published in Great Britain by Bloomsbury Circus,
Bloomsbury Publishing Plc, 50 Bedford Square, London, WCIB 3DP, UK
29 Earlsfort Terrace, Dublin 2, Ireland

www.penguinrandomhouse.ca

*Publisher's note: This book is a work of fiction. Names, characters, places and incidents either
are the product of the author's imagination or are used fictitiously, and any resemblance to
actual persons living or dead, events, or locales is entirely coincidental.*

LIBRARY AND ARCHIVES CANADA CATALOGUING IN PUBLICATION

Title: Tenderness / Alison MacLeod.
Names: MacLeod, Alison, 1964- author.
Identifiers: Canadiana (print) 20200233246 | Canadiana (ebook) 20200233297 |
ISBN 9780735233782 (softcover) | ISBN 9780735233799 (EPUB)
Classification: LCC PS8575.L4589 C66 2021 | DDC C813/.54—dc23

Cover design by Greg Heinimann
Cover image © Trent Parke / Magnum Photos

Printed in the United States of America

10 9 8 7 6 5 4 3 2

Penguin
Random House
PENGUIN CANADA

For my aunts, Jean MacLeod Kelley (1927–2020)
and Miriam MacLeod (1929–2008),
who gave us 'the Cape'

Ours is the universe of the unfolded rose,
The explicit,
The candid revelation.

D. H. Lawrence

'If they want to renounce Lawrence, then let them,
for pity's sake, renounce life.'

Gwyn Thomas to Michael Rubinstein,
Defence Solicitor for Penguin Books

Contents

These Hidden Things

'I wondered at his courage and daring to face and write these hidden things that people dare not write or say.'

Frieda Lawrence

The Exile

The dead could look after the afterwards, but here, here was the quick of the universe: the town lifted from sleep in a vast net of light, and the Mediterranean, five miles away at Cagnes, flickering like a great opal. He'd woken early and had watched the dark gravity of the night yield to daybreak. Now the streets were a mirage, half-dissolved in the dazzle of morning. Even the town's ancient walls were erased, while a barking dog in the road below was more bark than dog. On the balcony, among the geraniums, he squinted: the coastline as far as the Cap d'Antibes shook and shimmered. It was impossible to say where sea turned to sky. The smudge of an ocean-liner materialised at what might have been the horizon, while light streamed – the run-off from the warp and weft of the world. Nothing the day touched remained solid, nothing held, nothing except the geraniums and their defiant fists of red.

The previous day, upright in his underwear in the medical bay, the exile had learned that he was, even still, five feet nine inches tall, or that he was when the state of his lungs allowed him to straighten. He would have been cheered by this fact had he not weighed in at forty-five kilos on the French scales, and one hundred pounds on the imperial – or not quite seven stone. He had insisted on both scales, but the two nations were agreed.

It meant at least that he could go, almost literally, where the wind blew him. The almond trees of the town were a pink-and-white froth of blossom. The breeze, slight as it was, had a reviving salt tang. He needed only his hat and shoes. 'Are we ready?' he called into the room. Where was the release for the brake on the blasted bath-chair?

Frieda stepped onto the balcony, clicked her cigarette-case open and leaned, with Rubenesque languor, against the rail. She would not be rushed. At her feet, the tiles were littered with cigarette butts and orange peels, some blackened with age, for she was careless, and careless that she was careless. Below the balcony, shutters were opening to the day in good faith. A middle-aged man was washing himself at a barrel in a back garden, his braces trailing from his trousers, and, as if for her, he sang as he flung water at himself – Verdi's 'La donna è mobile'. Frieda's foot tapped along. She loved a vigorous tune.

Chickens, released from their coops, fattened and clucked. She could smell fresh bread from the baker's across the road; Monsieur Claudel always arrived at his premises before first light. Cats prowled. A woman, her hair still in its net, pegged out sheets on a line, and somewhere, a baby wailed.

Little by little, morning took possession of the medieval streets and the old Roman ways. Fountains bubbled forth again. Shop-owners winched their awnings high against the downpour of light, and the hooves of an approaching dray-horse smote the cobbles. Every few doors, its driver hopped down from the gig to heave a great block of ice to a chute on a shop or café wall.

The morning brimmed, the cafés began to fill, and she watched as holiday-makers tentatively joined the day. 'English,' she noted for the benefit of her husband. She had never lost her German inflections. 'One can tell by the faces. Pasty. Immistakably so.'

'Unmistakably,' he said.

She caught a whiff of something pungent – a blocked drain. 'I prefer "immistakable".' She turned, tapped ash into the pocket-spittoon on the low table by his chair, and resumed her position, gazing down. 'Isn't it curious? English babies are most beautiful. They are fat, rosy peaches. They are the glory of all babies. But something happens as they grow. I do not understand it.'

He bowed his head. 'May we go?'

'You love the Med, Lorenzo.' She drew deeply on her Gauloise. 'And this really is the most marvellous view. The manager did not lie.'

'You sound like a Baedeker.'

She'd thought she sounded merely cheerful. In England – though not the other English-speaking nations – one always had to think before one spoke. One had to compose first and speak second. English in England was a trap in which one revealed, without realising, the details of one's station: one's rung on the ladder of life, one's region – acceptable or not – and one's education, to be envied or pitied. One could unwittingly reveal, too, in a few casual utterances, an apparent lack of feeling or an excess of it; qualities of discernment, gullibility or culpability; as well as one's grasp of the code of belonging, or one's failure to do so. An English person might say, 'How interesting,' and one had to know that he or she was actually saying, 'How frightfully dull.'

It was a language for spies, Frieda thought, a means for its natives to find out what others were thinking, or who they truly were. German was matter-of-fact by comparison and, after all these years, she still craved its ease. One said what one meant. After marriages to two Englishmen, and the production of three English children by Husband Number One, she was a fluent speaker of English, *natürlich*. Yet still, she was deemed blunt or even rude in English where she would have been merely straightforward in German.

If this was a source of personal frustration, at least she side-stepped the traps the English set for each other, Lorenzo included. He had shaken off most of his Nottinghamshire inflections, though not his strong vowels. She had marvelled, years before, when she'd first heard him speak in his native dialect, to please Lady Ottoline at her elegant London dinner party. Afterwards, Frieda had told him that his voice mustn't be a mere party-trick, that he mustn't give up his true self, but he had merely shrugged. He wanted, he said, to move through society 'undetected'.

Indeed, surveillance was so much the habit of the English that they mistook it, she believed, for human nature, presuming all languages to be peepholes for the spy in every person. What a perfect irony that, during the War, *they* had accused *her* of that very thing – spying! As if *she* were capable of keeping any secret! No, she did not miss that little island. No, not at all!

The exile exhaled. Frieda smoked in silence, at last. She blocked his view but there was peace.

They were a thousand feet above sea level. The maritime air should have been fresh, but it was already hot for the early hour. He longed to be out and away. Hadn't he asked her, repeatedly, to get him released, to break him out? How could he know whether she actually had a plan to free him this morning or was about to cajole him again into a few more days in this place 'for his health'?

For her 'most marvellous view', rather.

'The English seaside,' he muttered, 'would have served us at least as well and at far less expense.' Money – how it gnawed. Even now, he couldn't trust it not to surprise him, like the jaw of a tiger. He'd had a good run with *Chatterley*, £1,400 in its first year, the most he'd earned from a book in his life. He'd felt quite jolly about that until his English agent told him that Arnold Bennett, whose reputation was finally – and belatedly in his view – on the down-turn, still managed to bring in £22,000 a year. Bennett was a pig in clover.

He watched Frieda light another cigarette. How he loathed her smoke. Why was he so often downwind of her?

In his more pragmatic moments, he accepted that she would not be budged from the Continent. She liked her Continental villas. She liked the endless oranges and European insouciance. She relied on French cigarettes and the presence of her Italian lover somewhere on the same land-mass. She'd be happy enough, he knew, never to see England again. England had been ruthless to them both. Even in his absence, it was ruthless – another novel seized (his last, his last!). Yet he missed it, England, pitiably.

Frieda, for her part, felt simply and happily grateful for the peace of her cigarette, for the view from his balcony, and for the prospect of a new villa – however temporary. What was Lorenzo's rush? As a young girl, on family visits to the Prussian court, she had observed that no person of importance rushed, and it was a lesson she had carried with her through life, no matter how straitened her circumstances.

She shifted on her hip and watched a striking, dark-haired young man, in cream-coloured flannel trousers and a crisp white shirt, pass below. He looked a little like a cavalry officer she'd once had in a Bavarian inn. Why hurry on a hot day? Their cases were in the taxi. She had paid the driver for his patience. A plan was not beyond her. She was German after all, and more than capable.

Now, as she leaned against the rail, she felt the knot of her hair slip loose against her neck. Were the man in the flannel trousers to look up to the balcony, she would smile beguilingly. She would make him glance back. Life's small pleasures saw one through.

The exile turned his head, cocking an ear, as an orderly entered his room and removed the breakfast he hadn't wanted. The 'Ad Astra Sanatorium' tried in vain to mimic a luxury hotel, and the clattering of trays was known as 'room service'. The motto of the place was nothing but an abuse of Latin. *Per aspera ad astra* – 'Through hardships to the stars'. He'd smirked at that. Through hardships to the sanatorium bar, more like. The resident consumptives played gay holiday-makers, and the odour of desperation in the dining-room each night would kill him, he thought, faster than his own lungs.

Only at his dogged insistence had Frieda found them a villa at last. At least she claimed she had. Sometimes she simply said what she imagined the day required. A full ten days ago, he'd said he wouldn't spend another night in the Sad Astra. He told her he'd die for lack of sleep; at night, the bouts of coughing from the neighbouring rooms shook the entire place. She told him the coughing that woke him was his own.

Now, she turned and tapped another full inch of ash into his spittoon.

'I wish you wouldn't do that,' he said. A string of muscle tightened across his shoulders.

'Perhaps we should take a trip to Nice one day,' she said.

'Nice isn't Brighton – and I'm fed up to the back teeth with France.'

Of course Nice is not Brighton, she thought. But who would not choose Nice over Brighton? He was in one of his contrary moods.

She watched the ribbon of her smoke rise into the day. It had been difficult, exceedingly difficult, to secure a place they might call home in Vence. Assorted villa-owners had refused her a lease, fearing contagion. For the last week, she and Barby, her most capable child – and now a young woman of twenty-five – had tried everything they could, from charm and guilt to desperation and bribes, but no one wanted a consumptive to expire on their property, and any journey beyond the radius of a taxi-ride was out of the question. Lorenzo was simply not up to it.

The morning's heat crept beneath his collar, and its studs burned like blisters against his neck. He suspected she enjoyed the fact he was helpless these days, neutered, an invalid requiring her assistance to survive. They needed only to get to Boulogne and catch the packet to Newhaven or Brighton. *'I am glad to be going to Sussex – it is so full of sky and wind and weather.'* He longed to see the white glow of the cliffs on the Channel coast. The sea-foam in the twilight. The yellow horned-poppies on the beach. He wanted to hear the noisy slap of the waves. All of it, now *verboten*.

'This coast,' he said, waving a hand, 'is full of riff-raffy expensive people.'

'People are simply enjoying the sun after a long winter, Lorenzo. Why shouldn't they?'

He tugged at his collar. 'No one's happiness in an English resort depends on all this endless sunshine.'

Which is just as well, she thought.

And why did he always go on as if she had no English memory of her own?

'In England, we think nothing of hopping over stones into a frigid sea. Bone marrow freezes on contact. Old hearts pack up. Testicles implode. But people are content. No one needs an eternally "marvellous view".'

She hoisted her bosom and wondered: would the man in the flannel trousers walk *back* up the road?

'We want a change of scene, a nice shell or two, a curio from some mouldering shop. We expect the ring-a-ding-ding of the pier, a day or two of fog, and ... and outside your lodgings, well' – he gripped his armrest – 'only the dustbin-men shouting to wake the dead.' A cough climbed out of his stomach. 'Damn it, if only some good old English bin-men would wake *me* when the time comes. If they failed, they could at least offer quick disposal. Whizz-bang!'

'Lorenzo, you mustn't tire yourself like this.'

'I am not tiring myself, Frieda. Imminent death tends to do that unaided, you see.'

She tilted a wrist. Her cigarette hovered elegantly.

His eyes burned. Was she meeting her lover, *Il Capitano*, these days? It was no great distance from the Italian Riviera to the French Riviera, and, one thing was certain, that man was stuffed full of spunk and gusto. The relationship had long ceased to be a secret between husband and wife; it was merely a subject they each knew to avoid.

At times such as these, he let himself wonder. What would life have been had he not walked down the hill that evening, through the olive grove, and away from *her*? *Darling R., Frieda to arrive in a week. She pesters from Baden-Baden.* What – who – would he have been now if, after those few weeks at San Gervasio with her, he had simply stayed?

Darling R. Together, they would have raised her three little girls. He might have fathered his own. Who could say? He would have written each morning in that ancient olive grove, with the view of the duomo shimmering on the plain below.

Frieda would have had her Angelo – even more than she did currently. There would have been no *Chatterley* because there would have been no need to write R., to conjure her and draw her close.

Well, so many words, because I can't touch you. If I could sleep with my arms round you, the ink could stay in the bottle.

He would have raised his head at the end of day to see her coming through the door with figs, cheese and bread from the market. He would have looked across the courtyard at Canovaia to see her red-brown head bent over her needlework or drawings. In bed at night, her body would have stretched to his. There would have been no need to reach for her through the welter of time.

That evening as he descended the hill, he did not turn to look back to her. He let her think him resolute. He sent a few cards, and did not see her again.

On the balcony at the Sad Astra, he tried now to turn his bath-chair from the sun, wresting thoughts of her, and that other far-away, Florentine balcony, from his mind. He resumed his theme: 'Brighton. Worthing …' he said to Frieda, fighting with a wheel. 'Littlehampton was jolly enough. Remember? Or Bognor. I'd be as happy as a trout in some dank Bognorian lodging-house. I'd fuck off there tomorrow if the knives weren't out for me.' He looked up. His wife was smiling and waving to a passer-by below, as if from an imperial balcony.

'No one has any knife out for you.' She turned and released the brake on his chair. 'You are a writer, not a fugitive.'

'I'd take a knife over prison.'

'You could write in prison. They feed you in prison. *Every cloud,* Lorenzo.'

He looked up. It was a brutally cloudless day in Vence. What hope was there for him here? Life flattened out into meaningless good cheer when the sun was so indiscriminate. That was the Riviera all over. Predictable. Promiscuous. *Popular.* It had once been his thrill and his sanctuary, but he hated the place now. People, people everywhere.

She cast her cigarette into the day and clapped her hands. 'Now then. Our taxi is around the corner. I hear the motor.'

His feet were pale, naked creatures – molluscs out of their shells. They looked absurd, he thought, on the foot-flaps of his bath-chair. 'Can we?' he said, staring at them. 'Can we actually?'

She emptied the ash in the spittoon over the rail, then stretched her arms luxuriously. She did not believe he believed that he was dying. Had he believed it, he would not have been able to speak of it so volubly. As he did not believe it, she would not believe it either. His death had been foretold for years, and they'd learned to dismiss the claims and diagnoses. His friends thought her reckless, irresponsible, even criminal. They despised her for it, and for more. Let them, she thought. He had defied every prognosis through the sheer force of their collective will, which meant she would not brood on the fact that he was now asking her to put on his stockings and shoes for him. For the first time, he said that bending over left him sick to his stomach and breathless.

The clip on his suspender wouldn't clip. She was bent double over his feet. As he waited, he looked away, studying the horizon, as if in search of some hairline crack in the bowl of the day. All those words, all that writing – now under arrest. *What had been the point?*

'I don't want to die in a taxi,' he said.

She told him he would have to accept a stocking at half-mast. For a moment, she considered unbuttoning his flies and fellating him, or offering him a weighty breast to calm him. But it was time to go, and his desires were no longer straightforward, if they had ever been. She rose, red-faced, and huffed a lock of blonde-grey hair from her eyes.

'My hat!' He gripped both wheels of the bath-chair.

'It is in the taxi, Lorenzo. If we don't go now, the driver will sell it and be gone. Please don't be unbearable.'

He said nothing. He was her dependant now. He needed her to live. Perhaps he always had. Any biddable wife would have tranquillised brain and soul. He'd needed the challenge of her. Perhaps he'd even needed the problem of her.

As husband and wife, they'd struggled from almost the first. She was at ease with her appetites, with the casually, merrily carnal. He thirsted for mystery, for the kindred who was also other; for the uncharted hinterland of the beloved. Illness had reduced him, while her appetite had made her stout. He was not enough for her, and she was too much for him. The force of their mutual frustration was their enduring bond and, in periods of relative harmony, she mothered; he was mothered. It was enough. Now it was. The end of their marriage had long been forecast by friends, yet here they were, familiars in a place they didn't know, on this narrow perch of life.

His shoes were tied. His tie was straight. Natty summer-grey suit. Laundered shirt with collar. A red handkerchief, so that no spattering of blood would show. Polished brown brogues. *'He might almost be a gentleman.'* Homburg hat. Coat folded over arm. He shunned the existential class of 'the invalid', the pyjama-ed person, the not-valid. Any day, he would open his passport to find a page stamped with it: 'In-valid'. He preferred 'Public Enemy'.

Frieda steered his bath-chair from the balcony through the thin curtains into the dreary room and out the door. 'If anyone asks,' she said as they waited for the lift, 'it is a beautiful day. That is reason enough.'

'Of course it's a beautiful day! It is always a beautiful day! That means nothing to these people. You might as well say, "The water is wet."' He felt as weak as a wilting white geranium in a pot.

She hit the call-button. 'We are taking the air,' she said calmly. 'That is all.'

He gripped his kneecaps. They rose like Golgothan hills of bone through his trousers. 'And if we meet my doctor?'

'Repeat, Lorenzo: we – are – taking – the – air.' Her r's rolled with Teutonic authority.

The lift arrived with a little ring.

Invalid, invalid, squeaked the wheels of his bath-chair.

The service-boy slid the cage, then the door, shut. He nodded good-day to the resident and his wife, and eased the crank to the left. The cab lurched horribly, and down they went.

All the while, using only his elbow, the exile clasped *The Life of Columbus* to him, a stowaway under his jacket. The library had been the only decent thing in the place.

'Yes?' she said to him. 'We are taking the air.'

He nodded, his jaw set, his knuckles white. The cables of the lift shunted and chirred. *The Life of the Life of the Life of*—

Then the cage opened, daylight rushed in, the bell of his heart rang out, and how glad he was, how eternally glad, to be on the move again.

The following day, the 2nd of March, 1930, the morning seeped through the shutters in bars of shadow and light. A wardrobe arose from the darkness. A wash-stand turned chalky blue, and stale water shone in a cup.

The day revealed, too, an enamelled chair in which a nurse dozed, her chin against her breast. It raised a dull gleam on her black oxfords and in the lank hair of her sleeping patient. It warmed the bare floorboards, and lingered on the nightstand, pooling in the open pages of *The Life of Columbus*.

At the end of the bed, a ginger cat flickered. In the jug on the nightstand, wildflowers strained towards the light. Above the narrow bed, a Virgin's frame flashed gold while, behind her, between the oval frame and the wall, a dry straggle of Palm Sunday leaves yearned in their fibres for green chlorophyll.

Outside, the day fell like the gaze of an old Provençal god, in haphazard benediction of everything and nothing. A breeze blew up, stirred by the heavy lids of that local god as they dipped and rose. It almost carried off the underwear from the line in the garden, but the charwoman ran out, charitably, and pegged it all down – two large ladies' vests, cambric drawers and men's knee-length underwear from *Angleterre*.

Far below the hilltop villa, the sea throbbed. Yet the bright, glittering light of the coast was tempered here in the hills by the earliness of the hour, by the tender hesitation of March, and by spring's memory of the contest with winter. The land was still dew-cold.

The exile lay on his side. His breath was a slow-burn in his chest. He dreamed, haltingly, of little boats, the prow of each painted with a single wide black eye. The flotilla had found him at last, surfacing from the subterranean walls of the Etruscan tombs he'd once explored in Tuscany. This morning, the boats had moored themselves at the dock of his bed.

He lay becalmed. His eyes were shadow-sockets. His head was reducing to skull, and his red beard was dimmed. The only permanent occupant of the villa, the ginger cat, had smelled illness on the newcomer and given up its aloofness to curl at his feet.

The pillow was a comfort. It had travelled with him, first to the Sad Astra, and thence to this, the Villa Robermond, their latest leased abode. Frieda and Barby had coaxed and cajoled, and on March 1st, after a jolting taxi-ride into the hills west of Vence, they were at last installed.

He surfaced slowly from sleep. Beneath his cheek, his pillow still smelled of the wild thyme and pine resin from the wood behind their old Tuscan farm villa, the Mirenda. A year ago now? Two? It had been square, solid and imposing, with marble floors. He'd paid £25 for the year's lease for the entire first floor, the *piano nobile*, and it had been their most serene home ever, on the crest of a steep hill, overlooking 400-year-old fields which fell away in silver (the olive trees) and gold (the wheat), on all sides, as beautifully configured as a Renaissance landscape by an Old Master.

At the front of the villa, clusters of green-black cypresses had stood sentry over his solitude. The rows of broom in the fields, covered in yellow petals, gave off a soft, warm, queer perfume. At the back, his wood awaited him, from eight o'clock each day. The wildflowers were plentiful. The surrounding fields were dotted with the match-stick dwellings of the sharecropper *contadini*. He had people nearby to nod to, but no one to pester him. No foreigners. Very few visitors who would ever make it up their forbidding hill.

Most days, he'd needed only his novel and its goodwill. There was Frieda too, of course. She had made an appreciative audience for each new chapter at their midday meal. Then came his paintings, each afternoon. Also fine company. At times, Barby, his step-daughter, a grown woman now, came to stay.

It had been bliss, or at least as much happiness as he'd felt entitled to – until he fell ill, or more ill, and had suddenly hated the Mirenda as much as every other residence where illness had got him. In the end, he couldn't leave the place fast enough.

In his half-sleep, under the watch of the English nurse, he could feel his feet slipping again into his old rope-soled sandals. His linen hat had a wide brim, and used to shade his eyes as he wrote behind the Mirenda. That final autumn in Tuscany, he'd decamped to the wood each morning, where he sat, pillow beneath his arse, spine supported by an umbrella pine, and hand flying fiercely across the pages as he out-ran his prognosis.

A novel into which one poured life became a life. He'd felt the force of his story coursing through its lines as blood courses through veins, as milk rises in a breast, as sap surges in wood.

Lizards ran across his feet, and birds hopped, heedless of him. Only his wrist moved. In the wind, the trunk of the pine flexed at his back, elastic and powerful. Violets spread at his feet in blue shadows. Moss breathed. A spring, banked in wild gladioli, bubbled up, dedicated to a neglected saint. On an overhanging branch, an enamel mug dangled for pilgrims and hot children.

He never saw either but, each morning, a priest in his black cassock nodded as he rushed through the wood on his way to celebrate Mass or bless the sheaves. A dog raced through the underbrush from time to time. Cicadas rattled, and in the neighbouring fields, girls sang as they cut the corn.

Far below, on the Arno's river-plain, Florence was a beautiful jigsaw of clay-pot roofs, cypresses and bright campaniles, while at the centre of the eternal world, the duomo rose up, benign and reticent.

To Secker, what had he written as his novel fattened?

'It's a bit of a revolution,' he said, 'a bit of a <u>bomb</u>.'

On their arrival at Robermond, following the escape from the Sad Astra, Frieda started unpacking their things in an uncharacteristic display of industry. As she made up his bed, she pointed to the blood-stains on his old pillow, but he refused to allow her, or their house-keeper, to take it, and Frieda, as happily slovenly here as anywhere, did not press the point, even in the face of the English nurse's discreet horror. Instead, she kicked off her shoes, stretched out on the cool marble floor, and instructed Barby to see to everything else.

In any other cottage, house or villa, he'd always set to work smack off, scrubbing floors – braces tied to waist – digging their kitchen garden, whitewashing walls, building shelves, running up curtains, making jam. *They used to say I had too much of the woman in me—* Frieda, by contrast, would never succumb to bourgeois necessity if she might stretch her limbs in the sun or on a cool floor, or sit at the piano and sing. She told him she knew what life was for, and he both loved and despised her for it. He used to quip to friends that, together, they made one great beast of burden; he was the beast, and she, the burden.

It was time. The nurse levered him up from his demi-monde of sleep. She felt for the galloping pulse in his wrist, silenced his complaints with a thermometer under his tongue, and pounded his pillow and bolster into submission. All the while, the strabismus-skew of her eyes studiously, if errantly, avoided his.

Had he been unkind? he wondered. Had he shouted at her? Perhaps. He hardly knew. He felt as weak as a lamb. But it had been a lucky body in spite of everything, a good body, energetic and wiry. A doctor had told Frieda he should have been dead years ago, but bloody-mindedness had preserved him until this, the advanced age of forty-four. He would not go quietly.

The English nurse reached for the shutters' handles, and her starched breast all but brushed the side of his head. He had a vague instinct to turn, open his mouth and suck. Instead a spasm of coughing overtook him. He and the bed-frame quaked.

'What's it all about?' he mumbled, breathless, breast-less, to the room.

His lungs burned hotter. He gaped like a fish. On the wall, a painting – a copy of a Raphael – of the Virgin gazed down at him in his struggle.

He knew those eyes. He knew them—

The English nurse was passing him a fresh cup of water. 'Mrs Lawrence and her daughter,' she ventured, 'left for the market an hour ago.'

He had no reply. His ribs ached.

She persuaded him to stand, or rather to stoop and cling, to rinse his clammy face at the basin and brush his teeth. In the square mirror, he re-assembled himself slowly: the mud-red hair, the potato nose, the narrow chin covered by its tawny beard, the small yellowing teeth, and the flattened, flushed plains of his cheeks. It was, he told himself, a mongrel face, a plebeian face, distinguished only by the deep-set challenge of his eyes.

He noted, with a curious sort of disinterest, that his pupils were wide – dilated presumably with fever – and he turned to look through the French doors, past the balcony to the olive trees and the indifferent sea. Then he collapsed into bed once more, and his nurse proceeded to trim his beard and hair.

Other women had seen to him in this way: his mother, his sister Ada – Frieda couldn't be trusted with scissors – and once, only once, R.

Almost a decade ago already – how was it possible?

The nurse finished by combing his hair and smoothing his crown under her palms. It was a beautiful thing, a luxury to be touched, and he wondered too: was it advance preparation for his laying-out? Easier to tidy him with him sitting up. 'Thank you,' he said. '*Thank you*.' Tears stood in his eyes.

Then he blinked and saw mimosa blossom stuffed in the breast-pocket of the blue cotton jacket he wore in bed. Pyjamas were the get-up of the louche, and he'd refused them. Who'd put the blossom there? Frieda? Barby? A gift.

He looked at his nurse's breast again and studied her upside-down fob-watch. It was fastened to her tabard by an enamel button, and had a retractable chain and a red second-hand which ticked loudly.

'When?' he asked vaguely. Morphia ran in his gills.

'Today is Sunday,' she said. 'It is half past ten.'

But that wasn't what he'd meant at all.

She looked past him, ticking.

Where had they found an English nurse? She was not like the ministering butterflies at the sanatorium, whose pleasing faces were meant to be both a lure and a tonic. She was another sort of creature altogether. Efficient. Inscrutable, with a skew-whiff eye.

His brain was baking in the oven of his head, and she ticked in her chair like a little time-bomb. Had that bastard of a Home Secretary sent her over to do him in? After the brouhaha in Parliament? He wouldn't put it past him or any of the Grey Elderlies.

A fit of coughing erupted within him. 'England,' he said, to the ceiling. 'Impossible.'

'Oh, yes. *Quite*,' the English nurse said, and her eyes crossed, as if to avoid the blue gas-flame of his.

He turned his face to the wall. She would never understand, he told himself, even had he the breath. England was impossible, not because of the disrepair of his body – the new doctor claimed he had but one working lung to his name. England was impossible because *it* was consuming him – *not* the 'consumption' or any of his own self-pronounced diagnoses: bronchial congestion, asthma, *la grippe*, the damned funk, a weak chest, a seedy few months, a ghastly winter, a touch of pneumonia, an Italian cold or his infernal cough.

He was dying of chagrin, of defeat, of a smashed heart. *England* was killing him. His love for it. His loathing of it. Fuck it, fuck his countrymen with their atrophied imaginations and their withered bollocks. Fuck his own heart for wanting it so.

I am English, and my Englishness is my very vision. More than anything, he wanted to see the larch trees of his boyhood. He, Jessie and sometimes Alan too, her oldest brother, used to set out early from Eastwood and walk to Whatstandwell, arriving three hours later, hungry to the bone. And between them – riches! Enough for a loaf which they'd set upon immediately with their shut-knives, hacking away. After they'd finished, they'd take the last bit of milk in their bottles and shake it hard until a beautiful piece of golden butter appeared at the bottom. It wasn't enough for more than a crust of bread, but a stranger passing might have thought they'd made gold from lead, so pleased were they with their efforts.

Once their stomachs were satisfied, they disappeared into their thoughts, hardly speaking as they sat on the wall near the village bridge, and watched the bright Derwent rushing by. Near the bridge, the brakes would pull up at the inn, laden with the trappings of some rich man's shooting-party. He always pitied the pheasants, raised to be shot *by fat men after breakfast.*

Then they'd cross the river and lose themselves on the green paths of Shining Cliff Woods, shouting 'Free warren! Free warren!' wherever they went. It was an ancient wood, and they didn't care who held its deeds, rich man or god.

At the highest point of the hill, by the thousand-year-old yew tree they knew well, they collapsed on the ground, which in the spring was still blanketed in pine-needles from the previous autumn. Jessie always rose first, going off to forage, for 'victuals' as she used to say. Then Alan sat up, knife in hand, and started to whittle, while he himself pulled out his sketchbook and began to draw the larches.

In his far-away sick-bed, the female flowers burst into life again like pink torches. The male flowers rose, pale and creamy. Those trees had been over two hundred years old when they were felled. Ada, his sister, had told him on his last visit to Eastwood – as if it were old, tired news – that they'd been felled *long* ago, early in the War, same as all the trees in that stretch of countryside along the Derwent and through the Amber Valley – all of it taken, she said, for trench struts and duckboards, for coffins and wooden crosses. Shining Cliff Woods had been denuded, stripped naked like a woman in war, and the happy ghosts of his youth had been felled with it.

There was too much pathos, too much beauty of old things passing away, and no new things coming. England's heart beat on, but only because it had been cauterised by the agonies of the War. Its people now had more and more – bigger houses, proud water-closets, stuffed furniture, new motor-cars – but they no longer knew how to feel alive in their lives.

The day would come, he knew it would, when they would champ at the bit for another fight, for another war, for a drama, a rush of blood to the head. And sooner rather than later. Another generation would be sacrificed to some new and deadly cock-a-hoop, while the Grey Elderly Ones signed declarations and treaties, and spouted clatfart in their clubs and chambers. Nothing would change. Caps would be doffed, knees bobbed, and everyone would defer for the sake of a crust.

God save the world from the Old Grey Men. He'd never be one of them, and that was something at least. Better to spend your life than to save it up for the obit-writers. His stories had scooped the stuffing out of him and chucked him aside. He could live with that. He could die with that. What he could not bear was the chucking of his stories.

His last novel, his 'English novel', his 'filth', his shite, his literary effluvia, had already been confiscated across the Channel, as had the manuscript of his new poems. British Customs and the Postmaster General had made it clear he was at the government's mercy – and there was apparently none to be had.

Almost fifteen years ago, all 1,011 copies of *The Rainbow* had gone up in smoke. He'd sent it to his literary agent with everything he had had in him: 'I hope you will like the book: also that it is not very improper … I could weep tears in my heart, when I read these pages.' He read of the 'destruction order' in the *Manchester Guardian* – the day after the bonfire.

Then, last summer, July '29, another disaster. His oils and water-colours – his nude paintings – were seized from Dorothy Warren's gallery in Mayfair. The pubic hair was the outrage. Yet which grown person didn't have it? What was its crime? Thirteen thousand people had been to see his canvases, if mostly to gawk, before the police arrived—

How hot he was. How wretchedly hot. Where was his nurse? Was it summer already? Had he missed the spring? What was this place? They would go to the Alps. He was decided. It would be cool. The mountain streams were icy even in high summer. The air was pure.

Only last month – was it last month? *when* were they? – the Home Secretary had stood up and denounced him, the author of the notorious novel, in the House of Commons. Afterwards, his agent had wired to say he was as sure as anyone could be that *Chatterley* had been blacklisted by Whitehall, too secretively to fight it in the courts. It was a double blow. A secret blacklisting also meant the newspapers couldn't report it. His novel was to be starved of oxygen, like his own feeble lungs.

Then, even worse news from his agent – how could it be? No one in London would provide assurances that he, the author and distributor, would not be arrested if he returned to England.

'AND IF I WERE TO ARRIVE BY BOX QUERY,' he'd cabled.

How hot he was, and no bed linen on him. He was burning up. 'Nurse!' he called.

The flowers in the jug were talking: 'So that's *that!* – And when one died, the last words to life would be: So that's *that!*'

'Take them away,' he said, and the inscrutable English nurse allowed herself a frown.

But no … He remembered. They were *Connie's* words. His Constance. His much-maligned Lady Chatterley. 'So that's *that!*' she said, early in her unhappiness – and late, now, in his. 'And when one died, the last words to life would be: So that's *that!*—'

The Virgin on the wall looked down, her head turned towards him. Her eyes were deep-set, alight with compassion. Could she understand? The nightstand would outlast him, he who loved life so. *Blasted* nightstand in its dovetail calm. Blasted sturdy chair by the miraculous window. Blasted wardrobe in all its heft and presence.

Even the jug of flowers, with its streaky white glaze, was unbearable. The glaze was luminous. He almost wept at the sight.

There were nights at two in the morning when his coughing was so bad he would have shot himself if he'd had a pistol. But this, the piercing loveliness of the everyday, would finish him off. He'd known despair, deep despair, but it seemed nothing to today's sudden, radiant apprehension of the life which goes on, beautifully, fuckingly heedless.

The English nurse duly removed the jug of flowers. He watched her now as she cast about the room, at a loss, before depositing the jug at the bottom of the wardrobe. Had he cursed aloud? Perhaps. He heard the cry of a door hinge. He watched her fold and hang a pair of his trousers. A hanger knocked uselessly against the rail.

Would she burn his clothes afterwards? Bonfires had blazed daily at the back of the Sad Astra, with dinner jackets, frocks and night-shirts. He should have liked to enter a plea on behalf of his corduroy jacket and hat, but to what end?

The familiar hallucination flickered again. He could see it laid out on the writing table at which he'd never written: his own body like a blank, useless sheet of paper: five foot nine, naked, thin as an El Greco, preternaturally pale, the white flame of him extinguished.

Where was Frieda?

With Angelo, her '*Il Capitano*'?

It was not impossible. The less life he had, the more she seemed to possess. Sir Clifford Chatterley, paralysed in his bath-chair, loomed before him. *Yet he was absolutely dependent on her – he needed her every moment... He could wheel himself about in a wheeled chair— But alone he was like a lost thing.*

His chest gurgled horribly.

The English nurse heaved open the windows, and the cat between his feet sat up. Outside, swifts screamed in the eaves. They mated for life, he recalled, and they screamed. The thought made him laugh – never good for his ribs.

He struggled for the cup of water. When the cramp eased, he asked his nurse to retrieve the flowers, for the anemones were companion-able after all, and he'd feel less alone.

He hadn't been hungry for weeks but now, he seemed to crave something, everything – the raw purple of the flowers, the lips of a woman, the soft, sweet pulp of a fig, the heady scent of a rose.

'You're feverish,' the nurse said, pressing a cool, damp cloth gently to his face.

And in that instant, he could have lived off the touch of the English nurse alone.

When he next awoke, he was propped and watered. He felt considerably better. His nurse suggested a game of pontoon. But no, he said, *The Life of Columbus* and his New World awaited. The cat licked his ankles. Above him, the Virgin on the wall was watchful and knowing.

Before turning to *Columbus*, however, he must work, he told his nurse. He asked for the tea-tray, his lap-desk. Where were the notes he'd made the previous week? Hadn't he started to compose a review?

No one can believe in their own death.

He resumed: 'Mr Gill is not a born writer. He is a crude and crass amateur. Still less is he a born thinker, in the reasoning and argumentative sense of the word.'

The English nurse opened the window wide, and her patient dozed again, recalling the landscape below the Mirenda. Each May, the tawny wheat fields had mesmerised him, like the pelt of an animal with the breeze moving through it. The stalks had bent under the weight of their seeds, and the air everywhere had carried their scent. Within the month, the sheaves lay tied on the fields like sleeping bodies, until evening when the girls came with their baskets to carry them home.

That evening, shortly before ten, he awoke to a tearing sensation.

Voices, high and low, crested and fell at the foot of his bed, washing over him, then receding. Beneath him, the sheets were soaked, and the tide was coming in fast on a pebbled shore. His little boat, listing on the beach, would lift soon with the incoming tide – what then? – but his eye was distracted by a stone that gleamed at his feet. He watched himself stoop and rub it dry: an eye-stone, with a smooth hole worn through.

He'd had one of these once … Where had he?

He closed one eye and pressed the stone to the other:

He saw his mother helping him with his Latin: '*nil desperandum*'. Dear Jessie in long-ago Eastwood was declaiming the words of their hero Maggie Tulliver: '*O Tom, please forgive me—I can't bear it—I will always be good—always remember things—do love me.*' His sister Ada was instructing him in jam-making: '*the same quantity of sugar to fruit*'. Even little Mary, his pupil at Greatham, was singing as lustily as she'd sung when he'd tutored her fifteen years before.

Yonder come the train, she coming down the line
Blowing every station, Mr. McKinley is a-dying
It's hard times, it's hard times

Look-it here, you rascal, you see what you've done
You shot my husband with that Iver-Johnson gun
I'm carrying you back, to Washington …

His ears rang with words, more words, his words.

The Sussex Downs: that was her England. In Italy, under his pine tree, his pen had inked those words onto a page – and *her* with them. *My dear Rosalind, I am weary*— Now, here in this far-off place he did not know, fleetingly, she seemed to return to him *Rosalind*, as if she had stepped from the white page of the snowy Sussex slope where he'd first sighted her on a January morning years before, when it had seemed as if the hill itself had dreamed her the *open-countenanced, skyward-smiling rose*—

Water and blood bubbled in his lungs.

He didn't hear Frieda cry out.

There had been life, a body, weight, sex, appetite, love, wonder and fear, and now, only the vessel of his little boat remained to him, bobbing like a cork in the tide.

The current took it, and him, quickly. He was without compass, oar or chart.

He took the stone from his pocket and looked through its hole of an eye, but it saw only the obsidian dark.

Slap, slap went the sea.

He was something apart at last, something inalienable, something beyond language. Where were the stars? Had even they left him for dead?

Oblivion came and went.

He felt no hunger.

All longing was snuffed out.

The end was endless, he realised. That was the truth of things. The Truth. He was adrift, and his eye-stone was blind.

He slept, dreamed, drifted, woke.

Then, after a long time or no time – how could he know? – some axis of the world tilted, the currents of dimensions clashed, a wave lifted his boat, and he saw something glimmering dimly at the rim of the night: a shoreline etching itself, patient and slow as scrimshaw; a faint scrawl of light, a last word, a first word, the New Worl—

Two days later, a small black horse drew a light hearse down the wooded hill into Vence. No service was read. The headstone was engraved with the exile's 'totem' creature, the phoenix. Ten mourners dropped sprays of mimosa, violets and primroses onto the coffin.

'Goodbye, Lorenzo,' Frieda said simply.

But it wasn't goodbye, not quite. The obituarists either sneered or damned with faint praise. The novelist E. M. Forster – to whom the exile had been cruel fifteen years before – would not have it. In his tribute to Lawrence, he observed that 'the low-brows whom he scandalized have united with the high-brows whom he bored to ignore his greatness.'

The exile had had a talent for alienating others, it was true.

In not quite phoenix-like fashion, he would rise up belatedly, five years after his burial, when Frieda had a change of heart. She issued instructions for her husband's exhumation, cremation and safe delivery to herself, in New Mexico, at the ranch he'd once loved, and her new home. Her longstanding Italian lover and third-husband-to-be, Angelo, was charged with the mission, and in the course of the epic journey, Lawrence travelled by urn rather than by *Nina*, *Pinta* or *Santa Maria*.

In his later years, after a few shots of bourbon, Angelo – who had regretfully but energetically cuckolded Lawrence – would claim he had done his friend and rival, 'David', the favour of tipping him out over the glory of the Mediterranean on a beautiful day in 1935. (David, he explained, had *loved* the Mediterranean.) He then promptly re-filled the urn, he said, with burnt wood-chips from a nearby fire-pit, fearing the great writer's ashes might be rejected by American Customs. Customs men weren't partial to the dead, and they had long had reservations 'about David'.

A fair point.

In this picaresque drama, the urn, whatever its contents, would be accidentally abandoned on a quiet train platform in New Mexico, where Angelo had felt the need to disembark to relieve himself. He then absentmindedly re-boarded the train, and twenty miles later, clapped his hands to his head in dismay. After rifling through the luggage rack – no! no! – he alighted to travel the twenty miles back to the forlorn station, where the exile, or the urn at least, was hastily retrieved.

Onward they travelled together, lover and notional husband.

Not long after Angelo's delivery of the deceased, Frieda would have the burnt offerings mixed with concrete, and the exile, or his wood-chip simulation, would be laid to rest in a small chapel of her design. Such was her husband's restlessness in life that only concrete, it seemed, would serve him in death. Moreover, only concrete, Frieda believed, would stop his devoted friends – and her devoted critics – from stealing his ashes and scattering them in the New Mexican desert.

Somewhere, the particles of the exile still flux and drift. A blazing molecule of blue iris. An atom of red beard. A neuron bearing a memory of a larch flower. Restlessness is his essence.

And what remains of each of us is story. Old yarns spun, then snipped.

Catch an end. Tug it gently.

Ignore the kinks, the interference, the contrapuntal crackle. That is always with us.

Time unravels with his story. See how its stitches fall away from the fabric of the world:

.niaga ecno – 0391, hcraM fo dn2 eht, gnineve ylrae si tI

It is early evening, the 2nd of March, 1930 – once again.

.dnomreboR alliV

Villa Robermond.

,deb worran eht eeS

See the narrow bed,

,dnatsthgin eht

the nightstand,

.guj rewolf dna yart-aet eht

the tea-tray and flower jug.

.tey ton era, doohilekil lla ni, uoY

You, in all likelihood, are not yet.

.si llits elixe ehT

The exile still is.

In three hours' time, the English nurse will close his eyes, consult the fob-watch ticking at her heart and record the time of death.

Against his stained pillow, his head turns, this way and that. His eyelids flicker. The Virgin on the wall gazes at him in the lamp-light.

He *knows* those eyes.

Unusual for a Madonna.

Raphael's *Alba Madonna*. That was the one. A reasonable copy.

Dark eyes. Deep-set. Wide. Both introspective and alight.

Through one face comes another ... *Dearest Ros—*

There she stands, watching him from her threshold of nearly a decade before: the 10th of September, 1920. Hers is the white house at the end of the terrace, high on the hill overlooking Florence, in the village of Fiesole. Her little villa lies at the end of a steep track that passes his borrowed abode, Villa Canovaia; the track climbs through the olive groves to her.

He arrived back in Italy the previous November, after five years trapped in England for the War. All borders shut with the Declaration, and his and Frieda's flying visit to London had turned, inadvertently, into a confinement, one they neither wanted nor could afford. When he landed, on his own, back in Italy – freedom, at last! – he had just £21 to his name.

It is the autumn of 1920. The Villa Canovaia is leased in her name *Rosalind Rose Ros rose-flame* but he has taken up occupancy for a few weeks. She decamped from it when she, her children and Ivy the nurse arrived home, after a mountain holiday that summer, to find its windows blown out. A nearby munitions store had blown sky-high.

The War never ends, it seems, although it is nearly two years since the Armistice. The War was won, but the Peace was lost. The blast damage, however, is his good fortune. Eleven rooms. A hill-side garden with a remarkable view of Florence. And Ros, a walk away.

Yes, she said, to his suggestion: of course. Why not? The house was his, if he wanted it. She could not remain there with three young children. Not in the state it was. And there was still the glory of a Tuscan September, cooler than the Sicilian south, the blaring heat of which she knew he and Frieda found so trying.

Frieda was in Germany that September with her family, and their last £3. She would have, he told his hostess, hated Villa Canovaia for its eyeless windows. She had little patience for the broken or defunct. The villa stood on a lane behind a high wall, with its own small courtyard and fountain, a balcony garlanded in vines, and a turret-room which overlooked Firenze.

The place had somehow been waiting for him. He felt he knew already its ochre-washed walls, its sombre green shutters, and its great tangled garden, full of fruit. The pear trees, a passing local man said, were 250 years old. Only olive trees lived longer. The apple trees were still fruiting, wild strawberries and violets ran rampant in the garden beds, and the courtyard was bright with terracotta pots from which lemon and orange trees sprung. He wrote and told Frieda, pointedly, he could breathe again.

On his first night in residence, a bat flew in one window and out the opposite. *And away he went! / Fear craven in his tail.* Bats were the only creatures which made his scalp creep. At the front of the villa, two resident goats nibbled the foliage. Excellent. He could milk a goat with the best of them. A puppy often waited at the kitchen door, and a motherless family of kittens mewed at the gate. He would mother them all.

In the grieving rooms that were, until the explosion, the servants' quarters, he found goat droppings and chickens roosting on an old cabinet top – with eggs laid daily in the couch's split upholstery. The two married elderly servants, who had long looked after the house, had moved up the hill to family in Fiesole once the influenza had seized Florence. Only their menagerie remained.

There he is now, again.

By night, he listens as the hillside breeze takes hold of the villa. A windy emptiness seizes the thirteenth-century house, and doors bang shut, like New Year's guns going off. By day, his mind is calmed by the mellow light of late afternoon. In the garden, the tortoises mate and shout in their extremis, and shell crashes upon shell.

The air smells of wild jasmine, and the place is slowly being re-claimed by nature. He will give it a good going-over before he leaves.

Each morning, he feasts on peaches from the tree in the garden by the gate; they are the best, the sweetest he has known. *I am thinking, of course, of the peach before I ate it. / Why so velvety, why so voluptuous heavy?* The blackberries will soon come on; he might try his hand at wine.

He is a resident voyeur in the world of the two tortoises. *Sex, which breaks us into voice, sets us calling across the deeps, calling, calling for the complement.* He is filled with a queer sort of happiness as he observes their ungainly, unsightly love. *This awkward, harrowing pursuit, / This grim necessity from within. / Does she know / As she moves eternally slowly away?* He loves the male's *Self-exposure, hard humiliation, need to add himself on to her.* He is half tortoise himself as he watches.

Since his arrival, the official tenant of Canovaia has visited him each day with her three small children. Their welcome party appeared on his first day, apparently so that the two little girls, Bridget and Chloë, could thank him for the sheepskin coats he made for them, for their sea voyage from England to Italy in bitter January. He was 'so clever with a needle!' their mother exclaimed. She smiled, her skin brown with the Italian summer, and her teeth flashing white.

The toddler, Nan, is not the child of the husband, Godwin Baynes. The exile understands that the youngest child is the consequence of his hostess's brief affair at the Savoy in London with a childhood friend.

Bertie Farjeon, Ros's playwright brother-in-law, discreetly suggested that the aim of the pre-meditated affair had been to create a scandal so incontrovertible that even a possessive husband would be unable to overlook it, and she would thereby bring about the divorce he would not otherwise allow. Bertie had revealed that she was in the process of helping her husband compile the evidence – love letters and whatnot – which would establish the grounds for Baynes's divorce petition.

When the exile suggested to his new writer-friend Bertie – not once but twice, in Sussex five years before, months before he met her – that they should co-author a novel or play based on the Bayneses' failing marriage, Bertie had simply changed the subject. The idea, however, was not without a spark of something, and it was one of those stubborn things in the exile's mind. He couldn't shake it off.

Today, on her visit to the courtyard of Canovaia, she, Mrs Baynes still – Rosalind – bends her head to smell a climbing rose. The blooms grow up a painted trellis in a profusion of deep red; they shake at her touch, spilling their scent.

She seats herself next to him on the cool stone bench. He pours tea. She knows the tortoises well, of course, from her own seven-month occupancy of Canovaia. She misses them, she says, smiling at her feet.

She has come today to check he has everything he needs in his – or her – windowless house. Crockery, flour, sugar, wine and other essentials. She has arrived, not only with children, but with bags of grapes and figs from her new garden up the hill in Fiesole. What is he writing in his notebook? she asks.

Poetry, he replies with a shrug. Jottings.

He captures her in four dashed lines as she sits, smiling quizzically at him.

So many fruits come from roses
From the rose of all roses
From the unfolded rose
Rose of all the world.

Words on a bit of paper were a sort of magic.

Across decades, dimensions and wind-shuffled drafts and pages, the fragments blow. *So many fruits come from roses / From the rose of all roses / From the unfolded rose / Rose of all the world.*

They laugh at the tortoises.

I heard a woman pitying her, pitying the Mère Tortue. / While I, I pity monsieur. / "He pesters her and torments her," said the woman. / How much more is he pestered and tormented, say I.

She tells him he mustn't always work. He must come for supper that evening. She has been to the market. She will put the children to bed early. The little girls, who are playing by the sluggish fountain, protest.

Yes, it is a plan: he must join them up the hill, she says, at Villino Belvedere. She slaps her thighs, rises from the bench and calls to her children.

He has waited. Since Sussex he has waited – since that snowy hilltop. Five years ago? Six? Although he is reluctant to admit it even

33

to himself, being without her, this woman he doesn't know, has been painful to him, an ache in the hollow of his chest.

On his way through the steep wood, he stops for breath. He leans against an old wall and listens to the rippling grey leaves of the olive trees, to the breeze moving in them, delicately sad. The evening is sultry. He can hear the deepening of the shadows of day. He hears the old Etruscan voices humming in the stone wall against which he rests. The vibrations move up his spine.

Listen.

In his sick-bed beneath the painting of the Virgin – as near now to death as he was that evening to life – he hears, from a decade away, the faint tambourine shake of those olive leaves. The door of her Villino Belvedere, when he finally locates it, is half-smothered in leaves and sweet, plump grapes. A small plaque of the Madonna peers at him through the vine.

Then the relief, the dizzying relief of her, as she appears – manifests: Rosalind, *Ros*, rose, her chestnut hair red with summer. Five years before, she was a rose-flame on a wintry Down. Now she is—

'Come through,' she is saying, again and for the first time. She rubs at a smear of yellow paint on her chin.

Beauty is a painful thing. He has to turn away.

He pretends to notice a painting on the wall as he composes himself. She brushes a mosquito from his cheek. 'Come,' she repeats, waving him forward. She picks up her shopping bags. She has only just arrived home herself. 'Goodness, you're out of breath! Have I killed you?'

Her voice is glad and she is open-faced, although she can't quite meet his eye. She is wearing a fine *grey woollen dress*, which, like herself, is splattered with paint from the room that will soon be her children's nursery. She shakes her head at the spectacle she imagines she must present, but she is *comely, almost beautiful, in her shyness.*

They first saw each other in Sussex, across nestled hilltops, on a January day in 1915. Now she too has escaped England and its sad claustrophobia. They have both broken free. 'Deserters, this way!' she says, ushering him in and up a staircase, but, for all her warm amusement, she is shy.

'Revolutionaries as well?' he says.

'I daresay the firing squad won't be fussy.'

As they arrive on the landing upstairs, she drops her bags, and he watches as she reaches up to knot the mass of her hair at the back of her head. Her body is both sturdy and graceful and, beneath her dress, her breasts rise. She isn't wearing a bodice.

'I'll leave the firing squad to you,' she says. 'I only ask that my new yellow wall is left out of it.'

He grins. He is never like this with anyone, so immediately free, so unencumbered by self-consciousness, plan or purpose. Had he remained a school-teacher, their lives would never have crossed. Yet even so, with the difference in their respective stations, she is entirely open. Other people *were always somewhat of a wonder to her, and when her sympathy was awake, she was quite devoid of class feeling.*

He passes her a bottle of Marsala, roses from Canovaia, a loaf of bread from a local woman, bought warm that morning, and a surprise in a basket for Bridget and Chloë.

'Did I say?' He is offhand – 'It's my birthday tomorrow.'

She doubles up her chin, brigadier-fashion. 'Your birthday, you say? Among *foreigners*? Lord! What a rum do.' Her eyes widen at her own antics. 'In that case – as it's now an *occasion* – you must assist me with our meal.'

'My last meal?'

'It may be.' She wrinkles her nose apologetically. 'I really am rather hopeless in the kitchen.'

He can smell the day's sunshine on her skin mingling with her scent. At the sink, by the nailbrush, he sees *a little bottle of Coty,* La Rose Jacqueminot. Together they unpack her shopping bags: goat's milk, nasturtiums, mortadella, anchovies, yeast. Their miscellaneous contents seem rather to prove her point about her culinary skills.

She tells him her plans: she is going to learn to make lace and will study Italian embroidery. She is embroidering cushion covers. She will get pens, paints and inks in Florence for her *little sketches.* She has a name for her work. A London publisher still wants her drawings, and hasn't been put off, mercifully, by the scandal of her forthcoming divorce, the courtroom drama to come, and all the talk. *'I know,' said Connie. 'Talk is beastly: especially if you live in society.'*

The divorce will indeed create talk: talk in *The Times*, in the *Daily Express*, the *Daily News*, the *Daily Mirror* and the *Daily Mail*. Personal letters will be read out in court and extracted for the papers. ('Decree Nisi Against Royal Academician's Daughter', 'Feminist Divorced!') She is longing, she says, to paint the duomo and Giotto's bell-tower from her new terrace.

Watching her, transfixed, he has to remember to listen.

Half a dozen years later, alone in a pine wood on the far side of the same river-valley, he will lovingly re-create her on the page. 'Constance' will have her chestnut hair and russet complexion. He will change her illustrations for children's books to 'old books'. He will alter the colour of her wide bright eyes from brown to dark blue, to disguise her.

Connie's husband, 'Sir Clifford Chatterley', like Ros's own husband, will be Cambridge-educated, a war-hero and, in the exile's terms, 'spiritually sterile' – an emotional 'cripple'. Sir Clifford's wheelchair will be the outward manifestation of an inward paralysis, the paralysis of an entire generation who closed their eyes to the truths of their war.

Connie Chatterley's Royal Academician father, the character 'Sir Malcolm', will feel as much contempt for her husband as Rosalind's own Royal Academician father, Sir Hamo, felt for his son-in-law. He *had always disliked Clifford*.

'Good heavens!' Ros says, and her hand flies to her breast. She has just opened the lid of his basket. Inside it, a salamander scampers.

'To amuse the three Young Graces,' he says.

Bridget and Chloë charge at him from the balcony, where they have been playing. On the sitting-room floor, Nan sleeps in a large zinc bath cushioned with a bolster. 'Sssh now, darlings!' their mother hushes as they coo over the salamander. 'Don't wake your sister!'

He could almost feel like the man of the house among them.

The floor of her new home is covered in rush matting. Here and there a few blue Persian rugs are scattered. On a wall in the sitting-room hang fine *reproductions of Renoir and Cézanne* – German, she says. She found them in Dresden on her travels before she was married. Also: a fine copy of a Raphael Madonna, a circular canvas in a battered oak frame.

'The *Alba Madonna*,' she remarks from the kitchen, when she sees him admiring it. 'It hung on the wall of my nursery when I was a child. I adored the Virgin then, and I dearly wished we were Catholics. My dear parents, however, always reminded my siblings and me that we were enlightened agnostics, and as such, we could love only the stories and art produced by the Church, be it the Old Church or the Church of England. We could not trust in its teachings.

'Yet I remained entranced by her head in this, and by the expression on her face – she's like one of Michelangelo's sibyl prophetesses. I went on loving her. Childish, I know, but she has travelled with me, and we remain close.' She smiles, amused by her admission, then flusters over the nasturtiums. 'Does one put them in water,' she asks, 'or eat them? I couldn't understand what the flower-woman was telling me.'

They step onto the balcony, over rag-dolls and a copy of Edmund Dulac's *Fairy Tales of the Allied Nations*. At the pale stone balustrade, window boxes glow with velvet-red geraniums. Far below them, in Florence's river-valley, the anchor of the duomo steadies the world.

…love can be wonderful; when you feel you live, and are in the very middle of creation.

Ivy, the children's young nurse, is away visiting chums in Siena. When the children are fed and tucked up at last in their mother's big bed, he cooks for her: a stew of tomatoes from her garden, olives, wine, garlic and mortadella. Then they walk up the hill in the pine-scented dark. Fireflies spark. Lights appear on the hillside below them, *like night flowers opening.*

She understands that he has written a study of the novels of Thomas Hardy. How wonderful, she says. They share their admiration enthusiastically, novel after novel. Her mother, she tells him, with undisguised delight, was adored by Thomas Hardy, and was, according to the great man himself, the model for Tess of the d'Urbervilles.

One only has to look at her, he thinks, to see it: she clearly has her mother's unaffected beauty, a luminous Tess-like freshness *a ruddy, country-looking girl with soft brown hair.* And he risks it then, an awkward effort at something closer. 'Were you ever in trouble, so to speak, before now, before the divorce? I mean, for living. For simply trying to live honestly – as now?'

Yes, she will say, *a soft, mild voice,* and that will be their bond.

'Good gracious, no!' She seems embarrassed by his question, by his earnestness, and she snatches up a handful of thyme from a rocky outcrop to press to her face, as if she would hide herself from him.

He feels the gulf of the night between them. She is drawing away, reminding him of their differences. Her tone is amiable: he is a friend, not a familiar.

'My parents were progressives, you see. My father is a sculptor, as I believe you know already, and he and my mother both were of the tribe of *cultured Fabians.* Travelling with my father was always wonderful. We learned German and French. My sisters and I were *taken to Paris and Florence and Rome, to breathe in art*— We used to copy in the galleries, and pretend we were orphans when kind souls would gently ask where our parents were.

'Growing up, we roamed, boys and girls together, in the country and in town. We could stay over when we liked in my father's studio in *Kensington.* We wore our hair loose and dressed in carefree home-made smocks – or sometimes, in exquisite costumes made by my mother for parties. I suppose we were *at once cosmopolitan and provincial.* We swam naked in the summers. We used to sleep out in the woods, unchaperoned.' She raises her face and seems to search the night. 'I don't imagine young people shall ever be as free again.

'But we thought nothing of it. We were *sent to Dresden at the age of fifteen, for music among other things. We lived freely among the students, and argued with men over philosophical and sociological and artistic matters, we were just as good as men themselves: only better, because we were women.* Then, when we were a little older, my sister – Joan, that is – she and I went off to walk in the Alps. That summer, we must have danced every night, in the moonlight, *and we tramped off to forests with sturdy youths bearing guitars – twangtwang! – we sang the Wandervogel songs*— Can you credit it?' Her laughter was warm and resonant.

'*In the Hague and Berlin,* we went to the opera and attended the *great socialist conventions.* I marvel now at the two girls who did all that. Who were they? Look!' She pointed to a falling star, its tail fizzing in the night. 'We sang endlessly and recited poems; we drew and composed. We were always, our little group, full of ideas and plans.

'When we were older and, by then, in London, the raucous, jolly gang of us would take up an entire row of the cheap seats at *Les Ballet Russes*. That was our favourite. Either that or Wagner at Covent Garden, organised by my Uncle George. There was cricket too, endless days of cricket and hockey.

'The Meynell girls – you remember Monica, Madeline and Viola, plus a younger one whose name I cannot recall – of course you do – they were on the Slade hockey team in those days, and wore great, voluminous medieval-style garments in which they played – not very well, I have to say. But who could play well in such trappings?!

'Their team captain was Caleb Saleeby, who became Dr Saleeby, he who later married and abandoned poor Monica Meynell. I'm sure you heard all about that unhappiness in your Greatham days with the Meynell "clan". Madeline, Monica's sister, was always so kind … We all played, you see, not only the boys. We were free, although we didn't know it. *Out in the open, out in the forests of the morning, free to do as we liked, to say what we liked. It was the talk that mattered supremely: the impassioned interchange of talk.*

'How alive we were. I can see that now. One never knew life could be anything but "living" and discovery, always new discoveries. One never imagined that it could … narrow so.'

She turns to him, shrugging something away.

He cannot imagine such a life.

Or rather, he can only imagine.

'We were spoiled, I expect,' she says, as if to vent his thought.

'You were loved.'

'Yes.' She turns her face to the sky again. 'I was once. Of course everything was possible before the War.' She quickens her stride and crickets fly from their path.

'I met my husband – he's still officially that – at one of my Uncle George's musical evenings in Hampstead. Godwin was a medical student at Barts. He had a superb voice, almost of professional quality. He sang Siegmund, and I tried my best with the part of Sieglinde. He was splendid. In everything Godwin takes on, he's a sort of sun-god. He's literally a towering figure – six feet four – and universally adored.'

'Did you adore him?'

'How could I not? He bent the air ... He was twice in the winning Cambridge boat for the Boat Race, beating both the Oxford and the Harvard teams. He introduced me to his Cambridge friends   *flannel-trousers Cambridge intransigents*   as a "stunner". I felt secretly flattered and resistant all at once. I promptly rolled up my hair, *most* unbecomingly, to give myself the look of a fifteenth-century pageboy. It didn't dissuade him.

'One snowy night in Hampstead, after tobogganing – that's to say, the whole gang of us – he walked me home. Halfway along, we found the road blocked by a great, endless snow-drift, so he simply picked me up, carried me the rest of the way, and delivered me to my father's door. Looking back, I think my future was decided on that walk home.'

'You loved him.'

'I certainly fell in love with him. He's an altogether overwhelming person, and I was absorbed in him completely. Nor is it really his fault, his not being able to— Sun-gods simply don't know how. Then Bridget was a toddler, and Chloë was on the way, when he abandoned us for the Front. He wasn't called up, you see. Doctors were exempted, as they were essential on the home front, so there was no need at all for him to go anywhere. But he actually believed in all that jingoistic nonsense.

'It infuriates me still. All those young men. All those dear hearts. And what was achieved? What was saved? But Godwin never was a very discerning thinker. He simply throws himself at anything that catches his eye. Regrettably, that used to include the dispensary girl in his medical practice – in our house in Wisbech.'

'Perhaps only people who are capable of real togetherness have that look of being alone in this universe,' said Connie. 'The others have a certain stickiness, they stick to the mass'—

'There were *many* who tempted him, but those episodes in our home were the most trying for me. I used to hear them in the larder, where they were ostensibly taking the inventory of the medicines stored there. They'd emerge flushed, in spite of the larder's coolness. After weeks of it, I took to opening the door to ask if they'd be so kind as to pass out the butter or a cooked ham.

'Yet, no matter how profligate, with women as well as men, he remained a jealous man, and refused to countenance a divorce. He adored me, apparently' – she rolls her eyes – 'and no one else was to have me. In some ways, Godwin, for all his heroism and medical achievements, is frightfully dim.' Her smile flickers. Then she looks to her guest, reading his face, and looks away again, as if she has said too much.

She turns, prematurely, back, and they step wordlessly into the Villino Belvedere. The house breathes with sleeping children. She checks on them, and he senses it is time for him to depart. She has drawn a line.

But, no – miraculously – as she returns to the sitting-room, she ushers him, with one fluid motion of her hand, onto the balcony, into the lantern-light, three hundred feet above Florence. Her hair smells of paint and onions. At the balustrade, they stare into the night as the stars shake.

He says, 'I feel one can come unstuck from England – from all the past – that it is possible to never go back, to never want to go back.'

Connie, belonging to the leisured classes, had clung to the remnants of the old England. It had taken her years to realise that it was really blotted out by this terrifying, new and gruesome England—

'I feel that sometimes,' she says, her voice low. 'Most days, I am full of hope but, even since the Peace, I haven't been able to shake off a vague sense of hopelessness. I am happy enough, but I walk about with an exaggerated feeling of vigilance. I don't understand it. I feel punch-drunk much of the time.'

The Armistice is a ceasefire, he says ruefully, nothing more. It's natural she feels as she does. Hostilities breed, and everywhere, he tells her, politicians stoke fear and resentment. So many who survived the trenches returned home only to be struck down by the influenza. Their own country, his and her 'green and pleasant land', is a haunted place.

England, my England! But which is my England?

It is the eve of his thirty-fifth birthday. It is, she tells him after a silence, the eve of her seventh wedding anniversary. The night air feels kinetic. The lanterns smoke. She has, she says, just turned twenty-nine; freedom is one thing, but she never expected to be one of those women who live 'unevenly'. And yet she's realised, too, that she never desired 'evenness' either.

At the balustrade, they lean in, shoulders touching.

Catch the strand. Unravel the year, day, moment.

.0291, rebmetpeS fo th01 ehT

The 10th of September, 1920.

Loop upon loop. Stitch upon stitch.

There:

On the plain below, Florence is dark, its lights extinguished. They sit, side by side, on the balcony's Roorkee couch. The red geraniums smoulder.

She takes up a lovely old shawl, *an emerald green shawl*, which she tells him she got for half a crown in the Caledonian Market in London, when she was newly married. She lifts her feet, in their *suede slippers*, onto the couch. His hands reach to take them into his lap. He cups her cold ankles. The bottle of Marsala sits on the little table, the dregs.

She raises a hand to the bare nape of his neck. His *thin cream flannel* shirt is collar-less. His hair, she notes, fingering its ends, is growing far past his ears. She laughs. 'How shaggy you are. When did you last have it cut?'

He cannot recall. 'I'll take the kitchen knife to it tomorrow.'

'Nonsense. You'll cut your own neck.' She assesses the length, well past his collar. Many barber shops in Florence are still closed, with the fear of the influenza not yet past. She caught it herself in the spring, but Ivy – the dear girl – saw to the children and kept bringing her damp, cool flannels and juices. It has claimed mostly men, healthy young men, men in their prime. Naturally he is wary. He has survived one bout already – remarkable given his lungs were weak even before the War. Some say one can catch it twice or even thrice.

The moment lengthens strangely, a bridge disappearing into a mist.

'I can trim it for you,' she says finally. 'I used to cut my father's hair after he'd spent too much time in the studio.'

Her touch on his neck runs him through.

'Why not?' he says.

In the darkness beyond, a nightjar chirrs.

She returns with her embroidery scissors and a flannel towel, and begins to snip. Her movements are calm and methodical. She studies him from the back and from the front, drawing the lantern close. He feels as assured as a boy in his mother's kitchen again, with a cloth on his shoulders to spare his clean shirt.

Finally, Ros runs her hand over his head, gathers up the towel and trimmings, and brushes him down with her shawl. She blows cool air along his neck, the most exquisite pleasure he has known in years. He longs to turn and take her to him, but instead, when she is seated again, he bends and lifts her feet onto his lap once more.

'Happy birthday for tomorrow,' she says. 'You are suitably spruced up!'

'I daresay the tortoises won't know me.'

Inside, the baby, Nan, cries out in her sleep. Ros turns an ear, listens – a bad dream – and straightens, poised to go to her.

Stay, he silently wills. Do not stir. *He felt his own unfinished condition of aloneness cruelly. He wanted her, to touch—*

The little girl goes quiet, and her mother sinks back into the couch. The spell is unbroken. She nods with her chin to her left ankle, still cupped in his hand. 'A snake bit me there,' she says, 'when I was a child. I had quite a fever, and nearly frightened my poor parents to death.'

As if there is nothing more natural, he bends his head and presses his lips to the spot; as if he would suck from it any residue of venom which could do her harm. Then he removes her slippers, turns to her and finds the gleam of her eyes.

She presses a heel lightly into his lap, and he feels himself harden. His hand moves slowly and blindly over her knee, under her dress, and up the fullness of her thigh to where she is soft   *brown maidenhair* petalled, dewy, silken   *the rose of all roses   from the unfolded rose.*

Every heart beats with its own secrets.

'I love thee,' he murmurs. It is his old voice, his native voice. 'I love thee an' th' touch on thee.'

'I love thee an' th' touch on thee.'

The Subversive

Readers are keepers of secrets: as an illicit page is turned, as a dangerous truth is inferred. The pulse quickens. Something explosive ticks between the lines. There is an intake of breath; the voyeur's silent flare of recognition. All the while, his or her face is impassive, unremarkable even, because like all subversives, readers lead careful double lives.

It was as she was about to leave, that it came to her. In the night, she'd dreamed of Constance Chatterley.

On the twelfth floor of the Marguery, in the empty family apartment, she checked herself again in her mother-in-law's mirror. The dress was new, suitable: a shift of raw silk, soft coral, knee-length. She slipped on the matching coat, tried again to fasten her purse, and eased on a pair of three-quarter-length white gloves.

'Goodness me, won't you mind traveling on your own?' Mrs. Clyde was their Scottish housekeeper. She'd been with the family for *years*.

'Not at all.'

Before leaving Irving Avenue, she had tried to devise a story that would allow her to ask Mrs. C. to pack, additionally, a raincoat, a plain wool skirt, a blouse and walking shoes. She would then have needed only to slip into Schrafft's on West 13th, near the Park, where she could have changed without fuss in the ladies.

But the trip was overnight only, and what excuse could she have made to justify a set of walking clothes and rainwear for the city? No one in the family ever packed a case for him- or herself. There were protocols which went back to the days of their Embassy travels as a family. And she had promised both Mrs. Clyde and her husband that she'd not walk anywhere on her own. She had to remember she was no longer anonymous, he said, biting into his sardines-on-toast as Mrs. Clyde smiled down on him.

She'd never *been* anonymous, she nearly replied. *No one* was anonymous. Others only saw them as such. But she knew she was in a mood, irritated that her clothes were not entirely her own to choose, and of course she knew what he meant.

At Schrafft's, in her girlhood, the hostesses had worn ankle-length gowns and had seemed to float, not walk, up the curving staircase of the restaurant, past Art Nouveau murals of women whose hair tangled around cornucopias of plenty. As a teenager, the first grown-up thing she'd ever bought herself was lunch in Schrafft's, the day after her graduation from Farmington – June '47 – on her return to New York.

She'd had money in a card from her father, and had ordered the Filet of Flounder with Creole Sauce, followed by the Custard Floating Island for dessert. It was a luxury to have a menu from which to choose, and to eat alone. At Farmington, the cooks would never have deigned to serve such a dessert, except perhaps to the girls at the Skinny Table. The girls at the Fat Table, by contrast, were generally given stewed prunes or something equally unappealing, while the rest of them were permitted tapioca, ginger cake with apple sauce, or blueberry cobbler. Wholesome food for active, growing girls.

In Schrafft's, she had studied the elegant, unescorted women of all ages in their well-made suits and hats – its typical lunchtime clientele. Some read books between mouthfuls of creamed chicken. Some contemplated address books, making notes with white mother-of-pearl pens. Others daydreamed through the bright plate-glass, or took corner tables and smoked, aloof as spies. Sometimes, too, they held the gaze of men who passed, with trenchcoats open to the warmth of June or suit jackets slung rakishly over a shoulder.

In '47, the war of course was still fresh in the collective memory, and there was, in those days, a particular expression on the faces of some who'd experienced it in their prime, a vague look of knowing; of unaffected, easy worldliness; of sophisticated nonchalance. It was a sultry, skeptical gaze in their new land of official post-war cheer.

It suggested too – in the black gleam of pupils or in the lingering slant of the gaze – a certain capacity for risk, or even an appetite for it. Surely, many must have surfaced from war, or from some edgy element of it, only to find themselves, as the forties yielded to the fifties, 'beached' in the new social order. Everyone was now expected to play house and, moreover, to enjoy it too. As a girl observing Schrafft's well-dressed customers from behind her Custard Island, she'd felt she was witnessing a discreetly organized Resistance movement.

It was the sort of woman seldom seen now, just twelve years later, and she couldn't help but feel she had come of age too late. She enjoyed small luxuries as much as the next person, but she knew she would have managed perfectly well in wartime Paris, with rationed food and coal, and limitless, exhilarating opportunities to *do* and to *be*.

At Farmington in '47, in the yearbook, she had declared her sole ambition was 'Not to be a housewife'. Now, Jack had his eye on the White House, and many of his campaign team were already unofficially in place. If he did declare next year, and if he were successful, she would become First Lady – or First Housewife– to the nation. She hated the title. It sounded like a top saddle-horse. Once upon a time, she had hoped to write fiction for the *New Yorker*. Now, she was the fiction.

Two years ago, Pat Nixon – who, as the Vice President's wife, was the so-called Second Lady (did titles get any worse?) – was named 'The Nation's Ideal Housewife'. In '53, Pat had also won 'Mother of the Year'. It was said she actually took pleasure in ironing her husband's shirts and suits on quiet evenings at home. How could she, Jackie, ever compete with a woman like that? How could she ever want to?

Her bill that day at Schrafft's had arrived with a miniature silver scoop of lemon sorbet on a white china plate and a mint-flavored toothpick. The total was 95¢. She'd had just enough for a tip.

The bed in the Marguery was vast. By night, she floated in it as if on the Dead Sea. The solitude was both effortless and alien.

Jack was somewhere in West Virginia, by way of Boston, and would then hop a flight to Florida. They were trying again, notionally, to conceive, but he was campaigning, and the truth was, she was afraid. She'd been pregnant three times in their six years of marriage. Before Caroline, she'd lost two babies. First, a miscarriage. Then Arabella.

When she'd hemorrhaged in her sleep that summer in '56, the pain had been primordial, as if she were being pulled inside out. She'd turned dumb and blind with it, clinging to the edge of their bed as if to a capsized keel. Jack was in Europe, and she felt sure that if it hadn't been for her step-sister's insistence that night, she would have bled to death.

Later, during the D & C, she had tried to tell the doctors the anesthetic wasn't getting through to her, but she'd been unable to make herself heard through the mask.

In the aftermath, she had blinked at the world, unable to assemble it. Nor would it ever assemble again, or not as it had been. Its shape would only ever be lumpen and awkward. Yet life, she now felt, was only truly loved if loved amid and for its misshapenness.

At some level, Jack was afraid too, as much as he wanted another child. He would never touch her when she was pregnant. Babies in the womb were sacred and, in her three pregnancies, the sheets of their marital bed had remained crisp and cool.

Not that it was all about her. Far from it. Jack had already had spinal surgery twice since they'd married. The risks, his doctors explained each time, were high. Both she and his father had pointed enthusiastically to the inspiration of F.D.R. – a leader who had led from a wheelchair – but Jack wouldn't hear of it. Even when the pain was close to crippling, he would hardly tolerate crutches, let alone a wheelchair.

Before his operations, she had never truly prayed. She was suspicious of it even, especially when it was muddied by self-interest. But suddenly she prayed. She prayed like hell. She ceased to be discriminating. She pleaded with Jack's Creator. Alone in St. Francis's in Hyannis, she knelt. She bent her forehead low, because to bow one's head – to humble oneself before life and its mysteries – was, finally, the only utterance one could make, something spoken by the body, in all its wordless human vulnerability.

After the first operation, Jack went down with an infection and slipped into a coma. He was expected to die. But he didn't – not Jack. He rallied. He was soon sitting up and reading newspapers and spy stories, with a new silver plate in his back. He grinned at her and said it would boost his personal magnetism.

Something did. In between operations, he criss-crossed the country, and people loved him.

He was easy to love.

Safety, she now knew, was an illusion and, as her gambling father had always said, nothing twisted you in the wind like hope. But Jack was determined his campaign was going to run on just that – hope, not fear – or he'd kill himself trying.

In August '56, when their unborn daughter died, he was on a yachting vacation, off the coast of Elba with assorted friends. Privately, she was never convinced he'd got the first flight back. No one was. His love of children and his fear of childlessness ran deep. He couldn't face it. Nor could he face his fear that he was to blame. Their family doctor had suggested to him and Joe Sr. that a venereal infection Jack had had at some point might have affected her fertility and her womb. Jack was apparently beside himself when the doctor said that, but Joe wouldn't hear of it: 'Nonsense. The girl's made of porcelain. That's the problem.'

Ethel, her sister-in-law, told her the truth, about the suspected infection. She said she couldn't bear to see her so low, thinking she'd let Jack and the Kennedys down – what with a childless man being unlikely to take the White House and all. That sort of worry wasn't good for her, Ethel said, her face duly glum. Jackie hadn't thought anything of that sort until Ethel had said so. The grief for Arabella had been enough to bring her low. But it was only Ethel trying to be kind, because it was how Ethel would have felt herself. Bobby and Ethel already had a brood of four, with a fifth on the way. She couldn't *stop* getting pregnant, Ethel said, and she puffed out her cheeks, in exaggerated comic exhaustion, as if to say Jackie didn't know the half of it.

Jackie didn't, she was sure, but she knew about Arabella.

Eight months old, perfect, and still as a closed, white bud.

She'd chosen a fairy-tale name for a child who could not be held.

When she was discharged from hospital, she found herself unable to return to their new house in Hickory Hill, with its silent, freshly painted nursery. So Jack sold it, at cost, to Bobby, and they themselves took a rented place near Washington, a three-story red-brick row house in Georgetown. Then, with Joe Sr.'s help, Jack bought Irving Avenue, next to the Big House, the Kennedy family home on the Cape, where they had all grown up. Before long, he was planning his 1958 campaign for re-election to the Senate. 'Already?' she said. He was hardly at home. When he was, the time was so precious that what else could they do but 'play house'?

On the Cape, venturing out at the end of that summer, after Arabella, she walked their stretch of beach, and the winds off the Sound blew at the gate of her heart. Clang, clang. The wind was wild company. It gusted in her ears and wouldn't let her think. It said, there is only this moment, here, now.

The drag of the tide was a sedative. The dunes made ramparts to keep the world out. That warm September, she swam by night in the amniotic dark of the Sound. Mrs. Clyde and her mother-in-law would not have approved, but Ethel and Bobby had produced their fifth child, a girl, and there was much rejoicing. The Kennedys were distracted. It was a mercy. The island of Nantucket blinked at her in the distance.

She had stopped herself from telling Jack that, in her mind, she'd named the baby 'Arabella'. It had never occurred to him that their daughter should have a name. Her gravestone simply said 'Daughter'. At Jack's request, Bobby had made the arrangements for the funeral while his brother traveled back via France.

One couldn't allow oneself to be overwhelmed by sadness.

And yet she was low, lower than she'd imagined possible. It was amazing how one's body could perform life to everyone's satisfaction but one's own.

At her sister Lee's insistence, Jackie traveled that fall to London to spend time with Lee and her husband Michael in their elegant new house on Chester Square. London provided the distraction of bright, fashionable parties. But it was among the ruins of the city, in the bleak rubble-scape, that she felt most at ease – because the rubble was inside her as much as it was out.

Little had changed in the city since she'd covered the Coronation for the *Herald-Tribune* in '53, her first proper job. Three years on, London was still devastated where bombs and rockets had knocked reality through. She found herself blinking at the wasteground of a lovely crescent or a formerly elegant row of Georgian houses. Saplings grew in once grand foundations. Internal walls reared up unexpectedly, dividing the day, and cellars gaped from the streets, dark as gullets.

The city was soot-stained, shell-pocked, haunted. Triumphal arches and monuments were covered in their strange, coal-black fur. Nothing swam in the Thames. In a bomb-crater off the Strand, a trolleybus had suddenly appeared after two heavy nights of rain and more than a decade under earth and sludge. She'd gone to see it for herself, vaguely thinking it was the route she had often taken during her stay in '53. When she arrived, a police constable was bearing a mud-caked purse away.

She stood and watched, like some sort of drifter, which, in effect, she was. Or one of those people who turn up at the scene after a disaster or murder to stare. Perhaps it made her feel more grateful for life. Perhaps it made her feel.

Londoners on their way to work wore gray, navy or brown – there was little else in shop windows – and most, she thought, looked under-fed, thin, and pinched tight as clothes pegs. Little wonder her glamorous younger sister turned heads. By the time Jackie arrived, Lee was conducting at least a few extramarital affairs, of one sort or another, with prominent men.

Once, she would have judged her sister sternly. Now, she let herself imagine ... Madame Bovary, Madame Récamier, Anna Karenina, Lady Chatterley. What if an affair was not always a form of cheating? What if it might *also*, sometimes, be about living as honestly as one could in a world which required men to be more than they were, and women to be far less? Was it any less honest than so many marriages, which were, as everyone knew, transactional by nature – a womb for one's children in return for a respectable home and security?

Three years into their marriage, her womb had failed to produce a child for the Kennedy clan, and Jack was rarely home. 'Home' was something one had within oneself, not bricks and mortar, and hers was gone. Irving Avenue was her bolt-hole, little more now. It was an open secret that she and Jack were estranged.

Conspicuously unattached in England, she was invited to week-end hunt-parties in Sussex. Lee wasn't keen, but she lent her sister the essentials: a hunt cap, tweed jacket, white shirt and buff breeches. The wife of someone else provided riding boots to fit her big feet, plus spurs, gloves and a crop.

When given the choice, she joined the non-jumping set, cantering across fallow fields and burnished woodland – going off on her own when she could. *She was like a forest, like the dark interlacing of the oakwood, humming inaudibly with myriad unfolding buds.* Sussex mornings were misty. The tree canopies, golden in the early weeks, faded to sepia by late October. She missed, more than she'd imagined possible, the fall colors of New England – the vivid crimsons, yellows and magentas – but her mood suited this muted Sussex gold. The branches embraced an emptiness. *From the old wood came an ancient melancholy, somehow soothing to her* ... Her horse kicked up leaves, bracken, chestnuts and mushroom caps. The scent on the breeze was one of resignation, the dying of summer, no matter how deceptively warm the day. White-bottomed rabbits beat a retreat as her horse approached. Squirrels watched from branches, beady-eyed. *The wood was her one refuge, her sanctuary.* Here, she was at home. The woodland was a home. She could have lived like this. No one watched. Her thoughts were her own.

When the downland hills reared into view, she felt their green kick of life. It was a kind of joy, a landscape into which she could imagine disappearing: the hills were intimate in scale. Their flanks rose up, unexpectedly smooth. Their haunches nestled tenderly. Often in the early mornings, the hilltops hovered strangely above rings of mist, as if they had broken away to float freely into the atmosphere.

Only the barking and whelping of the hounds in full cry disturbed the peace of those mornings – English foxhounds, perhaps fifty or more. Yet, the hunt, with its ritualized staging of civilization and animality, of restraint and blood-letting, fascinated her. She felt she understood it, even if nothing she'd known among the well-to-do of the American East Coast compared.

By the kennel, one of the keepers, a 'whipper-in', demonstrated for her, the American visitor, what made a fine hound: a well-muscled top-line along the spine, he said, holding the dog steady, and 'a straight stern'. The 'stern', she inferred, was the tail.

An intelligent head on a hound, he said, was neither too narrow nor too wide. It wanted a deep chest for good-sized lungs and a powerful engine of a heart. The nose mattered even more than the eyes, because it was the scent of the prey that drew the hounds on till they cornered or treed their prey.

After asking if it was alright to do so, she bent to pat it, but she stumbled back at the force of his muzzle in her crotch. She blushed hotly but the keeper laughed, saying something about 'scent' she couldn't make out, and irrationally, she hated him for his laughter, the intrusion, for the over-familiarity. He was handsome, confident on his feet, with a sly cock to his chin, and perhaps he'd imagined that gave him the right, with her there on her own. Had she not thought he would have been amused by her complaint, she would have reported him. To put him in his place. But that wasn't what she wanted. Not actually. As it was, she hated England for all its enforced 'places': its subservience; its infinite, tacit hierarchies; its taut smiles and simmering resentments. Yet, if she stayed in Europe much longer, its 'ways' would be *in* her, a part of her, and she would – were she then to return to the States – find her homeland, with its comparative immaturity, ease and easy affluence, forever wanting.

She and Jack spoke only as much as was necessary to avoid drawing the attention of his family. She was, officially, having a 'restful' time ('after the baby') with her sister. He was 'working hard'. He filled their brief long-distance calls with politics. The British and French had landed over a thousand paratroopers along the Suez Canal. The President was furious with Anthony Eden; Ike had warned the British not to invade, but, being the British, they had assumed they knew better. Privately, she couldn't bring herself to care.

Within a few weeks, rumors of a divorce no one had discussed reached the offices of *Time*. Joe Sr., not Jack, sent word via Lee. Jackie had to make up her mind.

She returned to Hyannis Port in mid-November, in time for the photograph for the Kennedy clan Christmas card of 1956. Inwardly, if not outwardly, she was changed. She carried a sense of another self she might have been, in France perhaps, or possibly England; of other truths glimpsed. Perhaps that was why, she realized only now, she'd not taken up the prize job with *Vogue Paris* when offered it years before, or the interview with the C.I.A.'s Paris office. She might never have returned.

It did mean, however, that she was no longer, in her own assessment of herself, consistent. Her 'porcelain' self had chips and cracks. She no longer recognized the woman who had formerly dispensed worthy advice and served as a winsome example to other young wives. Her sense of humor grew sharper, cleverer, and more wayward. She became, at once, less shy and more private. She minded loneliness less. She read endlessly while her husband traveled the country. She listened to fewer people in the Kennedy 'world'. It was a calming thing, self-possession. She had, too, come to understand the spell of bodies, of presence, and with it, the power of silence, including her own.

All the while, she grew more and more active behind-the-scenes in Jack's campaign. 'None of this means anything, anything at all, if you're not with me,' he'd said quietly, to her back one night, when he'd sensed she was awake.

She'd lain still and hadn't replied. They had agreed. He knew they had. Him as much as her. She didn't want to spoil his chances – and she wouldn't. But if he didn't win the Party nomination, they'd separate, officially.

Even so, as the campaign took shape, she helped him to see that, in the political sphere, it wasn't popularity he had to strive for, but an ability to convey sympathy, whether it was to a packed high-school gymnasium or a lone farmer when he shook his hand. As he rehearsed his speeches, she advised him how and when to gesture. She found fitting quotations and resonant phrases for him to incorporate. Jack never spoke down to anyone. It never occurred to him to do so – and she knew that was his greatest and most natural gift, one which neither Joe Sr. nor his team fully understood or appreciated.

For most of her life, she had got life right enough. She had been pleasing. She had pleased her teachers. She had pleased her college professors. She had pleased the magazines and the Kennedy press team. She had walked with the book always balancing on her head. Now she *was* the book, and all that lay unspoken between the lines troubled her dreams at night.

She didn't deceive herself. She knew that, even in all that was wrong with Jack's 'girling', there were probably times, with a naked stranger, when an enlargement of life *was* possible; of life feeling fuller, more than it could otherwise be in the day-to-day, year-in-year-out marathon of a marriage. The transience of those encounters didn't necessarily annul that 'enlargement' of experience, of life, as much as she might want it to; nor did the claims that such encounters were only about physical sensation or quick gratification. 'Society' simply needed to pretend it believed that. Everyone needed, collectively, to agree that such encounters were meaningless. In that way, although never quite sanctioned, they could continue.

Did most married men cheat on their wives? She was fairly sure the majority did – but the deception, she believed, lay as much in the words 'It meant nothing' as in the act itself. *Love, sex, all that sort of stuff, just water-ices. Lick it up and forget it. If you don't hang on to it in your mind, it's nothing. Sex especially – nothing.*

The unfortunate truth was that a fling or an affair didn't have to be deeply personal to be meaningful. The impersonal, it dawned on her, didn't preclude intimacy. Who didn't sometimes need the sudden flare of transformation? Who wasn't afraid of being cut off from the quick of life? Her husband was no different than others. Women and wives *also* wanted nothing less than life – a *felt* life – but the stakes for them, for her – were normally too great to risk. Even well-off women she knew depended on the clothing budgets and 'pin money' their husbands bestowed. And actually, when it came to it, she wanted transformation *with* Jack, her charismatic, adored husband, no one else. But sun-gods, she had come to understand, were – perhaps, by their very nature – incapable of singular beams of love.

She raged inwardly at some point most days, humiliated. But if she couldn't forgive her husband – and why should she? – she did understand him, better than she wanted to. Jack was a man who ran deep; he was a spiritual man, if not in the church-and-incense way that Bobby was. Jack, she knew, craved that rawest form of soul – the exclamation point of life-force, ejaculation, the transcendence of the body. Having come close to death, first in the war on his patrol-boat and then, twice, on the operating table, he needed – over and over again – the sensation of, the explosion of, life itself.

The intensity of physical pleasure was one thing; raw life shining back in the eyes of a complete stranger was, she imagined, another. Everything else in the world – including those traumatic moments of near-death – dissolved as he climaxed, as it did for others in the moments of a first requited love, or childbirth, or when a person received the last rites.

Including her, of course. She dissolved. Her body, her self, their marriage. She dissolved from his every thought at such times. How could she not when he was all 'exclamation', all life-force, all going-off-like-a-gun? She longed to be a romantic, but life had forced a realism – a hard-edged pragmatism – upon her.

The wound ran deep. Even so, she refused to pretend to herself that she didn't understand; she refused to lie to herself. She also refused to be a martyr to the pain, as some women were. She could actually understand the way a person might be changed by near-death, the way Jack might have been. She herself had felt that dark rip-tide, when she had survived death and her tiny daughter had not.

That black tide rushed in again before long, and claimed her beloved, dissolute father in August of '57, minutes before she arrived at his bedside.

Almost two years ago already.

Time was dizzying.

Then, Caroline was born a month before Christmas of that same year – their own small miracle – and Jack, euphoric. They both were. They were a family at last.

He made the cover of *Time* that December, thanks to a 'donation' of $75,000 by Joe Sr. to the magazine. At Christmas dinner, Jack had her doing her impressions of Castro, Nixon and the Queen. It was a talent she'd honed at school, when she'd impersonated the teachers for the girls, to compensate for the approval she won all too easily from the staff. Jack had laughed till he'd had to wipe tears away.

Within the year, he was preoccupied again, both restive and energized. The scent he trailed home, when he did come home, was L'Heure Bleue. Julie, his campaign's PR girl, wore it.

Jackie had always liked the younger woman's style.

She had liked it because it was her own.

In their house on Irving Avenue, the Nantucket Sound itself seemed, once more, to lie between them. It was a premature old age, she thought, the sexlessness, the not-being-touched. She was twenty-nine. They had not yet been married six years.

'Again, again, again!' Caroline had shouted yesterday as she'd dangled her daughter's red-booted feet in and out of the surf. They'd filled their pockets with delicate orange and yellow shells. Caroline's childish hands had grabbed and smacked at her arms, hips, legs and face. Her toddler's touch had earthed her and comforted her; it also made the physical hunger all the sharper.

I love thee, Mellors had said to Constance, *an' th' touch on thee*. It was enough. She could understand how Lady Chatterley could give up her 'life' – her marriage, title, status, even her country – to find a life. To be not only loved, but beloved. It didn't require Wragby Hall. It didn't require the White House.

Sometimes, when she looked at their endless photos, it was as if she were looking at another person's life. The more documented it was, the more unreal it grew.

After this flying visit to New York, when she returned to the Cape, there would be more pictures – for *Newsweek* this time. Jack was going to be their June cover. She'd chosen his suit. He might allow her to comb a little hairspray through his hair.

For her part, when necessary on those occasions, she knew how to hold the gaze of the lens and how to project herself within it. She knew how to position her hands to hide her nails, which were often bitten to the quick, an old habit she'd struggled to break in spite of the art mistress at Farmington painting them in something yellow and foul-tasting. She knew how to summon something of the inner while yielding to the outer; to the eye of the photographer. One had to let oneself be taken.

In her dream of the night before, she had been holding the hardback of the banned novel as Constance spoke to her directly. 'I myself was a figure somebody had read about.' It was Lady Chatterley's private thought in the novel, shared, almost conspiratorially, with her. They had stood face-to-face, wearing identical clothing: Lady Chatterley's gray woolen dress, her light coat, dark gray *All grey, all grey! The world looked worn out* and on their feet, Connie's rubber tennis-shoes. 'I myself *was a figure somebody had read about.*'

She didn't need a psychoanalyst to interpret her dream.

Yet what woman in her situation – with Jack, Caroline and Irving Avenue – could fail to be happy? *Connie was the hostess men liked so much, so modest, yet so attentive and aware, with big, wide blue eyes and a soft repose that sufficiently hid what she was really thinking. Connie had played this woman so much, it was almost second nature to her: but still, decidedly second.*

As Mrs. John F. Kennedy closed the door of the family apartment behind her, only one detail of her appearance suggested anything other than effortless composure. Only it pointed to a first nature, a first self, hiding within a second. The clasp of her purse wouldn't close over the contraband.

Normally a car arrived in the Marguery's inner courtyard to pick up members of Joseph Kennedy's family. Appearing at the main entrance, she had caught the elderly doorman off guard. He opened the door instantly and stepped quickly out after her to hail her a Checker cab. He looked concerned, but she shook her head. 'It's a short walk only, thank you,' she said. What else could he do but touch two fingers to his cap as she moved past him onto Park Avenue?

Fog sat like a lid on the corridors of the city. She turned onto East 47th. It had been overcast and raining on and off, for days, although up ahead, it seemed the sky might be clearing. She could make out the white towers of St. Patrick's, two still points above the stream of hats, briefcases, cars, trams, dripping trees, blinking lights and shoeshine boys wiping down their boxes.

Tires hissed against the wet street. She kept her head down and walked briskly, checking twice to make sure none of the Marguery's security men were following her. Would the doorman have said anything to anyone? It wasn't impossible. Her father-in-law was on a first-name basis with each of those men, and was often on the phone to the hotel manager. He'd taken two family apartments, plus he was in talks about renting twenty-five of their offices for Jack's leadership campaign.

She had to think fast. The lunch counters were filling up. At West 48th, two well-dressed girls waited beside one of the new photo booths: '4 poses for 25¢' – aspiring models or actresses. A man-sized Planters' Peanut tipped his top-hat to her and waved his cane as he proffered peanuts in shiny foil bags. *Pillow Talk* with Doris Day was still playing. At the theater, two Negro women in cleaners' smocks waited at the Colored Entrance. When she smiled hello in passing, they looked away.

She'd look away too if she were them. Had she imagined it would brighten their day, a nicely dressed white lady noticing them as she walked by? How ridiculous she was.

At the burnished door of the Bergdorf Goodman, she dashed in beneath its flag and plaster insignias, and took the elevator to the third floor, to Ladies' Outdoor Wear. It was mostly empty except for mature, wealthy women with nothing to do and nowhere to be. There were worse fates, she supposed, but, there and then, she couldn't think of any.

'Would you like to try one, madam?' She'd been scanning a rail of raincoats. 'We have a mirror over—'

'Thank you, no.' She produced a quick smile, glanced at her watch, then passed the girl a coat and pulled a few bills from the inside pocket of her purse. 'Just ring it up, would you, and clip the tags, please?'

At the cash, the three clerks looked on, smiling tightly. One of them checked the sky through the plate-glass window. She was buying a plain navy raincoat and a pair of deck-shoes. No one dared mention the exquisite coral coat she wore, the made-to-match dress, or the fact that the rain had stopped.

The most senior clerk found a pair of scissors and cut the tags.

'A large bag, if you wouldn't mind.' Then she removed her gloves and her triple-strand of pearls, slid out of her coat and pulled on the raincoat. The youngest girl stared, her jaw slack.

Finally, at the main door, the Senator's wife swapped her pumps for the deck-shoes, wiped her lipstick on a tissue, and fumbled for her sunglasses. Outside, she hailed a cab.

Jack would be on his way to Florida by now. On Monday, he was flying to Oregon. He confessed to being nervous there'd be no turn-out on the West Coast. She knew from Jerry, his 'advance man', that sometimes as few as ten people showed up at venues out there.

He'd flown her in for just one event last week. Then he'd taken her into a cubicle in a men's room in a steel plant in Gary, West Virginia. He'd dropped to his knees, to the dirty floor, and for a moment, the image of him on the kneeler in the Kennedy family pew at St. Francis's superimposed itself in her mind. He opened her coat and lifted her skirt. The coat-hook on the door prodded her back. She could see a scrap of toilet tissue stuck to the sole of his shoe. In the dingy light of the men's room, her husband – the country's most charismatic senator – looked older, hungry and almost weak with need.

Then he closed the toilet lid, unzipped his trousers and drew her onto him.

She hid her face in her husband's chest as he raised her hips and lowered them again, moving her fluently onto him. His hands weren't tender, but she'd marveled at the ease with which he maneuvred her, until he rolled forward, muffling his moan in her coat collar.

When he lifted his head, his eyes were cracked and glassy. His skin looked sallow. Her garter clip was broken. She'd have to go stockingless and hope no one noticed before their car came. It was lucky they were leaving. She had tried to give herself to the moment, but the experience was gone from his eyes before he opened the cubicle door.

Later, he was apologetic, about rumpling her clothes, about his mind being elsewhere, about his lack of delicacy, the rush, the location. That's why he needed others, she supposed. Girls. Or Julie. Usually Julie. No man wanted to apologize to his wife for wanting what he wanted, even if he'd only ever marry a woman who looked like she needed apologizing to.

She remembered now as she hopped into the cab with her shopping bag: in her dream of the night before, Lady Chatterley wasn't 'Lady Chatterley' or even 'Connie', but Constance.

Constance.

Constancy.

She dreamed of it.

On the heady night of Jack's election to his second term in the Senate in '58, Jerry had made a joke before he'd realized she'd entered the room. 'Oh, I'm the advance-man, alright. I make all the advances. Then Jack, the good-looking bastard, saunters in and lands all the girls!' Someone, Pierre, Jack's press secretary, laughed.

Of course she played dumb – the ingénue – the classic female act of damage-limitation. Pierre looked at his feet, crippled with embarrassment, although he'd only laughed at the joke. Jerry had cracked it. But it wasn't a joke, of course, and that's why Pierre couldn't meet her eye. She liked him. He played piano beautifully – he'd been trained at a conservatoire in Canada – but had told almost no one because it didn't seem patriotic, acquiring something so special in Canada.

'Has anyone seen my mint julep?' she said. All five men, Jack's 'Kitchen Cabinet', rushed to get her a drink.

On her wedding night, it had surprised her to learn that Jack said his prayers, on his knees by the bed, every night before he slept. She found herself moved by the sight, through half-closed eyes, of the deepening wrinkles on his face as his lips silently worked the air. It wasn't so much religious, she thought, as superstitious. He was half-consumed with guilt while the other half, she imagined, feared he might have to pay, if he didn't demonstrate due reverence, for his own great luck in life.

She found it ironic that his Catholicism was such a political hot-potato. Had it been Bobby running in the race, she would have understood, but Jack, by his own admission, was mostly a 'disinterested' Catholic. As for 'the girling', as his team called it, that was not Jack's biggest secret, not even as a supposedly good Catholic husband, nor was it the secret most carefully managed by his campaign team.

The real secret of course was the state of his health. In their courting days, seven years ago, in the back of his two-door Plymouth, she'd discovered his back brace – a tightly bound medical corset hidden by a wide bandage. He'd explained haltingly, telling her about the time he was blindsided in a tackle on the football field at Harvard; then came the war injury, his boat blown in two.

He'd been the patrol-boat's pilot when he navigated her one night bang in the middle of a Japanese destroyer's path. 'I got home expecting to be court-martialed,' he said, blushing. 'Instead my father spoke to some people in Washington and got them to say I was a hero.'

They'd met at a dinner party, hosted by a couple they were each friendly with in Washington. They chatted in passing over bowls of chicken casserole, and the meal was followed by charades, at which she excelled. He sought her out. He was attractive, she decided – tall, rangy with large gray-blue eyes and a tanned face. More than that, he had a lovely ease about him, a compelling nonchalance. He asked questions. Everything, everybody fascinated him, it seemed. He watched more than he spoke. He had a certain reserve, and she discovered he loved books. She could see he was a reader of people too, and shrewd with it; she could feel that in him – as if he had learned early in a big family how to measure needs and greed and hope. But if he was shrewd and watchful, he was generous too. And he loved a good joke. His laughter was quiet – a deep chuckling – but his eyes lit up with it. He had mischief in him.

She was not his usual 'bombshell' of a girl. She knew that. She was slim-hipped, small-breasted. She didn't know then that he'd told Bobby that Jacqueline Bouvier was 'fey'.

She promptly ended the relationship everyone had assumed would end in a gold band on her finger. But she only fell in love with Jack Kennedy months later, one night in his car, for the way he'd searched her face; for his worry over what she'd think about the truth of his war record and his grim back-brace.

He didn't tell her that, in spite of his injury, he'd swum out and towed a badly burned man back to the wreck of their boat, gripping the man's life-jacket with his teeth most of the way. Or that he'd then towed him another three-and-a-half miles to a remote island, while the other men followed, floating two of the crew, who couldn't swim, on planks from the wreckage. Bobby told her all that only much later.

Jack himself couldn't take any pride in his Purple Heart or any of the honors because two men died that day. His mistake had cost them their lives. Nor would he ever complain about the, at times, debilitating pain in his back. Only his doctors, Bobby and the closest members of his campaign team knew how bad it was, and they only knew because it was their job to keep everyone else from knowing. At home on Irving Avenue, away from the cameras, her husband favored a rocking chair.

The Addison's was making matters even worse. His muscles had started to waste. He was getting skinny and turning yellow. So she chose straight-collared white shirts for him, narrow, patterned ties, and conservative, double-breasted suits to give him more breadth and square shoulders.

She had him brush his teeth once a week with a peroxide rinse. She persuaded him to use the best face powder from Paris for his *Face the Nation* interview on CBS in February. He'd been in particular pain that day, but his brace had allowed him to sit up straight for just long enough to do the interview. She'd wrapped the bandage herself, to just below his nipples, in a tight figure-of-eight.

In time, with the cortisone prescribed for the Addison's, he began to put on weight, and she ensured he was the picture of sun-tanned health and boyish energy at the age of nearly forty-two.

He could strip an engine as easily as he could raise a sail, and he would enthusiastically shake hands on the campaign trail at farm shows, assembly halls and union canteens, as if each hand offered was the first of the night.

She also had no doubt that he could determine, with a hand on the small of a back, whether a call-girl was wearing a wire in her lingerie. She knew he liked sex in hotel pools, with that day's receptionist or the restaurant hostess. All that warm water on his back. Sometimes a sauna. In their early days, he'd told her that he got headaches if he didn't have sex every day, and in the Big House, she sometimes saw the bills for the private pool parties and the agency girls on Joe Sr.'s desk. At one big family barbecue, Joe Sr. had declared, with a bark of a laugh, that he should have had Jack gelded as a boy.

One night, when Jack was home on the Cape, in a fleeting break from the campaign trail, she had rolled onto him, tentatively, playfully. She'd sat up, straddling him, her stocking-tops pressed to his ribcage. She brought her hands to her breasts and ran her thumbs over her nipples. But an awkward look had crossed his face and he'd eased her off, saying, gently but unhappily, that she didn't have to do that, to make a show of herself, to degrade herself like that for him.

She hadn't realized she was.

Nor was it a conversation either of them knew how to have.

He was twelve years older. He loved the way other men looked at her. He said he loved her charm, her intelligence and her grace. But she knew he looked elsewhere for sex appeal. Mystique was not the same thing as allure. She knew that too. Mystique distanced. Allure beckoned.

She asked the cab driver to let her out at the corner of 7th Avenue. She wanted to walk the last block. She needed to clear her head and calm herself. On the corner, a street entertainer was thrusting his hat at passers-by, but he didn't miss a beat. He was singing 'The

Assassination of President McKinley', and its jaunty tune came back to her as she walked by. At Farmington, they'd often sung it over Saturday-night campfires.

Yonder come the train, she coming down the line
Blowing every station, Mr. McKinley is a-dying
It's hard times, it's hard times

Look-it here, you rascal, you see what you've done
You shot my husband with that Iver-Johnson gun
I'm carrying you back, to Washington …

The shopping bag with her coral coat was sweaty in her grip. She walked up West 31st, took a left onto 8th Avenue, and rushed up the G.P.O.'s fifteen-foot flight of steps. A wave of nerves overcame her in the Corinthian colonnade, and she had to pause to calm the knocking of her heart.

The contraband bulged in her purse. If she were among the last to arrive for the hearing she would be able to slip in the back unnoticed. Not that she was much in the habit of being recognized, or not at least when Jack wasn't with her.

She looked up to the ornate ceiling in the reception. She had last been here as a girl, before she was sent to school in Connecticut, waiting as her mother mailed Christmas parcels. It seemed no less grand now. The reception was a long gallery of Beaux Arts splendor and hush. It was like entering a temple.

At the desk, a security man with a deep voice and large, almost feminine, eyes asked if she would like to leave her coat and bag at the coat-check. It was a polite instruction to do so. Ahead of her, all the other arrivals were handing over their things. 'No, thank you,' she said, and she moved quickly past his desk, dipping her face.

Farmington had taught each of its pupils how to cultivate a persona – not to be false, but to present the exterior that would permit each girl, when she grew to be a woman, to pass through society without drawing attention. The aim, she came to understand, was not the effacement of the self, but rather, the creation of a private space *within*, the only truly private life most society women could hope to enjoy.

From the time the girls woke, the resilience of their public exteriors was tested daily, with routine reminders of one's faults, bad habits and physical flaws. She was too shy, she was told. She was a Roman Catholic; she would naturally refrain from any 'Catholic ways'. Did she know? In England, Catholics were not permitted to be Prime Ministers or members of the Royal Family, and divorced people could not attend Ascot. Her parents were both Catholic and divorced; it was a double stain, one which she would need to strive to overcome in her life.

She was lucky to be at Farmington, and they were sure she would work hard to make the school proud, in spite of her shortcomings. She liked too many solitary pursuits – horses and books. She must ask herself why. It was important to join in, to be a Farmington girl. She must ensure she had correct thoughts. She mustn't assume she was beautiful. She had a fine neck and shoulders but her calves were thick and, at size 10½, her feet were decidedly large. She was big-boned but she would appear slim if she chose her clothes carefully. Her eyebrows were heavy. She should tweeze. She would need to use depilatory cream on her legs. Dark-haired girls were unfortunate like that. Her diction was halting and her projection poor; she must see the elocution teacher in her own free time. Public speaking was a must at Farmington.

One of the maids, an Irish girl called Siobhan, glimpsed her behind her dressing-screen one morning – for each girl was expected to use the screen by her bed – and Siobhan whispered loudly to the other maid that Jackie had 'a right bush' – from which Jackie gleaned that her pubic hair was being discussed. Behind the screen, she shrank. Siobhan called to her that hopefully it wouldn't 'spook horse or lad!' Jackie remained crouched where she was for at least twenty minutes, until she was sure the maids had moved to the other end of the corridor.

Each Farmington girl's special quality was meant to be 'grace under pressure', as *Vogue* magazine described it. They were permitted *Vogue* and *Town & Country* but not *Mademoiselle* or *True Stories*. They were to learn by implication – not by instruction – that the more adept one was at *seeming*, the more allowance one would have, privately, to *be*.

The alumnae, or the 'Ancients' of Farmington, were a source of apparently undiluted pride for the school, and the headmistress had written to her personally after reading the news of her engagement to a senator in the society pages. 'I knew the very day I met you that you would be a shining example of a "Farmington girl".'

Upstairs in the G.P.O., she entered the long hall where the hearing was about to start. The sun streamed through arched windows, making the space unexpectedly warm. Or perhaps it was the press of bodies. The floors were waxed and polished. The ceiling was high and studded with keystones and ceiling roses. It was larger and more impressive than most courtrooms, not that she'd seen any to know.

There was a crowd. For *a book*. Who would have thought? A few chairs were empty in the back row but only a few. She sat at last, after all the rush. She couldn't slip out of or even unbutton her new – dry – raincoat, because who would wear a coral silk dress to a G.P.O. hearing?

A cordon-rope separated the public from the table of judicial recorders. The gallery seemed to be filled with publishing people, the friends, she supposed, of the publisher Barney Rosset and Grove Press, plus eccentrics from the Village, and perhaps a few academics. Professor Trilling himself, from Columbia, sat beside her. How remarkable. She tried to steal sidelong glances. She'd seen his photo in the literary press.

A pan-handler in sodden clothes was looking for a place to dry out after the morning rain. National representatives of the Catholic

Women's League sat in a somber row. But mostly it was press and legal types.

She spotted Judith Crist from the *Herald-Tribune* and felt a hot flicker of envy. She'd had plans herself before she was married. Being a reporter had seemed like a ticket to the world.

At one point, after her study-abroad year in Paris, she'd almost started a career in the C.I.A. The fear was that France would succumb, post-war, to Communism, as an estimated third of its population was Communist. It was a risk the C.I.A. had wanted to counter quickly and, where possible, through art, literature and liberal values. She had easily imagined herself as a part of that mission, in the Paris bureau.

Her French was still quite fluent in those days, and she'd been determined to perfect it. For an entire year, she'd already been steeped in Art History and French Literature. She still marveled at the way the knowledge of another language was a magic door to a second life, a second self. At Farmington, she had always tried to hide her thirst for knowledge, but in Paris, in her study year, she'd learned not to be ashamed of it. The freedom had been exhilarating.

She missed Paris even now, all of it: the gritty stories of the Resistance; the street artists and potters she used to speak to on her way to her lectures – on Existentialism, Camus and Sartre – at the Sorbonne and at Reid Hall. She missed the elegant society of Faubourg Saint-Germain; the bells of Paris ringing the angelus; the strange ease of being Catholic in a Catholic country; the horse-riding in the Bois de Boulogne; *picon-citron* and gossip at Le Select, where Fitzgerald and Hemingway had once lingered; lunches at the Brasserie Balzar on the rue des Écoles. She even missed her ration card and the dreaded adventure of Turkish toilets in cafés and restaurants.

Evenings had been spent at the theater, or dancing to records by Claude Luter and Edith Piaf. Weekend afternoons were gallery time … She discovered a love of Corot, of his quiet, silvery landscapes, tender and melancholy. When asked by a friend which painting she would remove from a gallery wall and take home if she could, she chose Corot's *Diana and Actaeon*, based on the story from Ovid's *Metamorphoses* and set in a muted but verdant woodland. She still loved the enigma of Diana: her sacred privacy, her woman's sensuality.

The head of the C.I.A., Allen Dulles, was a friend of her stepfather, and after graduating with her B.A. in French Literature, she'd gone so far as to fill out the application for the Paris bureau and its new team. Then, another idea struck. She submitted a short story for a competition and, somehow, incredibly, won first prize – a job with *Paris Vogue*.

But again, she prevaricated until it was too late. Perhaps she'd feared she'd go and never come back. What if she had? Who was that other self who never was? Did that woman dream in French? Did she make witty asides at Parisian dinner parties?

Upstairs in the G.P.O., there was no jury for the hearing. It was a hearing and not a trial, she heard the *New York Times* man explain to the cub reporter beside him. Charles D. Ablard, a Post Office functionary, was to hear the case. He was generally well-liked and respected – he 'ran a good hearing', the *New York Times* man said. The case had been brought against Grove Press by the New York Postmaster, Ablard's own boss.

'In other words, a perfectly level playing field,' the *Times* man smirked.

Barney Rosset, the publisher, was accused of using the U.S. Mails to ship his dirty books, and he didn't, the *Times* man predicted, 'have a hope in hell'. The book was banned from the mails thirty years before, and the Postmaster General wasn't about to change things now, whatever Rosset had got into his mind to try in 1959, and no matter how good a hearing Mr. Ablard ran. Officialdom, the *Times* journalist said, only had time for lazy thinking: obscenity was obscenity was obscenity. So the Postmaster General of the U.S. Mails had duly instructed the New York Postmaster, and a few days later, Rosset was sent his hearing date: May 14th. None of it was remotely surprising – except the eye-watering speed of the action.

Rosset's lawyer, a Charles Rembar, had never tried a case before, and had had just two weeks to prepare. He and Rosset knew each other, apparently, 'from some weekend tennis court' in the Hamptons. But Saul Mindel, acting for the New York Postmaster, was 'an old hand at this sort of case'.

She opened her purse. Apart from a bit of cash, a lipstick and a compact, the book, square and solid, filled it. It might have been an academic tome, with its dull beige cover. Yet she'd somehow spotted it in the bookstore on Main Street in Hyannis before all the brou-haha had broken out. She had always loved Lawrence's work – she used to study his short stories, and of course she'd read his better-known novels, including *Lady Chatterley's Lover* in the censored edition Farmington had had in its library, a book which only girls over sixteen were allowed to take out.

Once the Post Office action hit the news, the owner of the Hyannis bookstore told the local paper that the New York Postmaster had no business interfering with his trade there on Cape Cod. Just let them *try* to confiscate his stock, he fumed. *His* shipment had not trav-eled through the U.S. Mails but by car, his own, a non-commercial vehicle, in four journeys from New York City to Hyannis. Only the G.P.O. and American Customs had bans on the book. Commercial delivery trucks might get stopped, but a man's car, the bookstore man said, was nobody's business but his own.

It was a loophole, and he'd used it, reducing the quantities per journey so he could claim 'personal use' if his car was ever stopped crossing a state border. 'Souvenirs, Officer!' That was going to be his line, but, in the end, he hadn't needed it. God, he told his customers, had been watching over their 'porn'.

She paid the paperboy to go into Hyannis and buy her a copy before they sold out. The next morning, it was wrapped in the *Cape Cod Times* and sitting in their mailbox on Irving Avenue. Jack passed it to her with a wry, warm smile. 'Don't let Mrs. Clyde catch you or she'll be dragging you off to Confession.'

That morning, she managed to avoid both Mrs. Clyde and the Secret Service Agent who patrolled their patio and flower beds. She walked across the lawns to the Big House, with its wide views of the Sound. The water had been churned up by the storm of the night before, but the sky was pewter-bright. She cloistered herself in the sun-room and read the novel straight through in a day and a morn-ing. 'Was it actually her destiny,' Connie mused on her marriage, 'to go on weaving herself into his life all the rest of her life?'

Jack was biding his time before he declared his candidacy for the Democratic nomination. Would they separate, as planned, if he didn't succeed? She was unsure what she felt from one day to the next, but she did know that, in this moment as she waited for the hearing to begin, she felt excited in a way she hadn't since her days on the

Herald-Tribune. There in the back row at the end of the aisle, she felt something fizz, bright and angry-hot, within.

The hearing recorders and the lawyers entered the hall from a side door and took their seats behind long, gleaming tables at the front. Then, all rose and the room fell silent for Mr. Ablard, the Hearing Examiner.

She laid her book, like a missal, on her chair and stood, noticing as she turned back, at the other end of her row, seven or eight seats away, a man in a gray woolen overcoat. He clutched a folded umbrella. Like her, he had not surrendered his things at the coat-check, and oddly, for the day was warm, he also kept his coat on and buttoned.

He was forty perhaps. Tall, of average build. She couldn't see anything distinctive about his face. But his hands on the umbrella caught her attention. They were cracked and scaly with what looked like eczema and, as if he felt her assessment, he turned toward her in that moment, and she turned away.

Everyone was taking their seats. *Yonder come the train, she comin' down the line.* That tune again, in her head. Above them all, the gilt on the keystones flashed in a surge of midday light.

Mr. Charles D. Ablard formally opened the proceedings from his desk on a low stage at the front of the room. From the back row, she could hardly see him, but his voice resonated, she could hear every word, her plan had worked and, within moments – while her face expressed sober interest only – she was absorbed.

Constance Chatterley was married to an injured war-hero – a hero in a wheelchair, if not a back-brace. Sir Clifford loved his wife for the excellence of her company and her grace as a hostess, but he did not know her, and Connie had a dead ache within.

The heroine of the novel would be twenty-nine years old when she finally succeeded in making a life, *her* life, for herself; when she gave birth to her first child, her lover Mellors's child; when they made a home together, far away from Wragby Hall, in Canada, in British Columbia, a new Britain for them perhaps. Jackie knew English people had been flocking to that coast since the days of Empire. Its woodland was supposed to be ancient and beautiful, the winters mild, the soil rich. Connie, she liked to imagine, would be able to roam. She'd paint and sketch – she'd carry on. Vancouver

Island. Victoria. Prince George. The Queen Charlotte Islands. She knew the names because Jack sometimes used to pull out the charts; he had a dream of sailing that coast one day.

Twenty-nine was her own age. It was the age a woman was supposed to remain for ever.

That morning, first thing, she'd found the back-street bookie's her late father, 'Black Jack' Bouvier III – a New Yorker by both birth and inclination – had faithfully visited years before. The place was still there, with the Mission soup kitchen across the street and the barber shop next door. It was a spot where she'd waited many times as a teenager on the sidewalk outside. Nothing had changed except the sign on the bookie's door, lit up now in electric-blue.

A woman has to live her life, or live to repent not having lived it.

They gave her thirty-to-one odds against Lady Chatterley.

The Ladies' Home Journal
At issue today is whether this particular book can go through the mails. To that end, I have one question I would like to ask you with reference to your role as an esteemed literary critic. Does the reading of Lady Chatterley's Lover *in its entirety tend to excite lustful thoughts?*

I must preface my response by saying that Lawrence is considered to be the most significant English novelist after Joseph Conrad. He developed a consistent social and moral philosophy, one of 'naturalness', that is to say that the mind and body should not be separate. It was his last novel and he was trying—

Would you say that the description of sexual encounters in this book is germane to the expression of those ideas?

There is no language in the book that is <u>extrinsic</u> to the purpose. Moreover, I do not find anything in Lady Chatterley's Lover *that essentially I can't find in the* Ladies' Home Journal.

Silence, please, silence. The witness will continue.

I only mean that it is what marriage counselors are telling their counselees five days a week. The idea of fulfillment in the marriage state has become enormously common. At the present time, there is not one word printed in Lady Chatterley's Lover *that has not heretofore appeared in a reputable work of fiction. I would contend that there no longer exists a … a secret language of males. That has been abolished.*

Objection! Your witness, Mr. Rembar, is a literary critic. He is in no way qualified to give an opinion on obscenity and impact upon the average individual.

May I in turn point out, Mr. Mindel, that we don't have a jury here!

And may I say, Examiner, that I don't especially appreciate the personal comments of the Defense.

Mr. Mindel, I in no way meant to imply— I know neither of us is in the business of performing. I was not suggesting—

Then I will repeat my question to your witness. Does the reading of Lady Chatterley's Lover *in its entirety tend to excite lustful thoughts?*

The Encyclopedia Britannica
You are familiar with all the words in the novel? The so-called Anglo-Saxon words, as we politely refer to them? Would you agree with the Encyclopedia

Britannica's conclusion that Lawrence as an author was obsessed by the problems of sex?

I would disagree with the Encyclopedia Britannica. *His thought was very much concentrated on the subject of sex relationships but I would not call it an obsession—*

On behalf of my witness, I must strenuously object, Examiner! We don't even know if that is what it says in the Encyclopedia Britannica.

Would the recorders please note: Counsel have stipulated that this type-written page, purporting to be an excerpt from the Encyclopedia Britannica, Volume 13, 1946, page 796, may be received in evidence.

There we have it, Mr. Rembar. We are enlightened.

The Caretaker?
As I understand this book, the principal character, Lady Chatterley, obtained no fulfillment of her marriage, and that was why she was engaged in these sexual encounters with Mr. Mellors, the caretaker; also, with a writer and a visitor at her own home, the home of Lord Chatterley; and earlier than that with certain young men while she was staying in Germany—

Objection! That was prior to her marriage.

Yes, Mr. Rembar: I said 'earlier'. I put it to your witness: How does that fit into your concept that this thematic line drives the reader towards the idea of fulfillment, sexual fulfillment, in marriage?

It does in that she and Mellors are trying very hard to get married.

Isn't it a fact that for a while she thought she was in love with yet another man, the writer … Machells?

Yes, but that is the promiscuity that Lawrence feels makes people unhappy; it is this unhappiness that he is revealing rather than recommending.

Yet when she began her alliance with Mellors, the caretaker, you say there was then love between them also, and that this new relationship is excused as part of the theme of the book?

Not excused: it became a very deep relationship. Lawrence considered it a true marriage, whether or not they were able to be formally married.

Mixed Company
Is it your feeling that the so-called four-letter words are vital and indispensable?

Yes. Lawrence was trying to remove sentimentality – a false sort of emotion – from the sexual act and, at the same time, to reveal passion and tenderness.

Tenderness *was the original title of this book. He used the dirty words in a way that nobody who was used to using dirty words would use them.*

So, in your view then, they are no longer 'the secret language of men' – as you described it earlier?

No, not any longer.

And yet you would be terribly reluctant to use such language here today, wouldn't you?

...

Please answer the question.

Yes.

Yes, you would be?

Yes.

Do you recall the description of the type of sexual performance that went on, where Lady Chatterley has her last night with Mellors before leaving for the Continent?

I object!

Over-ruled. Continue, Mr. Mindel.

For the record, I now ask the witness to re-read the relevant passage starting on page 297 ... Allow me now to read it aloud. 'Though a little frightened, she let him have his way, and the reckless, shameless sensuality shook her to her foundations, stripped her to the very last, and made a different woman of her. It was not really love.' Is this *the tenderness to which you refer?*

It is a complex tenderness.

'Complex,' you say? Not obscene?

I'm afraid you put me into the rather embarrassing position of having to be unable to discuss this in mixed company.

I'm sorry – would you speak up? I could not hear the last part of your statement.

I must object, Examiner!

I am merely trying to get some indication from your witness in a concrete, specific manner with relation to parts of the book in support of the statements he made. In this section, Constance Chatterley was a person almost attacked, or at least a recipient rather than jointly engaging.

The witness will reply.

I disagree. It is not obscene. Judging from the amount of genuine love she felt for her lover, she didn't feel assaulted.

Please explain then how this 'congress' fits into your concept of the natural *marital relationship, which you say is the purpose of the author.*

Lawrence said that we have no language for expressing our feelings. The whole purpose he has as a novelist here was to find a language for our feelings, a language which is usually embarrassing, for feelings which are usually left out, because our words are unequal to them. It is the sort of thing that goes beyond language, but of course he only had language. That was the challenge he embarked on in this novel and in this scene. Moreover, I must point out that it is but one aspect of one scene.

L&M Cigarettes
Examiner, if I may interrupt the cross-examination in illustration of my witness's last statement, I would like the record to show that I am calling attention to a poster advertising L&M Cigarettes, which is displayed. It is a very good example of what is abroad in the year 1959—
Objection! There is no relevance nor any similarity between the content of Lady Chatterley's Lover *with regard to sexual interest and a picture of a girl in a bathing suit.*
If I may continue? As I said, I use this by way of illustration. So far as taking words or passages out of context, if you or anyone here assembled took a particular square inch of this picture, most of us would feel we were looking at something obscene, and yet—
Objection!

Lady Constance Chatterley on Trial
Do you think Connie was ever shameless?
I think she had experiences which surprised her.
Do you think she was ever shameless?
From whose point of view?
Her own.
No, I don't.
May I draw your attention to page 298, where Lady Chatterley herself says that 'she was shameless'. What are we to make of that?
That she had cast off inhibition and shame.
And on page 267? Are we to applaud Mellors's view of her here? If you would please refresh your memory ...
All he is saying is that he is glad he is in love and living with a real woman, a woman not afraid of life.
Do the marriage counsels and the Ladies' Home Journal *advise their readers to seek extramarital sex relationships?*

Lawrence doesn't regard the relation of Lady Chatterley and Oliver Mellors as extramarital. It is a true marriage.

Despite the fact that her marriage to Lord Chatterley was still legal and binding?

Well, we might note that impotence is a ground for annulment in very many states of this, our own country.

To return to the point, do you recall the Ladies' Home Journal *advising any wife who is unable to have a child by her husband to seek an heir by someone outside her marital relationship?*

Is There an Average Reader in the House?

May I emphasize the point, Examiner, that you are to judge this book with regard to its effect <u>on the average reader</u>.

Thank you, Mr. Mindel, for reminding me of my duties. Perhaps we should get someone in the audience to identify themselves as 'an average reader' and call upon them to testify … Silence, please. Silence. Would the witness please answer the question? As a successful literary critic, are you able to determine, let alone comment on, the effect of such a novel on the <u>average</u> reader? On, in other words, the ordinary person?

Perhaps not.

Would you speak up, please?

Objection! This line of questioning is—

Over-ruled.

Let us be absolutely clear: would the witness confirm for the hearing what he just stated, namely, that as a member of an elite profession, he is not able to comment on the effect of this book <u>on ordinary people</u>?

Silence, silence, please, or I will be forced to call a recess.

I would simply say that the very fact that this book has been read and admired by thousands of people in Europe and in this country would suggest that perhaps there aren't any ordinary people; that when anybody reads a book like this, perhaps they are extraordinary.

A recess was called. She sat, blinking as the words re-arranged her. She'd never heard anyone – not in a church, not in a lecture hall – say anything quite so beautiful.

Somewhere in the corridor outside, a clock bell chimed. She glanced at her watch. She had to leave. The Examiner was unlikely to make his decision that afternoon anyway, the *Times* man said. She'd been following along in her copy, page by page, but now she closed it, wedged it under her arm, and reached for her purse.

Others in the gallery were sitting back, like amused theatergoers in the intermission. Lionel Trilling, the celebrated Columbia Professor, even turned to her, as his nearest neighbor, with a puffing of his cheeks and a shy smile, as if to say, '*Well.*' She recalled in that moment that there was a line in his *Liberal Imagination* that had mystified her. 'Unless we insist that politics is imagination and mind, we will learn that imagination and mind are politics, and of a kind we will not like.'

The imagination. He, too, was here to lend it his support.

At the front of the room, Mr. Rembar, for the Defense, sat slumped in his chair, his knuckles almost brushing the floor. But he was dynamic on his feet, she'd give him that. His witnesses, it seemed to her, had held their own against the accomplished Mr. Mindel.

A buzz of voices grew. There was the sound of chairs scraping, coughing, laughter and all the small noises which are typically made to break the spell of any ritual. She rose, dazed by – almost vibrating with – the surprise of the words spoken aloud in the G.P.O.

'Madam, don't forget your shopping!'

She turned. It was Professor Trilling, of all people.

'Thank you,' she breathed, beaming. Under her raincoat, she was hot. Her dress clung to her, and her forehead was sticky.

Then the man in the woolen coat was at the door, holding it for her. She noticed his red, sore-looking hand on the door frame. The other still gripped his umbrella. If he were leaving now, they were the only two who were. She lowered her eyes and nodded her thanks as she passed. He seemed to fiddle with the button on his umbrella. Perhaps he was going out for a smoke. Was it raining again?

She hadn't quite meant to say it out loud: 'Bad luck to open an umbrella indoors.' It was stupid of her to say, to risk drawing attention like that. Yet what could she do after she'd said it but smile tentatively and move past? Others were spilling out into the corridor, reaching for lighters, notepads and cigarettes. Was he a reporter? She thought yes, probably. Well, if he had noticed her, he hadn't seemed to recognize her.

Even so, she couldn't go into the ladies' room, as she'd planned, to change back into her coat and good shoes. He might make sense of her as she walked back up the corridor.

She'd have to change in the taxi. She'd leave the bag with the raincoat and deck-shoes on the back seat, and she would cease to be the average – no, the extraordinary – reader to whom Professor Lionel Trilling had spoken just minutes before. She would turn herself back into a junior senator's wife.

Yonder come the …

Over breakfast the next day at the Marguery, she studied the morning editions of the papers, in search of any reports of the hearing. *It's hard times, it's hard times …* It appeared in one side column, a mere four inches of print. The report said there was no decision yet from the Hearing Examiner. And thank goodness, there were no pictures either.

She relaxed and turned to an edited transcript of President Eisenhower's speech on page 2 of the *Herald-Tribune*. She needed to know what had been said. Jack might wonder.

Political differences aside, they liked the General and Mrs. Eisenhower. Once, at a Capitol Hill Thanksgiving celebration in '53, when they were still new newly-weds, the General had even crossed the lawn to congratulate them, insisting they must join him 'and Mamie' for one of their Saturday bridge nights at the White House. He said all this even though Jack had ascended into Congress, in part at least, by attacking his policies.

The General hadn't meant it of course, about the bridge nights, but it was friendly all the same. 'Ike, call me Ike.' His grin had been warm and sincere. She'd felt terribly shy of him at first, the man who had commanded the Allied forces on D-Day. But then they discovered they shared a hobby – painting. She talked about her love of watercolors; he, about his preference for oils. She told him she wasn't skillful enough for oils. Watercolors were more forgiving.

Since that chat, she and Jack always had invitations from the President's office to anything 'cultural' she in particular might enjoy. The timing of the Lincoln Center invitation – the coincidence of the day – was perfect. She could have kissed the old man.

'Here in the heart of our greatest metropolitan center, men of vision are executing a redevelopment of purpose, utility, and taste. At the Lincoln Center, Americans will have new and expanded opportunities for acquiring a real community of interest through common contact with the performing arts. American technology, labor, industry, and business are responsible for the twentieth-century freedom of the individual – making free a greater portion of his time in which to improve the mind, the body and the spirit.' She liked to think of Ike bent over his easel, concentrating on a grandchild's head, or perhaps a crab-apple tree in the Rose Garden.

'The beneficial influence of this great cultural adventure will not be limited to our borders. Here will occur a true interchange of the fruits of national cultures. From this will develop a growth that will spread to the corners of the earth, bringing with it the kind of human message that only individuals – not governments – can transmit ...'

The secret goal these days, Jack had said, was to smuggle American ideas into other countries through American talent and entertainment. Minds and souls were the new front-line. 'Soft power'. Eisenhower was a practical man, more interested in highways than concert halls, but if there was a new race of any kind, the General was not going to lose it.

The Russians, Jack said, had their own methods. They weren't stupid. They knew their modern art and entertainment would never win mass appeal – it was stuffed too full with party-approved messages. She told him she'd grown up reading the stories of Chekhov, one of her heroes. Jack told her the days of Chekhov, Tolstoy and Dostoevsky were long gone in Russia. Writers couldn't get away with actual literature anymore. That left the Soviets with one big problem: they couldn't compete with art and entertainment from the West. Which was one reason why, he told her, they had initiated – as far back as the twenties – what they called, or what was translated as, 'Active Measures'.

The aim of these 'Active Measures' was to exploit American domestic tensions, and to sow discord in the West; to weaken, frame or even bring down the democratic Establishment. The Russians were looking for the cracks, the faultlines in which to lay their slim sticks of dynamite.

Who could have imagined, she'd said, that damage on such a scale could be so nuanced?

Jack said the Soviets gave money to legitimate democratic protests, then sent in so-called supporters to agitate or use violence to discredit the activists. Opinion would then be torn, and that was the whole point. It would become distracting at best and divisive at worst.

Why bother to attack your enemy when you could get the citizens of that nation to turn on each other? It was clever, for sure. Jack said Russia had huge offices of bureaucrats dedicated to that very job. They were pouring millions into it, and the American government was running to catch up.

Eisenhower's silver shovel, she thought, must have glinted in the midday light of the Lincoln Center construction site. 'And so we break ground for the first of your great halls ...' That's what he'd said.

She wondered who had written the speech. He'd been relying more and more on speechwriters since the stroke. According to Mamie, when the General collapsed, Nixon had loitered throughout the day, waiting and expectant in the White House parlor until Mamie had finally had to ask him to leave. Then the General had surprised everyone and bounced back.

She'd always thought there was something gauche and ungainly about Nixon, in spite of all his obvious cleverness. His brooding ambition distorted his personality in some way that always made her pity him. He struck her as not just unusually private for a politician, but profoundly lonely, even when things appeared to be going his way. Pat Nixon once told her at a White House tea-party that, in his determined courtship of her, he used to drive her to and from her other dates. They hardly spoke a word in the car, Pat said, but he'd refused to give up.

That was the sort of contender he'd be, Jackie thought. Dogged, with his jaw locked around the bone of the Presidency. Unlike most men, he was someone who would humiliate himself rather than lose the prize.

Yonder come the train, she coming down the line ...

It would be months yet before Jack would even declare his candidacy, but already he was sizing up the competition, and Vice President Nixon seemed likely.

Blowing every station, Mr. McKinley is a-dying
It's hard times, it's hard times

Look-it here, you rascal, you see what you've done ...
You shot my husband with that Iver-Johnson gun

That tune, that silly tune, was going around in her head again. She shook herself, sipped her coffee, and turned to the society pages to find the pictures of the reception.

And *yes*. There she was – in pearls, silk dress and gloves – leaning in, speaking to Mrs. Eisenhower, in black-and-white, for anyone to see.

It hadn't been difficult for him to get into the hearing, even with the revolver bulging under his coat. He hadn't needed to flash his badge. After all, the Bureau had been freely intercepting mail at the General Post Office for years. The Associate Director must have sent word ahead.

The G.P.O. was one of the usual places in which the New York Field Office tested the patience of its trainee agents as they EoD'ed, or Entered on Duty. He remembered it still, the interceptions. The trick was to *not* get distracted — that's to say, entertained — by the love letters, dirty pictures, chain letters, bribery checks, suicide notes, blackmail demands and poison-pen missives which flowed from the unquiet breast of the metropolis.

Information was power.

To read the minds of the enemy was to anticipate a move before it was made.

If there wasn't an enemy, it was the Bureau's job to find one.

If an enemy couldn't be found, an enemy had to be created.

Facts could not stand in the way.

Each agent was made to understand that the F.B.I. was never to be incriminated or embarrassed. That was the cardinal rule. A badge was never to be carried during illegal break-ins, for example. If an agent was caught by local police in a black-bag job, a wet-job or a wire-tap, he understood he was on his own.

They had three weeks at the Academy in Quantico for fitness and firearms training. To qualify as a trainee, a man's vision and hearing had to be near-perfect. He had to be able to shoot by day or night, left hand or right hand, standing, kneeling, prone, or in a moving car. He had to be, and remain capable of, performing a 300-yard sprint — in a suit.

From Quantico, Harding had been transferred to the Lab in Washington for thirteen weeks of further training, Monday to Friday, from 9 a.m. to 9 p.m. On weekends, they were allowed to take Sunday morning off — for church, they were told.

He did the basic training first, choosing from the Bureau's many divisions, units and offices: field investigation, covert technical engineering, document analysis, handwriting analysis, identifications,

Bureau statistics, record-keeping, speed-typing, finger-printing, moulage-making, blood serum testing, the polygraph program, forensics, bomb data and surveillance photography. Instructions were rarely given twice. A man had to be quick, with excellent recall and good shorthand.

There were short courses on everything an agent could aspire to: Information Conveyance (live drops), Information Transfers (dead drops), Audio Enhancement (wire-taps), Safe-Cracking (soup-jobs), Device Installment (bug-planting), Necessitated Entry (break-ins), Concealed Security (booby-trapping), Evidence Collection (black-bag jobs), Lethality Ramifications (wet-jobs), and finally, the most wide-ranging of the courses, Data Composition, which covered – you name it – controlled leaks, hate mail, intimidation, false reporting, disinformation and public-alarm dissemination.

As a boy, he'd loved making pin-hole cameras. As a teenager, he'd had an old Brownie camera he'd picked up in a junk shop. He'd replaced the cracked viewfinder and fixed the stuck lever for the shutter-release. He was better with a camera than any revolver. He liked the Photo Processing Unit above all, and they'd recognized his knack.

He passed his general Bureau training, if only just, with the requisite B grade of 85 percent. It was stipulated that he was to return for refresher training every five to twelve months in the field, but he was at last awarded the agent's kit: his badge, two large notebooks which masked *The Manual of Rules and Regulations* and *The Manual of Instructions*, plus a holster and a .38-caliber revolver. He was to carry a weapon at all times.

New special agents in the New York Field Office, whatever their specialism, were tasked in their first year with mail interception at the G.P.O., with hate mail and written harassment mostly; also with trumped-up tax audit orders and the creation of and sending of forged documents. The standard aim was to sow self-destruction among the left-wing groups the Bureau, and particularly the Director, suspected. The list was endless. Only after a New York trainee had done his time at the G.P.O. was he allowed out into the field.

Agents were to be models of the clean, manly life. They were to set examples for the ranks below them. They were not to eat or drink at their desks. It was understood that 'voluntary overtime' was required. Paperwork was to be accomplished each evening and not during working hours. The Bureau required its men to file reports daily, including Sunday. Disciplinary cautions were issued for hair that was too long or too short, for five-o'clock shadows and fedoras without snap-brims, or ties that didn't match the lining of a suit jacket.

The Director himself instituted a weight reduction program, with weekly weigh-ins for all agents and dismissals for men who failed to achieve their mandatory goals. A New York agent, on a crash diet, collapsed and died at his desk. There were also written reprimands for white shirts that were not pristine, trousers without vertical creases, and reports or memoranda with grammatical or spelling errors.

'An institution is the lengthened shadow of one man.' That tenet of faith was drilled into them. The man who owned the shadow was of course J. Edgar Hoover, the Director of the Bureau. It was said that if a man walked by his side on the street, Mr. Hoover insisted that no man stepped on his shadow. There had to be a distance. He had a force-field.

So it was no coincidence that, of all the Field Offices across the nation, it was the Washington Vice Squad – near the Bureau's HQ and Hoover's office – that confiscated the uncensored Grove Press edition of *Lady Chatterley's Lover*, hot off the steamy press.

Nor was it any secret in-house that Hoover had been watching Grove Press and Barney Rosset for years, even before Senator Joe McCarthy got up and started his finger-pointing in the nightly 'Un-American' show-trials on television. Harding had seen for himself the fat file on Rosset and the directive straight from Hoover's pen.

In preparation for the G.P.O. hearing, Harding had dutifully read each Bureau memo and postal intercept, and he'd listened to the audio from the assorted tapped calls. He even saw a copy of a letter, written to Rosset by the author's widow in '54, from New Mexico of all places. Rosset had been planning this maneuver for five whole years. 'Dear Mr. Rosset,' she wrote. 'It is very bold of you to try and publish the unexpurgated Lady C. ... I wish you all good luck with this problem child.'

It was her letter that tipped them off. The trainee agent at the G.P.O. had recognized the name on the envelope, Mrs. *Frieda Lawrence Ravagli*. On the off-chance, he'd plucked it from the sorting rack.

Before the *Chatterley* books were impounded in Washington, Hoover had instructed a Field Office halfway across the country – the Chicago office – to 'discreetly obtain' a copy of this 'highly controversial book for analysis, without disclosing the Bureau's interest'. So that nothing could be trailed back to Washington HQ.

It was fundamental, everyone knew, from the most senior agent to the most junior: the F.B.I. must never be implicated.

The Chicago Special Agent in Charge found the new, uncensored Grove Press edition in a university bookstore, paid the $6 in cash, and filed the receipt. The Chicago Field Office had the book delivered – by Bureau courier – to Hoover's home within a day of his instruction. Thirtieth Place in Forest Hills – north-west Washington – was a tranquil, leafy street lined with spacious stone properties.

Hoover took possession of the contraband over his hard-boiled egg, served always in one of the porcelain egg-cups he had inherited from his mother. He liked white toast – the whiter, the better – with softened butter and black coffee in a flowered tea-cup. He read the Lawrence book, cover to cover, in four hours, in his living-room, surrounded by family pictures, framed photos of himself from the papers – some with Clyde – and three stuffed stags' heads. He'd done a speed-reading course once at night college, and he prided himself on not actually having to read a book to know what was in it.

Those pouchy eyes of his must have lit up, thought Harding, when the subversive Barney Rosset moved so publicly into his sights. Hoover had had Rosset on his list since at least the early fifties when the Director had first declared war on the national contagion of 'dangerous radicals'.

Where prosecution wasn't a straightforward option, the F.B.I. policy was to monitor, disrupt, blackmail and harass. The mission for the Bureau was no longer law enforcement alone. Leave that to the G-men and the literal-minded chiefs of police. *Intelligence* work was about rooting out 'dangerousness' – which included, for the Bureau, the *potential* for danger and subversion.

It was also about planting the *right* thoughts among the American people, and stopping the Soviets from meddling in the American

Way. The Bureau was even learning a few tricks from the Soviets and the German Stasi. It was thorough like that. The bar could always be raised, Hoover said in his monthly in-house newsletter. He was good at his job. No one said otherwise. In his career, Hoover had transformed the Bureau from a bunch of glorified detective snoops into one of the most professional and respected security organizations the world had ever known.

Harding had heard that, for all the college degrees in frames on their walls, the C.I.A. guys had had no idea what they were doing when they first set up. Zero. Hoover had predicted they'd arrive at his door with their begging bowl, and sure enough they did. They wanted access to Bureau training.

After his morning at home with the dirty book, Hoover had reached for his pen and scribbled a DO NOT FILE memo. Harding had seen it for himself. In the confidential memo, Hoover informed the Lab's Porn Section of its 'forthcoming indictment' of the book; the guys in the Lab were, in other words, to write the report that produced that judgment. It was like ordering a take-out meal.

Then Hoover must have sealed the book in a Bureau carton, ready for the courier, picked up the phone, and told the Washington squad to raid as many local bookshops as it took. In less than an hour, they had twenty-four boxes of the book from Grove Press. Evidence aplenty.

Hoover got on the blower again, this time to the Postmaster General, at his second home in Florida. He would have asked solicitously after Mr. Montgomery's new grandson, born that very month at a Palm Beach Hospital in a private room. The Postmaster would have known, merely from the tone of the Director's voice, that the family secret was out, and that Hoover knew: the child was mulatto. Apparently, as if it were all in the nature of an informative 'chat', Hoover had noted that it 'had come to his attention' that the U.S. Mails were shipping obscenity country-wide via its New York mailrooms; countless boxes from New York had been impounded in D.C. alone. He expected immediate action.

An Agent in Charge finished the job by cabling the Postmaster General an anonymous reminder of the criminality of inter-racial sex in several states, including the state of Florida, namely that 'Any Negro man and white woman, or any white man and Negro woman, who shall habitually live in and occupy in the night-time the same room, shall each be punished by imprisonment not exceeding twelve months, or by fine not exceeding five hundred dollars.' Hoover had the Postmaster General exactly where he wanted him.

Of course that Agent in Charge knew only too well that the same rumor – about 'mulattoism' – circulated in the Bureau about Hoover himself. Some said it was the reason for the Director's obsession with inter-racial anything. The rumors always referred to his father's side – the father who was rumored to have ended his days in an insane asylum. Hoover mentioned his late mother often to staff, but never his father. Even middle-rank agents knew that Hoover was the only Bureau employee for whom no personal records were held, not even a copy of his birth certificate. But as the agent arranged the anonymous threat by cable to the new grandfather, none of that mattered a damn.

The following day, the Postmaster General received, right on cue, his instruction from Hoover to provide 'clear guidance' to his subordinate, the New York Postmaster, on the subject of *Lady Chatterley's Lover* and Grove Press.

The summons was served. The date for the G.P.O. hearing was set with breathtaking efficiency. Grove Press *would* be dealt with.

The Director relaxed as he looked out from his office window as far as Capitol Hill. He watched the usual reassuring trail of smoke rise up from the bowels of the building. Jonah, who worked the incinerator, was the oldest and most reliable employee Hoover had. One day, Hoover reminded himself, he must get Miss Gandy to organize some sort of raise for poor old Jonah. Maybe a small pension.

He reached back to his in-tray for the creamy sheet of stationery. Expensive stuff. He'd kept it on his desk for weeks now, in much the same way as he used to pin his grade-school report cards to his bedroom wall.

March 7th, 1959

Dear Mr. Hoover,

It was most kind of you to send me your congratulations on my dame-hood or dameship. I haven't myself yet grasped what it should be called! I am proud of my honour, and proud too that the F.B.I. should send me their good wishes. Long may they establish law and order.

Yours sincerely,
Rebecca West

His personal congratulations had merely seemed the courteous thing to do, given the correspondence and mutual respect she and the Bureau had enjoyed. In fact, Miss West was not a 'Miss' or a 'West' at all, but writers, Hoover knew, were rarely straightforward. Miss West's husband had long been a friend of Allen Dulles, Head of the C.I.A. They went all the way back to Wall Street in the twenties. Rebecca West and Dulles were on friendly terms. They socialized. They exchanged 'news' and views.

She was almost certainly a C.I.A. informant as well, but Hoover was discreet and a gentleman. He was never going to put her on the spot about that. Or hold it against her. The Bureau had her file, with a little more in it than she knew. He was still busy assessing how she might be useful. More useful.

Dame Rebecca liked to communicate directly with Hoover or, if not Hoover, then his deputy, Clyde Tolson. They indulged her in this respect, even though she never passed on the incriminating details they would most have appreciated about her liberal American friends. Still, the relationship was one of confidence, trust and even a shared passion for certain values.

She took the common-sense view that the endless claims of job losses and blacklisting under Senator Joe McCarthy had been greatly exaggerated and even hysterical. She ought to know, he thought; she had her own sources, including her very own pipeline of information straight out of the House Committee on Un-American Activities. The 'pipeline' was an old pal of hers, a Doris Stevens, who had given McCarthy her devoted support after seeing for herself that the New Deal bureaucrats had been infiltrated by Communists and liberals of easy virtue.

As Miss West rightly pointed out in one cable, *McCarthy* was not murdering anti-Communists – the Communists were. She called it like it was. One cannot, she said, murder society to save it. Whatever the wartime alliances had once been, she was absolutely clear: it had to be recognized that Stalin was a far greater threat to the world than a burly American senator who drank too much and had a temper.

One day, Hoover thought, history would prove them both right, whatever the so-called intellectuals claimed now. In fact, history would prove all three of them right: Miss West, Joe McCarthy and Hoover himself.

What a woman Rebecca West was. If she'd had a regrettable start in her young adult life, first as a socialistic 'Fabian', then as a 'feminist', and then as mother to H.G. Wells's bastard son, well, who hadn't made mistakes? She had certainly come good.

Hoover imagined the pleasure of introducing her to President Eisenhower one day. Or maybe to Shirley Temple. He wanted to ask her if they got *The Lawrence Welk Show* on television in England, but he felt unusually shy. He'd only ever known dames before, never a 'Dame'.

Yet *she* had sought him out. It was an honor. She had even admitted, in one of her London 'chats' with the Bureau attaché there, that she trusted the F.B.I. far more than she trusted England's security services. In the past, she said, she'd offered valuable information to London, but its authorities had ignored it – or her, in other words – *and* her impressive roll-call of contacts. Dummies. She had informants in key government agencies, in the highest legal echelons, and even in the British Foreign Office.

She was a friend. She warned them of 'unhelpful' representations of the Bureau which appeared in new books crossing her desk. She reported that her former lover, Charlie Chaplin, with whom she'd had an angry dinner one night, was dangerously Communist and 'crazy'. Chaplin was added to the Bureau's Subversives Watch List.

He and Clyde had agreed: she was to be given a place on their Special Correspondents List, a select compilation of individuals trusted by the Bureau to receive leaked information for the purpose of influencing public opinion. They were choosy, but Miss West had won their trust.

Hoover patted his chin with a hanky. He was actually drooling, like some sort of old hound dog, he thought, laughing. He folded up her thank-you note. Clyde once said that he, Hoover, was incapable of laughing at himself, but he just had, hadn't he? Only dear Clyde could get away with ribbing him like that!

Hoover was loyal. Clyde always said so. No one, Clyde said, was as stubbornly loyal as he was to anyone who had helped him or needed his protection. He almost felt the affront to Miss West personally, MI5 snubbing her like that. Those guys were plain arrogant. British intelligence tried their best to ignore the Bureau, except when they wanted something, of course. They viewed the Americans as 'latecomers' to the surveillance game, as 'juniors' who needed to watch and learn. One of their guys had once boasted to him that they – the Brits – had been doing it since the days of the Tudors. What the hell was Hoover supposed to say to that?

Hoover found their agents louche. They drank too much, and were prone to intellectual leanings and nervous breakdowns. The hard-working minority of MI5 men were, as it turned out, *too* hard-working. Double-agents. More traitors than you could shake a stick at.

If that wasn't bad enough, the Bureau had good, if not conclusive, intelligence which suggested that deep-cover Soviet agents had already penetrated the heart of the British Establishment – the Royal

Navy, specifically. The K.G.B. were, it seemed, right under the nose of MI5, but those English pansies were too busy knocking it back in gentlemen's clubs and indulging in orgies. That's what the Bureau intelligence said, and frankly, that's what you got when you didn't put discipline and loyalty to the fore. Soon, there were going to be a lot of red faces in Merrie Olde England.

Like most English men of a certain class, MI5 agents displayed homosexual tendencies. Not that they didn't like their high-class call-girls too. Hoover's informants said those agents had even shared the girls with leading members of the government in England. Well, that was one way to stay 'abreast' of intelligence. That's what he'd said to Clyde, with a snort and a laugh. Hoover had more and more information coming in about those girls and their uses – all neatly transcribed by his secretary, the ever-dependable Miss Gandy, on Bureau index cards. He was assessing it … for blackmail operations.

To make matters worse, most British agents were slippery atheists. Amoral types. Weak on allegiances. MI5, it seemed, required only the right Oxford or Cambridge college pedigree, and the right tailor. Once in the Ministry, its agents were on long leashes – too long. He'd never let his own men run amok like the MI5 snoops did. Had he been in charge over there, he would have made examples of at least a few.

In fact, it was not surprising that the famous Rebecca West – the famously *well-connected* author Rebecca West – had chosen, not London, but Washington, and Hoover's Bureau. She had put on the record her strong belief in the 'Rule of Law'. She liked *order*. Also, like him, he discovered, she believed in national purpose, in national tradition, and in the national *character* of a people.

The Bureau attaché in England said that every good right-wing paper that published her work – in essay form or a serialization – sold out on the street-stands. Hoover scribbled a note to himself; he wanted his team to get some of her articles re-printed in the States. A dose of realism, that's what the country needed. The woman could write. Not that he'd read her books. Agents didn't read stories. They manufactured them. But he'd heard. And now she was a Dame.

She'd lost many of her old friends on the Left, those who loved Communism. Good riddance, as far as he was concerned – even if it meant that potential sources, potentially rich pickings, were lost to the Bureau. At least it showed her who her real friends were.

Not that she was always popular with the Right either, or not since she'd denounced Prime Minister Chamberlain in the run-up to the last war, along with all 'the appeasers' and the 'see-nothing, do-nothing' witnesses to injustice. Well, good for her, he thought. It wasn't about being popular. It was about being right.

Her thank-you note was handwritten on a sheet of her *personal* stationery. Cream-colored, embossed. Very nice – even if her penmanship needed work. But she was a busy woman. An important woman. She needed a secretary or a wife, same as a man.

He would tell Miss Gandy to add it to his personal scrapbook. He only wished his mother were still alive to see it. He'd show Annie instead. Annie always handled his mother's egg-cups with such care.

The problem – The *Problem* – remained that bastard Barney Rosset, and would until the day the New York Postmaster assured him, Hoover, in writing, that Charles Ablard, the G.P.O.'s Hearing Examiner, knew right from wrong.

Hoover still hadn't had a reply to his personal cable. Something had to be done. He knew better than anyone that the Post Office Department was often thwarted by smut-peddlers who knew how to exploit the shortcomings or loopholes of the legal system.

Rosset was thirty-seven and from a sedate Jewish middle-class banking family in Chicago – on his father's side. His maternal grand-parents, however, had been terrorists for Irish Independence, and he appeared to have inherited their trouble-making streak. At school, he'd edited a student magazine called *The Anti-Everything*. Later, he gave up on three colleges, set out on his own – *with* his father's money of course – moved to New York and started picking fights.

He published anyone – pinkos, avant-garde Europeans, provo-cateurs, subversives, blacks, Jews, poseurs, iconoclasts, homosexuals, sleazes and deviants – or, as Hoover saw it, the whole goddamned un-American bunch. Grove Press operated out of someone's dining-room in a house on West 59th, with a view over clothes-lines, a shabby lawn and a crumbling brick wall. Jazz – that dirty-sounding sax music – poured out of windows in that neighborhood when most normal people were in bed for the night.

Few people in the Village even seemed to hold down regular jobs. One of his agents had infiltrated a so-called art exhibition there. The paintings, he'd said, had to be hung ten feet up, just so no one put out a butt on a canvas or sloshed a drink over it. It was a far cry from the art exhibition he, Hoover, had attended: the President's no less, the Paint-by-Numbers Exhibition in which his – J. Edgar Hoover's – signed work had hung across the room from Ike's own canvas.

Grove Press stank with the dirt of the Village. But even 'Barney Lee Rosset' had gone too far this time. Well, if he thought he was going to get away with it, let him try.

At the double-door of Hoover's comfortable home, his black maid, Annie, had signed for the contraband from the Bureau's courier. That morning, as Hoover rifled through the pages of the Grove Press book, he was convinced: he had Barney Rosset by the balls.

The Bureau had fixed Harding up with a run-down apartment in a brownstone in Queens, for a week only – so he could complete his assignment and file his report on the G.P.O. hearing before heading back to Butte. He'd spent half the afternoon taping up every crack and splinter of light in the dingy bathroom. He used black electrical tape for the cracks and chinks, and cut-up body-bags for blackout blinds. There was nowhere he felt more himself than in the solitude of a darkroom, watching the ineffable stuff of being materialize. It still felt like magic. How did the spirit of a person, in heat and lightwaves, touch and change a piece of film?

He'd almost turned down the assignment. On paper, it had seemed – it *was* – too junior a job for an agent who had twelve years in the Bureau: recording a public hearing for a banned book. No skills were required except the usual discretion and some basic photography. It was a job for a trainee. But he'd swallowed his pride. He liked fiddling with the Bureau's new gadgets. He was good with them too. The Bureau's Lab was at the forefront of everything technological and forensic, and he liked trying out the latest gear.

Besides, it meant a week back in New York, a week away from Butte. It meant Central Park. The reprieve of spring, that prayerful sort of light. The cherry blossom on Pilgrim Hill. He used to take his mother there in her last years, to get the sunlight on her face. He'd almost feel alive again, and, for a while, he could forget his life was only a negative strip of what a man's life was supposed to be – the reverse or inverse, and flimsy with it.

The hearing itself went more or less as expected – until, that is, the moment of the 'No Decision'. There had been an audible intake of breath in the gallery and entire rows of blank faces.

Interesting, but none of his business. He didn't care. He'd laid down the audio easily enough, gotten the pictures – prohibited in any hearing or trial – of all the major players, witnesses and attendees. No one suspected. The umbrella-camera-gadget was fussy to handle but not difficult. Professor Trilling's shots were going to be blurry, but they'd do as evidence of his attendance. The F.B.I. had a file on him going way back, as heavy as a Bible.

What he hadn't expected – moments before the doors shut, before the hearing started, in the back row of the public gallery – was *her*.

Any good photo is a secret of a secret. It's the unknowable glimpsed within a glimpse, the puzzle in plain sight. It's the question that makes us look for an answer we're never going to find. An open case. An unsolved mystery. A good still is never still – it's restive, alive.

He could hardly believe his luck when her face appeared on the negative strip – clear, bright, startled – in his loupe. The angle had worked, even without a viewfinder.

On previous occasions, from '56 to '57, he'd worked with a Robot Star II camera concealed in a satchel-style briefcase. The camera itself was a beauty. On faster shutter speeds, it could fire off four frames a second. The lenses were small but great quality. You got twenty-five frames on a full winding of the spring motor, and sometimes fifty or even sixty shots on a roll of thirty-six.

It was, at the time, the latest out of Germany. The Lab in New York had found a way to silence the shutter. The camera had a steel body, a little heavy, but compact enough – about three inches long – to fit in a custom-made briefcase. Some agents found it complicated to load the film, but he was a natural.

The case was the problem. You shot through a concealed lens on the side of the case, which meant you had to remember to slide back the strap from the lens, clutch the thing under your arm to get the best angle, tip it up usually, then squeeze a cable-release in the handle. The right-angle viewfinder was awkward. You had to rely mostly on instinct, what with holding the thing under your arm, and even with 20/20 vision, he usually discovered he'd mostly shot trees, sidewalks and car doors.

Occasionally, something interesting turned up among these accidents. Sometimes he printed and kept them: a woman's profile of despair under a sign advertising Ex-Lax, the gleaming shoes of a Latin dancer behind a dirty men's-room stall door, a child in mid-air over a street-game of hopscotch, the hands of middle-aged lovers against the cracked upholstery of a Greyhound seat.

The Russian F-21, on the other hand, was any agent's dream. The Lab replicated it. Three inches long, it weighed just six ounces, and had a quiet spring-advance mechanism. It was easily concealed in the gutted handle of an umbrella, with a cable-control connected to a button on the umbrella handle. No viewfinder but a small umbrella was much easier to aim than a damn briefcase. You could set the lens so it was continually open, slide back the button-cap, and shoot a hundred quick frames on a standard 21mm film. The images were usually good and sharp. He had to give the K.G.B. their due; they knew how to do covert operations.

In the dingy darkness of the bathroom, he switched on the safelight.

He'd forgotten to buy tongs for the trays. Again. He could hardly remember what it was like not to have raw hands. His eczema hated the chemicals, but he'd live.

The washing-line above the bathtub was pegged and ready. The enlarger fit on the countertop.

In the red-orange glow of the safelight, he turned the lens's aperture ring until he felt the clicks and saw a faint darkening of the projected image. The timer ticked. He checked the sharpness and ran a test strip. Then he placed the strip in the developer, set the timer again, and rocked the tray back and forth, sloshing it as usual.

She emerged slowly, alchemically. A black-and-white poem of a woman.

Dark lustrous eyes, widely spaced.

A beauty that was more exotic than American.

A cool, flower-like stillness, even in her surprise.

Her face was square, with a strong jaw, but the effect was delicate.

Lips parted. No lipstick. A large mouth.

Dark tendrils of hair against a white sweaty brow.

If she'd been hot, why had her coat been buttoned up during the hearing?

She looked preoccupied, even startled. Yet there was also, in the depths of her eyes, a fundamental quietude which made it hard to look away.

Remove. Drain. And into the fix – tick, tick, tick – then the stop-bath, with its vinegar stink – the timer buzzed – and finally, into the wash.

He pegged the strip onto the line above the tub, blinking.

The camera in the umbrella had been ingenious. He'd never dreamed his efforts at the door of the G.P.O. – on the hoof – would actually have yielded anything. Yet here she was.

She was photogenic, not only because she was easy on the eye, but because – he could see it now – she gave herself to the camera effortlessly, even when she didn't know it was watching her. It was a physical gift some people had, like opening your mouth and producing a perfect note; a quality which transcended logic, and something bigger than the set of circumstances in which she happened to be shot.

Film 'goddesses' sometimes came undone when you found their 'bad side'. Beautiful people sometimes didn't translate to film. Who knew the alchemy of it – the unique light of someone hitting the silvery crystals of a film's emulsion? But she had something which made bad sides and good sides irrelevant. If that something was random, it was also – what was that word? – *numinous*.

He bent closer to the image. Below her lower lip, he saw a small horizontal mark, where she'd been biting it with her two front teeth.

Nerves.

Yet she'd been bold enough to murmur something to him, a witticism about it being bad luck to put up an umbrella indoors. She'd been soft-spoken, with a less pronounced version of the Boston drawl her Senator husband had. Her words had been both a droll one-liner and a curse or a warning; her reflex way of letting him know she suspected he was not merely a stranger getting the door for her. 'Bad luck to put up an umbrella indoors.' She knew nothing about the truth of the umbrella. She'd barely looked him in the eye. But the phrase was over-familiar. Deliberately so. It suggested they shared something. A momentary complicity. A secret in passing. As if she was telling him she knew what she couldn't know.

The Bureau had intelligence on bigger fish, of course – on First and Second Ladies. Hoover even had a bulging file on Eleanor Roosevelt. Rumor had it that Miss Helen Gandy, his private secretary for forty years, guarded the most classified files in an ottoman foot-stool under her desk.

And the word in Washington was that Kennedy was going to declare his candidacy for the Democratic nomination by January. If Kennedy was aiming for the White House – and there was hardly any 'if' about it – Hoover would be gunning for Kennedy.

That was common knowledge in the Bureau. Lyndon B. Johnson and Richard Nixon, Kennedy's rivals, were going to cooperate with Hoover. The alliances were in place. The Director didn't particularly care about party colors. Nixon was sound. He'd started his political career as a dedicated anti-Communist member of the House Committee on Un-American Activities and was still a fervent defender of American values.

If there had to be a Democrat in power, Lyndon Johnson was Hoover's man. Ten years ago, they had been neighbors in Washington. Hoover would even recount, when feeling jocular with his agents, how he used to help Lyndon track down his runaway dogs, finding them before the dog-catcher from the pound could. 'It takes a hound to find a hound!' Lyndon used to say, with a friendly thump to Hoover's back. Hoover liked quoting that. Now and then, apparently, Hoover had chili con carne with the whole Johnson family on Sunday nights. 'I think you and all your men are tops.' That's what Hoover said Lyndon J. had said. Another favorite line. Who knew whether it was true? Who cared? The reality was the two men were useful to each other, and Johnson knew it as well as Hoover, especially when it came to the allegations of ballot-rigging in the '48 Senate race, allegations Hoover made disappear. So Johnson was 'indebted' to the F.B.I.

All of it meant that Johnson would take 'advice' from the Bureau. Besides, he had plenty to hide: not just the close-shave of '48, but all the women going in and out of his Senate office – otherwise known as 'The Johnson Ranch East' – plus some dirty business dealings.

'Insurance policies', all of it. Hoover had the records, plus his own card-catalog for quick reference. In Bureau lore, it was said that Hoover, as a young man, had got himself a job at the Library of Congress as a messenger boy, and there he'd learned the value of card-catalogs and comprehensive, well-indexed information.

It seemed Hoover actually liked Johnson too. Nice family. Once, he'd even filled in for a babysitter for the Johnson daughters on a Saturday night. Whether the next president was Nixon or Johnson, the key thing was that each man understood the 'gray areas' of Bureau business.

Kennedy, on the other hand, was young, inexperienced and 'liberal' – which, in Hoover's terms, was just another way of saying 'immoral'. Hoover had been friendly enough with the father, Joe Kennedy Sr., but his Senator son was no chip off the old block. He never even wore a hat, and that, as Hoover told his agents with a smirk, said it all.

After more than a year marooned in the Butte office, with only the occasional secondment when some Field Office somewhere couldn't find a photographer with the right clearances, Harding knew it in his gut: the picture of the Senator's wife leaving the hearing was his one-way ticket out of Butte, and the only one he was ever going to get.

Even the Ivy League liberals of the C.I.A. weren't going to touch that dirty Lawrence book. They didn't give a damn about the sex or perversion, but they couldn't overlook the fact that it was anti-capitalist, anti-materialist, anti-industrial and anti-war. Un-American, whichever way you cut it.

He'd read the literary analysis compiled by the Lab – its team read the books agents needed to know about. The report had been thorough. It itemized a whole pile of the author's outrages. 'Democracy in America,' he'd apparently claimed, 'was never the same as Liberty in Europe. In Europe Liberty was a great life-throb. But in America Democracy was always something anti-life.' That was for starters.

Oh America / The sun sets in you. / Are you the grave of our day?

The Lab had even obtained a copy of MI5's old Lawrence file; the author's mail had apparently been intercepted in the early years of the first War, when he and his German wife had been suspected of spying in England for the Kaiser. The only problem was that Mr. D. H. Lawrence had frustrated all conclusive analysis with his 'sheer inconsistency', according to the report.

The author had variously made arguments for the nationalization of industry, with pensions for every working man, *and* for the end of democracy. To the left-wing intellectual Bertrand Russell in 1915, he'd said: 'You must drop all your democracy. You must not believe in "the people".' He'd argued for a benign, patrician ruling class, and also for a Communist community of like-minded intellectuals. Then, just three years later, he was fearful that the end of democracy was coming.

The writer had escaped England for a ranch in New Mexico – of all the unlikely places for a skinny Englishman. But he was, it seemed, all for wide open spaces and freedom. At the same time, he despised 'bourgeois Republics with their presidents' and he damned America as 'the Sodom and Gomorrah of industrial materialism'.

Harding chuckled. That was quite the turn of phrase.

The dirty novel's so-called hero was a rich man's gamekeeper called Mellors. Mellors 'disbelieved in the dollar utterly' – which was odd, given the guy didn't even earn or spend in dollars. Hypocritical too because his author didn't 'disbelieve' in any currency, it seemed. According to the report, Lawrence had regularly scratched around for cash and freeloaded off friends. According to one MI5 'listener': 'One acquaintance of the Lawrences remarks that Lawrence never walks into a friend's country cottage or empty London flat without his eyes sizing it up for curtains.'

Harding could see, from Hoover's initials and date-line, that he'd ignored almost everything in the report, and had underlined, in heavy pencil, just one word: 'Communist'.

Harding closed the toilet lid, seated himself and stared at her, at this secret D. H. Lawrence admirer. She'd gone out on a limb for an author who was thirty years dead.

He tried to assess what he could reasonably expect from the Bureau for the photo. Only a couple of weeks before, the Bureau had obtained what appeared to be a picture of Jack Kennedy leaving his PR girl Julie Goodwin's apartment at one in the morning. It was also known in-house that Hoover had one of the fifty letters – an original – sent by Miss Goodwin's landlord and landlady to the nation's newspaper editors. The affair between the Senator and Goodwin had apparently been going on for months, maybe much longer. The middle-aged, God-fearing landlord-and-lady, the Steeles, were outraged. Mr. Steele had even provided a reel-to-reel recording of the sounds of the couple's lovemaking.

Hoover, it was said, had chosen his moment carefully and informed Senator Kennedy, personally, of 'rumors'.

A sure-fire strategy. Even a wealthy, well-heeled senator could be rattled.

Hoover had the strongbox with six copies of that original letter, the late-night snapshot of Kennedy looking furtive as he left what was alleged to be Goodwin's apartment, plus the sex recording. 'Insurance policies'. That was the designation in-house. The agent who'd obtained the 1 a.m. picture had been promoted straight to the rank of S.A.C.

The Washington Field Office Deputy S.A.C., a guy called Franklin, had stopped by Harding's office in Butte a couple of months before.

He knew the area, he said – had family in Montana – and was passing through. At the Director's personal instruction, he'd tailed Kennedy the previous spring and fall on the campaign trail for re-election to the Senate, all the way from Utah to Idaho to Montana. Butte, Harding's own patch, had been the last stop. The Senator was to give a speech at some Democrats' dinner. Harding hadn't been allowed to see the Secret Service guys' schedules and protocols for that dinner, even though he *was* the Butte Bureau and only up the road. He was informed the Bureau had it all covered. It turns out the Bureau, on that occasion, was Franklin.

After he managed to stop resenting the guy, he kicked a chair Franklin's way, and they opened bottles of beer against the gunmetal edge of his desk. He found beer caps around the office for months afterwards.

On that visit, Franklin claimed he'd seen the Kennedy box-file for himself, or one of them anyway. The truth was, even most Special Agents *knew about* 'Hoover's files', the Director's personal collection of derogatory information on cabinet officials, members of Congress and presidents. They knew because Hoover's collection of intelligence was something every Special Agent worth his badge aspired to contribute to. That's how a man got promoted. Make Hoover happy.

With his 're-location' to the Butte office in '58, Harding had been demoted, from his brand-new rank of 'Supervisory Special Agent' in the Washington Field Office – earned only after a decade in the heat of the New York office. He was downgraded to 'Senior Special Agent', a rank which existed mostly for the agents over thirty-five who weren't destined to climb to the lofty ranks of Assistant Special Agent in Charge, Deputy Special Agent in Charge, or Special Agent in Charge.

Harding was only glad that there was no one else in Butte to rub it in.

Franklin was diplomatic, he'd give him that. He didn't ask questions or crack the usual one-liners.

After their fourth beer, Franklin said he had no doubt that Kennedy's box-file was one of the files stored, not just in Hoover's office, but in the stack in the ottoman foot-stool under his secretary's desk. She never left her post without locking every door that could be locked.

But Franklin *was* shown the Kennedy file before setting out on the Midwest trail to tail Kennedy. Hoover had wanted him to know, apparently, how low he should be prepared to go. He'd wanted him enticed by the precedents. He wanted Franklin to better them, to go lower.

'And did you,' said Harding, 'get anything?'

Franklin shrugged. 'The Senator had his car pull over once. I thought, here we go. There was a local beauty queen accompanying him to a formal dinner in Idaho. Well, not accompanying him as such, but, you know, *available*. I pulled off the road behind them. Pretended to be checking a map at the wheel. Expected his driver to be told to get out of the car to admire the view for ten minutes.'

'And?'

'Turns out Kennedy actually wanted to see an elk the girl had spotted in the woods as they passed.'

'You had a wire on the driver.'

'Nope. On the girl. But' – he kicked the desk lightly – 'nyet, zilch. Which means, I figure, that Kennedy must have actually fallen for that Julie Goodwin.' He whistled low. 'It's not at all what Hoover was after on that occasion, but still, it was … of interest to the Bureau. Put it that way. It indicated that the Senator was "in love".'

Harding leaned forward again to stare at the image, drying over the tub. Whatever the unrest of the Senator's heart, this shot of his young wife was something altogether different, and possibly more valuable than any grainy snapshot of Kennedy leaving his PR girl's apartment. Here was a demure, Catholic, potential First Lady covertly supporting a perverted book.

If there were to be a leak, the American people would be less forgiving of a First Lady with a dedication to dirty books than a good-looking, likable President with a weakness for pretty girls. Hoover would recognize that instantly.

He'd understand, too, that Kennedy's wife could, unwittingly, do 'the job' for the Bureau, with minimum effort or risk for the Bureau. *She* could bring her husband down for them. They could sit back, put their feet up, and watch the Senator eliminated from any future presidential race by a possible First Lady who was secretly taking risks for a scandalous, un-American book.

It wasn't impossible.

At the Bureau, the Director, Deputy Director and Assistant Directors had amassed, with the help of their agents, over 400,000 files on American subversives. In addition, each and every federal employee was now checked for possible disloyalty, aberration or risk. Political leaders and their families were not spared. They experienced more prolonged investigations than they would ever know.

A man called Jonah stoked and fed the F.B.I. incinerator in the D.C. basement. The smoke of endless documents, seen and then committed to senior F.B.I. officials' memories, blew high over Capitol Hill. Jonah was hired long ago as a boy of fourteen because he was illiterate – and he was never out of work.

The specter of a First Lady subversive – holding a dirty book by a Communist-inspired writer, and printed by a renegade publisher – would fire Hoover's imagination.

The Senator's young wife was beautiful but unshowy. In the picture, her eyes were wide and sharply focused. The wedding band on her finger gleamed. Her hands were big for a woman. Her nails looked bitten. The tendons stood out on the hand that clasped the book.

He'd send the audio and classified pictures – of Barney Rosset and Professor Trilling particularly – from the hearing to the New York office of the Assistant Director, as instructed. But the print, the 'specimen', was going straight to the Special File Room at F.B.I. headquarters, a room always maintained under lock and key. He'd mark it 'JUNE', the most confidential protocol. Then he'd mark the envelope within the Manila envelope 'OBSCENE', for the centralized Obscene File. He'd bypass the Assistant Director, as well as the HQ's examiners, and mark the photo for Hoover himself.

Because he'd blow out his brains in the gun vault of his own Field Office if he had to go another year in Butte.

Here was hope. Last year, even the Special Agent in Charge who'd documented the *rumor* about President Eisenhower had been promoted to the rank of Assistant Director, with his pick of Field Offices. According to that rumor, Ike had tried to have sex with the wife of a Washington lawyer. Suddenly that lawyer had his fingers in official pies, not to mention affairs of state.

Harding couldn't take his eyes off her. Even after all these years behind a camera, it surprised him that no two subjects radiated light in the same way. He wasn't religious, not anymore he wasn't, but, on photographic paper, there was a reactive physics of light that looked to him something like soul.

His mother used to 'borrow' glossy magazines from the doctors' and dentists' offices she cleaned and, as a kid at the kitchen table, he would stare at the faces, trying to understand the expressions of light. The Senator's young wife didn't dazzle like a Grace Kelly or burn with the white heat of Vivien Leigh. She wasn't sunny like Doris Day or midnight-sexy like Elizabeth Taylor. She wasn't radiant like Monroe or luminous like Deneuve. The Senator's wife was like a vigil candle – that was the only way he could describe it – the sort you find in a basilica, flickering in the darkness of stone and shadow.

Her image dangled above the dirt-rimmed tub. What had she been up to that afternoon at the G.P.O.? If she'd been bold to turn up for the hearing – and she had been, no doubt – she had also seemed vulnerable in a way that was difficult to decipher in those dark, wide eyes.

Hoover was alert to every rumor and report of the Democratic race-to-be, and Agents in Charge had standing orders to report anything and everything they picked up on Jack Kennedy. Harding wasn't going to disappoint. He couldn't afford to. What other kind of work was he ever going to get? Everything out in the world these days was about 'team work', while the Bureau was like the Catholic priesthood. It liked lone operators. It moved you around so you didn't put down roots. That suited him. He was messed up – he knew he was. Rootless.

How was he to have known that day last year when he walked into the Mayflower Hotel that Butte was to be his fate? He hadn't had the slightest interest in what he saw …

As for Butte, a once prosperous town, its fortunes had declined until it was known in the Bureau simply as the Back of Beyond, or more commonly, the Butt of Beyond. That was the joke. The Butte of the joke. Banished to Butte. You poor bugger. I hear you're taking it up the Butte these days.

Franklin told him Kennedy's file was overflowing with white 5 x 7 index cards, with file references to his past and present. It even had naval intelligence going back to the war. Keyhole intelligence, Franklin called it. Hoover's favorite kind, he said with a smirk.

In '42, he said, Senator Kennedy, then a young Naval Intelligence officer, had had a passionate romance with a Danish journalist and socialist. She was a former Miss Europe, crowned by the actor Maurice Chevalier no less. It so happened she had even attended the wedding of Hermann Göring, where she was introduced to his best man, Adolf Hitler, who later gave her three exclusive interviews. There were audio recordings from Room 132, a bugged room in a Charleston, South Carolina hotel.

The report was delivered by hand to the Director. Kennedy, who had fallen big-time for Inga Arvad, the beautiful Dane, suddenly decided he wanted to marry her – even though she was still married to some movie director. She was almost certainly a Nazi spy – even if they couldn't land the proof. His family was horrified. Jack Kennedy's father and Hoover worked together behind the scenes to get Jack K. transferred as far from South Carolina as they could. They got him all the way to the South Pacific – where his P-T boat was hit and sunk.

Hoover was now determined, along with a few well-placed, rabid anti-Catholics, to stop Kennedy getting anywhere near the White House. He had media contacts working on the anti-Catholic alarm. No matter how clearly Kennedy promoted his view of the necessary separation of church and state, Hoover's paid-off media men were whipping up fear of a possible presidential candidate who would kiss and slobber over the ring of the Pope.

Hoover had several instances of the Senator, clearly identifiable, climaxing on tape, going right back to the Inga Arvad – the alleged Nazi – affair in '42 – plus all 628 pages of notes, plus the audio conversations. The Director knew Kennedy as few others did. Even if the sabotage mission were to fail to keep Kennedy out of the White House, Kennedy, as President, would be too afraid *not* to reappoint Hoover. The Director had him where he wanted him. 'Insurance policies'. Still, Hoover knew that both Jack Kennedy and his brother despised him, and that alone made Nixon and Johnson the men to trust.

But this – Harding lifted the photo off the wash-line – this trump card of a shot could, with a little careful execution, knock Kennedy right out of the presidential race before it even started. What candidate could live down the scandal of a wife with a dirty mind, secret behavior and un-American taste? No one was beyond scrutiny, and the F.B.I. was educating the nation with a call to do its duty.

The Bureau, in public messages penned by the Director himself, called on the citizens of America to play their role in saving the country from obscenity, just as the Bureau itself had already helped to root out sexual deviants from the institutions of the nation. The public had to be zealous in protecting standards of decency. It had to stand against the floodtide of moral corruption and support the national crusade. All Americans, if they cared about the youth of the country, had to be alert to the new spiritual decay.

Pornography had been proven, by psychiatrists and the best medical minds, to be an insidious threat to moral, mental and physical health. 'Did *you* know ...?' One teenager had become a prostitute after reading a number of cheap novels. 'Did *you* know ... ?' Rapes and assaults were statistically more likely after the reading of lurid books. 'Did *you* know ... ?' 'Soft porn' was no defense. Public authorities agreed that there was a link between many crimes of sex and violence, and smut literature, especially among juveniles.

Harding knew the patter.

He stood, turned off the safelight, hit the switch on the wall, and admired his ... accident. It was perfect. He only needed to print it. Newspaper editors would love it, if Hoover dangled it under their noses. There it was – the book under her arm, pressed to her breast, the title clear.

The address was stamped like a sweepstakes ticket number on his brain: HQFBI Internal Mail, c/o Secretary to the Director, Miss Helen Gandy, Attn: JEH, Code: JUNE, Special File Room: Obscene/ File 80–662, Cabinet 9 of 11, Section 8A/OBSCENE READERS.

The Senator's wife, an 'obscene reader' like no other, was on her way to the Director himself.

Harding turned to the sink.

His hands were burning.

The Exile

i

It was only meant to have been a short jaunt back to England in 1914, for a quick summer wedding in London – and respectability at last.

Frieda and Lawrence arrived at the Kensington Register Office, with Katherine Mansfield and Jack Murry for witnesses. The exile had never worn a boater before; it belonged to the ever-dapper Jack. Frieda was kitted out in a suit of sorts, which made her look, in even her groom's estimation, stouter and more matronly than she actually was.

Afterwards, they returned to Jack's rooms by bus for a wedding breakfast in his landlady's back garden. The informal wedding-day photograph *showed a clean-shaven, alert, very young-looking young man in a rather high collar, and a somewhat plump, bold young woman not altogether a bully, though her jowl was heavy she was years older than he ...*

Years later, the exile would turn to that photograph as he wrote the account of the gamekeeper Oliver Mellors's wedding to the unappealing Bertha Coutts, a woman to whom Lawrence's gamekeeper-character was to discover he was never suited, temperamentally or sexually.

After the wedding photo, Frieda changed into a flowing Isadora Duncan-like creation, and the neighbour-children stared at the four of them over the brick wall, as if they were creatures in a zoo. Poppies bloomed from paving slabs. Katherine produced plates of toast, honey and boiled eggs. On an impulse, Jack seized a sheet from the line and ripped it in two to cover the sooty garden table. His good friend, D. H. Lawrence, was now a married man, with prospects. In the London offices of Methuen & Co., the contract for the exile's next novel, *The Rainbow*, was prepared and ready to be signed.

Six months later, on a road seemingly to Nowhere one gusty January night, the exile thought enviously of their former selves and their happy ignorance. The peace of that back garden, a peace which had been the great gift of the day, was torn as decisively as Jack's landlady's sheet by the Declaration of War. Their lives – and his peace of mind – were riven into a before and after.

The borders with and through Europe had closed immediately. His sources in London confirmed there would be no getting back to Italy. Yet he, the newly respectable married man, could not afford anything but Italy. He hardly had a sixpence to his name.

With the help of friends, the Lawrences moved into The Triangle, a dark, mouldering cottage in Chesham, Buckinghamshire. Having no other option, he applied to a charitable fund for down-at-heel authors and, on receiving a cheque, wrote warmly to the Board to express his gratitude, while inwardly cursing their meanness.

The five months in Chesham were as oppressive as the grave. He got ill with it: black in spirit, weak in body. He sat endlessly by the stove, heedless of anything but the horrors of the daily bulletins as he rocked to and fro, exhaling gloom, and slowly breaking down.

When the local duck-pond flooded, as it often did, their cottage was cut off from what passed for civilisation in Chesham. Somehow, through the misery, he still scratched away at both his Thomas Hardy volume and *The Rainbow* – Frieda's suggested title. But every page exhausted him and he was slow. Their marriage did not thrive. There were days when they resented each other as never before.

Then came the chance to chuck Chesham. A writer acquaintance, Viola Meynell, invited them to take her little cottage, on her father's property – in a place called Greatham – an ancient hamlet in the wilds of Sussex. Her father, she said, would send the family's driver to fetch them.

If it was the road to Nowhere, then so be it, he thought. There was nowhere to be. 'Somewhere' usually disappointed while 'Nowhere' held every possibility.

Beside him in the motor, Frieda's mouth had fallen open in her sleep. Up front, their driver craned forward to peer for the road through the drifting snow. Lawrence cracked the film of ice on his window and forced it down. Frieda frowned in her sleep. He didn't care that the snow blew in; it felt good on his face, and his new beard protected his throat. He liked it, and felt rather proud it had grown so well. Moreover, a beard would distinguish him from all the servicemen, regulation clean-shaven. Let there be no confusion. He looked, he thought with a raffish smile, like a satyr released from a Roman urn.

His spirits lifted with the promise of Sussex – with the Downs, the sea. It wasn't the Italian Riviera, but Sussex was full of sky and wind and weather. Life was moving forward again, through the January night, down sunken roads which followed ancient Roman ways; they were going through the past to find a future. *I have such a terrible mistrust of the future.* The snow that night was already deep, and the slopes of the Downs glowed like phosphor in the darkness.

Sussex had, in its not so distant past, been cut off from the rest of the country by the area known as the 'Weald', a wild woodland which ran between the hills of the North and South Downs. The county had been the last to be Christianised, and even if dormant beneath the snow that night, some elemental spirit was alive in its dark-bright hills.

The car shimmied onward. *Lentissimo, lentissimo.* Their driver possessed a stalwart neck and excellent reflexes. In her half-sleep, Frieda clung to the exile's arm. 'Please close the window, Lorenzo!' she begged. 'Your chest!'

He ignored her. The snow blocked farm lanes, and the wind had sculpted the boundary hedges into haunted battlements. They passed a herd of cows huddling by a windbreak in a field, their silhouettes primordial. Poor beasts, he thought.

Frieda's brother-in-law, an aide-de-camp in the German court, had told him years ago – in those innocent days when Zeppelins were merely a new form of travel for people with too much money – that the gas-bags, the things which kept the bloated monsters afloat, were made from cow intestines. A single Zeppelin required more than 250,000 cows. It was obscene, industrial-scale madness.

Only a few nights before, two had appeared over East Anglia and metamorphosed into terror. Civilians were targeted and attacked. The morning news reported that a soldier's widow was killed by one of the bombs. A lad of fourteen died as he slept. A shoemaker was blown apart as he closed up his workshop and, in the morning, an old lady was found lifeless, half in and half out of a window, by passing schoolchildren. The sky itself – that dimension of Constable's heaven-lit clouds and Blake's strange angels – had been invaded. England's sky had fallen.

Sometimes, the black heat of revenge flared up and his soul fizzed savagely. But, on most days, he was of the mind that if the Germans wanted some house of his, he'd rather give it than fight them for it. If another man must fight for his house, well, that was his affair.

As it was, with his seedy chest, he'd probably never see the Front, unless conscription came and they scraped the barrel for the likes of him. He was not a pacifist. If anything, this war disgusted him because it wasn't war enough. Its machines and bureaucracies were a parody of war, a parody of an honest fight.

Those 'in the know' claimed that modern warfare methods were so terrible that the War *could not* go on beyond a few weeks. But of course it was not won by Christmas, as so many had predicted.

Christmas 1914 had been all tinkle, tinsel and shine – the last little trumpet-blast of a lost era. He had revived in spirits enough to cook, boil, roast and bake for miscellaneous friends in the dank, damp Triangle. They had swigged Chianti, danced, played charades and sung with gusto. Everything was hectic. Frieda fretted loudly that she might be seized 'at any moment' as a spy and 'enemy alien'. The men feared conscription, if mostly in silence. Their celebration had been cheerful, though at least half unreal.

The Expeditionary Force had already retreated from Mons and Antwerp. Fifty thousand of their countrymen had fallen at Ypres. The numbers surpassed all meaning. Men were the butt ends of rifles. They were cogs, rivets and spokes; their lifeless bodies, traction for gun carriages in the mud.

Lawrence family legend had it that his great-grandfather had been found as a small boy on the battlefield at Waterloo, dazed and adrift in the sea of the dead. Had he been an English soldier's bastard child? Or a Belgian farmboy who'd lost his way in a field so suddenly hellish it was beyond recognition? Whoever he was, he was rescued by English soldiers, or so it was said, and taken to Birmingham.

Since Lawrence's own boyhood, even before he'd first heard the story of his great-grandfather, he'd felt, in his history lessons at school, that he could smell that scene from Waterloo of a century before: the waterlogged ground after the storm, the crows at the intestines, the mangled horses, the human scavengers pulling the teeth of the dead and dying. Could mute horror, he wondered, be passed down the line, from father to son, and from father to son again? He didn't know, but his heart had turned as cold as a dead lump of earth the day he'd heard the news of war declared.

In late July and the first days of August, he'd been climbing with four others in Westmorland. He was newly married and pleased with himself. Two of the men were new to him, fellow walkers he'd met on the train platform. The other, Lewis, was an engineer he knew slightly from Italy. The revelation was Lewis's chum, Samuel Koteliansky – Kot – who was excellent company, and full of talk of Russian literature and his plans to translate it.

As they climbed, Kot demonstrated how, in Russia, he'd honed his ability to howl like a wolf, to see off the wild dogs of Kiev as he walked home from his university classes at night. It was a remarkably good impression, and Lawrence liked him immediately for it.

On their final day, the two of them stopped to rest halfway to the peak. They swam in a mountain pool, then pulled up its water lilies, twisted them around their hats, and doffed them to girls at the window of the hillside inn. The girls shrieked with laughter and sloshed the tea from their cups.

As they reached the peak, a downpour came. They sheltered, crouching against a low stone wall. Then, bugger it, he thought. Soaked to the skin, he stripped off and raced through the high yellow gorse, singing a music-hall tune. Koteliansky called him an imbecile, then stripped off too, joyously bellowing out sombre Hebrew songs as the rain bounced off the black hedge of his hair. 'Ranani Zadikim Zadikim!'

When they descended into the town, they heard it, on the stone bridge, before they saw it: men, as far as the eye could see, streaming in their thousands in ramshackle formations. In the time it had taken to go up a mountain and come down, the world had collapsed into a dark mirror-image of itself. Where *was* he?

The people of Barrow clapped and whistled as the recruits marched over the cobbles in their mismatched uniforms. They carried old muskets, pitchforks and broom handles. Their complexions were pale and their chests weedy from years in the local munitions factory. Now they were marching – rushing pell-mell – into the Factory of War.

The way to the station was blocked. Recruitment posters lined the route. WHO'S ABSENT? Is it <u>You</u>? Someone in the crowd knocked off Lawrence's hat of lilies. They feared they'd be battered before they made it aboard any train.

Kot, as a foreigner, felt he could risk it. He said he'd pretend he only spoke Russian. Later, Lawrence heard he'd made it to London. The other three holed up in Lewis's cottage in Barrow. But the exile couldn't bear its claustrophobia, and he fled down the coast in search of a boat going south.

There, the sands glowed in the mellow light of August. He watched a French onion boat come into shore, beating valiantly against a strong sea. Its white sails were painful in their splendour, the boat already a relic of the past.

He was not yet twenty-nine, and he knew that day that he could never hate any nation en bloc. *He could no more have been aggressive on the score of his Englishness than a rose can be aggressive on the score of its rosiness.*

In the back seat of the motor, Frieda drooled on his jacket lapel. She slept, her head on his chest, in the ineffable familiarity of souls cast, and miscast, together. They had railed at each other almost endlessly in recent months, and had had little pleasure as man and wife, and yet the wedding – legitimacy – had been the sole reason they'd left Italy, that and so Frieda could try, as an acceptably married woman once again, to see her children. But her plan failed. In the eyes of society, she was still the scandalous woman who had abandoned her children for a younger lover. To make matters worse, they were trapped in an England they had resoundingly fled.

He adjusted the rug on their knees.

When they were first drawn together, it had hardly mattered to him that Frieda had already been a wife. Her marriage to Weekley had not been a marriage of true selves, and it therefore followed that he could not 'steal' a woman from a union that never was.

Now, they were gradually resigning themselves to the knowledge that they were mismatched. Frieda was worldly, experienced, and he – he would not deceive himself – was narrow. Narrow in build and unworthy of her soft, ample femaleness. Narrow with a working-class anxiety he could not throw off. Narrow in the bright intensity of his focus.

He made her happiest when they sang together or when he found her a new home. If he resented her appetite for life and that elemental need in her he could not fulfil, he refused to police it; she'd already run from the authoritarian eye of one husband to be with him. If he couldn't satisfy her as a lover, he knew at least that his growing recognition and society connections were a source of endless pleasure to her.

In Nottingham, where they'd met in the early days of March, 1912, he'd simply arrived at an appointed hour at the home of his former professor for lunch and professional advice. But Weekley was late to arrive, so Mrs Weekley received him and sat opposite, leaning forward beguilingly – to better understand his Nottinghamshire English – and speaking wondrously in her matter-of-fact German rhythms.

They laughed a good deal at their mutual misunderstandings. Then she asked with a surprising directness about the black armband he wore. 'Who has died?' He explained that his mother, to whom he owed most, had died a little over a year before. 'More than a year ago, you say?' Her eyes narrowed, and she changed the subject to Sophocles's *Oedipus*. She was six years his senior, and his blood pounded in his ears.

She uncrossed her ankles and stroked her calf absent-mindedly. The day was warm. Behind her, the red velvet curtains blew out from the French windows, as if framing her, it seemed to him, in a rich labial shape, all folds and softness. He could think only of the ample cradle of her thighs.

He believed her then to be the finest woman he'd ever met. He would learn in time that he was her third extramarital affair. Frieda was honest and did not labour under English hypocrisies and flusterings.

Yet she was *his*, he told himself, as decreed by Nature. He believed in marriage, in its sacred fusion of forms, and he was glad, finally, to leave off all craving and raving and feeling only half of himself. But she was a free spirit. In even her most mundane decisions, she carried the confidence of her class. She was a von Richthofen, as she liked to remind others, and she emanated her own powerful sense of 'unclaimability', in the way, ironically, that virgins did. It entranced and infuriated him.

On their lovers' flight through her German homeland and onward to Italy, she was true to her impulses. When he went out for supplies at a local market one day, she chose to relax on a bank of the River Isar. On his return, she confessed that she'd 'relaxed' rather more than she should have. In fact, she'd swum across the cold river – it was a chilly May – and had offered herself to a woodcutter on the opposite bank. 'He looked lonely,' she explained.

The following week, as they travelled south, she had sex upstairs with a German cavalry officer whom she met on the stairs of their inn. The same evening, she told her English lover that the man had been nice, and it had been good to hear endearments again in her mother tongue, but now she was hungry and in need of dinner. Privately he marvelled at her spirit and daring, even as he heaped scorn upon her.

By August, six months after their first encounter by the velvet curtains, they were travelling to Italy on foot. Near the border, they were joined by the exile's young friend and protégé, David Garnett, and his student-friend, Harold Hobson. From the meeting point onward, Frieda flirted flamboyantly with Harold. When she later admitted that 'He had me in the hay hut', the exile disappeared, raging and morose.

Most of his lust for his lover was burned away on that journey to Italy. If his feelings for Frieda von Richthofen were not ultimately the stuff of Wagnerian passion, he nevertheless refused to be cast as the eunuch of her world, or a cipher of a man. Two summers later, when they could finally afford the passage back to London from Italy, he took her in hand, if only literally, and married her.

In song at least, they were a joyous pair. Frieda professed to like his singing, although his voice was rather too high – like the 'hooting of an owl', she declared. But *she* sang well and she loved company. Together they sang German lieder, American folk songs, Hebridean folk songs, arias, music-hall tunes, hymns and Negro spirituals.

Her presence made him long for children for the first time. Hadn't she produced three already? She was a broad-hipped, big-breasted fertility goddess, and he made his offerings. If he was thin, he was not yet quenched.

In the motor, Frieda snorted and shifted under the rug. Snow swirled in the tapered light of the headlamps. They were passing a small

Saxon church, where the lantern at the lych-gate blinked and beck-oned like a wrecker's lamp to a ship. *Believe*, it said, *believe*.

He rolled up his window. The Church of England was little more than a recruitment office these days. The Meynell family, by contrast, were not wanting in moral courage. Few other families would have offered a home, not only to a von Richthofen 'Hun', but to a couple suspected of spying for the Kaiser – suspected by Wellington House in London and, more routinely, by the children, publicans, post-mistresses and local constabulary of Chesham.

Spies! Frieda had often seen the Kaiser in the German court in her youth and had disliked him always. These days, she feared for her sister, who was married to the Crown Prince's aide-de-camp. Admittedly, she did admire her cousins who had joined the German air force, but that meant nothing. She freely acknowledged that her countrymen had no sense of what the English described as 'fair play'. Her people were simply logical in any task they chose to execute, and if the task at hand was a war, well, they were logical about that too.

Scotland Yard started investigating them, just after Asquith declared war. Lawrence remembered the night they left David Garnett's flat in Chelsea, calling out their farewells, all very innocently and gaily in German. Later they were informed that one of David's – Bunny's – neighbours had heard and reported them. That was the begin-ning. The Yard was getting hundreds of letters every day from people reporting their neighbours. Each case had to be investigated, the detective said. The future of the nation depended on it.

Later, Bunny alleged that Ford Madox Ford, or 'Fat Fordie' as he was also known, was writing propaganda for Wellington House, and had reported Lawrence and Frieda's 'German sympathies' to his superiors – to atone, Bunny suggested, for the fact of his own German father.

It wasn't impossible. Ford had championed Lawrence's novels four or five years previously, but that was a world away now.

Yes, the Meynells were brave and generous to take them in. Even so, he could only hope that, in Greatham, there wouldn't be too many of them flustering about the place. The kindness of Viola and her parents had saved him from the penury that stalked him, but he needed to work, not to be wheeled out for family occasions and the usual social bosh.

The Meynells were a clan. Viola's father Wilfrid, the *paterfamilias*, had provided each of his grown daughters with a cottage at Greatham. A few sons popped up too on occasion. There seemed to be seven offspring. The mother, Alice Meynell, was an Establishment poetess figure known for her benevolence to younger and less fortunate writers. Famously, she and Wilfrid had saved the down-at-heel Catholic poet Francis Thompson from myriad demons and vices. They'd literally rescued him from the streets, published his work themselves, and ensured it an elevated readership. Whether history would thank them for it or not, he had remarked to Viola, was another matter.

In the way of many religious converts, Wilfrid and Alice Meynell made devout Catholics and had raised their children in the Old Church. The exile assumed – that is to say, he fervently hoped – he and Frieda would be let off the Latin mumblings and incense. Bad for his chest, he'd say. But the Meynells seemed, from all he'd been told, *cheerful*. Almost unfashionably cheerful. How was that possible? He was intrigued by large, exuberant families, if only because his own had been so pinched and fraught.

Viola, one of the younger daughters, was a fellow novelist, doing rather well, and charming with it. She had declared herself a great admirer of his *Sons and Lovers*, and had sweetly, without hesitation, insisted they take her cottage on her father's property – a converted cattle shed.

Frieda burst out laughing, as only Frieda would – 'Do you think us in some way *bovine*, my dear?' – and Viola nervously explained that the cottage was now converted for human habitation, and really quite comfortable. The Meynells, she said, had dubbed it 'Shed Hall', but the designation was merely a family joke which had somehow stuck. She would, she said, happily move into the main house, Winborn's, with her parents, who divided their time between Sussex and London.

Shed Hall, if not the stuff of enviable letterheads, could be no worse, he decided, than the miserable, muddy cottage in Chesham. Frieda, for her part, was of the view that it would be a flimsy shack on the south coast, and they would be friendless. But in a perfectly timed afterthought, Viola sent word that he and Frieda would have a housemaid; the woman would be provided by her parents.

Frieda started packing.

The stubborn question remained of how to pay for his wife's divorce. It was unexpectedly costly, he'd discovered, to steal another man's wife; costly to the tune of £150, and in this, the Year of Our Lord, 1915, he didn't have £5 to rub together.

As they negotiated the snowy road, his typewriter, a recent gift from his new American poet-friend Amy Lowell, bounced and rattled in the footwell, between his feet. He'd lost time on the novel, with his five months numb in the grave of Chesham, and now he would miss spring publication, even with Viola Meynell's offer to type up the manuscript professionally for him. He didn't care. What was the use, he'd said only that morning to Frieda, of giving books to the swinish public in its present, hell-bent, war-mongering state?

We have to live, she said, with her characteristic shrug.

He was a married man, that shrug said. He had responsibilities. *She* was his responsibility, she, her handsome Prussian face, and its happiness. In Chesham, between the arguments, the depression, the bouts of fury, and the mutual threats of separation, he'd bought her a new hat, a new coat, and a necklace made of lapis lazuli. Of the £50 his publisher, Methuen, had advanced him, almost nothing remained.

He didn't tell his wife that his £90 on publication would be claimed directly by her Husband-Professor's lawyers before he, Lawrence, saw any of it. Why frighten her? The court had granted the divorce, but bankruptcy loomed.

And he badly needed new collars.

In the storm, there wasn't another soul on the road. They crept on, ever deeper into old Sussex. Their driver whistled a nervous jingle as the snow drove at the car. Once, they teetered over a ditch, and the exile had to get out to push. Then they skidded onward, down twisting roads and lanes.

Frieda was heavy against his side. With his free arm, he made a porthole in the window's frost and peered up at the fretwork of branches; they closed over the road, wrought in bright snow.

Near the hamlet of Greatham, the storm gave out. The sky cleared. The gabled roof of the old farmhouse, Winborn's, came into view. He straightened to see over a snow-topped hedge, and something within him warmed. Viola had said that a good fire, jugged hare and wine would await them, whatever the hour. He was hungry. He couldn't remember when he'd last had an appetite.

As the motor crept up the lane, he forced his frozen window down again. The stars swam above them like silver seed – reckless, rampant and yearning – in the dark womb of the night. The sky pulsed and here, he observed, in the beautiful middle of nowhere, the Milky Way was as thick as empyrean jizz; as bright, as glorious, as the wanks of the old gods.

The spirits of this place weren't dead as they were in Buckinghamshire. He could feel them, and he could feel life returning. *Libre, libero.* For the first time in months, he thought that he and his wife – who had just awoken with pink cheeks and shining eyes – might even manage a warm-hearted fuck.

The next morning, he found his old school-teacher's overcoat in one of their cases, having conceded that his corduroy jacket was unequal to the day's gusts. On their maid Hilda's advice, he tied potato sacks around his shoes, and accepted Wilfrid Meynell's kind offer of a pair of field-glasses. Frieda fussed at his neck with a muffler, offered by Viola, while Viola passed him a pair of her brother's gloves. He rewarded her with a warm smile over Frieda's shoulder.

Meynell children jumped like frogs from some hidden pond and pleaded to be allowed to go. Hilda shooed them away, and 'Off, quick as you like,' she instructed. He grabbed his old slouch hat.

He'd hardly started climbing when a gust took it, and he had to stomp through the drifts to catch its brim with a foot. He felt his face flatten as he walked into the wind and turned from it, looking down on what the Meynells, amongst themselves, called the Colony. He could see the roof of his new home. He was, in truth, delighted with Viola's cow-shed. Already his mind was composing a scene for a story – about he knew not what. It was a reflex, a turn of mind.

On one side of this quadrangle was the long, long barn or shed which Marshall had made into a cottage for his youngest daughter Priscilla.

The cow-shed was a long, low building made of brick and stone, with a lovely little plaque by the door of the Holy Family in blue-and-white plaster. The Virgin's face was caught in a sombre dream, and he felt irrationally glad of her company. The priest from Amberley, the nearest village, was a Meynell family friend, and had, said Viola, blessed Winborn's and each of the dwellings in the Colony.

On his way out of his own door that morning, he'd raised a hand and touched the Virgin with two fingers. He wasn't inclined towards Catholicism, but he was intrigued and comforted by its Madonnas. The Church of England believed it could do away with imagery and femaleness and mystery, and therein lay its greatest delusion. It was an immature Church, just a few hundred years old; it put a naïve faith in the rational study of the eternally irrational. That rationality had led his generation only to the trenches.

Inside their cow-shed, on first waking that morning, he and Frieda had discovered whitewashed walls, four working fireplaces, a grate loaded with logs, and solid, tree-like criss-crossings of dark beams; grand old timbers high-pitched. The sitting-room was austere and splendid, with a long, polished table. One could breathe in such a room. It reminded him of a refectory in a monastery, except, that is, when Frieda took to mooing like a cow, which she did, she said, both to amuse and 'un-frighten' herself. She found their new home 'stark'.

One saw little blue-and-white check curtains at the long windows.

She let the kitchen curtains fall back. 'It is so very rural, Lorenzo,' she said, looking as if she might cry.

He conceded that they would indeed be more isolated than they had been in Chesham – farther from London, certainly – but there was no duck-pond to flood under their door, and Sussex was far more beautiful than Buckinghamshire. Their new home was only in want of a good bookcase, and he would start building one directly. He would lay linoleum as well. The main bedroom was a good size, and – luxury! – they had not one but two guest rooms. Hilda, their maid, was a marvel and a dear, the train service from London to Pulborough was surprisingly good, the walk from there to Greatham not so very far, and friends *would* come. He didn't mention that he'd already written to Koteliansky, ignoring the fact that Kot didn't like Frieda, nor she him.

Mein Lieber Kot,

> *Will you come down on Saturday – write and tell us the train. I think only Viola Meynell will be here. I will walk down to meet you – but come in the daylight. The cottage is not yet quite finished – there are many things to do in the way of furnishing and so on. But this is really a place with a beauty of character. Frieda likes the Meynells but is a bit frightened of the cloistral severity of this place. I must say I love it.*

> *auf wiedersehn,*
> *D. H. Lawrence*

Miraculously, there was even a bathroom, with blue Delft tiles, a piped-in tub and gloriously hot water. He'd bathed very late the night before, after supper and failed relations with Frieda. He'd sat up to his neck, observing the outcrop of his ribs and the soft nub of his cock, while Frieda called 'Moo! Moo!' from the bedroom, half to entertain and half to beseech. 'Where is my bull?' she called. Her great gift was her eternal optimism.

As he climbed the snowy slope that first morning, the downland slept on, its flanks, bosoms and rumps blanketed in white-gold. The way was steep, and the snow knee-deep. He had to stop often to catch his breath in the gusts, bending double at times, and once lingering to exchange a few words with a shepherd. Each struggled to understand the other but the man, Lawrence finally deduced, had been digging out his flock since first light.

The exile looped the field-glasses over a pine bough and took off the fine Meynell gloves. Then he plunged his hands deep into the drift, where he felt almost immediately the cold, hard bone of a shin. With the shepherd at the other end, he got hold of a pair of legs and together they heaved, until a shaggy ewe emerged, like a yellow-eyed Lazarus from the tomb.

In his youth, he'd always enjoyed farm-labouring, especially when it came to tending the animals or milking the cows. He had, people always said in those days, a way with creatures. The shepherd looked up, mumbled terse thanks and an oath, then began pounding the animal back to life.

The exile had first come to Sussex, in May of 1909, in his former life as a Croydon school-teacher, on a walking holiday from Brighton to Newhaven, over the sea-cliffs, with Helen Corke. She'd been a colleague whom he might have taken as a wife had he not been determined to escape both Croydon and the school as fast as he could. On their holiday that year, it had been all easy sunshine, with frothy waves in the distance. Brighton was stately and magnificent, with its royal pavilion, a pleasure-palace which might have been dreamed up for 'Kubla Khan'.

They slept in a hazel brake, deep in bluebells. They laughed at the Rottingdean windmill, squat and awkward. The sunshine, for the entire nine miles, there and back, was unbroken, with a gentle breeze to cool them as they walked.

Now, in the sudden grip of winter, the wind was the kind that took your skin off. The evergreens were silent, with boughs drooping beneath their cauls of snow. In the distance, the local waterway of the Channel, known as the Solent, was leaden grey.

He trudged on and clambered higher, sensing the footpath rather than seeing it. After eons of erosion and wear, the hillside slopes were smooth, like children's drawings of hills, save for their 'tumuli', the burial mounds of ancient Britons. He remembered them, powerfully, from his previous trip, and he was determined to find them again, come spring. Before the Roman occupation of Britain, the people of Sussex had populated its high ground as much as modern people now did its lowlands.

He steadied himself on frozen branches as he climbed, stopping only when something caught his eye: fox dung on the snow, dense and dark with the fur of a creature consumed; a crossbill's nest high in a pine – the chicks often hatched in the winter with snow on their backs. On the ground below the nest lay the remnants of the pine-cones from which the mother or father had prised the seeds. Higher still was a profusion of holly and berries, blood-bright against the drifts.

In the distance, on the tablelands of the Weald, the snow muffled everything, and the River Arun ran through it, a sluggish artery of silver. Beyond its south bank, the parallel tracks of the railway line, where they weren't choked by snow, glinted with the illusion of infinity.

He heard a shrill 'kee-kee-kee' and turned his face skyward. The kestrel was not a big bird of prey but its stillness was magisterial, and free of all strain as it glided, then hovered, reading him as he read it, its wings gently beating the sky. Using the glasses, he made out the grey-blue underside of its wings and the white fan of its tail-feathers. Its peace, its wind-hovering patience, was briefly his.

Then it plummeted out of view, as if a string somewhere had been cut. The hunter dropped from a thousand feet to the ground within a matter of seconds. A vole or a field mouse must have run across the white of the hillside, as terrified, he imagined, as an infantryman sprinting across No-Man's-Land.

From the hilltop, the hamlet of Greatham, a mile away, seemed not so much to have been established as to have been cast at the foot of the Downs, like a child's abandoned toy bricks. According to Wilfrid Meynell, the parish was recorded in the Domesday Book and, if it had ever thrived, it was nearly extinct now, although still beautiful with a vestigial, fading life. A few chimneys puffed from the great manor house. Its glass-houses blinked.

Next to the manor house, and also apart from it, stood a twelfth-century, single-roomed church, as modest as a haystack. Meynell told him it had been built for Saxon shepherds, and that its walls were made with rubble from the Roman ruins of Sussex.

Nearby farm buildings lay dormant under the snow. He spotted the long, low rectangle of an ancient tithe barn and, not far from it, the steeply tiled roof of Winborn's, glowing red against the white.

Winborn's, as he'd discovered on arrival, was a seventeenth-century farmhouse with timbered walls, broody wings, and dark oak beams throughout. *Not far from the tiny church of the almost extinct hamlet stood his own house, a commodious old farmhouse standing back from the road across a bare grassed yard.* Meynell had added the library, which served as a reception room, and he had an ambition, Viola said, to build a family chapel. The whole arrangement was a pastoral idyll: eighty acres in span and, when not covered in snow, a patchwork of oak and elm, of wide lawns and rose bushes. It had a good-sized orchard too, plus shady woodland, and a dyke-bank with a beguiling ridge of dark pines.

When the River Arun overflowed its banks, as it did each winter, the family's parcel of land was lapped by an inland sea, which made the soil of only haphazard use for agriculture. For that reason, when Meynell was first shown the property, it had been in want of a buyer for many months. It was also four miles from the nearest village. Yet its very uselessness and dilapidation charmed the literary clan. They had no understanding of the farming life, but they possessed fertile imaginations and quickly grasped what the place could be.

Meynell, a Catholic editor and newspaper publisher, took possession in 1911. That June, he and Alice the poetess, his lady-wife, were transported in a fly from Pulborough Station up the rutted lane.

Their approach to Winborn's was skimmed by nodding corn and crimson poppies. On the property's far side, a herd of deer skittered across the scrubby heath of common land.

In time, the deer would encroach, eating their way through the family's kitchen garden over successive seasons. Bracken and gorse invaded the tennis lawn. Field mice nested in tennis shoes. A thriving population of grass-snakes made London visitors yelp and jump. As tea was poured at the outdoor table in autumn sunshine, family and guests alike chose to ignore the skirmishes and guttural barks of the rutting deer.

The challenges, however, rooted the Meynells ever more deeply to the place, and the peace of Greatham became their sanctuary from London, especially once the National Madness was declared. Where did all the sane people go these days? Where could they put themselves? To speak against the War and the country's self-inflicted wound was to be branded unpatriotic.

Viola explained that her father had been a Quaker until he converted to Catholicism at the age of eighteen. But he had stayed true to his pacifism. A quiet man of business and faith, he had no faith that the War could lead to anything but more war. On that, he and his new guest were entirely agreed. These days, Greatham was no longer merely the Meynells' summer retreat from the bustle and aspirations of Kensington life; it was a pocket of peaceful resistance.

And how the exile craved peace. Fragments, whole chunks, of him had flown off by the day – into the rain of Chesham. They got trampled in its mud. He had holes in him, and not only in his clothes. The cold of the rain got in; the muck too. Yet if there was still a grief in his brokenness, there was also a queer new energy and intent, now that he had landed in Sussex. Something bigger pulsed within. It was not a clarion call – no, it was certainly not that – but a life-hum sounded through his cracked spirit. His novel, for him the bright book of life, might even carry him forward.

A good story was a form of communication, mind to mind, spirit to spirit. It sent life sparking from stranger to stranger, across space, decades and centuries. Human sympathy – human attention – had magic in it. Any real story fizzed with sympathy – the writer's and reader's – across time, over rows of typographical marks; those low boundary fences of the imagination, hurdled.

He wasn't interested in the polished hard bricks of creation; of life trapped in edifices; in perfect symmetries on the page. True life held a looseness, a flux and influx, floods and barren fields, frozen winter and spring's green pulse. He'd risk jerkiness, the errant, the raw on the page. Other men risked far more daily – he'd seen that in the dark mines of his boyhood. Many were broken, with nothing more to mark their lives than a gaping maw of earth.

He felt a failure most days, it was true, but here, among the old gods of Sussex, life seemed possible. The air was so startlingly clear, and anyway, only the dead were ever safe.

'*I ought*' He turned again towards the rooftops of Greatham. He was lucky to be in possession of a novel to finish, a cottage, a maid, a bath and a typist.

How impossible it would have been   '*I ought never*'   in that moment to grasp his own words, blowing back at him from the future   '*I ought never, never to have gone to live at Greatham.*'

Earlier that same morning, they'd breakfasted with the Meynells – a veritable horde of them – over a bountiful table of food. Wilfrid Meynell, the clan patriarch, was a short but robust northerner in a good grey suit; a smoky torch of a man, puffing on a clay pipe, full of life and generosity. He enjoyed, evidently, the sentimentality of big family life and the cultivation of a genteel, cultured home. But he was quick, canny and clear-eyed. The exile could see as much in his gaze. As they spoke, Lawrence sketched his host in his mind's eye.

He was a business man, but by nature he was sensual, and he was on his knees before a piece of poetry that really gratified him. Consequently, whilst he was establishing a prosperous business, at home he diffused the old Quaker righteousness with a new, aesthetic sensuousness, and his children were brought up in this sensuous, aesthetic heat, which was always, at the same time, kept in the iron grate of conventional ethics.

His wife, Alice, was as small and delicate as her husband was robust. She was dark-eyed and dark in complexion, with a subtlety of perception which impressed the exile. Her poems were too distant – generationally and stylistically – for his liking; she was fond of sonnets, quatrains and a certain elevation of form, but her reputation was still going strong. She had, only a year or two before, been proposed by some for the role of Poet Laureate, for a second time, and her *Collected Poems* had recently been published.

Viola explained that her mother loved Greatham but had been down from London only little of late because of poor health – migraines usually, which Alice called 'wheels'. 'I'm down with one of my wheels, alas.' But her gladness at the sight of new visitors was heartier than she herself was, and she insisted that he and Frieda finish off a box of French chocolates, bought for the holiday season but opened only the evening before. 'You had a long, trying journey last night, and you must be restored!' Frieda readily agreed, although they had not yet breakfasted. Alice Meynell winked, as if she were colluding with a greedy child whom she couldn't help but indulge.

The introductions at the long breakfast table were complex. There were not only many names to learn but nicknames, married names and myriad branches of the family tree. The clan seemed to treble and swell, almost queasily as the exile ate, and the room was full of various dark, madonna-like Meynell women, moving in and out. *They themselves had their own grace, but it was slow, rather heavy. They had every one of them strong, heavy limbs and darkish skins, and they were short in stature.*

Afterwards, Viola played hostess in the library while a younger married sister arranged coffee, trays and armchairs around the great hearth. That sister – whose name he'd forgotten – was, apparently, a fine painter; she'd studied, Viola said, at the Slade School and still painted actively, though now a mother; a sweet-faced toddler slept on a cushion in a willow basket on the sideboard. Frieda asked if she might pick her up, and Lawrence had had to remind her that the child was sleeping.

The library was a large, book-lined sitting-room dominated by a cheery fire, and busy with Italian bric-a-brac and William Morris wallpaper. Alice took Frieda – the new, if not blushing, bride – by the hand and told her that they were most welcome.

The older woman had a natural warmth. She hoped that he, 'Mr Lawrence', would be able to get on with his book 'here in the wilds of Sussex', and that he would not find her family *too* overwhelming. She confessed – and he liked her immediately for it – that she often had to take to the water-closet when she needed to compose a poem.

She congratulated him on his objections to the War. Francis, her son, was of the same sound mind. She seemed to emphasise the word 'sound', and he wondered if Viola had told her mother, out of kindness, about his breakdown in Chesham.

As guests, they were shown miscellaneous family photographs and portraits, including a framed drawing by John Singer Sargent. The celebrated American had made a study of Alice in her youth.

The exile nodded politely as he assessed it. He said he enjoyed a little drawing and painted himself, or had in his youth; that he had taught painting, drawing and botany to the boys at the school in Croydon.

'You were a teacher?' asked Viola, joining them, and he nodded, remembering that former self.

Of the Sargent study of her mother, for courtesy's sake, he expressed no view. The Americans, like the English, he thought, painted clothes rather than bodies. Both nations were lacking a single artist of the human body to compare to Picasso, Michelangelo or Degas. It was an emotionally stunted artistic history. Renoir, for all his limitations, knew how to paint with his penis.

Frieda, always bored by conventionally polite occasions, separated from the group and moved to the library window to signal to her husband her desire to leave. She looked out to where Madeline's three little girls were playing in the snow, making snow-angels. She sorely missed her own three.

When she had appeared at the school gates, a few months before, shortly after her Register Office wedding, they had looked positively frightened of her. Even dear Monty, her eldest, her only son, had turned pale. Elsa, in her panic, had tried to pretend, in front of her chums, that she didn't know who 'the woman' was. After two years away from them, ten-year-old Barby, the youngest, seemed actually *not* to know her. She'd burst into tears at the sight of the woman reaching for her through the bars.

What on earth had the Weekleys been telling them about her? She asked Lawrence, but although he loved children, he hardly knew hers, and the problem for him was mostly a theoretical one. At times, he ran out of patience with her altogether. He had married her, hadn't he? He was scrambling to find the money for her divorce, wasn't he? He couldn't fix everything! If he could have 'magicked up her children', he would have, without hesitation. He would have been a second father to them.

As it was, he said, there was only one thing for it: she must ask for Lady Ottoline's help. *She* might exert influence on Professor Weekley. But Frieda would have to be *kind* to her. He would invite her to stay. What more could he do?

When Wilfrid Meynell joined Frieda at the window and asked after her, she blinked away a tear and declared that the fire was making her sleepy, which is when the exile saw poor Meynell tug on his short grey beard, as unsure in that moment how to entertain the golden-haired daughter of a German Baron as he would have been a Teutonic goddess.

Viola was quick to intercede. Most of the family were returning to London that afternoon, she told Frieda, casually but reassuringly. They had been *so* pleased to meet the new residents of the Colony, but they couldn't stay. She and Lawrence would have peace and quiet. She would herself stay, of course, as arranged, and she would make a start the next day on Lawrence's manuscript.

The exile departed Alice's company, to spare Viola the problem of his wife. He was, he declared, most grateful for her help with the manuscript. Privately, he knew there were hundreds of handwritten pages. Six hundred perhaps. He told her he'd have it all 'out of him' by the end of February. He had promised his publisher that there would be no *flagrant* love-passages in it, but he admitted to Viola that he and the Messrs Methuen might see things differently. She nodded and said she would mark up passages he might wish to 're-consider'.

Viola's sister Madeline crossed the room to them, with her three little girls in tow. Madeline explained to the guests that she, her husband and their family had, until quite recently, occupied a primitive place, called Rackham Cottage, at the far edge of the Colony, in a sunny dell, under a sprawl of old oak trees. The property marked the border where the Meynells' cultivated acreage met the shaggy land of the public common.

Madeline was thirty-one or thirty-two, he estimated, and had a husband, Perceval Lucas – Percy – who had been stationed for training in Epsom since September, when he'd volunteered for active service. Madeline passed the guest a framed photograph which stood on the sideboard. It had been taken the summer before – by 'our little niece Mary', Viola added. The photograph was of a cricket team, or rather half a team. In July, Percy Lucas had been playing cricket on the green and, afterwards, 'Mary, our sister Monica's only child' had asked the men if she might take their picture with her new Brownie camera.

In time, a few chairs and stools were pulled up. It was a relaxed assembly agreed for the benefit of an eager child. Standing a little nervously before the men, she had gripped her camera by her waist, turned it on its side to peer down into the side-viewfinder – in order to make a rectangular picture. Then she'd composed her subject, kept her belly very still, and – flip! – pulled the lever.

Madeline was distracted at that moment by her own pleading children. In the interval, Viola informed the exile that 'dear Percy', Madeline's Percy, was 'a gentle man' – 'thoughtful if a little indifferent to things,' she said with a smile.

'Oh?' he said.

She reached after words, still smiling brightly. 'A little adrift, I suppose one might say, in his own world.'

He gathered that Perceval Lucas had taken the entire family by surprise that summer when word of the Declaration of War reached Greatham. It was not thought that married men, and particularly not married men with children, would be conscripted, although the regular army was on the verge of being quickly outnumbered on the Continent, or would be, certainly, without new British recruits in their tens of thousands. The authorities were targeting boys and young men, but Percy Lucas, along with his cricket friends, presented himself, on the first day, at the recruiting office. 'It was a noble thing to do,' Viola said – and 'I'll leave it at that,' said her face.

Madeline re-joined their conversation. For the benefit of their guests, she pointed out her husband in the photo, seated on the ground at the end of the front row. He was tall, slender but strong in build, with long supple legs pulled up into the frame. His pose was both concentrated and languid. He possessed a handsome face, with the aquiline nose of an old county family. The gaze was intelligent, sensitive, reserved. An eyebrow was raised, suggesting a capacity for irony. He had a head of fine, silky hair, the kind that had ripened from blond to brown with age; he wore it oiled and parted sharply in the middle.

Percy Lucas, the exile saw, was even-featured, clean-shaven and effortless in his cricket flannels. Here was the flower of English manhood. Here was a man who was entirely at ease in his land, free from incongruities and intensities. He had the look of a calm, clever batsman, one who knew how to conserve his energy and react instinctively. Percy stared back at Mary's lens, and his gaze said: 'I am precisely where I am meant to be − I could only ever have been here.'

It seemed to the exile something near magical, such a sense of belonging; of rightness, of assurance in the ground beneath one's feet. He returned the picture to Madeline, stood and reached for a bowl of walnuts.

It was a job to crack them. He felt the weakness of his hands − small hands on long arms. Everything about him was dispropor-tioned: his hands, his clubby nose, his narrow chin. When he was young, he had been lithe and milky-white. Now he was merely thin and pale.

What sort of man, he asked himself, would willingly throw himself headlong into a war which had neither required nor demanded him? Perceval Lucas had to be either bloodthirsty or morbidly selfless. Which was it?

And from that morning forth, the mystery of Perceval Lucas was an irritation which scratched away at the exile's brain. 'A gentle man,' Viola had said of her brother-in-law − 'thoughtful if a little indiffer-ent to things. Adrift in his own world.' Why run at a war? What *was* the man running from? In his absence from the gathering, Perceval Lucas suddenly seemed to the exile to be more forcibly present than anyone in the room.

And so a story of England, of Perceval Lucas's England, flickered strangely to life in those otherwise inconsequential minutes of a convivial breakfast in 1915 − 'England, My England' − a powerful story which was unknown even to its author as he laughed, cracked walnuts and joked with the Meynells. A powerful, poison-dart of a story soon to fly − decades into the future.

Madeline Meynell Lucas, Viola's sister and Perceval's wife, was a warm-hearted, pretty woman, and capable too by all accounts. Her family was generous. Their children were beautiful. Percy Lucas clearly lived in peace, thought the exile, and with enviable ease. He had a flat in Bayswater *and the young couple must transfer themselves from time to time from the country to the city. In town they had plenty of friends, of the same ineffectual sort as himself, tampering with the arts*— He also had a little paradise there in Sussex with Madeline's family, in his cottage in the sunny dell.

At the window, Wilfrid Meynell had somehow managed to sustain the attention of Frieda, who, unknown to him, actually enjoyed the company of any man of distinction. Lawrence, Viola and Madeline now crossed from window to hearth, and he, their guest, chatted away, tossing shells onto the fire. But even as he happily proffered walnut halves to each woman in turn, he felt something queer cut through him, a hot knife from breastbone to bowel; a curious, seeping hatred for a seemingly virtuous man he did not know and had never met. What a peculiar thing hatred was – and yet no less real for that. He was not blind to the truth of himself: he had, he knew, a large but crooked heart.

Madeline took up the poker and prodded a burning log deep into the grate. As she did, she admitted to him, in a quiet tone, that, since her husband's departure for the army, she preferred their London flat to Rackham Cottage, which was too lonely and remote for her liking. Nor could she keep up with the garden 'dear Percy' had dug and devoted himself to. In fact, her husband had been repairing the log-bridge over their brook when he found he had to report for duties. The bridge was left unfinished. She worried it was unsafe, especially for the local children. The exile assured her he'd be glad to have a look at it once the snow was melted. He was handy with a hammer and nails.

Percy had, she said, in reply to his question before it came, joined up with men he'd known since his schooldays, even though some were a good deal younger than he. They'd been on the local cricket team together and in the same Morris-dance group, and although none of them could recall who'd first had the idea of joining up, one had somehow inspired the next 'and so on', she said with a vague wave of her hand. They had responded decisively to Lord Kitchener's call for volunteers. Now, incredibly, they were in training as officers in the Public School Brigade. She blinked, as if her brain could not catch up. It was so unexpected, she said. Her husband never argued with a soul, nor could he even bring himself to kill a snake! 'Let be,' she said. 'That is always Percy's golden rule, "Let be."'

She shook her head, banishing tears. Then she lowered her voice again and confided to the exile that Percy's decision *had* taken her aback at first. Before he had converted to Catholicism in order to marry her, he, like her own family previously, had been a committed Quaker. A pacifist, in other words. Also, their girls were still *so* young and they needed— She stopped herself. The idea of war was simply so far removed from all she – from all *they* as a couple – knew and held dear.

She was very proud of her husband, of course. She didn't mean to suggest that she wasn't. They all were. He had even 'cheated at' his army eye-test a little, memorising in advance the lines of an eye-chart, when he might have, legitimately, accepted a 'fail' and stayed at home. Yet he'd been determined not to break his promise to his old friends, given they were already through.

The exile's immediate thought was of the man's promise – his vow – to *her*, his wife, and as if sensing it, Madeline conceded that his going had been an 'adjustment'. After his departure for the army camp, Rackham Cottage – on her own with the three children, the nurse and governess – had become simply too difficult, even with others often nearby at Winborn's. These days she and the children visited from London instead, on school holidays and for special occasions, of which the Lawrences' visit was one! She and her girls tended to stay in the main house, now that Percy was away, but this time, the children had hankered after their old cottage for the weekend, and Arthur, her father's man, had left them a heap of dry wood on the hearth. Only they hadn't realised they'd be snowed-in by morning!

The two older little girls, who clearly took after their father with their blonde thistle-down heads, re-appeared now and spoke to the exile shyly at first, clutching at their mother's skirts. But soon, the middle child, Christian, was babbling away, describing to him how they'd had to dig themselves *out* of the snow to get to Winborn's for the special breakfast with the important guests. 'That's you!' she said, hugging herself with delight, as if she didn't quite believe it herself. Then, she grew serious: '*Why* are you important?'

'Why do you think I'm important?'

'Because you have a beard and because your wife used to be at a royal court. Are my cheeks still rosy?' she asked.

'They are.'

'That's because, just before we came indoors, we lay down with Florrie, our governess, and made angels in the snow – for you and Mrs Lawrence. I even got snow in my drawers!'

He grinned and said he would admire their angels on his way out.

'Mine is the best.' She must have been five or six. 'Barbara, my sister, is too little to understand how to do it properly, although Florrie *tried* to show her,' she said haughtily, 'and Sylvia, my big sister, could only use her good leg, couldn't you, Sylv?' She looked to her sister, then back to The Guest: 'Will you take us sledging today after Father Patrick comes?'

'Hush,' said Madeline, smiling. 'Go and see if Cook will make you hot cocoa in the kitchen.'

He watched the three little Lucas girls exit the library with their governess, and noticed for the first time Sylvia, the eldest. She had been too shy to do more than nod as her younger sister spoke for them. But now, he could see the shape of the leg-iron under her dark winter stockings as she limped away. Her right leg did not bend at the knee.

Later, as he left, he spotted her angel on the snowy lawn. The weight and effort of the leg in the brace had dragged up the mud from the ground, making for a mucky angel. A happier one, perhaps.

Viola's brother, Francis, and his wife moved vaguely in and out of the gathering too that morning. He must have been the pacifist son his mother had mentioned earlier. Was he a bookbinder? Or a printer? There was too much Meynelling to keep up with. Looking at him, it became quickly clear that Francis had married young. 'Whatever for?' the exile asked him over the piano-top. 'Nearly all marriages are frauds or failures.' He threw him a walnut. 'Is it because you were afraid of yourself?'

'I was rather in love,' Francis replied, blushing.

An older sibling, another brother, was retrieving logs from a snow-drift and heaving them inside, one heap at a time, to dry by the fire. The old spaniel, Careless, trotted to and fro after him, his tail knocking knick-knacks as he went.

Careless seemed to approve of the guests, to the extent that he was inspired on more than one occasion to hump Lawrence's leg. 'You have an admirer!' Francis declared. Everyone, including Lawrence and Frieda, laughed, and the exile bent to touch the dog's silky ear.

The remaining sister, Monica, sat in a winged armchair at some distance from the fire, her face mostly hidden. How odd, he thought, to sit so insistently alone at a family gathering. Francis observed the concern on the exile's face. 'She's got the morbs,' he said with a shrug.

Viola approached and shooed her brother away. Their eldest sister, she murmured, had been abandoned by her learned husband, a respected doctor of biology and eugenics. The exile nodded. Too rational a man, a man who measured the circumference of heads, he said, could only make a woman miserable. Poor thing, he said.

Viola, who was nearly thirty, the exile's own age, was engaged to be married to the editor Martin Secker and, perhaps because of her auspicious state of being, displayed a most sincere but, in his view, unwarranted optimism about the state of her elder sister's mind. In low tones, Viola informed her friend, and also his wife who joined them now, that Monica suffered with her 'nerves' – but that she was 'most certainly on the mend' in her own cosy cottage.

He saw Frieda's eyes narrow at Viola's appraisal of Monica. His wife had little patience for illness, or even much belief in most illnesses, but in that moment, she managed at least to refrain from making her usual, blunt diagnosis of 'hysteria'.

For his part, he could see quite plainly that Monica was *not* 'on the mend'. She carried some deep bruise within and was, almost certainly, in the middle of a nervous breakdown. At the breakfast table earlier, he'd recognised the strain of her mouth, the flat, slow monotones of her speech, the purpled shadows under her eyes, and their glaze, at once febrile and deadened. Hadn't he only just pulled himself back from that brink? He could hardly bear to look at her. She reminded him of the corrosive darkness he wanted to believe he'd cast off for good.

On the quadrangle of the Colony, Monica had the pretty cottage next to Winborn's, built for her by her father, as she could not, given her husband's abandonment of her, bear London society. Her cottage *with the vegetable garden stretching away to the oak copse* lay fifty yards away from their own cow-shed. Monica 'Magdalen' lived there with her ten-year-old daughter, Mary, who was not at school.

From what he could gather from Viola, her niece Mary more or less ran wild in Greatham, collecting birds' nests, keeping silk-worms, playing with the local village children, and taking endless pictures with the Brownie camera her absent father had bought for her last summer, so that he might otherwise ignore her.

She was clever, Viola told him. The girl had even taught herself how to develop and print the pictures herself in the old garden shed Arthur, Meynell's driver and gardener, had let her have. Together, they had covered its door, windows and internal walls in Turkey-red twill, two bolts of which her grandfather had purchased for her; it was the ideal fabric for keeping sunlight out. It even smelled lovely, Viola said, redolent with the fragrance of pot-pourri trailed all the way from the shop shelves of Liberty.

Viola showed him another of the girl's recent photographs, from the summer before, of the 71-year-old Henry James and his philosopher-brother William's daughter. They had called in to meet and pay their regards to Alice, the celebrated poet. Little Mary had insisted they pose on either side of Rory, the children's beloved pony – as if, said Viola, the two guests had failed, in the photographer's estimation, to be sufficiently interesting in their own right.

Lawrence grinned at that. Henry James had given him a bad review in the *Times Literary Supplement* the year before, and the absurd pony pose did his heart good to see. The sunlight struck Henry's bald pate, giving his stout form a comically mystical aura. Careless, the spaniel, was open-mouthed and barking at them from the background. William's mouth looked both strained and stained, as if with lip rouge.

Too many cherries, Viola explained.

As for the girl's whereabouts at breakfast, Mary had disappeared first thing that morning, apparently, when she saw the fresh snowfall. No one had seen her since. Miss Turner – Florrie – the Lucas girls' governess, thought she must have run off to check on Rory, who was pastured in Hawtins's field at the manor house. Mary and Florrie were the only ones who could catch him, and Mary had been worried he had frozen to death.

Throughout the year, on the neighbouring farms, she milked, mucked out after, and sang to the various animals. She wanted to be a farmer, Viola said. The exile thought she sounded like the most interesting Meynell of the lot, even if she did have the misfortune of her father's name – Saleeby, the eminent father-eugenicist who had bolted, abandoning wife and daughter. The very thought set his teeth on edge.

Viola then came to the nub of what – it now seemed – she had been trying to ask him all along ... When Monica had proved too unwell to make a plan for Mary's future, her grandmamma – Alice the poet – had booked her wild granddaughter into St Paul's School for Girls in London, for the coming autumn. But Mary, Viola confessed, had a great deal of catching up to do. The child had taught herself to read and could *just* write, but she had never been to school. The girl possessed quite original gifts, and Viola mused aloud about whether he, a former teacher, might be in a position to help her get through the entrance examination. In this way, the topic was at last broached.

He said, yes, of course, he could offer Mary tuition, once his novel was safely delivered. Privately, after his novel was complete, he longed only to be left alone to the writing of his 'philosophy' and his walks, but he knew equally that the tutoring would ease his conscience of the debt he owed to the Meynells – not that anyone in that room had or would ever make him conscious of it. He knew that too. But ... his nature wouldn't allow him to forget a good turn, or to forgive it. Life had reduced him, and the generosity of friends only made that fact more painfully obvious. Charity was humiliating to a man of nearly thirty, and he'd do almost anything to free himself of it.

He was convincing as he replied, 'Of course. I'd be happy to.'

Viola looked again, fretfully, to Monica, little Mary's mother, morose in her armchair. Viola leaned in and whispered that their father had expressly purchased the motor-car for Monica's sake, to at least get her out of doors each day. Everyone was trying to encourage her to sight-see as much as possible, if only to take the air. Viola hoped he and Frieda might also encourage such outings. As if on cue, Frieda set down her coffee and proceeded to the armchair in the dim corner. She felt that her natural place in life was a well-upholstered car seat behind a capped chauffeur. 'Monica,' Lawrence heard his wife ooze, 'how very good it is to meet you ...'

She would, he knew, intrude on poor Monica's misery long enough to win her affection and, with it, a chauffeur. Fortunately for Monica, the priest from Amberley arrived at that moment, stamping snow from his boots. So they all bundled up, took a mug of hot cider served by Hilda, and stepped into the orchard, where Arthur was busy tying slices of bread to an apple tree's snowy boughs.

Mary, Monica's wild-child, appeared suddenly then, red-cheeked and bright-eyed. Lawrence felt her curious, sidelong glances as Father Patrick blessed the orchard, splashing each tree with the holy wassail. 'Stand fast root, bear well top,' he said. 'Pray the God send us a howling good crop. Every twig, apples big. Every bough, apples now.' He made the Sign of the Cross, and everyone repeated: 'Every bough, apples now,' followed by 'Amen'. Then they crossed themselves too, raised their steaming mugs, and toasted the oldest tree in the orchard, the Old Apple.

'Well, where *are* they?' demanded Barbara, the littlest Lucas, as she clutched her baby-doll.

'Where are what, my darling?' said Madeline.

'The apples *now*!'

She cried and would not be consoled by the promise of apples come autumn.

He had made his excuses and a quick get-away. The mile uphill in the snow had been a trudge, but there on the hilltop the wind had dropped, and suddenly all was lustre and freshness. Through Wilfrid Meynell's field-glasses, he could see the shepherd, still on the slope below, digging out his sheep. He felt his lungs creak. The furnace of his heart burned.

On a mound swept clear of snow by the wind in the night, a frozen dew-pond stared back at him, winking in the sun. At its rim, catkins were golden husks, gloved in snow. As he walked, the only sound he heard was a crump-crump. Above him, the sky was so bright a bowl of blue that a coin tossed high would have rung out against it.

His words-to-come were still inconceivable that morning. *'I ought never, never to have—'* On three sides of him, the hills bucked up sharply from the tablelands. This was land that not even the Romans had tamed. *The spear of modern invention had not yet passed through it—* Its gods were wilder *and it lay there secret, primitive, savage as when the Saxons first came.* Only the scale reassured the human eye, for here was an intimate congress of weald and downland, of flatlands and hilltop.

He wiped the lenses of the glasses with his muffler. To the south, he could see the heraldic flag of Arundel Castle. Beyond, the sea stretched out like a blade with the sun on it. For once, he didn't let himself brood on the agonies and privations unfolding on the other side of the Channel. All around him, the deep drifts made a new page of the world and, in that moment, a flock of crows – as if harbingers of something – dropped from the sky to the ground ahead. He had wiped the glasses of his breath again, when another sudden commotion of movement and colour made him turn – and what-ho! A party of five was coming over the brow of the neighbouring hill, towing two Canadian-style toboggans.

For several minutes he spied through the field-glasses. Then, quite literally out of the blue, one of the group – a man – raised an arm high and waved at him.

He peered again. Surely not. What were the—

David Garnett!

He was certain it was him.

He'd last seen David – 'Bunny' to his friends – in the painter Duncan Grant's London studio a few weeks before. According to Frieda, he, the exile, had, on that occasion, made his feelings about Grant's latest work all too clear.

Well, what had they expected? At first, he'd said nothing. He'd gritted his teeth while the others oozed flattery, coaxed by Lady Ottoline. Finally, when asked his view, he was merely honest. He said Grant's paintings were bad, hopelessly bad. In fact, they were worse than bad because Grant, as he explained to the artist himself, was full of the wrong ideas about art.

A dozen years from Sussex, as Lawrence invents on the page the social circle of Lady Constance Chatterley, he will return in memory to Grant's studio that day. It will be a scene in which his characters Mellors and Constance dine with a friend, her friend, the painter Duncan 'Forbes'. The exile will confer upon Oliver Mellors, the gamekeeper, his own strong feelings about art: *His art was all tubes and valves and spirals and strange colours, ultra-modern, yet with a certain power, even a certain purity of form and tone: only Mellors thought it cruel and repellent. He didn't venture to say so, for Duncan was almost insane on the point of his art; it was a personal cult, a personal religion with him.*

Grant's abstract canvases that day were the worst of all. They had made him fume! Both Bunny and Frieda, apparently, had been acutely embarrassed as he launched into his critique. Forster – that's to say, Morgan – was also in attendance, and left at the first opportunity. Grant himself had merely sat with his hands on his knees, rocking gently, as if he had terrible toothache. Yet why invite them to look if he didn't want to hear the truth?

The exile *had* liked meeting Grant two nights before that. His dancing at Lady Ottoline's party had been vigorous. Grant and Ottoline had been improvising free steps across the drawing-room floor, when Grant caught his toe in the train of her dress, and down they went, crashing onto the parquet tiles. Grant, far less statuesque than Lady O., gallantly broke her fall, but he couldn't quite disguise the fact that he was shaken and badly bruised. The exile suspected he'd sprained or broken something. Ottoline insisted on feeding him brandy from a spoon as she cooed. How irritating she could be. Then she felt compelled to make it up to him in some way, and proposed the visit to his studio. Everyone would, she said, swoon at his work as she had.

Did Bunny – his and Duncan Grant's 'Mutual Friend' – realise now, at the distance of two Downs, that it was *him*, here, Lawrence, newly bearded and transplanted, without notice, to Sussex? Or was Bunny – he *thought* it was Bunny – merely greeting a fellow explorer on a neighbouring hill?

The exile waved an arm in reply. He called out, but snow muffled the world. He could make out a second man, taller than the others and square-shouldered. A third bent over the toboggans, steadying them on the brink of the slope. Not Duncan Grant. Too broad. There seemed also to be three women, although they were impossible to identify under all their wrappings.

Then, unexpectedly, one of them stepped away from the group's frolicking for no apparent reason. She wanted to take in the view, he supposed. The wind caught her hair; he watched her reach up to draw the nut-brown tangle back from her face and eyes, and the moment arrested him.

His centre of gravity went. He had to plant his boots hard in the snow. She was a woman sweeping her hair from her face – that was all – yet the view of her, of the Down, of the blade-sharp light, and her arm lifting— It cleaved him through.

The moment was of no consequence, and it was visionary. It hit him in the middle of his body. He felt a terrible vertigo – dread, elation, churning. She stared out over the hill, her stance steady on the icy drifts, and her face quiescent to the day, as if she herself had been raised from the downland, like some Diana of the wilderness.

She wore a man's tweed coat with deep patch pockets, a game-keeper's sort of jacket, buttoned up to her neck, and what looked like a man's thick breeches – practical in the weather. In the frame of his field-glasses' view, she turned, as if to study him, the stranger whom her friend – Bunny? – had hailed just moments before.

Her red-brown head was flame-like in the winter sunshine. She shielded her eyes with both hands against the sun, or he thought she did until he realised she too was gripping a pair of field-glasses – or opera-glasses, rather. At the top of downland, the air was crystalline, snow-flecked, a queer looking-glass. In stance and gaze, they mirrored each other strangely.

Until the man – *was* it Bunny Garnett? – beckoned her away.

He looked on still, but she returned the glasses to her pocket and pulled a hat with earflaps over her head, almost covering her eyes. Their moment dissolved. Lawrence felt a squeeze of loneliness to his heart; the cold iron shunt of bereavement.

What had happened?

There had been something ravelled in that moment as they looked. An uncanny density. A charge sparking from hilltop to hilltop.

She was about to disappear. Someone waited for her on the first of the two toboggans, anchoring it to the slope, another woman with arms rigid at each of her sides as she held it against the slip of the snow.

The flaming woman was supple in her movements as she lowered herself onto it, and drew her legs up and in. Still he watched. She radiated a stillness, a slow grace which seemed inseparable from the blue-skied peace of the day. The crows lifted off and landed again, this time only yards away from him. They composed themselves into black-winged hieroglyphs; his mind's eye blinked, the words formed.

The Sussex Downs: that was her England—

Then the toboggans launched, the flock lifted off and, as quickly as the words had formed on the white page of the hilltop, the birds dispersed, raucously.

Why was he on *this* side of the looking-glass? Why was he not speeding along on a Canadian toboggan? Was the waving man Garnett or merely a fellow hill-walker in high spirits?

It was a painful wrench – from strangers perhaps. Yet as he descended, the happy camaraderie he'd observed through Wilfrid Meynell's field-glasses left him feeling adrift.

Not for the first time he understood that it was a treacherously fine line between the freedom he needed to live and write, and the sensation that he could be anywhere in the world because he belonged increasingly nowhere. He had no home, no place to be, no new manuscript ready for delivery, no children. *Crippled for ever, knowing he could never have any children—* His only ballast was Frieda.

He needed her *to be there, to assure him that he existed at all*. She was a formidable burden, and she was all he had.

His knees stiffened on the steep descent. All the while, the words vibrated in his core, and his heart beat out their rhythm. *The Sussex Downs*, they said, *that was her England*.

The sentence signified nothing in that moment, in that year, or if it did, it eluded him as decisively as the woman who was coursing down a snowy slope out of view. He made his way on clumsy, potato-sack feet, listening to the receding whoops and cries of the sledging party.

His own day held only the prospect of a visit to the cow-shed by Father Patrick. The man was jolly enough, but the exile had no need of church or priests. He knew where the old gods lived.

In Greatham *'I ought never, never'* the water-meadows were a silver sea that February, and the trees were covered in the earliest buds of purple-red, each silent with the percussive force yet to come – the bud bursting, the vernal surge. Winter, however, had not yet loosed its grip, and cold stars bit the night sky while, in the cow-shed, the exile remained firmly of the view that any form of heating other than an open fire was immoral.

Little wonder, reflected Lady Ottoline on her first night as his and Frieda's guest, that a thin man kept a stout wife, no matter how difficult said wife. Frieda had been really quite irritating over supper, perpetually seeking attention.

In the better of the two guest rooms, the aristocrat and society hostess, Lady Ottoline Morrell, could not sleep at all, on account of the cold. If she despised the values of her class, and she generally did, she nevertheless missed, in the small hours of the 2nd of February, 1915, her good feather eiderdown and the luxury of her gas fire.

She plumped, then battered her bolster again. Her meagre supply of kindling was gone. She wondered if she should try to re-light the fire with the tissue-paper from her hat-box.

She had arrived by train earlier that day, presenting a vision never before seen in public in rural Sussex. Travellers at the small Pulborough Station Hotel emerged, vaguely amazed, to watch a middle-aged, mannish noblewoman descend into, and then depart the station in a hired fly. She was strikingly tall, and wore a purple velvet frock and a platter-sized hat.

'Don't let the wind get hold of that,' grumbled the driver, 'or you'll be arriving by air.' He feared he would be made to run headlong through the floods when the ruddy hat flew off her head; or, as he later expressed it to a fellow driver, when her 'get-up' got up and went.

She looked through him imperiously but adjusted a pin to anchor the platter securely to her mass of cropped, dyed auburn hair. Multiple strands of pearls gleamed at her neck and bosom. As the driver battened down her valise, she buttoned a cape over her frock and availed herself of a rug for her knees. They then together confronted the four flooded miles. It did not inspire confidence, Lady O. silently noted, that the driver had a black patch over one eye, and the day was dim. Well wrapped, she was at least able to ignore the spray from the wheels, and she munched contentedly on prunes from a little bag. Her nerve specialist, she called to her driver, assured her prunes were 'life-changing', but the man waived her offer.

As one society tattle page put it, Lady Ottoline was 'indiscriminately devoted to' the arts. In her own bedecked bosom, she wanted only to support the best of modern art and belles-lettres. To that end, she was a generous hostess and patron.

The Lawrences first attended one of her well-populated dinner parties the previous summer – the occasion at which Katherine Mansfield was first introduced to Lawrence. Later that same night in her diary, Mansfield decided he was 'perceptibly over-eager in aristocratic company'.

That eagerness had worked, however, for Lady Ottoline was now keen to be better acquainted with the Nottinghamshire author of *Sons and Lovers* and *The Prussian Officer*, and was on her way, through field and flood, to she knew-not-where.

The cow-shed.

She herself was Nottinghamshire born-and-bred, and had turned, rapt, when her ever-alert ears discerned, from across the dinner table, the phrases and music of her native dialect, long lost to her.

Later, to Bertrand Russell, her not-very-secret secret lover, she opined that Lawrence was a man of great passion, a person wholly alert to life, both inward and outward. He was, in short, a *revelation*.

She accepted forthwith his and Frieda's invitation to their new Sussex abode.

The morning after her arrival, she emerged, ravaged by sleeplessness.

Little Mary, who had loitered expectantly in the cow-shed kitchen for over an hour, waiting for the noblewoman to appear, ran now to fetch her beloved Brownie.

'You don't mind, do you?' the exile asked his guest.

Lady Ottoline smiled weakly.

Frieda sulked. She was also a noblewoman, but the child hadn't asked *her* to pose.

In a photo that will be destroyed later that year, in the wake of events undreamed of on this February day, Ottoline stands on the spot Mary has chosen for her, in the kitchen, next to a tall roll of green linoleum by the window. In the eventual photo, it is as if the glamorous Lady O. is standing in the shade of a great, leaning Riviera palm tree that has burst up through the cow-shed floor.

Her face is long, with a square chin and jawline. She wears a flowing, ivory crêpe jacket with a cameo pinned to the ruffle-collar at her neck. Her eyes are small, dark and deep-set, and her hair springs from her head like a wire-brush. She looks, not at Mary, but to her right, to the edge of the frame, where the exile is a blurred sliver of corduroy, an extended arm, and the back of half a head.

From this fragment, we can infer thin shoulders and a head smaller than we might have imagined on those shoulders. In the photo-to-be, his hand is upturned, its palm exposed. He is offering his guest the gift of her own prunes, as if he might feed her by hand. Ottoline laughs from the shade of the palm tree, raising her hand to cover her mouth, or more specifically, her teeth, which are large and show a great deal when she laughs. Her eyes, though shadowed by sleeplessness and self-doubt, are as bright as a magpie's.

Instants before this moment by the linoleum tree is captured, Lady Ottoline knocks up against the heavy roll. 'Timber!' shouts Frieda unhelpfully from the other side of the kitchen. The exile lurches and catches it just in time, and Mary gushes excitedly that Lady O. was nearly killed. Out of shot, Frieda sips her coffee and allows herself a wry smile behind her cup, while the exile offers Lady O. her own life-changing prunes by way of comic apology.

When she contemplated Lawrence, her new friend, she felt she had seldom met anyone so lovable. She was both disconcerted and thrilled by the directness of his gaze, by their blue-flamed spell. Those eyes said to their subject that no one and nothing else mattered as much as they. His warmth seemed boundless.

He, for his part, was sincere in his affection for her and, as was his wont, he was also already storing up impressions – word-pictures – of her flaws and physical defects. They would emerge subsequently in the form of the ostentatious society figure, Hermione, in *Women in Love*. Hermione would be a stubborn flirt and a well-bred pest. Recognising herself on the page, Ottoline would be laid low by both that shock of recognition and by her friend's betrayal. In this respect, she would join an ever-expanding 'club' of the aggrieved.

Mary gripped her camera at waist-level, her eyes trained on the viewfinder. She liked Lady Ottoline's teeth, which were strong and as surprising to her as a camel's. She composed her picture quickly and pulled the lever before Lady O.'s hand could fly to her mouth. Mary felt sure it would be as good as her photo of Rory the pony, flanked by old Mr James and his niece who ate all their cherries.

The snap taken, Lawrence stepped away from the frame, still beaming at his house-guest, like sunlight through a magnifying glass. Ottoline warmed, and her spirit expanded under his gaze. Only her eyes flickered with a nascent insight that would crystallise in her mind years later. *His insight was indeed very intense, but sometimes so bright it distorted those it focused.*

She watched him as he spoke softly to the girl both she and Frieda regarded as a ragamuffin. The girl – who *was* the child? – grinned, nodded and scratched her knee before flying out the door with the souls of the two of them, salon hostess and author, upside-down in her dark little box.

E. M. Forster, whom the Lawrences also met at Ottoline's dinner party the summer before, was next to arrive. He stepped across their threshold, bearing unwelcome news from civilisation: the Boots Lending Library, he'd been informed, was to refuse to take Lawrence's book of stories, *The Prussian Officer*, on grounds of moral indecency. Apparently, he glumly announced, the brutal depiction of the officer in the title story, Prussian or not, had been deemed unacceptable. Forster offered his heartfelt, if characteristically restrained, sympathy.

It made a bad start. The exile resented his guest for the gloom he had carried into their new home. 'A bottle of red would have sufficed,' Lawrence muttered to Frieda later that night in bed.

In Mary's staging of the requisite 'guest' photograph, she insisted, with childish percipience, on a tableau in which the two men were to clutch a catkin each and face off.

In the picture, Forster, then thirty-six, seven years the senior, appears mild-mannered and morose. He has sloped shoulders, a receding chin, a drooping moustache and curiously flattened features. He feels ludicrous and wonders why Lawrence indulges the child. He holds his catkin husk reluctantly, impotently, and will not take direction. By contrast, the exile, who always loves a charade or sketch, assumes a mock-fencing position and presses the tip of his catkin to Forster's throat. 'Right-o!' he calls.

The sea was bright that day, and the Downs in mid-February alive with noisy starlings and the sweeter song of warblers. Halfway up the nearest hill, Lawrence and Forster stopped and surveyed, side by side, the blue water lapping at the toy-villages on the river-plain, and the lonely train steaming along through a perilous gap in the floods. How vulnerable everything was, thought the exile.

At the sight of the train, the old American folk song came into his head.

Yonder come the train, she coming down the line
Blowing every station, Mr. McKinley is a-dying
It's hard times, it's hard times …

As they climbed higher, he reached after the other lyrics in his mind; a London music-hall impresario had given him the sheet-music in his long-ago teaching days in Croydon. He'd sung it often with the boys.

The forked pennants of snowdrops trembled along the track, their hope as fragile as ever that cold winter. A starling advanced ahead of them, a hopping guide. Forster remarked on the beauty of its black sheen, while Lawrence pointed out that every colour, even black, held others. It was his painter's sensibility. He showed his companion the lustrous greens among the black on the bird's head, and the deep purple feathers on its neck. 'Now watch this,' and he began to make whistling sounds.

Astonishingly, the starling, without pausing in its progress up the track, proceeded to mimic his pips. Forster laughed heartily for the first time in he-didn't-know-how-long, marvelling when his friend even coaxed from the bird a 'toodle-pip!' All seemed right again with the world, and Forster understood what Lady Ottoline had meant: Lawrence had a wonderful, child-like quality of excitement – excitement over the small things, as well as the great ones. Forster relaxed into his visit, or rather he did until later that afternoon as they sat down to tea, and all the small, bright things of life were suddenly eclipsed.

Hilda ran into the room. She stood, just over the threshold, clutching her sides as if she'd been slain. 'Oh, ma'am,' she said to Frieda, not feeling it proper to bother the men, 'they've gone and killed my brother at the War!'

All three swivelled on their chairs. Frieda leaned forward and began to speak, 'Oh, my dear—' but it was Lawrence who stood immediately and extended his arms to her. He took her into the kitchen, made her sweet tea, fed her her own freshly baked biscuits, and spoke to her soothingly.

Forster and Frieda sat in respectful silence, listening with heads bowed to the sounds of her sobs. Untouched, their tea and toast went cold. The exile had, Forster realised as they listened, a remarkable gift for tenderness. He himself would have struggled to do much more than offer Hilda his chair.

When the exile joined them once more, an hour later, Forster saw that his eyes were red-rimmed: 'I could wring the neck of humanity for it.'

The following day, his host worked on *The Rainbow* in his room, while Frieda played Beethoven on the piano, and Forster himself wrote letters at the long refectory table. 'The Lawrences I like – especially him. We have had a two hours walk in the glorious country between here and Arundel, and he told me all about his people – drunken father, sister who married a tailor: most gay and friendly, with breaks to look at birds, catkins.'

Lawrence emerged from his room, dazed from his labours over a novel which *had* to succeed. And to succeed, it had to get past the censors. Would it? He couldn't begin to say. He was incapable of reading as censors read; of thinking in the crude manner they did. He would have to ask dear Viola to 'filth-check' it for him before sending it off.

He sank into a chair across from Forster and stared through the sitting-room window into the deepening twilight. It was dark by four o'clock. 'If I can bash on to the page even a little of what grips me, I don't care whether I'm rich, poor, celebrated or forgotten when I finally cough off this mortal coil.' Forster looked up, smiled mildly, and returned to his page. Lawrence picked up a scrap of fur from a work-basket. He was making Frieda a winter hat, a sort of Russian toque.

The attack came that night.

Frieda, unable to divert or cajole her husband from his outburst, retreated to her room and listened through the bedroom door as he lit into the faults of Forster's novels – *all*, incidentally, sought after by the Boots Lending Library. Then he started on Forster, the man.

Why did he, Forster, recoil from passion and intimacy? Was he still a virgin? At thirty-six? No wonder he, Forster, was so utterly cramped and miserable in his manhood! Why couldn't he act? Why did he dodge himself? Why couldn't he take a woman and fight clear to his own basic, primal being?

'Is there anything you value in my work?' said Forster quietly, returning to that which mattered most to him. 'Anything at all?'

'The character of Leonard Bast.'

Forster waited. Nothing more came. At that, he nodded and, trembling slightly, took his candle and retired without saying goodnight.

Lawrence shouted after him. 'Why do you object to me telling you about yourself?'

The door closed.

'Yes! Go! Go fuck yourself, Forster! Then run back to your little patch of life and see if you can scratch out some meaning as easily as you do a living – if you call *that* life!'

The next morning, Forster rose early, before first light, before his hosts were up. As Hilda arrived at Winborn's, he raised his arm in a salute to her, and she watched him go. The sky was a soft grey, the moon a lantern, and the water-meadows glimmered. He walked the four miles in semi-darkness, through drifts of snow on the fields and knee-high floods in the lanes. He passed only a shepherd moving his flock to higher ground. Half-soaked, he narrowly made the 8.20 a.m. train to London.

The visit left him shaken. In the years to come, he and Lawrence would exchange occasional notes and cards. Lawrence would even encourage him to visit again, quite cheerfully, as if nothing of consequence had happened that February in 1915, as if he had no recollection.

Forster would meet him only once or twice again, in the safety of polite company. But he would not forget the starling on their walk, beloved of his host; or Lawrence's patience with Mary, the little girl with the camera; or poor Hilda, bereft and grieving, in Lawrence's unfaltering embrace.

February 16th. Lady Cynthia Asquith, the daughter-in-law of the Prime Minister, and the pre-eminent English beauty of her time, was fair-haired and classical in her features, with wide, intelligent eyes of rare – turquoise – blue. She'd met the Lawrences in Margate on a seaside holiday two years before, when Lawrence had been enormously kind to her children, including John. Her elder son, a boy of six, was a highly unusual child who made animal noises, shouted or cried uncontrollably at family gatherings and in public, and apparently troubled his grandfather, the PM, nearly as much as the War.

Her husband, Herbert – or 'Beb' as he was known – was at the Front, and she was very much alone these days. Lawrence believed he knew just the thing for it. He dashed off a note informing her he would meet her off the 12.10 at Pulborough. She would enjoy the four-mile walk to Greatham. That was the plan – unless the telegram boy rushed in or the heavens gave way.

For the photo, Mary assembles Lady Cynthia, Lawrence, Frieda, her own mother Monica, and, at Mary's insistence, Arthur. They stand in a row in front of Wilfrid Meynell's shined and waxed motor-car. Lady Cynthia parts her lips and stares into the blue distance, chastely flirtatious with the future viewer.

Frieda grips sad Monica by the waist, as if simultaneously to prop her up and make her smile. The Lawrences, contrary to their own initial expectations, have grown very fond of Monica. She is a sensitive woman, original in her thinking, and an honest observer of herself and others. In the photo, she peers up shyly. The exile turns from the camera to listen to a burst of birdsong. A blackbird is going hard at it, to get his whistle clear of winter rustiness. Frieda elbows her husband in the ribs, he grimaces, and, at her suggestion, on the count of three everyone except Arthur says: 'Moo!'

Mary pulls the lever.

Beyond the frame, later that day in the small cathedral-city of Chichester – a nearby market-town – they observed perhaps as many as a hundred soldiers in uniform sitting, laughing and smoking at the Market Cross. They were waiting for the army transit, and Lawrence could imagine, only too well, where – what horrors – they were off to.

Monica, Frieda and Lady Cynthia moved in and out of dress shops, although Lady Cynthia had already confided to the exile that she, like him, was cash-strapped. She asked if he would stand guard outside each shop, because she 'could not be seen buying off-the-peg'.

'She wearies me a bit,' he murmured to Monica and Frieda as they waited with him, outside the best ladies' shop in Chichester. 'Pip-pip!' he called to his guest, hurrying her as much as he dared.

Frieda was inclined to agree. 'She is quite nice, but – I feel sorry for her. She is poor in feeling.' Even so, Frieda was canny enough to know that a PM's daughter-in-law was never poor in connections, and before Lady Cynthia drove off from the Colony – in a car sent by Downing Street for her safe return – Frieda clasped her hand and made her promise she would visit again 'soon!'

February 17th. Jack Middleton Murry, the young writer, editor and lover of Katherine Mansfield, visited next, bereaved at his beloved's departure for the Continent, full of 'unutterable' miseries. He arrived in Pulborough in darkness and stumbled through the floods, only to succumb that first evening to a cold sweat and mucous fever.

The exile made an excellent nurse. He took matters in hand, rubbing his friend down with camphorated oil, an event which Jack Murry would later find recounted in close detail in *Aaron's Rod*. *For a long time he rubbed finely and steadily, then went over the whole of the lower body, mindless, as if in a sort of incantation. He rubbed every speck of the man's lower body – the abdomen, the buttocks, the thighs and knees, down to the feet, rubbed it all warm and glowing with camphorated oil, every bit of it, chafing the toes swiftly, till he was almost exhausted.*

It would be a truthful account, so truthful it would bring Murry up short as he read. He *had* glowed. They both had, and their friendship grew closer and warmer as a consequence of his new-found dependence on Lawrence.

Yet the following day, when Jack Murry declared himself 'out of the woods', his host-turned-nurse proceeded – in Jack's words – to 'crucify' him, both for his neglect of his lover Katherine *and* for her infidelity, which was unfolding in Paris, he confessed, even as he and Lawrence spoke. When Murry ruefully compared her infidelity to Frieda's own long history, his host glared: Frieda's infidelities were *not* true infidelities for 'they mean nothing to her'.

The corner of Murry's mouth twitched.

'And your point is?' asked the exile.

'It's high time you enjoyed a little meaninglessness of your own.'

'It wouldn't suit me.' It was *he* who dispensed the advice, not the reverse.

'Not tempted?'

'I am a happily married Puritan, who lives by my conscience and will not stoop to mere gratification.' More to the point, he knew Frieda would not tolerate it, for she was quickly jealous.

Later that week, the two friends walked up Rackham Hill into the Downs. The first primroses shook brightly on the breeze, flickering like candle stubs in the afternoon gloom.

In the meantime, Frieda took to her bed with what she sulkily claimed was Murry's cold, but in reality, it was a deep sense of injury; her husband had raged at her again – a horrible, explosive episode. First, he threw two plates at the wall. In response, Frieda hurled one of Jack's walking boots and accidentally hit her target in the head. To Murry's eyes, Lawrence was suddenly nothing less than demented; a raving demon. His entire countenance altered strangely.

The younger man stepped between the raging-weeping pair but to no avail. Only when Hilda entered, to prepare supper, did Lawrence bow his head and lope past her, through the door into the cold shock of night.

Lady Ottoline came again that February, this time with her lover Bertrand Russell, the philosopher-son of an Earl. Very kind, decided Lawrence. Dignified. Quite ugly. A forthright face with intent, honest eyes. A weak chin and an unusual shape of head, as if packed with additional brain-power at the back. A clever-jacks, by all accounts. A maths whizz.

In Mary's photograph, Russell holds a piece of ploughland chalkstone and, with it, he draws the symbol for infinity on her mother's garage door, where the motor-car is kept. Although faint in the photo, Russell's drawing covers most of the door.

Monica came out to see the assembled, and smiled wanly. No, she would not, she told her daughter, join any photograph.

The exile, a bystander to the moment, can be seen at the edge of the frame, a synecdoche of himself, a pair of trouser-legs and brogues.

Later, in the kitchen, Russell would suck his pipe and nod over the gravy Lawrence made at the stove. They spoke easily, through the steam of boiled vegetables. The exile spoke of the Ancient Constitution and The Levellers, of Blake and 'Jerusalem', the radical hymn, and its 'arrow of desire'; of his own formation in the Nonconformist church; of the Tolpuddle Martyrs – pardoned by Russell's own 'clear-sighted grandfather PM', who was, two years after their scandalously harsh sentence, Home Secretary of the realm. Russell nodded and recalled the rough-whiskered, gentle old man from his childhood. He had kept peppermints for his grandson in an old snuff-box.

The exile clung even now, he said, to the tradition and spirit of British radicalism, of freeborn men, of Common Law and Common Land. It was all they had, he said. It was the best of what they had. Unusually, he spoke with a restrained passion – the moderating effect, perhaps, of Russell's quiet gravitas. Redemption, the exile said, had first to be imagined. Healing would never spring from horror. A broken country knew only how to go on breaking, and it risked being forever at the mercy of opportunists, industrialists and political predators. Words alone – honest words, compassionate words, respectful exchanges – could begin to mend it.

Russell tasted the gravy at the end of Lawrence's spoon and nodded. He was a pacifist, he said. He suspected he was being watched by MI5 and murmured that he might be 'excommunicated' by Trinity College for his pacifism. Before bed that night, Russell told Ottoline that Lawrence had helped him to understand many things.

In the sitting-room, Jack Murry had been allocated to the refectory table to entertain the ladies. He sat, trying to hide his jealousy of the devotion Lady Ottoline heaped on the absent Lawrence. Wasn't he, Jack, also a writer of merit? At the same time, he eavesdropped on the kitchen tête-à-tête, jealous of Lawrence's new affection for the tête of Bertrand Russell. And still, he felt utterly wretched about Katherine running away to her new French lover.

Even as Jack yearned for attention from Ottoline or Lawrence, Frieda craved the attention of handsome Jack Murry – with his deep-set eyes, his even features, and his strikingly dark widow's peak. The day would come when he would succumb wholly to her attentions, but on this particular evening, he ignored her whenever politely possible, and seemed only to bother to come to life when Ottoline spoke.

Frieda pouted. Wasn't she, Frieda von Richthofen, also high-born? She resented Ottoline, while also privately, fervently hoping that their guest, one of the grandest women in England, might help her, a fellow noblewoman, find a way to spend time with the children from whom she had been cruelly separated by her ex-Husband-Professor. She railed at the injustice and started to weep at the table. She also coveted her guest's pearls.

Ottoline, for her part, said only that she would do what she could – she would write Professor Weekley a letter, pleading Frieda's case – and she wondered privately when Russell might emerge from gravy-making to save her.

Her hope was dashed as Frieda clapped her hands. 'You must think me a very poor hostess indeed, Ottoline. You and Russell must stay the night!'

Ottoline blanched.

'That way,' continued her hostess, 'you may take your time and enjoy dinner, without the worry of the long journey back.'

Of course, there was still the pretence to be respected, the one in which everyone conspired – namely, that Russell was *not* sleeping with Lady O., for each was married. Frieda turned to Jack, instructing him. 'Murry, you will sleep with us. Ottoline, you will have the room you had last time, our best, and Russell shall have Jack's room. Jack shan't mind.' She glanced his way. Jack made a guttural, stammering noise. 'Lorenzo and I have a double bed,' she added reassuringly, 'and Lorenzo is only thin.'

Lady Ottoline remembered her cold sleeplessness of earlier that month, and the silverfish in the bathroom. She declined 'aristocrat-ically', which is to say, with neither explanation nor apology. And that was that.

In the ghost of Mary's photo, Jack Murry and the exile are laying the green linoleum in the long sitting-room of the cow-shed, in a wash of morning light. The roll of lino has been felled and is a palm tree no more. The two men are at their most content, their closest – and their blurriest too – as the snap is taken. They would not be still! complained Mary. Their sleeves are up. Murry cuts the lino, and the exile is on his knees, banging each sheet into place, with one arm raised high and a pencil behind his ear.

What are arguably John Middleton Murry's most memorable words are yet to be written. As he unrolls the lino, that particular work of criticism is still unimaginable, as is the bomb of a book to which it refers, *as is* the courtroom drama in which Murry's words will aid and abet the attack on the final novel of his former friend. By the time of the infamous courtroom scene, both men will be dead, and yet their words will clash.

In Greatham, we are still forty-five years away from that drama, but reality is porous. Time seeps. In Mary's viewfinder, Jack Murry adopts a wicked face as he slashes at the lino, like The Ripper himself and, behind the neat triangle of his beard, Lawrence laughs, his eyes alight.

Together they beat the new flooring into submission in a triumph of a morning. The following day, Murry was gone at first light, without so much as a goodbye to anyone. Why the sudden departure?

Katherine Mansfield's train was due in Victoria Station at 8 a.m., and her cast-aside lover was determined to be there on the platform to woo her.

The exile was bereft. Jack was gone, gone. He'd gone running back to Katherine like a whipped dog.

A knock came on the door, early. The exile leaped from his chair. Jack had changed his mind! But no, it was only Mary, saying she needed to practise her copperplate letters in preparation for her lessons with the exile, which were to begin 'soon'. He told her, 'No, not soon – not until May.' But she sailed past him, over the threshold, her little dark head held high. Then she glanced up at him, reading his features cautiously, and poured herself a cup of tea from their morning pot.

In truth, Lawrence, in his gloom, *was* glad of her company. Perhaps her mother, Monica, had sent her over to the cow-shed to give herself an hour or two of peace; Monica was always slow to 'right herself' in the morning.

He joined the girl at the refectory table and set her to writing out lines: 'Jack Murry is a bad boy because he does not stay here long enough. Jack Murry is a bad boy because he does not stay here long enough.' He instructed her to continue, down the page and onto the next, until he lost track, and the edge of her hand was smeared with black ink.

The dictation was interrupted at last by Hilda, eyes darting with nervousness as Lawrence opened the door to her. She was clutching something behind her back. A telegram, as it turned out. It had been delivered moments before to Winborn's – for Mrs Lawrence.

Frieda read, then collapsed at the table. Mary fled. Lawrence stood above his wife, cupping her head to his stomach.

Her father, the Baron, was gravely ill. The doctor said he wouldn't survive the month.

'You must go to him, madam,' said Hilda.

'I must, Lorenzo,' she said.

'Of course you must.'

Sometimes, it was still possible to forget, momentarily, that the War was on, that borders were closed, and that it was, in fact, impossible to go to her family – or it was if she wanted to return to England. No one's mind could catch up quickly enough with the new reality. The world had turned inside-out.

Uncharacteristically for Frieda, she was so despondent that she neither wept nor railed against the War, nor bemoaned her fate in a country which had confined her free spirit to rural Greatham. She merely disappeared into their bedroom, refusing to come out all day and night, even for dinner. At last, the exile called to her that he had made a shepherd's pie.

'Lamb?' she said quietly, her eyes dull as he entered their room with her plate on a tray. 'We can't afford lamb.'

'Don't fret. Not lamb,' he said. 'Shepherd. I went out and killed one myself.'

A smile got the better of her mouth.

Then he sat down by her side and fed her, forkful by forkful.

The following day, when Frieda was feeling more like herself, it was he who was overcome by the fluey-cold bug which, as she reminded him, his fair-weather-friend Jack Murry had brought to their door.

She persuaded Monica to lend her Arthur and the car so that she could go to Chichester to buy herself two quality black frocks – a day-dress and a gown – for her mourning. The exile imagined their bills of sale in the post, and his temperature soared. Frieda said she would get him something for it at Boots Cash Chemist, the dispensary in Chichester.

'What can they give me for *you*?' he growled.

Frieda missed the point altogether. 'Oh, I'm feeling quite well again, dear Lorenzo. The shopping trip shall revive *me*.'

Propped up in their guest-room bed, in a flannel shirt buttoned to the neck, he felt miserable and alone. The bug had reduced him to a churl of an invalid, and he wanted no one to see him. Even Wilfrid Meynell, his Greatham benefactor, was turned away. For the sake of his novel, he conceded only to receive Viola, his typist, and her friend, the fledgling poet Eleanor Farjeon.

Eleanor was lively and she loved hill-walking. He liked her immediately. She was plain, with heavy eyebrows, thick specs, and a chin which doubled as she spoke, although she was thin and not yet jowly or middle-aged. She was, he feared, the sort of endearingly vibrant young woman whose destiny was bound to be one of unrequited love of the most intense variety, followed, ultimately, by spinsterdom. It was all wrong, he decided, for she possessed a wondrous smile which made him sit up and forget he was ill. How hard the world could be on women.

Bunny Garnett would have to marry her. That was the solution. He would tell Bunny as much himself. She was too marvellous not to be seized by life.

Eleanor had kindly agreed to help Viola type up the remainder of the manuscript. Viola refrained from saying that she herself was struggling with eye strain.

Eleanor, as well as her brother Herbert Farjeon – a London playwright he knew something of – was in the Bax brothers' circle of friends. As the exile understood it, the Bax gang favoured the opera, Russian ballet and cricket above all. David – Bunny – was a member of that circle too, and Eleanor spoke fondly of him. She had been glad, she remarked, through her friendship with Viola, to find at least a few decidedly literary people of her own age.

The patient set down his cup of Ovaltine. 'Were you on a Canadian toboggan in the Downs, near here, last month?' he asked.

Eleanor's face went blank, then she laughed at the oddity of the question. A strange intent was etched on the author's wan features. 'Yes, I daresay I was,' she replied.

'With David?' His eyes were an avid blue.

'Bunny,' she said. 'Yes. He was with us.' Why such interest in a day's sledging?

'And?' he said.

'And?'

'Who else?'

'Oh, I see! Let me think … Maitland Radford – yes, he was with us too. We were all feeling a bit cooped up, you see, after the Christmas hols and what with the war bulletins, so grim each day.'

Viola chimed in. 'I expect you'll meet Maitland before long when—'

He fixed his gaze on Eleanor. 'Do you mean the Maitland who saved little Sylvia's life when she hurt her leg in the accident?'

'Yes.' Eleanor paused. 'That was the summer before last.'

'Madeline mentioned it …' he murmured.

He lied. She hadn't. Hilda had said a little about the incident, but only a little. He'd deduced that there was something everyone knew about the child's accident, but were not saying. What was it?

Notably, no one referred to *the father*, to Percy Lucas. That was curious. Why hadn't Percy, the child's father, taken charge of the situation himself? Hilda had only said that, as time passed, *Madeline* was beside herself. Why not Lucas as well? It was most peculiar. Hilda said the doctor from Storrington had come *a fat country practitioner, pleasant and kind.*

Yes, there was inflammation. Yes, there might be a little septic poisoning – there might. So a fortnight passed by.

Then this Maitland person, a godsend apparently, arrived at Winborn's by complete coincidence, with Eleanor *and looked grave.*

The child might be lame for life. Up went the fire of fear and anger in every heart.

Eleanor's friend Maitland, *not* Percy, had taken charge of the day.

At the foot of his bed, Eleanor recalled the peril. 'Maitland was completing his medical training at the time,' she said. 'We were on a ramble in Sussex, and had stopped at Winborn's to say hallo to everyone. But of course, we never got farther. At Madeline's request, Maitland examined Sylvia and immediately spotted what the local doctor had failed to see two days before. Maitland got on the telephone directly to the senior consultant – the surgeon – in London, and Sylvia was rushed up in a special motor. I can still hear her desperate cries.' No mention of the father still, he noted. 'I'll never forget her little face, or Madeline's. Madeline was positively stricken,' Eleanor said. 'We feared—'

Viola interrupted. 'It was dreadful. But all's well that ends—'

'Who else was on the toboggans that day?' he asked, cutting across her.

Eleanor and Viola exchanged sidelong glances. 'Goodness! I can hardly recall.' The poor man was clearly fevered, and like a dog with a bone. She and Viola had to make allowances. 'Maitland's colleague, Dr Godwin Baynes. Yes, Godwin was there.'

'And?'

'Mrs Baynes, too. In fact, I shall be visiting them next—'

'Do you know her?'

'Ros? Of course – though not well. She's a good friend of Bunny's, and of the Bax brothers, too. Both she and her husband are. Rosalind Baynes. Née Thornycroft. I know her a little. She's a dear heart. My brother Herbert recently married her sister, Joan, also a lovely woman. Maitland was at school with Joan and Ros's brother. Maitland is a dear friend of mine – indeed of my entire family. We all go back a long way, you see, one way or the other. Maitland and Godwin Baynes are partners in a new medical practice in Wisbech. Why do you ask?'

The Sussex Downs:

'I waved – to all of you, that is – from Rackham Hill that day.'

that was her England.

'Ah! I see! Or rather, I didn't!' She pointed to her bottle-glass specs. 'One can't wear specs and toboggan at the same time! Have you and the Bayneses met, then?'

A rose-flame in the winter sunshine. 'I don't believe we have.'

He knew they hadn't.

He coughed and asked Viola to adjust his pillows. Then he pointed to the second half of the manuscript, on a narrow table in his room, and he allowed his eyes to close.

He had her name. It was a strange form of possession. Rosalind. *Ros.* Rose, rose-flame. Of course that was her name. The gods had raised her, a flame, a winter-rose, from the snow of Sussex.

In the days and weeks to come, in the grip of illness, the exile's brain will snap shut and open, open and shut, like the shutter of Mary's box-camera. He will be unable to leave his bed until March, struck down by fever and an overwhelming sense of doom, a doom darkened by the awareness that Rosalind Thornycroft Baynes was fleeting, a vision; a married person to whom he had neither the right nor the means of approach. He would not know her, the only woman who had ever fascinated him, in the old sense of the word. She wasn't merely 'enchanting'; she *had* enchanted him, across the cleft of two hills.

When Frieda returned finally that day, with her shopping and her funereal extravagances, he would tell her, 'No more visitors,' although he would be clear on the point of one exception: if Perceval Lucas should appear in the Colony, whatever the reason or time of day, he must be roused.

A fortnight later, the exile emerged from his bed – not yet well, but restive – and left the cow-shed early, walking across the Colony's lawns, past Alice's rose bushes, and along a flattened track of shaggy grass in the direction of the distant ridge of pines. No one knew his destination. No one saw him leave.

The day seemed to darken as the fir trees closed in, and he pulled pale drops of sap from their bark as he went, sucking them like an old woodsman. He side-stepped a sudden bog, then dropped to his haunches to watch three fallow deer skitter through the undergrowth. At last he arrived at the scattering of oaks which sheltered the hollow where Rackham Cottage brooded, primitive and stalwart.

Strange how the savage England lingers in patches: as here near the foot of the South Downs. The spirit of the place lingering on primeval, as when the Saxons came, so long ago.

The cottage was about a mile from Winborn's and was a solid, timbered construction, with a sloping, cloak-like roof and a heavy oaken door. It was its own squat fairy tale, planted in the dell and keeping its own counsel, with the unyielding indifference of three centuries of life. He surveyed the land. The cottage was neighbourless, except for the deer on the common, a chuckling stream, and the birds of the Downs beyond.

As he walked, the lash of an adder uncoiled and flashed by his feet. He felt like a poacher but did not hesitate as he surveyed *the dream* the dream of a garden: a wide rolling lawn and several beds, pocked now with rabbit-holes. Bracken, gorse and briars had spread from the common and, begrudgingly, he admitted it. It was a marvel that Percy Lucas had succeeded in establishing any sort of garden from such rough turf, let alone a garden such as this.

The exile discovered, too, the wooden tub, nailbrush and watering-can, where the gardener-husband must have washed himself down after his labours. An old wheelback chair with a missing leg listed under the lean-to beside a few damp logs. Percy had also built a fire-pit, planted an apple tree, and made a good-sized kitchen garden, with a fruit cage. Rackham Cottage was a small corner of paradise.

Fragments of what was not yet a story arose in the trespasser's mind. There on the land a stranger had tamed, he found himself conjuring Perceval Lucas, adding inference to intimation until he believed in nothing so much as his own figment. *It was not that he was idle. He was not idle. He was always doing something, always working away, down at Crockham, doing little jobs.* One only had to glance at the scrub of the common to imagine the pride Percy must have taken in his idyll. *But, oh dear, the little jobs—the garden paths – the gorgeous flowers – the chairs to mend, old chairs to mend!*

It was a pleasure to behold, of course it was, but what else was a man of thirty-five to do with his time and energy when he, his young family, their nurse and governess were kept by his father-in-law? And what did dear Madeline *actually* feel about the man she had harnessed herself to for life?

Her ostensible grievance against him was that he made no money to keep his family; that, because he had an income of a hundred and fifty a year, he made no effort to do anything at all—he merely lived from day to day. Not that she accused him of being lazy; it was not that; he was always at work in the garden; he had made the place beautiful. But was this all it amounted to? They had three children; she had said to him, savagely, she would have no more. Already her father was paying for the children's nurse, and helping the family at every turn.

Fragments. Glimpses. Not a story yet.

The exile knew better than to say it to anyone, even to Frieda who often savoured his bitterness for others, but he knew what he felt about Perceval Lucas. *It was that he stood for nothing.* Lucas was an ineffectual man running into a futile war, and the man who now stood in his garden despised him for it.

Hatred is sometimes an alloy of love, the dark matter of lit souls. If its heat has the power to burn its object, its flame can burn its subject too, its source, as relentlessly. Perhaps the exile, the trespasser, also loved Perceval Lucas, as one may love a rival. Had he fallen in love with that effortless quality he'd immediately discerned in the man in Mary's photo; the husband-father with the long limbs and fair hair, unself-consciously elegant in his cricket flannels; the man who belonged to England, their England, without any sense he could ever be otherwise?

What the exile wouldn't have given to possess such *evenness*, the evenness and ease of old breeding. But why rave after it? He knew there could be no great art without cracks, without crookedness and incongruity. Without strangeness, no enchantment came. *Percy* would never produce great music, stories or dance; he would only ever catalogue it in his ledgers and safeboxes of papers. Percy was, Viola had said, a 'genealogist of English folk-song' and had transcribed old local tunes at every opportunity. When he, the new resident of the Colony, had registered mild amusement, even she had suppressed a smile.

The windows of the Lucas cottage winked in the dappled light, and the trespasser pressed his face to a thin, warped pane. Inside, furnishings under dust-sheets made phantom shapes, and the beams and lintels loured. He put his back into the door, but it didn't yield. Rackham *Crockham* Cottage kept its secrets.

Near the fire-pit, he seated himself on an old stump between two grave elms. Ahead, an unfinished stone path, mossy and neglected, was marked out in mud-hardened sticks as far as the stream. As straight a man as Percy was himself, he couldn't manage a straight path; he should have dug out the roots of a great toppled pine before starting. Instead he'd tried to dodge the real labour.

On the path, a skipping rope lay abandoned, and the exile could almost hear again the childish sing-song of the little Lucas girls. From his sick-bed, he'd listened to them playing outside Winborn's. They had sweet voices.

The cuckoo is a pretty bird,
She sings as she flies;
She bringeth good tidings,
She telleth no lies ...

Neither the rose bushes nor the lone apple tree had been pruned back. The roses had grown twiggy, and needed an arbour to train them. The apple tree was in bud but was stunted and struggling. Red squirrels scolded him from the branches. He gazed high, studying their small clawed hands and the parabolic perfection of their jumps from tree to tree.

In the shadows below, pale crocuses bloomed, and beyond, in the thicket, columbines pushed up through the thin grey soil. He stood and walked as far as the stream to examine the repairs to the bridge – Percy's haphazard handiwork again, and Madeline's worry. Rotting planks scarcely held back the gardener's dug-out mounds of earth, and now, after the rain and snow of winter, those mounds threatened to collapse. He hoped the man was a better Morris-dancer than he was a labourer. The bridge was rotting too. Naturally, Madeline was concerned about the safety of the place for children. One would have thought that one accident – Sylvia's – would have been lesson enough for Percy.

Had he taught his little ones the rhymes they'd been singing that day as the exile burned up in his bed with fever?

The leaf it will wither,
The root will decay;
Alack! I'm forsaken
And wasting away.

The exile was decided. Once he completed the herbaceous border for Viola outside the cow-shed, he would start on *the dream* the garden at Rackham. He would dig out the roots, straighten and lay the path, shore up the banks of the stream, mend the bridge, clear the overgrowth, re-plant the beds, and generally pick up after the would-be war-hero.

He was of course an amateur – a born amateur. He worked so hard, and did so little, and nothing he ever did would hold together for long. If he terraced the garden, he held up the earth with a couple of long narrow planks that would soon begin to bend with the pressure from behind, and would not need many years to rot through and break and let the soil slither all down again in a heap towards the stream-bed. But there you are.

Madeline would be able to lease the cottage out, and would no longer have to worry about it sitting empty. The work would suit him, for he enjoyed plants far more than people these days and, if he chipped away at his moral debt to the Meynells, he would feel the burden of their kindness less. More than anything, he'd welcome the physical challenge after the many months at his desk.

As he explored Perceval Lucas's little house in the dell, he felt their two fates tangle inexorably, like the ivy and brambles at his feet, and all the while, the story, his Greatham story, spread and twisted within him.

The dream was still stronger than the reality. In the dream he was at home on a hot summer afternoon, working across the little stream at the bottom of the garden, carrying the garden path in continuation on to the common. He had cut the rough turf and the bracken, and left the grey, dryish soil bare. He was troubled because he could not get the path straight. He had set up his sticks, and taken the sights between the big pine-trees, but for some unknown reason everything was wrong.

Everything *was* wrong in Percy's paradise.

A crooked path.

A stunted apple tree.

A snake in the grass.

Mary's photographs of the comings and goings of 1915 multiplied. She was only indulged, the exile concluded, because she was otherwise neglected. No one had wanted to add to Monica's worries by insisting the girl needed schooling and civilising, and yet everyone in the Meynell clan now felt the relief: Mr Lawrence would get her through her entrance exam for St Paul's School in London. All might still come right.

Mary's own plan that spring was to produce a hand-stitched flip-book of her photographs, like the one that showed a horse racing and jumping, which she'd won at the fair in Arundel for Best Pony-Riding. After her Brownie camera, her own, new flip-book was to become her most prized possession.

She was careful to write the date in pencil on the back of each photograph.

Flip, flip—

March 6th. Mary's camera's eye alights on three heads. An unusual composition. The window catches the sun. The writer Ford Madox Ford, the suffragette Violet Hunt and Mrs H. G. Wells are peering into the sitting-room of the cow-shed. Their backsides rise like parsnips in a garden row. Their feet are planted in Lawrence's newly dug border.

The two women wear pale ankle-length frocks. Violet Hunt, Ford's mistress, has a stack of dark, dyed hair, confected in the Pre-Raphaelite style of her youth, although she is no longer young. Mrs Wells, of a similar age – in her fifties – is looking, not through the window, but at her pretty leather shoes – sinking in the mud.

Ford is in his early forties. His backside is broader than the women's. In the photo, he can be seen pressing his hands to the sides of his head, the better to see through the window. Though Mary will never know it, it is an inspired shot, for she has caught them in their act of spying, and the irony will not be lost on the exile when he returns from his trip to Cambridge.

Frieda did not accompany him. She is at home – or nearby, rather, visiting Monica in her cottage. The new arrivals were simply passing, they announce, and they thought they would call in.

No one is ever 'simply passing' Greatham. It requires an act of determination and navigation to locate the Colony, in the woodland criss-crossing of lanes and tracks, and there was no invitation from either Lawrence or Frieda.

Frieda only just manages to hold her tongue; Ford, she knows perfectly well, has come, under the guise of friendship, to spy on her and Lorenzo, after assuring his boss and friend, Charles Masterman of Wellington House, that he will supply an update on the couple's alleged pro-German sympathies – alleged, originally, by none other than Ford himself.

Ford is in the debt of Masterman, the Minister of Propaganda and a golfing crony. Masterman intervened at the proverbial eleventh hour when the Chief Constable of West Sussex wanted to expel Ford, as a supposed German sympathiser, from his home on the coast at Selsey. So Ford *Hueffer* suddenly metamorphosed into Ford Madox Ford.

Emerging from Monica's cottage, Frieda frowns, shoos Mary away from the scene, and folds her arms across her breast. The three intruders turn, red-faced, and stumble back through the mucky garden bed. 'My dear!' fumbles Ford. 'We knocked but thought perhaps you hadn't heard us.'

'We started to wonder if you might be away,' adds Violet, her smile fluttering.

Frieda opens the door and gives them short shrift. She is most certainly at home, as they can see for themselves, but her husband is in Cambridge, the guest of Bertrand Russell and John Maynard Keynes. He will not be back for a day or two. 'I do hope you enjoy the remainder of your Sussex outing,' she tells them, closing the door.

'Mr Wells,' says Mrs H. G., piping up, 'was *so* sorry he was unable to come on this occasion.' She drops her voice to a whisper: '*Polyuria*.' Then she resumes her bright tone. 'He sends his regards.'

Before Frieda knows it, the trio have followed her into her kitchen. Why do they stay? What are they after? She wants only a nap after listening to Monica's long, sad account of her marriage to and abandonment by Mary's brilliant father, Dr Caleb Saleeby.

With the long car journey, Violet and Mrs Wells are delighted to find the cow-shed boasts an indoor lavatory. As Frieda searches, wearily, for the tea-leaves and pot, Ford replies, pointedly, in English to Frieda's German. Although his father was German and he himself is fluent, he is at pains to resurrect his *Dutch* and *Russian* heritage for her now. Frieda tells him he looks more German than Hindenburg.

They move into the sitting-room. Violet emerges from the lavatory and joins them at the refectory table, where Frieda remarks, with mischief in her gold-green eyes, how touching it was that Ford should have dedicated his last book to the Kaiser himself, or as he expressed it on the dedication page, to their 'august sovereign'. He must have been caught off guard by the war, she says, smiling wickedly. Violet flushes and remonstrates on her lover's behalf.

Mrs Wells sails into the room, and pauses to take in the view at the window through which she was latterly spying. Doubtless Frieda is enjoying the beautiful *English* spring. Frieda replies only to say that she sorely misses alpine flowers.

She does not serve the brandy-apple cake, a cake which Hilda made only that morning, and which Ford admired conspicuously on his way through the kitchen.

Before the week is out, Frieda's failure to serve the coveted cake, and her impertinence as a guest of the English nation, will manifest as a 'black mark' on the Lawrences' official record at Wellington House – for Fordie *loved* his food.

Flip, flip—

March 9th. On Lawrence's return from Cambridge, Mary poses him in his favourite room of the cow-shed – on the edge of the bathtub. He appears thinner than ever, and he still has not shaken the bug which laid him low the month before. His face is blade-sharp. His beard is tidy and pointed. Even in black-and-white, his pale blue eyes burn.

To Mary, he looks in that moment like an angry faun or a fox-man, and indeed her photo reveals a peculiar menagerie to which he seems, in this moment, to belong. The tiles above the bath are Delft blue, and on them are designs of the paradoxical and misbegotten: a hog-like creature with the needles of a porcupine and the horn of a rhino; a dog with the ears of a rabbit; a pony with the bill of a duck; a fish standing on land on its tail-fins.

'Is it nice to be home?' asks Mary.

The exile regards her wearily.

She shrugs, then pulls the lever.

If we were to tunnel backwards through the dark, dilated pupils of Mary's subject, we might see his nervous departure for Cambridge a few days before: 'What if,' he fretted to Frieda, 'I am required to wear a dinner jacket?'

We might see him meeting Bertrand Russell, John Maynard Keynes and Co. at Trinity College, in the grandeur of the Senior Common Room. We might witness his tetchy discomfort, as well as their affability, their patrician ease and lightness of touch. They admired his passion. He was privately impressed – and worried – by their cleverness. His education, in conventional terms, was limited. More than anything, he was annoyed by their nonchalance and irony; by their endless rationalism; by the sense he had, more acute – or paranoid – with every hour, of the cultural kingdoms over which they reigned.

He had decided to make the journey to Cambridge to advance his philosophy of the sexes; of true marriage and expanded consciousness; of the regeneration of the nation. He'd scribbled notes on the train: 'Love is, that I go to a woman to know myself, and knowing myself, to go further, to explore in to the unknown, which is the woman, venture in upon the coasts of the unknown, and open my discovery to all humanity... But knowing myself is only preparing myself. What for? For the adventure into the unexplored...'

Insofar as his philosophy concerned *women*, he was barking up the wrong tree ... Yet Keynes, for his part, thought the novelist fine company. Later, he would be surprised to learn, from Russell, the intense degree of Lawrence's agitation and resentment. Nevertheless, and to Keynes's credit – years later, in 1928 – he was to be counted by Lawrence as the only member of 'the Bloomsbury Group' who supported him by subscribing to the private publication of *Lady Chatterley's Lover*.

That was not quite true. The painter Duncan Grant *Duncan Forbes*, whose art had been verbally vandalised by Lawrence in Grant's own studio that long-ago day before the outbreak of war, had also – rather generously under the circumstances – subscribed.

People had a habit of going on being kind to Lawrence, whatever the rancour or spite he served up.

Flip.

March 13th. Kot, Lawrence's Russian writer-translator friend, arrives at the Colony with the ailing Katherine Mansfield. She writes to Jack Murry from the refectory table as soon as she installs herself in the cow-shed, in the better of the two guest rooms. It seems that she and Jack Murry are 'on' again:

> *Greatham*
> *Saturday afternoon*

> *Darling Jack,*

> *I came here by a fly driven by a man with a black patch on his eye. It was a most complicated journey. I kept thinking of my 'wandering boy' and the journey in the dark that you told me of, and when we took the tenth turning, my hand flew out to you. This is a very nice cottage and I feel like you that ours is sordid in comparison. The bathroom! The fresh whitewash! And a fire in one's bedroom all dancy in the dark.*

> *I gave Lawrence your love, and he sends his and so does Frieda. They love you, both of them. I have talked a good deal of your book. Lawrence wants to review it. It's a good idea, I think.*

> *I have seen Mrs. Monica Saleeby. She called me Katherine. I don't know why that touched me. I like her but she seems to me unhappy: she appeals to me. Little Mary keeps your photo under her pillow, but you said you were coming here soon, and Mrs. Saleeby says if the promise is not kept 'there will be no holding Mary'.*

> *The country is lovely – sand and pine hills, daffodils in flower, violets and primrose in plenty, and on the marshes this morning there were almost as many seagulls as we saw in Rye. The downs so free are lovely – but I cannot walk quite there. Far for me. But I <u>am</u> much better – the air is so good. And the hot baths in the bathroom – with sea salt – very sumptuous!*

I am sitting writing to you, and Frieda and Kot are talking. My brain is wispy a little, my precious dear. Two little quick kisses.

Your
Tig

Privately, Frieda concludes that Katherine is only *with* Jack when Jack is within earshot. Otherwise, her head turns for any admirer. Frieda is of the view that Kot is slowly seducing Katherine with his translations of Chekhov's stories, and that Katherine is only too happy to be seduced. *Poor* Murry. There is also, apparently, the gift of a Russian dress from Kot, which Katherine told Murry she bought for herself in Paris. Frieda likes the dress, which Katherine wears for dinner that first evening; she likes Katherine too, although she suspects her endlessly.

On the train to Pulborough, Katherine leaned against Kot in the carriage and murmured: 'You, Koteliansky, are a kindred, and that is why I know I can confide in you. The weekend will be a tonic but, between us two, I feel ancient – a crone, 500 years old. The truth is, I am often reduced to a hobble these days. I cannot even dress myself without bewailing my bones. Only vanity makes me struggle on. I have spent every penny I have on a corset of violet silk, which is so exquisite it pains me that there is no one to admire it. Frieda would say I am a tease, confessing these things to you, but you understand, don't you, dear Kot?' On arrival, he duly lifted her down from the fly, whereupon Katherine announced that the Colony was 'Paradise itself', and that she could not, and would not, walk as far as the Downs.

She and Kot are, Frieda decides, a gloomy pair of guests, pining for each other's every word, though Katherine loves only the attention. Moreover, she has taken two baths already and is like a greedy child with the bath-salts.

The exile, for his part, is still depleted after his trip to Cambridge. He grumbles that he can shake neither his winter bug, nor his mood. Over dinner, he informs his guests that he has come to think of 'Evil' as an active principle in the affairs of men.

Kot and Katherine exchange a glance, half-mocking and half-nervous of him. He lectures Kot: 'Really it is a disgrace to be as inert as you are.'

Frieda chuckles. She enjoys it when 'her Lorenzo' skewers others. In the end, only little Mary can distract him from himself. The following day, in the lane outside, she draws a game of hopscotch, then insists they play. Play, for Mary, is a serious matter, and she is impatient with their slow recall of the rules. They must pay attention!

In Mary's photo, Katherine's pain, it seems, has subsided sufficiently for her to follow Mary's lead. She teeters on one leg on Square 3, gay and teasing. Her marker-stone can be seen on Square 2, and she has proudly hopped past it, charming and bird-like. Frieda looks on from the verge. She wears her mourning day-dress, and her eyes narrow as she watches her guest's spirits revive so winsomely. Lawrence and Kot crouch and grin from the side-lines, delighted by Katherine's verve. In the snap, a shadow makes the hedge of Kot's hair appear even higher than it actually is. Lawrence tells Katherine that if she can hop, she can certainly write, and that she has no excuse.

'Didn't I say?' She glances over her shoulder. 'I shall be hopping away again next week – to Paris to write.'

Mary holds her breath, gripping her camera so that it doesn't wobble. Then she pulls the lever, and in that instant, Kot looks away, lost – Katherine will not be his, after all.

April 1st. Bertrand Russell returns to the Colony *sans* Ottoline and stays until Easter Saturday. On this occasion, Mary asks him to pose with a wild rabbit she has tamed. In the photo, there is a curious resemblance between the renowned mathematician and the rabbit; perhaps it is the teeth.

As the photographer composes her picture, Russell tells Mary, sweetly and without irony, that she must entitle his portrait *April Fool*.

She does.

Flip, flip.

Easter Sunday, April 4th.

Viola's friend and co-typist, Eleanor Farjeon – whom Lawrence previously interrogated over his sick-bed – is visiting Viola at Winborn's. Both say a hearty 'yes' to joining in the Lawrences' Easter Sunday dinner celebration, the rival to Wilfrid and Alice Meynell's more civilised gathering.

In reply to Lawrence's sudden question, 'No,' Viola says, bemused: there is no sign of Percy, though Percy's nearest and dearest are down from London – that's to say, Madeline; the three children; Percy's bachelor brother, the literary man Edward Lucas; plus, the Nelsons, friends of Percy and Madeline. 'Perhaps Percy will yet be granted leave this month?' Lawrence ventures. But Viola says, no, she thinks not.

Alice Meynell's poet-friend Dollie – mother to Maitland Radford, the doctor-hero who saved Sylvia's life – is also staying at Winborn's. It is a full house.

Dollie pops across the quadrangle to meet Mr D. H. Lawrence, the writer, and his wife, and to thank Lawrence for his work in the cottage garden at Rackham. She plans to lease it from Madeline later in the summer, for 'the young ones', she tells him as he mashes potatoes, 'my daughter and her friends.' *The cottage was shut up – or lent to friends.*

Maitland, she says, is serving at a field hospital in France. Lawrence stops his mashing and says what an agony that must be, sewing up blown-apart men. How good of Maitland to bear it, he says.

Dollie finds Lawrence not 'rough' at all, as she'd heard, but touchingly child-like, and 'brim full' of sensibility and perception. 'Are you a pacifist, perchance?' she asks.

At that moment, on the little desk in the exile's room, his letter to Aldous Huxley waits, not yet sealed. In it, apropos of everything and nothing, he has written: 'Sometimes I wish I could let go and be really wicked – kill and murder – but kill chiefly. I do want to kill. But I want to select whom I shall kill. Then I shall enjoy it.'

In time, in a manner of speaking, he will make his selection.

He was lying with a great mass of bloody earth thrown over his thighs. He looked at it vaguely, and thought it must be heavy over him. He was anxious, with a very heavy anxiety, like a load on his life. Why was the earth on his thighs so soaked with blood? The leg lay diverted. He tried to move a little. The leg did not move. There seemed a great gap in his being. He knew that part of his thigh was blown away. He could not think of the great bloody mess. It seemed to be himself, a wet, smashed, red mass.

At the stove, Lawrence gingerly raises the lamb roast from the pan. 'A pacifist?' he replies to Dollie. 'Alas, no.' There is menace in his smile. 'I'm afraid I lack the requisite peace of mind.'

Dollie warms to Frieda, and sympathises with the agony of her estrangement from her children, as well as the death of her father, the Baron. Together, they pick daffodils in the orchard for a centre-piece. Viola lays the table. Eleanor chops chives and informs the exile that the typing of his manuscript is nearly complete. He bastes the lamb and stirs the onion sauce. Kot sings mournfully for Passover; he is still love-lorn for Katherine. Mary rushes in, wanting to join *their* Easter feast, but her Aunt Viola tells her no; a special treat awaits the children in her grandparents' house, and she must have her dinner *there*.

Frieda is relieved. The girl is a pest.

Mary is permitted, however, to take one picture. In it, Lawrence stands at the head of the long table in a striped pinny, clutching a gravy boat. Mary looks down and composes the group in her view-finder. The lamb roast smells sweet and strong. On the count of three, 'Baa!' they say, and Mary pulls the lever—

April 14th.

Jack Murry limps back to Greatham. Like Kot, he is heartbroken with Katherine gone again. Lawrence, the married man, castigates him for accepting her departure so fatalistically. He lectures his protégé on sex, the otherness 'of Woman', the ideal of simultaneous consummation, as well as the need, through sex, to 'die to' the personal self.

Murry begins to regret his visit. He cannot suppress a yawn.

'I am *trying* to get you to understand sex in relation to the widening of one's consciousness.'

Murry tells Lawrence he needs to get himself a new jacket.

They are off to Rackham Cottage for tea with Eleanor, Viola and some of Eleanor's friends, down from London. They are all crowded into Rackham.

Before they set out, the exile admits to Murry: 'This old cold I've had never really gets better. It feels like a sore throat in my stomach. The cow-shed is damp,' he says. 'I didn't know it at first but I know it now. Don't say anything to Viola, but we will move on by the end of summer. I don't know where we'll go, but I'm tired of the place and I'm tired of the wash of visitors under our door.'

'You seem to get on jolly well with them.'

'What choice do I have?'

Murry says Lawrence must get the doctor in Storrington to listen to his lungs. The exile turns, hot-faced, and asks if he is mad. '*That* was the doctor who almost killed the Lucas girl!' The two men step outside and examine the sky. Is it about to rain? The air feels charged, loaded with something the exile cannot see or smell but can feel across the back of his neck; a presentiment or an intimation; something not yet wet in the ink of his imagination.

Then the little group is underway. Frieda joins Lawrence and Jack and, in no time, husband and wife have turned on each other. They carry on, arguing bitterly for most of the mile-long walk. At one point, Lawrence grips Frieda by the arm, although he looks so thin, and she so solid, that no one is especially concerned. It is simply what the Lawrences *do*.

Up ahead, Viola chats with Jack. She, for one, has become accustomed to overlooking and 'under hearing' the Lawrences. 'How very odd,' she says, with a mischievous tilt to her chin, 'that his *Rainbow* is a veritable hymn to marriage!'

Frieda starts to weep in Wagnerian proportions. Viola murmurs to Jack that she can't help but feel Frieda is play-acting. Lawrence, on the other hand, is the dearest soul *almost all* the time, and abominable the rest. She and Jack stride on. 'But how interesting he makes everything generally,' she says. 'We Meynells have grown very fond. He is so eager for life, and every one of us feels more alive in his company. He sees all of that which passes most people by. Birds. Trees. Flowers. Stones. And the children positively adore him, although he never indulges them as the rest of us do.'

On their arrival at Rackham Cottage, Mary, already there, skips around the exile, her camera bouncing from the strap at her neck. Lawrence holds up a grass-snake gently for her to see. It is over two feet long, with vertical bars of black. It coils around his wrist, and he smiles, as relaxed as any snake-charmer. Mary holds her breath, steadies her hands and pulls the lever.

Flip—

And in that same moment, at her desk, Lady Ottoline, one of the first readers of *The Rainbow* in manuscript, is writing to tell Bertrand Russell that she finds Lawrence's new novel decidedly too sexual.

April 17th–18th.

David – Bunny – Garnett and a university friend have come to stay at the Colony, with little notice. Although it is only mid-April, it is as hot as midsummer. The exile emerges from the cow-shed to find the pair throwing coins in a gambling game on the lawn behind Winborn's. Miscellaneous Meynells join in. It is, the exile concludes, a veritable 'Meynellage'. Yet in Mary's photograph of the group, he appears happy and at ease. No one could have known otherwise.

Eleanor Farjeon came over earlier in the day from Rackham Cottage, where Madeline is again in residence for the Easter hols. Eleanor's brother, Herbert Farjeon, and his new wife, Joan, are also staying with Madeline. With a little squeezing in at Rackham, there is room for guests, especially with Percy away in training.

Eleanor, Madeline, Herbert and Joan walked over together. Now, they mill about the lawns and quadrangle, enjoying the fine weather. Joan, Lawrence recalls – not that he could forget – is the sister of the woman he beheld that snowy day on Rackham Hill. *Rosalind. Ros. Rose-flame of winter.* He can see a passing resemblance between the two sisters, and he makes a point of introducing himself to the brother-in-law, Herbert Farjeon.

That is the way to do it.

It is a happy, youthful gang. Viola's fiancé, Martin Secker, is visiting; so too Maitland Radford, the hero-doctor. Frieda flirts gaily with both. Lawrence listens instead to the call of a cuckoo; to its melancholy, minor descending third. As always with the cuckoo, the call seems to come from everywhere and nowhere.

He watches Maitland bend down to speak kindly to Sylvia, whose young life he saved. Still no one has told Lawrence precisely what happened that day. A veil has been drawn over the accident, but it is notable that Percy, the errant father, has not taken leave from his army training to join his friends. He must have *some* leave, surely. What is the man avoiding?

The children are the only truly interesting company. In the orchard, he shows them a wagtail on a stone wall, then produces a bag of brandy-balls from his pocket, and makes his apologies to the entire group. He must cobble together some supper, he says, for David Garnett and David's newcomer friend. Winborn's is full for the night, and the two visitors are to stay in the cow-shed.

Inside, he does not cobble supper. He goes to the long table and seizes his pen:

Dear Kot, to hear David and Frankie talking really fills me with black fury: they talk endlessly, but endlessly — and never, never a good or real thing said. Not a crumb or grain of reverence. I had rather be alone. I like David Garnett, but there is something wrong with him. Why won't he have Eleanor? I long for Italy. Sometimes I think I can't stand this England this England any longer.

From the other side of the open window, he eavesdrops on the private exchange of two of the Meynell sisters. Madeline is showing Viola a letter from Percy; it arrived that morning. The training, he wrote, is intensifying. It did him a world of good, seeing her and the girls in London. He is to be sent to the Front any week now. Not Belgium. He is permitted to say that much, to put her mind at rest. He hopes Monica's health continues to improve, and that Alice is feeling stronger now that spring has arrived. Madeline is to give his love to Viola and his regards to Secker. It saddens him to say that he won't get to Greatham before his regiment is shipped out. He will miss the children more than he can express, and her above all of course; he will hold her close in his every thought. He aches for her, and now, he is only down the coast at Seaford! How will he cope when he is across the Channel? He hopes she will forgive him his absence. He will return to her a better man for it, although his love cannot be greater than it is already, and this, he knows she knows.

More coins are tossed — heads and tails — across the lawn, small bets are wagered, and the luminous spring day drifts with pollen and bumblebees. Indeed, it is impossible to imagine that, in just four days, the Kaiser's troops will deploy the horror of chlorine gas, to drive the Allied forces from their trenches — before they open fire. The Second Battle of Ypres, that man-made apocalypse, will unfold in the time it takes for the apple blossom of Greatham to bloom and fall.

Mary arrived before breakfast was finished, bearing a fistful of anemones torn from the woodland floor for her tutor. It was the morning of her first lesson.

Ruffian, thought Frieda.

In the sitting-room, Lawrence began Mary's instruction in composition, while, at the distant end of the table, Frieda wrote letters home to Baden-Baden, repeatedly forgetting not to kick the table leg with her idle foot. She hated being left out.

'Mrs Weekley!' shouted Lawrence.

It was his habit in such moments to disown her.

'Moo!' she mouthed back at him, sulkily.

In her rural loneliness, she had asked tutor and pupil if they might permit her to sit at the end of the table during lessons. She was no good in her own company, unless it involved a sunny spot in which she could nap.

She did not need an inner life, she would reply to her husband, because she had married a writer, and he had inner-life enough for them both. She, on the other hand, needed distractions – and company! Warm-hearted company. Was it too much to ask?

In a few hours, when their neighbour, Monica, had excavated herself from sleep, Frieda would stroll across the quadrangle and propose that she join her for her daily, chauffeured excursion.

Lorenzo, when he was pleased with her, used to tell friends that she lived only in the moment, like a glorious cat.

'Like a goldfish, rather,' Koteliansky once retorted. 'With a similar attention span.'

What was Frieda supposed to say to that? Her husband's Ruski friend was always full of disdain for her. Yet she was, in her own way, as remarkable and important as Lorenzo, and she had no hesitation in reminding her husband's friends of that fact.

In their Chesham cottage, one afternoon the autumn before, torrents of rain had poured down outside, and the local duck-pond had slowly flooded their property. Inside, rain streamed down the walls of their miserable kitchen, and they'd moved pots and bowls to catch what they could, but it was hopeless. That day, all the tears in her had seemed to arrive with the flood. She could not be happy, she sobbed to the two men, without her children!

Kot, who'd sat eating his way through their only loaf of bread and last block of cheese, was indifferent to the water lapping at his ankles. As the water gushed and her tears flowed, he had taken it upon himself to reproach her: 'Frieda, you have left your children to marry Lawrence. You must choose either your children or Lawrence – and if you choose Lawrence, you must *stop* complaining about the children!'

She'd fled to Katherine and Jack's nearby cottage. Then, she sent Katherine back through the rain with the message that she would not return. Lorenzo exploded at Katherine, as Frieda knew he would: 'Tell Frieda I never want to see her again!'

Katherine shrugged, turned, and went back into the rain, her skirts already sodden and mud-caked. It was the first time Kot had laid eyes on her, and from that point on, he seemed to Frieda to dismiss any woman who failed to be Katherine Mansfield.

Yet – 'and this is where it gets spicy,' she wrote to her sister in Baden-Baden:

> only a few weeks later, Katherine <u>ran out</u> on dear, handsome, poor Jack Murry and left him broken, utterly heart-broken. Katherine believes Jack is too child-like and unformed for her. But here's the rub. She abandoned Jack, <u>not</u> for clever, adoring Koteliansky – mais non! – but for a young Parisian lover!

Frieda enjoyed sending her sister the latest gossip from their not inconsiderable bohemian circle. Lorenzo often asserted that he was no bohemian – it was true, she conceded, that he worked too hard to qualify – but she could happily 'do' Bohemia for them both. By doing very little.

When she looked up from her page, Lorenzo and Mary were staring at her sternly. She had, apparently, been laughing aloud.

She returned, *in her own time*, to her letter.

Frieda's sisters had confirmed that her letters *were* getting through these days, via Switzerland, although they were 'thoughtfully pre-opened', they said, and only on occasion re-glued. The Lawrences' post, even out of tiny Greatham, was intercepted. The thoroughness of the Royal Mail, Frieda noted to her sister, was a marvel. Let the spies read that!

She looked up from her morning coffee to observe her husband. He was making elegant copperplate letters in Mary's exercise book for her to imitate. The girl idolised him. He was neither excessively polite to her, in the falsely distant way of most adults, nor did he patronise her. He was generous and, when they weren't concentrating on her lessons, he was merely himself and full of fun. Mary was, in his view, and clearly in her own, his smaller equal, and he liked her company, whatever the toll on his writing time.

For Frieda, the girl was more gnome than child. Why should Lorenzo take such a fond interest in Mary when he cared so little for the plight of *her* three motherless children? He didn't care a tuppence for them! It was cruel. To her. To them. *He* was cruel. Moreover, the Mary-child made her uncomfortable *in her own* cow-shed.

But Frieda kept her discomfort to herself. It was important that Lorenzo earned their keep and kept the roof above their heads, even if it meant he had to civilise the wild-child of Sussex. The lessons, thankfully, seemed to be a success, and perhaps Mr Meynell might even give Lorenzo a bonus of cold, hard cash if Mary passed her exam. It was lovely that Papa Meynell had supplied Hilda – that was all well and good – but they had to eat as well.

'Must we gnaw our fists?' she'd asked her husband tearfully one night. He'd pointed to the vast bag of lentils in the kitchen and said, without even looking up from the book review he was writing, that, when the lentils were finished, like so many grains of sand in an hour-glass, he would send her out to *forage* on the Downs, whatever the weather. He'd already gathered all the chickweed and mallow within miles. It was her turn, he said coldly, to provide.

She'd grabbed the nearest cushion to muffle her sobs.

Her spirits were revived by her discovery that Mary was booked in for St Paul's School for Girls in London in September. Two of her own three children, dearest Barby and Elsa, were at St Paul's. With any luck, if she and Lorenzo could but maintain a cordial Meynell connection, she, the heartbroken mother, could send secret notes to Barby and Elsa *through* Mary the Gnome. Indeed, with things as dire as they were between her, the sinned-against mother, and their hard-hearted father, this little urchin might be the only lifeline she would have to her dear ones.

She tried to keep the agony of the separation from them to herself. Yes, she howled, as Lorenzo said, but only when he was in his nightly bath with the door shut. He was growing ever more jealous of them, which was most unjust, and he had all but given up trying to understand the tumult of her heart. Their arguments were turning fierce again, and nearly as horrid as they had been in their Chesham days.

Frieda resolved to think strategically. She would find a way to bribe the girl. What did gnomes like to eat?

Her coffee cup clinked loudly in its saucer.

'Sshh!' the pair said.

Such an unpleasant child.

Lawrence was doing dictation with her, to improve her handwriting and spelling. "'Under the calm ascension of the night / We heard the mellow lapsing and return / Of night-owls purring in their groundless flight / Through lanes of darkling fern.'" It was a poem about Greatham by a poet-friend of the family who had stayed at the Colony before the War. Lorenzo was sniffy about the verse, from 'On Greatham', but it would do for a child's dictation, he said.

He deducted five points when she wrote 'herd' for 'heard'.

'An easy mistake to make!' Frieda opined, and she indicated their cow-shed setting with a flourish of her arm. She had to try to win the Gnome's affection, but they both ignored her.

So she picked up her pen and wrote to her sister Else about the death of the poet Rupert Brooke.

Of sunstroke on the way to Gallipoli, the papers say. Yet <u>we</u> have it, via Eleanor Farjeon, who had it via her sister-in-law – Mrs Rosalind Baynes, who knew Brooke well in the 'neo-pagan' days of their youth – that he <u>actually</u> died of a gnat-bite. Blood poisoning. But a gnat seemed too ignominious a death for so handsome a soldier-poet, so the official cause of death is sunstroke. Apollo carried him off, in other words – and before he ever saw action. Poor, lovely Rupert. I met him once in London before the War. He was so beautiful, Else, it took your breath away. You would think some people must be untouchable in this War, but no ...

To her mother, the Baroness, Frieda could not bring herself to confess that she was not permitted to see her own children. The loss of the Baron was already enough for them all to bear. Instead, she would amuse her dowager mother, Scotland Yard and her sorrowing self in one communiqué.

Dearest Mamma,

In these sad days of strife and tribulation, I cannot help but recollect the stories with which Wilhelm once regaled us — of his happy boyhood so-journs at Windsor Castle visiting his Queen-grandmamma, of putting his little hand up the skirts of the ladies-in-waiting, and changing the clocks to worry the cooks and courtiers. I seem to recall he played hide-and-seek with his nurse in all one-thousand rooms. Do you remember how, each year, his nurse would leave Berlin stout and well, and then return — yes, precisely! — a thin shadow of her former self. What a monkey he was!

No doubt Willie feels a great and abiding affection for Windsor Castle. He always looked upon it as his second home. Is it not wonderful to recall that the English are in fact Saxe-Coburgs, whatever this 'House of Windsor' bosh now? I confess, I don't understand the sudden fashion in England for re-naming <u>German</u> Shepherds 'Alsatians'. It grieves my soul. Why should any creature — King of England or cur — be separated from his true nature? Even the homage to the Kaiser at Madame Tussaud's has been, I am in-formed, relegated to an annexe near the public lavatories. It cannot be borne. Why must we be at war when we are one great, jolly, bejowled family?

Wilhelm wept most pitiably, I understand, at his cousin King Bertie the Seventh's funeral not five years ago, and Queen Mary, it is said, still sounds very German indeed, in spite of the elocution lessons. She does us proud even, if I'm told, she is not much let out these days. They are keen, you see, Mamma, to get the new surname to <u>stick</u>.

This whole War business is getting very messy indeed, and you know I am congenitally incapable of dealing with mess. I simply can't think on it — I have to plait my hair so I don't pull it out.

I must bid you adieu here, for 'I spy with my little eye' (<u>such</u> a charm-ing English idiom) the postman through the window. He frowns most miserably when he sees the destinations of my letters, but I tell him how marvellously efficient the state interception is — I tell him I never realised *the Royal Mail was so efficient – and he departs, suitably congratulated, and in far better spirits than when he arrived.*

I remain your peace-loving daughter,
Frieda

For every grade Lorenzo gave Mary of seven out of ten or higher, the child was allowed to stop her lesson and learn a new song. She had a good voice and could carry a tune – Frieda couldn't deny that – and Lawrence's high-pitched voice, one which initially surprised those he met, blended well with Mary's young one, even if his chest was still sore.

Mary went merrily 'at' the tune, which was too maudlin for her years, although Frieda herself greatly enjoyed singing 'Barbara Allen', and would have accompanied the pair at the piano had they not insisted, jointly, that she remain 'invisible' or leave the room. Even in her own cow-shed, she must be treated like an enemy alien.

Not that anything could be worse than their months in Chesham. There, the locals had claimed she was poisoning the blackberries of the most popular bushes! Then they reported her for flashing lights. Apparently, she was signalling to the Zeppelins to bomb the village in which she herself lived!

Spy? She wasn't the spy. *Lorenzo* was. She knew exactly what he was up to as he set Mary off on 'a composition'. Today's topic was … 'Rackham Cottage'.

Of course it was.

He was still fascinated by Percy and Madeline Lucas, and the tragedy of Sylvia, their little crippled girl. Frieda observed him from her end of the table, as she pretended to blot her letters. While the girl wrote in her exercise book, he worked on his Hardy volume. The time passed slowly. Frieda deplored silences.

Then, the dark-headed gnome-child straightened on her mushroom and glanced up at her tutor. He nodded and, shyly but proudly, she began to read her composition:

Rackham Cottage

Uncle Percy says the Cottage is as old as the hills but not really. Its from the sixteen hundreds, only with a nursery, bedroom and bathroom added to it. My cousins live there with there mother, father and nurse. The children are Sylvia, Christian and Barbara Lucas. Also Barbara has a baby-doll. There are many snakes at Rackham Cottage. There is also a little brook and when I play there, we dig in the garden and find rubbish people used to bury, such as broken crockery from the olden days. Once we found a coin but they wouldn't take it in the shop when we wanted to buy toffee.

There father will be going to the War, he is tall with fair hair and kind. When its raining, he teaches us folk songs. He came back yesterday from the camp to see his garden which he dug by himself, not even with Arthur to help. Its very flowery now. There is a big lawn with hedgehogs in the morning when its dewy and an apple tree.

Sylvia hurt herself on a fag-hook not last summer but the one before, she was six. Sometimes we all look for snakes to frighten their nurse with—

'With which to frighten their nurse.'
'Oh, yes.' Mary pushed the hair out of her eyes and licked her lips.

That day, Christian and Barbara were looking for snakes. Robert and Cicely Nelson were playing too. Robert, Cicely and their parents were visiting at Rackham. Cicely screams a good deal. She is frightened of snakes. When she screamed very loud, Sylvia ran out to see. Then there was blood everywhere. A fag-hook was in the tall grass. Sylvia didn't scream at all. She just went very white and trembled. She was brave, her mother said, who is Aunt Madeline. Sylvia had to change her frock and wear a bandage. Then we all went to Storrington. The doctor in Storrington gave Sylvia a bigger bandage and a bag of humbugs.

The next day, Aunt Viola told Mother that Sylvia had a fever. Aunt Viola went to Rackham and played the piano for Sylvia to sing along. Sylvia had tapioca for a treat. Sometimes she cried because her leg was very sore. Another doctor came, a friend of Aunt Viola's. They were on a walk but didn't go. Then a special motor-car came to take Sylvia away. Christian said the doctor in London almost cut off Sylvia's leg. Then he didn't. Sylvia stayed in London in the hospital for many months. Granny sent Sylvia letters to cheer her up. I helped her. We wrote 'Dear dear price-less Mrs Badleg'. Now Sylvie is the slowest of us all but she can hop-run. She has to wear an iron which she is only allowed to take off at night and when we go swimming at The Quell.

189

She looked up. 'The End.'

The exile's face had been sober as he listened to Mary. Frieda watched him take her exercise book and read it again for himself. He crossed and uncrossed his legs. He uncapped his fountain pen and made a few marks.

'Seven out of ten?' she asked.

Frieda waited too. The girl always had seven out of ten. Enough to encourage her, but not enough for her to think she didn't have to work very hard.

Frieda watched her husband's face.

'Mr Lawrence?' Mary said.

His heart went back to the savage old spirit of the place: the desire for old gods, old, lost passions, the passion of the cold-blooded, darting snakes that hissed and shot away from him, the mystery of blood-sacrifices, all the lost, intense sensations of the primeval people of the place, whose passions seethed in the air still, from those long ago days before the Romans came. The seethe of a lost, dark passion, in the air. The presence of unseen snakes.

'Eight,' he announced, blinking.

Mary clapped.

Frieda sat back in her chair, her eyes narrowing. How long would it take before he prodded at the question of Perceval Lucas?

A fit of coughing shook him. Then it came: 'I hadn't realised Sylvia's father was here yesterday.' He returned her composition and held his ribs as he stood. 'I will make a pot of tea.'

The girl stared after him.

'Can I—'

'May I …' he called.

'—sing the President song? I remember it already.'

'You may *if* you can write down the history I taught you. You have five minutes. You must imagine it is a question in your written test for St Paul's.'

She picked up her pencil, and off it went across her page.

In the kitchen, he opened and closed cupboard doors, distracted.

Frieda knew by what.

'Was Mrs McKinley in mourning?' the girl called to him, checking her facts.

'Naturally.' He stood in the doorway, drying a tea-cup. 'Four minutes!'

She crossed out a line and carried on.

'The time is up. Put down your pencil.' He returned to the table with mismatched cups. 'Is Mr Lucas still at Rackham?' he said in an offhand fashion.

Frieda looked at him. Spy, spy, spy.

The Gnome shook her head. 'He had to go back to the army, my cousin Christian said, to do his duty and serve England. I'm glad you're staying with us and not doing yours.'

Frieda could feel the white-heat of his silence as he set the cups out with the jug of milk. She could see it as he took his seat: he was boiling it all up in his mind. The carelessly abandoned fag-hook. The garden in which children always played. His hatred of those who ran at the War.

Mary chose the brightest tea-cup. Then she took a deep breath and began to read at speed.

Mr McKinley was once the President of the United States. He was nice, Mrs Mckinley loved him, and most people thought he was a friendly chap. One day in 1901 he had to go to a place called Buffalo. He was greeting people at a meeting, then a man called Leon Cholgosh, an archer—

'An anarchist.'
She grinned and nodded.

—an anarchist fired at Mr McKinley with his Iver-Johnson gun. ~~Down he went~~. The first bullet bounced off his coat button but the second got him. The train rushed him back to Washington D.C. but no doctor could save him. Mrs McKinley cried till her eyes were red and swolen. She was sad and wore a black veil over her face. Cholgosh was locked up in Sing-Sing. Sing-Sing is not in China, its in New York state. Everyone in America was angry at the murderer, they told him he had to stay in gaol. After that day, important people in Washington agreed the President must always be protected so that no one would ever shoot him again.

She closed her exercise book and plunged into the song, her legs swinging under the table.

Look here, little children, don't waste your breath
You'll draw a pension at your papa's death
From Buffalo to Washington

Yonder come the train, she coming down the line
Blowing every station, Mr. McKinley is a-dying
It's hard times, hard times

Look-it here, you rascal, you see what you've done
You shot my husband with that Iver-Johnson gun
I'm carrying you back, to Washington ...

Doc come a-running, takes off his specs
Said 'Mr McKinley, better pass in your checks
You're bound to die, bound to die.'

She turned in her chair and scolded her teacher. 'You're not singing!' He loved the tune as much as she did.

But something stopped her from starting up again. She assessed
his face in the unguarded, fixed manner of children. 'Are you sick?'
she asked. She frowned at the way he clutched his ribs. Then she
ducked her head under the table to look at his legs, as if something
might have escaped her notice. 'Or are you crippled?'

He pushed back the blue-and-white curtains in the sitting-room and wiped the condensation from the pane. Madeline and Percy's lame daughter, Sylvia, was in the orchard, jumping at the new blossom. She was stuffing her coat pockets with it.

Mary had told him that Sylvia was recovering from measles, not a bad case of it, but nevertheless she was staying at Winborn's with her mother until it was safe for her to return to her sisters in London. The girl's face was pale and drawn against the green velvet collar of her coat, but she was jumping, fierce as any plunderer, at the Old Apple.

He seated himself at the long table, where the view to the orchard was clear. The surface of the table was a jumble of paints and brushes. He was decorating Viola's kitchen pots and jars with bright stripes and spots. From time to time, he looked up from his work and observed Sylvia again. How stubborn she was, throwing herself at that tree.

Her mother or her governess must have allowed her outside for fresh air. For every second or third fistful of blossom she managed to snatch from a bough, she fell to the ground, sometimes backwards. The leg-brace threw her off, but up she got each time.

It was a miracle she'd survived the accident with the fag-hook. She'd only been six, and the cut to her leg had turned to septicaemia of the bone. They'd nearly amputated. In the end, both she and the leg survived but it had been, said Madeline, an utterly desperate few weeks, followed by a long convalescence for the girl.

She hadn't said more.

He watched Sylvia haul herself up once again, if rigidly, grabbing hold of the tree's gnarled trunk, and then surging higher, as if she were a white hyacinth bulb in a forcing jar, sending out the slender shoot of herself. The sunlight tangled in her yellow hair. The blossom fell about her like paper-wishes. She was beautiful as she jumped, *like a little poem in herself.* Yet if she were a lamb in the field with a withered leg, the crows would have had her.

She, the eldest Lucas child, most resembled Percy her father, and they had been very close, according to Viola. Madeline Lucas was a lovely woman, too precious with her children, but that was the vogue among middle-class English parents. As a mother, she was warm-hearted and refreshingly self-possessed. It was as if, in confronting the prospect of her first-born's death, she had got the measure of life and would never not know it again. Unlike her various siblings, she appeared to have no artistic affectations, and he liked her all the more for it. She was true only to life and to her god, and was full of an entirely honest sort of love.

Her sister Monica was, officially, the abandoned wife, but Madeline, too, he thought, had been abandoned by Lucas, perhaps more suddenly than Monica had been dropped by her husband, Dr Saleeby – 'the head-measurer'.

Percy, as Madeline had proudly explained to him and Frieda over morning coffee earlier that day on the lawn, had recently been commissioned and promoted to Second Lieutenant. That's why he was transferred to Seaford, just down the coast – for advanced training. She had seen him, but only fleetingly, the week before, at Rackham, she told them.

Frieda watched her husband lean in closer from their side of the table. 'Oh?' he said.

It was pure coincidence, Madeline said, smiling happily, that she had been in the cottage at all as his army transit travelled along the nearby logging road. His men had been using trees in the area for target practice, and Percy had persuaded the officer in charge to stop for half an hour, simply so he might dash up the track and cut through the woods to her. It was bittersweet, Madeline said. Percy had hardly been home at all when he had to turn back for the transit.

In Seaford, he was tantalisingly close, and yet unable to take leave. His new responsibilities, she said. It really was quite 'a step up' to be made Second Lieutenant. Yet he would have *so* enjoyed meeting them, the new residents of the Colony. He had no literary gifts himself, but he was, she assured them, an avid reader.

Madeline poured coffee for them from her mother's silver pot. Then Frieda reached across and took Madeline's hand, causing the poor woman to drop the sugar-tongs. 'Oh, my dear,' Frieda said, cocking her head sympathetically, 'how *awfully* difficult for you.' The exile looked away, ostensibly to allow the women their private exchange of wifely feeling. In reality, he cringed at Frieda's ham acting.

Perhaps Madeline was relieved, he thought, that Percy finally had an occupation in the world and 'responsibilities'. After all, was it not easier for her, in company, to speak of his war service than it had been, previously, to explain his gardening efforts or his folk-song cataloguing, or his dedication to the bells and sticks of Morris-dancing?

He had no profession: he earned nothing. But he talked of literature and music, he had a passion for old folk-music, collecting folk-songs and folk-dances, studying the Morris-dance and the old customs.

Was it not easier to be married to an absent Second Lieutenant than to awake each day beside a dilettante?

Like her parents, Madeline did not herself believe in the moral purpose of the War, but nor did she seem to begrudge the War her husband. *Her soul was fierce as iron against him, thrusting him away, always away.* In fact, the exile suspected that Madeline was secretly *glad* her husband was away; glad he was acquiring definition in the world; glad he would match her own energy at last. No matter that she publicly lamented his absence; their intimate life, Lawrence deduced, must surely have depended on Perceval Lucas's decision to move into a wider arena.

Even Viola, his fond sister-in-law, had discreetly suggested that Madeline was so eminently capable in their home life that Percy, a 'sweet-tempered, gentle soul', had been rather excess to requirements. *Her passion gradually hardened into dissatisfaction. She wanted some result, some production, some new active output into the world of man* ... The words of the story of Greatham were, that morning, still unknown – even to its author – but his inner eye watched.

Perceval Lucas was, by all accounts, entirely 'unwarlike', and yet he had thrown himself, absurdly, at the War – on Day One, no less. What else was he doing but pleasing his wife by wedding himself to 'manly' purpose?

It was folly. What sense of purpose could anyone find in a sham war? Percy Lucas was a lost man, a cipher of a man, and the truth would out.

What did he stand for? She had started with a strange reverence for him. But gradually a sense of frustration came up strong in her. He was so strangely inconclusive. The War could not confer upon Perceval Lucas any greater sense of soul or manhood. The reality was that he had abandoned his wife and children when he should have taken a profession and *worked* to provide for them.

Then there was the matter of the fag-hook.

And the iron brace on his little girl's leg.

The exile said nothing. He let Frieda witter on. 'In any event, my dear, who wants a man at home under her feet?'

The exile did not point out that, in their home, *he* did most of the housework, as well as the outdoor work, the sewing, the painting and repairs – and that, strictly speaking, *she* was under *his* feet, especially when she stretched out on floors and lawns to sleep or lounge.

Lawrence sipped his coffee. He was not unacquainted with his own thoughts and warps of mind. How he deplored that good man, Perceval Lucas. He didn't deceive himself on that score. And how he loved the green, broken shoot of the girl who jumped after apple blossom. Perceval Lucas did not deserve her. But human reproduction had nothing to do with natural justice.

Frieda had given Professor Weekley three children. Where were his? One thing was certain: once he had his own, he would not abandon them as easily as Perceval Lucas had his. Nor would he be so stupid as to leave a fag-hook in a garden where children played.

He surveyed the garden of Winborn's. That morning, the orchard was still in shadow, but the back lawn was lit with daisies and buttercups. He waved away a bee. The lily-of-the-valley were out early after the burst of heat in April, their rows of crowned blooms as white and perfect as babies' teeth.

Mary appeared with her camera. He watched her grip its box at her waist, composing the view of the three grown-ups at the outdoor table in the May sunshine. He met the camera's gaze directly and offered a rare smile, for Mary was devoted to him, and when all was said and done, he enjoyed teaching her. She was an intelligent child, and moreover, she was good company – his highest praise for a person of any age.

But his smile was for naught, because Mary's beloved Brownie was falling to the grassy ground. The picture would never be taken. She was running, running at speed towards the orchard.

Madeline turned, astonished by the commotion. Then she clambered to her feet and lifted her hem.

'Uncle Percy!' Mary shouted, waving an arm high. 'Over here! We're over here!'

The Subversive

Agent Mel Harding arrived on Hoover's doorstep at 8 a.m. sharp. He'd hardly slept. The flight from Butte the night before had been delayed. The hotel – on FBI expenses – was necessarily cheap, with flimsy walls. He'd paid a small fortune – not on expenses – to the guy at the front desk to ensure his suit and tie were pressed, and his shirt starched for the morning. The bedside clock had ticked like a woodpecker at his head most of the night. At five, unable to sleep, he got up to clip his fingernails and clean them with a pin from the hotel's sewing kit. He'd been told that Hoover often checked.

The morning was a deluge of light. The tree canopies were lush with a spring far more advanced than in Montana. He felt unworthy of it. It was odd being away from Butte. He'd grown accustomed to its narrowness. He had lived so much between the four plywood walls of his office that he usually managed to forget how much of his time was dedicated to the petty dirt of small-town life; to spotting it, tracking it, and filing the same old reports, week in, week out.

In reality, the local cops dealt with most of it: the stolen cars, usually driven by teenaged joy-riders; the bootleggers and crooks; the traveling swindlers pretending to be preachers. He couldn't sniff out so much as a single Communist in Butte, or even, say, a few plain old subversives intercepting church picnics. It was hardly worth the Bureau's time. There had been rumors of an underground porn ring, but that turned out to be nothing more than a Friday-night basement poker club which showed blue movies after the game. He investigated the local casino's interstate dealings. He stumbled across a marijuana farm. He put out feelers about three Butte families who wanted to move to Canada. Why? He dealt with two domestic homicides and some tax evasion. It wasn't New York.

On Hoover's peaceful street, every new leaf that morning was like some green, flickering flame, a pentecostal tongue of spring fire speaking at a pitch he could no longer hear. As a boy, he'd liked that Bible story, the one about the tongues of fire appearing over the Apostles' heads. In fact, he'd liked lots of the stories he and his mother had listened to, from their side pew at the back of their church. His mother had always wanted to lie low – she didn't want anymore questions about his father.

In the end, she lay so low for so long, she almost disappeared. She told so many lies about her husband's whereabouts, she couldn't keep them straight, and even he sometimes confused his mother's lies and fantasies with the truth of what had happened. They'd kept moving, from cheap apartment to cheaper apartment. She had cleaning jobs, initially in doctors' and dentists' offices, and then, as the years took their toll, in laundromats and public conveniences.

Today, as he walked to Hoover's house in the spring sunshine, it was as if the whole world had been rinsed clean. If he was no longer a part of it, he could at least look on and lift his face to the day.

He'd had the taxi drop him off two streets away so he could stretch his legs and shake off his nerves. His eczema had flared up again, and the sores on his hands oozed and bled. *Sensitive*, his mother used to say to him as he took his pictures or stared at the images in her magazines. She'd look at him as if he were a species of male she'd never come across before. *You're sensitive.*

His shoe stuck to the sidewalk. Bubble-gum. Of all days. He seated himself on the curb and scraped with a rock at the pink goo on his sole, with his holster digging into his thigh. He was sweaty already – the only man in a twice-buttoned suit jacket on a hot Friday in early June.

He felt conspicuous, even with his fedora and the prop of the businessman's briefcase. He wasn't anyone's father on his way to work or anyone's husband kissing his wife goodbye at the door. Children passed him on their way to school: the girls in skirts and white knee-socks; the boys with cow-licks, pin-on ties, and teeth they hadn't grown into.

Hoover, legend had it, had had his own teeth removed as a young man and replaced with 'perfect' dentures. Even so, he never smiled for Bureau photos or press photos, not even the time he arranged to have his picture taken with Shirley Temple at the height of her *Heidi* fame. It was said he kept that shot in a gilt frame on his desk, in the place where other men displayed photos of their children and wives.

The more weight Hoover put on, the jowlier his face grew, and the harder he worked to impersonate the no-nonsense demeanor of a Bureau G-man. On rare occasions, his features seemed to soften into what Hoover must have imagined was a 'benign' or paternal expression, but it never convinced. You only had to look at the eyes. The brain behind them was always whirring, calculating and grinding, and the eyes photographed as flat as the caps on a strip – black pops of gunpowder ready to go off.

A year ago, on the day everything went wrong, Harding had only just been promoted to the Washington Field Office from the New York F.O. His new rank was Supervisory Special Agent. He'd worked hard for twelve years to get there. He wasn't a 'natural', not the way many agents were, but he was good with the gismos at least. New ones were always being rolled out by the Lab, and they required a knack.

He hadn't been in Washington even a month when he was sent to the Mayflower Hotel by the local F.O.'s Special Agent in Charge, Howard Johnson. Harding was to deliver an analysis. That was the assignment. Hoover had been urgently waiting for it from the Lab. Easy. That's what they told him. The hotel was on Connecticut Street.

Everyone in the W.F.O. knew that Hoover and Tolson, the Director and Associate Director, lunched together every day at noon at the Mayflower. They took a quiet table in a corner. The entire squad seemed to know their favorites on the menu. They each ordered the same, and it rarely changed. Cream of mushroom soup, with plenty of Saltines. Toasted turkey, bacon and cheese sandwiches stabbed with a pickle. Piping-hot coffee. Canned fruit cocktail for dessert. Hoover would send his back if he didn't get a maraschino cherry in his bowl.

The first thing which struck Harding that lunchtime was that Tolson wasn't sitting in the chair across from Hoover, as you'd expect, but next to him on the red banquette. That's when Harding should have turned around and got the hell out of there. That's when he should have realized the joke was on him. But he was stupid – eager to please, eager to make an impression, like some kid-trainee. When he saw Hoover smile at Tolson, he was foolish enough to take that as a sign that they were relaxed; that it was an acceptable time to interrupt.

He arrived at their table and reached for the analysis it was his honor to deliver. He might have been a waiter topping up their mugs of coffee. Neither felt the need to register his presence. Whoever he was, he was not significant. The hotel staff knew to keep members of the public away; they knew the drill. They had long enjoyed Hoover's custom as well as his trust.

The two men continued their conversation in low tones, their heads close. Harding fiddled with his briefcase, flipping the central buckle and inserting the small key into each punch-latch before popping them. But nothing happened, dammit. Nothing. The latches didn't pop. He hoisted the case, got the strap out of his way, and hit everything he could.

Only when he moved a little closer – close enough to smell the sickly steam coming off the mushroom soup – did he see it: the Director's small, meaty hand clasping Tolson's. Hoover was stroking the Associate Director's hand lightly with his thumb.

Then he remembered – oh God, the relief – the case had false latches, and the key was a dummy. There *was* no standard compartment in the case, only the false bottom where he'd stowed the analysis, and the false bottom was opened by a release-button on the bottom of the case.

It was the latest in the Lab's customized line of manufacture. There were umbrellas with gutted handles for cameras – not that he'd trialed one of those yet – plus pens with tiny bugs, shoes with hollow heels for message storage, and microphones stitched into ties. The new briefcase had the false bottom, plus a miniature camera in a side compartment, with a lens covered by a satchel-strap you had to lift free. They had a similar arrangement in purses for female agents, the few employed by the Bureau – for honey-traps, not standard work, not with Hoover in charge.

Harding had initially hoped to trial-run a wristwatch device that connected to a wire, which in turn ran up a man's sleeve to a neat little reel-to-reel recorder. But when the Washington S.A.C., Howard Johnson, asked him to deliver the analysis, the briefcase he'd been trialing was ideal – beautiful leather, professional quality. Except, on the spot in the Mayflower, in front of the Director, Harding's nerves had scrambled his brain.

Hoover had looked up, staring at him vaguely, almost dreamily. Then, as if a hypnotist somewhere had snapped his fingers, he blinked. His eyes were dark, with the dull luster of old coins, but he had thick black lashes that, in his boyhood, must have endeared him to mothers and childless women alike.

Harding felt hot rings of sweat breaking out under his arms. He hadn't wanted to see those two clasped hands on the table. He'd only wanted to do his job, get noticed and get out of there. As he struggled to find the release, his brain was in free-fall. Then at last, the hidden compartment of the case opened. Thank Christ. He passed the Director the sealed report. 'Sir,' he said.

What he *wanted* to say was that he didn't care. Didn't give a damn. Live and let live. He was nobody, and their business was no business of his. To each his own. He believed that. Who was he to judge? He'd never judge anyone – not least because he never fit in anywhere himself.

But there was nothing that could be said.

Hoover leaned forward slowly, as if only the most minimal effort could be spared for the likes of Agent Mel Harding. With the same hand that had, an instant before, been stroking Tolson's, he received the Manila envelope. He hardly glanced at Harding's face. Instead, he looked past him, even through him. Then he picked up a thick wedge of Saltines.

Tolson reached for his glass of water. The ice cubes clinked. Hoover didn't ask for Harding's name, rank or Field Office. He scarcely paused in what he'd been saying to the Associate Director.

'Dismissed,' he said, as he broke the wedge of Saltines into his soup.

And Harding was, by the end of the day.

To Butte.

He'd been in Washington for a grand total of eighteen days. Now, he was to be the only agent in Butte, running a deadbeat office on his own – so small an operation, the Bureau had decided that it didn't even require a Special Agent in Charge. With the transfer to Butte, he was simultaneously *demoted* to the rank of Senior Special Agent.

At the age of forty, after a dozen years with the Bureau – he'd started his training just after being de-mobbed from the army – after twelve years, it was a humiliation. The rank of Senior Special Agent might have been labeled 'Senior Junior'. It existed to send that message out, stuck to your back like a high-school joke. It said to everyone in the Bureau that you were middle-aged and you hadn't cut it.

Annie, the maid, opened the door and showed Harding through to the dining-room, where Hoover sat alone at a long dining table, spooning out the last of his hard-boiled egg from a porcelain egg-cup. Bits of shell were scattered over the place mat, and he had crumbs of yolk on his shirt. A pressed blue suit jacket hung on the chair behind him.

As Annie picked up his plate, she clicked her tongue maternally at the shell and abandoned toast crusts on the table. When she returned from the kitchen, she took the bib of Hoover's linen napkin and brushed gently at his shirt while he smiled up to her, compliant as a small boy. Then she placed an orange, a blood orange, on a dessert plate in front of him, and his smile hardened with pleasure. For the first time, Harding saw the white-plastic gleam of the dentures.

Annie asked Harding if he'd like a coffee, but Hoover thanked her, 'nothing more was required', and could she slide the door closed on her way out?

The ritual dressing-down was about to begin. That's what the breakfast slot in Hoover's home was known for: 'disciplinary action' – in cases where witnesses weren't wanted.

'What's wrong with your hands?'

'A mild skin condition, sir.' Harding stared straight ahead, at the wall above Hoover's head, military-style.

'It doesn't look mild. It looks unclean. It looks like you've caught something off some whore's—' He paused, heard Annie departing the kitchen, and brushed toast crumbs from the tablecloth.

'Does it hurt?'

Harding hadn't expected a show of concern. 'I have to watch it.'

'Do you like the picture?'

He blinked. He hadn't noticed any picture. The taxidermied creatures on the walls and their glass eyes had been enough to take in as Annie showed him through the living-room and into the dining-room.

The picture on the wall above Hoover's head was, he now saw, a simple oil painting of what looked like a Swiss mountain village. Competent but amateur, he would have guessed. 'Yes, sir. I do. It's very nice.'

Hoover put down his egg-spoon. His smile was like lock-jaw. 'It's a Paint-by-Numbers. Eisenhower got a group of us doing them a few years ago. He paints, you know. He's got a thing for it. He passed out some box-sets to select members of staff. He even put the results in a special exhibition in the White House.' Hoover swiveled in his chair to take in his handiwork. 'You know, I didn't realize I was so good. I bet you didn't guess I was the artist.'

'No, sir, I didn't.'

Hoover tipped his head, almost whimsically. 'I like how pure everything looks, as if Heidi herself could just walk out of that church. See what I mean? There's not even a goat or a cow to shit anywhere. No people. And it's all so still. Almost frozen. I think I'd like Switzerland. Not the rest of Europe. It's still a goddamn mess over there from the war. But Switzerland. That's a good place, from what I hear. Tidy. Organized. Lots of nice scenery. Clean. Do you know what I have in here?' He waved an arm to indicate his entire home. 'Air-filtration. It electrocutes poisonous particles invisible to the eye.'

He reached into a drawer in the desk behind him and dropped Harding's prize photo on the table.

'Caught red-handed,' Hoover said. His face was inscrutable; his voice toneless.

Only speak if asked a question.

Hoover leaned forward and tapped the picture – Mrs. Kennedy's face, the book she carried – with his stubby finger. 'Is that a fair summation?'

'Yes, I suppose it is, sir.' He felt sorry for her now. But what the hell *had* she been doing? She'd been at a hearing for a banned book – and now, he had to get out of Butte.

'Yes, you say?'

'Yes, sir. It was a big surprise to see her there that day. I suppose,' he tried, 'that she must really like that bo—'

Hoover picked up the orange on his plate and flung it at him. Harding caught it, just before it hit a lamp. 'You,' Hoover snarled. 'Not her. We caught *you* red-handed. You informed on yourself, you dumb bastard.'

His neck went cold. 'Sir?'

Hoover nodded to the blood orange in Harding's hand. 'Peel it.'

His fingers were clumsy. He couldn't get the skin to peel. His newly clipped nails were too short. Then the skin of the orange broke at last, and juice started running like acid into his hand where the skin was raw and broken.

'Eat.' He watched Harding put a segment in his mouth. 'It's a nice and juicy one. Am I right?'

Harding broke off another segment. Red juice squirted over his starched white shirt. His hands dripped and the juice ran under his cuffs onto the broken skin of his inner wrists.

'You were *asked* to photograph and tape the G.P.O. hearing in New York. You were *asked* to keep tabs on Barney Rosset and his filthy Commie bastard publishing pals. You weren't *asked* to photograph the pretty, young wife of a senator of this country's Congress.'

'No, sir.'

The photo of Mrs. Kennedy's startled, lovely face lay between them. He felt ashamed now, not that he'd failed to stick to specific orders, but that he'd shot her like prey. You could steal a soul with a camera, and he'd given hers to Hoover.

'With this assignment, we gave you a chance to better yourself. We gave you a chance to watch Rosset. But you couldn't simply follow orders. Did anyone ask you to think for yourself?'

'No, sir.' He'd fucked up. He'd be in Butte for another year at least. Maybe he'd never get out. Not only that, he was, more than ever before, in Hoover's sights, and that was never a place anyone wanted to be.

Hoover tapped her face again.

'Enjoy jerking off to her, did you?'

Harding swallowed a segment of orange, whole.

'I asked you a question.'

'No, sir.'

'Why not?' He leaned back in his chair and crossed his arms, with the air of a man who was about to enjoy a show. 'What's wrong with you, Harding? A pretty lady. A *private* photo ...' He let the word hang in the air.

The corners of Hoover's mouth lifted. 'I ask because it's my job to know these things. It's thanks to my unilateral efforts that faggots have been almost totally eliminated from government service. Whatever else they are — and don't get me started on *that* — they're "black-mailable", and that's nothing but a risk for our national security. I authorized the checks personally. The "Sex Deviates Program". Ring a bell? Miss Gandy sent out memos to every department and F.O. Now, every day, we're sent anonymous allegations, from colleagues, employees and neighbors, concerning the past and present of more people than we can keep up with. It's been such a success, I've even rolled it out to places of so-called "higher" education and the law enforcement agencies. We're having a good clean sweep of this country's institutions. You wouldn't want an allegation to turn up about you, would you, Harding? Not with that peeping-Tom camera of yours.'

Harding stared ahead at the dead Swiss village.

'It's better, for your sake, if I know what there is to know. So I'll ask you again: what's wrong with you?'

'I'm fine, sir.' He gripped the orange.

The Director pushed back his chair, put on his suit jacket, and walked over to Harding's end of the table. 'What do you do out there in Butte for kicks?'

He kept his voice neutral. 'There's nothing to do, sir.'

'I suppose you have to make your own fun.'

Hoover moved to within inches of Harding, unbuttoned his employee's jacket and removed the .38-caliber revolver from its holster. 'So you jerk off over the Senator's pretty wife, and you develop another nice clean print for us at HQ. Barney Rosset – as in Barney Rosset, *the Person of Interest* you were asked to watch – just too damn ugly, or what?'

'I misunderstood, sir. I'm sorry. I thought she *was* a Person of Interest. I'd understood there was a Bureau-wide memorandum procedure for the compilation of background information on members of Congress and their families.'

Hoover pressed the mouth of the revolver against the fly of Harding's trousers. Harding flinched.

Hoover glanced at the photo. His black eyes protruded. 'What do you think Senator Kennedy would say if he knew we were tailing his wife?'

'As I say, sir, she just appeared at the hearing. I wasn't following her. I didn't expect—'

'He'd tell me to fire you. That's what he'd say. Forget Butte. He'd want you sent to Timbuktu. Do you *know* who his father is? Joseph Kennedy Sr. A former ambassador to England, no less, and one who has bought himself more friends than even women in his time, which is saying something, believe me.'

'I understand, Mr. Hoover.'

The Director looked past him – as if there were a mathematical puzzle hovering over Harding's right shoulder – and, with his gun-free hand, he began to work a crumb out of his teeth. 'What if young Mrs. Kennedy figured it out that day in New York? You watching her, the Bureau ...'

'I give you my word, sir. There was no way she could have. She didn't notice me.' A lie, or half-lie. She'd never remember him and that's what mattered. 'I—'

'Was it smart to get a picture of her, Harding? How would that make the Bureau look if it did get out?' The muzzle of the gun nudged Harding's groin again. 'I asked you: was that *smart*, Harding?'

'No, sir.'

'*No, sir,*' he mocked in a falsetto.

The doorbell rang. They heard Annie's steps on the stairs and then in the hall. Hoover coolly returned the gun to Harding's holster, stepped back, adjusted his trousers and checked his nails.

Annie showed Clyde Tolson in. 'Mr. Hoover, Mr. Tolson has arrived.'

'So I see, so I see. Thank you, Annie.'

It was common knowledge. The Director and the Associate Director drove into work in Hoover's car most mornings. In-house, among the younger agents especially, they were known as 'J. Edna' and 'Mother Tolson'.

Harding looked straight ahead, expressionless. At the threshold of the dining-room, Hoover chatted with Tolson. On the wall between them, a stag's head bared its teeth. The Associate Director seemed to be wearing the same blue summer suit jacket as Hoover, with a near-identical tie, a tie which matched the lining of their jackets, as stipulated in the F.B.I. manual.

Hoover turned back to him. 'What color is my jacket, Harding?'

It was like some sort of trick question. The Director didn't say 'our jackets'. Yet the match between his and Tolson's, right down to the buttons, was exact. 'I'd say your suit is ... blue, sir.'

Hoover rolled his eyes and buttoned the jacket over his paunch. 'Clyde, what color do you call this?'

'Chambray blue,' said Tolson.

'That's what I thought.' Hoover seemed to take pleasure in the luxury of the word. 'Chambray ... chambray ...' He picked up the print of the Senator's wife and slid it into his briefcase.

Annie re-appeared and said his chauffeur was waiting on the step outside.

Hoover looked back at Harding, as if with sheer disgust. 'Finish the damn orange now you've started it. Annie will show you out.' He turned to her. 'Annie, I won't be back tonight but I'll be home tomorrow night in time for *Lawrence Welk*, as usual.'

'Yes, Mr. Hoover,' she said, dusting down his shoulders. 'There'll be a nice mug of hot milk waiting for you by the television set.'

They picked him up just before he boarded the flight back to Butte, two agents in snap-brim fedoras and suit jackets which bulged over their holsters. He was being driven back into the heart of Washington. No one spoke on the journey. The agent in the front passenger seat switched on the radio and sang along quietly. 'Smoke Gets in Your Eyes'. In his mind's eye, Harding saw a gun going off in his face.

He had never been good in the back seat of moving vehicles; hadn't been since he was a kid. His mother had never had a car, and he'd never grown accustomed to the motion. He just hoped to God he wasn't going to throw up before they arrived wherever he was being taken. He rolled down his window. The evening light was golden, the clouds gilded. The 'sweet light' – that's what photographers called it. The liquid light just before sunset that makes the world sharp and soft at the same time. You saw the full beauty of the day just before it was gone.

The air blowing in smelled of warm asphalt and Friday-evening mown grass. A girl in an eye-patch and lime-green shorts was playing on the sidewalk with a plastic 'hula hoop'. That's what they called the things. Her chubby little face was serious, almost entranced as she hula-ed, but even so, as the black Cadillac progressed in stately gloom up her street, she seemed to hold Harding's gaze with her one good eye while her hoop went round and round.

The people they passed – sitting on front porches or bending to adjust lawn-sprinklers – looked free. If he hadn't known it before, he knew it now. He'd never be free again.

He was delivered to the Washington Field Office's Special Agent in Charge. His secretary was gone for the day. In fact, almost everyone was gone for the day, except for a few sweaty agents still trying to get their reports typed and filed before clocking off. One of them stared frantically at his corrector-ribbon. Hoover was a bastard about typos and spelling mistakes.

As soon as Harding walked into the S.A.C.'s office, there she was: Mrs. Kennedy looking up from the desk, startled all over again, with the smudge of Hoover's prints all over her.

Something must have happened. Something else. They had brought him back for round two.

The room smelled of cigarettes, sweat and deodorant. The flag in the corner was too big for the space, and the white stripes had turned nicotine-yellow. A large framed photo of President Eisenhower stared down from the wall.

The S.A.C. was Howard Johnson – 'Howard Johnson', as in the roadside restaurant chain with the orange roofs and weather-vanes. 'Make it a fried clams for me, sir!' The jokes followed him through the office on any given day, and Johnson had a lot of pent-up frustration.

Harding had worked for him just those eighteen days last year.

'You look green,' Johnson said. 'What's the matter with you?' He threw Harding a pack of Winston's and dug in his pocket for a lighter. It was a concession. Johnson was the one who'd sent him to the Mayflower Hotel that day with the delivery – the so-called 'urgent analysis requested by Hoover'.

'Sorry about Butte,' he said, clicking and clicking the lighter head. 'It was out of my hands.' The flame leaped, he lit up, then he leaned forward, clicking and clicking again.

Harding could smell the lighter fluid off Johnson's fingertips. The flame finally took. He thought he could feel his nostril hair burn. But he drew hard on the cigarette, to seem grateful. If it made him feel more nauseous, it was the only thing to do. Because when you think things can't get any worse, they always can.

He saw them again: the two men, Hoover and Tolson, seated on the same banquette, their oiled, clean-cut heads bent towards each other. The shaved roll of fat on Hoover's neck had bulged over his collar, and under his jacket the white shirt buttons strained. But it was the sight of Hoover's small, pudgy hand stroking Tolson's that had shut down his brain.

In those stammering moments, he could make out Tolson's long, fine fingers, and the high-school ring gleaming on his ring-finger. He could see wiry black hair on the back of Hoover's hand and the liver spots. Each man's nails were neatly clipped. Harding saw all the detail in close-up.

Now, he watched Johnson roll down his sleeves, close his office blinds, and kick a desk drawer shut. He was a few years younger than Harding and three ranks ahead. 'I should have been out of here two hours ago,' he said, 'but Hoover called. I'm offering you a new assignment.'

Harding blinked.

'Shut your mouth or you'll catch flies.'

'I'm finished in Butte?'

'You are.'

The Director had been toying with him that morning. He was a sadist in a chambray-blue suit.

Johnson pushed an ashtray across the desk. 'You'll report to me again.'

'I'm back in Washington?'

'I didn't say that. It's a surveillance job. Out-of-office, but low-risk. Easy.' He tapped Mrs. Kennedy's forehead with a blunt index finger. 'Hoover liked this. Good job. Call this new posting a reward.' Johnson turned the glossy print and her face his way. 'For Christ's sake, what did she think she was doing at that goddamn hearing?'

Harding played along. 'God knows.' But he was bad at improvising, at bullshitting. Always had been. 'Maybe she gets her kicks that way.'

Johnson looked up sharply. 'What do you mean by that?' His eyes narrowed into pale blue slots into which Harding's answer was meant to drop.

Harding didn't know what he'd meant. He hadn't meant anything. He'd said what he'd guessed Johnson wanted to hear; what Hoover had wanted to hear. Make Mrs. Kennedy the target. He just wanted out of Butte. He wanted – literally – to be left to his own devices again. His cameras. To be left alone.

'Did you see her get up to anything else, Harding? Because if you did, it could be important. Important to us. And helpful to *you*.'

'No …' Not that he wouldn't have betrayed her in that moment had his mind come up with anything. 'I only meant that that nice reception at the Lincoln Center, at the President's personal invitation, wasn't enough for her that day. She had to get mixed up with that hearing and some dirty book. It makes you wonder. That's all.' He breathed. He was putting on quite the show.

The ashtray on Johnson's desk was molded into the shape of the U.S.A. Johnson stubbed out his cigarette in California. 'I saw their file a couple of weeks ago. The Kennedys. An agent tailed them through Georgetown, on and off last year. They double-dated with friends one night. Went to a movie. But not any movie. A soft-porn flick, if you can believe it. The *wives* too.'

Harding shook his head, as if dismayed. It was a novelty – this moral high ground. Sometimes he'd thought about going to church in Butte on Sundays, because he'd be able to stand in a row with other people and look like any other guy, like any other upstanding citizen. More than that, he'd look like he existed.

He never did – go. Women could go places on their own. But middle-aged, unmarried men couldn't be alone anywhere without someone somewhere wondering if you were a pervert. A pervert who happened to like taking pictures.

He changed the subject. He told Howard Johnson that, back in Butte, he'd been checking on the outcome of the Post Office hearing. 'I read in the papers that the Hearing Examiner returned a "No Decision" on the case.'

'Not exactly,' said Johnson. 'Charles Ablard, the Post Office guy in charge, *did* reach a decision that day ...' He looked up. 'It just wasn't the *right* decision. It wasn't *our* decision. Hoover had to intervene before the verdict was returned. So it got turned into a "No Decision". We required him to kick the can up the road to his boss's boss – the Postmaster General. Dick Montgomery. Hoover's got stuff on Montgomery. Family stuff. Black–white *relations*, family stuff.'

'That ought to do it.' He couldn't believe what was coming out of his mouth. He didn't care who was with who. Leave people alone. Let them live their lives. That was his own view – in the 22-inch private space of his own skull. Every F.B.I. man knew his hat measurement as well as he knew the caliber of his gun. A gun needed a holster and the flap of a jacket or a coat. Private thoughts needed the cover of a snap-brim. No detail was overlooked. No cover *wasn't* maintained. It was the First Commandment. Maintain your cover. Don't draw attention. Don't deviate from Bureau-think. Never, under any circumstances, let the Bureau look bad.

Smoke streamed from Howard Johnson's nostrils. 'We're delaying the actual decision, so it has the appearance of due process. In reality, Montgomery is enjoying some fly-fishing in Florida. The bonus is that the publisher – Rosset – and his brief are getting hot under the collar with the delay. Rembar, the lawyer, applied for a suspension of the Post Office shipping ban *while* they wait for the decision, but it's a decision we're in no rush to give, of course. Rembar applied first by letter, and again by telegram today. They're panicking, in other words.' Johnson laughed, shaking his head.

'Hoover phoned up the Postmaster General personally. Told him that under no circumstances was he to reply to Rosset's lawyer. Can't be easy for a small publishing company in that sort of limbo ...' He took another drag on his cigarette and smiled. 'Rosset's losing money by the day, with that dirty book of his sitting in crates. That's how Hoover wants to keep it. With any luck, the delay will bankrupt him. Which would be the cleanest way for us to take him down. No fingerprints anywhere.'

'I suppose Rosset could, technically, sue the Post Office? In the federal court.'

'If he tries, the Bureau will be steps ahead. Our lawyers know exactly what to do.'

Harding thought back to the hearing that day. Compared to other stuff on the book stands, the novel hadn't sounded so bad to him. It had sounded – he didn't know the right word – *emotional*. Embarrassing maybe. But not sick. Not twisted. 'What's the Director's problem with the book exactly?'

Johnson looked up, surprised. 'It's a filthy book.'

'You've read it?'

'Of course I haven't read it. How am I going to read a book that's sitting in crates? Besides, I don't need to read it. You don't need to read it. No one reads in Intelligence. I skimmed the report produced by the Porn Section. And what did the President himself say?'

'I don't know.'

'He said it's "dreadful". He said we can't allow it.'

'It's just that Ablard, the Hearing Examiner, didn't seem so sure it was *that* bad.'

'Which is why Ablard was taken off the job. The book is un-American. Rosset's on our Subversives Index. The *book* is how we bring him down.'

'Sure. I get that ...'

'But what?'

'Four hundred thousand people are on our Index. I mean, obviously, he's scum. I'm just trying to get a better grip on procedure, on matters of Bureau assessment. To learn ...'

Johnson screwed up one eye. He spoke slowly. 'The *difference* between the 399,999 on the list and Rosset is this: Rosset is a renegade publisher. Rosset will *publish* any subversive shit out there, any pervert. People *read* that shit. Impressionable teenagers and students *read* that shit. It gets *into* their brains, and the Commies' job is done. They hardly need to lift a finger to stir up shit in the country *we're* supposed to be protecting.'

'Sure.' Harding scratched at his hands. Flakes of him drifted to the floor. His thumb started to bleed. 'But Barney Rosset … you know he's not actually a card-carrying Commie. I've seen his file.'

'That doesn't mean he's *not* supporting a Russian plot to stir up trouble over here. That's Russian policy. Get people angry. Better still, get 'em confused. That tends to work best for the silent majority. Get 'em confused, set them at each other's throats, then split the country. Weaken it. "Active Measures". That's what it's called. They're active, alright. And it's cheaper than any war. You get that memo, Harding?'

'Yeah. I got it.'

'You hear about something called a *federal election* next year?'

He swallowed. 'Sure.'

'Well, then, what does that mean?'

'The Russians are busy.'

'You bet they are. They want to play with American heads. They want to make Americans think they don't know what is and what isn't the American Way. They want *to get to us*, to fuck us over. It's not just some crazy memo on a desk in Moscow, Harding. It's real, and it's here. So don't let some book with a nice English accent and some aristocratic bit of cunt fool you into thinking that the book is harmless – or that Barney Rosset is a stupid rebel without a cause. He has a cause, alright. And I wouldn't be surprised if the Soviets were funding it.'

Johnson sat down on the edge of his desk. He sucked in his top lip and made a popping noise as he released it. 'Anyway, you *don't want* that book to be harmless, Harding. Remember that. You want it to be "*Time* magazine's Dirty Book of the Century". You understand me? You scored big with this picture of the Senator's wife. Hoover wants to add it to his personal collection. You could score bigger still.'

He leaned in and spoke as if he was addressing a simpleton. 'Hoover told me to say, well – done – at – the – hearing.' He nodded at the photo. 'He said, keep – up – the – good – work.' He offered Harding the state of Texas for his ashes. 'Take it from me. That means: "Don't fuck up and make me send you back to Butte."'

Howard Johnson leaned back and flipped a stick of Wrigley's in his mouth. A stick of gum had to follow a cigarette. It was in the conduct manual. He stretched his arms high, revealing sweat-marks halfway down his ribs. 'Do you want to be a Senior Special Agent forever, Harding?'

Harding looked to the desktop. He looked into the Senator's wife's dark, anxious eyes.

'I asked you a question, Harding. Do you want to be a Senior Special Agent forever?'

'No.'

'So stop already with the grade-school questions and have some self-respect.'

He took Harding's cigarette, stubbed it out, and offered him a stick of gum. 'I'll tell you this for nothing. Hoover wanted us, the Washington Field Office no less, to check you out – under the Deviates Protocol. He wanted it done before we – before Yours Truly – offered you this new assignment. But I vouched for you. I figured maybe I owed you. Plus, you remind me of my wife's brother. I like my wife's brother. He's shy – gawky – like you. A misfit but a decent enough guy. I help him out when I can. The Mayflower Hotel that day was only ever supposed to be a joke on the new guy in the office. Hoover hates having his meals interrupted. He says it's bad for his digestion. But the joke went further than planned. All the way to Butte. I felt a little bad about that. I hold my hands up. So I told the Director you were A-okay. I told him I found out you used a discreet little whorehouse downtown, and that seemed to put his mind at rest.'

He crossed his arms. 'What are you now? Forty? No family. No home. No girlfriend even. You don't go anywhere on your vacation-time. You just fiddle about with your goddamn cameras. I know about you, Harding. I couldn't offer you this job if I didn't. Once a week, you go to the shoeshine. Every three weeks, you get your hair cut and your eyebrows trimmed. Sometimes you take a book out of the public library. You like to read about the lives of the great explorers. Marco Polo. Captain Cook. Christopher Columbus.

Am I right? Your father sold encyclopedias across the country and was last heard of in Milwaukee. You think he had another family somewhere. You suspect he was a bigamist. You wanted to become a detective so you could track him down. Give him a piece of your mind. You buy a postcard in every state you visit for a collection you keep in photo albums under your bed. You were going to send the cards to your mother but she died before you got round to it. You kept buying them anyway.

'You're a creature of habit, Harding. You wanted to find your father to tell him how your mother used to cry into her pillow at nights; how hard she worked, cleaning offices just to keep the two of you in food-stamps. Am I right? I'm right, aren't I? You tracked down a record of gambling debts for him, but the trail dried up. You never did find him. He and what you suspect was his other family used to change addresses in the middle of the night. You heard about that more than once from angry landlords. But here you are anyway. You beat the odds. You're not some two-bit detective. You made it all the way to the Bureau. You're one of those fatherless men who craves a strong leader – like the Director – and who rebels, like a weak and stupid teenager, from time to time. Like a teenager with what the quacks call "arrested development".

'I know the psychometrics, Harding. You're more predictable than you realize. We all are. You secretly think you're "different", clever, artistic even. Your school reports called you "shy". You wonder if you're maybe a bit on the sensitive side, but in a funny way, you've just as much of an ego as the next guy. Secretly, you think you're smarter than most people, that you see more than they can. You think you're "smarter" than most men in the Bureau, even if you can't handle the field work as well as most. In fact, you don't really like people. But you do like women. You genuinely *like* them. A shame you're afraid of them up close. See? I'm right again, aren't I? I'm sounding like a mind-reader. I know the "Dark Arts". Stuff you never had in your basic training. You have to get promoted to S.A.C. to be let in on what I know. The fact is, you're not "different", Harding. You're a "profile", and I've got your number.

'You're in bed by nine thirty most nights. You subscribe to *National Geographic* and *Life*. You like going to the pictures. You sit in the middle row, on the aisle, so no one mistakes you for one of the perverts in the back rows, and so you can exit fast. You don't do sports. You can't even swim. When you were a kid, the chlorine in pools made your skin blister, and saltwater made you cry. I've seen your medical records. God knows when you last had a woman.

'On your birthday, you treat yourself to a three-course meal in a steakhouse and then a peep-show. Last year, the girl on the other side was heavily pregnant. You never spoke to her but she got to know your eyeball, and she used to smile and speak to you from her side of the slot. You sent her money for baby clothes and the hospital bill. It wasn't even your kid. Of course it wasn't. Now that might be your idea of sweet, but most people would say it was screwball. I don't have an opinion. Maybe it was touching – I don't know – but for crying out loud, drop the questions, Harding, and show a little gratitude. I got you a new assignment. What else do you have in your little life except the Bureau? What would you be without it?'

He reached behind for something, then dropped a heavy file, a legal wallet tied in green string, into Harding's lap. The intelligence for the new assignment.

'Don't think. Just do. You've got exactly one chance to get things right this time. To be' – he hesitated – 'normal.' He glanced down. 'And do something about those hands of yours. You're peeling all over my goddamn floor.'

There were, she told herself, two kinds of women: those who wanted power in the world, and those who wanted power in bed. She herself had little interest in 'the world' or in worldly titles, 'First Lady' or otherwise. She could understand, as few others did, how Lady Chatterley could give up the society she knew, as the wife of a baronet, along with her title and status.

Sex was the only state in which a woman could achieve – not the power of high ambition or the power of 'power games', which were mere manipulation and fakery – but the power which came with vitality. It was something far greater than color to the cheeks after sex. It was the power of self-possession, of being alive in one's self and one's body. Very few achieved it. Most only idolized or envied it.

Her own experience was limited, but she knew instinctively that such power came only with intimacy; with the secret act of beholding the public, daily person – the lover, sanctioned or illicit – transformed in one's presence into a private, raw spirit. That was power: to be a part of such life-force, or even the conduit of it. The power to transform; to return someone to the person they always actually were, their innermost. Everything else was only the animal drive to reproduce.

Lawrence's heroine, Jackie believed, had never been a woman who'd wanted to 'bed history' in the form of a titled husband. Lady Chatterley wanted life for life's sake, and if her desire was to be, for a time, her downfall, it was also the source of the healing she would bring to her gray and broken post-war world.

Her very desire made her a threat, of course – because she didn't need history, bedded or otherwise. She was beyond history. Constance Chatterley was nothing less than a native English goddess.

England was gray once again – austere and haunted. Fifteen years on from the most recent war, London was still pitted with bomb-sites, a desolate cityscape. Jackie saw again in her mind's eye that red London bus raised, during her stay in '56, from the mud of a bomb-crater.

In her own land, shiny suburbs and highways spread as never before. Could an English goddess transcend England? She wanted out, certainly, but could she roam free? Not if the United States Mails had anything to do with it – or more accurately, not if the federal government did. But *who* was out to stop Lady C.? Which office? Which men in suits?

'No Decision'.

She had checked the record of the hearing herself. Grove Press *could* take action on an actual judgment from the Hearing Examiner, but a 'No Decision' simply left Barney Rosset in limbo, with his new edition of the novel locked up.

Perhaps that was the point.

What to say? She sent the note on her personal stationery, drafting it twice and including her card. She wrote that it had been such a pleasant surprise to meet him – 'almost!' – at the hearing. She wondered if he might remember her. He had, very kindly, passed her the shopping bag she'd forgotten, between their chairs. She told him how disappointed she was by the outcome – the non-outcome, rather. Did he think there might yet be room for maneuver? Should they meet, she wondered, to discuss whether there was any way to assist the publisher – 'and Lawrence's cause, of course!'?

She was not really one for exclamation points, but she mustn't sound too serious or determined. She never ruled out the possibility that her and Jack's private mail was being opened.

She told Professor Trilling that she was unlikely to be in New York in the foreseeable future. She wondered if he ever visited the Cape? If so, she would be honored if he would join her at home in Hyannis Port for a modest lunch.

She had no illusions. When he received her invitation, he might take her for a society hostess with time on her hands. But Jack's name was everywhere these days, certainly on the East Coast, and in this instance, she was not above hoping that the connection might appeal, to the Professor's curiosity, if nothing more.

He replied warmly on the day he received her card. 'I would be delighted.'

It was one of those June mornings, radiant and sluiced by wind. She strolled bare-foot to the far edge of the Big House lawn, coffee in hand. The grass was cold and sharp underfoot, and the breeze was fresh. Ahead, wild roses shook on their bushes, their deep pinks vivid against the dunes. Her heart always lifted at the first sight of them, the petals of each bloom as wrinkled as a newborn's face.

Beyond the dunes, the blue expanse of the Nantucket Sound was endless, while under its wind-beaten, sun-hammered surface, the cold Labrador currents and the warm Gulf Stream clashed.

The sunshine was heavy on her eyelids as she stood in the embrace of the new day. When she opened them, it was to the sight of a sea osprey banking directly above, with a live fish gripped in its talons, as if it wanted to be admired by her for its hunting prowess.

Beyond the beach and out of sight, turtles paddled in the shallows. Farther out, imaginable only, whales burst from the depths.

She'd met the eye of a humpback once, as the top of its monumental head surfaced beside the hull of the Kennedy sloop, the *Victura*. She remembered, still, the rank-fish spray of its breath, and the primordial intelligence alert in its single eye as it held her gaze. She'd taken off her sunglasses to meet that eye, crusted in barnacles, and she felt something mute pass between them. The humpback could easily have overturned the yacht, like driftwood in its path, but instead it had slipped fluently beneath the keel, taking with it, she felt, some trace of her in its huge, inscrutable pupil. She, too, carried some trace of it back to the shore, and was pensive with it as Jack's family launched themselves into a game of touch-football.

Now, the tide was on its way in. Boats bobbed. At the Yacht Club's anchorage, masts tinkled and knocked, their music borne on the breeze. Beyond, frail isthmuses and sandbars glittered, and fishermen with reels moved across them, like men walking on water.

The wind ruffled the long dune grass. On this part of the Cape, the dunes could change shape overnight. Everything was impermanent, and only the impermanence was abiding. The Cape taught you that. Don't hold on, it said. Whatever it is. Don't hold on.

A few miles inland, kettle-ponds, in craters hollowed out by ancient glaciers, blinked myopically. The topography of the interior seemed to change beneath your feet as you walked, while the air, sweet with the resin of heated pine sap, could suddenly blow tangy with marsh-rot or salt spray.

From midsummer on, the days snapped like sheets on the line and, in the strong Cape light, every blade of grass pulsed, the dunes glowed, and the blue skin of the Sound flexed and glistened.

In a sketchbook perched on her knee, she tried to capture the liberty-blue of the summer sky or the stripped-white shine of a shell or bone. She was painting outdoors again – small studies mostly – but she was rarely satisfied with her efforts.

She drove Jack's old Plymouth on her painting excursions, and the entire peninsula, she realized, was a fretwork of sandy back-roads with a mind of its own. She loved the unmanned fruit and vegetable stands that waited patiently at the end of tracks and driveways, their trust-boxes intact. She loved the surprises of church steeples – their white exhortations – and the kites which skittered over the beaches, valiantly high.

Every year, islands of marsh-grass and saltwater channels re-shaped one another, so that local maps were quickly outdated, and bearings lost. Meanwhile, the cranberry bogs of the Cape bloomed in the deep red of dreams – until they too disappeared under the first snow. Then, the fog-horns sounded their seasonal lament, and the houses, gray-shingled and weather-beaten, stood square to the Atlantic gales.

By spring, the dunes were hardly recognizable to the fair-weather visitors of the year before, and there were always revelations: an old burial-ground emerging from a sandy pine forest; the bog-preserved stumps of some colonial palisade; ancient stepping-stones discovered in a forgotten creek. Occasionally, in a spring thaw, even the rock foundations of an old Puritan house might be exposed, its granite slabs gripping the twentieth century like knuckles.

Whatever the season, the earliest morning light of the Cape, when not obliterated by fog, was pearly-soft. 'Beautiful morning,' a neighbor might say as they passed on the beach, and she'd reply, 'It is. We've been so lucky with the weather.' Any ordinary exchange was enough in that absolving light. No matter how much she enjoyed the intelligent chatter of New York and Washington, it was the wordless eloquence of the Sound which restored her.

Jack was on his way to Maryland, on the trail again, gathering support. She'd set the date for lunch, knowing it was Mrs. Clyde's day off. Caroline was with her grandmother for the day, in the Big House, with Nanny Maud to assist.

She baked buttermilk biscuits, sliced tomatoes and steamed asparagus. She made a pot of chowder with haddock fresh from the wharf at Barnstable that morning. Only after she'd added the salt pork did she remember that Professor Trilling was Jewish. Had she spoiled things before he'd even arrived? She imagined the awkward embarrassment, their mutual protestations. She reached into the freezer and found the only thing that would thaw in time, hamburger patties and buns for the Kennedy children's parties.

She'd asked the Secret Service man – lately, a new man every week, it seemed – if he might vacate his standard position – in the flower bed on the lawn at the back of the house – so that she could have an old friend to lunch on the patio. They agreed he'd situate himself at the front of the house, on Irving Avenue, for just a few hours, without the usual 360-degree checks.

The man wore a lightweight navy summer suit and sunglasses, and carried a transistor radio in a leather case on a shoulder-strap. Because of the length of his shifts, he was permitted to listen to sports games and news bulletins to keep himself alert, although not, he reassured her, popular music stations. He kept the volume low and used the jack and an earpiece. When she asked what the latest was, he told her the news was still full of Khrushchev's demands that the Americans, French and British remove their armies from West Berlin.

The agent appeared, oddly, both formal and informal as she addressed him. He stood upright, his shoulders square and his manner respectful and distant; she was only surprised that, rather like a teenaged boy, he removed neither his sunglasses nor his hands from his pockets as he spoke to her. A small Hilroy notebook poked out above his breast-pocket. He saw her notice it – 'I try to get down the day's scores when it's quiet,' he said.

An 'old friend', she'd told him. A white lie. She hadn't met Professor Trilling, not properly of course, but the ambiguity of the phrase was useful as she arranged her clandestine lunch, and of course she knew the Professor posed no security threat whatsoever.

Trilling was in his mid- to late fifties, she supposed. That's what she'd say to Jack if the Secret Service man quoted her to anyone. 'I was referring to his age!' She'd explain there had been no intention to deceive; that she hadn't realized that *any* visitor who was new to them on the Cape was supposed to be vetted first, and even if she had, she would have resisted protocol for the sake of a respected man of letters who had come all the way from New York at her invitation.

She felt she knew Professor Trilling better from his essay collection than she knew some of her own relatives. *The Liberal Imagination* was a book of striking openness and, in her view, a work of heroic criticism. Trilling was a humanist who believed that works of literature were not inert, but had the power to speak across time and space.

His voice as an essayist spoke to her in a way that few other critics or academics ever had, even during her revelatory time at the Sorbonne. Professor Trilling took into account, not esthetics alone, but the full human experience. He resisted false and rigid categorizations. He argued that the emotional sphere could not be separated from the political sphere, and that the political could not be separated from the world of art and literature. How many other leading academics had turned up at the G.P.O. that day last month to support a banned book and a small publisher? Few, if any.

She cleared Caroline's alphabet-blocks and shells from the living-room floor, and swept away the latest issue of *Newsweek* with her husband's face on it. Thank God she'd noticed it in time. It would have looked show-offy. Outside, the Secret Service man moved the patio furniture into place for her. It was kind of him.

She cut peonies for the table. In the vase, the ivory petals fattened on the morning light. She only hoped that the sight of an agent in sunglasses and a suit outside her front door wouldn't make the Professor turn on his heels and head straight back to New York. Few intellectuals were entirely at ease with checks and questions these days, not since the televised specter of Senator McCarthy's show trials in '54. Thank goodness Justice Warren had finally given the Senator the heave-ho.

She'd worked out that Jack's family, in particular, were keen to move past any political association with Joe McCarthy, although Bobby was still a little conflicted, because of old loyalties – McCarthy had once employed him. Nor did it help that two of Jack's sisters had once dated the man.

But if Joe Kennedy Sr. and even Bobby had had business dealings with McCarthy, Jack was a different breed of thinker. He was politic, naturally, but he regretted the fact he hadn't been more of a voice in Congress against McCarthy. He was also determined that poets, novelists, philosophers, film-makers and artists would thrive in modern America; that they would be actively encouraged to question, provoke and challenge those in charge. He believed that's what honest politics was about. They both did.

She'd left a bookmark at a particular page in her copy of *Lady Chatterley's Lover*, and had underlined Lawrence's words in pencil, as if she were a student again: 'It is the way our sympathy flows and recoils that really determines our lives. And here lies the vast importance of the novel, properly handled. It can inform and lead into new places the flow of our sympathetic consciousness, and it can lead our sympathy away in recoil from things gone dead. Therefore the novel, properly handled, can reveal the most secret places of life … the *passional* secret places of life …'

The 'passional secret places'. She wasn't sure exactly what or where those places were, but it was those she sought.

She had spent much of her life concealing her hunger for learning. In '52, she'd started as the *Washington Times-Herald*'s 'Inquiring Photographer', surveying public opinion on the streets, and snapping her respondents' pictures, all for $42.50 a week. One time, her 'Question of the Week' had been: 'Do you think a wife should let her husband think he's smarter than she is?' 'Yes,' came the unanimous verdict: if a man wasn't smarter than his wife, then she should be smart enough to make sure he seemed smarter than she was.

If Professor Trilling had, on receiving her invitation, taken her for a breezy socialite or a docile Senator's wife, she hoped she might make him understand: not so much that appearances were deceptive, which of course he already knew, but rather that she maintained an excellent cover.

Once she'd checked that the Secret Service man was in position at the front of the house, she laid her prized contraband on the patio table, in a pool of sunshine next to the biscuit basket.

The Professor arrived late and was charmingly flustered. His hair was mostly white and his eyes were ringed by dark circles, but they were as large and alert as a child's.

He passed her a 'small gift', a used book, he explained bashfully – 'I do hope you will excuse the underlinings.' It was an old academic edition of Lawrence's stories, the Professor's own from the thirties, something he thought she might not have. It was rare, he explained, only in that it was the sole collection he'd ever come across with *both* versions of the story 'England, My England', the 1915 version *and* the revised, extended version of 1922. 'Lawrence was fixated on that story!'

She must have returned a bemused expression, but she thanked him, accepted the gift and pressed his hand.

'Forgive me,' he said. 'My wife assures me that I routinely blather on – and she is a fine critic, unerring in her judgment.'

She smiled nervously, not quite knowing how to reply, and felt herself blush as she ushered him inside. Then, as they moved through the narrow entry, they were wrong-footed again as his shoulder bumped a picture on the wall, which was falling to the floor when, remarkably and against the odds, she caught it.

The Professor stumbled over his words, relieved and embarrassed.

'No, please don't apologize!' she said, summoning a quick smile. 'My husband often bumps into it too!'

'Corot?' he said.

'Yes,' and she liked him straightaway. 'A little-known one, and only a copy of course. I "commissioned" a street painter, during my exchange-year in Paris. The gilt frame is a little overstated for it, and too big. You've done an excellent thing, Professor. You've reminded me I must either move it or re-frame it. Jack *will* be relieved!'

She was about to lead him onward, when he put on his glasses and peered. 'Diana and Actaeon,' he said with pleasure.

'*Yes*,' and she found herself looking at it, with him, afresh.

The virgin goddess Diana was bathing with her companion nymphs in a woodland pool when they were surprised by an approaching hunter. It was springtime, and the foliage was silvery-green. The wood Corot painted was a real place, not a fashionably mythological one, and that was something Jackie had admired from the first. He'd loved the forests of Fontainebleau, outside Paris, as she had herself during her Paris study-year.

In the moment Diana spotted Actaeon, the intruder, she was surfacing from the pool in her full-breasted nakedness. What could she do but rush to cover herself in the only way possible? She cast a torrent of water into the air, as great as her fury. In the same instant, the Dryads opened their mouths to scream a warning at the hunter – like gulls, Jackie imagined, when they see off a crow. But it was too late.

For the ancients, a man's direct gaze upon a mortal woman was an act of over-familiarity at best, and a claim at worst, a wordless declaration of possession. But to spy upon a *goddess* was to trespass upon deity; on the private sphere of an immortal. It was a violation of the sacred, and nothing less than profane.

Professor Trilling's finger pointed to Actaeon, small and goggle-eyed in the woodland. 'There he is!' he said with glee. 'You could almost miss him, the spy!'

Did Diana in that moment, Jackie wondered, know the power of her own curse?

When she uttered it, the metamorphosis began, in all its uncanny kinetics. Actaeon's hands and feet shed their skin, and gnarled into hooves. His spine lengthened to that of a beast's, and his jaw stretched into mandibles. He must have felt his rump suddenly bare – the air oddly cool upon it – as he bucked, startled by the swish of his new tail.

Within moments of Corot's scene, Actaeon's hooves were to crash to the earth, his antlers knocking and cracking against tree-bark as he thundered away on four legs – fleeing himself, trying to out-run the horror of his new shape, and his fate.

For the pack was not far behind, and the first was already within the frame. Soon, poor Actaeon, cursed by a goddess, would be devoured by his own hounds.

They surfaced from the drama.

'*Wonderful*,' Professor Trilling pronounced. 'Sometimes my clumsiness does have its advantages!'

She took the opportunity to confess the error of her fish chowder – spoiled, she said blushing again, by pork.

She was not to fret, he said. His Jewishness carried more signif-icance for others than it did for him – 'But please don't tell the F.B.I.! My dossier must be dull, but it keeps agents in work, and no doubt entire families fed!' He patted his forehead with his handker-chief and said he'd enjoyed the novelty of being frisked as he passed through the front gate. It had made him feel important.

She said, 'I am *so* sorry. I can assure you it's only our Security – the Secret Service. *Not* the F.B.I., you'll be pleased to hear!' He laughed and waved away her apologies. She said she was honored he'd come. She'd never had lunch with an esteemed Professor of English Literature before, let alone the most famous one in the country. She and her husband had admired *The Liberal Imagination* very much.

She was, he observed only now, soft-spoken and a little breathless as she tried to put him at his ease.

He chuckled, leaning towards her conspiratorially. 'In the thirties, I had the distinction of being turned down for tenure at Columbia because, I was told, a Jew could not fully understand *English* Literature.'

'And *now,*' she said, 'you are venerable!' She guided him from the front of the house to the back, and out onto the patio. He straight-ened to marvel at the view of the Sound: its cobalt-blue expanse, the spangled light, the wide horizon. At the table, a corner of the tablecloth snapped in the breeze. He lit a cigarette. Jackie filled his glass and passed him an ashtray. 'If I may ask, what made the tenure committee see sense?'

He sipped his beer. 'My *Matthew Arnold* in '39 did the trick – though not, I must add, on its merits alone. There was an unexpected review, a commanding piece by an English critic, John Middleton Murry, which changed my fortunes.'

'He approved!'

'Better, even. Coincidentally and apropos of our discussion today, he'd once been a friend of Lawrence's. They were close in a certain period, then they fell out badly. Murry died just two years ago. He was an editor, a reviewer, and a prolific writer, if only a middling novelist – much like myself!'

She tsk-tsked and offered him the chair at the table with the best view. 'You are too modest!'

'And *you*, Mrs. Kennedy, are more indulgent than either of my novel's *two* reviewers. But I digress. Of my *Arnold* biography, John

Middleton Murry was sweet enough to write: "Mr. Trilling, who is an American professor, has written the best – the most comprehensive and critical – book on Matthew Arnold that exists. It is a little saddening to us that this particular glory should fall to the United States." Imagine my delight! His words were meant, of course, only in a teasing, light-hearted way, but at Columbia, they couldn't sign me up fast enough.' He shrugged. 'Today, on the subject of the Academy, I remain …'

'Skeptical?'

'Bitter!' He laughed with genial ease, then admired her peonies. She insisted he help himself to the meal. 'I exaggerate,' he said, pinioning a spear of asparagus on his fork. 'On a good day, I am merely disenchanted.'

She offered him a warm biscuit. 'By?'

'Well, when I first joined the ranks of academe, I discovered something quite unsavoury behind the hallowed walls.'

'Corruption?' She ladled steaming chowder from the tureen into his bowl. 'Scandal?' She smiled.

'Worse.' He wiped butter from his chin. '*Mediocrity.*' He grinned like a white-haired imp. 'It was breathtaking – if mediocrity can be, that is!'

He tasted the chowder and looked up, smiling appreciatively.

Were they flirting? she wondered.

'Do you know my secret?' he asked.

She arched an eyebrow.

'I am the most mediocre of them all. I wanted to be a great novelist, not some paragon of the Academy. I play-act at "professing" … at professor-ing.'

'I wanted to be a writer too once …' She looked away. 'Not a senator's wife.'

He reached across and clinked her iced-tea glass with his beer glass. 'To a fellow paragon!' Then he sighed, contented with the moment, with his company, with their perch on the blue edge of the Cape. The smoke of his cigarette rose into the air, vague as a thought. 'The only notable fiction of my life is my so-called acclaim. I don't understand it. I am lazy in every sense that matters. I am, quite rightly, accused of social passivity, of too little activism, of insufficient critical bite.

'Apparently, I trade in an excess of faith in the transcendent power of literature. I admit to you that I don't even understand the charge. Faith, by definition, exists only in excess. Don't you think? I know only that I love those books which "possess" me … the ones that disorient me. I am no different than I was when I was a child – I think literature is *wondrous*. And strange as well – because it is somehow alive. True literature defies our efforts at analysis, paraphrase and thematic interpretation. I believe books read us as much as we read them. Don't ask me what I mean by that. I won't be able to say, and yet I feel as sure of that as I do of anything. In short, I am an oddity, Mrs. Kennedy.'

'Well, if you are, that makes two of us.'

'My learned peers would like me to stick to stylistics and narratology. But which novelists ever *think* about "style"? They might think about the music or rhythm of their prose. Indeed, that mysterious vessel of sound might come before the characters or plot. But "style" is usually the gift of the things a novelist cannot *help* but do, and those things, unique to his or her own quirks of vision and voice, are what make a book come to life. As a minor novelist, I had many competencies, plenty of style, a great deal of technique, and no gift!'

'You protest too much!'

He pressed his napkin to his face, and his cheeks swelled briefly with gas. 'No, I promise you. I am a failed novelist and an academic impostor. I refuse to take on Ph.D. students. They are so … obedient. And there are days when I'd rather do almost anything than read a book.' He accepted another brimming ladle of chowder. 'One day, before I retire, I must try to be better behaved.' He waggled his eyebrows.

She replaced the lid of the tureen, and because it came into her mind at that moment, she dared say it: '"We have all in some degree become anarchistic."'

'I'm afraid I can't recall who said that …'

'You!' she said jubilantly, and offered him another biscuit.

'Ah!' He nodded and leaned back, as if to ponder his own previous thought, turning his face to the high, cotton-ball clouds while she cleared their plates.

She returned with a cake-stand, and he stood to hold her chair, gripping his cigarette between his lips.

'I used to dream,' she said, leaning in slightly, 'of being published in the *New Yorker*. In my teens, I read countless stories by Chekhov. I read and wrote and painted all the time in those days. At college I even took an extra-curricular writing class, in short stories – I've told nobody that, not even Jack. That's when I first read Lawrence's stories.

'It was so wonderful that you should give me his collection. I couldn't find the words earlier. I'll look forward to both "England, My Englands"! I don't know that story. "The Odour of Chrysanthemums" is a favorite of mine. I see that's in your collection, and I'm going to re-read it before bedtime tonight. I'll never forget that scene of the woman washing her dead husband's body. She and his mother, they do it together, until finally the mother leaves and she is left alone with her husband. I still can see the terrible, raw intimacy of that scene. I don't think it will ever leave me.' *He was blond, full-fleshed, with fine limbs. But he was dead.*

She slipped on a pair of dark glasses.

'You could still write stories … You're young!' Trilling cast his arm out to the lawn, to the freedom of the shore. 'Here. Look at all this … space, this openness.'

Her face was downcast, then she reached for her iced tea. 'My world is narrower than it might appear. Not that I'm complaining at all. But yes, here, on the Cape, when I'm alone, or with Caroline, my little girl, sometimes it … widens again.' She shook herself, picked up the pie-server and smiled her best hostess smile. 'Now, Professor Trilling, may I—'

'Lionel, please.'

'Goodness, I couldn't possibly! You are eminent.'

'And you are polite. The sorry truth, as we both know, is that "Lionel" doesn't trip off anyone's tongue. I would go so far as to say that it is a name which makes people vaguely uncomfortable. When I was growing up, do you know what I longed to be called?'

She passed him a piece of peach crisp on a white china plate. 'Tell me.'

He pulled at his ear-lobe. 'You'll laugh.'

'Of course I won't laugh.'

'I wanted to be called … Jack.'

She drew in her lips, to force back the smile, but her effort had only limited success. The pie-server trembled in mid-air.

He nodded slowly and spoke with mock-seriousness. 'No tragedy is complete without its quality of farce.'

She laid down the pie-server and hid her face behind her napkin.

He cut into his peach crisp with gusto. 'I rest my case.'

She had to take off her sunglasses to catch her tears with the sides of her fingers.

'"Trilling. Jack Trilling here,"' he rehearsed, as if answering an important phone call. 'That could have been *me*!'

'Oh my goodness!'

'It has a ring to it, don't you think? "Jack Trilling". I sound like a famous movie actor!'

She pressed her palms to her cheeks.

She had perhaps an hour before Caroline would come toddling across the wide lawn, with her regal grandmother, Rose, and Maud, their aging English nanny, in tow. Jackie cleared the table hastily and returned with her notebook. 'Thank you for indulging me.' She checked her notes, as if she were about to move once again into her old interviewer mode.

'Politics, you say, needs the imaginative qualities of literature … I like that very much, if that is not too trite a thing to say.'

'I am flattered, Mrs. Kennedy—'

'Jacqueline, please. I'm not trying to flatter. I'm trying to understand.'

'—by which I mean, please continue.'

'Liberalism, you argue, needs literature's sense of "variousness, possibility, complexity, and difficulty" … Yet you say that "In the American metaphysic, reality is always material reality, hard, resistant, unformed, impenetrable, and unpleasant."'

'It's a relief when one actually agrees with oneself.'

But she was reaching for something more, staring into the wide, untroubled sky as if she might draw her question from its resounding blue. '*How* then does our native metaphysic evolve into something less hard, less "resistant", and more … nuanced? How can we as a people come to love variousness and difficulty – in the way we do in literature and stories and poetry – when we are in love with modern conveniences, with … endlessly straight highways, with … segregated lives and perpetual economic growth?'

'In some ways, it's simple. Books. Good books, bad books. They are "conversations", after all. Dialogues. Not theses. Not sermons or ideologies. Or novels aren't, at least. Nor poems or plays. They're different beasts altogether.

'We need bad books so we understand the power of good books. Good books so we can talk to ourselves; so we can see ourselves as we are; so we come to understand – no, to *experience* in the live unfolding of a story – the reality that others are rarely "other". Only with such understanding can our sympathies, as a nation-state, mature.

'Remember, we *do* have a great tradition, a *founding* tradition, of nonconformism in this country. The Pilgrims of Cape Cod were nonconformists, after all. They took great risks and made big sacrifices to be nonconformists and to establish an early form of democracy, a form of self-rule no longer based on subservience, as it had been in seventeenth-century England. We need to revive that tradition – of many voices, of true dialogue, of dissent.'

'You say that "Unless we insist that politics is imagination and mind, we will learn that imagination and mind are politics, and of a kind we will not like." Those last words in particular, from' – she checked – 'from your 1946 introduction to—'

'Mrs. Kennedy—'

'Jacqueline, *please*.' She looked at her hands, at their bitten nails. For a moment, she regretted her entire plan. It meant too much to her. 'I'm embarrassing you. Forgive me.'

'Jacqueline, we are friends. Ask your questions. I know nothing, but I am at your service.'

She laid down her notes. 'What did you mean when you said that?' Her hands were clasped tight. '" … we will learn that imagination and mind are politics, and of a kind we will not like."'

'I suppose I meant that if we don't understand that the emotions govern the political, if we trust only to the conceptual – be it crass ideology or one-track idealism, or even pure reason or pure logic—'

'—we will be lost to our emotions.'

'Our emotions will grow monstrous and bite us from behind. We won't even see them coming. Even the facts will be devoured by them if those emotions are not understood in their complexity and integrated; if, in other words, we ignore the education of our imaginations and our sensibilities, as individuals and as a nation. This is my long-winded way of saying, yes: if we don't *imagine* the politics we need, politics will imagine us. And we won't much like it. Some dark projection will be cast – such as this new concept of the "un-American" or the impure citizen.'

She shivered in the breeze.

'In my view, we don't need "purity". We need to be mature enough to admit the contradictory, the various. Crazy as it sounds, I'd like to see a politics for this country that never strays far from poetry. Or from poetic truth, at least. We need its complexity. We need its simplicity. Poetry keeps us honest. It admits all that is human and it lets us see it, love it and wrestle with it. With education in poetic truth and in the human complexities we find in great novels and plays, our emotions are less likely to run rings around us and wreak havoc, as we saw happen in Germany after its deep national humiliation following the First World War. The education of *all* our faculties is everything. If we glorify the conceptual or the rational at the expense of all the rest, we do so at our peril. Manipulators and predators will exploit our emotions. It's the one truth which the Academy, as magnificent as it often is, often fails to spot. It's too invested in that glorification of the rational above all else.'

'Jack loves the work of Robert Frost. He's a great reader. When he was young, he was so bookish his father didn't think he was cut out for politics.'

'Then we're lucky to have him in the Senate. Above all, we have to be wary of jingles, jargon and slogans. The truth is never so easy.'

'Literature is subversive.' She flipped through her notes. 'You say that somewhere ... As if *it's* dangerous. As if it might overwhelm us.'

'Yes.' He met her eyes. 'Or apprehend us. But *that's* the sort of danger we need. To wake us up. To help us keep our wits about us. To remind us of what it is to be human, for good and for ill.'

'I think I understand ... I hope I do.'

'Let me give you an example of what I *don't* mean.' He looked tired suddenly, older, under the bright bulb of the midday sun. 'My own weakling novel was all concept, you see, all schema, with too little life. I couldn't "bring life down". Do you understand? A great book, at its most essential, is a summoning or a visitation. Some academics pretend they master literature – the frauds do – but a great book masters us, even its author.

'You can strip away a great novel's esthetic shortcomings. You can spot the wayward tangents of prose, the blinkered vision of the times in which that novel was written, and the personal limitations of the author … The gamekeeper – Mellors – for example, makes a sickening comment about black women in Chapter Fourteen, and he has an absurd view of lesbians. There's an unpleasant remark or two about Jews as well.'

He shrugs. 'We must be honest: these comments may belong to the character Mellors only, or they may represent Lawrence's own vileness and ignorance. Sometimes there's no denying the dross of an author's biography, and the cultural impurities we all carry at some point in our lives, but I would contend that there remains something in a *great* work of literature which is indelible and animate. Something mysterious which exceeds the author. Something big-spirited and alive. It vibrates with life, across time, and *that*, for me, is literature. That's what we need to hold onto.'

He tapped her copy of *Lady Chatterley* on the table. 'Lawrence emptied the last of his life into that book. He worked high up a hill, in a pine wood. Wildflowers grew at his feet. Peasants sang in the neighboring fields. A spring bubbled away. And he was dying.

'My colleagues tell me I do not pay enough attention when I teach to style, esthetics and technique; that I fail to isolate sufficient themes and concepts for my students before they take their exams. Yet, for the writer, these things do not arrive in parcels of theme and form. They arrive in a wave, in a shimmer. They are experienced as a feeling across the back of the neck, or as a pressure in the heart during the deep "excavation" of a story. One cannot isolate an "effect" on the page or "lift out" a literary intention, as if it is a tooth to be pulled. Not even in Lawrence, who sometimes liked to preach his philosophy at his readers. Each part contains the whole. The wildflowers at his feet – as much as the spring and the song of the peasant girls – are as fundamental to the prose "style" of *Lady Chatterley's Lover* as Lawrence's despair about the Great War and his hopes for the healing of his country.

'A story is not a concept or a scheme or a theme. It is an author's breath, heat and heartbeat – and when I say that, I don't mean to suggest that the process is primitive or unsophisticated. Quite the opposite, in fact.'

She picked up her edition, and a shadow crossed her face. 'I can't understand why the Hearing Examiner delayed the decision. When I left the G.P.O. that day, at the recess, I was sure Grove Press was going to win.' She shrugged, fatalistically.

He sighed. 'The news is not good. I'm afraid I heard the latest yesterday, from someone in the Law Department at Columbia. The top man, Richard Montgomery, the Postmaster General, *has* now decided. He's upholding the postal ban. He has found that the novel is "obscene and filthy", although he has also, rather proudly, noted that he isn't accustomed to reading fiction. He prefers articles on fishing, apparently. Nevertheless, he is sure that "filth is filth".'

She tossed her napkin on the table. 'Of course he is.'

'The headlines will come tomorrow.'

'But the – sex – is merely …'

'Human.'

'Yes.'

'And the book,' he added, finishing his peach crisp, 'is as much about war and grief as it is about sex.'

'She is astonishing.'

'Constance?'

She picked up her sunglasses, as if she might disappear behind them again – a reflex – then changed her mind. 'She simply wants to be known.' She blinked. 'In both the biblical sense, *and* in the more ordinary sense too. She simply wants to be known, in her self, for who she is. She wants only to know that she will be *known* in this life.'

Her voice was low but urgent. He was unsure whether she was speaking about Lady Chatterley or herself. 'Lawrence,' he replied, 'had a rare awareness of the female principle, of its force.'

'I read somewhere that his wife was the model for Lady Chatterley. I thought that was touching.'

'It is sometimes *said* that Frieda was the model for Constance, and of course it might be true in the most literal sense – an aristocratic woman who ran away with a working-class man – but in reality, theirs was a very trying marriage. I suspect the "cover-story" of Frieda "as Lady Chatterley" suited them both. Frieda was certainly the force behind *The Rainbow*, in the first flush of their love, but *Lady Chatterley*—' He shrugged. 'It's doubtful. Frieda had taken a lover by the time Lawrence was writing *Chatterley*, a man called Angelo Ravagli, whom she married after Lawrence died. In that illicit relationship, we find another *superficial* parallel. But the character of Oliver Mellors is undoubtedly Lawrence himself, as is Sir Clifford, as is even Constance in many of her aspects – in her desire for a child especially, but also in her struggle toward an honest life and freedom.'

'So there was no "real" Lady Chatterley … That's a shame.'

'We may never know. I'm inclined to think there was. You see, Lawrence usually needed the "clay" of lived experience in order to create.'

She turned and looked out to the Sound. 'I'd hoped we might come up with an idea today, to help Grove Press, even if I were to have to disguise my role in any plan. Yet, from what you say, we're too late.'

'Don't give up just yet. Rosset's taking the case to the federal court. He filed his suit yesterday.'

Trilling watched her close her notebook. How interesting it was that no one ever knew what youth was while they had it. She was only half-formed still, and mysterious with it, perhaps above all to herself. He placed his hand lightly over hers. 'Humor me while I tell you about one last thing.'

'No humoring is required.'

'E. M. Forster and Lawrence,' he began, 'fell out, just as he and John Middleton Murry did. Lawrence was always falling out with people. He was a wonderful friend but he also turned on friends – and viciously. Be that as it may, and as different as they were, Forster and Lawrence were of the same mind in several important ways; they each rejected imperial might, imperial nostalgia, the intellectual domination empires accord themselves in the world, and they rejected, too, the Machine Age. They shared a vision, in other words, a passionate one. At his death, Lawrence was, at best, ignored and, at worst, derided, but in the obituary press, Forster – who had fallen out with Lawrence, remember – defended him. Have you ever come across it?'

She shook her head.

'I believe I still know the pertinent bit. Forster wrote: "All that we can do is to say straight out that he was the greatest imaginative novelist of our generation."' He raised a finger and looked at her meaningfully, his gaze warm. "'The rest must be left where he would have wished it to be left – *in the hands of the young*.'"

She nodded and smiled falteringly, as if with both gratitude and modesty, as if she couldn't make too great a claim for either her generation or herself. But yes, her eyes seemed to say, she would allow herself to hope, and to stay true to the book. 'Do you think Rosset can beat the Post Office's lawyers in court?'

'It's hard to say. In my understanding of these things, when a court reviews the decision of a government agency, such as the Post Office, there is almost always a presumption that the government agency is right. Even if the judge might have decided things differently if the issue had been with him from the start, it's another matter to over-turn the decision of a respected government authority. To do so, he would have to disagree very strongly – which means the odds are against it. But no doubt, Barney Rosset and that lawyer of his are going to throw everything they have at it. They'll be up against some heavyweight government lawyers, but sometimes, youth and energy *do* win the day.'

He passed her copy to her. 'Now, before I take my leave, you must read me a passage – simply to round off the pleasure of this after-noon. And because I am neither youthful nor energetic, we must simply skip over the bit where you demur and I insist.'

She smiled at the table, then eyed him over the rim of her iced tea. He held her gaze. Both gave up any last vestige of shyness.

The osprey, whose nest must have been nearby, circled again over the lawn, watching. She took the illicit book and opened it to a turned-down corner, one of several pages she had marked. She straightened in her chair. Her voice was typically whispery and soft, and often the target of teasing from Jack's sisters, who called her 'Babydoll' because of it, when they thought she was out of earshot. But as she began to read, her voice grew steady and resonant. She found her pitch:

'*At the back of the cottage, the land rose rather steeply, so the back yard was sunken and enclosed in a low stone wall. She turned the corner of the house, and stopped. In the little yard two paces beyond her, the man was washing himself, utterly unaware. He was naked to the hips, his velveteen breeches slipping down under his slender loins. And his white, slender back was curved over a big bowl of soapy water, in which he ducked his head, shaking his head with a queer, quick little motion, lifting his slender white arms and pressing the soapy water from his ears: quick, subtle as a weasel playing with water, and utterly alone.*

Connie backed away from the corner of the house, and hurried away to the wood. In spite of herself, she had had a shock. After all, merely a man washing himself! Commonplace enough, heaven knows.

Yet, in some curious way, it was a visionary experience: it had hit her in the middle of her body. She saw the clumsy breeches slipping away over the pure, delicate white loins, the bones showing a little, and the sense of aloneness, of a creature purely alone, overwhelmed her. Perfect, white solitary nudity of a creature that lives alone, and inwardly alone.'

The band was 940–980 MHz. The bug was no bigger than a silver dollar – it had been easy to fix to the underside of the Kennedys' patio table. All he'd needed, apart from the transistor receiver, was the miniature hand-cranked drill from the kit and a bit of wire.

Like the bug itself, he was a plant – in the Secret Service – and had been dropped into Hyannis Port. Hoover had set it up personally, through Howard Johnson and the Washington Field Office. It was a perk of an assignment and Agent Mel Harding's last chance to get things right.

At the front of the house on the quiet street, he hovered now by the wind-bent picket fence. Sand glittered at the edge of the road. A gull wheeled overhead. Earlier, he had moved across the front lawn, experimenting with the reception. The fence, where it met the paved walk up to the front of the house, seemed the best location. *She turned the corner of the house, and stopped—*

The radio, the bug, the drill kit and earpiece had been delivered on his arrival in Hyannis Port by an agent in a plumber's van. The radio had a case with a shoulder-strap. In his right hand, he held a pocket notebook, the kind often used for scores and sports results; in his left hand was the stub of the pencil he kept behind his ear. *Commonplace enough, heaven knows* His shorthand was good. Part of his training. Alone, in the heat of the day, he had let himself take off his suit jacket. Mrs. Kennedy and Professor Trilling had been talking for nearly two hours, the radio-strap dug into his shoulder, and he *a creature that lives alone, and inwardly alone* held on to every word.

Hoover had that day's report from Hyannis Port by the time he sat down to *The Lawrence Welk Show* at 9 p.m. Eastern Time. *'Literature is subversive. You say that somewhere ...'* They had a fat 'Bufile' – Bureau file – already on Professor Trilling, but even so, something made Hoover sit up in his La-Z-Boy recliner. A whiff of something. A scent.

Mrs. Kennedy's visit to the G.P.O. hearing hadn't merely been some misguided adventure. Today proved that. She should have been out shopping on a Saturday, like other ladies, or hosting some charity tea-party. Instead she had invited, to a very private lunch, a fellow sympathizer, a Jew with connections, a known subversive – a one-time Trotskyite and an officer of the Authors' League of America, a group which the Bureau had been monitoring for the last decade. Of course she wouldn't have known all that – she had no idea, whatever the jokes the Professor cracked about the F.B.I. and keeping agents in work. But ignorance was no excuse. She was using whatever thin political influence she could muster to champion a book which had been publicly judged to be obscene; a book that celebrated an upper-class woman's affair with her husband's servant; a so-called heroine who abandons her husband, a war-hero for Christ's sake, in a wheelchair. Mrs. Kennedy just wouldn't let it drop.

She and the Senator were known to have spent the autumn of '56 apart. She'd taken off to England. God knows what she got up to over there. MI5 claimed not to have a file. Of course they had a file.

Her Bufile was growing with new intelligence, almost weekly. It was said in some circles that her father, Black Jack Bouvier, was part Negro. The Bureau had even bribed the emergency-room doctor to obtain her permission for an autopsy. The doctor did ask, in the elevator supposedly, as he escorted her and the Senator to a private exit, but then he bungled the conversation and they sensed something was up.

Harding had managed to get a clear shot of Mrs. Kennedy and the Professor, at the front door as she welcomed Trilling into the house. He'd got a number of shots, in fact, before she'd shut the door, as the pair looked at something in the entry. A picture maybe. Hoover had to give credit where credit was due. It had been a good day's hunting. Harding had done well.

He looked up from the report and the enclosures in his lap. Lawrence Welk was introducing the next number, an old ballad, he said. When he spoke to the audience in the studio and at home, he sounded German. Or like a German trying not to be German. It was too bad. But every Saturday night, the country forgave him. World War Two was over. Forgive and forget. Americans were big-hearted, and Mr. Welk was a kind father figure to all those beautiful young people onstage.

Annie had left Hoover's mug of hot milk on the side-table, with a dash of vanilla, just the way he liked it. On the television, bubbles streamed over the bandstand. Bobby – toothy, strong and all-American – crooned to the camera in a striped blazer *naked to the hips* and a boater. Cissy twirled around him in a dress stiff with crinolines. The studio-set was of a church picnic, with a white steeple in the distance and the outlines of rolling hills. As the chorus appeared, plastic flowers popped up from a shiny black-and-white meadow. Big-eyed singing girls in long, pale dresses walked by with handsome tenors, two by two. The girls carried parasols; the boys picnic baskets. Hoover sipped his milk. Bobby *velveteen breeches slipping* sang on. Out of view, the bubble-machine ejaculated.

Prior to Harding's arrival in Hyannis Port, Hoover had *personally* instructed the plants team to refrain from bugging the bedrooms and bathrooms on Irving Avenue. Mrs. Kennedy was a Person of Interest, but she was also a lady – and he was a gentleman who had been raised in the South.

On the studio's bandstand, the saxes, trombones and trumpets flashed and gleamed. Mr. Welk waved his conductor's baton. The flowers popped. The parasols went up. Hoover wondered how Senator Kennedy liked best to take his wife. He wondered what suit he and Clyde should wear on Monday; he'd have to let Annie know tomorrow after she got back from church; they planned his suits three days in advance. After *Lawrence Welk*, before bed, he'd give Clyde a call. Clyde was watching too.

At last, when Bobby's heart was full, and the words of the song were no longer enough, he seized Cissy's waist and lifted her high. Her smile lit up the picnic. It lit up the television studio. It lit up the whole nation, from sea to shining sea, on Saturday night. That was art, Hoover thought. That was love.

The Exile

At the top of Rackham Hill, he had hoped for peace and the company of only the Downs, but the jingle of a recruitment band near Parham House had pursued him up the slope and wouldn't let him be. Empire Day was almost upon them, and the springtime loveliness of England was a recruiter's dream. Who wouldn't rush to defend it?

Not that the recruiting officers would have had him, not with his chest. He was not the fine specimen Perceval Lucas was. He woke most nights in a sweat, and only last night he'd dreamed that Careless – the patriarch's spaniel – had run off with his cock in his mouth.

Careless, careless, careless, the dream scolded him. How he raged in his sleep at the injustice, for he wasn't careless at all. *He* could never *afford* to be careless – easy-going – leisured – effortless. That was the point! And yet his manhood had been taken from him anyway. Wilfrid Meynell, his patron, had taken it; the dog was merely his dogsbody, doing the work of the *paterfamilias*. The Colony was colonising him, unmanning him, just as it had unmanned Percy Lucas before him. No wonder Lucas had fled to the evils of war. But he, Lawrence, wanted to live his life as a life should be lived so that his nights were not wakeful with regrets.

Far below, Greatham was looped and noosed with red-white-and-blue bunting for the Empire Day celebrations. The government was preparing for gas attacks on British soil, but no matter! The spirits of His Majesty's subjects remained insanely high. The hope was the Italians were on the brink of joining the Allied forces. Everyone had it on reliable authority that they would, and that their action was sure to be swift.

It was as if no one had ever *been* to Italy.

History unfolded day by day, like a creaking concertina. Who could even say what the country was fighting for? The Belgians were suffering most pitiably. That was true. Was further suffering the answer?

Now the *Lusitania* had been torpedoed, and all *that* suffering – the innocents washed up on the beaches of Ireland – seemed to prove to his countrymen that, yes! More suffering *was* the answer. Let's throw all the horror we can at it!

As he descended, his mood descended with him. Yet he couldn't not feel it: Sussex was luminous. The meadows winked with daisies and cowslips, and moorhens nested at the edges, clucking over their broods. In the woods, trees reached for each other, weaving canopies of green over the tracks and lumber-roads.

In the lane outside Winborn's, the hawthorn and the old man's beard glowed like fresh snowfall on the hedges. At the back of the house, the laburnum tree in the garden was tasselled in gold, and the beds he'd dug tumbled jubilantly with wallflowers and purple heliotrope.

The Meynells were Londoners through and through: impractical and therefore easily impressed by the sight of a boot on a spade. He often rolled up his shirt-sleeves and worked with Arthur, pruning the trees in the orchard or spreading manure. Their joint efforts had been rewarded. Everything looked splendid – everything, that is, except the endless people, people, people.

That weekend, Rackham Cottage, the Lucases' place, and Winborn's too, had turned into a *seething pot* of visitors. Word of Percy's surprise arrival had spread, and Arthur had had to give up work on the raspberry canes to ferry miscellaneous visitors from the station.

The Meynells, pacifists though they were, were thrilled, and quietly proud, to have their son-in-law in residence with them for twenty-four hours. He had told no one that he'd been granted leave, not even Madeline. 'What a surprise!' That was the phrase *du jour*. Lawrence had glimpsed the man upon his arrival: a tall figure in khaki, puttees and a cap. *Recruiting Now! How do you want your wife to view you?* Lucas had crossed the orchard in long, effortless strides.

Madeline had run to him, naturally enough. *Winifred waited for him in a little passion of duty and sacrifice, willing to serve the soldier, if not the man.* Then there were quick introductions and greetings before the couple disappeared.

At the outdoor table where they had been, until that moment, awaiting Mary's photographic direction, Viola confided in him and Frieda that her sister and brother-in-law were hoping for 'glad tidings' before Percy was sent to the Front.

Lawrence silently forgave Viola the silly euphemism. The Lucases had gone off, rather sweetly, for a fuck. *For a few hours, perhaps, they ceased to be in opposition; they let the love come forth that was in them.*

Then the love blazed and filled the old, silent hollow where the cottage stood,
with satisfaction and magnificence. But it passed in a few hours.

All manner of friends of the family arrived. Frieda, who feared
nothing but housework, claimed she was afraid to step out of doors
lest she was accosted by yet another visitor. They threw themselves
at her 'like grenades', she said. She didn't know where to walk, which
path was safe. He claimed she must do her duty, be sociable for them
both, and not give offence; he required the cow-shed to write – to
earn – and he would be far more productive if she would simply
surrender it to him for the weekend. She must join Monica and the
other Meynells for whatever activities they had planned.

She stared. What was this? her face said. Normally, her husband
wrote either with her in the cow-shed or, if the weather was fine,
out of doors, with his pad of foolscap. No other arrangement had
ever been proposed. She had never disturbed him before – at least
not when he was writing. What *was* he up to?

'Is it a new piece?'

He stared back, unapologetic. 'A notion of a piece … We will see.'

As soon as she left, he would hide his typewriter and the new
manuscript in a cupboard with the mop and cleaning bucket. She'd
never look there, not as long as she lived.

For the time being, he tried to interest her, with false enthusiasm, in the Meynell family visit to Queen Alexandra's yacht on
the Bank Holiday Monday. The vessel was berthed in Brighton,
just offshore of the Palace Pier, and the general public was to be
allowed on board to inspect its new Red Cross hospital. They were
all going. She would enjoy that, he said. The pomp. The beach.
Empire Day.

She regarded her husband, sucking in her cheeks with suspicion.

That spring, his mornings typically began with the two daily columns
of body counts in *The Times* – one for Officers, and the other for
N.C.O.s and 'Men'. Under each column were sub-headings: 'Killed',
'Died of Wounds', 'Accidentally Killed', 'Died', 'Wounded', 'Suffering
from Gas Poisoning', 'Wounded and Missing', 'Missing', and finally
and most intriguingly, 'Previously Reported Dead Now Not Dead'.
He identified strangely with the latter, and between all the lines of
print, he imagined the suck of the mud, the stink of old blood, and

the bite of lice at his head. There were mornings when he could almost feel them latching hold of his brain.

That day, Wilfrid Meynell's edition of *The Times* reported that St George's Hospital alone was preparing a mile-and-a-quarter of beds. Coffin-makers, it was reported, couldn't meet the demand.

The exile's depression was worsening again, as if he were being pulled down into the mud he could imagine all too keenly. But he was at least decided: it was time to escape Greatham and all the Meynell jollity. He'd feel so much better, he assured himself, once he could afford his own house or flat again.

On sending *The Rainbow* to his agent in early March, he had written, feverishly, from the depths of his flu: 'I hope you will like the book: also that it is not very improper … I could weep tears in my heart, when I read these pages.' Whatever his agent did or did not like, the manuscript was returned to him a month later with lashings of blue pencil. Cuts to the 'explicitly sensual' were demanded by Messrs Methuen.

'I hope you are willing to fight for this novel,' he fired off to his agent. 'It must be stood up for.'

He ignored Methuen's demands, but revised and chipped away, sculpting the novel into being. As for its numerous alleged offences, he could not judge those at all because he could not *feel* their offence. He gave it to Viola, with Methuen's notes, and asked her, once again, to act upon the least of their demands, so that he might appear, in some degree, compliant.

Percy Lucas's brother, Edward, visited the Colony from time to time and spoke to Viola in low, conspiratorial tones, no doubt trying to persuade her to go more ruthlessly at the book – to maim it. Edward – or E.V. Lucas, as he was more widely known – was a reader for Methuen, and the exile suspected his visits to Greatham were not merely to offer greetings to his sister-in-law's family, as claimed. He was a double-agent for Methuen, meddling, and meddling again. The exile came to resent Perceval Lucas all the more for the fact of his brother.

On the domestic front – and what a 'Front' it was! – he and Frieda had managed to agree on one thing: their separation would be an immense relief. She was to take a room or a small flat in London – Hampstead, with a bit of luck. Publicly, they would say to friends that the separate London residence was to be a base from which she would endeavour to make contact with her children when Monty, Elsa and Barby were in London, in term-time. The following winter, he himself would need to be in London a good deal – 'for work', he would say. There was a chance it might even be true.

In the short-term, he would, discreetly, find himself an alternative room or cottage – a bolt-hole far from Greatham. He had to escape. He might stay in Sussex or he might go farther afield. Friends might help again … Ottoline *had* offered him a cottage on her husband's estate, but then had wanted to charge him – an imminent bankrupt! – for the cottage's renovations. The wealthy were wealthy for a reason.

Who could he trust? Kot, always – but Kot had nothing. Murry, but Murry was always running off after Katherine and their latest melodrama. Viola's cow-shed was damp – blast and hang it! – *it* was the problem – but he would shake off this flu as soon as he was elsewhere. Anywhere else!

In his own mind, he classified himself as the 'Now Not Dead' – there were worse states – and it was high time he limped away from Greatham. He had promised to complete Mary's tuition in time for her August entrance exam, and he would not let her down. He would miss Mary's company, Hilda's affection, Viola's charm and Madeline's great warmth. In his estimation, she was the only Meynell truly capable of a natural, honest, unaffected love. He had watched with a stab of envy as she'd run headlong at the first glimpse of her husband in the orchard. In her rush, the hem of her frock had caught on her heel and she'd nearly gone over, but the joy never left her face.

Who was Perceval Lucas before he was in uniform? A man who preferred Morris-dancing to any actual occupation. To work! A man who lived off his wife's father. A dilettante who compiled folk tunes and called himself a genealogist. No wonder he'd gone off to train for war, to do *something* at last. *It did not suit him to be a modern soldier. In the thick, gritty, hideous khaki his subtle physique was extinguished as if he had been killed. In the ugly intimacy of the camp his thoroughbred sensibilities were just degraded.* Still – the exile couldn't *not* see it – how fine, how effortlessly fine, Perceval Lucas was in person, just as he was in Mary's cricket photograph in the library of Winborn's.

One final writing task remained to him before he fled Greatham. He was a painfully slow typist, but if he could make a reasonable manuscript, he could send it off without anyone knowing. It was unlikely any editor in England would touch the story, but in America there was a chance, and now, with Second Lieutenant Lucas's surprise appearance in the orchard and their introduction, the vital battle scene came to him, as if with a will of its own: *He turned round with difficulty as he lay. But he was struck again, and a sort of paralysis came over him. He saw the red face of a German with blue, staring eyes coming upon him, and he knew a knife was striking him.*

He didn't stop at his character's leg, for it was the handsome face from the photo in the library which preoccupied him, above all. *The German cut and mutilated the face of the dead man as if he must obliterate it. He slashed it across, as if it must not be a face any more; it must be removed.*

The exile felt aggrieved about the garden at Rackham Cottage. He had cleared brambles and briars. He had mended the path and the bridge over the stream. For weeks, he had cultivated pots and bell-jars of new summer shoots – sweet peas, larkspur, gladioli – and had been looking forward to planting-out this weekend. But Percy Lucas's unexpected appearance had spoiled his plans. The gentleman-warrior had laid claim to his Sussex plot once more, and Lawrence was suddenly, in his own eyes, a mere poacher, snatching at another man's life.

He disliked Second Lieutenant Perceval Lucas in proportions equal to his desire to live in his house, to be loved by his wife, to father his children, and to walk on his strong, lean legs. He wanted to swing the man's cricket bat, tend his earthly paradise, and put down roots in his patch of old England. His own England was gone – razed, violated and industrialised – so that the likes of Percy Lucas and the Meynells could have their verdant slice of Sussex: their Colony retreat, away from their comfortable London house; their peace of mind; their eighty acres; their Downs overlooking the silver sea.

He did at last succeed in getting rid of Frieda that day; a shopping trip to Chichester with Monica and Mary was planned in the motor. He reminded his wife that they had not a shilling to spend. Wasn't she still in mourning? Why couldn't she wear her black day-frock? Why did she always need more? He told Monica through the passenger window that 'Mrs Lawrence' was 'under no circumstances to borrow' from either her or Arthur – or from Mary, for that matter. She was not, he said, above defrauding the child of her egg-money. Frieda had blushed deeply. But why should he bear the humiliation alone? He worked at everything tirelessly while she strove only for new hats and frocks, and gave him no children. He felt sure she was withholding her womb from him in some act of visceral resistance. And still he was making her a summer hat!

Their finances haunted him. The week before he had presented himself to the High Court at Somerset House in London, and he was still waiting to learn whether he'd be declared a bankrupt, with his name in the papers for all to see. The Registrars of the High Court might as well cut his knees out from under him. He'd be crippled by it. He'd never recover.

That dark day in London, the only distraction from his own woes had come when he'd crossed the river on a rumour. The rumour had proved true. He heard the riots, near the East India Dock, before he saw them. A woman in her apron told him that the uproar had started with a crowd of boys looting a pastry-cook's shop. They'd smashed the front pane and had descended, eating everything in sight. The German owners had run for their lives. In that part of town, every second butcher's or baker's was German.

It was just as well he'd sent Frieda off to leafy Hampstead to investigate a bed-sit, although it was impossible to say what sort of reception she would have there. The *Lusitania* had gone down only three days before. She might be out on her ear.

Boys as young as ten picked up bricks and stones. Women arrived on the scene, followed by men from the docks. Later, the papers said German shop-owners were dragged out from under their beds. While he watched at the edge of the crowd, a looted piano was rolled into the streets and the crowd started to sing 'Rule Britannia'.

Police with truncheons arrived but were quickly outnumbered. At the front of the crowd, a German man was stripped in the street. Another was ducked in a horse-trough as he pleaded in broken English: 'I am Russian!'

Lawrence worried for Kot. The masses often didn't bother to distinguish between 'foreigners'. It was a contagion. Grief twisted up with rage; rage at the atrocities in Belgium, at the gas attacks at the Front, at the death of 1,200 souls at sea, and so many women and children among them. The images from the papers – of their eyes still open to the shock of the sea – wouldn't leave him, or anyone else who had looked on them. He paced at the perimeter of the crowd, walking and seething, feeling himself drawn into the tide of hatred. Never had he felt smaller or more futile than he had that year. It made him want to kill – a million, two million, Germans.

Or at least Frieda.

How infuriating she was. Only the day before, he'd had to disabuse her of the notion that she would take a three-bedroom house in the best part of Hampstead.

Husband and wife met up at Victoria Station. Frieda had not secured the Hampstead bed-sit – the mood of the day was against her.

Returning from London to Greatham, they travelled via Brighton, and joined Lady Cynthia and her children on their seaside break, for two days as planned. They somehow succeeded in hiding their strife, and Cynthia was unusual among the exile's friends in that she seemed not to mind Frieda. She even grew fond of her.

Herbert Asquith, the PM's son, was still in Flanders. Cynthia found herself often alone, and anxious. Her debts were growing, and it was not easy to travel freely between friends' houses with the burden of her little son, an unusual and uncontrollable child.

How deceptive her sort of calm, classical beauty was. Viola thought her the prettiest woman she had ever seen, and Cynthia's photograph often appeared in the illustrated news. She had a wide-eyed dreaminess worthy of the Lady of Shalott, and a mesmerising poise. Yet she was eternally anxious.

How layered, how fascinating women were. They seemed better at accepting the flux of their own contradictions than most men, who either lied like cheap rugs or spoke utter bunk.

He and Frieda decided to offer Cynthia an afternoon's respite from her children. Although it was a very gusty day, threatening rain, they took the two little ones to the beach and pleasure-pier, tiring out the older boy and cooing over the younger – a toddler – until tea-time. The four-year-old, John, was the abnormal son, rigid in his wishes, defiant, and so remote as to be other-worldly.

Cynthia, they could see, did her best to weather his rages and tears, but the boy was a force of nature. He used his food as missiles at each meal; he had tantrums if his mother used what he deemed to be a 'wrong' word, or if she failed to provide the response he judged to be correct. Once upset, he would not allow anyone to touch or hold him, not even his nurse. He would not be consoled and, for a child, he had a peculiar stamina for bearing a grudge over weeks or even months. His speech was minimal, with a strangely flattened rhythm. He frequently made animal-like noises. Worst of all, his rages gave him the air of a boy possessed, and, at times, if he was not pacified, they intensified into shaking fits. Yet the doctors could only recommend discipline, firm routines, cold baths, and fresh air, the more bracing, the better.

Two years before, when they all met on the beach in Margate, Lady Cynthia saw immediately that Lawrence was better able to communicate with her son than any person she'd known. Now, both she and the nurse were relieved beyond words when her guests volunteered to take the children for the day.

In Brighton, the exile stood with John on the beach, where the waves pounded the shingle. Together they ran at the churned-up green sea, while Frieda, in the lee of the promenade, bounced the little one, Michael, in her arms, and watched the Pierrot show on its wooden stage on the beach. It was a bright gusty day and, with the War, the audience for the show was woefully depleted. A few soldiers sat, dazed and indifferent; some had heads that were heavily bandaged. Rows of empty deck-chairs were slumped and mournful, many were blown over, and the words of the actors were snatched by the wind.

In the distance, she watched her husband and the boy shouting and running. Lorenzo seemed to care for all children but her three. Why?

At the tide-mark, he positioned the boy next to him and made him stand up straight. Then, on a count of three, they roared. They roared at the sea like lions, bears, and gorillas. They grunted like hippos and wildebeests. Finally, at his instruction, they growled like themselves, like John-beasts and Lawrence-beasts, and those were the loudest utterances of all, noisy with bestial anguish.

The exile had been scanning the pebbles on the shore, and now he stooped low: 'A-ha!' he said. 'That makes a pair.'

'A pair of what?' asked the boy.

He took one stone from his pocket and bounced the other, still wet, in his palm. Then he laid them over his eyes. 'A pair of eye-stones.'

'But they have *holes* in them. They're no good. Throw them away.'

He smiled, as if to taunt the child with mystery.

The boy stamped his foot. 'I *said*, throw them away!'

He kept the larger one and gave the other to the boy. He showed him how to close one eye and peer with the other through the perfect hole. They did it together, looking out across the wind-threshed sea.

'What do you see?' said the exile.

'Secrets,' said the boy.

'Yes,' said the exile.

'I spy ...' said John.

'With my third eye ...'

'I'm not telling.'

'Nor am I.'

Rain started up, and they pocketed their eyes. Then they found Frieda and the baby, and off they went in search of ice-cream, heedless of the weather.

John didn't throw his eye-stone or his ice-cream at anyone, which his mother, upon their return, was ecstatic to hear. To celebrate, she insisted that they, the adults, dine out. Her treat. The nurse took receipt of two sleepy, peaceful children.

As Lady Cynthia and her guests walked through the town, the exile remarked that there seemed to be a Red Cross van at every other street corner. Over dinner in a dim restaurant – a consequence of the new light restrictions with the bombing threat – he advised her on John and the way she should handle him. She marvelled, not for the first time, at his uncanny ability to see people, to grasp everyone. That night before bed, she wrote in her diary, 'The Lawrences were riveted by the freakishness of John, about whom they showed extraordinary interest and sympathy.'

The following morning, after a late breakfast, the adults left for a walk to the top of the nearest sea-cliff. The gusts of the previous day had softened into a warm breeze. It was going to be a day of mild May sunshine.

On the rocky shore, they assessed the cliff. The stone face pulsed and glowed. Heaps of chalk scored the narrow strip of beach – recent rock-falls. Yellow sea-poppies pushed through the rubble, and all three glanced up anxiously, as if England itself was crumbling.

But the tide was coming in faster than they'd expected, and the beach would soon be flooded, which meant it was time to climb. Frieda went first, because she was the slowest. As she clambered, she sang German folk songs, and Cynthia was charmed, which encouraged Frieda to continue all the way to the top. The lung-power of his wife, the exile remarked, never failed her.

He struggled, over Frieda's volume, to converse with their host, who enquired politely about his 'philosophy' – the ideas he'd advanced with Bertrand Russell and John Maynard Keynes during his visit to Cambridge earlier that spring. '*I believe in being warm-hearted. I believe especially in being warm-hearted in love, in fucking with a warm heart. I believe if men could fuck with warm hearts, and the women take it warm-heartedly, everything would come all right.*' She listened carefully, her turquoise eyes intrigued – and sceptical, he thought.

By the time they reached the top, his confidence was shot. Perhaps it had been the reminder of Cambridge; of the searing sense of anger and inadequacy he'd felt in the company of Keynes, Russell and their colleagues. Perhaps it was his sudden awareness that Lady Cynthia was accustomed to the conversation of highly educated men of rank and distinction. 'Probably everything I say is pure bosh,' he said.

'Not at all!' she declared generously.

The memory of his Cambridge humiliation resurrected another. As they climbed, he felt himself shrinking again under the black-browed stare of the Chief Registrar in London. The whole matter of Frieda's divorce and their extramarital affair had been reviewed by the officials of the High Court, with a column of evidence in a ledger listed as 'Monies Owed'. He, a man who had striven endlessly for respect and respectability, was now on the public record as a disreputable lover who'd stolen his friend's wife and was living off charity.

For all the struggle and sacrifices of marriage, the truth was that he longed, for the time being at least, to be shot of his wife. The situation was shaming after so short a marriage – not yet a year. He and Frieda usually hid the truth as well as they could, but when they were alone, their unhappiness seemed to redouble, as if their masquerade cost them dearly.

They had reached the top of the cliff and revelled now in the bright endlessness of the view, and the variegated canvas of the sea: silver-green near the shore, cerulean-blue beyond it, and slate at its greatest depth. Fishing boats – blue, black and red – daubed the horizon, and the shadow of a vast, low-bellied cloud moved in the far distance. They cocked their ears and stopped their chatter. Was it? Was it actually?

Yes. They heard, faintly, the pounding of the guns across the Channel.

The exile's blood ran cold.

No one mentioned Flanders or Neuve Chapelle – or Cynthia's husband Beb 'over there' with the Royal Artillery. No one had to. A curious, collective inertia overcame them, like chloroform, and they sat on the grassy turf, silent for entire minutes and lost to their thoughts.

At that cliff edge, he saw the visible world – the striped sea, the bright boats – and also that which lay beyond them – the charred landscapes of Belgium and France, the innumerable miseries unfolding, a legion of dead. *He was hopeless at the very core of him, and he wanted to be hopeless. He rather hated hope.* He watched the low-bellied cloud approach, entranced by its cumulous mass and its gravid, Zeppelin-like menace.

Cynthia broke the spell of gloom, remarking how beautifully hot it was, even with the breeze. On the cliff-top, they reclined in the grass, wove daisy chains, then wandered, chatting amiably with an unforced warmth. Butterflies sunned themselves. The exile rolled up his shirt-sleeves. The breeze was silken on his skin. When the two women turned to peer at the surprise of early orchids, he felt a little better, stronger – strong enough.

The cliff edge was soft under his boots. The tide had risen to cover the beach below. The sea crashed against the cliff, then retreated in a long sibilant hush – crash and hush, hush and crash.

Would he lose consciousness, he wondered, before he hit?

Crash – and hush.

It was the discovery of the eye-stone in his pocket that stopped him; the stone from his beach-walk with Cynthia's lad. Its solidness in his hand reminded him of the boy, who had insisted that morning, dictatorially, on knowing precisely what time they three would return. The boy was all but fatherless and spoke little, but his face softened back into that of a child's when Lawrence said, 'Tea-time.'

The stone, tide-worn, said: 'Patience.'

Its weight was ballast.

He stepped back, blinking.

And: 'Orchids,' he said, 'already?'

Back in Greatham, he seated himself at the refectory table, then got up again to close the window and draw the curtains – so that his typewriter would be neither seen nor heard. Viola was his designated typist, and he didn't want questions.

Outside, he heard the Lucases and their friends, the Nelsons, pass on their way to the lane. The children were clamouring for a swim at The Quell. Madeline, along with Florrie the governess, was gently insisting it was still too early in the season. The waters of the Arun had not had time to warm up! Percy laughed and said, why not let them have a paddle? Thud, thud went Sylvia's leg on the path.

Lawrence bent his head and re-read his story, where it was gripped in the roller. 'He was lying with a great mass of bloody earth thrown over his thighs. He looked at it vaguely, and thought it must be heavy over him. He was anxious, with a very heavy anxiety, like a load on his life. Why was the earth on his thighs so soaked with blood?' Then, down the page, 'The leg lay diverted. He tried to move a little. The leg did not move. There seemed a great gap in his being.'

It was taking shape … his mine, his little bomb-blast of words. *'If only one could sweep clear this England of all its houses and pavements, so that we could all begin again!'*

But softly, softly—

Which is when he spotted it: an eggshell-blue envelope against the green linoleum. Someone had slid it under the door.

He walked over, bent, opened it, and tugged at his beard.

It was true: he was fed up with visitors but he *did* enjoy a party.

The Lawrences arrived at Rackham Cottage that evening looking unusually cheerful, with the secret knowledge they were soon to separate. The exile had steered a wheelbarrow all the way from the cow-shed to the Lucases' door. He wore a light, red-striped Eton jacket and a straw hat, for even the end of the day was still hot. Frieda wore a pale green linen tunic. Rather a sack, her husband thought, but he was feeling cheerful at the prospect of a party, and said only that it made her gold-green eyes flash.

Madeline greeted them at the oaken door, and Lawrence lifted a cover of canvas to reveal an array of gifts: pots of sweet peas for planting-out – he would make a trellis for their garden, he said. A jar of apple compote. A loaf of bread he'd baked that morning – 'not as nice as Hilda's, but nicer than the baker's in Storrington'. A bottle of French wine (left by Jack Murry). Plus – and he produced these, like an illusionist, from his jacket's inside pocket – six peacock tail-feathers, one for each child in the house: Sylvia, Christian and little Barbara Lucas, Mary and the visitors' boy and girl. Barbara wailed because he didn't have one for her baby-doll.

He'd had the feathers since the previous year in Chesham, from a neighbour who'd kept all manner of fowl. The man had explained that his peacock typically dropped most of its tail-feathers as soon as the mating-season was over. 'By that stage, the poor fellow is positively blasted!' Lawrence declared.

Percy joined his wife at the door, looking neither blasted nor spent. He rolled down his shirt-sleeves. His hair was fair with the sun, his face was ruddy, and he looked fighting-fit. Madeline, whose eyes still glittered with the lovemaking of the afternoon, peered into the wheelbarrow and said she'd never seen such a trove. Frieda insisted that Madeline '*must* take it all!' What else was she to do with it? Lawrence wondered. Frieda never could resist hyperbole and overstatement.

'And look!' Frieda gestured to the one-wheeled vehicle. She was, she said, to be conveyed home by the very same wheelbarrow at the end of the evening!

Lawrence grimaced comically, but with feeling. Much later, before they blew out their bedside candle, Frieda would comment to Lawrence that Madeline and Percy were, no doubt 'at it' again. She would laugh but Lawrence would roll over, away from her. At times, she revolted him. Yet it was true: other people were endlessly fascinating. In the silent darkness, each would imagine the beautiful jigsaw of Percy and Madeline's bodies.

Now, at the cottage door, the evening in Rackham was only just underway. Lucas shook the exile's hand, for the second time that day. Frieda extended her hand for Percy to kiss, and he obliged. The exile entered the cottage, bending his head to avoid a particularly low beam. The world inside was dim after the dappled brightness of early evening. 'Something smells delicious,' he said.

'Veal-and-ham pie,' said Madeline. 'Somehow I managed to make six!'

The house was hot with the heat from the oven, and noisy with the pell-mell of children, who came thumping now, down the steep, narrow staircase, to see who and what had arrived. Frieda cooed over each child, even the gnome Mary. Little Barbara showed Frieda her baby-doll, and Frieda encouraged the little girl not to hold her baby in a head-lock. The Nelson boy stared hard at Frieda – 'Are you a Hun?' – and his father promptly marched him outside. Sylvia came last, slow and methodical on each stair.

Christian, the middle Lucas girl, said she wanted to wear her peacock feather in her hair. Barbara insisted tearfully that her dolly *must* have one too. She pounded her father's leg. Sylvia told her mother she was going to make a quill with her feather for writing. Mary was more interested in the sweet peas and when they would flower. When she grew up and became a farmer, she was going to grow fields of flowers too. Barbara began to cry again because she wanted to eat the apple compote and would not be distracted from it.

The exile heard Frieda tell Madeline that she was going to take a place in London so she could insist on seeing her children in term-time. She would wait day and night by their school gates if that's what it required. 'And Lawrence?' asked Madeline.

'He has work to finish and needs his solitude, but of course he will visit in Hampstead. We're so accustomed to travel, it's no distance at all for us.'

Lovely, plain Eleanor Farjeon, who had become the exile's fond companion for long walks, moved self-consciously across the room to greet him, and her brother joined them. 'You remember my brother, Herbert, from Easter weekend?'

'Of course,' he said. 'Good to see you.' And it was, truly, for Herbert Farjeon's wife Joan was the sister of the woman who had appeared to him on that snowy, January Down: Rosalind, she who had watched him from the hilltop, as if through a looking-glass, dressed in a man's jacket and breeches.

Were the two sisters also here at Rackham somewhere? He craned. Yes, there was Joan, Bertie's wife, heavily pregnant, and next to her – his heart dropped – Ivy Low, another friend of Viola's. The girl was a creeping vine.

Joan approached him with Ivy, who was eager to know when she might obtain a copy of his forthcoming novel. He said he wondered the same thing himself.

Viola joined them, saying she was proud to be one of its first readers, and recommended it highly.

He gestured to her with an open palm:'Corrupted, as you can see for yourselves. Apparently, my books and I have that effect.'

Joan laughed. He did, as well. No one of course could have imagined the bonfire, only a few months in the future; or his words lifting off, ashen, into the air of London, at the order of a magistrate. 'The book in question is a mass of obscenity of thought, idea and action throughout.' Messrs Methuen & Co. will be ordered to pay £10 10s. costs. They will do so promptly, and with their apologies. Nor will they waste any time in revoking Lawrence's £300 advance.

Hard times were about to get worse.

But on that late-May evening at the Lucases' party, the exile's mood was nearly optimistic. Viola turned to Joan and asked after Joan's sister, Rosalind. Joan murmured a pleasantry and told Viola she would remember her to her sister. Viola turned to the exile and explained the connections. Dr Maitland Radford was a close friend of them all, *and* a colleague of Joan's sister's – Rosalind's – husband, Dr Godwin Baynes.

Normally, he would have struggled to suppress a yawn, but in that moment, his eyes were alight. 'Ah, yes,' he replied, 'the doctor who—'

'Yes,' replied Viola quickly, mindful of Sylvia seated nearby on her father's lap. The little girl was showing Percy her peacock feather. Soon, Second Lieutenant Lucas would return to the army camp at Seaford.

The exile watched Sylvia tickle her father's chin with the feather, and he felt the gut-punch of grief. Perceval Lucas had all a man could want. What had he?

He turned to Joan, and guided her towards a view of the stream and the common. 'Now you must tell me: are you also new to "the Colony" or am I the only stray?' His voice was warm but wry. He was quite sure that she, too, was a little lost amid the Meynellage.

'I am indeed.' Her eyes were clear; her expression reserved but calm. Her right hand rested lightly on her pregnant belly.

They must have made an odd pair standing there, he thought, their heads bent, each to the other. She was as full and ripe as a piece of fruit, and he was thinner and paler by the day, no matter the season.

Her words came only tentatively, but her voice was pleasingly resonant. 'My father, coincidentally, is an old acquaintance of Mr Meynell's. In the '80s, Mr Meynell edited a volume of essays about modern art, and he visited my father in his studio, in a family property in Kensington. I'm told he arrived for a meeting, but my entry into the world that very morning meant he had a wasted journey. I apologised to him earlier today.' She smiled, and her faced bloomed.

She was dull, but sweet. 'You upstaged Meynell!'

'Well, not so much as that, but apparently, I did send him back through London, after he'd arrived – and on a day when the roads were chaotic with snow! Even the doctor hadn't reached us in time.'

'Did Mr Meynell accept your apology?'

She smiled again, in the soft, secretive way of pregnant women. 'He did. He said I am to give his warm regards to my father, and that I am to return with this little one' – she glanced down – 'in the future.'

Suddenly he wished he were a heavily pregnant woman, with a rightful place in the world. 'Well then,' he said, getting hold of himself, 'you must return and soon, now that your sister-in-law, dear Eleanor, is such a familiar at Rackham. She tells me, too, that she visits your sister – Mrs Baynes, is it? – in Wisbech sometimes. Indeed, you must *all* come to Greatham very soon. The weather is splendid now, and there is plenty of room. Mrs Lawrence and I have two guest rooms which are often empty ...'

To live to live to live—

'Eleanor will certainly be back and forth to Greatham, and I might indeed join her. Bertie is having a very good run with his latest play, so I'll need more company when it's just the baby and me. Ros absolutely loves this part of Sussex' – she hesitated, smiling weakly – 'although I don't expect the timing will be quite right at present for her and Dr Baynes.'

By mid-evening, he had winkled it out of Herbert, the playwright. Bertie was sociable, and knew everyone and everyone's story, it seemed. He was easy to trust, a dependable sort, and the exile liked him very much, even if his speaking voice was rather affected. But he was as genial as his sister Eleanor.

Lawrence nudged the subject round to that of the fabled Bayneses as the two men threw logs onto a smouldering blaze. The cottage sitting-room was too small for everyone, and Madeline's plan was that the gathering should decamp to the fire-pit after supper.

The Bayneses' marriage, Bertie confided in a low voice, was most unhappy. Dr Baynes, a handsome, strapping man – six feet four inches in his bare feet – had never been able to' – Herbert lowered his voice – 'rein himself in.' Flirtations. Affairs. With women. With men. He simply loved to be loved, and he was enormously attractive.

Across the fire, the exile cupped his ear.

Unfortunately, Dr Baynes imagined himself to be in love with the young woman who dispensed the medicines for his practice. Naturally, Baynes adored Ros – she was, her brother-in-law loyally declared, 'made to be adored' – but Baynes was making it intolerable for her, given their house was also his surgery, and the dispensary was at the back of the kitchen. Ros had found the pair 'inseparable' on more than one occasion. She claimed he no longer desired her now that they had their two children.

The exile felt a testy impatience for the charismatic people of this world – the Godwin Bayneses, the Friedas, the Katherine Mansfields. What damage they wreaked with their easy, careless charm. Yet something else bucked, exultant, at his core. Rosalind Baynes had a husband who didn't deserve her. Rosalind Baynes was unhappy in her marriage.

He kicked a log back into the fire. Sparks rose high, lighting up Bertie Farjeon's spectacles.

The sun was dropping fast, and glow-worms were lighting their miniature lanterns in the long grass. Percy's beds of white stock glowed magically, and the evening primrose lifted to the twilight.

Under the sloping roof of the cottage, the nursery window was lit. Madeline arrived at the fire with a plate of bread and long forks. Would they toast it for the children, before they were put down for the night?

They pulled over logs and seated themselves.

'It all sounds rather tough,' he said to Bertie, his face appropriately sober.

'Quite. Ros and Joan's father, Sir Hamo, fumes to us about Baynes's "wild animalism", about him spoiling the life of his dear girl. Joan gets frightfully upset, on her sister's account.'

The words would travel far, along the synapses of the exile's brain into the following decade:

She thought he made use of Connie shamefully and impudently. She had hoped her sister would leave him. But being solid… middle-class, she loathed any 'lowering' of oneself, or the family.

'Sir Hamo,' Bertie added, 'doesn't appreciate how much Joan worries about everyone. I worry about her in turn.'

'Particularly in her condition,' said Lawrence. 'She's sensitive. I knew as soon as I spoke to her. How many children have the Bayneses?'

'Two. Girls. They are sometimes only upstairs when all … *that* is going on. And yet, unless Godwin actually deserts Ros, she can't rid herself of him. Such is the law.'

'Of course. How horrid for her.'

The two men stared into the fire. In their silence, it crackled and spat. Something more was on Bertie's mind. 'You see, we no longer know if Rosalind will be able to …'

'Endure it.'

'Precisely. Joan fears she will be tempted to "devise" a scandal.'

'I see … Her own affair. A co-respondent who might allow himself to be named.' It was not an uncommon story.

'That is what Joan believes she will do.'

'Mrs Baynes doesn't fear the newspapers?'

'She does, naturally. But she believes a scandal might be the lesser of two evils. She says she must be allowed to live, without all this anguish. She fears for her children too. Baynes is a devoted father, but all the upset between Ros and Godwin … I daresay the children have not been spared the unpleasantness.

'Ros tells us she might leave the country for a time, to get away from the wagging tongues, but that's not possible for us, of course. *We* would have to stay in London and weather the attention Baynes's divorce petition would undoubtedly draw. My dear Joan especially.'

Herbert Farjeon straightened and lit a cigarette, offering it to Lawrence, but the exile shook his head, tapping his chest.

'I know what the London press is like,' Bertie said, 'and it will simply be too much to bear if Joan is left to be the family's lightning rod.'

'I must say, the Bayneses' difficulties – the account you give – it has something of the character of our times.'

The playwright tipped his head back and blew smoke high. 'Does it?' He turned and seemed to assess the exile. 'I expect the papers might try to *make* it mean as much as that, if it does go as far as—'

'Court? The Divorce News?'

'Worse, I'm afraid. If she leaves him, if she forces his hand, there will be full-blown headlines. Her father is a Royal Academician, after all. You've probably heard of him: *Old* Sir Hamo *Sir Malcolm* Thornycroft.'

the once well-known R.A.   still handsome and robust.

Here were the earliest imaginative flickerings: Rosalind *Constance*. A woman trapped in an unhappy, sexless marriage. From a family of distinction – the daughter of a Royal Academician *his favourite daughter*. Married to a war-hero and a Cambridge graduate, a man who stood for little, as the author judged it, and was crippled in his soul.

The exile offered his new friend a piece of toast. 'I've an idea. For a collaboration between us two.'

Herbert Farjeon looked up. 'Oh?'

It was a gamble of an idea, but when was an important idea ever not a gamble? 'We must co-author a play based on the collapse of the Bayneses' marriage. A serious play. An allegory of our times. The story of a nation's breakdown in the wake of—'

The whites of the other man's eyes widened in the dark.

Then, 'Look!' a voice shouted from inside, and both men sprang up, as if a boar were about to crash out of the woods. Lawrence's proposal was lost in the commotion. 'No! *Up!*' called Eleanor again. 'Look up!'

From Parham House, the great manor house across the wood, a light streaked across the sky, then another. A beautiful volley of golden lights followed. Pops and bangs sounded. Everyone inside the cottage stepped outside and craned their heads to see the Empire Day fireworks over the boundary tree-line. The children came tumbling out onto the lawn again.

Rockets went up, whistling and shrieking. A Catherine wheel, evidently mounted high on a stand, spun itself into a fire-storm, spitting and blazing. Ooh, they said. Ahh, they said. 'Ding-ding-ding, ding-ding-ding!' sang the Nelson boy, seated in Arthur's wheelbarrow as his father bumped him about the lawn. Together they made a human fire engine.

Then something cracked, like the egg of Creation, the sky flashed yellow, and a mock-Zeppelin rose above the trees. Sylvia and Christian leaned into their mother. The Nelson boy leaped from the wheelbarrow, tipped it over, and hid beneath. Exploding cargo fell from the airship's belly to the earth. The night was coming down – the roof of the world.

There was a shocked silence, except for the whimpering of the children, who were gathered and hushed.

'Well then,' sighed Madeline, because someone needed to speak. Smoke gusted across the sky, all yellowy-grey. *All grey, all grey! The world looked worn out …*

'You've had enough toast, my darling,' murmured Madeline to Sylvia, 'and it's time for bed.'

Mary, the eldest of the cousins, insisted it was not late at all. Monica, her mother, was still fixed on the night sky, her upturned face pale, and her eyes brimming. The spectacle had done nothing for her nerves.

The little group was making for the brightness of the cottage when something high overhead blazed into life again. An unexpected finale.

A faint burst of applause was heard. Then, above the tree-line, a grinning phosphor skeleton arose.

Sylvia frowned up at it, as if her glare would see it off. Christian, the middle Lucas sister, sprinted across the lawn, fleeing indoors. On the other side of the wood, a fuse was lit, and the skeleton-man kicked one sizzling leg in a clumsy quick-step, then the other. Within moments, each leg had fallen from him and was plummeting to the earth. A flaming arm floated free, and a hand waved as it fell. Its mate gave way next and dropped. Finally, the skull popped off, like a burning cork.

Beside the ancient cottage, the turned-up faces were strangely lit in the yellow gunpowder light. Frieda's mouth, normally the first to laugh, was set in a grim rictus. Barbara asked in a loud voice why the dead in Heaven were falling out of it. She gripped her baby-doll hard by the arm. Percy got down on his haunches and murmured in her ear.

'It is!' she said to him, pointing heavenward. 'It *is* falling. Just as in "Chicken Licken"!'

He spoke softly to her again.

'But will *we* be dead too tomorrow when we wake up?' She shook her doll.

Percy picked them both up – the doll dangling disconsolately – and carried them inside. The darkness ticked, and the guests drifted across the lawn at a loss, until Lawrence reminded everyone that it was a party *We've got to live, no matter how—* and that they must have singing!

Madeline beamed her relief at him. Frieda clapped and drew herself up to her full height, as if she were about to walk from the wings of a stage. The others – Herbert and Joan, Eleanor, Viola, Lawrence, the visitors Robert and Mary Nelson, and Madeline – hauled chairs and logs to the fire.

When the candle in the nursery was out, Percy joined them, although he sat a little apart, as if preoccupied. *Then he sat by the fire with the friends and with Winifred's sisters, and they sang the folk-songs. He put on thin civilian clothes and his charm and his beauty and the supple dominancy of his body glowed out again.* The exile observed him, unobserved. Tomorrow, Perceval Lucas would be gone again. Madeline, he noticed, looked over to her husband but could not catch his eye. They appeared not unhappy, but the ember of their earlier lovemaking had gone out. *He seemed to her almost like a pale creature of negation, detached and cold and reserved, with his abstracted face and mouth.*

Frieda unpinned her hair, climbed on a stump, clasped her hands to her breast, and sang from Schubert's 'Gretchen at the Spinning Wheel'. Lawrence dutifully murmured the translations. *Meine Ruh' ist hin. / Mein Herz ist schwer.* My peace is lost. My heart is heavy. *Ich finde sie nimmer / Und nimmermehr.* I will find it never, never more. *Wo ich ihn nicht hab' / Ist mir das Grab.* Where I do not have him, that

269

is the grave. *Die ganze Welt / Ist mir vergällt.* The whole world is laid waste to me.

Lawrence seemed to chuckle, as part of the double-act, but when Bertie's flask went around, he seized it.

In a few days' time, he would send a postcard to Forster, his first communication since their unhappy evening in February: Frieda, he said pithily, was in town again searching for a flat, unless, that is, a bomb had fallen and she'd been flattened by her own people.

Then he stood to sing, a traditional Negro spiritual, the first such song any of them had heard. Privately, each was embarrassed by his soulful delivery, but they applauded energetically, to vent their misgivings, and pronounced his choice 'Jolly interesting!'. Encouraged, he moved on to his favourite American ballad, already too well known among some of them as a consequence of his and little Mary's peculiar dedication to it.

Roosevelt in the White House, drinking out of a silver cup
McKinley in the graveyard, he'll never wake up
He's gone a long, long time.

'Lord, that tune hangs on like a flea,' Eleanor whispered to her brother, but in her next letter to Lawrence, she will ask him to write out the lyrics and send them.

Ain't but one thing that grieves my mind
That is to die and leave my poor wife behind
I'm gone a long, long time.

Herbert and Eleanor Farjeon – brother and sister – stood up next and performed from their 'nonsense repertoire'. 'Hands, Knees – and Whoops-a-Daisy!' was a hit.

Requests were made for a duet by Madeline and Percy, but Percy claimed he couldn't carry a tune these days. The drills on parade had made him deaf, he said, not very convincingly. He had a tenor voice and, as he spoke, it sounded worn, after calming the nerves of the little ones in the nursery. 'I'm a stick at entertaining,' he murmured with a faltering smile. 'The children made that quite clear just now.'

The exile leaned towards Bertie. 'Lucas is not himself,' although they both knew he hardly knew the man. He and Percy had only exchanged pleasantries all evening but, as ever, Lawrence trusted his instincts entirely. *And on his face a slightly impure look, a little sore on his lip, as if he had eaten too much or drunk too much or let his blood become a little unclean. He was almost uglily healthy, with the camp life. It did not suit him.*

His confidant surprised Lawrence by agreeing with him. Bertie nodded. 'Yes ... Being back. Seeing the children. Leaving tomorrow, being pulled away. Not to mention all that is to come ... Yet funnily enough, what's troubling him most is that Sylvia refused a swim at The Quell this afternoon with the other children. That was a first, apparently. She's suddenly grown shy about others seeing her gammy leg.'

The exile's mind's eye flashed to the page of his unfolding story, as he'd last seen it in his typewriter *the father could not bear it; he was nullified in the midst of life.*

He shook his head. 'It can't be easy, her injury, especially as he's very much the agile sort.'

'*Before* ... she was the child who most resembled him in that way.'

The exile edged closer to the events of two summers ago. 'He must curse himself.'

Bertie's brow lifted in puzzlement.

Lawrence dropped his voice. 'That sad business with the fag-hook.'

Bertie pushed his specs up his nose. 'I say, that wasn't—'

'Well, no, naturally. It was an acci—'

'Percy was in *Italy* at the time. It was poor Robert Nelson who dropped the thing. He and his family were visiting. Nelson offered to help in the garden, to cut it back. As I say, Percy was away and the garden was getting too much for Madeline. But Nelson's own little girl, on the other side of the cottage, let out a great scream. Nelson ran to her, dropping the scythe. He never dreamed that Sylvia, who was only six herself at the time, would run from the kitchen at that same moment, to save her friend. It really is all so terribly sad. No one could have predicted it. As it happened, the little Nelson girl had only seen a snake.'

Something sank within the exile, like a log falling – dead and cold – from a grate. 'I see.'

Bertie mistook his disappointment for sympathy. 'It took the Nelsons a long time to return to Rackham, although they and the Lucases are old friends. For all I know, this might be their first visit since the accident. Naturally they helped Madeline in absolutely every way they could while Sylvia was in hospital for all those months. Poor chap. It was a tragic accident, and no one is to blame, but I don't imagine Nelson will ever forgive himself for' – he chose the word carefully – 'injuring a child.'

For crippling a child. Bertie didn't need to say the word for them each to know.

Lawrence shook his head slowly, as if to say, what a sorry tale.

Nelson. The fault was Nelson's. The revelation moved across his brain like an eclipse.

And that should have been an end to it. 'The End'. Percy was not to blame, after all. Lawrence knew that finally.

But the story was not to end here.

Trust the tale, not the teller.

Perceval Lucas must still be punished for his war, the War; for his passivity and moral paralysis when faced with the defining event of their generation. *The leg did not move. There seemed a great gap in his being.* The outer life *neutered, neutered* must be made to match the inner.

And so the story of their paralysed generation began in the little English paradise of Rackham Cottage in 1915, with a cipher of a husband and father – a soldier to whom Lawrence would give life, only to strike him down on the page.

The story would end, finally, in 1928, in another ancient English wood, in the tale of Sir Clifford Chatterley, a paralysed war-hero and an 'emotional cripple' of a man; of his gamekeeper, Mellors, a stubborn loner lost to life; and of Lady Constance Chatterley, who longed to love and be loved. More than a decade away from the revels and fireworks of Rackham Wood, Lawrence, approaching death and never out of the woods himself, would try to dream his country whole.

The following week, Lady Cynthia Asquith visited Greatham in the Downing Street motor, with Beb, home on medical leave, and their little boy John. Notwithstanding the Lawrences' open invitation, her return was unexpected. On her previous visit that spring, she had commented to Lawrence that she had never seen anything as pretentious as the Colony.

She had sniffed at its 'library', with books by Alice, Viola, and the family's friend Francis Thompson, displayed on a shelf beneath the John Singer Sargent study of Alice – a study in pencil. Cynthia was – discreetly – surprised to find artistic ephemera framed and hung, though she refrained from remarking that her own dear mamma and aunts had been painted by Sargent in their family home on Belgrave Square, a monumental canvas widely thought to be one of Singer's finest.

Unusually for him, Lawrence remained circumspect. He suspected his guest envied the Meynells their idyllic Sussex retreat, their ease and peace of mind. Poor Lady Cynthia hadn't known peace for some time. Beb Asquith 'was no longer her dear old Beb', not since the outbreak of the War. Her little boy John was wrong in the head and did not improve. Motherhood was trying, even with a nurse. Cynthia wanted only to read, edit and write; to hear fine ideas and the best political gossip. Above all, her money worries were persistent, and that was a burdensome secret for her to bear.

As she and the child stepped from the car into the quadrangle, they were received by Lawrence – Frieda had already departed for Hampstead – and Lady Cynthia noted immediately that her friend had lost still more weight, even in the three weeks since Brighton. Wilfrid Meynell emerged to greet the visitors. The day was hot, and John was fractious and unruly after the long drive.

The boy's father walked away from the welcome party, with hardly a word, to pace in the lane. 'Stretching his legs,' said Cynthia. He seemed to Lawrence to be, not merely reserved, but distracted and queer in mood. He had been granted leave to sort out his teeth – smashed in an explosion of some sort – and no one, Cynthia warned in her note of the previous week, must commiserate or seem to notice. Beb *could* speak, but his words, she said, were rather slurred. After his dentist appointment, the first of three, they would set out, directly, for Sussex.

Beb joined them at last, and John set upon his father, pounding his leg over some perceived injustice. Beb hardly reacted, and Cynthia, crouching down by the child's side, was unable to calm him. 'I'm not sure what's worse,' she said under her breath to Lawrence, 'his beating poor Beb or the kicking he gave earlier to the Prime Minister's car.' Lawrence suggested Cynthia should take John into the kitchen of the cow-shed for a cool drink at the kitchen tap.

Inside, at the refectory table, Cynthia took the liberty of picking up a thin sheaf of manuscript pages as she waited for her son, who had insisted on drinking straight from the tap without her help. She had only been allowed to haul a stool into place so that he could reach. Then he shouted that she must stand in the sitting-room, and not look at him while he had his drink.

'You're looking!' he accused.

'I am not! I swear!' She took two steps back, receding around the corner. He was a little terrorist, and how she wanted to run from him.

She turned to the manuscript. Lawrence, evidently, was typing – though not well – for himself; there were numerous scorings-out and corrections. He had added a title by hand, with a question mark: 'England, My England?' Was the title in question or his country? Both, perhaps.

She was reading the opening page when John presented himself. She hadn't heard him get down from the sink, so absorbed was she in the story. His shirt was sodden and dripping. 'One moment, darling.' She read on, mesmerised.

The dream was still stronger than the reality. In the dream, he was at home on a hot summer afternoon, working across the little stream at the bottom of the garden, carrying the garden path in continuation on to the common. He had cut the rough turf and the bracken, and left the grey, dryish soil bare. He was troubled because he could not get the path straight. He had set up his sticks, and taken the sights between the big pine-trees, but for some unknown reason everything was wrong.

Her little boy stood, staring fixedly at her. How he simmered, she thought. At times, they disliked each other intensely. Their greatest difficulty, however, was that she did not know how to love him, and he knew that she did not.

In the boot of the great Downing Street car lay a rocking-horse for the nursery. An expensive purchase earlier that day, but it might appease him – or allow him to burn off some of his wild energy. Beb had no view on John's behaviour, or on anything much these days. On the way to Greatham, he'd stared out the window at Sussex as if the scenery were made of card and paste. The phantasmagoria of life in the trenches had overtaken the reality of everything else.

In the car, beside her on the back seat, he'd kept touching his mouth where his teeth had been, and it revolted her. The dentist had informed them that there was nothing else for it; the cracked stumps would have to go. Beb had simply stared at the ceiling, twisting in the chair as the dentist gripped and pulled, but the pain had hardly registered on his face. The contradiction of his agonised body and his emotionless features had been most disturbing. She'd never forget it. Her husband was somewhere else, and didn't know how to come back.

Which left her to cope with their abnormal son, a cold and raging child. Yet John was unnervingly perceptive. In the cow-shed, he glowered as she read from Lawrence's pages. 'Are you a thief, Mother?'

His dripping shirt was making a puddle on the floor.

She felt herself blush and returned the pages to their place beside the typewriter. She had to resist the urge to pat her son dry, for she knew he must not be touched if it could be helped. He'd go rigid as a board and shout or wail as if he were being murdered.

She feared she had no affection left for this small, fierce boy who would show her no love or affection, nor even any love of the life she'd given him. She resented him all the more for having made her arrive at this fear of herself, the fear that she could not love her own child; that *she* was the unnatural one, because at times she found him so repellent, she wished him gone. Gone where, or by what means, her brain would not permit her to imagine.

Beb was lost to her; her true friend Lawrence, typically, had already observed as much for himself. Her husband was still in the trenches, he'd told her gently, or his soul was, rather. She'd almost wept at his words, at his understanding. She had been, until Lawrence, so alone with her problems and the shame.

Beb was strapping in build, but a poet by inclination, and too sensitive for any war. Now, they had no money, and Beb couldn't grasp that fact at all. He wouldn't ask his father for help. He didn't seem even to hear her pleas. 'As you like,' he often said. 'As you like.' Their future, and that of their two small children, fell to her.

When she and John emerged from the cow-shed, her husband, Lawrence and Wilfrid Meynell were standing nearby, their heads bowed over Beb's slow, spluttering account of a recent military offensive. The men listened thoughtfully. She wondered if Beb was even halfway intelligible. The dentist had promised false teeth.

Lawrence turned to her as she and John approached. Her friend's corduroy jacket hung off his shoulders, but he was full of his old warmth and vitality, with those curiously significant blue eyes and an easy smile for her uneasy son. He instructed the boy to run around the orchard to dry himself off and, miraculously, the boy did as he was told. Careless the spaniel ran after, and John seemed glad of his canine company.

Wilfrid Meynell smiled at Beb. 'Lawrence has a way with children, does he not? We shall miss him greatly when he leaves.'

Somewhere, turtle doves purred, casting the drowsy spell of an English summer. A tremor spread across Beb's cheek.

'His teeth,' Cynthia said, joining them. 'They've been an ordeal, I'm afraid. Time for us to be off.'

They had only just arrived. Lawrence said they must at least tour the area in their motor. He would be happy to show them. Then, he would hop out, their man could drive on, and he would walk back.

How cheerful he looked, Cynthia thought, even with Frieda away.

Later that day, Lawrence scribbled additions to his story and skimmed its pages, satisfied. It began as a Sussex fairy tale might.

They had three children, three fair-haired flitting creatures, all girls. The youngest was still a baby. The eldest, their love-child, was the favourite … Then one day this eldest child fell on a sharp old iron in the garden and cut her knee. Because they were so remote in the country she did not have the very best attention. Blood-poisoning set in. She was driven in a motorcar to London, and she lay, in dreadful suffering, in the hospital, at the edge of death. They thought she must die. And yet in the end she pulled through.

But every tale must darken.

In this dreadful time, when Winifred thought that if only they had had a better doctor at the first all this might have been averted, when she was suffering an agony every day, her husband only seemed to get more futile and more false. He stood always in the background, like an exempt, untouched presence …

They were separate, hostile. She hated his passivity as if it were something evil.

She taunted him that her father was having to pay the heavy bills for the child, whilst he, Evelyn, was idle, earning nothing. She asked him, did he not intend to keep his own children; did he intend her father to support them all their lives? She told him, her six brothers and sisters were not pleased to see all the patrimony going on her children.

The author approved of his choice of names: 'Winifred' for Madeline, which had an internal echo of 'Wilfrid', Madeline's father's name. That was fitting, as she *was* of her father, her father who kept her family; she did not belong to her husband. Perceval was rechristened 'Evelyn', and Lawrence liked, not only the coincidence of '-eval' and 'Evel-', but also the subtle *double entendre* of 'Evelyn' and 'evil'.

She hated his passivity as if it were something evil … He was not idle; why, then, would he not take some regular job? Winifred spoke of another offer—would he accept that? He would not. But why? Because he did not think it was suitable, and he did not want it. Then Winifred was very angry. They were living in London, at double expense; the child was being massaged by an expensive doctor; her father was plainly dissatisfied; and still Evelyn would not accept the offers that were made him. He just dodged everything, and went down to the cottage …

The child … was a cripple; it was horrible to see her swing and fling herself along, a young, swift, flame-like child working her shoulders like a deformed thing. Yet the mother could bear it. The child would have other compensation. She was alive and strong; she would have her own life. Her mind and soul should be fulfilled. That which was lost to the body should be replaced in the soul. And the mother watched over, endlessly and relentlessly brought up the child when she used the side of her foot, or when she hopped, things which the doctor had forbidden …

But the father could not bear it; he was nullified in the midst of life. The beautiful physical life was all to him. When he looked at his distorted child, the crippledness seemed malignant, a triumph of evil and of nothingness. Henceforward he was a cipher. Yet he lived …

His wife was set fast against him …

There was a state of intense hard hatred between them.

He wrote the story and, as the magic of the words made contact with the page, it was suddenly so.

He did not spare himself his own harsh judgement. He knew what he was. He made up stories about other people's lives while men suffocated in the mud of France. He was shamefully dependent on the charity of others – the very weakness for which he damned Percy Lucas. Moreover, unlike Lucas, he was weak in body – and at times weak in soul as well. He failed to control his temper. He was weary of his wife. They had, together, wearied others. Frieda was fecund enough, but he had proved unable to father children. His seed was bad.

He shook himself and concentrated. Back he went to the old cottage in the dell, adding a line by hand: *The children were tentative and uncertain, or else defiant and ugly. The house was hard and sterile with negation.*

Slowly the story came to life.

The family was down at the cottage when war was declared …

There, in the absolute peace of his sloping garden, he was aware of the positive activity of destruction, the seethe of friction, the waves of destruction seething to meet, the armies moving forward to fight.

The next time he went indoors he said to his wife, with the same thin flame in his voice:

'I'd better join, hadn't I?'

'Yes, you had,' she replied; 'that's just the very thing. You're just the man they want. You can ride and shoot, and you're so healthy and strong, and nothing to keep you at home.' ...

Evelyn Daughtry enlisted in a regiment which was stationed at Chichester ...

He was her lover for twenty-four hours. There was even a moment of the beautiful tenderness of their first love. But it was gone again. When he was satisfied he turned away from her again. The hardness against her was there just the same. At the bottom of his soul he only hated her for loving him now he was a soldier ...

He was a potential destructive force, ready to be destroyed ...

All he could feel was that at best it was a case of kill or be killed ... We're all out to kill, so don't let us call it anything else.

So he took leave of his family and went to France.

The following day, the draft complete, Lawrence sent 'England, My England' – *sans* question mark – to his agent. Then he packed up his typewriter. It had been worth the battle with the keys and his cough, even if the story would only ever find a home in America. At least it would be out in the world. At least it would have a life of its own.

He left the ranks of the Now Not Dead. He felt, quite suddenly, born anew as a writer. He was also free of Frieda, if temporarily. His chest improved with the dry weather. Larks sang in the barley, crimson poppies splashed the fields, and thanks to his efforts, Mary passed the entrance exam for St Paul's School for Girls.

Privately, he was immensely proud of her, and to show it, he let her sing her summer away and take as many pictures as she liked for her photographic flip-book. She followed him in the early mornings to Rackham Cottage, where he had taken charge, as promised, of the Lucases' neglected paradise. Percy was gone again. The garden was coming along. The hollyhocks, eight feet tall, swayed on the breeze. Forget-me-nots, blue and lacy, covered the perimeter beds.

In the days and weeks he laboured there, assorted women, Viola's friends, came to stay in the old cottage to enjoy the fine weather. He found women endlessly interesting, and was happy to pause in his work to chat, commiserate and pry.

Eleanor, visiting again, reported that her sister-in-law, Joan, was safely delivered of her baby, if now rather lonely because Bertie seemed to live at the theatre when he had a play on. Eleanor did not mention Joan's sister, Rosalind Baynes. Not a word or casual remark. Six months on, he still felt the loss of this woman he did not know, as tenderly as a scar.

Yet how *to* know her? In spite of the mutual connections he had deliberately forged, she had not appeared.

He possessed only her story, that of her marital history. He wrote again to Bertie Farjeon, her brother-in-law, proposing for the second time a collaboration based on the real-life story of the Bayneses' marital breakdown. It would be a 'state of the nation piece' – a play or a novel. Pre-war England would be depicted in the character of the warm and natural wife who had been betrayed by the modern husband, a 'rational', sterile man of means and education, who knew not how to honour his wife or to see her for who she truly was. The renewal of the nation, he told Farjeon, could only begin with the renewal of men and women; with true relations, true marriages, not social contracts. *That* could be their novel or play.

He didn't hear back.

Yet the idea would not leave him.

At Rackham Cottage, when Mary wasn't looking for snakes and rabbits, she took pictures. She photographed the exile mulching the roses and hammering a new arbour. She caught him chopping down a tree and scything brambles. She even mischievously stole a picture at the side of the cottage, his bare back turned, as he scrubbed himself at the tub.

Madeline was grateful for his efforts. The entire family was.

Above all, with Mary's education now assured, he felt he had re-paid his debt to the clan, and to Wilfrid Meynell in particular.

He no longer owed them a thing.

In his final weeks in Greatham *I ought never, never have gone* he felt alive in his being for the first time since he'd walked in the Lake District with Kot; since those innocent hours before they'd heard the news of war declared.

The Rainbow was moving at last towards publication – a payment was forthcoming – and his new story, 'England, My England' *was* to be published. His agent had placed it in the *English Review* no less – the exile could have kissed its Covent Garden floorboards.

Instead, he wrote cheerfully to Lady Cynthia: 'You will find in the October issue of the *English Review* a story about the Lucases. No doubt you remember we passed by their garden on your last brief visit.'

The landmine had been laid.

E. V. Lucas – Edward – Percy's literary brother, was the first to feel the blast. He'd had an early warning from a colleague who read manuscripts for the *English Review*. The colleague wrote: 'Sorry to say, and strictly on the QT, D. H. Lawrence's story for the October issue will be of interest to you.'

Edward Lucas flipped through the proof-copy.

Later that very day, in the Tavistock Street office of the *English Review*, he made threats on behalf of his brother, who, isolated from the world on his army base, knew nothing of the story. The editors coolly informed him no changes would be made.

What was to be done? His brother was preparing for battle, for the trenches. He could not burden him with such worry, yet the story was a damnable defamation.

> *He was not idle; why, then, would he not take some regular job? Winifred spoke of another offer—would he accept that? He would not. But why? Because he did not think it was suitable, and he did not want it. Then Winifred was very angry. They were living in London, at double expense; the child was being massaged by an expensive doctor; her father was plainly dissatisfied; and still Evelyn would not accept the offers that were made him. He just dodged everything, and went down to the cottage.*

The details were plentiful, instantly recognisable and shockingly untrue, which made it the cleverest sort of libel. Lawrence had betrayed Percy and the Meynell family utterly.

The *English Review* enjoyed a healthy circulation among the Meynells' *the Marshalls* friends and associates. The family would have to be warned. He would go to Greatham directly to break the news to Wilfrid Meynell. With any luck, Percy, Madeline and the children might yet be spared all knowledge of the story. That's what he and Meynell would have to ensure.

Had poor Mr Meynell been shot? As Hilda entered the library with her duster, the great man himself was doubled-over in his armchair. Careless, the spaniel, trotted anxiously to and fro. 'Are you unwell, Mr Meynell, sir?'

He spoke into his lap. 'Forgive me, Hilda dear, but might the dusting wait?'

She promptly turned and left.

The words still swelled and swam before Wilfrid's eyes, although they had seemed nothing short of impossible as he turned the pages. Inconceivable. Yet, not only had they been conceived, they were about to be printed for all of London – and beyond – to read. It would break Alice. As it was, she was no stronger than a button on a thread. How could he tell her that this, *this*, awaited their beloved brood?

It didn't require a careful study of 'likenesses'. All of the Colony was laid out with careful malice in Lawrence's story: each of them, but most emphatically Madeline, Percy and, unbearably, sweet Sylvia. Lawrence had even brought to life again the terror and grief of the accident. How had he done it? Who had told him? It was obscene – a violation he would not have believed possible were the evidence not staring at him in black-and-white.

She was a cripple; it was horrible to see her swing and fling herself along, a young, swift, flame-like child working her shoulders like a deformed thing.

Wilfrid forced himself to read the story through a second time. The character modelled after Percy died a most horrible death on the battlefield. The detail was as malign as it was sensational. 'Evelyn' was wounded in the leg and groin. Then, most gratuitously, he was attacked by a marauding band of German infantrymen, and his face was hacked away by their machetes.

What artistic purpose did such horror serve? He could see none! It made him feel sorry even for the Germans, to be made so monstrous. His stomach fell out of him when he thought of his kind, strong daughter reading the story in all its intimate detail; not to mention Percy in the officers' quarters at Seaford. According to

Percy's brother, the *English Review* was sent free to all the army's reading-rooms.

Who had been living among them these six months?

That morning, he wrote a letter to Lawrence care of his new Hampstead address, outlining his grave concerns, and appealing to his former guest's better nature. The letter was returned unopened. His son's angry letter was also returned.

He discussed it with his sons and sons-in-law. Together they decided to give it time. What else could they give it? They were helpless in the face of such an accomplished fiction. The names had been changed, but little else. Their identities were strikingly clear, events were clear – Sylvia's injury, Percy going off to war, Meynell's own acquisition of the Colony, its every geographical detail – while nearly everything else was a grotesque invention.

The summer issue of the *English Review* would be published at the end of September, for October distribution. It attracted serious readers of literature and letters – everyone they knew, in other words. Something had to be done, but what?

In late July, Wilfrid Meynell dispatched his two sons-in-law to 1 Byron Villas, Hampstead, the terraced house the Lawrences had taken following Lawrence's departure – nay, flight – from Greatham. He chose his sons-in-law over his sons because their heads were cooler, and because they could speak, Wilfrid believed, with greater detachment and reason.

The two men, Lawrence's peers, stood in the vestibule of the house and appealed to the exile to withdraw the story, for the sake of Madeline and the children, above all. At first, the author had appeared to listen patiently. Then a change overcame him. Colour came into his cheeks, his eyes blazed blue, and his face twisted, for suddenly he had realised he was speaking to Dr Caleb Saleeby, Monica's faithless husband and Mary's neglectful father.

The sight of the man – handsome, upright, arrogant and uninvited – enraged Lawrence. How *dare* Saleeby appear at his door lecturing him on the welfare of women and children? Here was the man who had turned poor Monica into the shadow of herself. Here was the man who had ignored Mary and her education. Here was the man whose wrongs he, Lawrence himself, had had to set right!

In the vestibule, a skirmish broke out and spilled onto the quiet road. Lawrence, the weakest of the three men, did most of the shoving and shouting, or did until he stumbled and fell on the front path. 'Out!' he hollered. 'Out of my sight!'

The story would not be withdrawn by either author or publisher. Wilfrid Meynell had no choice but to inform his fragile wife. Madeline would also have to be told.

Alice trimmed rose stems as she listened. By the end of her husband's account, a sticky trickle of blood ran from her palm down her white muslin sleeve. So full was her mind, she had forgotten the thorns.

The account Alice gave to Madeline was both stark and tender. She extracted from her beloved daughter a vow that she would never read the horrid story. Then they gently agreed they would not speak of it again.

Soft-hearted Alice had never issued a family-wide decree, but on the subject of 'England, My England', she did so now: *no* Meynell was ever to read it. In this way, when it was mentioned by friends, acquaintances, guests or strangers, as it certainly would be, they would remain free of the fiendish story. Mr Lawrence's malice might have flowered terribly, but it would not bear fruit. Furthermore, Alice made it clear to the entire family that Mr Lawrence's name was not to be spoken again at the Colony, nor in any of their houses. Never. It remained only to confess to her priest that she could not forgive the man.

In the days that followed, Madeline's sister Viola, Lawrence's devoted protégée, would feel the injury to the family deeply. It had been she, after all, who had invited the Lawrences to stay in Greatham. It was she who had so admired both the author and the man.

Martin Secker, Viola's fiancé, would attempt a defence of their friend to her – for Lawrence's sake, for Viola's, for the sake of literature, and in an effort to minimise the family's worry. His words, however, would engender a rift, and the pair would grow gradually more estranged until Viola decided their engagement should be ended.

In the months to come, Lawrence's publisher, Methuen & Co., will fail to defend *The Rainbow*, and Secker will step in to publish it, though he will simultaneously question his own judgement of both the novel and Lawrence himself. Lawrence was dangerous, and his books, Secker suspected, would never sell widely. Why gamble? But he did. For the sake of literature, if not necessarily for Lawrence.

Sweet Alice Meynell, the lauded poet-mother *whose poetry won some fame in the narrow world of letters* who had so enjoyed the lively company of her guests, will ask Arthur to dismantle the rose arbour Lawrence built at Rackham Cottage. It will be too sad a reminder for Madeline, and for Percy too in the future, when he returns from the Front and learns of the betrayal.

Alice will go over everything in her migrained head, and her 'wheels' will spin. How often the Lawrences enjoyed the hospitality at Rackham Cottage and Winborn's. Not that anyone gave it a thought. No one had measured or begrudged them a thing. Wilfrid, certainly, had never entertained the notion of any debt, be it financial or moral. In life, one simply gave if one could, and one felt happy – nay, blessed – to be in a position to do so.

As for Mary, Lawrence's devoted pupil, she will never forget the words of 'The Assassination of President McKinley' or the tutor and friend who transformed her prospects. After St Paul's School, she will not fulfil her farming ambitions, but she will, by way of Cambridge University, qualify as a doctor of medicine in 1930, the year of Lawrence's death.

On hearing of his death, she will remember suddenly, and with a peculiar joy, the frank exchanges they used to share during her lessons in the spring and summer of 1915. She will remember, too, his shuddering cough and his feeble walk. *'Are you sick?' she asked. She frowned at the way he clutched his ribs. Then she ducked her head under the table to look at his legs, as if something might have escaped her notice. 'Or are you crippled?'*

When taken to one side and told by Monica, her mother, that she must be a big girl and give something up for the good of her cousins Sylvia, Christian and Barbara, Mary will cry, as she rarely did. She will tell her mother she *cannot* throw out her book of photos. She *will* not. It is her most precious thing. Look! Here, she will say, here is Mr Lawrence duelling with Mr Forster – flip – here he hammers linoleum with Jack Murry – flip – now he poses in front of the bathroom beasty-tiles – and he's grinning by the hopscotch with Miss

Mansfield – then he serves Easter dinner in his pinny – and here he is, cuddling a snake by the apple tree.

She will promise her mother that she will hide her photos for ever from Aunt Madeline and her Lucas cousins; that they will never ever see them. But when Mary is at school in London, Monica will find the album in Mary's room and instruct Arthur to destroy it on his bonfire.

How will her lovely, warm-hearted sister Madeline be seen in the world now? 'Winifred', her fictional re-creation, relies on her father more than her husband. It has the ring of the unnatural about it. Lawrence has drawn a portrait of their most intimate life. Percy is defamed, detail by grotesque detail. As for dear little Sylvia, Monica cannot bear to imagine her niece reading the description in years to come. It is as cruel as it is untrue. Sylvia could never be 'ugly' to anyone. Monica does not believe Sylvia ever was even to Lawrence himself. On the contrary, Monica suspects he adored the little girl and her great stubbornness for life.

For her own part, Monica had been so fond. They had shared an understanding of what it was to feel too much. He alone had been able to make her laugh again; to restore her after her husband's abandonment. He had transformed her wild daughter into a proud schoolgirl. He'd been unfailingly kind and generous – kind enough to tell her about a time, while living at Greatham, when he'd almost ended his life in Brighton, from a sea-cliff. He'd wanted her to understand that he understood: how unbearable life could be. He hadn't wanted her to be alone with it, because that was the worst of all, he said.

Could you ever know another person? Could you ever truly trust? Had he thought so very little of them all? It was a stone slab on her heart.

Now, his name could not be spoken. All evidence of him had been removed or destroyed, everything except the fitted bookcase he'd built so solidly in Shed Hall. Viola conceded that the bookcase had to stay *in situ*, or the entire wall of her cottage would come down with it.

A clan is not merely a large family. It is a family with an inborn knowledge of the fragility of life and the need, above all, to endure – with a collective strength when that of any individual is unequal to life's blasts.

What of Percy? Would Perceval Lucas of Rackham Cottage ever read the story he had unwittingly inspired?

At the time of the story's publication in October 1915, he was remote from the world, on a windswept infantry base in Seaford, on the Sussex coast. As Second Lieutenant, he answered to one Lieutenant Clarence Gormley, an officer whom some of the men in the platoon had dubbed Lieutenant Gormless, although Percy himself deemed the moniker unduly harsh. Gormley, a man of sixty, had distinguished himself as a young man in both the First and Second Boer Wars. The long peace had meant that experienced, capable officers were now thin on the ground, so Clarence Gormley's generation were called to arms. Desperate times required desperate measures.

Gormley was a decent man but no leader. He understood infantry 'manoeuvres', not the new trench warfare. Few did. He was pale, even in summer, with a permanently bruised look under his eyes. He frequently had to gargle with ginger beer before barking orders. By nature, he was a shy man, especially in his later years, and he deplored all barking. Only a fringe of greying red hair remained on his head.

Until 1914, Clarence Gormley had been destined for the calm of the village green, for ruminative games of bowls with old chums, and for smoky afternoons in his well-appointed, comfortably upholstered London club. The man's fate – his quiet, slow progress towards a distant, peaceable conclusion – forked like summer lightning with the declaration of war.

Now, the trenches ran without a break from Switzerland to the North Sea. Who could have imagined that a single segment of the Front, between Ypres and Verdun – 150 miles as the crow flies – would be the landscape of men's nightmares for the remainder of the century?

After a series of false starts and changes to orders, Gormley and Lucas's platoon of fifty-three men was dispatched to the Front, at the end of June, 1916, by which time the offending issue of the *English Review* had been, one might have safely assumed, relegated to bonfires and wall insulation. That summer, Edward Lucas could finally rest easy in the knowledge that his brother, a dedicated reader, had not come across the humiliating story at his base in Seaford; after all, he'd had precious little time for reading.

Before Perceval Lucas lay the chasm of the century.

On the platoon's arrival in France, it joined the company, which progressed steadily at two miles per hour until the march came to an enforced halt at the sight of great clouds of dust hanging in the air. Maps were consulted, tea made, and tobacco chewed and spat. A post-bag was delivered and letters were read aloud. He received a letter from Madeline and opened it expectantly. They had quietly hoped, but no – it grieved his heart – she was not pregnant.

Later that day, as his platoon organised itself in the crowded support-trench, he and his men watched with sidelong glances as the lowest ranks, already veterans of the Front, collected body parts in sand-bags, in an effort to 'clean up' for the new reinforcements. Two gunners, laughing, threw a jellied eye between them.

If, earlier in the day, the clouds of dust had seemed harbingers of some unspecified dread, that dread now realised itself in the devastated landscape of mud which awaited Percy's platoon.

He tried to sleep that first night in the dug-out, on a bed made of struts and wire-netting. The walls stank overwhelmingly of creosote. The flies were beastly. He gave up on sleep and studied his *Field Service Pocket Book* by the light of his electric torch, but couldn't concentrate. Rats scrabbled in the darkness. He sat upright when three shells whistled overhead and burst in rapid succession. Shrapnel rained down.

In the middle of the night, he woke again and, this time, he rose and walked the length of the trench, searching for stars, the same stars which studded the sky of Rackham. But the night was grimy with the day's bombardments, and he saw nothing.

Or not quite nothing. He saw eyes – gleaming amid the bunks in the stubby candlelight, men awake, just as he was, in the small hours. A few had torches, but most relied on candles. One boy was rubbing hard at the buttons of his tunic with his toothbrush and the cleaner, which you had to buy for yourself. He looked no older than fifteen. Scores had signed up under-age, wanting to escape the grinding tedium of the factories. They had done that, all right. Suddenly they were marching with packs of seventy pounds on their backs. In some cases, they themselves didn't weigh more than a hundred.

England was strong, they told him. The Empire was big. England couldn't lose. 'I just want to have a go at a Gerry,' one said.

Percy knew they were afraid, secretly, of what it might take to take a life at the end of a bayonet.

No one knew what the War was about. What was it to stop? One fought so it would finish faster, but no one could quite remember what it was about.

As the company had approached the Front, they'd been instructed to lighten their kit to a maximum of thirty-five pounds – the pressure of space, of accommodation. Comforts were jettisoned.

In the trench, Percy saw a man who lay reading in his bunk wearing only his jacket and shirt-tails. By the light of the man's candle, Percy could see his legs were covered in angry sores.

'My puttees,' the man said, though no question had been put. He had barely looked up to see who he was addressing, and he had a sly-sounding voice, with menace in it, as if warning the officer off from any idea of lingering. It was his territory, that sly voice said. The man's eyes, when he did raise them, were hyper-alert, too awake, glittery. He was one of the men Percy had seen gathering up body parts.

Because Percy hovered, uncertain whether he should inquire or move on, the man elaborated: 'They go solid with the mud, the ruddy things. Never dry out.'

Percy left, and returned minutes later, laying his own spare pair at the end of the man's bunk before turning again to go. But the soldier sat up all of a sudden, rolled the clean, new puttees into a bolster for his head, and reached into his pack. 'Go on,' he said, in his sly, cold voice. 'Have it. Fritz made it.'

In the palm of his hand was a coin of chocolate, wrapped in silver foil. Percy blinked, bemused.

'I won't tell no one, if that's what you're Hamletting about. Fair's fair.'

Percy shrugged and took the chocolate while the man continued in his cold, hard voice. At noon that day, he said, three of his number had met three German soldiers halfway across No-Man's-Land. Each party brought with them an interpreter, who had previously agreed the terms of the exchange.

On offer were sweets, souvenirs, reading glasses, wool stockings, fine-tooth combs, playing cards and periodicals. 'Their lot read

English, and are keen on our magazines and such. We don't want their magazines, but their chocolate, now that's another matter.' He looked at the officer by his bunk, who seemed to be assessing the chocolate coin. 'Go on. Better than a girl's nipple, that is.'

He unwrapped it. The chocolate dissolved exquisitely on his tongue.

'Well then?' The soldier studied his face in the candlelight.

Percy swallowed. '*Sehr gut.*'

The soldier smirked, amused. Then he reclined again, unpeeled two damp pages of his periodical, and folded back the front page. In the light from the candle stub, Percy could easily make out the headlined message across the top: 'You can send this Review free to the Troops from any Post Office. See page iii.' Evidently, someone had.

Miscellaneous journals and magazines made their way down the miles of trenches. Depending on demand, they could take anything from a few weeks to a year to travel the length of a single trench.

'My old man was a printer, and I could read from the time I was big enough to see over his press. Loved the old thump-thump, didn't I? Like a heartbeat, it was, at the back of our house.'

(Lean in. Can you see in the dim light?)

The periodical was grubby and man-handled, but Percy recognised names on the front page … W. H. Davies, Austin Harrison, Mary Webb, whose work he admired, and—

When they'd said goodbye that evening at Rackham over a year ago now, on a fine Empire Day weekend, Percy had told Lawrence, his author-guest, that he very much hoped to obtain and read a copy of *The Rainbow* as soon as it was published. Frieda had already started walking back to the cow-shed after the party. Viola joined the two men by the door. Lawrence had smiled and nodded his thanks over his wheelbarrow. Viola turned to Percy and promised she'd send him a copy of the novel herself, wherever he was posted. Then, at some point, months later, Madeline wrote to Percy, with news of various friends, including the sorry news that Lawrence's book had been confiscated by the police.

'What a blow,' he'd replied to his wife. 'Poor chap. Poor old Lawrence.' He'd felt for him.

But clearly Lawrence had *not* been universally rejected, for here he was in the *English Review*. Lawrence was not a man who was easily stopped or dissuaded. Percy had discerned that much that night by the fire-pit. Lawrence had sung his 'Assassination of the President' song with remarkable gusto for someone with so bad a chest.

In the quaking night, another shell burst somewhere, and Percy remembered too the fireworks of that weekend: the burning skeleton, the mock-Zeppelin, and his little Barbara, frightened and angry that the sky was falling.

'I'll give it you tomorrow,' said the soldier to him, tapping his *English Review.* He mistook Percy's silence for covetousness.

'That's decent of you,' Percy replied, allowing himself a hint of a smile. 'Right you are. I'll see you here, in this spot, tomorrow.'

The soldier peered over the top of the journal. 'You're a new arrival, aren't you, sir?'

'I am indeed.'

The man nodded quickly, and kept his eyes on the open page. 'Watch out for the crump-holes, sir – that's the craters. Gerry sometimes waits in there, to ambush you.'

'I understand.'

'If Gerry gases us, piss on your handkerchief and stuff it 'round your nose and mouth. But don't try to run back here, even if you can still see, because you'll be shot – by our side, that is. You want to collect your fortnightly pay, don't you, sir. I'll be damned if they're getting their mitts on mine.' He smiled. Most of his front teeth were missing.

'Thank you. That's good of you.' Percy reached over and touched the man's shoulder.

'What's more, the mud and the water are knee-deep in places out there. You'll see men in mud up to their eyes. Whatever you do, watch your step on those duckboards. Slippier than they look, and men drown. It's a queer, sucking kind of mud out here, sir. It's not like English mud. If you're ever offered a piece of rubber over a game of cards, or from Shyster Bob, take it, whatever the price, then split it in two and hammer it to the soles of your boots.'

'Ah – yes. I see …'

'There'll be men, at your feet, sir. That's what I'm saying. I want you to be smart about that. You can't not run over 'em. I just try to miss the faces when I can.'

Percy nodded.

The man's eyes moved left to right, across the page.

The earth was torn. He wanted to see it all.

In his frail, clear being he raised himself a little to look, and found himself looking at his own body. He was lying with a great mass of bloody earth thrown over his thighs. He looked at it vaguely, and thought it must be heavy over him. He was anxious, with a very heavy anxiety, like a load on his life. Why was the earth on his thighs so soaked with blood?

The man had disappeared back into the story he was reading. Second Lieutenant Perceval Lucas patted the man's puttee-bolster and turned to go.

Without looking up from his page, the man extended the length of his arm, like a toll-barrier. 'Touch me for luck, sir. All's that can, do. I'm Victor,' he said, 'as in "Victory". See you tomorrow night, right here, same time.' He rattled the *Review*. 'You're in luck. You've just jumped the queue.'

'Jolly good. I'll look forward to it.' He wanted to offer the man – Victor – something, something more than the puttees. 'Mind how you go,' he said, quietly.

It was all he had.

They waited in position, bayonets fixed, on the morning of July 1st, and listened to the mines go, on schedule at 7.25 a.m. In the distant village of Fricourt, the church bell rang clamorously as its tower collapsed.

The weird sound unnerved the men as they waited in their trench, as if the clanging of the bell were the terrible gabble of their own mute fear. Then the whistle went, and they surged forward, over the top into a world of noise.

There was no logic that carried Perceval Lucas forth as he ran on those strong, lean legs of his; no discernible path that had taken him from his garden by the stream at Rackham Cottage to one of the bloodiest battles in human history, there on the upper reaches of the River Somme.

The following morning, his company entered the village square, and kicked away, underfoot, the stone fragments of saints. The church was a smoking stump, and they saw that its bell-tower had crushed two houses as it fell. Cows wandered the streets, mad and fevered with not having been milked. No one else was seen, for the German garrisons had retreated from the village under the cover of darkness. Yet to the men of Percy's company, the Allied victory seemed as make-believe as that of children who mark territory in a field by dragging a stick across mud. For a further two years, the front-line would not alter by more than a few miles.

After the bombardment of thousands of shells, the air of the village was choked. The landscape that surrounded Fricourt was dumb-founded. Haystacks smouldered. There was no birdsong. Houses stood disembowelled.

As for Percy, he was not to take possession of Victor's copy of the *English Review* that night in the trench. He did not jump any queue of would-be readers. Nor did he see the village square, the broken church, or the fevered cows. Half an hour after the whistle went, metal blazed through his thigh, and another bullet lodged in his groin.

When he came to, he wondered dreamily if he were in his grave. It was a quiet, soft place. A few green leaves – five, he counted – rippled like frail pennants on a charred branch. He levered himself up on his elbows. He was hot, then he was cold.

He could see the village in the distance, still flaring under the day's bombardment. Such noise. He could hardly hear himself think.

He had run, fallen, into a crump-hole, a crater. But no – not a crater from a mortar charge. He was, he realised, in a natural hollow in the woodland floor. The wood had saved him.

How peaceful it was here. He wanted for nothing. Nothing, save sleep. Nobody. He was hot, cold.

The trees above him smoked. Where is your trunk? they said to him. *Where is your trunk?* He brushed away earth. He saw a khaki tunic. His. The body was his own. *I am here*, he said.

They said, *Search search root and branch.*

He surveyed himself. A chunk had been blown from his thigh, but the leg was still attached.

I am here, he said to the trees and the hole of sky.

His bowels gave way. The earth was cold and dank on his legs.

A burnt limb of a tree gestured. *Root and branch, root and branch.*

He managed to sit halfway up, to examine himself. He removed his mud-heavy coat and tied the clean side around his leg to staunch the flow.

Agony.

Elevate wounds. Expect snipers. Anticipate enemy retreat. Lie supine or prone until help comes.

He vomited. Then he fell back.

The trees said, *Stump rot black fuse green spark.*

They asked, *Stump, where be your buds?*

In Rackham Wood. White-blonde daisy heads

Over the stream, across the plank-bridge, their voices called.

When he awoke, the shadows on the forest floor had lengthened. The trees were silent. His teeth were stuck to his lips. He tasted grit on his tongue and in his molars, as if he and the earth were already becoming one.

He was lying with a great mass of bloody earth thrown over his thighs. He looked at it vaguely, and thought it must be heavy over him. He was anxious, with a very heavy anxiety, like a load on his life. Why was the earth on his thighs so soaked with blood? The leg lay diverted. He tried to move a little. The leg did not move. There seemed a great gap in his being. He knew that part of his thigh was blown away.

He would never read the words.

It was a mercy, and it was not.

He lifted his head and strained to see over the edge of the hollow. Bodies were strewn, like wood after a great storm. On the ground not far from him, a man twitched. 'They're coming,' he called as clearly as he could. Stretcher-bearers from the Regimental Aid Post – they arrived after an offensive to pick up those who were still alive and could not hobble. 'Basket-cases'. That was the designation. His throat was wretchedly dry. 'The stretchers. They'll be—'

He tried to steady his gaze. He knew the top of the man's head, its thin fringe of red and grey hair. He raised himself on his elbows. The man's chest was torn open and a lung was hanging out.

'Lieutenant Gormley, sir?'

Chiff-chaff, chiff-chaff, chiff-chaff.

A lone bird answered.

He would have shot him through the head had he been capable. 'Bless you, sir,' he called. His lips worked the air but only a rasp came. 'Bless you, I say.'

The moment was stark and holy. Trees creaked. Something ran over his feet. Then he slept in his cradle like a small boy and had bad dreams. In one, his face was cut away by a blade, and his blue, horrified eyes stared out at the enemy from the red muscle of his face. He understood perfectly well what had happened: he had lost his face. Lost face. That was the revelation that came with the dream.

True, he told himself as he woke with the shock of it. He had fallen so very quickly. It was his first morning at the Front, his first battle, his first hour.

He had left his family. No edict had required him to go.

That morning, he had only run. Nothing more.

His achievement, after the months of training and sacrifice, had been to cost the enemy two bullets.

There seemed a great gap in his being   *a   great   g   ap*

He woke, dreamed, remembered. A trembling shock overwhelmed him each time he surfaced.

He was like a flower in the garden, trembling in the wind of life, and then gone, leaving nothing to show.

The sound of the shelling grew fainter and more erratic.

He smelled something sickly sweet – the gore of his leg.

Flies buzzed.

There was something he strained to remember. What was it?

Someone would come. Wait. Elevate wounds.

He was hot. Cold. His body shivered. So did his soul. Sometimes he was in his body, sometimes adrift from it. Expect snipers. His hand was sticky – he couldn't remember why. Had he fallen from a tree? He'd gone down so fast, so suddenly. And yet he'd seemed to be falling for a very long time, as when the toe of your boot catches in a cobble in the road.

His teeth chattered. His brain was on fire. And his children were singing. Three voices. A bridge of sound over the stream from

Rackham Wood. He could see the stream again. The water was as clear as tear-drops. He could hear his girls: 'Where the bee sucks, there lurk I ... In a cowslip's bell I lie. There I couch when owls do cry. When owls do cry, when owls do cry.' But he could not cross to them.

He lay in the hollow. He had no voice. In the gusting smoke, he stared back at the hole of sky, at the eye of God, calm and unblinking.

In the Casualty Clearing Station, he learned that his body was smashed. The medical team diagnosed a comminuted compound fracture of the left thigh and pelvis. His femur and pelvic bone had not merely broken; they had shattered.

He watched wounded men stagger and totter in, bent-backed under the weight of their greatcoats and packs. Some toppled over repeatedly. Others had been sitting in water for three days. Their faces were white and haggard, or their eyes glared out from masks of mud. Most stank with the rot of their feet, and if they walked at all, they paced, in trances, and the mud in the bristles of their unshaven faces gave them the appearance of wounded feral things.

The medics operated. The type of injury, the position of the bullets, the effect on a running man, was still relatively new to them, but it wouldn't be for long. Wheelchair manufacture would boom, mobilising a paralysed generation.

The bullets in Perceval Lucas's leg were found and extracted, and a new sort of experimental splint was fitted. The thing was torture, but he said nothing, not to the nurse. Then he was transferred.

At the Base Hospital, a new nurse explained he was to be sent to London as soon as the traction transport unit could be arranged. The injuries to his pelvis complicated matters. He would not see action again. That much was obvious, even to him. But no doctor would discuss his chances of walking.

He vomited onto the floor.

He felt more anxious and alone in his hospital bed, in traction, than he had in the crater, in the smoking ruins of Fricourt Wood. The man next to him did not speak, but only stared at the ceiling, catatonic. He could see the man had bedsores, but there weren't enough staff to keep turning him, and he stank and oozed.

Percy found himself wondering about Victor with his sore-ridden legs and his borrowed puttees. Where was he now? Back in the trench? Had he out-run the bullets?

He himself had run when the whistle went, and on he ran. For thirty minutes of war, he had sprinted, agile, through mud, blood and water. He'd hurdled bodies. He'd felt the slap of his boots on duck-boards; the mud in his teeth; the noise of the guns in his marrow. The earth itself was cracking open, but he'd stayed upright, sure-footed, his heart drumming in his ears, until the first bullet blazed through him, and it felt as if he'd fall for ever.

He had been a calm batsman, steady when confronted by fast bowl-ers and late bowlers alike. He could hit a ball for six, with good height on it. He could play a pull shot. The swing always began in his legs.

He had climbed over the top and run when the whistle went. He had good balance and a strong stride. He concentrated only on the burnt remains of the tree-line that composed the village's eastern boundary. He did not think about the combat to come in the village, man-to-man. After the months of training and the confinement of the trench, the run itself was a strange liberation.

Now, in the ward, alone and formally *hors de combat*, he started to shake. His body had disengaged from his will, and the cogs of himself were sliding to the floor.

A nurse pressed his hand, then changed his dressing. His wound stank of paraffin. An orderly left a cup of ginger beer on the metal nightstand by his bed. He remembered Gormley, gargling with it before orders on parade. Percy asked the nurse how long a man could live with a lung hanging out. She didn't know.

She helped him to hold the cup. She reminded him he would see his family in London soon. He must inform them he was to be trans-ported so that they would be there to meet him when he arrived.

He imagined Madeline as he'd last seen her in their low-ceilinged bedroom: naked by the window, her skin flushed, her hips full and womanly as she bent to wipe his seed from her thigh. No child was made that day, nor would be now.

His little girls had sung to him as he lay blasted in the crater.

The nurse moved a chair to his bedside and prepared to take down a letter. She said she would listen to what he said but that she would not *hear*.

Dear Brother,

As everything is in the papers, there is no harm telling you that I was between Fricourt and Mametz. I 'went over the top' in the first line of my battalion as I indicated to you in my last letter, leaving at 7.27 a.m. and lying out in front between our shell-bursts and theirs. Ours stopped at 7.30 and we dashed on, but I was hit at about 8 by two machine-gun bullets from the flank which broke my thigh high up, going right through but missing blood vessels and nerves. So I sat where I was for nearly 8 hours till a doctor & stretcher-bearers came. I was fortunately in a sort of natural crater, so, though shells were bursting quite near all the time, I was under cover. The battalion swung past me very quickly, but there was a fair amount to watch.

Then an agonising journey of about two miles on a stretcher to the first dressing station. Then in ambulance wagon to another dressing station where I spent the night & went under chloroform.

Then two tedious days down the Somme in barges.

Now at a base Hospital, where I shall stay until considered fit for England. The wounds don't tire me so much as the splint, which is hellish. And I have had no sleep for days & a lot of acute biliousness & dyspepsia. However I am getting on to the food again now, and all things considered am not feeling too bad. My nerves are a bit rocky but probably owing to lack of sleep. My eyes are funny & my mouth permanently dry. I hoped to cross tonight but have just heard it is not to be. Shall probably go somewhere in London & will notify you on arrival.

Yours ever,
P.

The letter was sent out with the next transport, but its author was not. Within hours of the letter's composition, gas gangrene set in. Percy's fever intensified into a delirium; his left leg turned pale and then brownish-red. The smell of pus grew strong, and his leg swelled so quickly, it was actually observable to the nurse as she stood by his bed.

So many things go out of consciousness before we come to the end of consciousness.

The leg was amputated.

There seemed a   great g   a   p—

The gap stretched into a void, and there was the plank-bridge by the brook. He walked across it, over the common and farther still, onto the green of Greatham. It didn't matter that his cricket flannels were soaked in blood. No one seemed to notice. He had both his legs. That was the thing.

The match was finishing for the day, and he could hear the rattle of tea-cups from the marquee. Mary, his sister-in-law Monica's girl, stood gawky and nervous before him once again, asking if she would be allowed to take a photograph of the Greatham team.

He rallied the others. The chairs and stools were pulled out. He took a seat on the ground in the front row, drawing his long legs into the frame at Mary's instruction. On the count of three, he stared into the lens again, as if to say, 'I am precisely where I am meant to be – I could only ever have been here.'

The shutter opened and closed.

Let be, let be—

And Perceval Lucas did not regain consciousness.

Edward, Perceval Lucas's brother, had always been both predictable and precise in his movements, but on this particular morning, after the first post of the day, his housekeeper had no choice but to call for the man next door to help lever her employer off the floor of his study. The letter had arrived after the telegram.

I hoped to cross tonight but have just heard it is not to be. Shall probably go somewhere in London & will notify you on arrival.

Dear God.

Oh, Perce.

Later that day, Edward will travel from London to Greatham, bearing the sealed letter Percy wrote for his wife before he embarked for France. His sister-in-law, Madeline, will take it without a word. She will retire to her sister Monica's cottage and will hardly step outside that cottage for months. The news of Percy's death will knock a hole through the future in which she had never before failed to trust.

She is informed that Second Lieutenant Perceval Lucas will be buried in France. There will be no body for her to behold a final time – no silky hair, no calloused palms or smooth flanks, no arms or stump of a leg to wash and touch in that terrible inventory of love. Nor will there be a chest for her cheek, or a stopped heart for her to pound. Wake, *wake*!

It will be months before any thought of the story will occur to her. 'England, My England' will be of no consequence, given everything that followed. So what could it matter, she will ask herself, if it is read or ignored? Nevertheless, she will keep her promise to her mother. She will not read the unspeakable story.

Or she will not until fifteen years after her husband's death, when she comes upon 'England, my England' – Lawrence's second, expanded version of the story – in a volume on a friend's bookshelf in Italy.

Her mother is long dead.

Her husband is longer dead.

Madeline herself is nearly fifty when she yields to curiosity and opens the collection. Her three daughters are grown and married, with lives of their own.

She has recently learned of Lawrence's death, in France that very spring, only two months before. She was sorry to hear of it, in spite of the betrayal and the bitter falling-out with her family. He and she had been so easily fond.

She knows the true proportions of life. She knows, too, that the truths of love and life cannot be written over, no matter how able the author.

She turns to the opening pages, and beholds 'Crockham Cottage'.

She smiles. How droll.

Only it is not. It is *them*. Their own dear selves. As they were.

The timbered cottage with its sloping, cloak-like roof was old and forgotten. It belonged to the old England of hamlets and yeomen. Lost all alone on the edge of the common, at the end of a wide, grassy, briar-entangled lane shaded with oak, it had never known the world of to-day. Not till Egbert came with his bride. And he had come to fill it with flowers.

She is brought up short – by the sweetness of the detail, by the bright clarity of the prose. The story is alive as she reads. Even in far-away Italy, she can see again the green flanks of the Downs, the swaying pines, the brooding oaks, and the shaggy common. She can see the pink hollyhocks and the purple-and-white columbines, blooms her husband coaxed from the stubborn turf.

And how he had wanted her: Winifred! She was young and beautiful and strong with life, like a flame in sunshine ... Her hair was nut-brown and all in energic curls and tendrils. Her eyes were nut-brown, too, like a robin's for brightness.

The description of the woman is not of her; she does not delude herself. She was never any 'flame in sunshine'; she was dark of complexion, rather small, and dark-haired too, without beguiling tendrils. But her character's appearance, from whomever it is borrowed, is incidental, for here is her young husband, so vividly drawn, alive again, *tall and slim and agile, like an English archer with his long supple legs and fine movements.*
She turns the page.

And he was white-skinned with fine, silky hair that had darkened from fair, and a slightly arched nose of an old country family. They were a beautiful couple ...
He was not clever, nor even 'literary'. No, but the intonation of his voice, and the movement of his supple, handsome body, and the fine texture of his flesh and his hair, the slight arch of his nose, the quickness of his blue eyes would easily take the place of poetry. Winifred loved him, loved him, this southerner, as a higher being. A <u>higher</u> being, mind you. Not a deeper. And as for him, he loved her in passion with every fibre of him. She was the very warm stuff of life to him.

She will never know or need to know the import of the story. She has no interest in its author's purpose, moral, didactic or artistic. Its ending, she understands, is horrid and sad. But she needs no protection from its inventions and distortions. Indeed she is grateful to Lawrence. He has, briefly, returned her husband to her, something the army never did.

She has not known a sense of home – of deep intimacy, of body beside body, familiar to familiar – since his death. Perhaps she'll not know it again. Whatever Lawrence's theft from their lives, however unspeakable the fabled story, the author has allowed her to be with her husband again as she turns its pages.

She is proud, for it is their love and no one else's which charges his words, and that love cannot be bent to any purpose. It cannot be anything but itself. It defies both analysis and invention.

As she skims the words on the page, it is not the force of memory she experiences, but of *contact*. Across half a continent and almost fifteen years, she sees her husband's limbs in motion again and feels the warmth of his glance. She knows again, too, the silky hair, the strong line of the nose, the vein that rose in the middle of his milky brow, and the salt-sweet smell of his neck. She knows the piston-force of his lean legs, and the long weight of him bearing down on her until she broke open.

Love is so little understood.

Let be, he used to say mildly to her or to the children. *Let be.*

They were beknown and beloved.

It is rare, and it is enough.

'It upsets me very much to hear of Percy Lucas. I did not know he was dead.' Although those are his own words-to-be, Lawrence is not yet troubled. On this, the day of the exile's departure from Greatham, the death of Second Lieutenant Perceval Lucas is still almost a year away, and the strange divinatory power of 'England, My England' is known to no one, not even its author.

Before closing the door on the cow-shed for a final time, he sends friends dashed notes with his new Hampstead address, declaring he will never return to Greatham. Nor will he see the Meynells again, not any of them!

As is his wont, he gives in to an old superstition – which requires him to leave an offering in each place that has provided a roof for his head. He reaches into his case and removes the eye-stone he found on Brighton beach in May. There at the tide-line, he and Cynthia's boy had each closed one eye and looked through the sea-polished hole with the other, peering across worlds and dimensions.

'What do you see?' he'd asked the boy.

'Secrets,' said John.

It was the ballast of the eye-stone in his pocket the following day that had coaxed him away from the cliff edge, back to life.

He goes to the bookcase he made, gets down on his haunches, and finds the place where he failed to get the case to stand flush with the wall. In the cranny between wall and bookcase, he deposits the eye-stone, his offering. Then he reaches for his hat, hoists the cases and typewriter, and closes the door, stopping only to touch two fingers to the Madonna.

The family emerge, one and two at a time, from respective doors into the quadrangle. He flushes. He said his hasty goodbyes the previous afternoon and had expected to make his get-away without further ado. It is a misty, muggy morning. The trees drip, and Madeline and the three little girls, still on their summer holiday, are waiting to see him off when he appears. 'Of course we must say a proper goodbye!' she says when he protests at how damp she and the children look.

Wilfrid Meynell is next to join the farewell party, munching on a piece of toast. Careless trots alongside him, his tail wagging cheerfully.

'Alice,' says the patriarch in his warm, smoky voice, 'sends her affection and her fondest wishes to both you and Mrs Lawrence. She says you are to visit us in Kensington at your earliest convenience.'

Always moving on – from place to place, friend to friend: and always swinging away from sympathy. As soon as sympathy, like a soft hand, was reached out to touch him, away he swerved, instinctively, as a harmless snake swerves and swerves and swerves away from an out-stretched hand. Away he must go.

The story nudges at him again. It is a strong story. He has no regrets. Overhead, black rain-clouds sit strangely among banks of eerie white. The heavens bear down.

Hilda comes hurrying, with a wrapped paper parcel: buttered bread, she explains, with cheese and gherkins for his journey. 'You must get fat for me,' she tells him, and he lowers his cases to hug her soundly.

Mary and Monica emerge from 'Regreatham' Cottage, looking forlorn with faltering smiles. If he allows himself to linger, he will be gripped by emotion for this mother and child, as if they, Monica and Mary Saleeby, and not Frieda, are his true family. They need him and have come to depend on him. Why, he thinks suddenly, *is* he going? What is he going *to*? The same tiresome rows with Frieda, only in Hampstead. What old gods can survive there, in London's mighty shadow? None.

Mary grips her Brownie but when he removes his hat and stands still for her, she says she is too sad to take a photo. Then, 'Wait!' she insists and, remembering something, she runs back inside.

'I'm so sorry,' says Monica, over-apologetic as usual, and scratching nervously at her head. 'I explained to her it would be difficult for you on the train, with your cases and typewriter and whatnot, but I couldn't dissuade her.'

Careless has started to hump his leg.

Mary re-appears, bearing a brown card box. 'This is for you,' she says, blushing.

He throws Careless a stick and peers inside.

'What a beauty,' he says. His eyes flash with mirth, and wickedness too. 'I love it – and Mrs Lawrence will hate it!'

Mary shines with joy, standing on her tiptoes to examine her gift with a new pride. Wilfrid Meynell looks over the top of the box and his laughter booms out. 'An empty birds' nest. How apposite! The cow-shed shall be empty without you, dear Lawrence.'

Mary frowns as her grandfather laughs, and is suddenly unsure: 'Will you keep it or throw it out?'

'A chaffinch's nest?' he says.

She nods. 'Both broods have flown. I watched and made sure.'

'What do you take me for? Chaffinches make the loveliest nests.'

Her blush deepens, and she bends quickly to throw the slobbery stick Careless has returned.

'But how will you carry it all?' asks Monica. Her old fretful anxiety is rearing up again at the prospect of his departure. 'You mustn't feel obliged to—'

A commotion goes up in the orchard behind them. Then, out of the misty day, Viola appears, along with her friend Margaret – Dollie Radford's daughter and the hero-doctor's sister. The two women take everyone in the courtyard by surprise. It seems an entire group of Viola and Margaret's friends landed the evening before at Rackham Cottage, and a walk is planned to Petworth House. In the near distance, he can hear Ivy Low approaching. One can always hear Ivy Low. She is chattering to, or rather at – he turns and squints –

Eleanor!

It was only earlier that week that he posted her poems back to her with his admiration and encouragement. He didn't expect to see her again before he departed Greatham.

The four women are kitted out in macs and walking boots, with a rucksack each. They are intrepid, given the threatening sky, and he keenly wishes he were going with them.

'Remember,' he says warmly to Eleanor. 'Don't let your map get wet again! You are hopeless without a map!'

'You were as lost as I was on our walk to Chichester! More so!'

'I had no idea you were arriving today.'

'And you – leaving? Shame!'

The exile loves her face, open, unaffected, radiant.

Eleanor watches Arthur struggle with the cases. 'Frieda's things, I take it?' She cocks her eyebrow.

He growls.

She nods to Mary's gift. 'The nest, however, is essential.'

'It is.' He glances to the ground. 'Which is why *you* are to have my typewriter.'

'What?' she exclaims. '*Me?*' and she takes a step back. 'Are you not long for this world, Mr D. H. Lawrence?'

'Not if I have to hump my chattels as far as Hampstead. Have it, please – typing crucifies me at best. Be sure to visit me in our new abode. I expect you to come bearing wet maps, songs and poems. I shall be lost if you don't. Come see me through this unbearable war, won't you?'

She nods, and he squeezes her arm.

He goes next to Viola and draws her to him. 'Thank you for your cow-shed, my dear friend,' he murmurs. 'Thank you for putting up with us – with me especially.'

She smiles up at him. 'It was a pleasure and an honour.'

'Give my best to Martin, won't you?'

'Give it to him yourself! We shall see you soon enough in Hampstead!'

He nods, steps back and looks away. 'I hope so,' he says. And he does in that moment. He does earnestly hope. Tears prick at his eyes. Why is his life so transient? Where are the roots of himself? Will Viola ever speak to him again once the story is out? He can feel it now – reality snapping at his heels. He presses her hand. 'I couldn't have finished The Tome without you.'

'Nonsense,' she says and quickly kisses his cheek.

Rain starts to blow through the quadrangle, and he suppresses a cough. Viola takes the hat from his grip and places it on his head. 'I cannot wait till The Tome appears.'

He looks about him, at the red-tiled roof, the garden beds, at the cornfield across the lane where the stalks are bowing under their golden weight. 'I feel as if I've been born afresh here,' he tells her quietly.

Viola nods to the door of the cow-shed, to its blue-and-white plaque. 'I do hope you bid *au revoir* to your little Madonna. She will be sad – even sadder, that is! – if you haven't.'

He has laid his mine.

'I shall miss both her and you nearly as much as your bathtub!'

Viola slaps his arm.

'Well, at last!' Eleanor declares abruptly. 'You slow-coach!'

Another friend emerges from the orchard's veil of mist. Everyone in the courtyard turns to see.

'Luckily,' Eleanor explains to the newcomer, 'we've managed to delay Lawrence before he heartlessly abandons us. He should really be joining us for our walk, but apparently, he has his sights set on a dry train carriage, if you can credit it!'

Joan Farjeon *demure and maidenly as ever* smiles and nods to the assembly. Her hair is covered in droplets, and she clutches a handkerchief as if she might have a summer cold. At least the day is mild. She is down from London with neither husband Bertie, nor baby, it would seem. The exile takes off his hat to her, but Arthur is waiting, there is no time to speak or do anything more— when her sister arrives and takes her place at Joan's side.

'All present and correct,' says Eleanor to Viola.

Rosalind.

Ros.

The woman from the snowy hilltop. The vision of that January day. He with Wilfrid Meynell's field-glasses; she with her opera-glasses.

That wordless, dizzying exchange at the top of Sussex while the downland dreamed them both.

He feels a rush to the head, a wind knocking at his soul.

'Mr Meynell, may I present,' says Joan, 'my sister, Mrs Rosalind Baynes.'

'How do you do?' says Mrs Baynes to the crowd of Meynells and friends.

Time cleaves into past and future.

Arthur revs the motor.

'Yet another daughter,' Wilfrid Meynell declares, 'of the good Sir Hamo Thornycroft! You are most welcome, my dear.'

Mrs Baynes greets the Meynell sisters, with whom she was acquainted in their youth, on school hockey fields. Only then does she turn towards him, her expression intent but enigmatic. He is the departing guest of a family with whom she is slightly acquainted; he is a man she knows and knows not.

She is in her early twenties, perhaps six or seven years younger than he. Her gaze is veiled by the memory they share – she is shy, almost embarrassed – but that gaze is also direct. He cannot seem to separate himself from it, from her – and, unknown even to him, a study for a portrait in words forms in the gleaming strata of his imagination. *She was young and beautiful and strong with life, like a flame in sunshine.*

He can see the memory of the snowy day move across her eyes, in shafts of light and shadow, and there in the quad, strangely, he feels himself seen, truly seen, so unfaltering is her gaze. *He was rather frail, really. Curiously full of vitality, but a little frail, and quenched. Her woman's instinct sensed it.* He is discomfited, and magnetised to the spot.

Arthur climbs out of his driver's seat and takes the birds'-nest box from the exile. 'That's everything, Mr Lawrence.' Which is to say: you are about to miss your train.

Wilfrid brushes himself of crumbs and offers his strong hand. 'God speed, Lawrence. Don't forget us – Palace Court, Kensington! Never far!'

Lawrence turns to Hilda. He thinks of the day she rushed into the cow-shed, overwhelmed by the news of her brother's death. He remembers how slight her frame was in his arms.

'Your lunch is on the car seat, Mr Lawrence. Mind you don't sit on it!' She reaches for his hand.

He kisses her forehead, as if she is the dearest of them all, and doubtless she is, for she knows the beautiful fragility of life better than any of them. Her brother was not yet eighteen when he was buried alive in a collapsed trench.

Everyone pretends not to mind the rain, which is heavier now. Madeline and the three girls walk him to the car. He hears the iambic thud of Sylvia's heavy leg as they cross the front courtyard. He feels its echo in his heart as he goes.

He never got to know the girl. She was always too 'apart', too unto herself, mysterious, injured and remarkable. He had been moved by her – by *her* more than by the plight of her leg – and, unusually for him, it had made him shy to approach in the familiar way of kindly adults. Nor did she ever clamour after his affection in the way the other children did.

She possesses a powerful independence of spirit, and is luminous with it. Indeed, in some peculiar way, as he stands in the courtyard now, he almost loves her as his own, and he regrets she is not.

Ros ... *rose-flame.* Has he imagined her? His eyes seek her out as he calls his final goodbyes and cheerios. But what can he possibly say? He is aware of his own passions; they are often tangled in farce. And he is a married man, a point of principle he values perhaps more than his wife herself.

He has almost certainly imagined her. Ros. Does that falsify his impressions? Or make them more true?

He will not know for another five years: Italy, the 10th of September, 1920. Hers will be the white house at the end of the terraced row, high on a hill overlooking Florence – a house and hill unimaginable to them now. The house will lie at the end of a steep track, above a flickering olive grove. Lights will arise in the balmy dark beyond her balcony, *like night flowers opening*. They will be new to one another, no longer the detainees of a country spellbound by war.

As the two stand – poised on the brink of an inscrutable future – in the grassy courtyard among the Meynell clan, something in their neurons, primitive and plasmic, something which admits no difference between memory and presentiment, brims with that September night to be, for such are the secret, unchartable transfigurations of love.

He forces himself to move along, smiling for all. He knows he won't have children. He knows he won't make an old man. He knows he won't be back. Everyone is suddenly both precious and ghostly; charged with vitality and significance, and fading as he beholds them. But it's too late to change his mind, and his nature will not brook indecision or vacillation.

Onward.

What choice does he have but 'onward'?

'I told Percy you were leaving us this week,' says Madeline, taking his arm as they walk to the motor.

It would be rude to turn away from her as she speaks, to see if Rosalind still watches. He cannot think clearly, cannot hear. His heart is in his gullet, and she, Ros, is a miracle and a catastrophe both.

'Percy said I am to thank you "most heartily" for looking after our garden. He asked me to send his goodbye and his great good wishes.' She kisses his cheek, and Lawrence, confounded, climbs into the car.

Arthur releases the brake, and the exile pokes his head through the window. He salutes the little Lucas girls, who wait sternly in the rain for their mother. His eyes find her again, Mrs Rosalind Baynes. *Her hair was nut-brown and all in energic curls and tendrils.*

309

Who is she?

Joan has turned to speak to Monica, but Rosalind doesn't join their conversation. She clasps her hands and stands as peaceably as she stood on that hilltop, returning his gaze.

The Meynellage begins to follow the motor as it pulls heavily into the lane. Rosalind disappears from view. A newcomer, she can only stand back as the family wave off their guest and dear friend.

England, the English people, make me so sad, I could leave them forever. He swivels in his seat for a final glimpse of the Colony. Mary has caught hold of Careless by the neck so that he can't run after the car. The three little daisy-headed Lucas girls are scratching at the midge bites on their bare legs. Viola and Eleanor are performing a farewell mock-Morris-dance in the lane, knocking big sticks together to make him laugh as he drives off. He does laugh. Arthur watches in the rear-view mirror and he grins too. Monica joins the group waving in the lane. In the rain, she looks like a long-faced weeping Madonna. He sees Hilda pat her arm as she waves fiercely to him. Wilfrid Meynell rocks on his heels, thumbs in his waistcoat. In the field across the lane, Rory, the children's pony, raises his head.

The exile feels disoriented, both buoyed up and jangled, as this vision of the Meynellage recedes. Madeline lifts her arm high as if to say, 'Do *not* forget – we are here.'

In this moment of leave-taking, he suddenly feels as if they are indeed his family, a true family who will offer him, for life, their company and warmth. He wonders again what he's about, what he's doing, why he's going, why did he write that story – and he is briefly overcome with an indecision that is alien to him. *Go back, go back*, a voice says. Eleanor, Viola, Hilda, Monica, little Mary – he misses them all already. And Rosalind: here, now, manifested. He will go back. He will withdraw his story.

Frieda seems to him in this moment like a lump, a growth which has been surgically removed from his person; once a part of him but now a foreign body.

He loves this place. He loves the Meynells. He loves them as if they are his own people.

Yet he does not turn back, and in little more than a month, when the proof-copy of his story 'England, My England' travels into the world, his name will be unspeakable in the Colony, and Mary's book of photos from 1915, the Year of Our Special Guest, will be destroyed.

The car is moving slowly up the lane when Barbara, the youngest Lucas, is seized by a childish impulse. She breaks away from Madeline and begins to run – on plump legs clutching her doll – through the rain and puddles towards the car. She cannot reach it, of course, but the exile watches her stubby exertions through the rear window. Her bright cheeky face is earnest and, as she runs, she holds her baby-doll upright by its ankles, as if the doll, also, must watch him go, or bid him goodbye, or see him off the premises. Perceval Lucas's youngest child holds her baby high, as if the doll is the last witness to the history they have all just become.

Daughter of the House

On the 10 a.m. London to Pulborough, Bernardine – better known as Dina – had just uncapped her pen when a large family burst into the empty carriage and seemed suddenly to be everywhere. She smiled brightly at the children, who bounced into their seats, excited at the prospect of a rural adventure beyond London. They had inherited their father's big ears, which shone on each fair little head, as translucent as petals.

She turned to the window where the last of summer flickered by like the fly-end of a film reel. On the embankments, plumes of buddleia tangled with wild sweet peas. Coca-Cola bottles winked and flashed and an old, green iron mangle surrendered to rust. She checked her watch. Half past already.

Time flew.

The child beside her pressed in to see whatever there was to be seen. Behind them, a brother and sister kicked and squirmed.

She bit her lip and shoved her manuscript – that's to say, half of what she tried to convince herself was a novel – into her satchel. Modern novels could be very slim, she consoled herself. Surely, she could manage a hundred and fifty pages, the length of a Virginia Woolf novel – if not with the brilliance of Woolf. Her Great-Aunt Viola had produced respected novels. But could she? If only she knew about something – about anything at all, really – or had something to say. Then the task might not have seemed so difficult.

One had to make up such *a lot*.

It was infuriating being young, and being forever told that novelists needed age and wisdom. What was she supposed *to do* for the next twenty years? Resign herself to mediocrity until brilliance finally dropped? She had stamina but she was no masochist.

She had tried sending off stories to the university review, but the editors were all very clever young men, and the last story had been returned with a one-word dismissal: 'Florid!' She sent others off to a few small but choice literary journals, but these, too, were all returned. 'Not for us'. 'Not sufficiently convinced'. The most encouraging reply was 'Try again'.

It was a depressing sight each month: the 'returns' envelopes in her pigeonhole in Peile Hall poking out at her like fat tongues. The porter would often look up from his desk, understand that the next instalment of her unhappiness had just arrived, and offer wordless commiseration with a glance over his specs, as if to say, 'No luck? Well, damn them.' She liked the porters of Peile Hall. They knew when to offer a hanky and when to turn a blind eye.

She thought she should begin her post-mortem assessment of her latest rejection, a short story which brooded in her satchel alongside her half-novel. Even her name looked wrong on the return envelope. It didn't *sound* like a writer's name. 'Bernardine Wall'. Was there, she asked herself, any less evocative name for a novelist than 'Wall'? She sounded like something one crashed into. Why couldn't she be a 'Meynell', as Granny Madeline had been, and Great-Aunt Viola, and her great-grandmother too – Alice, who had nearly been appointed Poet Laureate, *twice*.

She couldn't help but think, a little disloyally, that *not* to get that honour *twice* was almost worse than never having been noticed at all – a plight she understood – except that Alice Meynell probably hadn't felt the slight as she herself would have. Everyone among her elders remembered Alice as a 'gentle soul', with neither ego nor selfishness. But Dina, while not *entitled* to any ego – by dint of talent or position – was not gentle either, and, moreover, did not want to be gentle. She wanted to see things, do things and have 'experiences'. She wanted *life*, not a soft retreat from it.

Why, she wondered, did each generation always profess, in its grandiloquent way, that hope rested with the next generation, before passing the baton on so feebly? Then they, the same, down the decades. What good was that? It was a failure of courage, and a failure of imagination too.

She was twenty years old, and she went to parties, of course she did, but she could not bear to stand and smile for even *one* more garden-party, which were never really parties at all. Everyone nibbled like mice at crustless sandwiches and wrote thank-you notes afterwards, lying and saying they'd enjoyed it immensely. Worse still were her parents' drinks parties, where everyone stood sipping sherry and murmuring vaguely.

Was she really to wait a further twenty years for significance to arrive in her life and on her pages? In the meantime, did she have to function as a smiling handmaiden to everyone else, discreetly accumulating 'wisdom', only to be told in twenty years' time that she had missed a boat she didn't even know was sailing?

But she couldn't deceive herself. There was a problem, and *she* was it. Her nature was too passionate. Sometimes it made the 'society' of others seem mild to the point of sedation. Almost everyone else seemed content enough. What was wrong with her?

Only children, she decided, knew truly what life was for. As a child in the woods of Greatham and Rackham, she had known what it was to be alive under her skin, and she was determined not to forget it. Old people sometimes knew as well. Her grandmother, Granny Madeline, waiting for her now at Winborn's, certainly did. She possessed a playful, irreverent streak that was ageless.

But Dina's life to date, while outwardly fortunate and correct, had been sheltered: at Winborn's with her grandmother till the age of seven; then to her convent school in Bayswater; now, at Newnham College, Cambridge. The most eye-opening sights she'd experienced were of the animals of Greatham, both domesticated and wild: roosting, rutting, laying, cantering, giving birth and dying in stables, woods and fields.

Outside Winborn's, the bulls and stallions were still led up the lane each spring, decked in harnesses with red ribbon and bells, for the annual mating ritual. Everyone, from manor house and cottage alike, lined the route to clap and cheer. Sometimes, after the animal had passed, they raised a glass or fired an old revolver into the air. In its slow parade, the bull or stallion would snort and stomp, while under its ribbon and bells, its flanks rippled with muscle, and its undercarriage swung heavily to and fro.

In recent years, if she were visiting her grandmother during the break in the Lent term, she felt increasingly conscious of her own 'stasis' as the procession passed. She was well aware that the Greatham girls with whom she'd played as a child in the war years had 'beaux' and husbands now. Some had children as well. She had to be the only virgin left among them. Even the Virgin Mary, on the plaque on Shed Hall, seemed to look at her sorrowfully these days.

At Cambridge – at her all-female college – boys were forever being sneaked in and out of her residence, Peile Hall, with drainpipes the principal mode of transport. But she herself had never felt sufficient inspiration or motivation to take that risk, not even by her third year, when any self-respecting Newnhamite had the measure of things. What if she were rusticated? Sent down? Her father would have been furious, and her mother deeply disappointed. Only her grandmother, in rural Greatham, would have laughed and shrugged it off.

She was 'pretty enough', the other girls assured her, although she did wonder if that was 'damning with faint praise'. Her parents had never encouraged vanity or self-consciousness in their children, and as a family they had an unspoken policy in which they simply did not comment on the appearances of others. It was, she knew, beneath them, but it had left her ill-equipped among most her age.

She couldn't objectively see anything *wrong* with herself. She was tall, but not too tall; slim but not skinny. She had the thick, dark hair and wide eyes of the Meynells, and the fair skin and long legs of the Lucases. From her grandfather, she had inherited her 'aquiline nose' – or so said Granny Madeline. In the inventory of herself, she did not discover beauty, but she did not fare badly. It was not impossible, or even unlikely, she decided, that a boy might feel attracted to her. Would she feel the same? It seemed against the odds, two people not only liking each other, but wanting each other. What magic.

There had been no boys at her school, of course. Nor were there any at Newnham. She had joined 'societies': the Drama Society, the Ramblers' Society, and the Christian Society which, she was surprised to discover, was the most louche of the lot. The problem was that she had not *wanted* to 'go off' with just anyone, or even a friend of a friend from her year-group for the sake of it. She didn't want to 'have done with it', as other girls had for curiosity's sake, although she *was* curious.

She'd heard mixed reviews from the girls on her corridor. Four or five of them would gather on Sunday afternoons over crumpets and tea, often around the fireplace in Verity's rooms. Verity was a striking, auburn-haired girl who revealed to the others that, at the critical moment, 'it' had been so big, she'd half-expected a kidney to pop from her mouth.

Verity *was* thought to be an inveterate liar.

'Where does one *put* it all?' said another girl, Rosemary, her lower lip trembling. An awkward silence followed. Unlike Verity, who had maintained a smile throughout her account, Rosemary had made a schoolgirl error. *Don't show fear.* Everyone knew that. People could be merciless to those of their own age and sex and, predictably, after she left the room, Rosemary was dismissed as 'brainy' but lacking in sophistication and 'sex appeal'.

Verity and Diana were confident that 'sex appeal' was something they could identify as easily as a permanent soft wave.

Dina's bob wasn't waved; her hair was thick and straight. She lay low in Peile Hall and adopted a blasé persona. Privately, she didn't expect her first experience of sex to be the stuff of 'souls conjoined', but nor could she accept it was merely a hurdle to get past, or a sacred duty to be performed on her wedding night. If she waited, as her Church instructed, she might find she'd made a dreadful mistake, and the gate of Life would crash shut. She would have 'made her bed', her marital bed, and that would be that.

It made complete sense to her that Othello had wooed Desdemona with his stories. She only wanted someone who might catch her imagination. She only wanted 'a story'. Perhaps she even wanted to be *in* a story. Briefly. She wasn't greedy.

Her mind was made up: she *did* want to have sex, and sooner rather than later.

At that very moment, the high-spirited family in the carriage burst out laughing, as if all those ears had been listening to her every thought.

As she walked from the station, the fields of Greatham were shorn and gold-stubbled. The harvest was in. Somewhere a bonfire was burning – she could smell the sweetness of the smoke – and, in the hedgerows, the blackberries were ripe. She'd take a pail out later and pick for her grandmother.

Great-Uncle Francis was visiting too. As she arrived in the library, Dina surprised him with a kiss to his bald head before she had even dropped her satchel and overnight bag. Then Granny Madeline wheeled in the tea-trolley and seated herself in the winged armchair, where she proceeded to slice lemons for the tea and great slabs of lemon sponge. Dina, she said with a nod of approval, had timed her arrival perfectly.

Great-Uncle Francis, ever the man of letters, quizzed her about her reading for the English Tripos exam. She swallowed a forkful of cake, and projected her voice in the direction of the ear-trumpet he clamped to his head: 'The Moderns!' she called.

Francis sniffed. 'The Moderns.' His lot, in other words. It was hard to take one's own contemporaries seriously. One had seen them, close up and from afar, in too many compromising positions over the years. Were there actually any Greats among them? One was aware, he told his great-niece, of the cliques and lucky breaks; of the random breakthroughs and the flash-in-the-pans; of the inflated reviews and the overlooked talent – of which, it went without saying, he considered himself one.

Cambridge had just gone down a notch in his estimation. 'The *Moderns*!' he declared again with a harrumph. As a designation for academic study, it lacked rigour and distinction. What would follow it? The *post*-moderns? And the *post*-*post*-moderns?

'And who might these "Greats" be?'

Dina called out again for the benefit of his ear-trumpet. 'Virginia Woolf, Joseph Conrad, Katherine Mansfield if I'm permitted—'

His face crumpled, as if with a minor stroke. 'Do you remember Katherine, Madeline?'

'I do indeed. She was full of life. A *piquant* mind, as I recall, and an alert intelligence. Not that I knew her well …' Madeline leaned forward to pour herself more tea. Her eyes, when she looked up again, were veiled, as if the past were processing before them. 'She and I were only ever introduced.' She refrained from stating by whom – Lawrence, or He-Whose-Name-Must-Not-Be-Spoken. 'I like her stories very much. "The Daughters of the Late Colonel" makes me roar every time.'

'"The little colonial",' Francis muttered.

'*No*,' called Madeline, craning forward. 'The "*Late Colonel*"! It's a short story.'

'I know it is!' he said, vexed. 'The "*little colonial*" is what *some* used to call Katherine M. That's what she was, after all. Small in stature and from Australia. Or was it New Zealand?'

'Uncle Francis!' scolded Dina.

'I didn't say *I* called her that!'

'Well,' said Madeline, '*I* approve of your choice, Dina, whatever Francis and your don might say. It was heartbreaking to learn she died so young. In her early thirties, as I recall.'

'I always thought she must have caught it off *him*,' opined Great-Uncle Francis. 'The tuberculosis, I mean.'

'Off who?' asked Dina.

After all these years, he still couldn't say it. 'Oh, you know … That bearded chap. *Sons and Lovers … Lady Chatterley*.' Francis waved his hand impatiently.

'D. H. Lawrence!'

He looked up, slightly shaken.

'D. H. Lawrence,' Dina repeated happily. 'He's my "specialism" this year.'

Her great-uncle coughed into his napkin.

'Are you quite all right, Francis, dear?' Madeline's gaze was steely over the rim of her tea-cup.

'Shall I pound your back?' offered Dina.

'Francis, take a drink of your tea, for heaven's sake.'

He did as his sister instructed. The utterance of the accursed name had not brought down the roof of Winborn's. *How* had it not?

Dina poured herself more tea. 'I love his novels, those I've read, that is, and, if my proposal is approved by my tutor, I'll read absolutely everything by him.' She put down her cup, sprang to her feet and started searching the library's bookshelves. 'In fact, I thought he might be here somewhere …'

Francis scowled.

'You know …' she called over her shoulder. 'Old editions and whatnot.'

'Well, *you* prepared the card-catalogue for the library, so you should know. I *rather doubt* it myself.' Francis marvelled at his own powers of restraint.

Madeline would not meet his eye.

'I was seventeen when I did that job! I can't be expected to remember every book!'

Behind her back, Francis looked meaningfully across to his sister, as if to say, *Books here, by that man? When Hell freezes!*

Madeline shook her head. A warning. He was to hold his tongue. *She doesn't need to know about all that,* her eyes said. *Let her enjoy his books if she wants to.*

Yet the man, thought Francis – if man he was, and not devil – had wantonly injured their family. He had betrayed their parents' warm-hearted hospitality. He had humiliated dear Madeline and Percy, Dina's own grandparents. He had dreamed up that horrible death for Percy on the page of his evil story, a death that subsequently and sickeningly came true, in part at least, at the Somme. He had written grotesque words about Sylvia. 'Distorted'. 'Crippled'. 'Ugly'. How dared he?

He – Lawrence – had been the stunted excuse for a man. It was true: more than forty years had passed, but Francis still didn't know how Madeline could remain so calm.

For his part, he would honour his promise to his mother, Alice. He would refuse to speak the man's name. Yes, he would keep the truth from Dina, and let her pursue her own path. But he couldn't be expected to encourage it! 'His prose is far too preachy for my taste, and overdone.'

At the bookshelves, Dina turned, ingenuous. 'Gosh. Do you think? I've never read more wonderful descriptions. He breathes life into every primrose, larch and squirrel.'

'Dangerous,' muttered Francis. 'A *dangerous* man.'

'He grows more interesting all the time!' She joined them again at the hearth. 'Dangerous, how exactly?'

'With people. He's dangerous with people.'

Madeline shot her brother a look.

'With characters, that is. I always felt rather sorry for poor wounded Sir Clifford Chatterley, relegated to that mechanical bath-chair, and then vilified by both his wife and his author! Insult to injury. That's what I call it.'

'Uncle Francis!' Dina chided. 'Lawrence isn't hard on him *because* he's in a wheelchair! He's hard on him because he's mean-spirited. Sir Clifford is morally paralysed.'

Well, his creator knew all about *that*.

'The wheelchair is only the outward manifestation of his soul.'

'Is that so?' Francis grimaced.

'Moreover, Lawrence has given Lady Chatterley a war-hero husband in a wheelchair whom she wants to divorce. He deliberately stacks our sympathies against her – but we still love her! That alone is a triumph!'

'Well, I don't know if I'd go so far as to say I loved Lady Chatterley …'

'No?' Dina framed an inch of air with her thumb and index finger. 'Not just a little?'

A hint of a smile appeared on her great-uncle's face. 'I suppose it's possible I once lusted after her – a little.'

Dina took a swig of tea. 'Well, I should hope so!'

'Madeline,' he said, as if to save himself, 'I think I will have another piece of cake.'

'But *why*,' asked Dina, exasperated, 'is he – or was he – "dangerous"?'

Her great-uncle cleared his throat. 'Oh, that was just something Martin Secker, his publisher, used to say. Lord knows what he meant, but that man had a talent for trouble.' He stared into the fire, remembering. 'Charming at first. Offensive as soon as your guard was down.'

'Did you ever meet him?'

Francis had clearly married young. 'Whatever for?' the exile asked him over the piano-top. 'Nearly all marriages are frauds or failures.' He threw him a walnut. 'Is it because you were afraid of yourself?'

'I was rather in love,' Francis replied, blushing.

'I'm not sure …' He looked across to his sister, fiddling with his shirt cuffs. 'He might have passed through. Our parents were generous to all manner of artists and writers who needed a meal, a roof – or a bath, more often than not.'

Madeline sighed loudly.

'I believe my friend David – Bunny – Garnett knew him. I suppose I *might* have met him … But, as I did not "take to" his work, his impression was not, shall we say, lasting.'

Even Dina's grandfather, who had died in the Great War, long before she was born, seemed to stare out sceptically from his photograph as he listened to Francis.

Dina turned to Madeline. 'Did you ever meet him, Granny?'

Madeline greeted them at the oaken door, and Lawrence removed a piece of canvas to reveal an array of gifts: pots of sweet peas for planting-out in the garden – he would make a trellis for them, he said. A jar of apple compote. A loaf of bread he'd baked that morning – 'not as nice as Hilda's, but nicer than the baker's in Storrington'. A bottle of French wine.

Uncle Francis straightened in his armchair and cut across Dina's question, to save his sister: 'Now, *here's* a story for a girl reading English Literature. Henry James himself once retrieved a fan my sister dropped at a ball and returned it to her.'

Dina blinked. What else was Henry James to do with a fan? He was hardly likely to use it himself.

H. G. Wells was the host of the occasion and would later compare the sight of the portly Mr James stooping for the fan to an elephant trying to collect a pea.

Uncle Francis continued undimmed, in his efforts, to entertain and distract. He claimed that Virginia Woolf, on 'her throne' in the Bloomsbury Group, was always a tad superior when it came to their mother Alice's poetry, and also about the family's Catholicism. But what was less known was the fact that Woolf had once observed to a mutual friend: 'Well, at least the Meynells believe in *something*.' Atheism, said Francis, with a touch of superiority himself, did become rather sterile in the end, and the 'Bloomsbury lot' had always laboured under what he believed to be 'a barren intellectualism'.

Uncle Francis did witter on, Dina thought. But secretly, she regretted missing out on the Colony in its heyday. She'd have loved all the comings and goings, all the *interesting* people: Virginia Woolf, who had lived in Sussex as well, and all those writers roaming, hither and thither over the Downs, or so it now seemed to her. Her seminar tutor, the great F. R. Leavis, told her not to give it much thought: Woolf was 'rather over-boiled', and she was better off reading Conrad and Lawrence.

Of the latter she had read, chronologically – so as to travel through time with him – *The White Peacock, The Trespasser, Sons and Lovers, The Rainbow* and *Women in Love*, plus the censored version of *Lady Chatterley's Lover*, the only version her school library had owned – any other being, one, illegal and two, 'corrupting'. She had enjoyed its melancholy romance. At the same time, she'd felt rather cheated – of what, she still didn't know exactly. It had been like reading with dark spots swimming in front of one's eyes.

When she'd leaped up to scan the shelves in Winborn's library, she'd been searching in the secret hope that her grandparents might have purchased, in the twenties or thirties, a copy of the rare, original 1928 version, and that she might find it, before term started. But no one in the family seemed to have been a Lawrence fan.

In time, she'd have to read all his stories and poems too. Even the search was exciting.

She hadn't forgotten that Granny Madeline had not replied to her question. But the next thing she knew, her grandmother was on her feet, saying she might nap before supper. She squeezed Dina's hand and said she expected *her* to finish the last piece of cake. At that, Great-Uncle Francis crossed his arms and pouted.

In family life, we all revert.

Was Dina's novel doomed to be ordinary? This was the question which went around and around in her mind. She expected it was. What was there left to write? Who was there left to be? She was only another bright, middle-class 'Newnhamite', a girl with a good convent-school education and a great-grandmother who might have been Poet Laureate once upon a time – *twice* upon a time – but wasn't.

As students of Literature at Cambridge, her generation was expected to admire the Greats, but never to aspire to be one of them. That would have been foolish, and not only foolish, but laughable if you happened to be female. She was out of her depth when it came to her novel, and she knew it. She needed experience. She needed a life.

Other girls on her wing in Peile Hall had taken work as 'hotel-girls' at the Swan, the establishment in Cambridge known, she was informed, for its discreetly staged scenes of adultery; for help, in other words, with those divorce cases in which the co-respondent's name had to be kept out of the courts and the Divorce News. Verity and Diana 'educated' her on the subject one Sunday afternoon, strewn across a pair of nun-like beds, in the room of a shy girl called Judith.

Verity slid a Gitane expertly from the box with the dancer on the front – a slender silhouette of a woman in a gypsy dress, who raised a tambourine high. Dina was by no means averse to smoking, but she knew better than to attempt it for the first time in company.

Diana, who was as glacially beautiful as Verity was striking, explained that, as a 'hotel-girl', you only had to sit up straight, fully clothed, on the edge of a double bed in a perfectly nice hotel room, and be photographed, expressionless, as a photographer burst into the room on schedule.

The others agreed. They earned good pocket-money, and were in demand as Newnham was one of only four colleges for women. The Swan Hotel wanted respectable, middle-class girls for the respectable, middle-class men who could afford the tidy, middle-class arrangement.

After the photo was taken, the hotel manager simply assigned your photo an alias name and forwarded it to the client for his wife to use as 'evidence', in principle against him, but really so that he could free himself, usually to run off with his 29-year-old 'bit on the side'. The false name assigned to one's photograph was never traced, it was all 'perfectly legal', and off you went with two guineas in your pocket!

Dina thought it might not only be easy work, but good experience for her novel, which was, she hoped, to be an examination of the secret lives and restless hearts of a sedate English academic town. What did she know of restless hearts other than her own? It was one thing to invent; it was quite another to *have no idea*.

She was aware she was rather 'unformed' in the eyes of the world, even if she felt fully formed – brimmingly so – in herself. She had read so much throughout her life that she felt she possessed the glittering sediment of countless lives and experiences in the bedrock of herself. Not that she could convey as much as that. By the start of her third year, she had reached the conclusion that her mind did not interest her tutors; they found her ideas competent but bland. One day, she'd taken a chance and digressed from her essay, about *The Golden Bowl*, as she read it aloud to Mr Leavis across the seminar table in his study. She'd looked up and remarked, in a seemingly offhand way, that the elderly Henry James had once visited her family's place in Sussex and posed for a photo with the family pony! Mr Leavis's eyes had returned a flat stare.

How could she have been so trivial? She'd be lucky to scrape an upper-second degree. Soon she'd be back in London, turning the crank of Great-Uncle Francis's hand-press for titles few would buy. Then, in time, whatever she did, no matter how hard she worked or how capable she proved herself, he'd hire and promote some boy to Editorial.

The following morning, Great-Aunt Viola arrived at the Colony and took up temporary residence in Shed Hall. She and Dina had a plan to whitewash the interiors, and lift and remove the old green linoleum. Aunt Viola was seventy-four but, although small in stature, she was hale and sturdy, like all the Meynell women. In fact, she and Dina had to insist to Granny Madeline, who was almost eighty, that there *were* upper-age limits, and they would only permit her to supervise.

Francis, for his part, had already disappeared – for a walk, he'd said, to the local shop to buy the papers and get news 'of the outside world'. Khrushchev and his wife, he told them over breakfast, were touring the United States as guests of the President. It all seemed very far away, thought Dina.

She was still perplexed as to why she hadn't been able to find a single thing by Lawrence in any of the Colony's dwellings. And why had Granny Madeline avoided her question about him? Had they ever met? Why else would her grandmother be so unusually sphinx-like?

Dina let her imagination wander as she slapped the walls with whitewash. The weather was dry and fine, and as she and Great-Aunt Viola painted, they left the windows and doors of Shed Hall open to the day and the welter of warm September light.

Soon, the first coat was complete, and her dark hair was streaked white. She kept forgetting *not* to lean against the walls her great-aunt had already painted. When she spotted something gleaming darkly in the dust, in the crevice between the sitting-room wall and the bookcase, she assumed it was a door-stop, or a child's toy, lost as someone moved house.

She bent low, her arm and fingers straining, but whatever it was, it was wedged just out of reach. Finally, she got down on the bare floorboards and stretched herself out to her full length. The person who'd lodged it there had had arms longer than hers …

She got to her knees and turned it over in her hands: a stone, with a smooth hole in its centre. She blew the dust of the years off it, and rubbed it against her overalls until the gleam came up.

Her great-aunt looked puzzled and couldn't imagine where it had come from. 'Evidently, it's been waiting for you. But tell me this: how are we ever to get rid of all this linoleum?'

When her Granny Madeline examined Dina's discovery, she nodded and called it by its local name. According to the lore of Sussex, where such stones were often found, 'eye-stones' allowed one to see into other realms.

'Finders, keepers,' she said. 'I only wonder if it might show us where that wayward old uncle of yours has got to.'

A week before the start of the Michaelmas term, staff, new and old alike, arrived at the University Library, shaking out brollies and macs. It was the annual 'Commencement' glass of sherry for the librarians, to be followed by speeches and introductions. Dina had only just begun work as a Saturday assistant, and had been in two minds about taking the job at all. She would have earned more as a 'hotel-girl' at the Swan. Instead she'd turned it down and applied for an assistant's job, the advertisement for which she saw tacked to a board in Peile Hall.

The University Library was looking for an 'Assistant to the Director of Special Collections', a position which seemed made for her. She was from a bookish family and, as she explained in her letter of application, she'd been around libraries, presses and page-proofs all her life. She also had good knowledge of card-catalogues and both the Dewey and the L.C. classification systems.

She wasn't invited for an interview. Instead she found a three-line letter in her pigeonhole offering her a job as a Saturday 'shelver'. Anyone could re-shelve books – but her Great-Uncle Francis, via her mother Barbara, urged her to accept it. He still ran Nonesuch, the small press he'd founded in London in the twenties with his old friend David Garnett. Uncle Francis, her mother told her down the phone line, had promised that Dina could start at Nonesuch and work her way up to *Editorial*, if she got herself some experience first. Cambridge University Library was a start, even if hers was to be only a lowly position among the stacks.

The library was majestic, six storeys high, with a vaulted roof and stained-glass windows which made a place of books seem like a place of worship, austere and magnificent. In row after row, gold letters flickered from faded leather spines, and even familiar smells were redolent of mystery as she pushed her book-trolley. The smell of floor polish mingled with the dust of book decay. The odour of old glue arose from aged bindings.

The 'Commencement' gathering, she decided, was – at last – a drinks party she might enjoy. In Catalogue Hall, at the top of the great stone staircase, the sherry was served by senior staff. Then glasses were raised, smiles bestowed, and introductions hastily made before the speeches began.

She observed the assembled, the women in particular. Had she missed a dress-code on the invitation? She seemed to be the only woman in trousers – sleek black cigarette trousers from Sayle's, new for the occasion.

While everyone listened and applauded politely, she'd hardly noticed him. She was concentrating on the speech of the Director of Special Collections, the man who *hadn't* invited her for interview. She couldn't see him well, but he sounded affable enough. Her view was limited by a mountain of a man, with dandruff, like snowfall on his shoulders. She dipped her face and found herself pleased again by the sight of her black ballet-style flats. New, like her trousers. Then she found herself absentmindedly assessing the neighbouring shoes, to the right of hers on the polished floor.

Their owner was in possession of a long pair of feet and good brogues. She'd deduced that much before she looked up again. A new speaker was taking to the floor, and all the staff pressed in close, there at the top of the staircase. The brogued man's elbow hovered within an inch of hers, and she was dimly aware of the navy wool of a jacket sleeve.

Then, for no reason, he bent towards her and his voice came spinning into her ear – a sentence, a gentle quip of some sort at the expense of the latest speaker. She laughed, not because she wanted to please, but because, she realised only moments later, she wanted to conspire.

She couldn't have described his eyes or his face. He'd only bent to her ear. She'd smelled the sherry on his breath, and his elbow had nearly brushed hers. But hadn't. She had a vague impression of height. Then he'd said something. She hadn't actually heard what. In reply, she'd offered a smile, a low ripple of laughter, but she hadn't turned to look. She carried on, craning to see, pretending to focus on the speech, all the while aware that she was charged with something – some new resonance.

Then the Chief Librarian appeared at the rostrum to conclude the evening. As she and her neighbour stood, in their gravitational field of two, he leaned towards her again, bending his head, his mouth close to her ear. She felt the vibrato of his voice at her ear-lobe. His lips hovered near the small hoop of her earring.

They hadn't made eye contact. She didn't know the colour of his eyes. She knew his brogues better than his face. That was all. Yet as the speeches drew to a close, she felt her core hum, as if a current had passed through, from her inner ear to the soles of her feet.

She wasn't silly. It was obvious he'd only murmured a friendly aside or two during a series of predictable speeches. Everyone in the room was applauding the Commencement of the new academic year. How did one clap and hold sherry at the same time? Her glass was still full – sherry, she'd decided, was sickly.

'Hallo,' he said, extending a hand. 'Nicholas – Nick.'

She blinked. 'Bernardine.' She nodded apologetically to the glass in her right hand. 'Dina.' She could smell the damp-woollen smell of the rain off his jacket. He wore one of the new style of ties. He might have been younger than her. His eyes were small, a hazel brown perhaps. His smile was reserved but sincere.

'Are you new here?' he said.

'Gosh, yes,' she said. 'As a staff member, that is.'

'Which section?'

'Oh, any section I'm told to go to. I'm only a shelver. Saturday work.' Perhaps he was as well. 'You?'

'Assistant to the Director of Special Collections. Lord knows how. I walked in last week, inquired, met the Director, and he simply said the job was mine. He had a pile of applications sitting on his desk, and my turning up when I did apparently "spared him all that".' He laughed with palms upturned, as if to say he was as mystified as anyone.

He was easygoing, with a likeable face and intelligent eyes. And a quality wool jacket.

Of course he'd got the job. She shrugged her arms into her mac. It had never occurred to her to turn up in person and ask about the position.

He consulted his watch. 'It's still early … I wonder if you might like—'

'So sorry,' she said, cutting him off. 'I'm on tomorrow. Have to be up bright and early.' Her smile tightened and her eyes flashed darkly. 'Life at the coal-face and all that!'

Then she escaped down the great staircase and out the doors, wanting only the hit of the cool evening air.

Three Saturdays later, the clock on the library wall was nearing six – would the day never end? – and she had just one last book to return to its shelf. *No Exit* by Jean-Paul Sartre.

It rather summed up her day.

In the gap to which Jean-Paul was to be returned, an eye and half a mouth appeared, as if escapees from a surrealist painting.

She managed not to jump.

'Found you,' the mouth said. 'How do librarians flirt?'

She ignored it.

'They ask for your call number.'

A moment later, both eyes appeared, on her side of the stacks, in the aisle for 840, 'Literature of French and Romance Languages'.

'Couldn't resist,' he said, with a wry grimace. 'If I fail in this job, I'm going to start writing jokes for Christmas crackers.'

She scarcely turned. 'Come to see how the other half live?'

'Excellent! You remember me then.'

'Nick, was it?' She knew it was.

She put Jean-Paul to bed. 'I'm just "clocking off", as we shelvers say. Must get to my locker before the porter shuts up shop.'

He didn't move aside to let her pass. 'I'm sorry you didn't get the job.'

She looked up, her eyes wide, her composure blown.

He took a seat on the step-ladder she'd hauled into the aisle a few minutes earlier. 'The Director, my boss, he asked me to return the stack of applications to the Personnel Office. Yours was on top, I'm afraid.'

'Oh.'

His face brightened. 'Maybe that was a good sign – it being on top, I mean.'

She felt a squeeze of humiliation at her throat.

It would pass.

'I really had better get to my locker.'

But instead of moving his legs to clear the way, he carried on. 'The Special Collections thing is actually a cataloguing job. Dull work. Only fit for Second Years. Third Years are never interested.'

She turned again, pretending to re-arrange books. 'It's really okay. I'm not a child you need to humour.' It wasn't his fault he'd got the job she'd badly wanted. She knew it. But her application had been private, and no one's business but her own.

'I have a stuffy box-room without a view, more dust than in a mummy's tomb, and no heating.'

'I catalogued my great-grandparents' entire library.'

'It wouldn't matter if you'd catalogued the lost library of Alexandria.'

She refused to ask 'why not?', to play along.

'You're a girl, you see.'

She forced a book into place on the shelf. 'Breasts. Gosh. Is *that* what they mean?' Sometimes she couldn't help herself.

But he only laughed genially – an 'own goal' for her – and shifted on the step-ladder, too long for it. Why didn't he simply stand up? Unless he was *trying* to block her exit. As it was, she would have to clamber over him, and no doubt that would amuse him even more.

'What I was trying to say,' he said, 'is that they couldn't hire a girl.'

'What century *are* you in?'

'The job is with the Arc Collection, you see. "Arc" as in "arcana". The arcane. The mysteries.'

She offered a bitter smile. 'I know what *arcana* means.'

'Well, here, it's posh university code for "Dirty Book Collection". Female students aren't allowed to request its titles, let alone be trusted with the catalogue.'

'You're not serious?' Sometimes, sly humour did actually sail over her head.

'Did you really not know?'

Overhead, a row of lights buzzed and went dark.

She *was* about to get locked out of the cloakroom – and into the library with him.

After a few tries, he struck a match off the stacks. 'Ciggie?'

Under all the so-called 'charm', he was smug. She could feel the heat rising in her neck. 'I turned down another perfectly good job.'

'For one you didn't have? Well, that was a little foolish. What are you reading?'

'English. I can read, you see, as well as shelve books.'

He paused, showily. 'And me? Thank you for asking. History and Classics. As I was saying, second-year history students generally get the cataloguing jobs. It's nothing personal.' He turned his head and exhaled.

It went without saying that it was against the rules to smoke in a library. He was provoking her into saying so; so she would sound like a prude he could laugh at. How puerile he was.

'History students?'

He nodded.

'*Male* history students.'

'Yes, but only because you, as a member of the gentler sex, might be corrupted if exposed to dirty books. You'd lose your wits, you see.' He grinned.

'*Move*,' she said.

At the end of their aisle, three rows of desk-lamps blinked and went out. She heard a heavy key turn in a distant lock. 'My God. Run, will you? Tell them we're in here.'

'You run,' he said. He formed a smoke-ring and watched it rise.

She raised one leg. She'd simply climb over the obstacle he was.

'A word of warning,' he said.

Her leg hovered.

'In the last few weeks, I've learned that the porters are not *at all* happy when they have to turn back in their patrol and free people who didn't exit at the ten-minute warning.'

She arrived on the other side. Thank God she'd chosen slacks that morning. 'I'll tell them we were looking for an author; that we didn't realise it was throwing-out time.'

'Which? Let's at least get our story straight.' He stood up – now that she was past – and leaned against the stacks, as if they had all the time in the world.

The truth was, she had sometimes thought of him in the last few weeks. Once, she'd even made a detour with her book-trolley to Special Collections, to see if he might have been working. Now, she'd gone off him entirely.

He was tapping ash onto the floor. He was like a teenager. 'All right,' she said, her patience wearing thin, 'I will say we were looking for Lawrence. Will that do?'

'T. E.?'

'D. H. He's my specialism this year.'

'I started reading Lawrence's works when I went up to Cambridge and studied him for Part I of the Tripos ... I can confirm for the court ... I am now twenty-one.'

'It's not really a lie,' she added. 'I *had* planned to come in tomorrow, to do a full search for his work.'

He walked towards her, blowing smoke over his shoulder. Then he lifted the flap of his jacket and pointed with his chin. A large brass ring was fixed to his belt loop. Attached to it were at least a dozen keys. What was he? Bluebeard in tweed?

She adopted a weary face. Secretly, she was relieved. At least they might not be locked in.

'D. H. Lawrence?' he began. 'For God's sake, why didn't you say?' Then he looked up. 'Blast! Is that the time?'

She turned to the clock on the wall and panicked. In the fleeting interval, he seized her hand. How lovely it felt.

'I have tea, toast – and Lawrence – upstairs.'

The Arc Collection lay at the top of a steep, winding staircase, in what was, as he'd reported, a box-room. He unlocked the door, held it for her and – 'With your permission?' – locked it again behind them. 'Sorry. We can't risk a porter bursting in. We'd be out on our ears.'

Ramshackle cartons of books were stacked high in every corner. The floorboards were bare. A long, narrow desk was covered in index cards, and an anglepoise lamp teetered at its edge. Another stood lopsided on the floor, while a toaster and a kettle gathered dust in a far corner – at a prudent distance, at least, from the books. She'd be surprised if either was permitted.

'My lair!' he said.

He opened a broom cupboard, dragged out a threadbare oriental rug and unrolled it across the old floorboards, kicking boxes of books out of his way as he did so. Up went clouds of dust.

Was 'lair' another word for 'sex-den'?

He was rinsing out a teapot in a sink in the broom cupboard. She climbed a step-ladder to look out the only window, a small rectangle of glass, high up. The moon was out, golden and recumbent – a woman's face in profile, tipped back, as if she were about to be kissed. Picasso might have drawn her. Then Dina descended and, still uncertain – why had she followed him? – turned to the books at her feet.

They appeared random: an Edwardian sex manual; a folio of seventeenth-century Venetian 'pornography', not *very* pornographic; an illustrated *Decameron*; Casanova's memoir; a novel entitled *Why? A Story of Great Longing*; and the *Ars Amatoria*, Ovid's guide to love.

Nick busied himself making toast and finding something – a heavy sheet of card – that might serve as a second plate. Then he reversed a packing crate for a table and smoothed out his jacket on the rug to make a seat for her. Draughts whistled through the floorboards. The wet night outside had turned gusty.

She wasn't unaware. She knew why he was buttering her toast and popping open a fresh jar of jam. But his box-room was stuffed full of treasures. She hit the pedal-switch of the lamp and opened a book of gilt-edged pages: '*Odi concubitus, qui non utrumque resolvunt.*' She started to translate aloud before stopping herself: Ovid, it seemed, wasn't keen on copulation which didn't satisfy both lovers. Best keep that to herself.

'A good egg, Ovid,' he said, enjoying his *double entendre*, 'but sorry.' He pointed to the window and stepped on the lamp-switch. The room went dim again. 'No blackout curtains here. We can't risk a lamp being spotted by someone outside. Not unless you fancy a porter confiscating our only rations.'

'You locked the door.'

'There's such a thing as a skeleton key.'

'Oh, God. What if they find us?'

'You'll hide in the broom cupboard over there, and I'll say I'm working late.'

Hiding in broom cupboards … It all seemed so … low. Like a bad sketch from a 1940s comedy revue. 'You said we'd find Lawrence. That's why I've come.' She wasn't lying, but she wasn't being entirely honest either.

'Wait there.' He pointed to her 'seat' of honour, on his jacket.

She did as instructed.

For nearly half an hour, he foraged, in his spectacles, by the half-light of the moon – until 'Ah ha!' he declared.

He joined her at the table and slowly slid a book across to her.

She gasped.

'1928. Signed,' he said.

Lady Chatterley. The original. Between terracotta covers that were still bright.

She traced the phoenix insignia, engraved on the front.

He tried not to look as pleased with himself as he was. 'Lawrence drew that phoenix.'

She looked up. 'Really?'

'Open it.'

'Oh! What a beautiful signature ...'

'One of just a thousand copies produced – privately published in Italy, to bypass the censors. Not that *that* worked out especially well. I assembled and recorded the full provenance.'

In the moonlit room, her eyes shone. Something gusted within her, and she felt suddenly fully awake, in spite of her long day. 'I've only read the censored version. At school.'

'That's about to change – for starters.'

'You mean I can actually read it?'

He scratched his head. 'Actually ...'

Her mind whirred. 'I could read it in the broom cupboard while you work – when it's convenient for you.' Suddenly the broom cupboard was no longer the sordid prospect it had been minutes before.

'In all honesty, I don't think it's a good idea.'

The wind clattered at the window. It seemed to her a little mean of him to dangle the book, then withdraw it. At the table, her back stiffened. She returned the book – 'Thank you all the same.'

He nodded, sombre. 'I don't think it's a good idea because it's rather dusty in that cupboard.' He took a big bite of toast. 'I expect your room is a more suitable location.'

She gasped again. 'Really?'

'Who will ever know?'

'I'll guard it with my life.'

'Well, if you could avoid doodling in the margins, that will do. I can't tell you how much of my time is spent erasing.' He winked. 'Specialist work.'

'I don't know how to thank you.'

His eyes flashed with cartoon wickedness. 'I suspect you do.'

She ignored him and opened the book to a random page and started to read aloud, suddenly strangely unselfconscious in front of a boy – a man – who stared and wouldn't look away:

"And are you sorry?" she said.
"In a way!" he replied, looking up at the sky. "I thought I'd done with it all. Now I've begun again."
"Begun what?"
"Life."
"Life!" she re-echoed, with a queer thrill.'

She leaned across the crate and kissed Nick's cheek.
He half-rose from the floor and kissed her, slowly.

Over tea, he explained the provenance of – 'no', he corrected himself – the *story* of 'her' copy of *Chatterley*, pieced together from multiple index cards.

He'd had to do some extra 'digging', he said, because, as a Classics student, he'd been tasked by his tutor to research the work of the late Cambridge classicist, Sir Stephen Gaselee. Sir Stephen had led him unexpectedly to Lawrence. Lawrence, in turn, had led him to the 1928 *Chatterley* in the Arc Collection.

In the dig, Nick had excavated the volume and even cleaned the dust from its phoenix engraving with a fine horsehair brush. He said the history and travails of that single volume was going to help him to fill a 'Sources' essay he had to prepare for his history tutor. So it was, 'Sir Stephen for Classics. Tick! And a hunt through the archive for history. Tick! Two birds, one stone'

'Three, if you count me,' she replied, her eyes glinting over the chipped tea-cup.

'I didn't want to presume.'

'Which is why I'm still here.'

'After I met you, I had rather hoped you might be reading English. I was determined to find you, and to *try* at least to dazzle you. I hoped you might be keen on Lawrence. Frankly, I hadn't expected you'd be quite *this* easy to please.'

She kicked his shin.

He couldn't help himself: '*Dewey* look good together or Dewey not?'

She groaned.

He smiled to himself, pouring the dregs from the pot. Then he grew subdued. 'Actually, I thought you'd never speak to me again, after I saw your CV sitting on top of that pile of applications.'

She bit her lip. 'I thought I never would either.'

'Will you stay?' he said simply.

She felt a rush of exhilaration, of dread. 'What if a porter *does* find us? We'll be sent down..'

'I'll put the desk against the door. No one will come in. I swear.'

She winced as she asked. 'Do you have … "something"?'

He understood. 'Yes.'

Her eyes searched the ceiling. 'Be honest. Is this your … sex-den? Do you bring girls here?'

He slapped the crate and laughed. 'How many rare 1928 editions of *Chatterley* do you think I have?' And as if to answer the doubt on her face, he shouted, 'One!'

'*Do* you bring girls here?' she said, her brow wrinkling.

'No.' He reached for her hand. 'But give a chap time, will you? I *have* only been in post a few weeks.'

She was killing the moment with seriousness, but she couldn't help it. 'Am I the first?'

He took a big spoonful of jam from the jar, as if he needed it to sustain him through her interrogation. 'Here, or ever?'

'Here.'

'Yes.' He leaned across. 'What's *actually* on your mind?'

She hesitated. 'I've never … "stayed" before.'

He nodded contemplatively. 'Well then I would be honoured. And happy. Will you?'

She watched him pull at a hangnail. He was nervous too, she realised, and he had, she saw in that moment, beautiful hands – strong with long fingers.

'On one condition.' She leaned across and kissed his neck softly.

'Name it.'

'No more Christmas cracker jokes.'

The September moon had risen high over the Arc Collection, and had taken with it much of its light. Draughts of wind still whistled through the floorboards, where the rug didn't stretch, and the room was cold. She could see his eyes in the semi-darkness – small, brown-green, she thought, direct in their gaze – not beautiful eyes, yet beautiful, she thought, as they directed their warmth at her. Two calm points.

She opened to another page in the rare book in her lap. She would not censor or edit her selection. That would be against the spirit of the book. She would read 'as she found':

"'Shall I tell you?" she said, looking into his face. "Shall I tell you what you have that other men don't have, and that will make the future? Shall I tell you?"

"'Tell me then," he replied.

"'It's the courage of your own tenderness, that's what it is: like when you put your hand on my tail and say I've got a pretty tail."'

Strangely for her, she didn't blush.

'You do,' he murmured. 'I confess, it was one of the first things I noticed at the Commencement drinks. It's why I stood next to you. I wasn't going to tell you that. All rather adolescent. Which I am, of course.' He picked up the greasy butter knife and shook it like a finger. 'I blame those trousers of yours.' He deepened his voice and adopted a clipped, old-fashioned diction: 'Damned temptress!'

'My cigarette trousers!'

'Smoking, indeed.'

He took the book from her, replaced the plain yellow dust jacket and the glassine wrapper, and laid it on the desk. Then he returned to the rug, pushed away the crate, and wrapped her in his arms.

She forgot books and novels and words as she entered the trance of her body. In the semi-darkness, his voice was a warm frequency travelling through her, as it had at the Commencement drinks. What was carried in the current of a human voice?

'May I?' he said, and he tugged gently at her blouse. They sat up, and off it went, over her head. Her dark hair rose with it, in a nimbus of static. Their eyes had adjusted, to the darkness, to each other. 'Look at you,' he said quietly, blinking.

Gusts rattled at the window as his lips swept her – cheek, neck, eyelid, collarbone, throat. It was dim among the mysteries of the Arc Collection, but the night sky outside the window was moon-bright.

In time, they stretched out on the threadbare rug, and she had a new sense of his height, of his slim build. Lanky. That was the word.

He had a long face, unguarded. A high forehead. Patchy stubble. Uneven teeth. She put her arms around him, closing the circuit of his arms. He smelled of tweed, smoke, hair oil – and something that was only him.

Their breath stirred the dust. His lips were dry and hard, and tasted of tobacco and toast. His neck was sweet with the scent of shaving foam, and she breathed in his laundered collar. He unbuttoned his shirt and pulled her to him again, more fiercely now. Her brain couldn't keep up, but her body moulded itself to his, lip to lip, nipple to nipple. The soft convex of her belly met the hard concave of his. She raised her face, breathing, to look: he was all alien pupil, cheekbones, muscle, shadow and tendon.

The old floorboards of the room had aged into mounds and warps. Kiss, clasp, cleave. Their legs reached and pinioned, and how wet she was. He lifted her breasts to his mouth and she heard his low moan, which touched her deeply. She reached up to stroke the crown of his head, and he boosted her in his arms.

Her slacks gave off shocks of static. 'Sorry,' she said. 'Sorry.' She felt an eyelash on her tongue and saw the tiny craters in his face where he'd scratched his chicken-pox as a child. When he laid her down again, his weight upon her was as pleasurable, as delicious, as any drug she'd never had.

'Yes?' he murmured. She nodded and he fumbled for the rubber tucked in his wallet. 'In his memoir over there,' he said with a smile, 'Casanova uses animal intestine, but I promise you, this is preferable.'

She smiled to show him she wasn't nervous, though of course she was – and he was, again, because she was, and it was all rather momentous. The edge of her trouser leg caught him in the eye as it came off. His belt was tricky for her to unfasten, so he stripped himself and, for some reason known only to him, he stood and ran widdershins around the little room, smiling like a village idiot before collapsing beside her.

'Might it be an idea to take off your socks?' she ventured.

'Next time, I'll wear sandals – with socks. Utter turn-on.'

She plucked a curl of his chest hair.

'Oi!' He seized her and kissed her again, deeply.

High above, the oracle of the moon rose in the watchful night. Their breath was a mist on the window. The room was cold but neither felt it. Under their weight, the floorboards creaked at their every turn, and they suppressed raucous, giddy laughter.

'Sssh!' she said, lifting her head suddenly. 'A porter?'

But no footsteps came.

He sat up, turned to her and stroked her hip and belly. Then his mouth, his tongue, hungry and delicate, travelled up her calf and along the inner curve of her thigh, where the stubble of his cheek rasped and tingled.

She held his head lightly, in the cradle of her legs, and her hands moved through his fine hair, stroking his ears, and softly scratching the back of his neck. Pulses of warmth moved through and through her, until the current swelled in her thighs, and rolled higher, pulling her – from toes to the top of her head – through some bright loop of being. His mouth moved to her breasts, and he raised himself, above her, on his arms. With her fingers, she opened herself, and slowly, haltingly, he filled her.

She grimaced and tensed, yet the sensation of another body in hers overwhelmed her – a strange completion, mysterious and satis-fying. Then the pain subsided, her thoughts dissolved, she cleaved to him, he quivered and shook and was elsewhere.

What spell had her body cast?

When he returned to her, lifting her hips to him, the flame took, and she was seized, life-lit, as he held her; until the riddle of her cry, uncanny even to her, arose from some new-fathomed depth of herself.

How good it was, she realised, to rest in the crook of a lover's arms, to be shepherded into sleep by another body. Her mind was hushed. She knew only that his chest hair tickled her cheek; that his cock was small again and dewy in its nest. He pulled the dusty edge of the rug over her to keep her bottom warm, and still half-aware, he gripped it in place with his leg as he dozed.

The raw light of the new day seeped through the window, and pigeons purred in the guttering outside.

When she woke, she toyed with him idly while he half-slept. She was both amused and touched by the human penis's motor-skills: by its blind yearning and exposed vulnerability in the world. Its single eye seemed to stare at her lazily, dreamily. The turkey-neck skin of his testicles made her smile. If male genitalia had not evolved, no one could have dreamed them up.

She stretched out an arm and grabbed a leg of her slacks. Then, reluctantly, she peeled herself from the warmth of him, stood, and began to dress.

Her whole body buzzed.

He opened one eye and pointed to her knickers – on the staff desk. 'Best, probably, if those aren't catalogued today.' He rubbed his eyes. 'Fuck, how lovely you are.'

With one leg in her trousers, she almost fell over as she scooped up her underwear belatedly. She surveyed the box-room. 'I'm afraid we've made a mess of your index cards.'

'Will we do this again?' he asked through a yawn. But his voice had feeling in it he couldn't disguise.

Her cheeks burned from the chafing of his stubble. 'Here, you mean?'

'My key-ring is large.' He jingled his trousers.

She bent to his belly-button and kissed it.

His cock woke and climbed to her.

'Jingle, jingle,' he tried.

'Very subtle,' she said.

'Penises are incapable of subtlety.'

She retrieved her gift from the desk that blocked the door – her illicit library loan – as if it were a present left by elves. 'I really didn't believe you when you said you'd find Lawrence for me.'

He propped his head on his hand. 'I don't disappoint.'

She smoothed the wrapper lovingly. 'I'll return it by end of week, I promise.'

He turned over, reached for a stack of index cards and cleared his throat. 'Sit down for a few minutes and listen to this. Then I'll break you out of this place.'

She fastened her bra. 'E. M. Forster himself is giving the Lawrence lecture. Apparently, they knew each other – *centuries* ago.' She stared at her new acquisition: 'With any luck, I might even be corrupted.'

'My work here is not done, clearly!'

She still hadn't conceded to sit. She nudged his armpit with her big toe. 'You don't *do* any work up here, do you? I bet you're wanking away over' – she waved an arm at the assorted stacks – 'all this.'

He fished for his specs in a case in his trouser pocket. 'Why do you think I'm already half-blind?' Then he patted the rug, determined to delay her departure.

So she stopped fretting about porters and keys, and seated herself again, rapt as her lover narrated for her, from assorted index cards, the journey of a single book, from Italy to England.

'That was wonderful,' she said, blinking, when he finished. '*Thank you.*' She smoothed her hair. 'Right. Up! – or we'll both be sent down.' She stuffed her knickers into her trouser waistband.

He rose at last, scratched his chest, ran his hands through his hair, and stumbled into his clothes. He was lean and pale-skinned, now that she could see him properly. Her eyes lingered on the clean hollows above his buttocks; the strong strips of muscle in his legs; the beautiful movement of his shoulder blades. She loved the naked nape of a man's neck; they were still children there somehow.

'And they're off!' he said, pivoting suddenly and slapping her bottom.

She slapped his back.

Together they moved in stealth, down corridors and through reading-rooms. At each door, he studied the keys on his ring and, in trial-and-error, on they went, until they arrived at her locker, where she hurriedly buttoned and belted her mac over her 'library loan'. Finally, at the top of the stone staircase where his lips had first brushed the lobe of her ear, they stood, unsure, dazzled by each other, and embarrassed.

He broke the silence, patting the illicit book and bending to speak to its bump under the belt of her buttoned coat. 'Be sure to grow big and strong for Mamma and Papa.'

Then she kissed him, urgently on the lips, turned and dashed down the stairs, expectant.

The red-brick chimney stacks of Newnham College surveyed her approach. Trinity's clock had just chimed the hour – 5 a.m. – which meant the gates were still locked. She stood, her face pressed to the wrought-iron sunflowers, wondering how long she might have to wait before a porter passed. And then, what to say? Would she be fined? Or worse?

She resigned herself to the hidey-hole passage, through the gap in the hedge by the bike sheds – every renegade Newnhamite's last resort. It meant crawling on all fours, and in this instance, with the added challenge of a stolen rare book smuggled in her coat.

When she emerged, the college grounds were transformed. In the night, she and Nick had registered the high winds outside his tower, but their world had reduced to the dimensions of that box-room. Now, she saw the white petals of the great rose garden everywhere. The blooms had been blasted and, in their blown abundance, they looked, that late-September morning, like the first snow of the year.

She passed Sidgwick Hall, hurried down the mossy stone steps, and crossed the sunken garden. The circular pool at its centre was occult and murky. Early-morning mist had erased the box-hedges and benches, and the yew trees brooded over her. Yet at her feet, the earth itself seemed to surge and swell with life, as if it were a vast sheet billowing out irrepressibly.

She'd had little sleep and was still caught in the heady uplift of the night. Not 'rapture', but fullness. She had liked being re-made in her lover's hands into an object of desire, a yearned-for body. Perhaps she wasn't supposed to like being objectified, but she had. She'd loved his touch, his hunger, and as she walked, she felt again the electricity of that first clasping of palms as he led her up the stairs.

She crossed the lawns of Clough Hall. Its ground floor was uncharacteristically sober and quiet – no clatter of breakfast plates yet. Ahead, the windows of Peile Hall blinked. She checked herself before she entered: the belt of her mac was still firmly knotted and her book was in place beneath it. At the main door, she composed her face, inserted her key and slipped inside, passing the porter as he blew on his first cup of tea of the day and, thoughtfully, turned a blind eye.

On she went, past the pigeonholes, where no literary rejections waited to spoil her happiness. Then: up her staircase to her new room for her final year, Room 213. As she climbed, she was still unaware that her knickers had fallen from her person, somewhere between the college gates and the door of her room.

Inside, she unbuttoned her coat, released the book, and crossed quickly to the oak bureau, as if, even now, a determined senior librarian might be hot on her heels. She had never stolen anything – not that it was theft, she reasoned, if you planned to return it. She had merely 'liberated' a book which wanted to be read. The author, she assured herself, would have *wanted* her to have it – or would have certainly if she'd crossed his palm with two guineas.

And she remembered again her Great-Uncle Francis's words during her most recent Greatham visit – 'A *dangerous* man' – while her Granny Madeline had avoided the topic of Lawrence altogether. Why?

Beside her narrow bed, the oak bureau was generously proportioned and somehow benign. On taking up residence in her new room, she'd discovered the decades of former residents' signatures on its back panel, dating all the way back to 1910, the year Peile was opened. There was a quiet comfort in that. *You are not alone,* all those names said. *You are in good company.* There was even a bent compass kept in the drawer for the purpose of signing. It was the first thing she did on taking up occupancy.

The autographs, however, weren't the bureau's most intriguing feature. The furniture of Peile Hall was known for its quirks and anomalies, and in the bureau she'd discovered a secret compartment at its bottom.

She prised off its cover now, and into the compartment slid Lawrence's banned novel, a prized 1928 first edition. It would be a friend, she told herself, to her own small collection stashed there: a copy of Whitman's *Leaves of Grass,* the erotic stories of Anaïs Nin, the manuscript pages of her own fledgling novel, plus the eye-stone, which had travelled back with her from Greatham.

She laid the stone on top of her library 'loan', *Lady Chatterley,* and replaced the compartment's cover. Then she slipped out of her slacks, found fresh knickers, and lay down for a few hours. Breakfast was at nine sharp and she was hungry.

Should she take the job as a hotel-girl, after all? she wondered sleepily. Perhaps her novel demanded it. Perhaps she needed world-liness; glimpses of that which, otherwise, she'd never see or know, or not if 'society' could help it.

She could still smell Nick on her – his hair oil on her fingers, the light yeasty smell of his balls on her palm.

Her nipples were sore.

She closed her eyes, content in the knowledge that she had a lover, that she had lost her virginity amid the erotically arcane, and that locked in a secret compartment in her college room was a rare, unexpurgated edition of *Lady Chatterley's Lover*.

She rolled onto her stomach. Her lover, literally, had the key to the arcane. To the mysteries.

He had an appendix scar. A scrawl of light-brown chest hair. The hair under his arms was unexpectedly soft. Eyes – green or brown? She still wasn't sure. Notes scribbled in ink on his hand, illegible. A high, pale forehead. Thick specs.

How delicious his touch had been.

Fuck, she breathed, trying the word out.

It was good to have words at her disposal. All words. To have that 'f'. The soft 'ck'. To be unafraid.

'Fuck, how lovely you are,' he'd said.

Her body had moved him to expletives.

She smiled into her pillow.

It was difficult to think of E. M. Forster, a shy, short man with a receding chin – a kindly but desiccated figure – reading aloud from *Lady Chatterley*, or lecturing on Lawrence's philosophy of men, women and the 'sacred-sexual'.

She had passed Mr Forster once outside the university concert hall. He'd seemed too unprepossessing a figure to have written *A Room with a View*. She could never imagine old people any younger than they were, just as she could never see bomb-sites in London and imagine them as anything but waste ground or car-parks, not even when her parents described the great buildings that had once filled those gaps. In the same way, she could see only the *octogenarian* Forster – the weeds growing from his ears and nose; the uncleared rubble of a long life.

If she was unable to imagine a *young* Mr Forster, perhaps she'd never be capable of a novel at all.

Certainly her tutors, in the reverence they communicated for the 'Greats', had managed to stymie hers and most of her peers' hopes of achieving anything more than a respectful appreciation of their betters. Even so, she was determined that she should have more, and be more.

In Cambridge, she had now passed a 'great writer' outside a concert hall: Mr E. M. Forster. That was exciting, no matter his age. *That* was at least a start to life.

Somewhere within that small, balding head were brain cells which held the residue of old conversations with Lawrence himself. She almost wished she could press that elderly, liver-spotted pate between her palms, and listen for Lawrence's voice as she'd once listened, as a child, for voices through a tin can on a string.

'Why so cramped and miserable in your being, Forster? Why do you not act? Why do you dodge yourself? Why a virgin?'

We cannot see Forster's blind tramping through four miles of semi-darkness, across the floods of Sussex, to catch the train that morning in February 1915. His own novel of illicit love, already written by the time he visited Lawrence – his love story of the stockbroker Maurice Hall and the gamekeeper Alec Scudder – was to remain a secret and unpublished, at Forster's instruction, until after his death.

For the forthcoming lecture, Dina wished she could summon the courage to stand and propose her thesis to this genteel don and celebrated author. She should like to suggest that Lawrence's notion of 'tenderness' – significant enough to have once been the working title of *Lady Chatterley's Lover* – was, in fact, the very concept upon which the novel, his 'bright book of life', depended; that he and his friend Katherine Mansfield had shared this notion of 'tenderness' in relation, not only to life, but to art itself.

Lawrence, she would argue – in her fantasy lecture-hall scenario – derived *his* notion of tenderness from his writer-hero (heroine) George Eliot, from her artistic devotion to 'sympathy', or the imaginative 'entering into' the mind, soul, spirit or body of another. The life of the body was not, for Lawrence, separate from those other things. Rather, it was the way *to* those other things, and could not be divided from them. It was only Christianity which had cut them asunder.

Her thoughts rushed on as she spoke from her place in the imaginary lecture hall.

It was this fundamental principle of sympathy or 'tenderness' – namely, the recognition that we all share a human form and spirit, and are vulnerable – and *not* merely the development of social realism in literature in the eighteenth and nineteenth centuries – which had, in her opinion, allowed the novel to become *the* most profound vehicle for the expression of human consciousness.

The great power of the form lay in the tenderness of the novel's 'eye'; in it, and also in the fact that, as Lawrence himself had said, the novel, as a form, was entirely *in*capable of absolutes. Yet in that 'incapability' lay its power.

In her imagined scene, she reads aloud, in a clear voice, to Mr Forster from her notes: "'All vital truth,' Lawrence said, "contains the memory of all that for which it is not true."' Wasn't that a wonderful thing to say? she would venture.

It seemed to her that *systems* of thought, which, by definition, must aim for a purity of absolute thought, so often went terribly wrong. One only had to look at the French Revolution, she would say, as if off the top of her head – or Nazism or Stalinism or McCarthyism. If only the world wanted *novels* as much as it wanted ideologues, pure 'philosophies', and so-called great 'systems' of thought!

She was digressing – apologies, Mr Forster, she would say. If he would permit it, she would like to argue that Lawrence had departed from his hero George Eliot's 'formulation' of sympathy only, but crucially, in one sense: *Lawrence's* view of tenderness was a form of 'coming through' – a coming-through from shame, a confronting of the human predilection for violence, a painful stripping away to truth, the truth of human need, frailty and longing. Lawrence believed *that* was the tender point at which change was possible. Real change. Metamorphosis. And healing too, she added. The war, the Great War, had 'killed', or at least crippled, Lawrence's England. She did not need to tell Mr Forster that, of course, for it had been his England too.

It could be healed, Lawrence had believed. She did as well. It could stand free again, but not on the back of jingoism and false glories. It had been D. H. Lawrence's dying effort to say it could be healed, but to say so *un*-absolutely. And *that* was *Lady Chatterley*.

Dina concluded her imaginary disquisition with Lawrence's own words: 'We should ask for no absolutes, or absolute. Once and for all and for ever, let us have done with the ugly imperialism of any absolute.'

As she lay on her bed, Forster quietly commended her from the lectern. In reality, she knew she hadn't a hope of a First.

Her room was cold. The heating of Peile Hall would not be turned on until November, and her room had no fireplace. But she could not let herself get under the bedcovers. She'd fall asleep and miss the breakfast hour. Instead she leaped up, grabbed her academic gown from its peg, and draped it over herself, wishing she were back at Greatham, dozing by the fire in the library – or out in the day's gusts, picking beans and tomatoes for lunch with her grandmother.

As she lay down again, wrapped in black, she thought of Granny Madeline at Winborn's before she, Dina, had left the last time. Her grandmother had insisted she take a bag of supplies: a pot of Greatham honey, farm butter in a jar, and crumpets for toasting on her arrival back in Peile Hall.

She adored her grandmother, having spent most of her first seven years of life with her, as her parents travelled back and forth, to Italy and London, for literary and war-work. In fact, Greatham still seemed like her true home, not Bayswater at all. When in London, a deep part of her missed the green cradle of the Downs.

At least, she thought, she had finally had a lover.

At least she'd experienced 'mysteries'. The arcane.

At least she'd smuggled out the most dangerous D. H. Lawrence novel for her private education.

As she lay in her Newnham bed, she could not imagine that, in a year's time, she would be standing in a court of law, telling the world about that education – and stretching a point, just occasionally, as she did so:

'The influence of the book, in unexpurgated form, on me, and on my many friends with whom I discussed it at the time, was to turn our thought entirely against experimental sexual relations and in favour of a settled and lifelong one ...'

She felt languorously post-coital. Then sleep ambushed her.

Twenty past eight, said her bedside clock. Her stomach rumbled but it was still too early for breakfast. She got to her feet and retrieved her treasure from her bureau.

'Her' copy, Nick had narrated, was one of only a thousand printed in Florence by a friend of Lawrence, the 'broadminded' Florentine bookseller 'Pino' Orioli, whom he first met in England, and who had helped the Lawrences to find their Tuscan 'Villa Mirenda' to lease. Lawrence's first typist in Italy had objected to the 'language' in the manuscript, then quit. Aldous Huxley's wife, Maria, took over.

In February 1928, Lawrence wrote to Orioli: 'I am going to make expurgated copies for Secker and Alfred Knopf' – his publishers – 'then we can go ahead with Florence edition, for I am determined to do it.'

'It' being – Nick explained – the full, living story. But Lawrence simply couldn't do the deed. He couldn't bring himself to start chopping. *I cannot expurgate the real one – physical impossibility. I might as well try to clip my own nose into shape with scissors. The book bleeds …*

A plan was agreed, namely to sell the novel through private subscription only – which would be, they hoped, Lawrence's means of bypassing all publicity and, with it, the worry of another ban. He had not forgotten the experience of *The Rainbow*. Nor the penury which followed.

The novel was typeset by hand, by Italian printers who could not read English and take offence – Orioli made sure of that. Predictably, the proofs were full of typographical errors, and Lawrence was almost driven mad over the corrections. 'Progress was slow in Orioli's dark little shop' – and here, Nick struggled to read his own index cards – 'at 6 Lungarno Corsini.'

'We must go,' she appealed, 'before the library wakes up!' But she made no move. Nick had a beautiful voice, deep and resonant, and she was ensnared.

Lawrence's health, he told her, was in rapid and irreversible decline, but the thousand copies were finally printed in July of '28. The boards were emblazoned. *I've made my favourite phoenix rising from a nest of flames (I rise up) for the cover – and it will be a nice book.* He was happy with the terracotta colour of the cover. Each copy was signed by the author himself. Then he helped parcel up the books for the post: plain wrapping, false titles and secret shipments to evade both British and American Customs. *I've got to sell my thousand, or I'm a lost soul*. One hundred and forty copies were ordered by American subscribers, but many were confiscated at the ports, American and English, although it was impossible for Lawrence and Orioli to prove it without drawing attention to the very thing they sought to hide.

In London, W. & G. Foyle Ltd of Charing Cross Road, the city's most popular bookshop, promptly returned its six copies to the Florentine shop. The enclosure was brief: 'a book we could not handle in any way'. As if he and Orioli had pushed a grenade through their letterbox.

The book must be read – it's a bomb, but to the living, a flood of urge – and I must sell it.

Other copies were ordered and paid for, at two guineas apiece. *I've got to sell it: for I've got to live*. Again, they were never received. It was as if the book was as contagious as Lawrence's own body; as if both he and his progeny were to be rejected in every English-speaking land.

And of course it will in a way set me apart even more definitely than I am already set apart. It's destiny.

The ailing author, Nick narrated, weathered it all, but he was battered. Reviewers got hold of the book and decried his diseased mind. It was 'one of the filthiest books ever written'. Nevertheless, in March 1929, Lawrence travelled to Paris to agree a popular, cheap edition, simply to beat the pirate publishers at their own game, and reap whatever profits he could. He was conscious that he had to provide for Frieda, alive or dead, and it was a duty he took very seriously.

A young American writer who spotted him in Sylvia Beach's bookshop on rue Dupuytren was shocked at the sight of him. Lawrence, he reported to friends, was dying on his feet.

The year got worse. That July, thirteen of his twenty-five paintings – in other words, any which featured a penis or pubic hair – were seized by London's Metropolitan Police at his first exhibition. At the time, he lay fevered and writhing with tubercular cramps in Orioli's Florentine flat.

His paintings were only saved from destruction by fire because his lawyer, in his absence, agreed they would never again be shown in Great Britain. Lawrence was devastated – and furious at the concession. Nor did Frieda – then in London – even write to him to break the news. He felt abandoned by all, and learned of the grim compromise only by telegram from his lawyer.

His manuscript of poems, sent through the post to his agent, was next to be manhandled. Individual poems were confiscated by an anonymous postmaster and retained as evidence. 'Of what?' he might have shouted.

Then—

Savage rumours that Lady Chatterley is to be suppressed in London; and that it is stopped from entering America. Oh, dear thing!

Nick told her that his heart must have died a little more when, on January 18th, 1930, two months from his death, Scotland Yard announced that they themselves – and not merely the Customs Department – had seized six copies of *Chatterley*. The Yard examined it and deemed it an 'indecent publication'.

This was now potentially a criminal matter; the writer and publisher had used the Royal Mail to ship obscenity. The copies were to be destroyed, along with any others found. Naturally enough, others *were* soon found: specifically, six which had been posted to the writer Brigit Patmore's home in Bedford Row, London. Scotland Yard had all it needed.

The police seizure of unpublished pages from his poetry manuscript, *Pansies*, was raised as a matter of concern in the House of Commons, but the issue went no further. Scotland Yard had the upper hand. Its detectives warned Lawrence's agent that the author would face arrest were he to return to Britain.

And so he was exiled, made fugitive, a 'man on the run' – only he no longer had the breath with which to run.

Lawrence wondered, in a letter to Orioli, if he could make an earlier version of his novel, his first slender draft, acceptable for the general public, and for Scotland Yard. *I wish you would just glance through the so-called hot parts and tell me how hot they are. I'm sure they are barely warm – whereas our Lady C., I cannot, absolutely cannot, even begin to expurgate.*

'So he died abroad,' said Nick to Dina. 'In France. Not even in Italy, which he knew and had once loved.'

'What a lonely phrase,' said Dina. '"Died abroad." It sounds so … adrift.'

Nick held the title page of the Arc copy to the morning light; he said that what appeared to be foxing on the page – brown speckles of damp or age above the signature – might in fact be splatters of Lawrence's blood!

She had laughed. But now in her bed, she peered again through her eye-stone. Could it be true?

'As for *your* copy' – she loved it when he called it that – 'this is its own little tale.'

Two copies were collected one day in 1929 from Lawrence himself, in Orioli's bookshop, by a Sir Stephen Gaselee. Sir Stephen had been a first-rate classicist at Cambridge, and was a distinguished eccentric. He was known, for example, to wear a hair-net when he played tennis, and he hosted a dining club to which all members – men, naturally – were required to wear purple dinner jackets with lilac silk lining. He owned numerous Siamese cats; it was difficult, by all accounts, to keep them off the table or out of his guests' laps when they dined. He was mad about bridge and shooting, and had tutored Queen Victoria's grandson. Sir Stephen was, in short, an editor, a bibliographer, a renowned librarian, a speaker of ancient Coptic, and a lover of church vestments, rare books – and vodka.

Crucially, he was also Keeper of the Papers at the Foreign Office. *That* was crucial because, in 1929, he 'transported' two copies of *Lady Chatterley* out of Italy. One for Cambridge's Rare Books Collection. One for Oxford's. Both travelled in his diplomatic bag, a sort of attaché case. *It* meant that neither he nor the bag could be seized, or even so much as searched, at any border.

All of which meant in turn, Nick said, drawing his story to a close, that she had Sir Stephen Gaselee to thank for her moral corruption.

Sitting up in bed, she opened *Lady Chatterley*, and bounced the eye-stone in the palm of her hand. What did it see, across space and time?

A girl of twenty-one bearing witness in a court, with a stone like a secret in her pocket: *'The story of Lady Chatterley gave hope of a less cramped and sordid mode of existence from a full, and fully developed, description of a human relationship. This I found—'*

She turned again to a random page and read through the eye of her stone, as if it were a photographer's loupe:

He began to put on his boots. She stared at him.

'Wait!' she faltered. 'Wait! What's come between us?'

He was bent over, lacing his boot, and did not reply. The moments passed. A dimness came over her, like a swoon. All her consciousness died, and she stood there wide-eyed, looking at him from the unknown, knowing nothing any more.

He looked up, because of the silence, and saw her wide-eyed and lost.

'This I found—'

And as if a wind tossed him he got up and hobbled over to her, one shoe off and one shoe on, and took her in his arms, pressing her against his body, which somehow felt hurt right through. And there he held her, and there she remained.

Till his hands reached blindly down and felt for her, and felt under her clothing to where she was smooth and warm.

'Ma lass!' he murmured. 'Ma little lass! Dunna let's fight! Dunna let's niver fight! I love thee an' th' touch on thee.'

'This I found deeply moving.'

The Subversive

The sign pointing to the beach must have been hammered to the tree ten or even twenty years before. 'Swim At Own Risk'. The red paint had faded almost clean out of sight.

Harding had never learned to swim. His skin was over-sensitive, and it flared up in saltwater or chlorine if he was in it for too long. The shore wasn't his natural element – he was a city guy, a people-watcher – but he had to do something on his Sunday mornings off. He needed to be taking his own pictures again – so he didn't go stir-crazy – but he couldn't go far with just one morning off each week.

The beach below the Kennedy compound wasn't private, but most families, visiting or resident, had avoided it that Labor Day weekend in favor of hamburger stands, lifeguards and beaches with less seaweed. That was good. No people was good. Because he stuck out. But here, he could enjoy his own company, the freedom – away from the world, off duty. Even half a day made a difference. Anyway, too much time on his own and he was at loose ends.

He wore his Bureau-approved summer trousers with their sharp vertical creases, his weekday work-shoes and, in a rare concession to the holiday weekend, a well-pressed, short-sleeved shirt. It was odd to feel the breeze on his skin. Usually he wore his shirt- and jacket-sleeves extra long, to obscure the flare-ups on his hands and wrists. Otherwise he relied on deep pockets.

But there was hardly anyone around that morning, which was just as well. 'Nature' wasn't his usual subject matter, and he wasn't sure what he was doing. He gripped his tripod and looped his camera case over a shoulder. It was his own beloved camera, not a Bureau gadget – one of just four-hundred-and-some Leica MPs, made for the professional, and specifically the photojournalist. It had an electric motor drive, ideal for quick sequences. It hadn't even been marketed. He'd heard about it from another photographer at the Bureau and had paid two months' salary for it. He didn't get to take it out nearly often enough. Today was perfect though. The light, the ease of the morning, the blue solitude of the Sound.

He had the beach to himself except for two older women who appeared to be reading under a vast umbrella. He passed the charred wood of someone's cook-out, and a kite anchored under a rock. Otherwise, the beach was untouched. The surf roared. Channels of water, like silver gelatin, carved the sand into continents.

He stopped, rolled up his trousers and made his way to the water's edge. Bladderwrack popped underfoot, and small holes pocked the beach where clams slept, six inches below. He liked the lobster claws, washed up and estranged from their bodies. Over here, they seemed to beckon, loner to loner. Over here.

He could do this.

Agents always had Sunday mornings off so they could go to church with their families and set a moral example. The Bureau was all about setting an example.

He wasn't going to any church, of course, but the Kennedys would be in their family pew by now at St. Francis's — overflowing it, in fact, because Bobby and Ethel were visiting with their brood. Eunice, one of the sisters, had stayed home with her dog and the toy-dog she was looking after for a friend, as well as Bobby's slobbering St. Bernard.

Ted was down for the weekend too. He'd be in church as well. The guy always had the look of an over-sized kid, as if his mother had just combed his hair, spat on a tissue and wiped his face. Joseph Kennedy and Rose never missed Sunday Mass, nor, for that matter, did Jackie and little Caroline.

Five to nine. It was about to start.

Jack Kennedy was on his way to San Francisco, for some speech or another, but Jack Kennedy wasn't his business. His wife was. He often saw the Senator come and go. Sometimes they exchanged a few quick words in passing, but Mr. Kennedy was on the campaign trail — genial and down to earth, but preoccupied, as you'd expect. When he was out of town, his calls to his wife every evening were short and sweet. Sometimes Caroline baby-talked down the line. Afterwards, Harding would remove his earpiece, close his notebook and head for his motel. His shorthand, he was glad to discover, was still serviceable.

Currents off the Cape could change without warning in September, and that year, the change came early to the Nantucket Sound, driving rogue waves and more weed than usual onto the beach. At the tide-mark, sandpipers skittered, and a new volume of energy crashed down. Summer was on its way out.

Harding knew that view, the whole vista, well by now. He'd been on duty – on surveillance – at the Kennedys' house since June, with little to do except walk the lawns, pat down visitors, check the day's tapes, and file his nightly reports from his motel, Pilgrims Motor Inn on Route 6A.

He was supposed to ask the neighbors, covertly, about Mrs. Kennedy's staff – specifically, Mrs. Clyde, the Scottish housekeeper, and Maud Shaw, the English nanny. The Bureau discovered things about the Person of Interest that way, without drawing undue attention. The comings and goings of Mrs. Clyde and the English nanny might turn up the volume on Mrs. Kennedy. That's what Howard Johnson, the S.A.C. in Washington, said. That's what Howard Johnson wanted.

So far, Harding had managed to avoid it, to delay. But sure, he knew the sort of thing. How long has she (Maud Shaw/Mavis Clyde) been with the Kennedy family? Any strange-looking visitors? Was she foreign? British, you say? Any idea why she hadn't tried to become an American citizen? Any idea why she might not want to become an American? Did she do Mrs. Kennedy's shopping? What stores? What kind of errands? What did she do with herself on her day off? Ever happen to notice? Ever see her drunk? Ever get her mail by mistake? Ever see her with a man? No? A woman? A foreigner? What sort of accent?

He'd tell the neighbor he only wanted to keep the Senator and Mrs. Kennedy safe – that was his job. Certain checks were necessary and helpful. They understood, he'd say, before they did. They were good neighbors, he'd assure them. He knew he could rely on their eyes and ears. 'Thank you for your cooperation.'

He'd get round to it. One day.

His room at Pilgrims Motor Inn was basic but it had all he required: housekeeping, a laundry service, a hot-plate. Sometimes he sat in his car, listening to the radio, or not listening as such but letting the wash of human voices wipe his brain. In the motel's front office, he bought Cape Cod postcards – with images of wild, windswept beaches and cartoons of the Pilgrims eating turkey – for his collection, which he still had in storage in New York. At night, he read for thirty minutes, then turned out the light.

He'd recently told Howard Johnson he needed a copy of 'the book', so he could pick out any references Mrs. Kennedy might be making to it on the tapes. He'd been caught short, without a copy, he pointed out, when Professor Trilling visited. Didn't the Bureau have at least two dozen boxes of the thing sitting in the vice-squad lock-up?

The Post Office intercept in Hyannis revealed that the Professor and Mrs. Kennedy were still following the Federal Court case about the novel, exchanging news clippings and so on. 'Government Lawyer Says the Lady is a "Tramp"'. So ran one headline. According to the same report, the government's lawyer had claimed he loved both literature and the First Amendment. 'I'm no censor!' he told the court, but he warned the jury that well-written obscenity was the most dangerous obscenity of all. Maybe he had a point. Harding didn't know.

In their notes and cards – opened, re-sealed and sent on – Mrs. Kennedy and Trilling were jubilant when, in late July, just over a month ago, Federal Judge Frederick van Pelt Bryan – what a mouthful – found in favor of Barney Rosset and Grove Press, and overturned the Post Office ban. Hoover must have seethed.

Of course the judgment didn't do Harding any favors. It meant his prize photo immediately lost its currency inside the Bureau. The banned book was redeemed. His photo was no longer a picture of a possible First Lady secretly supporting a dirty book – *and* going against the official government position.

A bit of him was glad. His photographic offering to Hoover would be consigned to the Bureau's incinerator. Easy come, easy go. At least he was out of Butte. That was all he'd wanted in the first place.

In her letter to Trilling about the Rosset victory, the Senator's wife had underlined passages in a *New York Times* piece before enclosing it for the Professor's information: 'The Postmaster General, while expert in matters of moving the mail, was not qualified to pronounce on the literary merit of the book. "Therefore," said the judge, "the Postmaster General was not qualified to say that the book's literary merit was outweighed by its allegedly pornographic features. D. H. Lawrence," Judge Bryan concluded, "was an author, not a pornographer."'

In one of her intercepted letters, Mrs. Kennedy had scribbled a line at the top of the clipping: 'Lady Chatterley walks free!' She told

Trilling – whom she often addressed jokily as 'Jack' – that the news had come in that morning like an early birthday present. 'Dear Jack T., A week today, I turn thirty. Perhaps Lady C. might drop into my party on her way to her new life in Canada!'

Professor Trilling replied in kind: 'Tell her Bon Voyage for me. She'll love all that fresh air. She won't know what's hit her after stuffy old Albion! Give her my regards!'

The following week, there was another flutter of correspondence. Their mood was now downcast and subdued. The government had lodged an appeal. Mrs. Kennedy was, she said, incredulous. 'How can it be?'

The Professor was 'very saddened' to hear the news. These things, he conceded, could drag on for a long time, and in that way, good books were simply 'disappeared' out of circulation, and small publishers went under. Red tape was the easiest form of censorship.

It was Hoover behind the appeal, of course. Harding knew the Director was not going to give up. The Bureau had his secret picture of Mrs. Kennedy; the gift which he, Harding, had given; the gift that would go on giving if the Bureau, under the guise of the U.S. Mails and 'the government', stuck to its guns. They had the big lawyers. Hoover was determined that the book which Mrs. Kennedy clutched in glossy black-and-white would still be proven to be, not merely scandalous, but obscene.

He hadn't given up his hope of getting her popular husband off the scene before the Senator could declare his candidacy for the presidential race. Of course he hadn't. The Director was tenacious to the point of obsession, and the scandal of a scandalous wife *could* pull Jack Kennedy down in a way his womanizing probably never would.

If the latter got out, American men would feel sorry for young, pretty Mrs. Kennedy, having to put up with her husband's infidelities, but they'd admire and envy handsome Jack Kennedy. They'd want to be him, and *that* might just be his ticket into the White House. Hoover's greatest hope lay in Mrs. Kennedy's dirty secret.

It wasn't only politics. Hoover believed in 'right' and 'wrong', and he was sure he knew which was which. What other government employee, he would ask himself, was allowed to indulge in un-American activity? Why should the wife of a rich-kid Senator get away with it? She'd been caught red-handed with a banned book.

Why wasn't she supporting the government position? Why was she sneaking around?

Jackie Kennedy, according to Hoover's own notes in her Bufile, 'put on airs'. She liked to be called 'Jacqueline'. Queen Jacqueline! That's what he'd penciled in one margin. In another, he dubbed her 'Lady Kennedy', and in another, not 'Lady C.' but 'Lady K.' He must have smirked at his own wit.

In Bureau-think, she and her husband needed to be dealt with. And soon. The New York Field Office had reported that Papa Joe Kennedy was already taking out leases on two whole floors of new office space in the Marguery Hotel, the family's New York base. His son's declaration for the Democratic nomination contest was a foregone conclusion. The only question was when he came out with it.

In mid-August, Harding's personal copy of the contraband book arrived in thick brown paper in the motel mail, marked 'Strictly Confidential'. The owner of Pilgrims Motor Inn looked at him hard over his yellowing bi-focals, but the man knew not to say anything. Mr. Harding always paid his bills right on time, and he seemed to have no plans to move on.

After Harding's long banishment to Butte, the open space of the Sound that summer, the play of light, and the bedrock peace of the Cape seemed eternal. Harding knew it was as illusory as anything else; that, under the skin of the world, all of life was restless. Change was the only constant. When he was seven, his father kissed his mother goodbye, popped a quarter in his son's pajama-shirt pocket, hoisted his encyclopedia case, and never returned.

He and his mother watched for him – silently sometimes, giddily at others. They'd watched at the living-room window for months, ducking out of sight when neighbors appeared on the front step and rang the bell, to ask after them. Once, they even made popcorn and sat watching the living-room window, as if it were the big screen at the movie theater. After that night, he never could stand the smell of popcorn. But it was in those months, staked out behind that window, that he learned how to watch, how to see, and how to work out truth from appearances. The two didn't line up as often as people thought, and knowing that, in the gut, is what made a good agent.

It sure was something how the brain could play tricks – with another man's height or his gait or even the back of his head. He saw his father for years, on street corners, in barber shops, at gas pumps, and at the far end of drugstore counters. Maybe the truth was that everyone was marked, randomly or miraculously, with the traces of strangers; that no one was ever only themselves. Maybe that meant no one was ever truly alone either.

It was the kind of thing that could turn a person's wits. It was also the closest thing to religion he could muster these days, a thin belief in the stray but seemingly inevitable connections between strangers; a sense that everyone was only a thread, a frayed stitch or a loose end in some design too big for any of us to ever see clear of.

On the beach, at the tide-line, a roller crashed at his feet, soaking his shoes. He'd have a flare-up on his feet by the time he unlaced them, but he couldn't always avoid everything. Besides, sandals were unacceptable on a man, and he certainly wasn't about to go barefoot, not even on a beach. He agreed with the Bureau conduct manual on both points. There had to be standards.

The weight of the camera felt good in his hands. He fixed the base-plate to the tripod – loosely, in case he needed to pluck the camera from the path of an approaching wave or a splashing swimmer. He didn't usually photograph 'shore scenes'. Breaking waves were the stuff of a million Cape Cod postcards. But he wanted to see if he could capture *the wall* of a wave as it glided in to shore. He wanted the smooth, rolling stillness in the powerful upsurge; the glassy calm in the unstoppable force. It was the tug of two opposing elements that made a great picture.

In the shot of Mrs. Kennedy, say, it had been the vulnerability of her face combined with the defiance of that book clutched under her arm.

It felt odd knowing things about her, about her movements, her thoughts; things that even her husband didn't know.

Not that his respect for her changed anything. He was determined to do what Howard Johnson said – stick to the job. 'Don't get ideas.'

The Nantucket Sound seemed to draw in and hold its breath before each crashing release. Waves surged toward the shallows in thundering exhalations: pure power just before they broke.

He thought he could get that on film. If he were to stand more or less in the shallows, he'd get something special. He'd forget about his trousers getting wet and his skin going crazy tomorrow. Hell. So what?

The rhythm of the Sound was hypnotic. He felt his breathing deepen. Time stretched away, as far as the horizon, and he was up to his shins.

He anchored the legs of the tripod in the wet sand. Then he pocketed the lens cap, fitted a filter and selected a slow shutter speed. The tide was coming in fast, and his feet were already stinging, but he'd survive. He'd parked his car not far from the beach, on Irving Avenue by the Senator's house. He'd have time to change at the motel before his afternoon shift, and he could spring for another pair of shoes in Hyannis on Tuesday, when the stores opened again after the holiday.

It was as he took the first test-shot that the sea-floor pulled away.

A rogue wave.

The world tipped.

The horizon disappeared.

Later, he remembered only the arch of her back and the shadowy-white knots of her spine as she burst from the wave.

He nearly fell backwards at the wave's slap, but he got hold of the tripod and steadied himself. The wave flooded the shallows, crashing to shore, bearing its swimmer to the beach. Spray flew high. He was all thumbs, fumbling with the base-plate, with the already pointless lens cap.

Damn it, damn it.

Above him, gulls screeched.

She was struggling to stand in the surf, trying to get her balance. She was in a two-piece, a dark blue bikini, and a yellow-petaled swimming-cap. He tried not to watch as she sat down in the shallows and tugged off each flipper, like an angry child. She brought her hands to her face to wipe her eyes, and pulled off her cap, flinging it hard up the beach. Then she stood again, awkwardly. Her ribs heaved, and her hair was plastered to the sides of her head.

He reached for the sunglasses in his shirt pocket, for their safety, for cover, and nodded a neutral greeting.

She approached, gripping her flippers as if she wanted to clobber him. 'Why are you taking pictures?'

He shoved his hands in his pockets – a reflex action from his first day on the job in Hyannis Port. In case she remembered New York, the hearing at the G.P.O., his hands, *him* – which of course she was not about to do now, not after all these months. But the movement, his stance, seemed to strike her in that moment as rude or insubordinate. She glared.

He could still hear his grade-school teachers shouting at the boys: 'Hands – out – of – pockets!'

'I beg your pardon, Mrs. Kennedy. I didn't realize you were swimming this morning.'

She looked up the beach, and he turned too. The two older women, from the beach-umbrella shelter, were marching in their direction. It was Mrs. Clyde, the housekeeper, and Maud Shaw, Caroline's nanny. He could see their faces now.

'I was just trying,' he said slowly, 'to get a few shots of the Sound. Stupid idea. I'm a city-slicker by nature.' He could feel the saltwater biting the blisters on his hands. He wished she'd leave him be so he could check his camera for water damage.

Jackie Kennedy's dark eyes narrowed. He could see, without wanting to see, that her skin was goose-pimpling; that, beneath her top, her nipples had risen with the breeze. Her bikini bottoms looked too big for her, and her knuckles were white against her hip where she gripped their elastic edge. Sand was weighing them down at the back. Her trademark poise was gone.

'You have no right at all to be taking pictures,' she said, almost inaudibly. Of her, she meant, of her. But she couldn't come out and accuse him, as much as she wanted to. Her jaw was square and hard-set.

'I thought you were at church, Mrs. Kennedy, at nine o'clock Mass,' he said, 'with the family.'

Mrs. Clyde and Maud arrived breathily at the water's edge, and Mrs. Clyde stepped forward into the shallows on varicose legs to drape her charge in a large striped towel. The gulls dipped and squawked overhead. His heart flapped. He couldn't blow another assignment.

Jackie Kennedy didn't take her eyes off him as she spoke to the two women. 'Thank you, Mrs. Clyde. Thank you, Maud,' which meant, *Please leave us now.*

They retreated up the beach to wait, patient as sentries, by the dunes.

'I'm not *able* to go to Mass, Mr. Harding.'

'I apologize. I didn't—'

'I can't go into Hyannis now. I said as much to you already.' Her voice was low, breathy but insistent.

She was referring to the issue of *LIFE* magazine. A couple of weeks before. The cover story: 'Jackie Kennedy: A Front Runner's Appealing Wife'.

After that hit the stands, she couldn't walk down Main Street in Hyannis without drawing a crowd. Women wanted to know where she'd bought that pink dress she wore for the magazine cover; where she had her hair done locally. Men stared. A few had the presence of mind to ask after her husband, the local boy done good. She smiled always, but privately she felt overwhelmed by the attention, by the intrusions; by the way complete strangers addressed her as 'Jackie'. Only family and close friends called her that. Harding knew her mother-in-law worried she wasn't going to cope with political life, and Rose made no secret of her concerns. He had it all well documented on the audio.

'I'm sorry, Mrs. Kennedy,' he repeated. 'I assumed you still went to church with the family on Sundays. I didn't know anyone bothered you there. We'll put another Secret Service man outside the church if you like. I'd do it myself, only I'm not on the job on Sunday mornings.' *As you can see*, he almost added, but he stopped himself, in case it sounded sarcastic.

Her eyes were molten. 'I want that film, please.' She extended an arm and opened her palm. The elbow of her other arm gripped the flippers at her side. It was a balancing act: the towel slipping; her bikini bottoms sagging; the flippers heavy.

'Photography's just my hobby, Mrs. Kennedy. Mr. Kennedy Sr. said I could use the beach for picture-taking. I'm sorry if I surprised you. I was only trying to shoot the wa—'

'I'm waiting, Mr. Harding.' She eyed the camera. She seemed even to appraise it. He'd forgotten until that moment that she'd once been a photographer of sorts herself, the *Times-Herald*'s 'Inquiring Photographer'.

So neither of them saw it coming: the second wind-driven wall of water — at least five feet high, and powerful as it exploded in the shallows.

In that tumult – in the crashing indifference of the Nantucket Sound – she seemed, briefly, to care as much for his camera as he did. He saw concern flicker in her eyes. *Your Leica!* Then the tripod went over, the camera and base-plate went flying, and she leaped out, the full length of herself, to catch it, like a center-fielder.

He saw her flippers carried off in the backwash of the wave. The ground beneath his feet pulled away. He teetered again. His sunglasses plummeted into the tide. She rolled, somersaulting at the wallop of the next wave and, for a long moment, he couldn't see her. When he did, she was receding, not coming at him again. For a moment, he was relieved. He was in the clear.

Then the question came: what was she doing out there? Where was she? He stumbled forward and the cold smacked his chest. The volume of water was a strange sensation. As a kid at Coney Island, he used to wade out, but his mother had always warned him about his skin, about going out above his head. He was a tall guy, sturdy – no one would think to look at him he couldn't swim. What the hell had he been thinking? Now she was furious with him.

And gone.

He squinted into the sun, scanning the waves, but nothing. She was nowhere – Jesus Christ – when something brushed his leg. A foot?

He looked down but the water was no longer clear. Sand churned in the tide. He thought he saw a foot, pedaling. Had she come up for air?

A wave rolled over his head, almost knocking him off his feet.

The backwash was powerful.

He stumbled deeper into the tide, as deep as he dared. The waves buffeted. Another rolled over him. When they flattened out again, the water was up to his collarbone. How the hell had that happened?

And where was she? Most of his life he'd felt too numb to feel fear – worry, sure, he worried all the time – but fear was rare. Something in his head had scrambled the day his father didn't come home. A part of him had gone missing. But that hole within had often served him well as an agent.

Yet now he felt it. Fear. Fear for her. Fear for himself.

It was hard to stay upright, hard not to be drawn even deeper. He started taking off his belt – maybe he'd need some sort of tow-line. He had the thing off when, underwater, fingertips brushed his.

And disappeared again.

He groped the water.

His heart slammed out the seconds.

Until her hand locked on.

Only by virtue of his height and weight did he manage to drag them both back to shore. He checked she was steady on land before releasing her hand. Her face was pale. She turned away, coughing onto the beach. Was she throwing up? Seaweed was still tangled around one of her arms.

When she finally turned to him, something – an involuntary flash of sympathy or perhaps a receding sense of alarm – passed between them.

He saw again the startled expression he knew from the New York shot. But it was worse this time. Much worse. She was spooked.

She hauled her bikini bottoms up, and he turned away, embarrassed, as if he were again 'the intruder'. She bent, stony-faced, for the towel that floated in the shallows. His tripod was there too at the tide-mark, washed up. His Leica was long gone. He no longer cared. He only wanted to get back to his car, and back to the four walls of his motel room.

Her tone was stiff, formal – 'I'm sorry about your camera' – but her shoulders were stooped. She looked exhausted, defeated.

'I'm sorry for the confusion, Mrs. Kennedy. It was a stupid idea of mine.'

'Thank you,' she said, formally again.

It wasn't clear what she was thanking him for.

Another wave crashed at their feet. They both shuddered in the breeze. The silence was painful. Was she waiting for him to confess? What more could he say?

She straightened herself and strode up the beach, in the direction of her keepers and the Kennedy lawn. She'd been right to accuse him, of course, even if her timing had been wrong. He *had* secretly photographed her. Not today, but …

It was as if she'd intuited the truth of that day in New York, even if there was no way she could ever get at the facts of it. In some part of her, it must have been maddening.

There, alone on the beach, he hated himself, not for the first time. That morning, they'd both foundered, and it was his fault.

Only when she and her companions were out of sight did he fish his tripod out of the shallows and clamber, miserably, toward the dunes in the direction of Irving Avenue. He was soaked. He'd lost his belt in the confusion. His hands were red and raw, as if the dumb creature he actually was, was trying to burst through his thin-skinned hide.

In the distance, he heard car doors opening and slamming shut. The Kennedys were back from church. The pack of family dogs, tied to the wash-line at the back, set each other off. By the time he made it to his car, they were barking themselves into a frenzy. He gave it a day – two at best – until Hoover came for him.

ii

He glanced apprehensively at her. Her face was averted, and she was crying blindly, in all the anguish of her generation's forlornness. His heart melted suddenly, like a drop of fire, and he put out his hand and laid his fingers on her knee.

'You shouldn't cry!' he said softly.

But then she put her hands over her face, and felt that really her heart was broken, and nothing mattered any more.

He laid his hand on her shoulder, and softly, gently it began—

The call from the Bureau came that night at quarter to ten, as Harding read the banned book in bed. It had taken Hoover not even twenty-four hours.

It was Howard Johnson, from the Washington Field Office. The call lasted less than three minutes. Johnson's voice was impersonal, impatient. He was chewing gum.

'*The Director* just phoned,' he said, '*on a Sunday night.*'

Senator Kennedy had phoned Hoover direct that afternoon, from somewhere out in California.

Harding was to turn in his badge, revolver, holster and manuals. No, he wasn't to take them to Washington himself. There was a protocol. A Boston agent would be sent to the motel the following morning by ten. He was to have everything ready, including his motel receipts, up to but not including Labor Day. He'd be paid till the end of the month. The Bureau would not provide references.

As Johnson spoke, Harding saw her again as she first appeared that morning: the sluiced skin, her back breaching the wave, the knots of her spine.

It was pointless, but he said it anyway. 'It was a misunderstanding.'

'You were taking pictures of her as she swam. In broad daylight.'

'I'm not that stupid.' He scratched at the broken skin on his arm.

'Well, Harding, it turns out the Senator's wife isn't stupid either. Far from it. Senator Kennedy said there were witnesses. He checked with both himself. They saw it all from just up the beach. You think about that, why don't you? You think about how you fucked up an easy job I passed you on a silver platter.'

And that was it. Howard Johnson hung up.

Harding looked down to the book. His hand still held the novel open to the page he'd been reading before the faultline opened up in his life; the crazy, jagged boundary that divided everything into a Before and After. He'd expected a balling-out, sure – a reprimand, a formal warning.

Not this.

He felt limp, dazed, conscious only that his skin was burning.

On the page, a line swam up at him. 'Then she felt the soft, groping, helplessly desirous hand touching her body'—

Hand.

His *hands*.

Of course his hands.

As a new agent, he'd been deemed of average appearance, 'nondescript', not memorable. 'Nondescript' had been used in his Bu-profile. It was an advantage when he applied to the Bureau.

True, his hands and arms sometimes drew attention, but he'd learned how to compensate, how to dress; how to stay, literally, under cover. Until the hearing back in May, that is. Until the surprise of her words in passing: 'Bad luck to open an umbrella indoors.'

He'd been caught off guard by her that day. She'd had a disarming quality. Plus, he'd had to fumble with a camera hidden in an umbrella handle; it wasn't as if there was a viewfinder. When he found the shutter-release, he'd clicked off a few shots, with no real expectation of getting anything at all. She'd scarcely paused on her way out of the hearing.

She was a person who noticed things. Details. He knew that about her now. They had that in common. He could see it in the way she organized the shoots when the press photographers turned up on Irving Avenue.

She'd remembered – his hands.

Of course she had. That morning on the beach, once they were clear of the water, he hadn't let go of her hand, not till she was steady.

She'd said nothing. She knew how to maintain a cover too. She'd gone home with Mrs. Clyde and the nanny. Then she'd slipped away from the Kennedy family's Labor Day weekend homecoming brunch to phone her husband – mid-morning West Coast time – to sound the alarm.

Harding was back on duty at Irving Avenue by one o'clock. She'd used the phone in her father-in-law's 'den' to place the call, as if she suspected he, her 'security man', might be listening. Not that she knew about the bugs in her own place. But she now knew Agent Harding was, in her terms, a 'spy'. That's what she would have told her husband. She'd worked out he couldn't be Secret Service. She never would have suspected the Bureau, which was a law *enforcement* agency after all. The only explanation would have been that he was a spy. A Communist spy. Jack was the front-runner in the Democratic race.

'The Russians, they're following us,' she must have breathed into the phone.

Because of course it couldn't be *your own people.*

She couldn't have told her husband the entire story, not without revealing she'd secretly been at a hearing for a dirty book while he was on the trail, campaigning for every vote he could get in union halls and at county fairs. She would have told him only about the photos on the beach that morning, about the agent's flimsy excuse – 'Nature photos,' the man had said. The spy. The Soviet.

She'd probably exaggerated that morning's scene to ensure the result she needed. Harding wouldn't blame her if she had. But if her husband hadn't been told the full story, he'd certainly grasped enough. Kennedy had bypassed the Secret Service and gone straight to the Director himself, about an agent who was supposed to be Secret Service – any leading politician's peace of mind in the world.

To Kennedy's ears, his wife's account would have made it clear that 'Agent Harding' belonged to Hoover; that the man in their flower bed and at their front gate was not just watching his wife; he was following her, with help of the highest kind. *That* meant the Bureau, and it meant Hoover was violating even the privacy of their home life, for Christ's sake.

The conversation, coast to coast, must have gone something like that. The Senator would have wondered how much lower Hoover would go. Who wouldn't have under the circumstances? But it was a question, thought Harding, someone like the Senator should never ask.

He didn't want to know.

Kennedy might have threatened to expose Hoover's dark maneuvers, but both men would have known he couldn't threaten much.

The Senator knew Hoover had plenty on him, going way back. Countless files stuffed full. Miles of tape. He knew because Hoover had made sure he knew – enough, and not more.

Still, it couldn't have been a 'comfortable' conversation for the Director either. Even in his shock that night, Harding understood that much. Kennedy's call that afternoon would have caught Hoover on the back foot, and that would have enraged him, particularly as the call had probably interrupted the Sunday ritual of his and Tolson's backgammon game on Hoover's veranda.

The Director's rages were legendary. No quantity of his house-keeper Annie's hot milk was ever going to appease Hoover in a tantrum. All that mattered was the fact that the Bureau's cover was blown. A weakness had been exposed. A Bureau secret was out.

It was the only logical explanation for the speed of events; for Harding being fired at ten o'clock on a Sunday night on a Labor Day weekend at the order of the Director himself.

Never let the Bureau look bad.

That was the cardinal rule.

He went over it again: that wave knocking the two of them off balance; her feet churning in the current; that long, pounding heartbeat of time. Then her hand, underwater, gripping his, and the indescribable relief.

It had been a human bond. Fragile, but real.

And now it had passed.

She owed him nothing. Nothing at all.

When she'd first demanded the film in his camera, he'd wanted to confess to her then, about the hearing back in the spring. Not that he would have. Not that she wasn't about to put two and two together for herself. She was way ahead of him as she left the beach.

They'd dragged themselves from the Sound. He'd noticed her fingers, pale and wrinkled as she withdrew her hand from his. She'd stood, choking and spluttering at the tide-mark. Her shoulders had heaved.

'Are you okay? Mrs. Kennedy?' Was she throwing up? Was it mild shock? She was shaking. When she turned to him again, she looked drained, and her expression had changed. She was wary, in a way she hadn't been even at the G.P.O.

His brain had seized up as he'd looked at the loveliness of her, lovely in spite of the ordeal, in spite of her exhaustion, and he felt a dull pain in his chest; something swelling in his heart, in his lungs, as if it wanted out. Not desire or fear. Not pity or even his usual sense of shame. Tenderness maybe. A torrent of it.

In his bed, he saw again the concern that had come into her eyes as the rogue wave hit – *your camera, your wonderful camera!* – before she'd remembered she was furious with him, exposed, unnerved by his intrusion. How *dare* he take pictures?

That first soft, liquid expression in her eyes had stayed with him. He saw it now in the darkness behind his eyelids. He didn't switch off the bedside lamp. The night was too empty, too great a chasm, to invite darkness in.

Sleep didn't come, or when it did, it was a stupor; his brain shutting down against the scale of calamity he faced. No job, no family, no place to be, no purpose. The last thing his eyes registered that Sunday night was the hardback book, still open on the blanket to the page where the gamekeeper, Mellors, was speaking to Lady Chatterley.

'I could die for the touch of a woman like thee.'

Then his eyes closed, and he felt again her hand seizing hold. The shock of it. The force of it.

He couldn't remember when he had last been touched, by anyone.

iii

Mrs. Clyde had Labor Day Monday off and had caught the bus into Boston to meet relatives. Caroline was playing with her pull-along ducks in the living-room, overseen by Nanny Maud. Soon, Jackie and Caroline would cross the lawns and join everyone in the Big House, for 10 a.m. breakfast with the family.

She was in shorts and an over-sized sweater, long-sleeved to cover the bruise on her arm where their resident 'spy' had pulled her to safety. Jack had assured her yesterday afternoon that the man wouldn't be back.

She was on her way up the stairs to change when the bell went.

He spoke before she had time to protest. 'I'm sorry to disturb you, Mrs. Kennedy. I came to return your key. I understand you are to give it to my replacement when he arrives this morning.'

That was odd, she thought. She hadn't realized Agent Harding had been given a house-key. It didn't bear thinking about. His eyes met hers. He wasn't wearing his dark glasses for once. Nor were his hands stuffed in his pockets as they usually were, and perhaps because of that, he looked a little taller.

He had a piece of folded paper in his hand. He was offering it to her. She didn't understand. Was the key wrapped in it?

'All fine, Mrs. Kennedy?' called Maud from the living-room.

'Thank you, Maud,' she called back over her shoulder.

She took the folded-up offering. But it was only a sheet of stationery from a local motel, Pilgrims Motor Inn. There was no key at all.

Dear Mrs. Kennedy,

Please don't say anything. I am sorry to tell you, and to tell you in this manner, that your house, your telephone, and your patio are planted with listening devices: small microphones fitted with radio transmitters. I am unsure whether they are recording now or not. I am sorry about yesterday. It wasn't as you feared, at least not then it wasn't. I wasn't taking pictures of you. But I was previously, as I think you now realize. If you would agree to walk me to my car, which is parked outside, I have something you should have. It might be a help to you. It's all I can offer, to make amends. Then I will leave you in peace. I would be grateful if you would return this note to me now.

Sincerely yours,
Mel Harding

She searched his face. His eyes were cracked and red-rimmed. He hadn't shaven. His clothes looked as if he'd slept in them.

Her features wrinkled with disdain. She folded the note, returned it to him and closed the door behind them. Damage-limitation. Nothing more.

She crossed her arms as she walked up her own front path. She couldn't wait till this man was out of their lives. Perhaps he thrived on imagining he had some sort of hold on her and her family. Well, let him imagine all he liked. Yesterday, Jack had promised her he'd get the man fired, and he had done just that. The problem lay with the Bureau, her husband had explained. Fellow *Americans*. Not the Soviets. She'd hardly been able to take it in.

At the car, the man reached through the open window into the glove compartment and passed her a Manila envelope. She peered inside and saw a small paper sleeve, with a square negative inside. As it slipped out onto her palm, she looked up, blinking.

'The New York hearing,' he said. 'At the G.P.O. Hoover has the print. I sent it to him after. I'm sorry – I have no excuse. As you can see, he doesn't have the negative, but to be honest, that's beside the point. I wish I could undo what I've done, but this is the most I can do now. Remember – you need to tell your husband he must have your house swept for bugs – light fixtures, telephones, sockets, switches and so on.'

Her lips parted but words didn't come. Her sweater swam on her, and she looked cold in spite of the mild morning.

'Surely you're not serious,' she said finally.

'There are people in the Bureau who say the Director has the entire Department of Justice bugged, even the Attorney General's private elevator. One family dwelling is not a challenge, Mrs. Kennedy, although' – he looked embarrassed – 'I can assure you they left the … private spaces untouched. Your husband's people won't find anything there to worry you.' Then he nodded once, as if to say, I will bother you no further.

She felt her eyes filling – with the shock – and bent her head. She noticed his work-shoes, ruined by saltwater. Did the man not have another pair of decent shoes? His stray-dog quality irritated her. Repelled her even. 'Shoo!' she wanted to say to him. 'Shoo! Leave us be. We have nothing more for you.'

The shoes were nothing of course compared to the loss of that beautiful camera of his. She shook herself slightly. Agent Harding. Mel Harding. That was the man's name. He looked miserable – a sorry, shuffling thing – as he stood before her, under the weight of his belated regret.

Their stilted tableau seemed to require her to speak, to say *something*. 'I hope your next position is more ... straightforward,' she managed to say. *Shoo! Shoo now.* On the picket fence between them, pearls of dew trembled on autumn webs. How fragile everything was – all their fates hanging on threads – and how low she felt.

He couldn't bring himself to meet her eyes or speak. This wasn't how he'd rehearsed it in his head. A welter of grief and fear was pushing up behind the bones of his skull; a pressure behind the sockets of his eyes, as if his defenses had been stripped from him with his revolver, his holster and badge first thing that morning.

One of the family dogs in the yard of the Big House began barking riotously, and she jumped. Rabbits on the lawn must have set them off. She managed to extend her hand. The faster she brought things to a close, the sooner Mel Harding would disappear.

As her sleeve slipped back, he saw her wrist, ringed with a deep bruise, where he'd hauled her free of the current yesterday. He accepted the courtesy he knew he didn't deserve, extending his hand – risking it. She took it, red and sore-looking though it was. She didn't recoil. She shook his hand once, lightly, before turning.

Much of the time, he felt like a social leper, and here she was, the Senator's pretty young wife. Not just pretty but nice. She was a nice person. She tried hard at whatever she took on. She was surprisingly shy. He'd recognized that in her. She didn't find strangers easy. She wasn't as confident as all those boisterous Kennedy sisters. She was a little unusual, even. 'Fey', his mother might have said.

Before she had taken more than a few steps, he made himself say it, because he wanted it said: 'It's a good book, Mrs. Kennedy. I' – he felt his Adam's apple bob in his throat – 'I've been reading it. I hope … I hope it wins in court.'

She turned: a three-quarter profile shot. 'Yes.' She hesitated. 'I do too – Mel.'

The morning light was filmy-white, a long exposure, all pearly radiance. He raised a hand, less in a wave than a gesture of goodbye. 'Thank you, Mrs. Kennedy.'

She said it so quietly he almost missed it.

'Jacqueline.'

Then she disappeared inside.

From a corner of a window in the entry hall, she watched him as he sat in the driver's seat, his head bowed over the steering wheel. Finally, he swung his car around in the narrow road, skidding slightly on the sandy lip of a ditch, and drove off to she-didn't-know-where. She'd wished him well. It was the most she'd been able to muster. But in her anger at his confession – and in her desire to sever their peculiar intimacy – she'd withheld from him one truth.

In the water yesterday morning, as he'd hauled her up, the situation had been more frightening than she'd wanted him to know. For the second time, on his 'watch', she had been reckless. First, when she'd attended the hearing in secret; then, yesterday, when she'd leaped for that damn camera of his.

On the beach, she shouldn't have shown him her anger. She'd revealed too much. She should have simply bid him good-day, walked home and placed the call to her husband.

Perhaps none of it mattered now. Mr. Harding had been fired. He was no longer their problem. They'd never see him again.

How long had her panic underwater lasted? One minute? Two? She hadn't been able to get her head up for air. It was a cold-sweat of a nightmare, an impossibility she couldn't kick free of.

She'd been able to see the ocean floor – the water wasn't deep – but it was in her nose, her windpipe, then her lungs.

She often swam alone, and yesterday, Maud and Mrs. Clyde had been only up on the beach. The Sound was never a millpond, but she was a strong swimmer, and she liked a Sunday-morning swim, first thing, to clear her head.

She and Mel Harding had only been in the shallows. In fact, she'd been on her way in when the first wave crashed.

She dove – stupidly – thinking she might save the camera before it hit the water. But the wave itself hadn't been the problem. It was the power of the backwash; the dark grip of the undertow that had pulled her out.

Then her lungs had started to burn, and a terrible clarity had come over her. A person could drown in just four feet of water.

She'd thought of Caroline, in the pew at St. Francis's in that moment grinning among her cousins. Caroline loved the murals of the floating angel-heads on the wall above the altar. Had Jack already reached for his morning paper? She wondered vaguely, almost calmly, if she'd be a headline, the next day. She saw her husband's blue-gray eyes, their quiet depths, and the light of them, a gleaming line of being from him to her. *Grab hold!* he'd called. But when she'd tried, there was only weed brushing her face.

The tide was murky. Was that a leg ahead? That man's leg?

It was hard to see, hard to keep her eyes open in the saltwater. What was his name? Her brain was slowing down. His trouser legs had swollen up underwater, like a dead man's limbs. What had happened? Where was she? She couldn't recall. Jack was shouting to her again: the man was an anchor. *Grab hold!* She had to grab hold.

She swam again into the wall of water. Two feet maybe. Three? It was all that separated them. Her hands were cupped and her fingers closed and rigid as she swam, cleaving the tonnage of water; forcing the wall to part. Her knees flexed hard, her feet kicked out, over and over, but each time she drew near, she felt the current drawing her away.

Her chest was tight, as if her lungs would burst. She was tired, so tired suddenly, and dizzy too – was she facing up or down? A bare arm swept across her field of vision. Two arms threshed the current. A hand groped blindly. She thought she saw her little girl – Arabella? No, Caroline. *Caroline* was bending to pick up shells on the shore, at the tide-mark, so close.

She'd summoned the last of her energy – heat, oxygen, muscle, love – and had driven herself forward until—

Sunlight on her eyelids.

The mercy of it.

Something blue on the shore.

A beach umbrella – getting brighter and bigger.

And the green of dune grass.

After, she'd sat in her kitchen, still shaken, saying nothing to anyone. Bobby had come in from the beach to tell her the children's swimming party was off. There were reports all along the beach of a strong rip-tide. Two swimmers had been dragged out. They were lucky to be alive.

A few hours later, she was subdued at the family party in the Big House. She didn't have the energy to pretend. Instead, she watched the clock on the mantelpiece, waiting for the time when she could slip away to phone Jack in California.

That man, Mel Harding, was already back on duty, for his Sunday-afternoon shift. She knew as she waited that she had to say enough to Jack for him to understand that the man was a spy, an intruder, but not more. She mustn't mention New York and the G.P.O. in May. She couldn't say a word about that.

When she, Maud and Mrs. Clyde had set out for the beach yesterday morning, Mrs. Clyde had remarked that Agent Harding couldn't even swim. He'd told her as she'd tended the flower bed where he was often stationed. 'I do hope,' Mrs. Clyde said to Jackie, 'that the Secret Service provides *another* man for your and Mr. Kennedy's days on the *Victura*.' Mrs. Clyde often enjoyed her own snippy commentary.

Only as Jackie watched Mel Harding drive away from Irving Avenue for the last time did it dawn on her: he must have been terrified, in the water, with those waves up to his neck.

She wanted to blame him, to lock every door and window of her mind. If he hadn't been there on the beach with his damn camera, she would have simply enjoyed her swim and stretched out on her towel in blissful ignorance.

Yet it was also true that if he hadn't been there yesterday – if he hadn't, literally, held his ground – the Sound would have taken her.

Later that September, 3,000 miles across the Atlantic, an idea popped into the brain of Eunice Frost, like a message bobbing up in a bottle. She grabbed it.

Eunice Frost, Fiction Editor at Penguin Books in London, promptly sought a colleague's advice, dashing off a memo. 'Can you give me any guidance about the likely-to-be complex situation on the possibility and/or wisdom, perhaps, of considering publication over here of the unexpurgated version of Lady Chatterley's Lover?'

From what she could make out from that distance, the new Grove Press edition in America was languishing in the Court of Appeal. By November, Sir Allen Lane, Publishing Director at Penguin, was weighing up a possible addition to their 'commemorative edition' series of D. H. Lawrence's works. He tried out Eunice's idea on the Board. 'I wonder whether we might not include the *unexpurgated* Lady Chatterley's Lover as one of the group?'

In December, Professor Trilling scribbled a note to Jackie: 'I'm told by my sources in the Law Department that the Government's appeal will be heard this month. They're fighting the book hard all the way. I am cautioned that it will be months before the Appeals Judge reaches a decision. In the meantime, I hope Lady C. is not too melancholy as she waits it out at her sister's place in Scotland, and that Mellors is bearing their separation with fortitude. The New World beckons!'

In late January, 1960, a parcel arrived on Irving Avenue from Chester Square, London, stuffed with Christmas presents from her sister Lee and Lee's husband, Michael – although 'husband' for how much longer, it was impossible to say. The marriage was coming undone, and Lee confessed in her note to her sister that life was 'testing'. She had struggled even to write Christmas cards, and she apologized for not getting her parcel off till after the new year. She hoped the treats would at least come as a nice surprise, because they were so late.

The boxes inside the shipping carton were shop-wrapped, and the carton itself was stuffed with balled-up pages torn from the newspapers and magazines Lee and Michael had on subscription. *The Times of London. Homes & Gardens. Vogue. The Tatler. The Queen.* The

Bookseller and Trade News. The latter must have been Michael's. He was from a family firm of publishers of some sort, although Jackie could never quite ascertain his role. He seemed to be at lunch a great deal or at dinners in the West End, while Lee looked for, and found, attention elsewhere.

Jack's own smiling face appeared among the packing paper, in the news of him joining the race for the Democratic nomination. Had Lee packed the box herself or had she asked her housemaid to do it? Presumably the latter. She didn't think Lee would scrunch up Jack's face. If anything, she had, at times, seemed too enamoured of it.

It was an Associated Press piece, something picked up off the wire in London, late evening on January 2nd, in time for the British Sunday papers on the 3rd. She pressed it out on the kitchen table, smoothing her husband's brow. As she did, she could hear him playing with Caroline in the living-room. Tomorrow, he'd be off again.

Senator John F. Kennedy of Massachusetts moved formally into the Democratic Presidential Race Saturday with a challenge to potential rivals to meet him in the primaries. Kennedy has been campaigning actively for months. But he had declined to officially avow his intention.

He is generally regarded as the front runner for the nomination, but his backers concede he is now well short of the backing he would need for a first-ballot victory at the National Convention. The 42-year-old Senator told—

And there, his words were torn off. She gathered up the presents to deliver to Caroline and Jack. It was kind of Lee when she was struggling with her own life. Jackie was on her way out of the kitchen when she noticed a page from the *Bookseller*, trapped under her heel. Something made her set down the stack of gifts in her arms and bend for it.

Wonders never, she thought.

It was a full-page advertisement, dated the 9th of January. 'To mark the thirtieth anniversary of the death of D. H. Lawrence, Penguin will publish in June 1960 a group of seven Lawrence works, including the unexpurgated *Lady Chatterley's Lover*.'

Alone in the kitchen, she felt a rush of childish delight – and vindication. Let her own country get in the way of a great book. It was a young country and would have to be forgiven. But Lawrence's England had seen sense.

My dear Jack T.,

I thought you would enjoy this particular enclosure. Such a surprise, given the failings on our side of the Atlantic. You can't keep a good woman down!

A very happy new year – and decade – to you and Mrs. Trilling. May the sixties be kind to us all.

With deepest friendship,
Jacqueline

Fly Little Boat

But I stand by her: and am perfectly content she should do me harm with such people as take offence at her. I am out against such people. Fly little boat!

D. H. Lawrence

Less than a week after Jackie had posted her celebratory note to the Professor, *Lady Chatterley's* British publisher was checking that it was 'all systems go' for June publication. A question arose in the House of Commons: would the Attorney General of England and Wales, Sir Reginald Manningham-Buller, give his assurance to the Board of Directors of Penguin Books that their forthcoming publication of *Lady Chatterley's Lover*, by the late D. H. Lawrence, would not be the subject of criminal proceedings?

Among parliamentarians and the judiciary, the Attorney General was more commonly known as 'Bull'.

'NO,' Bull informed Parliament.

British obscenity law had recently softened – just six months before – to take into account a book's literary merit and public good as a work of art, but 'Bull', true to his moniker, remained unmoved.

Penguin's lawyer, Michael Rubinstein of the firm Rubinstein, Nash & Co., advised his client as well as the circumstances allowed. The new legal position, however, was untested, and therefore 'subject to interpretation'. Would Lady Chatterley be allowed to pass through the gates of the Establishment unchecked? Sir Allen Lane had, quite literally, wagered that she would. The advertisements had already appeared in the press. The printers were at the ready. But Michael Rubinstein wasn't as sanguine.

On the one hand, *Lady Chatterley* might be singled out 'sympathetically' for trial by the Director of Public Prosecutions – a test case through which the refinements and support of the new law could be demonstrated. On the other hand, the Director of Public Prosecutions might 'make an example' of Lady C. There was no telling which way his thoughts would go.

In his office in the old Georgian building known as Gray's Inn, Rubinstein lit his favourite Savinelli pipe and unbuttoned his waistcoat, as was his habit when he needed to concentrate on a legal case or, in more languorous moments, a sheaf of sheet-music. Manningham-Buller's single-word reply suggested that attitudes had not changed a jot since 1928, when Rubinstein's own father, Harold, took up the cause for the publisher Jonathan Cape in an infamous obscenity trial.

In '28, the story had ended with the destruction of all 1,500 copies of Radclyffe Hall's *Well of Loneliness*, a book declared by one newspaper editor of the day to be more dangerous to the nation's youth than a phial of prussic acid. Harold Rubinstein, Solicitor for the Defence, had marshalled some of the best literary expert witnesses, but they went unheard. They weren't even permitted to take the stand.

Michael Rubinstein was something of an oddity in the legal world. After losing his hearing in his right ear in the war, he had continued to play his beloved violin and cello as much, if not more, than previously. An avowed amateur, he had come, paradoxically, to better understand the full expression of string music with his hearing loss – not only its plaintive strains and sweetness, but also the elemental expressions of the particular instrument, its purring, its growling vibratos, its sonorous silences.

He had married a ballerina, after a few broken engagements in his youth. He was increasingly interested in Sufism and penned Japanese-style haiku poems. He could not remember when or where he had first read the controversial novel but, as time went on, he realised he felt an abiding affection for Lady Chatterley.

On re-reading Allen Lane's latest venture, he admired, more than he would have expected, Lady Chatterley's 'stillness', her self-possession and quiet courage; he felt he even understood the hidden turmoil of her heart. He had had a long wait in his own life, until the age of thirty-five, until he discovered a genuinely mutual love. Until then, he had gone through the motions, as society expected, and engagements had failed. Sex in itself was fine, but intimacy had eluded him. He wasn't even sure he knew what it was. His beloved mother had died when he was nineteen, and perhaps something within him had stopped with her. Re-reading *Lady Chatterley*, in the run-up to Penguin's press announcement, he had been strangely moved by Constance Chatterley's struggle for a life of true feeling. As Penguin was his client, however, and not Lady Chatterley, he was obliged to think as cautiously as the early information permitted. 'There can be, I think, no question of prison sentences for the Directors of your Company or anyone else concerned with the publication.'

In this way, he reassured Sir Allen Lane, publisher and family man, that a prison sentence was unlikely, and he simultaneously reminded him that it could not be ruled out. Rubinstein drafted his reply twice, adding the phrase 'I think' to the final copy. Then he scribbled his weekend telephone number, HAM. 9350, and awaited Sir Allen's call.

There were times in Michael Rubinstein's working days when, as his secretary observed, he would switch the telephone receiver to his deaf ear as he took a call, and stare out of the tall Georgian window, more taken with the view of the lawns and the work of the grounds-men than the discussion at the end of the line. There was something of the nonconformist in the highly regarded solicitor. Perhaps it was his streak of circumspect rebellion which best equipped him to face down 'the law' on behalf of the unruly book trade.

When Sir Allen Lane rang him at The Gables, on a Saturday, in the middle of a 1915 Debussy sonata, Rubinstein laid down his bow, nodded and said – as if he were still somewhere in 1915 – 'Indeed. It would seem that blighter Lawrence is relying on us, Lane.'

In the Hyannis Post Office, the Bureau's intercept had been slow to realize the significance of a clipping sent by Mrs. Kennedy to Professor Trilling. The item, an advertisement from something called the *Bookseller*, didn't directly concern the New York hearing, the federal court case against Grove Press, or the recent government appeal of the decision. It was, in fact, from an English magazine, so its relevance had initially been missed.

Hoover made no secret of his displeasure. The photostat of the January ad arrived at Washington HQ only in mid-April. The Boston S.A.C. had neglected to send it up the line. A verbal reprimand was issued.

J. Edgar Hoover and Clyde Tolson, Director and Associate Director, were enjoying toasted turkey sandwiches at the Mayflower when Hoover slid the clipping along the table to his deputy. They shared their usual corner table and the same comfortable banquette.

Clyde tssked. 'I thought the English were famous for their reserve.'

Penguin Books, the ad announced, was to publish the unexpurgated *Lady Chatterley's Lover* in June. It was a half-page ad. 'Not cheap,' Clyde remarked. He speared the pickle on Hoover's plate. 'I'd say that publisher is confident.'

Hoover fished from his breast-pocket something further, words telephoned through that morning by the Bureau's London attaché. It was a Letter to the Editor of one of the national papers in London, written by a member of the public after reading the Penguin announcement.

'Listen to this,' he said, settling back, well fed. '"Publisher Allen Lane and his fellow directors rightly look for a profit from their publications. I am sure this book will bring in a rich reward. But is it right to make money by debasing the moral standards of the nation? Are they familiar with the Communist technique of first undermining the moral standards of the nations they plan to take over? I am sure Penguin Books have no such purpose in mind. Nevertheless, the publication of *Lady Chatterley's Lover* will undoubtedly advance the Communist agenda in Britain."'

Hoover reached for a toothpick and eyed it. It had fine green streamers stuck to one end. Classy. You got what you paid for. 'Trust me. The Public Prosecution Office in London will have this in their sights, and I expect to hear more any day from our guy in London.'

He laid other clippings on their table for Clyde to see: a barrage of headlines from the British press.

'LADY CHATTERLEY IS <u>COMING</u> – AS A PAPERBACK'

'Chatterley Novel (Nothing Barred) for Britain'

'IT WILL BE A MISTAKE!'

'IS This a Wise Move?'

'I WISH LADY CHATTERLEY LUCK: It's What Might Follow That Bothers Me'

'CUSTOMS SEIZE COPY OF LADY CHATTERLEY'

In Britain, a copy of the uncensored *Lady Chatterley's Lover* could still get you three months in jail. Hoover had checked himself. British Customs even had a screened-off area dedicated to its confiscation. He liked that idea. Sometimes, the English really knew how to do things. The fruit cocktails arrived. As always, Hoover pushed to one side his maraschino cherry. He was good at waiting, and waiting games.

Back at HQ, he asked his secretary, Miss Gandy, to get a message to the Bureau's London attaché. 'The Director would be grateful if Dame Rebecca West would telephone Washington, reverse charge, when her schedule permits.'

Dame Rebecca phoned the following day. She was out of the country until June but yes, she *supposed* she could meet the Bureau's London attaché on her return. Hoover outlined his concerns for 'the free world'. Her voice was clipped and she gave little away, but she was not unhelpful.

There was no urgency, she assured him. She seemed to know. No prosecution case could be launched until *actual* publication – and the word in London was that Penguin was in difficulties. Its printer had pulled out, having taken legal advice about the controversial novel. They'd been warned off, apparently. June publication of *Chatterley*, her sources told her, had been delayed until August.

Dame Rebecca West had impeccable sources.

Behind his desk, Hoover unbuttoned his suit jacket. He knew she prided herself on her grasp of government policy and legalities. She was already proving a very useful ally. Moreover, her Bufile had turned up an unexpected gem. Dame Rebecca's personal attorney was none other than Sir Theobald Mathew, *Director of Public Prosecutions*. Chief Prosecutor for the Crown. The very man who would decide: trial or no trial for the book.

Better still, Theobald Mathew was not just her attorney but a personal friend. According to Bureau sources, back in the forties, he had been one of Dame Rebecca's expert guides through judicial matters as she prepared her book, an examination of loyalty, treachery, treason and betrayal. All the things that mattered, in other words. Hoover couldn't recall the title. The woman wrote too much to keep up with.

Naturally, he had no intention of discussing Mrs. Kennedy and *her* recent reading habits with anyone outside the Bureau. He didn't need to. It was enough to remind Dame Rebecca of the Soviets' Active Measures program and their very well-funded interest in Britain's moral confusion and decline.

He had done his homework. Over the crackling line, he read back to her her own words from an article in which she had warned her readers of the 'lethal threat' of Communism, and 'a new dictator' who 'steals on us undetected'. Britons, 'weary of austerity' post-war, would be too easily distracted by 'abusive words', 'brawls' and 'grievances'. Yet *that* was precisely the Soviet mission. Distraction. A moral weakening of her nation.

On the phone, Hoover congratulated her on her percipience – he'd looked up the word in advance. Her concerns about the Soviet threat in Britain, he said, were justified. The Communists were using any available controversy to drive a wedge into the heart of the West, and the scandal of this Lawrence book was, for the Soviets, a prime opportunity to do so. She said she understood. Yes, she would meet the legal attaché in London to consider the Bureau's request for assistance. She would, however, give no guarantee.

Hoover put the phone down. 'Bingo!' he said to his desktop picture of six-year-old Shirley Temple.

Jack Kennedy was still the Democratic front-runner for the presidential nomination, and July – the Democrats' decision time – wasn't far off. Kennedy had to be stopped. The Bureau was doing its best, and the Director was throwing everything he could at it. The Bureau's surveillance of the nominee-hopeful and his inner circle was piling up in classified files. Not that Dame Rebecca needed to know about that. Women of all descriptions liked Jack Kennedy. He had that effect.

In light of the growing threat posed to the Bureau by the Kennedy brothers, the Bureau was funneling cash, and plenty of it, into the Washington Field Office. In a move sanctioned by Hoover himself, the Washington Special Agent in Charge, Howard Johnson, was 'importing' call-girls from London to tempt Kennedy and his campaign team away from the straight and narrow. It was worth a shot.

Howard Johnson understood he was to keep HQ, and Hoover especially, above 'the fray'. Hoover wanted to know only the essentials: i.e., that the girls had had 'dealings' with high-flyers in London, dealings which were sure to turn the heads of Jack Kennedy's team. Who didn't want the cream of the gossip, especially when served up by gorgeous foreign girls?

Howard Johnson assured Hoover the girls could be flown over and 'returned to sender' at a moment's notice. They came highly recommended by someone trusted in the most discreet circles in London, a 'society doctor'. The Quorum Club in D.C. and the 21 Club in New York were, Johnson confirmed, turning out to be ideal locations for the after-hours meetings. Nice and private. Worth every penny of the Bureau budget.

Two girls were doing the pre-election rounds with Kennedy's team. Stunners, the pair of them. One was dark and exotic; the other, blonde and shapely. So far, Senator Kennedy hadn't taken the bait – but he was flirting. He was certainly flirting. Johnson said Hoover had to be patient, give it time. There were rumors that Mrs. Kennedy was expecting again, but even if she were, that had never stopped the Senator before.

Quite the opposite.

There were the old Jack Kennedy sex-tapes of course, still in the Bureau's safe. They were good for frightening the Senator, but the truth was, Hoover couldn't actually *release* anything like that on the airwaves, not without corrupting the innocence of the nation – and that wasn't in the Bureau's long-term interests. He wanted the whole country to go on believing in the world of *The Lawrence Welk Show*. Like Welk, he wanted to be a guiding father for his country. If he managed that he would have served his country well.

Yet without an actual leak of the sex-tapes, without hard proof, the allegations of extramarital affairs would be dismissed as spiteful rumors, or even worse, as a 'smear'. Even if the leftie journalists couldn't trace the rumors back to the Bureau, the very word 'smear' might bolster sympathy for Kennedy. It could all backfire.

So the London call-girls might just generate the scandal he needed. A few choice pictures. Not too much, but enough – especially if the Democratic front-runner had a pregnant wife at home. If Lady Kennedy *was* pregnant, women, from East Coast to West, would be outraged when the news of his adultery broke, and they'd brow-beat their husbands into being outraged too. There were only a few occasions when women got their way, and, in his experience, pregnancy was one of them.

On second thought, he hoped to God the Senator's wife *wasn't* pregnant. A baby on the way would be a bigger boost to the Kennedy campaign than Frank fucking Sinatra.

He had a hunch that the best bomb in his arsenal was still Mrs. Kennedy's picture, with the book – *that book* – under her arm.

He just had to ensure the bomb went off.

Back in March, things had gone belly-up in New York. The damned Appeals Court judge had upheld the first judge's decision *in favor* of Grove Press over the Post Office – over the government, *over the F.B.I.*, although only the Postmaster General knew about the Bureau's 'investment' in the trial.

Hoover had fumed for days. He'd announced to the New York Field Office that the government – meaning the Bureau – meaning *him* – would take the case all the way to the Supreme Court. But the New York S.A.C. had turned mealy-mouthed, and the government lawyer, also in the room at the time, had pointed out with an insolent shrug that the uncensored Grove Press edition of *Lady Chatterley's Lover* was already Number Two on the *New York Times* bestsellers list. As if to say, 'End of story, Hoover. Cut your losses and walk away.'

He wasn't about to cut anything, except that smug bastard of a lawyer. Instead, he'd bide his time. He could do that. He could do it because he could still imagine, vividly, the splash the photo of the 'front-runner's wife' would make on the front page of, say, the *Chicago Tribune*. He had the ear of men at the *Tribune*, and beyond. Now, England was his new battleground. God love England.

British Customs had responded to his call. They were on alert, impounding all copies of the new American edition. But a *trial* – a trial in London, England, if it could be made to happen – would draw the eyes of the world. The only difficulty was the timing: with the Penguin edition delayed till August, how fast could the Prosecution in London move and, more importantly, what could he do to guarantee the start of a trial before the federal election in November? Who did he know?

Great Britain was flat-broke after the war. On its knees, in fact. Poor old England was not very 'Merrie' at all these days, but it still had standards. The Director of Public Prosecutions – Dame Rebecca's personal friend – was there to ensure that it did. He rang the new London attaché himself. 'When Dame Rebecca is back in England in June, you're going to meet her at her convenience. There's a place called the American Garden. In London, yes, in London! Find it. Women like flowers. Send a car, meet her in the garden, have a nice chat, a discreet chat, then take her to a pricey restaurant. Get a table with the best view and buy her high tea. Buy her the highest tea they've got. Do you understand? If she has information, I want it by phone before the day is out. If she doesn't, make sure she knows: *you're* a friend, *I'm* a friend, the *United States* is a friend, and we're keeping the line open for her. Don't get clever. Don't mention that writer H. G. Wells or you'll be out on your ass. Don't try flattery, and check your facts. That woman is nobody's fool.'

In London, it's a muggy midsummer – humid, close, with not even a breath of a breeze off the river – and Lady Chatterley's future hangs in the balance.

As he wakes, Sir Allen Lane wonders if he hasn't been dreaming of her of late … How odd. Indeed, on this particular morning, he seems to recall a dream in which he bumped into her in Kensington High Street. The plane trees above them were wilted. A faint stench was blowing inland from the Thames. She fanned her hands before her face, saying, 'Heavens. One can hardly breathe.'

By the time he arrives at the breakfast table, a card from Hans Schmoller – Board member at Penguin Books and Sir Allen's right-hand man – awaits him by the toast-rack.

15 July, 1960

Dear A.L.,

Today's (Friday's) intelligence was that a nephew of Sir Theobald Mathew, Public Prosecutor, told Tony Rowe – owner of the new printer for Lady C – over dinner at the Travellers' Club, that his uncle was determined to prosecute. It seems to me very unlikely that a man in such a position – Sir Theobald – would gossip with his nephew about his plans, but Monty Weekley, D. H. Lawrence's stepson who happens to know Sir Toby, says he is the type of person who might. Perhaps the idea is 'to see off' Rowe as well?

Hans

The dining-room at the Travellers' Club had hummed, as ever, with the discreet conversation of the world's leading dignitaries and diplomats. Even at the start of the new decade, the Travellers' could still be relied on for the traditional values upon which the country stood: civility, good manners – and subterfuge.

Had Mathew's nephew – 'Mathew the Younger' we might call him – been planted in the Travellers' Club by his uncle, the Director of Public Prosecutions? *Was* the plan to 'see off' a *second* printing company and thereby scupper Penguin's new book, without the bother of a trial? The flight of another printer could well make the book 'untouchable'.

In any case, weren't *novels*, when it came to it, rather beneath the DPP's office? The magnificent private libraries of Sir Toby's peers were one thing – a blind eye could be turned for men of culture and learning – but a paperback which was to cost 3s. 6d., the price of little more than a pound of bacon, was another matter altogether. The nation's housewives would be able to buy the novel with their pin-money. Mob-capped girls in service would share it on the back-stairs. Public schoolboys would read soiled copies in dormitories up and down the country.

The Mathew family coat of arms featured a mythical beast with claws extended. Mathew the Younger ordered the loin of venison. 'It seems,' he said in a studiously offhand manner, 'that my uncle is determined to prosecute.'

Tony Rowe studied the menu and did not blanch.

It is the longest day of the year, and in Sir Theobald Mathew's estimation, it feels like it too. His desk overfloweth, and he hardly has time to turn his attention to the matter of a novel. Allen Lane could simply have published the damned book discreetly, as a costly limited edition, and saved Sir Toby's office all this stuff and nonsense. *As it is*, Sir Toby is now required, officially, to *seem* to care about the morality of the nation and the corruption of all youth in possession of pocket-money.

What a bore.

He exhales and sends a rare proof-copy of the new Penguin edition to 'Counsel to the Crown' at the Old Bailey, Mervyn Griffith-Jones. He requests Griffith-Jones's professional opinion on the matter. 'Worth our time?'

Griffith-Jones has a proven record in prosecuting obscenity cases, with four titles under his belt already. He also has a way with words. Griffith-Jones replies by return: 'If I get an erection, we prosecute.'

The following week, his view is re-phrased for the public record: 'In my opinion, the unexpurgated version of <u>Lady Chatterley's Lover</u> – a proof-copy of which I have read – is obscene, and a prosecution for publishing an obscene libel would be justified.'

His reading copy, a publisher's proof-copy, was lent to him by Sir Toby. The source of this copy remains a mystery. How did Sir Toby come by it? Let's re-trace its wayward path.

Publishers are not asked to avail would-be prosecutors of free copies of the books they might choose to prosecute. No defendant can reasonably be expected to facilitate his or her own downfall.

Griffith-Jones is clear in his statement that he has read a 'proof-copy'. Yet Penguin's plan to distribute advance proof-copies in the late spring and early summer of 1960 was cancelled, in light of growing concerns over the threat of prosecution. Penguin staff couldn't simply carry on, working towards a summer release date, as if there were no clouds darkening on the horizon. Nor were proof-copies sent abroad to any foreign publisher. No one, in other words, from Sir Toby's office could have nipped over to Paris or New York to collect a copy for the Office of Public Prosecutions.

Where *had* that advance-copy come from? Who was the mystery donor? Who might have oiled the wheels of the Prosecution?

Two advance-copies for reviewers – and strictly two – *had* been given, back in February, to *Lady Chatterley* enthusiast Leonard Russell, Literary Editor of the *Sunday Times*. It would have been entirely natural for Russell to pass a copy on, in turn, to one of the established reviewers on his roster – let us say a respected, big-name writer who had, thirty years before, composed a personal recollection of D. H. Lawrence for the publisher Martin Secker, following their mutual writer-friend's death.

Rebecca West would have been *the* natural choice for a rare proof-copy among Russell's stable of fiction reviewers. She was normally sought-after. In this case, she would have been wooed.

Had the American Garden worked its magic that summer's day in June as the FBI's London attaché escorted Dame Rebecca West down its lush and lovely paths? Had he steered the conversation with as much care?

The Bureau man would have told Dame Rebecca he had no doubt that Sir Allen Lane and the Penguin Board were well-meaning. But unlike *her*, they weren't privy to 'the intelligence'. They couldn't know that their plan to publish such a controversial novel was playing right into the Soviets' hands. That was the troubling context, which Mr Hoover was sure she appreciated. They valued her friend-ship greatly. If he might be so bold … she was a credit to her country. Might she know of any means by which she could help Mr Hoover to 'deactivate' the Soviets' 'Active Measures' work in London, partic-ularly with regards to *Lady Chatterley*?

6th July, 1960
Ibstone House

Dear Toby,

I am forwarding this proof-copy on behalf of a highly regarded Ameri-can friend. He believes it may be of interest to you in your official capacity. Lunch? Soon?

Yours,
R. W.

Did she send it?

July gives way sluggishly, in a torpor of heat, to August. Penguin's unexpurgated *Lady Chatterley's Lover* – a trove of 200,000 newly printed paperbacks – sits in a warehouse west of London, in the unlikely location of Harmondsworth, an otherwise quaint village, little used to excitement in a cricket match, let alone contraband. Two security guards are hired for a round-the-clock patrol. As the senior man hands the keys to the other at the end of the first shift, he shrugs off the younger man's question about the contents they guard. 'Explosive,' he says. 'If I tell you more, I'll have to kill you.'

The heat of summer goes tick – tick – tick, like the overworked engine of a year that is slow to cool. While most Londoners that August stick to the shade of awnings and trees, Literary Editor Leonard Russell is about to climb out on a dangerous limb. He is ready to declare that Penguin Books is unlikely to be prosecuted on publication day, August 25th. He has written a long editorial saying as much. In this way, he – or rather, the *Sunday Times* – might just influence Establishment opinion before it knows what its own opinion is.

Might.

He consults the two reviewers he selected in February for the rare advance-copies, trusted professionals, including Dame Rebecca. Is each agreed, he asks, on his statement – his nailing of their colours to the *Sunday Times* mast – namely, that Penguin Books won't face prosecution?

Something unexpected transpires in one of those conversations. In which of the two, we can only speculate. It would be safe to assume, however, that it was *not* the discussion, in the Russell kitchen, with *Lady Chatterley* admirer and *Sunday Times* reviewer, Dilys Powell – a.k.a. Mrs Leonard Russell, and in all likelihood the mystery-recipient of the second advance-copy. After all, why let a rare book – the rarest of the year – leave one's shelves when a literary couple could offer an unpublished orphan a perfectly good home?

Otherwise put: the second copy was never assigned.

Yet the records show only that, on Saturday, August 13th, Russell places an urgent telephone call to Penguin's offices. He is panicked. Sir Allen is away on a family holiday. Russell tells the members of the Board that he will look extremely foolish if the other Sunday papers carry news about the *likelihood* of a court case.

It appears he has been given early warning. By whom? A trusted source? Apparently, but what, he wonders, can he do about it now? He returns to his desk and a long round of Solitaire into the night while Dilys gently snores. He is not prepared for the surprise which awaits him on Sunday morning, first thing.

No other paper, not one, has so much as mentioned the story. He is a lone voice on an empty stage. No other literary editor has put his head above the parapet. The Establishment has decided to hold its breath and wait to see which way the obscenities blow.

By late that morning, Sunday, August 14th, Mrs Rackley, Sir Allen Lane's housekeeper, will find herself on the doorstep of the family home, informing reporters and members of the public – who clutch their *Sunday Times* – that Sir Allen is away. She grips an imposing broom. 'I have no idea where he is.' Now would they kindly 'remove themselves'? And with that, she begins to sweep the step, vigorously.

Tick – tick – tick. Twelve copies, deemed to be 'evidence enough' of publication, are volunteered by Penguin to Scotland Yard. Penguin's lawyer, Michael Rubinstein, has advised that it is best to demonstrate cooperation with the Yard or, more accurately, to head off trouble at the pass.

In a book-lined office in Penguin's premises, tea is offered to Detective Inspector Monahan of CID. Twelve orange-and-white paperbacks, priced at 3s. 6d. each, are presented in a three-magnum wooden box, stuffed with fresh straw – as if the books are the finest intoxication Penguin can offer.

DI Monahan nods appreciatively. 'Well, I ...' He is briefly lost for words. Like many working people, he feels indebted to Penguin paperbacks for a good deal of his own education.

The pot has been warmed. Tea is poured. 'Lemon or milk?'

It is an admirably English seizure of goods.

What follows is rather less composed.

Later that day, an urgent telegram is sent by the Board Directors to Sir Allen, who, as Mrs Rackley knows perfectly well, is holiday-ing in Spain. LEGAL ACTION IMMINENT STOP ADVISE YOUR IMMEDIATE RETURN.

'The Fight for Lady Chatterley's Honour Begins!'

'Would You Allow A CHILD to Read This Book?'

'PENGUIN CHIEF CUTS HOLIDAY SHORT'

Scotland Yard is waiting for Sir Allen as he comes through his own door, a compact, grey-haired man sporting a *bota* on his belt, a panama hat and a sunburn. A police constable waits in the sitting-room, like a new and ungainly piece of furniture. He informs Sir Allen, bashfully, 'that you, on the 16th day of August, 1960, did publish an obscene book entitled *Lady Chatterley's Lover*. You are therefore hereby summoned to appear before the Bow Street Magistrates' Court on Thursday, the 25th day of August, 1960 at the hour of 10.30 in the fore-noon to answer to the said information.'

Let us review the expert thinking.

On reading the offending novel, Mervyn Griffith-Jones, Counsel to the Crown, felt sufficiently roused or aroused – it is not clear which – to recommend prosecution to Sir Toby.

It is the job of Sir Toby Mathew, Director of Public Prosecutions, to assess the weight of evidence, for and against, prior to any court order. He is a busy man. He has not read the book. Give him an Ian Fleming any day. In fact, it was all only meant to be a roundabout favour for a literary lady friend. She is, as they say, a pistol – if a nuisance, as well.

In Sir Toby's defence, he *is* on the brink of reading it three months *after* the trial's conclusion, when a friend agrees to post him a copy of '*Lady Loverley's Chatter*' after a dinner party: 'It's not particularly good. I certainly don't think it's rude enough for you to play with.'

And what of Attorney General Reginald Manningham ('Bull') Buller?

It is Bull's responsibility to ensure due process. He oversees the Office of Public Prosecutions and, in this capacity, acts as the independent guardian of public interest. The prosecution of a serious offence requires his consent. The Attorney General must always be ready to answer to Parliament.

On a train to Southampton, where he is to catch a rather splendid ocean-liner, 'Bull' writes to Sir Toby Mathew, Director of Public Prosecutions, with his professional assessment, scribbling in haste on House of Commons stationery. Having persisted as far as Chapter IV, he declares: '... if the remainder of the book is of the same character I have no doubt that you were right to start proceedings & I hope you get a conviction.'

On the train, tea is served in First Class, along with fresh scones with clotted cream and jam. The china is fine bone. The train rumbles on. Bull posts the note from Southampton Station, and away he sails on the ocean blue.

Two days later, with the Attorney General's consent in hand, Sir Toby studies the calendar. He anticipates ... It will be October for the trial's launch at the Central Criminal Court, better known to the nation as the Old Bailey.

Mr Justice Laurence Byrne is appointed to judge the case. He recalls the history of the novel well enough to disapprove of it at first sight. He has little taste or time for fiction – for things 'made up'. What can a busy man do but delegate?

In bed, as Mr Justice Byrne reviews the day's committal papers, Lady Dorothy, in her Liberty nightdress, is propped beside him, cataloguing the novel's offences:

pages:

25–28 – lovemaking with Michaelis

34–41 – Conversation between men. Coarse. Lady C. present throughout

44–46 – discussion re. having a child by another man...

68 – man washing

71–73 – examination of her body in front of mirror...

118–124 – lovemaking

137–141 – lovemaking

178–185 – more lovemaking...

228 – coarse

Soon, her ledger will stretch to four pages of headed stationery from the Central Criminal Court.

As they switch off their bedside lamps, Lady Dorothy has but one unspoken concern. She is conscious of her husband's dignity. Photographers tend to appear when one is least expecting them. Yet brown-paper wrapping on a book only invites lewd jokes.

As she tosses and turns, her brain alights on a plan. In her sewing-box, she has an old damask-silk cushion cover. She will unpick its seams and run it up anew, on her Singer. A book-bag will be just the thing. She will make a drawstring from purple ribbon. And so, at last, she is able to sleep.

In this way, the 'Grey Elderly Ones', the Establishment figures of Lawrence's bad dreams, close ranks around their own; around an old order that is crumbling. They take up positions at the wheelchair of Sir Clifford, a man their fathers might have fought alongside in the Great War. They look down from the casements of Sir Clifford Chatterley's Wragby Hall, from which the mistress has bolted without leaving an heir.

Rotten luck.

Worse still is the fact that Sir Clifford has been humiliated by his gamekeeper. A servant.

It doesn't bear thinking about.

So they do not.

They will see Allen Lane in court.

iv

It was a Sunday afternoon in early September at The Gables. The light beyond Michael Rubinstein's study window was honeyed, and pale fronds of pampas grass dipped and swayed against the parched lawn. At the bottom of the sloping property, their patch of orchard had fared better. This year's apples were redder than usual – the good luck of the streak of hot days and cold nights they'd had of late. Where the front garden met the village lane, two ancient copper beeches leaned into their lament for the passage of summer.

He listened to Elgar and munched on ginger biscuits straight from the tin.

Rubinstein was almost forty. He had missed out on university, what with the war, but he had joined his grandfather's firm on his return, worked tirelessly, and now advised the nation's best publishers. He enjoyed the literary tribe in a way not everyone did. The Penguin case was his biggest gamble yet. Something peculiar in the book inspired loyalty; something bigger than the tragedy of the author's premature death. With every passing decade, Rubinstein found himself ever more the agnostic, yet on those pages, whatever their flaws, was life, and with it, something more, something – dare he think it? – sacred. Which was to say, he was bloody well going to do his best for Lady Chatterley. Everyone else could go hang.

The pile of notes and letters on the left side of his desk was substantial. In his own mind, he referred to these respondents as 'The Great & the Good'. The second pile, on the right, was thin by comparison, and these replies were from the pens of those he had privately dubbed the 'Dissenters'. He had written to them all, nearly three hundred hoped-for witnesses.

If he were to host a dinner party, he knew which lot he'd want at his table.

He lit his cherished pipe and turned to the Great & the Good. The Prosecution was sure to produce heavyweight witnesses such as these: Church leaders, government ministers, and leading critics who would be prepared to say the same as these respondents, if not worse.

F. R. Leavis, respected Cambridge University don and champion of Lawrence's fiction: 'I do not think that Sir Allen Lane does a service to literature, civilization or Lawrence in the business of <u>Lady Chatterley's Lover</u>.'

With champions such as Leavis, who needed enemies?

Rubinstein whistled for his dog. He needed company.

Novelist Evelyn Waugh: 'I am quite certain that no public or private "good" would be saved by its publication. Lawrence had very meagre literary gifts.'

While others had very meagre souls.

Poet Robert Graves: 'D. H. Lawrence, even at his purest, is the writer I least like of my contemporaries and I won't have a book of his on my shelves. I can't explain it.'

Envy?

Writer L. P. Hartley: 'I do think that many people would read it simply to stimulate their sexual desires. Whether it would matter much if they did is another question.'

Hartley at least, God bless him, had a sense of humour.

Actor Alec Guinness: 'I cannot honestly say that I consider the publication of this book to be of "particular importance for the public good".'

He'd been a long-shot.

Children's writer Enid Blyton's pen had leaked all over the page, nearly as much as she herself: 'My husband said NO at once. The thought of me standing up in Court solemnly advocating a book "like that" (his words, not mine – I feel he must have read the book!) made his hair stand on end.'

It was more likely that Enid was worried about being quizzed too closely on the subject of adultery …

Graham Greene, novelist: 'I can't imagine that even a minor could draw any other conclusion from the book than that sexual activity was at least enjoyable.' Rubinstein smiled. Greene could always be relied upon for dry wit. He found, however, some parts of the book 'rather absurd' and, for that reason, preferred not to be called as a witness in case he was forced to admit his true opinion and do harm to Penguin's case.

The most thoughtful rejection of the lot.

Huw Wheldon, BBC executive: 'It was as if the act of love had to be accepted as the act of worship too, and that a twin bed was a church as well.'

Did the Wheldons still sleep in twin beds? Rubinstein had assumed that fad had gone the way of cold showers and the withdrawal method.

The Manager of Students' Bookshops Ltd: 'You may try to tell me that this work has literary merit – as far as I am concerned it "stinks".' The Manager of Hatchards Bookshop was more civil. 'It would place Hatchards in a rather invidious position to take a stand on either side in this case for the simple reason that there is bound to be a great deal of publicity and we would surely displease either our liberal-minded customers or our stuffier ones.' Sir Basil Blackwell, of Blackwell's Bookshop: 'For me no honesty and beauty in writing can compensate for degrading human beings ethically and sexually to the level of the sparrow.'

Was the sparrow really so contemptible, or had Sir Basil led a sheltered life?

Reverend Leslie D. Weatherhead, theologian: 'It would get into the wrong hands, sell in millions and do immense harm both to young people, and to many frustrated older people also.'

How old was the Reverend, incidentally?

And so on …

'I found re-reading of this particular book an embarrassing experience.'

'I am afraid I found it funny, uproariously so.'

'It is more likely to put you off sex than to deprave or corrupt you.'

'It's not the banned bits I mind, it's the rest of the book!'

And finally, from a plain-speaking Lord Mayor: 'It was revolting.'

Rubinstein sighed, threw a biscuit to Fetch, and reached for another. Both felt the need of sustenance.

Among the Dissenters, Tom Eliot was, characteristically, anxious. Decades ago, as a young man, he had written critically of *Lady Chatterley's Lover*, but now, he was prepared to recant. 'I am glad of this opportunity to let it be known that I am not necessarily to be assumed to agree with all my earlier opinions, some of which I now regard as being immature, ill-considered, and too violent.'

Not a ringing endorsement but …

John Braine, writer: 'The general effect of the book upon the normal person would be to induce within him a deep reverence for the physical world, for the life of the senses … And for my own part

I cannot see anything but good in this conception of sex – or to use the better word, love.'

Bravo, John Braine.

Doris Lessing, novelist: 'I would reply that Lawrence is probably the greatest writer produced in this country, this century. That until recently he has been consistently represented as an indecent or immoral writer who advocated sexual licence; whereas the truth is that he was a very moral, not to say puritanical man, concerned to give sex dignity.'

Lessing had the makings of an excellent witness. Rubinstein made a note.

Iris Murdoch, novelist and philosopher: 'It seems to me to be the reverse of corrupting.'

Hear, hear.

Novelist Kingsley Amis felt much the same. He was confident that only 'the already corrupt' could find anything depraved or depraving in *Lady Chatterley*.

Good old Kingsley. He would dazzle a jury.

Mrs Mary Middleton Murry was the fourth wife, and widow, of John Middleton Murry. 'My late husband was associated with D. H. Lawrence in an almost legendary friendship. Lawrence's fundamental point is a need for tenderness in the man–woman relationship on which the fulfilment of what may be called a sacramental marriage depends. He was, as I am, a firm believer in monogamy, and if literature that helps to show how monogamy can be made to work has merit for the public good, <u>Lady Chatterley's Lover</u> certainly has that merit ... This must be of particular value to so many women who come to marriage frightened and apprehensive about the act of physical love.'

All this *fear*, thought Rubinstein.

Publisher Leonard Woolf, widower of Mrs Virginia Woolf, reported that his late wife had admired *Sons and Lovers* and *The Lost Girl* for their extraordinary sense of the physical world, but that 'Virginia' had not been engaged by Lawrence's late oeuvre. According to Leonard, she in no way *disapproved* of the significance Lawrence ascribed to sex, but she was disquieted by the focus he gave it.

Ah, well.

In a rather lovely digression, Woolf noted that V.W. and D.H.L. never actually met, although in '27, Virginia glimpsed Lawrence on a bench on the opposite platform, moments before her train departed a station in Italy.

It must have been a curious coincidence, Rubinstein thought, these two minds 'passing through' the station, aptly moving off in different directions – she for Rome, and he for Tuscany.

Apparently, Lawrence didn't see Mrs Woolf at the window of her compartment, but he'd stood out to her among the travellers on the platform: painfully thin, with a sharp, red, fox-like beard and, she'd noted to Leonard, a 'pierced and penetrated' quality. Within minutes, her train was in motion, and in less than three years, he was dead.

Not long before his death, Virginia, said Leonard, *had* offered to serve as a witness for the defence in the case brought against Lawrence's nude paintings in the summer of '29. She didn't much like the paintings – 'Did anyone?' Leonard mused – but she believed that Lawrence's mind was wholly original and she'd been sorry to learn he was so wretchedly ill. She had a great deal of sympathy for the bedridden.

Leonard was restrained in his own assessment of *Lady Chatterley's Lover*. 'The book in question, though not his best book, is a serious work of art and has no pornographic intention.'

Useful, but not enough.

John Lehmann, on the other hand –

'I have re-read Lady Chatterley's Lover and found it even more remarkable and moving than I did when I first read it some twenty-five years ago. It is a book of deeply serious intention, a work of art written with all Lawrence's marvellous feeling for the English language ... He wanted man to feel things again with his heart, as well as think them with his head; but he did not believe that even that was enough unless man recognized that sex was fundamental.'

Good man! How rare the truly generous were.

Christina Foyle was owner of W. & G. Foyle Ltd, the largest bookshop in the world, in Charing Cross Road. 'In my opinion, the only person who will find the book obscene is the person who is looking for obscenity – the psychopath, or the gentlemen of inelegant leisure who haunt the medical sections of bookshops.'

Ha!

Poet and *Encounter* Editor, Stephen Spender: 'I shall be glad to give all possible support to <u>Lady Chatterley's Lover</u> ... Lawrence's book is truthful and of course the truth is always dangerous: it has been made explosive by those who have repressed it ... If the young read it and took it to heart, they might well be saved the guilt and misery of some of their elders.'

In that Spenderian moment, Rubinstein realised something vital: he hadn't yet considered 'the young' ...

Of course! What better defence could there be than a well-educated young person who had read the book and emerged, unscathed and uncorrupted, to tell the tale?

A young woman, preferably ...

A bright young woman, one who could speak with 'expertise' on the view of her generation.

A Catholic would be ideal, to undermine the testimony of the Catholic bishops the Prosecutors were sure to invite to take the stand.

Intelligent, engaging, fresh-faced and *guileless*. That's what he needed.

When Michael Rubinstein pushed back his chair, Fetch likewise scrambled to his feet and sprang after his master, out the door and down the hall, his claws scratching wildly on the chequerboard tiles.

The previous year, Michael Rubinstein's friend Bernard Wall had declared to Rubinstein that he was in his debt, after Rubinstein had advised him *pro bono* on a libel threat to the *The Twentieth Century*, a problem Bernard had inherited as the magazine's new editor.

Rubinstein listened now, with his good ear to the brrng-brrng of the line, and felt the order of the universe reveal itself, like gold panned from a river. Bernard would want to help, and he was the only one who could. His daughter was *the* daughter. Rubinstein knew of no other.

The Walls' housekeeper said Bernard was away, working on a literary translation in Rome, but *Mrs* Wall could be reached at her parents' house in West Sussex. Rubinstein knew Barbara less well than Bernard of course, but ... 'Barbara!' he exclaimed, when she picked up at last. He'd almost rung off. She had been at work in her mother's vegetable garden, she said catching her breath.

'It's very kind of you to interrupt your dig for me. Your mother won't thank me, I'm sure, but I shan't monopolise you for long.'

He asked after Bernard and their daughters. Had Bernardine graduated from Cambridge yet? That very year? Heavens!

'Dina,' her mother said, 'was in fact on her way to 'the Colony' as they spoke, *with* her boyfriend in tow, a history major in his final year at Cambridge. The pair, Barbara said, had just been to see the Picasso exhibition at the Tate, for the *third* time. They'd queued for hours – what with the crowds – 'then loitered among Picasso's wonky bodies for another half a day!' She said she must be too old to understand all the excitement. She found herself rather in sympathy with the Duke of Edinburgh. 'Did you hear about that? Apparently, at the opening party, after glancing at a few of the portraits, he asked whether the artist drank!'

Rubinstein chuckled. 'I have it on reliable authority that Evelyn Waugh has taken to signing off his correspondence: "Death to Picasso"!'

Her voice was low and silvery-bright. 'Well, for the record, a few years ago, I sent Waugh a copy of one of my books, newly published, and I gathered that, after that, he rather thought death to me too!'

The pleasantries were accomplished. Rubinstein found her genial and refreshingly direct. He risked it: 'I was wondering if Dina might like a bit of a "role"?'

0691 0591 0491 0391 0291. Find the row, the decade. Don't let the gusts of time catch the strand. 1915. August.

The exile is there, in the Meynell family's car once again; he is the face in the rear window, receding. In the drizzle of the day, his red beard, more than anything else, is what the little girl notices. She does not like it. Her father's face − Perceval Lucas's face − is always smooth. In the pictures in their Children's Bible, the devil has a red beard. Her cousin Mary likes their Special Guest, but she does not. Nor does her dolly. The Special Guest and his wife don't have children. *Why* not? Also, he likes the snakes at Rackham Cottage, but snakes are horrid. He stares hard when she stares at him, but she is only small, and his eyes are bigger.

The car is moving slowly up the lane, when Barbara, the youngest Lucas, is seized by a childish impulse. She breaks away from Madeline and begins to run − on plump legs, clutching her doll − through the rain and puddles towards the car.

Rubinstein closed the phone-cupboard door tight as his children thundered past, tormenting poor Fetch. 'Dina,' Barbara was saying, something about Dina … With his bad ear, he could hardly make her out.

He explained the forthcoming case. He summarised the plight of Lawrence − the dead author − the plight of the book, and the courage of Penguin Books. The case would be tried in October, he said, which meant there was little time. He and the Defence team were preparing day and night.

Then came the '$64,000 question', as his American friends liked to say. He tried to sound light-hearted, yet sincere and sensitive. Might she and Bernard kindly 'lend' him Bernardine for a day of the trial?

Barbara's voice came back down the line like a warning note struck on a triangle. 'Dina, you say.'

'Naturally, we'd take excellent care of her − and she might even enjoy herself.'

'Michael, I'm afraid I must ring off. You see, I'm collecting Dina and Nick at the station shortly. As it is, I'm late, and the sky has rather started to heave here. It's kind of you to think of her.'

'Not at all.' Surely it was apparent that it was *her* kindness he was soliciting. Something had gone awry. He wished Bernard were in the country. What more could he say? 'I do hope you and Dina will consider my request.'

He heard Barbara forage for a pencil. She said she would take his number and ask Dina to ring. 'Got it. HAM. 9350 – I've made a note,' she said with brusque efficiency. 'Now, if you'll forgive me, I must set off.'

The penny had clearly dropped. Barbara didn't much like her daughter mingling with Picasso's odd-bodies at the Tate. Nor did she want her daughter standing up in a court of law to defend a scandalous novel.

The law had been amended to protect works of literature – to distinguish them readily from the S&M novels displayed on book stalls the length of Charing Cross Road. Prosecutions of obviously lurid novels would not turn a head or draw a crowd, whereas *this case* – about a work of literature – had the potential not only to draw a crowd, but to antagonise one too. That was something the Establishment would really not mind at all. A conservative backlash would be no bad thing, as far as some were concerned.

Perhaps it was not as straightforward a matter for Barbara Wall as he had hoped.

Make an example of Lawrence, draw a line, preserve the *status quo*. The action of the Public Prosecution Office was reminiscent of something he'd once witnessed as a child on Regent Street, when a group of public-school boys set upon a skinny grammar-school boy in his cheap blazer.

Rubinstein knew that Barbara Wall had intuited something of the jeopardy of the case, and whatever her husband might have said, it was a mother's judgement which counted most where a daughter was concerned. She didn't want a child of hers caught up in any public backlash. He supposed he couldn't blame her.

Dina did *not* ring the next day. He held onto a fragment of optimism till early evening, when Fetch, exhausted by the children, curled up with a whimper at his feet.

Outside his study window, a grave moon rose in an inky sky.

The following morning, a large envelope arrived at The Gables in the first post. Rubinstein had been on his way to Gray's Inn, late admittedly. When he opened the envelope, he turned back for his study.

To his surprise, out slid photostats of two stories, both by Lawrence. In fact, they appeared to be two versions of the same story.

The first was from a very old issue of the *English Review* – 1915 – entitled 'England, My England'. He'd heard of it, though he couldn't claim to know it. The second seemed to be a version of the same story, entitled 'England, my England'. It was hand-dated 1924. Its title had lost an upper-case 'M', but the story itself had expanded by several pages. Who was sending it and why?

Between the stories was a letter, a long letter, from Barbara Lucas Wall. How unexpected. Whatever was she unburdening herself of? He sat down at his desk, unbuttoned his coat and lit his pipe.

The first version of 'England, My England' pre-dated *Lady Chatterley's Lover* by thirteen years. What could its relevance possibly be? He got to his feet, shovelled coal on the grate, and sat down once again with Barbara's letter. What had happened in the interval since his telephone call?

The sheets of stationery were covered in a coursing hand, in blue ink with a strong pressure, as if a dam had given way.

> *6th September, 1960*
> *Winborn's*
> *Greatham*

Dear Michael,

Perhaps you will have guessed. I asked Dina not to ring you yesterday. I should like to explain.

The situation you unwittingly touched on with your request is more complex than you could possibly know. If you will bear with me in the coming pages, I should like you to understand, as we consider you a friend. I know that Bernard has been most grateful for your friendship and support.

By way of explanation, I enclose a story by D. H. Lawrence: 'England, My England'. Perhaps you know it, in one form or another? Its two versions speak more 'vividly' than I will here.

If you read it, you might spot the essential correspondences. The 'Marshalls' are modelled after my family, the Meynells, my mother's family – my family too of course – as we were in the Great War. We lived then, as we still do, between London and Sussex. Naturally, my grandparents, Wilfrid and Alice Meynell, are no longer with us, but my mother, their daughter Madeline Meynell – Madeline Lucas by marriage – is very much alive at nearly eighty years of age!

I was only a small child when Lawrence and his wife stayed in our little 'Colony' for about six months. The result was the final draft of _The Rainbow_, and 'England, My England'. Normally, Lawrence relied on my Aunt Viola and Eleanor Farjeon, a family friend, as typists in this period, but, at the end of that summer, he typed 'England, My England', in secret apparently, shortly before leaving us for good. We none of us saw him again.

Few readers of Lawrence give much thought to this history, nor should they. The story, 'England, My England', is finally free of the people and places that inspired it. It carries on into the world, to follow its own fate. But once upon a time, it was all terribly ... tangled up.

As any natural reader understands, writers often borrow the outward appearances of whomever they like, and they fill out those externals with the ectoplasm of invented feelings and motivations. Even so, once you read the two versions, I am sure you will be able to imagine the hurt and humiliation my family experienced on reading 'England, My England' on its publication in the autumn of 1915, shortly after Lawrence's departure.

It is all a very long time ago. But the present has deep pockets.

My mother, Madeline, was the unwitting model for 'Winifred' in both versions. My father, who was killed at the Somme not long after the first version was published, provided the 'model' for 'Evelyn' in the first version; his name is changed to 'Egbert' in the second. It is my theory that it was changed to Egbert because it carried the trace of the name 'Bert', David Herbert Lawrence's nickname from his youth.

In the story, Evelyn/Egbert is driven to war by the deep unhappiness of his marriage to Winifred – an invention the literary world at the time read as a revelation of the secret 'truth' of my parents' marriage, ostensibly observed while Lawrence stayed at Greatham. For a time, after I read the story in my teenaged years, even _I_ wondered if it was part of the reason *for my father's departure for war. You see, he was considerably older than most who joined up in 1914, and married men, as you may recall, were not conscripted until 1916.*

Every external appearance in the story was <u>almost</u> uncannily true to life. But not. And that was its menace.

Like Evelyn/Egbert, my poor father was to suffer a fatal blow to his thigh at the Somme in July 1916. Thankfully, the violent hacking away of Evelyn's face, described in the first version of the story (and removed from the next), has more to do, I believe, with the author's self-loathing; his own 'raw' nature is unmasked and exposed, in the horrid hacked visage, beneath the very pleasant face of my father's character. After all, can we ever be detached from our creations?

As something of a writer myself, I rather doubt it. I think there's a great deal of Lawrence's bitterness and envy mixed up in the depictions of Evelyn/Egbert, and yet I don't deny that it's a strangely powerful story.

What was not generally remembered at the time by those who knew us, or who knew of us, was that Lawrence had hardly met my father. My grandparents and my Aunt Viola had opened up their homes and hearts to the Lawrences, but <u>my father</u> was away at an army camp for most of the duration of their stay among us. The story suggests an intimate acquaintance with my parents, but in truth, Lawrence hardly knew my father. He knew my mother Madeline better, but mostly as the older sister of his 'literary friend', my Aunt Viola.

A violation by language is a difficult thing to describe to those who have not experienced it. One is helplessly re-made by the dark imagination of another — re-cast by a remote will. Words on the page confer a weird authority upon themselves, and they can have a malign magic.

Others will often breezily remind victims of defamation of the indelible power of the truth, and of course they are right, but that remote 'will', the dark imagination of the defamer leaves a sort of 'breath' on the air, and he or she knows it. It is a kind of haunting. His or her fingerprints mark the windows of one's home, but everything appears untouched.

Sometimes it seems to me — in cases where the victims are recklessly but convincingly re-cast — that there is evil in the betrayal. But of course you must not take me seriously. I grew up in a fairy-tale place, Rackham Wood, and at times, it is with me still!

I did used to wonder, most irrationally, if Lawrence had 'imagined into being' the fatal blow to my father's leg. It might have seemed to him, as it did to some of us, that he had somehow conjured that event with so acute a description in the story – six months before my father sustained the wound and died from it.

I understand that, for a time, after my father's early death, Lawrence did feel quite badly about the story and the injury to my family. Those feelings did not last. Five years later, in a second version, he added to the story, making my family and our place in Sussex even more recognisable!

All these things rushed through my head yesterday when you asked me on the telephone if I would 'lend' you our daughter – Madeline and Percy's grand-daughter – to help 'save' Lawrence. It brought me up short.

My sisters and I feature as small children in the story, a little younger than we actually were when the Lawrences stayed at Greatham – but it is true to the time of the dreadful accident which befell my eldest sister, and which is recounted in the story. I am the toddler 'Barbara' in both versions – evidently, I didn't inspire Lawrence's imagination to new heights of naming! Our Rackham Cottage is 'Crockham Cottage'. It was, then, precisely as it is described in the story. Indeed, the story could serve as a guided tour of our property.

My grandmother, Alice, was a tender soul. It was therefore a defining moment for my family when Alice forbade the entire family from uttering Lawrence's name again. What else could she do, poor woman? Neither author nor editor would withdraw the story. It was a wound – and it was opened again, when Lawrence re-published the expanded version in '22 in America, and again in '24, when Martin Secker published it in a new British selection of Lawrence's stories. (Secker had even once been engaged to my aunt, Viola.)

A solicitor friend suggested we had a perfect case for libel, but did we? Everyone knew the story was 'about' the Meynells, and particularly about the supposedly failing marriage of my own dear parents, Madeline and Percy. But Lawrence hadn't used our names, had he? And it _was_ a story.

It was not only the matter of my father's depiction as a man who was weak and purposeless. My elder sister, Sylvia (called 'Joyce' in the story), had, as I mentioned, a terrible accident when she was a child, two years before the Lawrences ever came to Greatham. She nearly died.

My family hadn't realised Lawrence even knew the details. Perhaps he had asked friends of ours about it. For my family, it was a private and very painful episode. It is indeed one of my first memories – my mother's face stricken in the car window as she departed Greatham with my feverish sister. I understood instinctively that I might not see my sister again.

My father was killed within months of first publication, but even so, Lawrence went on, in the second version, to make his character an even sorrier excuse for a man. He made the character of 'my father' responsible for the accident.

'Oh, Daddy, Daddy, Daddy!' She was terrified by the sight of the blood running from her own knee. 'She fell on that sickle thing which you left lying about after cutting the grass,' said Winifred, looking into his face with bitter accusation as he bent near.

My sister did cut her leg on a scythe which had been left lying in the grass. That was the nature of the accident. In the second telling, it is my father's character who made the mistake of leaving the scythe in the grass. Few would know that he hadn't done so, that he was out of the country at the time. Yet as a family we weren't about to start assigning blame to the person who <u>had</u> actually left it in the grass – a dreadful accident – or to air a private sorrow in public.

Madeline, my mother, was forbidden by her mother from reading either version of the story, but it was an ongoing anguish for my grandparents and for others in the family to see Sylvia's near-death experience 'reviewed' on subsequent occasions in the literary press.

Even I had once wondered if there might have been a 'cover-up' by the generation before me. I made that foolish accusation once in my youth, yet of course, in my ignorance, I only made the situation worse for my mother. I had assumed that Lawrence was exposing a truth or truths my elders refused to confront. Do you see how the poisons leak? My father was a wonderful father and a much-loved man.

I myself believe that the creation of my father's character was a mask for Lawrence's terror of his own futility and 'paralysis' – psychological, spiritual, and of course sexual. His work is haunted by the figure of the 'useless male', right up to the character of Sir Clifford Chatterley, impotent and 'trapped like a beast' in his wheelchair. Had my father returned from the war in a wheelchair, I can assure you he would have been anything but useless. He would have been adored and robust.

We don't know if he discovered the story before his death. Many in the army did used to take the <u>English Review</u>. It was often posted to the trenches. As you can imagine, we, his family, very much hope he never did see it. He was sensitive and loving, and it would have cut him to the quick.

Nor do I actually know if my mother – Madeline – has read it, or if she obeyed her mother's injunction. Frankly, I've never been able to ask. I have never wanted to trespass on her grief.

I suspect my sister, Sylvia (the injured girl in the story), read it when we were in our teenaged years. I hope she didn't, but she has always been one to confront challenges 'head-on'. The portrait of her as a child was – is – despicable. My sister was in no way 'deformed' in either body or mind. Very much the opposite. She is an inspiration, and has gone on to have a family of her own.

My elders could only try to pretend – among themselves, above all – that they had never known Lawrence. After what had happened, it <u>did</u> seem as if they had never actually known him.

I only told Dina today that, not only had Lawrence and Frieda visited us in Greatham, but that they had lived as friends in my Aunt Viola's cottage for about six months; that Lawrence himself had been treated like one of the family. Dina was a little stunned to learn the history. She has always thought of our 'Colony' as her first home, and she'd believed, until today, that she knew its every nook, cranny and tale.

Lawrence, it is said, had a gift with children. I hardly remember him, but apparently, I was the only child in my family who was always bad-tempered with him. Perhaps I was wise beyond my years! It must be said that he did do my cousin Mary and her mother, my Aunt Monica, a tremendous service by tutoring Mary and advancing her lamentable education in just three or four months, to the point where she passed the entrance examinations for St Paul's School for Girls.

The entire experience made my elders wonder if they had somehow stumbled on a scythe of their own making by welcoming him to the Colony; if they had been, like children, foolishly unguarded.

We were never quite as 'free' after Lawrence. I'm not sure we, as a family, ever recovered our full confidence, or faith, in the world. I think it's possible we became less easy somehow in the twentieth century, more private. If it had ever been 'our time', then our time passed, you could say, when 'England, My England' was published and hailed, critically, as one of the first indictments of the insanity of the First World War. Perhaps our time passed, along with the England Lawrence mourned. Indeed, he mapped out its ending on our little patch of Sussex. For all intents and purposes, our Colony was his England.

My Uncle Francis still refers to him as 'the snake in the grass', but I don't believe my grandmother, Alice, wanted him demonised. She simply wanted to be allowed to forget.

In any case, there are some undeniably lovely passages in the story, particularly in the second version. It is a beautiful elegy for a lost England.

Today I showed Dina the story, in both its incarnations. Your request made it necessary to do so, but I am glad she knows finally. I had vaguely wondered if she might have already come across the story at Cambridge – but no. She didn't study his stories, only his novels and poems.

She tells me that E. M. Forster lectured to them on Lawrence, and perhaps, in his recommendations and exclusions, he also avoided memories and mentions of Lawrence and Greatham. My mother said Forster was seen leaving on foot one early morning before first light. Lawrence had been heard tormenting him the night before. Thin windows, you see!

We understand the importance of your Penguins case and your reasons for wanting Dina to testify. I am, however, afraid we are unable to help you (or D. H. Lawrence) on this occasion. As you know, my mother, Madeline, is still alive, but not a little frail. We cannot trouble her with this. She is precious to us. I know you will understand.

Dina and I have agreed to say nothing of your request to my mother. We want to spare her the story and the sad memories of Lawrence. I believe she was once fond of him.

Dina and I are wholly sympathetic to the anti-censorship principle you seek to defend, and we wish you every success in court. Nor do I lose sight of the fact that Lawrence wrote valiantly and tirelessly until his death.

I can hear the lovely hooting of an owl in the orchard as I finish this letter. It is a comforting sound from childhood. My mother is reading by the fire. My Uncle Francis is regaling us with sweet (if repetitive!) stories from the old days. Dina and Nick are toasting crumpets for us all. Nick, it seems, is staying with us until the start of term. I have given

them adjacent rooms – I am a most modern mother! Dina hopes to find
editorial work soon. She tells me she has started writing a novel. Bernard
blames my side of the family!

Yours, with best wishes,
Barbara

Michael Rubinstein exhaled, returned the letter to its envelope
and, rather than starting out again for Gray's Inn, crossed the corridor
to the sitting-room where he selected from the concertos a recording of Albinoni's Adagio in G minor. But as Albinoni ascended from
the hi-fi, Fetch got to his feet and began to howl at the exquisite
pain of the violins.

Poor hound, thought Rubinstein – he struggled with his emotions.

Rubinstein's wife opened the door, wincing. Her face simply said,
'Please make it stop.'

He relented, stood and lifted the needle.

She glanced back over her shoulder. 'Any reason why you're wearing your bowler?'

He raised a hand to his head. 'Ah.'

Back in his study and hat-less, he gathered up the two versions
of the story and sank into a battered armchair. He read the second
version, the longer of the two 'Englands', first. *Not far from the tiny*
church of the almost extinct hamlet stood his own house – that's to say,
Rubinstein reminded himself, the house of 'Godfrey Marshall's', i.e.
Barbara's grandfather, Wilfrid Meynell – *a commodious old farmhouse*
standing back from the road across a bare grassed yard.

As he read, Michael Rubinstein felt he could see the whole of the
Colony, as if the story were a bright diorama of an ancient hamlet
into which he peered, through time. There was the long barn or shed,
which had accommodated cows or pigs before it had, in converted
form, accommodated the Lawrences. There in the bright hollow was
Rackham Cottage, on the edge of the shaggy common, where the
snakes darted. He could see a young Madeline Lucas calling for her
children from the threshold, and little Barbara toddling after her
sisters. He could see their father, Percy, hammering planks to make
a bridge.

Lawrence's story did indeed have a peculiar life to it; a sense of a world about to be stopped, like a pendulum, by the hand of war.

In his mind's eye, Rubinstein reached down and lifted off the roof of the old farmhouse, and there was Dina, curled on a rug by the fire in the library, reading for the first time of the *commodious old farmhouse standing back from the road* and of *Crockham Cottage* where her grandparents had once lived; where children had played in the long grass.

Old ghosts, he thought. Clearly, he had disturbed them, and however pressing the needs of the case, what choice did he have but to let them rest again?

Dina and Barbara were not the only ones with reservations. Rubinstein was discovering that various promising witnesses were either cryptic, conditional or 'otherwise committed'. The job of finding compelling experts was growing more difficult by the day, and time was running out.

Rubinstein had assumed that Rebecca West would be only too pleased to serve as a witness. He would have put money on it. Her interest in courts and trials was well documented, plus she had been acquainted with Lawrence, and had written a tribute to him shortly after his death in 1930, at the behest of his publisher, Secker.

On the first page of that tribute, she had made her feelings clear: 'Not even among his own caste was he honoured as much as he should have been. I realised with a shock how much of what I had always put down as Lawrence's persecution mania had a solid basis in fact, when I read obituaries in which not only was the homage due from the living to the dead genius meanly denied, but the courtesy paid to any corpse was so far as possible withheld.'

Now, here, thirty years later, Rebecca West had the perfect opportunity to right those wrongs; yet she had replied rather oddly to his request for support for Penguin Books. She'd left a brief telephone message with his secretary, courteous but terse. She said she had it on reliable authority from her 'informants' – *informants?* – that Lawrence himself had *not* wanted the full, unexpurgated version of *Chatterley* to be published for 'general consumption'. She was therefore doubtful she would be able to help. If she had further thoughts on the matter, her assistant would be in touch.

Not only was her lack of support for the Defence a blow, her assertion that the author had believed his book to be unsuitable for the general public was dangerous. A claim like that had the power to bring down the entire Defence case. If the Prosecution were to get hold of her thoughts – or worse, get hold of her – it could be 'curtains' for Penguin in court. There were many who wanted to see the book fail, and hers was a powerful voice.

Moreover, as much as he respected Dame Rebecca, he simply didn't believe her. Lawrence's own words showed that he viewed cuts to his manuscript as a form of mutilation. Even as late as 1930, weeks before he died, he had described his own efforts at removing the so-called 'offences' from his prose: 'I might as well try to clip my own nose into shape with scissors. The book bleeds.'

How could its author have wished to bequeath a 'bleeding' book to the public? Rubinstein checked with Martin Secker, and he confirmed: Lawrence most emphatically had wanted the full version published. Secker, as publisher, simply hadn't been 'inclined towards prison'. The private subscription plan had been Lawrence's only way to find readers and income – for Frieda – before he died. *Lady Chatterley* had never been intended for those with private libraries. The 'full, fine flower' of the novel, 'with pistil and stamens standing', was Lawrence's legacy to his people; to those who, like him, lived in the shadows of the Establishment. His story was a myth of renewal for a broken land.

Within a few hours of Dame Rebecca's message, Rubinstein had made a call, checked a source, and written his reply. He knew she would only 'yield' if he produced an 'informant' who 'out-informed' hers. Secker, in his late seventies, preferred to remain 'above the fray'. Would Monty Weekley be enough?

20th September, 1960
Gray's Inn

Dear Dame Rebecca,

Further to my letter of yesterday's date, I had a long conversation today with Mr Charles Montague Weekley who, as you may recall, is Lawrence's step-son – the 30-year-old son of Frieda Lawrence, and the eldest of her three children, all from her first marriage. In the light of Mr Weekley's many conversations with his mother, both before and after Lawrence's death, he expressed to me the definite view that Lawrence would always have wished the full version of Lady Chatterley's Lover to be published in England as soon as the intellectual and social climate permitted. I still think it inconceivable that your informants' suggestion to the contrary would have any basis in fact without the information having long since been published – and I am sure it has not been.

No one has yet communicated with me at your behest and I await anxiously further word from you with regard to the whole matter. You will know only too well what an embarrassing position I am placed in with my only information on the matter of this importance, regarding your informants, in effect anonymous. I am, of course, particularly appreciative of your having drawn my attention to this possibility so soon.

Yours sincerely,
Michael Rubinstein

Rubinstein added by hand: *P.S. Do you think it conceivable that it is a rumour put in circulation by someone on the other side?*

Dame Rebecca's response was delivered to his firm the following day. It was veiled, and strangely unconvincing, but it was progress at least!

21st September, 1960

Dear Mr. Rubinstein,

I have no doubt whatsoever that Lawrence did want <u>Lady Chatterley's Lover</u> to be published. I think that we had better let the matter drop. One of the informants plainly made the statement because of rapidly approaching senility, and the other one was obviously misled by a conversation that had taken place a long time ago. Neither of them could conceivably have <u>any</u> connection with the persons responsible for the prosecution.

I do imagine, however, that there is acute dissension among the powers that be. No one should be deceived.

I will later send you a copy of the letter I am addressing to one of my informants, neither of whom is in the least likely to repeat the rumour.

Yours sincerely,
Rebecca West

Rubinstein knew he'd never receive a copy of the purported letter-to-be. There was no 'senile' informant trying to speak on behalf of the dead author. The rumours had either been fabricated by Dame Rebecca – but why would she want to put Penguin off in its effort? – or they had been invented by someone else who did not want the Defence to succeed, and then repeated to her. But who could that be?

He promptly asked his secretary to ring Dame Rebecca's assistant to request a meeting, so that he might take her witness statement at her earliest convenience – before she came up with another excuse. She hadn't agreed to give him a statement of course, not yet, but she seemed to be on the brink of yielding. He would seize the moment before he lost it.

He was also keenly aware that she was a personal friend of none other than Sir Theobald Mathew, Director of Public Prosecutions. Sir Toby had even served as her attorney at some stage. It was vital that he, Rubinstein, won her over – in writing – before 'the other side' did.

Could the false rumour in Dame Rebecca's letter – a rumour which was so obviously *someone's* concoction – lead back to the Office of Public Prosecutions? Was 'the other side' prepared to win at any cost? And what – or rather, who – was he actually up against?

At Washington HQ, Miss Gandy, Hoover's secretary, took the call. It was Dame Rebecca. Miss Gandy reached for her shorthand pad and copied as Miss West dictated down the line from Buckinghamshire, England: 'Please tell Mr. Hoover that my efforts were not successful. I continue to share his concerns, but as the case is now scheduled, we have no choice but to let it take its course.' With that, she bid Miss Gandy 'Good-day'.

In keeping with the Bureau's Confidential Protocol, Helen Gandy placed the message on the Director's desk, sliding it beneath the picture of Shirley Temple, as was her habit for items which required his immediate attention. Then she locked his office door again, smoothed her box-pleat skirt, took her seat at her typewriter, and placed her feet neatly on the ottoman below her desk.

As she typed, she could not have imagined that a secret photo of a senator's wife awaited the world in the Manila envelope at the top of the stash *in* the ottoman.

Miss Gandy did not imagine.

A trusted servant of the Bureau was never curious.

Nor could she have dreamed that the picture – of a woman with a banned book under her arm – represented the F.B.I. Director's greatest hope. She did not dream. She had no dreams. She had confirmed that when Mr. Hoover hired her in March of 1918, forty-two years before. No, she said, she had no plans to marry. She liked children but did not need her own. She was not ambitious and would not seek advancement. She did not mind long hours.

Seated above her on the edge of his desk, Hoover asked her if she knew the etymology of the word 'secretary'. What could she do but admit that she did not know the meaning of the word 'etymology'? The interview was not going well. She was nervous, and the hem of her dress had been badly splashed by a passing motor-car on her way to the Justice Department that morning. A beautiful girl, with a lovely figure and perfectly crimped hair, was already sitting outside, waiting to be interviewed after her. At this rate, Helen Gandy thought, she'd be back behind the counter of the hosiery section at Garfinkle's before the week was out.

But Mr. Hoover, who was only a few years older than she was, surprised her. He praised the honesty of her admission, as if he were her father. She had never felt so grateful to anyone in all her twenty-one years. She was a plain girl of average intelligence, and no one had ever commended her before. But she was diligent, and she knew she had a capacity, not only for loyalty, but for devotion.

Mr. Hoover leaned forward and read from an index card he had prepared in advance. 'Secretary', he said, came from the Latin '*secretum*' for 'secret', and meant 'person entrusted with a secret'. He studied her with those black eyes of his that were like a midnight spell. Could she be that person he could always trust? She felt tears prick at her eyes. 'Yes, Mr. Hoover,' she replied. 'Yes. I am that person.' And the beautiful girl on the bench was sent away.

As she typed the Bureau memorandum, she made a quick note to remind herself to pick up Mr. Hoover's suit from the dry-cleaner's. His chauffeur would take it home and pass it to Annie. The Director liked his suits to be lined up and ready. Helen Gandy pondered her weekend plans for trout-fishing. It was a glorious September, and she favored Gunpowder River at this time of year, a little north of Baltimore and good for wild brown trout.

She had her mixed maggots ready in her refrigerator, and her hip-waders in the trunk. She generally tied her own flies, used a 12 hook, and added a little split-shot for weight. There would be a nice ripple on the water this month and still, with all the heat of late, a good hatch of flies – perfect for trout.

At Gunpowder River, nobody got too stubborn about their spots, and sometimes she even waved to one or two fellow anglers on the opposite bank. She never made conversation. Most people, she found, asked too many questions. She, for her part, had learned not to ask any. Even the inclination to do so was long gone. Mr. Hoover had once said she was his 'rock'. She seemed to recall he'd paid her that compliment in the early forties. True words lasted.

When the Director arrived back from his Friday lunch at the Mayflower, she put through a call from the New York Field Office. She heard Mr. Hoover speak – 'What have you got for me?' – then she gently put down the receiver.

In his office sanctum, Hoover listened to the update from New York. Senator Kennedy still hadn't actually had sex with either of the call-girls they'd flown in from London. He was flirting, sure, said the New York S.A.C. 'You bet he is.' He was enjoying himself. But maybe, suggested the S.A.C., he'd turned over a new leaf with his wife pregnant again.

Hoover laughed down the line in a hard staccato.

Of course he *could* approve a budget for new girls, different girls, more girls. But the strategy had failed, he said. That was the point. Kennedy's brother and his campaign team were obviously keeping the candidate on the straight and narrow, beyond reproach, until Election Day. Until the victor was decided: Kennedy or Nixon.

As fall overtook summer, it was too close to call, and far too close for Hoover's comfort. He'd had a heart attack two years before, and his blood pressure was soaring these days, what with Bobby Kennedy being lined up for the role of Attorney General – cocky Bobby Kennedy, the liberal, do-gooder lawyer who was already too curious about the dealings of the Bureau. The kid lawyer who'd never practiced law. Of course he hadn't! Now give him the top job in the Justice Department!

In July, Jack Kennedy had won the Democratic nomination on his father's money, with pictures of his pretty, expecting wife, and celebrity types like Sinatra and Harry Belafonte campaigning for him all over the country. Harry Bela-baloney. The Democrats had taken to wooing the Blacks. Even Adlai Stevenson hadn't scraped that barrel.

No one was more surprised than Hoover when his old neighbor, Lyndon B., had accepted the bone Kennedy threw: the offer of the Vice President spot on the ticket, in the wake of Johnson's defeat at the Convention. Johnson hated Kennedy. That was no secret. He called him 'the Boy'.

By all accounts, even Kennedy hadn't expected LBJ to accept the offer. In the Senate, Johnson hindered most anything Kennedy tried to push through. As the primaries approached, he'd even teamed up with other Democrats to actively block Kennedy.

But there was no denying it. The strategy had improved Kennedy's chances against Nixon and, with Johnson as his foil, Kennedy might even take Texas, where he didn't otherwise have a hope in hell.

Anyway, what did 'the Boy' care who his number two was? One of the Bureau's bugs, in the Democrats' convention hotel, had picked up an argument between Kennedy and his campaign scheduler: 'I'm forty-three,' Kennedy told the guy. 'I'm not going to die in office. So the vice-presidency doesn't mean anything.'

Now he had Johnson as a running mate. So what? Jack Kennedy was still trailing in the polls. His convention victory speech had been a dud. He'd looked wrung-out. Where was all that supposed charisma? Hoover hadn't seen any.

Even if Kennedy did manage to close the gap – and that was a big 'if' – he could still be knocked off his pedestal.

And by nothing more than a secret picture of his pretty wife.

Hoover had copies, if not the negative. His men in Boston had traveled to Cape Cod and turned over Mel Harding's motel room to find the thing, but they'd returned to the Field Office empty-handed, except for a tripod – no camera – and a copy of the banned novel, with a bookmark in it near the end.

Poor Mel Harding! He was going to miss the happy ending. He had missed his own happy ending, that was for sure. He was still living out of the same cheap motel room, somewhere in the Back of Beyond, on the Cape.

Before leaving the motel, the Bureau men had left money with the proprietor for damages to the room, taken a receipt, and filed it in their end-of-day report. They knew how to conduct themselves.

Periodically, on Hoover's instruction, the Boston S.A.C. sent a man down to tail Mel Harding's car, watch his room or follow him on his days off. Whether the agent was right on Harding's rear on the open highway, or turning up in the next booth in some diner on the 6A, ex-agent Harding was made to understand that the Bureau was never far.

Apparently, the dumb-bell had got himself a two-bit job at some drugstore in Hyannis. He was developing snapshots in the back room. Hoover had to smile. Harding had thought Butte was bad. Now he was printing wedding snaps and kids' birthday party pictures with Bozo the Clown. He'd be getting shots of the Grand Canyon and Niagara Falls *ad nauseam*. Most people didn't have any imagination. Most people didn't, because no one needed one. People with imaginations only got themselves in trouble.

Even with Harding out of action, the fact remained: no ex-agent was ever *not* a liability. So Hoover made sure the Bureau never lost an ex's scent. Wherever Harding went, Hoover's hounds would follow. The guy would never feel alone again.

You gave up certain comforts when you let the Bureau down. When you gave away Bureau secrets to Persons of Interest. To targets.

There was no forgiving that.

As for Mrs. Kennedy's 'delicate condition', Hoover felt bad about that, he really did. He didn't want to make trouble for any lady who was expecting, but Mrs. Kennedy had made trouble for herself, hadn't she? She'd got herself tangled up with a banned book, a filthy book. Even her husband didn't know what she had done, which only proved she knew her secret attendance of the New York hearing was wrong. All wrong.

Much as Hoover would have enjoyed it, he didn't *tell* Kennedy what his wife had been getting up to. Because the security of the Bureau's surveillance operations was paramount.

And Hoover's conscience was clear. If Mrs. Kennedy had the First Lady role in her sights, she had to be subject to the same F.B.I. background checks as any other federal employee. It could hardly be one rule for everyone and another for Mrs. Kennedy.

He wasn't unfeeling. If her un-American activity had ended with the hearing back in the spring, maybe, he told himself, just maybe he'd have dropped the whole thing and closed her file – at least he might have once he'd found out she was 'in the family way'. He'd been raised in the South, and he was always a gentleman where ladies were concerned. But she hadn't dropped it. Not at all. Her eyes were on the London trial now. She and Trilling were exchanging information and conspiring. Back and forth, to and fro, Cape Cod to Columbia U. The woman just *wouldn't stop.*

Well, if Mrs. Kennedy had her eyes on the London case, so had he. So did the weekend papers all around the world, and that meant a certain picture remained the best 'secret weapon' he had. He'd been turning the plan over and over in his mind. Clyde was in favor, and now he was decided too. They only needed a guilty verdict for that damned book. Then the picture could be discreetly leaked. The beauty of the plan was its simplicity.

They didn't need the expensive London call-girls. Clyde was right. Something less sensational would carry more punch: a shameful wife. A wife who read dirty books. An immoral, un-American First Lady-to-be who liked pornography. Who went against government decisions and even the view of the President.

'Dreadful.' That was Ike's statement about the book. 'We can't allow it.' Ike knew what he thought. Ike was his own man. Hoover had only suggested he make it public.

Now, they just needed that guilty verdict from London. Then, give it a day or two, and it would travel around the world.

The British Prosecution Office was getting on with the job, according to Dame Rebecca. She had certainly stepped up and played her part. Even if she was now withdrawing from the scene, he was grateful. Of course she still didn't know about the Bureau's Kennedy operation. Why complicate matters? The Soviets were watching the trial as closely as he was, and that had been enough to persuade Dame Rebecca to get involved.

He'd get Miss Gandy to send her a bunch of flowers. Pricey ones. Miss Gandy would have the flowers on their way and the receipt filed within the hour.

The timing of the London trial – a little before the American federal election on the 8th of November – was perfect. The plan was now in motion: 1. Get guilty verdict. 2. Leak photo to press. 3. Nixon to White House. 4. Winter vacation with Clyde in California.

He got the New York S.A.C. on the phone. 'Find me a Miss Katherine Anne Porter. She's a writer.' Her published output looked slender to him. His own published pages certainly exceeded hers. But that didn't matter. She was esteemed in academia, if nowhere else, and intellectual esteem was what was needed at this moment in time.

It helped that, according to his C.I.A. sources, Miss Porter was dependent on hand-outs from the Congress for Cultural Freedom – the biggest cultural exporter of American, liberal, anti-Communist art and ideas. If she was financially needy, all the better!

Miss Porter had toured Europe with their goddamn artsy road-show. Writers who couldn't afford bus tickets got flown around the world First Class, with limousines waiting and champagne receptions.

The Ivy League guys at the C.I.A. were able to tell him all about it because the Congress for Cultural Freedom was covertly funded by none other than the C.I.A. As was Britain's own elite literary maga-zine, *Encounter*. They had agents planted among the editors. Almost no one knew, even among the top staff. The C.I.A. presence was a time-saver. No one had to go to the trouble of censoring contribu-tors anymore – because most of the journal's writers, especially the American ones, were 'pre-approved'.

Whether she knew it or not, Miss Katherine Anne Porter had been pre-approved – and, looking at her gift of an article, Hoover could see why. Her recent review of *Lady Chatterley's Lover* was damning. Even the rarefied, literary types at the C.I.A. wanted D. H. Lawrence's anti-capitalist, anti-war novel stopped.

The Soviets were rubbing their hands over all the trouble a rene-gade novel was causing, and, same as him, the C.I.A. guys were determined to wipe the smiles off their faces. Hoover asked a C.I.A. contact straight up about Katherine Anne Porter's politics, especially regarding the upcoming election. 'She's a longstanding Democrat,' the contact said. 'She loved F.D.R. Likes Adlai. Has little time for Kennedy. Calls him a "young tough" and is not happy that the son of an erstwhile bootlegger might be on his way to the White House.'

Unbeknown to any of his C.I.A. contacts, Hoover had a Bureau man planted in their midst. *Encounter*, his guy was learning, allowed the Agency access to a better quality of international intelligence: who in London was pro-McCarthy, and who wouldn't dirty their hands in the anti-Communist fight. That sort of thing. *Encounter* was, it seemed, a successful, joint Anglo-American intelligence operation smuggled in under the cover of a high-brow magazine. Miss Porter had proved surprisingly useful when she denounced *Lady Chatterley* on its pages.

Hoover's plant read him a taste of her review over the phone. 'A woman like Lady Chatterley "often wears extremely well, physically. How long will it be before that enterprising man" – that's the pervert-gamekeeper,' added the agent – '"exhausts himself trying to be everything in that affair, both man and woman too, while she has nothing to do but be passive and enjoy whatever he wants her to have in the way he wants her to have it?" Blah, blah, blah. "I suppose she deserves anything she gets, really, but her just deserts are none of our affair."'

Only on that point did Hoover disagree. Lady Chatterley's just deserts were very much his affair.

His agent didn't know how much 'editorial' coaching Miss Porter had had at *Encounter*, but her article had been welcomed by the Agency. Hoover explained that her role was not yet complete. He wanted her on 'Bureau' business. The good news was that she'd known hard times since childhood, and no doubt she was smart enough to know which side her bread was buttered on. He let out a short, sharp laugh. Then he hung up.

He called for Miss Gandy. She was to send, pronto, a cable to the Bureau attaché in London: REQUEST FOR INFO RCVD FROM BRIT OFFICE OF PUBLIC PROS. RQST APPROVED. DESPATCH GROVE PRESS FED COURT TRANSCRIPT. ALSO K. PORTER/ ENCOUNTER MAG/FEB 60. LONDON-BU TO OFFER FULL ASSIST TO O.P.P. AS MATTER OF PRIORITY. E.J.H., DIRECTOR.

vii

In London, the press were busy speculating about the identity of the Prosecution's illustrious experts to come.

'PROSECUTION GUARDS SECRET LIST OF STAR WITNESSES!'

No one could have guessed that, with just five weeks to go, the names of their star witnesses were as great a mystery to the Prosecution as they were to the general public.

Around a mahogany table in Senior Counsel Mervyn Griffith-Jones's chambers, an articled clerk, a bony, concave young man called Mr Leaf, produced an old book – 'criticism from 1931,' he said, by one John Middleton Murry, who had been 'a close friend of Lawrence's until they had a falling-out'. Mr Leaf read aloud: '"a wearisome and oppressive book, the work of a weary and hopeless man".' He looked up. 'There is more,' he ventured.

Mervyn Griffith-Jones nodded, listened, and then raised a large, paddle-like hand. 'Mr Leaf, where is Mr Middleton Murry, pray?' His courtesy was withering.

'Deceased, sir, I'm afraid.'

The office clerk scratched a name off the list.

'Kipling?' tried another, from the end of the table. 'He was a witness for the Prosecution at the *Well of Loneliness* trial.'

'Dead,' called various voices.

'Henry James,' began a man with film-star looks and a weak grasp of literary history, 'gave a very mixed review to Lawrence early in his career. I have located a copy of it. Mr James will, in all likelihood, have an even lower opinion of Lawrence's work now ...'

No one spoke. No one threw him a life-line. Henry James was as dead as a door-nail.

Mr Griffith-Jones waited. The hinge of his jaw flexed.

Mr Leaf had boot-black hair and a blue-white pallor. His lips seemed permanently bluish too, as if he had been made to sleep in a pot-drawer as an infant. His suit was cheap but well pressed. He was the only 'grammar-school boy' at the table, and everyone knew it.

'And you are now waving Mr Eliot about, Mr Leaf, *because* ...?'

'Because he is alive, sir.'

433

'Go on, Leaf.'

'As you know, sir, Eliot is one of this country's major poets – and now *practically* English, if, regrettably, American by birth. He is also, arguably, the most distinguished lay-critic of our times, that's to say, the most respected critic outside the Academy.'

'I am acquainted with the meaning of "lay-critic", Mr Leaf.'

'Of course, sir. In this series of published lectures, entitled *After Strange Gods*, Mr Eliot denounces liberalism, individualism, D. H. Lawrence *and'* – Mr Leaf paused, a sort of rapture lighting up his pot-drawer pallor – '*Lady Chatterley's Lover.*'

Heads turned to assess anew the unprepossessing Mr Leaf. He continued boldly, if trembling like a— well, yes.

'Mr Eliot's series dates from …' He checked a note on his wrist. '1933. We'd only need ask him to repeat, or even simply read out, his text in court.'

'Well, what are you waiting for? Get on with it.'

'Unfortunately, attempts at gaining an introduction to Mr Eliot have not progressed.'

'Why not?'

'It would seem Mr Eliot does not wish to be introduced, sir. To us, that is. We have, however' – he lifted the book – 'his words.'

'Thank you for stating the obvious, Mr Leaf.' Griffith-Jones's pale lashless eyes blinked once. In shape, they resembled nothing so much as the curved tip of a pair of surgeon's scalpels. They had the fine, obdurate light of polished steel.

A young junior barrister called Blewitt sallied forth: 'In '32,' he began, 'in the *Spectator*, the biographer Lord David Cecil described Lawrence as an "uncontrolled egotist" and a "guttersnipe".'

Hungry, envious eyes lit up around the table.

'I take it, Mr Blewitt, that you have interviewed Lord Cecil?'

A shaving cut on Blewitt's throat started to bleed over his collar edge, as if in response to some pressure within. 'Regrettably, he has not yet returned our calls, sir, but I do have the full article here ready for your perusal.'

'The *full article*,' said Griffith-Jones, with *sotto voce* menace, 'would be *Lord – David – Cecil.*' He turned to his 'potential witnesses' list. 'What of Helen Gardner, Reader in Renaissance English Literature at St Hilda's College, Oxford?' He glanced at the faces around the table. 'Who has seen to her?' In a great stroke of luck, Miss Gardner had written disparagingly of *Chatterley*, and she mustn't elude their grasp.

The office clerk cleared his throat and read out her reply to the Prosecution request for support, received only that morning: '"<u>Lady Chatterley's Lover</u> is, whatever its merits or defects, the work of a writer of genius and complete integrity." Et cetera, et cetera. To summarise,' said the clerk, puffing out his cheeks, 'she is, and I quote, "unwilling to provide any assistance". In fact, rumour has it that she has offered herself to the other side.'

Trollop, they thought.

The despair in the room threatened like a landslide.

Then Mr Leaf rallied again. He *had*, he informed his colleagues, interviewed the publisher John Holroyd-Reece, and Mr Holroyd-Reece *was*, very nearly and almost certainly, prepared to say in court why he had *declined* to publish the novel when Lawrence offered it to him in the late twenties.

'Good, good,' said Mervyn Griffith-Jones. 'Make a note,' he instructed the clerk.

Things were on the up.

'The only difficulty,' continued Mr Leaf, 'is that Mr Holroyd-Reece tends to speak a *great* deal. It isn't entirely easy to get a word in, and I fear he might not be "guided" in court. He *did* assure me that he would consider giving evidence about the weaknesses of the novel' – here, the team sat up – 'but only if he can *also* say that he is *against* the prosecution.'

The clerk scratched another name off the list.

Two secretaries averted their eyes, as if the proceedings were now too shameful for women to witness.

In fact, the truth of that interview was worse than anyone knew. The Prosecution's only possible 'expert' so far that morning was Mr Holroyd-Reece, and Mr Holroyd-Reece was actually working for 'the other side'. The day after his interview with Mr Leaf, Holroyd-Reece wrote to his longstanding publisher friend:

My dear Lane, I promised to report to you about the visit of Mr C. H. G. Leaf from the Public Prosecutor's Office. I would describe him as an elderly young man, tall, slim, and more highly educated than I had assumed from my previous telephone discussion. Intellectually no giant. But rather pathetically well meaning. He asked me seven questions, which I outline below. They are pleased you have elected to go to trial by jury because they think the use and frequency of the four-letter words will horrify the jury and condemn the book. They are worried about how many eminent witnesses your side might produce – they fear you have Bertrand Russell on side. Do you? I was a reluctant interviewee for Mr Leaf. Happy, however, to be your Trojan horse in court if useful. And do come to dinner!

The office clerk took this opportunity to remind Mr Griffith-Jones that the press must be supplied with copies of the new Penguin paperback edition, so that they could follow the trial and quote accurately. Penguin had already provided a quantity for the jurors, but they could not be expected to offer more.

'Very well. Instruct HM Stationery Office to copy it.'

'Attempted already, sir,' said the clerk. 'But the Controller is reluctant to commit to the job, as his copying staff is composed entirely of young women, *unmarried* young women, and he cannot require them to handle such material.'

'I trust then that you will *overcome* his reluctance.' Griffith-Jones offered a thin smile. Each man felt it in his bowels.

It had grown progressively darker in the Prosecutor's chambers, although it was not yet three o'clock. A fug-like inertia had settled over the room, and no one seemed capable of rising to turn on a lamp. Mervyn Griffith-Jones was a tall, well-built man, and he presided over the heavy silence.

At last, he measured his words and began again: 'If it proves necessary in court to discredit the recent legal victory of the American edition, I will find a suitable way to remind the jury of "lax American morals", and I will point to the *proper* banning of the book in Canada. If neither *the book* nor *the author* can be sufficiently discredited, we will move to discredit the witnesses themselves. Researchers, please? Volunteers?'

Index fingers were raised. Their owners did not blush.

'Excellent.' Griffith-Jones shuffled his paperwork and turned to the matter of their FBI source, 'who shall remain nameless, gentlemen, for reasons you will no doubt appreciate.' The Bureau, he said, had been *most* helpful. Along with a copy of the American court transcript for Grove Press versus the New York Postmaster – 'which might, in theory, offer us pointers, I suppose' – he waved a desultory hand – 'they have forwarded an article by an American author called Katherine Anne Porter.'

He held up a photostat. 'Had the New York Appeals Court judge read *this*, I very much doubt he would have found in favour of Grove Press. The article, published in *Encounter* in February, is substantial, incisive, *and* highly critical of both the novel and the commercial efforts to publish the novel in its original form.'

Mr Griffith-Jones removed his half-moon spectacles from their case and read down his Roman nose: 'Miss Porter refers to the "air of evil which shrouds" *Lady Chatterley's Lover*. She describes Lady Chatterley as "a moral imbecile", and she points to Mr Lawrence's "blood-chilling anatomy of the activities of the rutting season between two rather dull persons".

'Most usefully, for our purposes, she identifies the form of "blackmail used by publishers and critics to choke their ambiguous wares down our throats. They say in effect, If you disapprove of this book, you are proved to be (1) illiterate, (2) insensitive, (3) unintelligent, (4) low-minded, (5) mean, (6) a hypocrite, (7) a prude, and other unattractive things. I happen to have known quite a number of decent persons," she says, "not too unintelligent or insensitive ... who were revolted by the book; and I do not propose to sit down under this kind of bullying ... This is the fevered day-dream of a dying man sitting under his umbrella pines in Italy indulging his sexual fantasies ... Lawrence was a very gifted, distraught man who continually overreached himself."'

Mervyn Griffith-Jones indicated he would take questions.

'Is *she* still alive, sir, Miss Porter?'

Mr Griffith-Jones leaned forward, unnervingly. 'I suggest that each of you pray that Miss Porter is not merely alive, but in *ruddy good health*. The FBI is trying to locate her now on our behalf. Sir Theobald will fly her to London to serve as our star witness. Our *only* expert witness.' He glowered. 'Next item!'

Copies of the list of the novel's wanton use of 'four-letter words' were distributed. The two secretaries were excused, in deference to female sensibilities.

'Now,' said Griffiths-Jones, pushing his specs up his nose, 'a cursory count has uncovered the following: forty-two uses of "fuck" or "fucking", fourteen "cunts", twelve "wombs", thirteen "balls", six "shits", ten "arses", "bottoms" or "tails", twenty-eight "penises" including the variants of "cod", "cock" and "phallus", plus three "pisses". "Feel" and "touch" are repeated nine times on a single page; "sensual" thirteen times on another. "Inside" is used repeatedly to compound certain salacious effects. A second-stage search is to be conducted for lewd colloquialisms, such as "going off" and "the ink could stay in the bottle".'

Henceforth, he said, their principal strategy would be two-fold: to demonstrate, in a so-called work of art, one, the obscene vulgarity of the gamekeeper Mellors, and two, the promiscuity of Lady Chatterley. 'Lady Chatterley, I'm afraid,' he said, with a smile which suddenly had teeth, 'has a great deal to answer for. A great deal indeed.'

He did not mention to his staff the note he'd received the week before.

14 Melbury Road
London W14
8th September, 1960

Dear Sir,

I understand that you might be requiring witnesses in the forthcoming case Crown v. Penguin Books Ltd. I place myself at your disposal.

Yours faithfully,
Constance Chatterley

The hand was elegant, with flourishing capitals. His secretary had prepared a standard reply, thanking 'Mrs Chatterley' for her offer of assistance. She'd brought it to his desk for his signature, when they'd spotted the joke and shared a little chuckle. In the current context, the word 'faithfully' had seemed especially droll.

And yet, oddly, he hadn't been able to resist. The action was entirely out of character, but the address was clear. On his way through town, he'd felt compelled to check, if only to satisfy his curiosity, for the words had echoed seductively – 'at your disposal'. He'd felt like a sleuth and a lover all at once.

The area was Kensington & Chelsea. Melbury Road was composed of large, gabled, red-brick Victorian houses nestled around Holland Park. Some were detached. Most were 'semis'. Some had been converted into smaller, higgledy-piggledy dwellings and flats. He could almost have imagined himself outside the Kensington house 'Lady Chatterley' might have inherited from her father, the Royal Academician, 'Sir Malcolm Reid' – were it not for the fact that Number 14 did not exist.

How clever.

The joke was indeed on him.

What should have been Number 14 was merely a house-shaped absence, a woman-shaped absence – a bomb-site, a patch of waste ground, with a roof of watery blue sky.

A tree had taken root in the gap between the neighbouring houses. Two children had crawled through the broken fencing and were playing beneath the tree.

One couldn't even call it a hoax. It was merely someone's sly wit at work, her notion of fun – 'her' because the handwriting was assuredly female. Yet, for a singular moment, as he'd read the signature at his desk for the second time – *Yours faithfully, Constance Chatterley* – his blood had thrilled to the name.

Like all the 'Lady Chatterley' headline-writers who wrote of her, not as a character, but as a woman on trial, he too had half-longed for her to come true.

Away from the case precedents, the court papers and the leather-bound tomes that lined his chambers, he was not unaware of his own narrowness. He knew that, beneath the Savile Row suit, the barristerial silk and wig, there shivered the man who stood naked under a cold shower each morning, and who, in spite of himself, wanted a woman like Constance to love him, to forgive him, and to release him from the person he didn't know how not to be.

viii

Time is so lightly stitched.
.7291, yluJ fo ht82 ehT
It unravels at the touch.
The 28th of July, 1927.
He has been writing all morning – in the company of Connie
dear Ros – in the secluded wood behind the Villa Mirenda, high
above the city of Florence. On the page, she's with him once
more.
larutan ylno si tI
It is only natural,
he thinks to himself,
Trapa em tes yaw a ni lliw levon siht taht
that this novel will in a way set me apart
.trapa tes ydaerla ma I naht yletinifed erom neve
even more definitely than I am already set apart.
.ynitsed s'tI
It's destiny.
When Lawrence retreats from the midday heat, he arrives in the
kitchen bearing fresh pages and a basket of peaches from the garden.
He has climbed the stairs to the *piano nobile* of the villa he and Frieda
lease.
It takes him several moments to catch his breath, but he's pleased
with his harvest. He wipes the sweat from his face with his shirt-tail,
then shows her. The peaches are perfect globes of rosy-yellow. He will
make jam. Do they have sugar? Not that she will know. He will read
her the latest chapter as they eat. What do they have in the larder?
When Giulia, the peasant girl, arrives to prepare their meal, he
goes to his room to scribble a note to Secker. 'Second draft. You'll
have to see what you think of the result. It's a bit of a revolution in
itself – a bit of a bomb.'
Giulia wants to show Frieda her new heeled shoes. When any
visitor comes, she dons a cap and apron, like a parlour-maid – and
now, she says, clapping her hands, there will be fine shoes! Usually
she arrives barefoot. She and Frieda laugh as she sashays across the
marble floor, practising her new walk, which means it is a moment
or two before Frieda registers the faint but curious sound.

She puts a hand to her ear and hushes Giulia.

A gurgling. A rasp.

In the bedroom, she finds the ink-pot overturned and her husband on the bed, his eyes wide with shock.

A thin stream of blood runs from his mouth.

It is strange – no, a marvel – to be so full of life, literally! she is saying.

Over the telephone, Jackie confirms for her husband that, yes, the baby is a kicker. He or she is already training for touch-football with the family.

In his Chicago hotel room at the Ambassador East, Jack Kennedy is playing Peggy Lee records and cramming for his 'Great Debate' that night – September 26th – with Nixon on CBS. Down the line, a thousand miles apart, they go over his choice of suit. The dark one, she tells him, for authority, and to make him stand out against the gray of the studio set.

At the Big House, she, Jack's mother and sisters watch on a television they've rented for the occasion. The furniture in the sun-room has been moved, and guests have been invited, including a few members of the press, at Rose's insistence. It is important that they as a family appear open, confident and natural, with nothing to hide. Several people sit on cushions on the floor. The mood is upbeat and informal. Jackie sits at the far end of her mother-in-law's lemon-yellow sofa, sensing that her every expression and reaction is side-eyed by the reporters. As the television set buzzes to life, she tries to imagine but can't: at that very moment, seventy million viewers are tuning in across the country to watch her husband and Nixon face off.

Jack looks good on screen – no question – and she relaxes a little. The steroids have filled him out, and the Addison's has one advantage at least; it's given him the appearance of a healthy tan, even in black-and-white. She telephoned one of his aides as they left the hotel and asked the man to go back to pick up Jack's pale blue shirt. Pale blue would appear white, but unlike white, it wouldn't reflect back the harsh studio lighting. 'Please tell him his wife insists that he lets someone dab some powder on his face. And make sure he's wearing *long* socks,' she adds, 'in case they're made to sit on those high stools.'

She watches her husband approach the studio podium. 'Mr. Smith, Mr. Nixon,' he begins, 'in the election of 1860, Abraham Lincoln said the question was whether this nation could exist half slave or half free. In the election of 1960, and with the world around us, the question is whether the world will exist half slave or half free, whether it will move in the direction of freedom, in the direction of the road that we are taking, or whether it will move in the direction of slavery. I think it will depend in great measure upon what we do here in the United States, on the kind of society that we build, on the kind of strength that we maintain. We discuss tonight domestic issues, but I would not want any implication to be given that this does not involve directly our struggle with Mr. Khrushchev for survival. Mr. Khrushchev is in New York and he maintains the Communist offensive throughout the world ...'

He's doing well, she decides, and she strokes her belly gently. The baby seems to have calmed to the sound of his or her father's voice. Jack looks straight into the camera. It's as if he's in the room. His gaze is steady and reassuring, and he radiates a quiet confidence. 'If we do well here, if we meet our obligations, if we are moving ahead, then I think freedom will be secure around the world. If we fail, then freedom fails.'

As the cut-and-thrust of the debate unfolds with Nixon, Jack is authoritative and even tough, but not combative. He has his facts at his fingertips, and he punctuates his significant points with hand gestures, as they rehearsed.

She actually feels sorry for Dick Nixon. He's lost weight – a recent bout of the flu, apparently – and his suit looks two sizes too big for him. It's light gray against the light gray set, his white shirt is too stark for his face, and all of Pat Nixon's ironing can't save him now. The whiskers of his beard look like a dark shadow across his face. Even worse, under the studio lights, the Lazy Shave foundation stick they've used on him – a standard repair tool on the campaign trail – is melting down his neck and marking his collar.

Throughout, Jack calmly but passionately evokes the promise of a new age, a new youthful spirit, and a new frontier of possibility. He emphasizes the need not only for a strong economy but also for access to education and good healthcare for all.

He speaks powerfully about the chances a black baby being born that year has, compared to those of a white baby – a baby like their own, she thinks. She's proud of him. This is where he shows the nation that he's cut from different cloth than Adlai Stevenson.

When Nixon is caught on camera as Jack speaks, he looks shifty and nervous, as if he doesn't realize the camera is on him while Jack is 'on'. It's not a face you could trust. A half hour under the lights, and beads of perspiration are dripping from his nose. The poor man has to take out his handkerchief to mop his face.

For the first time, she feels the force of it sweep through her – Jack might actually take the White House – and there, at the end of the low yellow sofa, she feels a kind of vertigo.

After, Maud arrives to let Jackie know that little Caroline is asleep upstairs. Is she alright where she is for the night, or should she be taken back to her own bed? Maud approaches the sofa and reports in low tones, so as not to disturb the others, that she read Caroline her *Madeline* book before sleep, and if she is no longer needed, she'll retire for the evening herself. But she lingers, uneasily.

'I'm grateful, Maud,' Jackie murmurs. 'Is there anything else?'

The older woman says nothing but opens her palm and shows her a pink paper stub. 'I dropped off the films today at Whelan's.'

Her employer smiles.

'Of the children's party, Mrs. Kennedy, from Labor Day …'

'Yes. Of course. Would you mind holding onto the ticket and picking them up for me when it's convenient? There's no rush at all.'

'I think it *is* best, Mrs. Kennedy, if I pick them up.'

'Oh?' Jackie adjusts the cushions at her back. She still has two and a half months to go, and she's bigger than she was with Caroline at full term. Her fingers have swollen and her wedding band is tight. She has one ear on the post-debate analysis and one on Maud.

Maud draws closer and drops her voice. 'Because I saw someone, ma'am, someone at the drugstore you might feel is best avoided.'

Jackie raises a finger, then heaves herself off the couch and joins Maud at the door which leads onto the lawn. 'Someone?'

'Mr. Harding, Mrs. Kennedy.' The woman pauses, uncertain whether she should elaborate. It is important that Mrs. Kennedy is not upset. Her pregnancies are delicate matters. The Kennedy sisters-in-law glance their way. Mrs. Joseph Kennedy does not. The proud mother sits on the edge of the sofa, in the grip of the studio analysis.

'When I dropped off the films, Mr. Harding of all people appeared for a moment behind the counter. He was wearing some sort of lab coat. I think he must be working in the film-processing room. Isn't that queer?'

'Did he say hello?'

'No. He looked away. I don't know if he saw me or, if he did, if he remembered who I was. Isn't it strange that he's still on the Cape, Mrs. Kennedy? Given that he was … let go.'

Jack's sister Pat arrives in the room, bearing frosted glasses of 7 Up and bowls of peanuts for the reporters. Rose Kennedy waves Pat out of the way of the set. Rose is telling a reporter how terribly sorry she feels for Richard Nixon's mother.

Maud waits. Jackie nods, assessing Maud's report. It is indeed a surprise – Mr. Harding still on the Cape, and only up the road in Hyannis. She certainly would have preferred him gone.

It is three weeks since she reported him to Jack, for trying to get those pictures of her as she swam that Sunday – a misunderstanding, he claimed. Whether it was or wasn't, he admitted he was one of Hoover's men, spying on them – a vile thought – and Mr. Hoover, everyone knew, was no fan of Jack's.

If she were to tell Jack that ex-agent Mel Harding was still in Hyannis, he'd go into that drugstore himself and tell him to pack his bags. But why make more trouble for the man? He'd tried to make amends in his own way. Hoover's horrible orders weren't actually his fault. Harding was doing a job, one which even he seemed to regret. He'd tried to atone. He'd given her a copy of her picture from the G.P.O., plus the negative. It hadn't fixed everything. As Mr. Harding explained, Hoover still had her picture, evidence of her attendance that day. He'd have made copies, with or without the original negative. The thought was sickening.

And there was Mel Harding's hand – in her mind again – his hand gripping hold and hauling her free of that rip-tide, even though he couldn't swim. Even though he must have been scared half to death.

So why did it still feel as if he'd caught her in the act of something shameful, when he snapped her at the Grove Press hearing back in May? Jack moved independently in the world. Why shouldn't she on occasion? She rarely knew his exact whereabouts. Why was she supposed to account for hers?

'Shall I get your films back for you, Mrs. Kennedy, before Agent Harding – I mean, Mr. Harding – develops them?'

'That's quite alright, Maud. If you could simply pick up the pictures for me, that would be a help. Leave it for a time. Perhaps his job at Whelan's is only temporary, until he moves on or back to wherever he came from.'

Best not to let Maud rush in and draw Harding's attention to the fact that she, his former 'charge', knew he was still in town. Best not to react. Jack was reassured that the man had been fired from the Bureau. Yet could Hoover still be using Mel Harding?

It made a kind of sense … let Jack and her imagine he'd been fired. Then keep him in the area to spy.

Well, let them do their worst. Mr. Harding was no longer allowed anywhere on Irving Avenue or on the beachfront. If she spotted him in Hyannis Port, Jackie was to report the incident to the Secret Service.

There was only one puzzle that remained. For some inexplicable reason, when Jack had telephoned Hoover to complain about the planting of one of the Bureau's agents – 'In my *house*, for Christ's sake' – Hoover didn't tell him about her attending the hearing for *Lady Chatterley*. She'd waited for the grenade to land, but it hadn't.

Why hadn't Hoover told Jack? After all, her presence at the G.P.O. was what seemed to have prompted Hoover to have her spied on in their home. *Had* he told Jack the truth of her whereabouts last May, Hoover could have used it to justify his ongoing surveillance: 'Your wife, Senator Kennedy, was found publicly supporting an action in defiance of the government position.' He would have had Jack on the back foot. So why didn't Hoover say anything? He had the evidence, and it wasn't kindness. She knew that much.

She looks back to the roomful of family and guests. Eunice is on her knees, bending the television's rabbit-ears this way and that while Rose directs. Jackie tells Maud she must return to them, and she bids her goodnight. As she takes her seat again on the couch, a reporter, a woman, from one of the Boston papers, asks her if her bracelet is real gold. She says she doesn't know. It was a gift. The reporter looks skeptical.

'I didn't ask,' she says tersely.

Another reporter asks her if it's true that Mr. Kennedy forgot their wedding anniversary on the 17th of that month. It is true, but she merely replies, 'How thoughtful of you to be concerned about our anniversary when there is *so* much going on in the world.'

Jackie accepts a handful of peanuts from Pat, although her hand is greasy now and she feels she'll be sick if she eats them. She watches Maud slip away onto the veranda and recede across the darkened lawn. She wishes she could disappear with her.

Another reporter says, 'Goodness! You bite your nails!'

She wonders how quickly she can exit the scene.

'What did you think of your husband's performance, Mrs. Kennedy?'

All the pencils and pocket-notebooks come out.

Rose turns, too, to listen, her smile vinegary. She thinks her daughter-in-law is too shy, too soft-spoken, to be the wife of a President – although she takes a lovely picture.

'My husband was brilliant,' Jackie says on cue, 'I'm very proud of him.'

They wait for something more. Her mother-in-law waits too, her smile fixed.

'Now if you'll excuse me, I must check on Caroline.'

Fifteen miles away, in his motel room on Route 6A, Mel Harding stands and switches off his transistor radio. Things are hotting up. For the first time, it's clear: Kennedy actually has a shot at the presidency. Hoover won't be a happy man tonight.

Which is when it starts again – the strobing of the flashlights through the cheap curtains.

So he knows they're there.

Once or twice a week.

When he finally sleeps, he dreams that yellow dog eyes are looking back at him in the night as he walks to Hyannis Port, to Irving Avenue. He has to keep moving. The dogs are downwind of him, and they've got his scent. So he dips off the road into the area known locally as the Great Marshes. He can smell the stagnation, the rot, but it's either the route of the stink, or risk the dogs. The ground gives way underfoot, he has no idea how deep the bog might get, or if he'll step into a murky pond and drown in the night – anonymous and known to no one, with no one to come looking – when he awakes to the sound of dogs, actual dogs, barking outside.

Each night, his new and seemingly permanent neighbors in the next room lock their hounds in their station wagon, with the windows wound down an inch or two for air. The car is parked right outside in the lot, outside his window. Nebraska plates. The four dogs sound like fifty. Something has startled them: Hunter, Killbuck, Racer and Snap.

'Great names,' he said, when he was 'introduced' the day before by the owners.

If you live in a horror movie.

Mr. and Mrs. Dagenhart are a tall, stooped couple in their mid- to late sixties. They were fixed on chatting, on being neighborly, as they prepared the bowls of 'feed' – butchers' off-cuts – on the low motel porch they shared. Mr. Dagenhart explained that the recommended blend was five percent liver, five percent other organs, ten percent bone, and eighty percent meat, fat and ligaments. On holidays, he said, the 'doggies' got ground venison.

The four go wild every time Harding goes in and out of his room.

He rolls over and pounds his pillow. His sheets are clammy with sweat. His hands are getting worse, what with the daily splashes of fixatives from the processing room at Whelan's. He thinks he might lose his mind if he has to develop one more snapshot of a kid on a swing. He wonders if he'll ever touch a woman again.

He can't get back to sleep. Let them shine their damned flashlights into his room. Let them tail his car. It was only standard Bureau harassment. The agents who were on the case were just following orders. It wasn't personal. 'You leave the Bureau but the Bureau never leaves you.' That wasn't news.

He only wished they'd left him his copy of the novel when they ransacked his room. It had calmed his brain when he couldn't sleep. Plus, he'd found himself actually enjoying the story of the solitary gamekeeper and Lady Chatterley. He'd even started to understand the gamekeeper's dialect. Would she leave her husband for a man like that?

Usually, he just read dime-store pocketbooks, detective novels mostly. Sometimes, they drove him crazy, getting the details wrong, but he kept his expectations low.

He had wanted to say more about the book to Mrs. Kennedy. He'd wanted to thank her, for introducing him to it, the day the Professor came for lunch. But of course, she hadn't introduced him to it. Not at all. She hadn't intended to read it aloud to him, of all people – not to her intruder.

In Gray's Inn, Michael Rubinstein, Instructing Solicitor for the Defence, was bent over his desk. The trial at the Old Bailey was to begin in less than a fortnight, and nothing could be taken for granted.

On the 'good news' side, both T. S. Eliot and Dame Rebecca West had 'come around' and submitted their respective witness statements. Dame Rebecca's was not as 'staunch' as he might have hoped, but he believed she would rise to the occasion when called to the witness box.

Tom Eliot, on the other hand, had been scrupulous and generous, if understandably strained, given the fact that his youthful criticism of the novel might well be flaunted in court by the Prosecution. It could, potentially, get quite embarrassing for him.

Tom had been a long-time friend of Jeremy Hutchinson's, the Junior Defence Counsel's, *father*, St John Hutchinson – otherwise known as 'Jack'. Indeed, Jeremy had helped Tom overcome his nerves and volunteer to testify. In a lovely quirk of fate, Jack Hutchinson had defended Lawrence's confiscated paintings in 1929, just as his son, Jeremy, was now to defend Lawrence's final novel. Lawrence had written *Lady C.* in the mornings and painted the controversial canvases in the afternoons, not realising he would one day rely upon the expertise and goodwill of both Hutchinson Senior and Junior. Rubinstein decided it was a good omen.

Altogether less welcome was a warning he'd had by letter three days before, from a trusted source, reminding him of something everyone on the Defence team had hoped to ignore, himself included: namely, Lawrence's references in *Lady Chatterley's Lover* to a sexual act 'which (I believe) English law holds to be criminal'.

Bugger, thought Rubinstein.

Precisely, said the Censor in his head.

The letter of caution referred him to, for example, page 280 in which Sir Clifford says, 'if a man likes to use his wife, as Benvenuto Cellini says "in the Italian way", well that is a matter of taste.'

On the day the information arrived, Rubinstein copied the letter and added a note for his researcher. Could he confirm, please, the meaning and etymology of the phrase 'in the Italian way'?

The answer arrived by the second post. Rubinstein quickly scribbled a few lines to Gerald Gardiner, Senior Counsel for the Defence. '"The Italian manner" is sodomy. See Penguin *Cellini*, pp. 280–283.' Then he noted: 'You are contacting Bull on this one.'

He felt quite sure that 'Bull' – Sir Reginald Manningham-Buller, Attorney General of England and Wales – had little sympathy for the plight of the book. Now he was likely to have even less.

As for the passages on pages 258, between Mellors and Lady Chatterley, well, Lawrence was hardly helping his own defence. 'It was not really love ... It cost her an effort to let him have his way and his will of her ...' Rubinstein sighed. What could any of them do but hope that the Counsel for the Prosecution's attention to detail might have wavered by this point in the novel; or that the references might be sufficiently veiled. If not, a jury would almost certainly return a guilty verdict. What choice would they have? To not do so would seem to sanction a 'criminal' act.

His own careful words to Sir Allen Lane tugged at the back of his mind. 'There can be, I think, no question of prison sentences for the Directors of your Company or anyone else concerned with the publication.' Perhaps he should have underscored 'I think'. But doubts would serve no one now. The case was in motion. What could they do but go forward and be of good courage?

He returned to the preparatory notes he had been dictating into his desktop Dictaphone, particularly for their lead barrister, Gerald Gardiner, QC. He pressed the record button on the reel-to-reel and resumed: 'Mellors tells Connie that the "right relation with a woman" is "the core" of his life (page 213) and then (page 215) says, he has no satisfaction, unless she "got hers of me ... It takes two." Worth noting. At the bottom of the page, "warm" is used seven times and "tender" twice. On page 216, Mellors says, "I'd rather die than do any more cold-hearted fucking", repeating what he has said earlier that if the "right relation" is not achieved, then he will do without. *This*, surely, is the profound point.

'The Prosecution is, of course, hypocritical among a body of men for whom the word "fuck" is a multi-purpose verb, used daily and with great feeling by all ranks. I think we all agree that the Prosecution will suggest that this commonly used but uncommonly printed word, "fuck", is obscene and therefore has the tendency to deprave and corrupt as printed and published in this book.

'What I *do* not understand is whether they assert that, when "fuck" appears ten times on a page, its tendency is to deprave or corrupt *ten* times over, *or* whether, after reading that page, the reader is likely to be ten times as depraved and corrupted as he or she was after reading the word once, *or* whether the law of diminishing returns might apply so that he or she is likely to be *less* depraved or corrupted, or even *ten times* less likely to be depraved or corrupted than the first time he or she read the word "fuck" on the page—'

He looked up, startled.

Four women were standing in his open doorway.

'I'm sorry to interrupt, Mr Rubinstein,' said his secretary, colouring. 'I did knock, but I don't believe you heard.'

It was evident, however, that *they* had heard, in full, his disquisition on the word 'fuck'.

At the threshold, the women presented an echoing trio of profiles: Barbara Lucas Wall, her daughter Bernadine Wall, and a woman who could only have been Barbara's eighty-year-old mother, Madeline Meynell Lucas.

He pressed the stop button and rose clumsily to his feet.

'Apologies, Michael,' said Barbara. 'We came only on the off-chance, but clearly we've chosen an inopportune—'

'Not at all, not at all! The apologies are all mine! Ladies, do forgive me – dicky ear since the war. Please, please come in. Barbara, it is a lovely surprise! Your timing' – he smiled – 'is impeccable.'

He quickly assessed his three visitors. Barbara Wall was embarrassed and would soon reach for any excuse to leave. The faces of Dina and her grandmother, however, were warmed by the same expression of glee at the accidental comedy of his 'textual analysis'.

Madeline Meynell Lucas of Greatham, Sussex, the widow of the slain and defamed Perceval Lucas, had arrived at this juncture of events, he knew, against all odds. She was breaking a vow she had made to her dead mother. She was overlooking the injury done to her husband, herself and her child. She was offering him, Rubinstein – and the traitor Lawrence himself – the gift of her bright, book-loving granddaughter.

Here was a moment he would not soon forget.

Indeed, he felt rather emotional.

'Tea?' he said.

Day One, Thursday, October 20th

The day had come at last, grey and soggy. October had been a wet month, with little of the crisp freshness he loved in a usual Hampstead autumn, and with still less of October's mellow light. The temperature had dipped, and mist clung on through the days, like a fog to the head or a bug one couldn't quite shake.

In town, a thick yellow murk obscured street kerbs and road signs, and sometimes one's own feet. People seemed to keep falling into the Thames these days, or riding their bicycles into it. The week before, with very low visibility, there had been a spate of burglaries, and cars abandoned along the length of the Mall. At Marble Arch, the police were directing traffic with flames. It wasn't the worst of the fogs he'd known, but it did seem as if the whole of the city needed a stiff breeze.

At The Gables, he'd woken too early, clammy, with a racing brain. Rather than lie awake, he'd risen at five and, tea made, he'd thrown a mac over his pyjamas and walked, balancing cup and pipe, to the bottom of the garden. Fetch trailed companionably after, and there they'd stood beneath the dripping beeches, between those massive trunks and their twin poles of calm. Their branches had been stripped of leaves in the storm of the previous week, but the great, exposed roots, three centuries deep, gripped the earth and steadied him.

In four or five hours' time, he would be seated alongside his client, Sir Allen Lane, in the well of the court, directly below the Judge's bench. But for this brief interlude, he did nothing more than sip and smoke, moving on in his day only when the quantity of rain in his cup exceeded the quantity of tea.

Court Number One of the Old Bailey was renowned as a theatre of justice, and it rivalled any one of London's beloved, historic stages for spectacle, intimacy and poor acoustics. It was the largest of the four courts that radiated off the Grand Hall of the Central Criminal Court, and it had seen more than its share of drama over the century. Yet for all its magnificence and its place in the moral imagination of the nation, it was a surprisingly small chamber, seating just two hundred – at a pinch.

As Solicitor for the Defence, Michael Rubinstein could do nothing more than wait for the performance to unfold. He had worked intensively, day and night, weekday and weekend, behind the scenes and above the parapet, for ten weeks. He had orchestrated the entire Defence case, and now he could only watch from 'the wings' as his cast took to the stage. Had he done enough?.

The be-wigged players – the barristers – knew their parts faithfully. As he'd assured Sir Allen from the outset, the Defence Counsel were three of the very best, and good men all: Lead Counsel, Gerald Gardiner, QC; Junior Counsel, Jeremy Hutchinson, QC; and Mr Richard Du Cann, the youngest and not yet QC.

The solicitors' table, in the well of the floor of the court, was a sort of trench or dug-out where one could only hold one's breath and keep one's wits. In the war, he had usually found he could *do* something when things got tough, but in this moment, seated beside Sir Allen and Board Director, Hans Schmoller, directly below the Judge's dais, he felt somehow cut off at the knees.

The architecture of any court is explicitly configured to raise up and to lower; to aggrandise and to humble. It provides the vessel for the flamboyant display of legal ritual. On rare occasions, a witness might be offered a chair in the witness box, or perhaps a moment to compose him or herself. A juror's eyes might widen in sympathy or shed a quiet tear but, in 1960, these were incidental details only, for Court One, literally, had little *room* for human sympathy. Notwithstanding its neo-classical grandeur, the swishing of robes, the white-gloved hands and wigged erudition, the court was still inseparable from its primitive rituals of captivity, debasement and punishment.

Someone had to be 'low' so that others could be 'high'. Or perhaps it was the other way around. Hierarchy, caste and rank still defined every social structure and interchange in the nation's consciousness, as assuredly as the columns, pediments and pilasters that propped up the Old Bailey itself.

Sir Allen and Hans Schmoller had been spared the humiliation of confinement to the huge dock at the centre of the court. It seemed a civilised token of goodwill, but was it? Was a jury more likely to give a verdict of 'Guilty' if the dock itself were empty? That was the risk, yet they would remain at the solicitors' table, seated to the right of Michael Rubinstein, closest to his good ear. His folders of notes and witness statements were stacked before him, should Mr Gerald Gardiner, Lead Counsel, need to check any point – or should Lane and Schmoller need, he thought with a grimace, to take cover. After all, in the narrow confines of Court One, the public gallery was only 'a stone's throw' away.

God help them.

Above him, on the Judge's bench, a series of high-backed chairs – like thrones on a dais – occupied the length of the rear wall of the court. These mighty chairs awaited not only the Judge, Mr Justice Laurence Byrne, but also the Sheriff of the City of London, City Aldermen, assorted judicial observers, and even the curious wife of any presiding judge. Mounted on the wall behind the Judge's chair, the golden Sword of State rose three feet into the air, from a scabbard of purple velvet.

Behind the solicitors' table, also in the well of the court, were the Counsel's Rows, a series of leather-upholstered seats for the barristerial bottoms, with the Prosecution Counsel positioned nearest the Judge's bench, and the Defence Counsel positioned nearest the dock. Barristers were permitted a modest desk and lectern, across which they were now, as the proceedings drew near, discreetly arranging their papers. Behind the Counsel's Rows, assorted dignitaries were propped like over-sized, obedient school-children who happened to be wearing medals, baronial chains of rank, and, in one case, a pair of house slippers.

The Clerk of the Court had received countless requests for admission tickets for the remaining seats on the floor. The requests had flooded in from the great, the good, the impassioned, the titillated, and the nosy. Even Mr Vyvyan Holland, Oscar Wilde's son, was in attendance that first day. The trial of *Lady C.* was the hottest ticket in town, and, now, shortly before half past ten in the morning, Michael Rubinstein could almost hear an invisible orchestra in the well of the court tuning up.

Court Number One, the principal courtroom of the most important criminal court in England, sacrificed nothing of its symbolic staging to the claims of convenience or comfort. The place was jammed full of woodwork which interrupted sight-lines and acoustics equally. It was a tight, three-dimensional puzzle of benches, panelling, desks, chairs, lecterns, tables, platforms and arches, not to mention the upper-storey box of the public gallery, a space so narrow, it most closely resembled a cupboard from which a superfluity of tea-cups might at any moment come crashing down.

In spite of their pending discomfort, the general public had been queuing for hours in the rain outside the Old Bailey for seats in this china cupboard. As the heating system choked and banged into operation, a fuggy smell of wet woollen coats and furs summoned the fond memory of family pets in the minds of many. Michael Rubinstein hoped, absentmindedly, that his wife had remembered to let Fetch in out of the rain.

In any concert hall or theatre, he was always struck by the impression that each member of the audience, be they in the royal box or 'in the gods', affected the performance in a way most would never dream. Similarly, the goodwill, or lack thereof, of those gathered in a courtroom was, he believed, a silent but genuine force.

Close to the Judge's bench and ahead of the Counsel's Rows was the jury box: two enclosed rows which seated six jurors apiece. This was 'front row of the stalls' for the twelve most important people in the court, citizens who, on the morning of Day One, had yet to be revealed. Watching on behalf of the nation were twelve tightly packed rows of members of the press.

The great dock itself, a box large enough to accommodate at least ten defendants, or ten specimens for the scrutiny of the court, was centre-stage and directly within the Judge's sights. In more usual cases, the defendant would ascend into the dock from the holding cells in the bowels of the Old Bailey. Also in the basement was the coal-room of the great edifice and a mighty heaving furnace. Beneath it and a hatch in the floor, the ancient River Fleet ran, culverted and unseen, through London's underworld, like a River Styx of ancient Britain.

On the stroke of half past ten, three loud raps sounded on a door of the court, and everyone straightened in their seats. The overture had begun. An usher appeared and, in a rousingly clear voice which defied the acoustics, he called upon everyone to be upstanding, and for God to save the Queen.

A door promptly opened on the Judge's bench-cum-dais, and from it, as if in a clockwork theatre, came the Sheriff of the City of London, ruffled in lace, glinting with hardware, and clutching a cocked hat. The Lord Mayor entered in full regalia, flanked by two City Aldermen in gold chains and midnight-blue furred robes. A silver-haired woman emerged, wearing a voluminous cape upon which a brooch glittered expensively. *That* was not paste! noted the editors of the Women's pages.

Finally, all stepped back, and Mr Justice Byrne appeared, a wizened figure in a cropped grey wig, white gloves and an ermine-trimmed, scarlet robe, girded at the waist by a gleaming black sash. It was a costume that wouldn't have looked out of place on a sorcerer, and Mr Justice Byrne carried not only the black cap of his office, but a nosegay of flowers – traditional relief from the rising stink of Newgate Prison, over which the Old Bailey had once stood. Ritual sprigs of rue had also been strewn on the Judge's bench, at the ends of the barristerial rows and, most plentifully, around the prisoners' dock.

The Judge bowed three times to the assembled barristers, who bowed back to him. Gowns fluttered as he and the court took their seats. His own Seat of Office was first held and then 'glided' into place by the Sheriff, an action facilitated by twin-tracks on the bench, to give the impression of a Judge infallibly at ease.

Lady Byrne, his caped spouse – also, reader, judge and annotator of the Judge's copy of the novel – was shown to the high-backed chair beside her husband. Then Mr Justice Byrne peered, not unkindly, over his spectacles at the assembly.

As Michael Rubinstein looked up at him, he observed that something unexpected dangled from the Judge's wrist – a blue-grey damask *bag*. I say, thought Rubinstein, that's a new bit of kit! From this bag, Mr Justice Byrne now produced, in solemn fashion, an orange-and-white item – as if it were an object anthropologists might one day identify as a fetish of some little-known, twentieth-century European rite.

The offending Penguin paperback, priced on the cover at the radical sum of 3s. 6d., radiated its own curious life as the Judge laid it upon the narrow desk before him. Only at this point did Sir Laurence Byrne nod to the Clerk of the Court, who stood on cue to initiate proceedings.

The spectre of the great dock was, for those gathered in Court Number One, a disappointingly hollow prospect. Not only did its oaken mass block many a view, without any compensatory glimpse of a prisoner, it was also oddly inert, like a ball at the start of a match, doomed never to leave the referee's hands. No prisoner had made the sickening ascent up the stairs from the holding cells below. No wretch had arisen, blinking into the light of justice. No defendant looked out upon the rows of impassive faces with the confusion of the wronged, or the cockiness of the congenitally criminal.

As the trial gets underway, the jury is called, one by one, from the back of the court where they wait out of sight. Each juror is sworn in, reading the oath from a printed card, or stumbling over the reading – *rather* worrying, thinks Michael Rubinstein, for a trial *about a book.*

Jurors are required to be property-owners, which means they are usually middle-class men with fairly standard middle-class views. Otherwise put, they are often compliant with the Prosecution and 'willing to convict'.

In the roll-call of jurors, Mr Gerald Gardiner, QC, Senior Counsel for the Defence, objects to the fifth man. 'Will you step down, please?' No reason is required. The tea-cups in the gallery look at each other, blank-faced. The man is instructed to come out of the jury box, and he is replaced.

The twelfth and final juror is just approaching the 'whole truth and nothing but the truth' when, once again: 'Will you please step down?'

Both men are left eternally to wonder. Did they appear untrustworthy? Unkempt? Unclean?

They cannot know that the Defence are of the view that women generally feel less need to disapprove for disapproval's sake. It is also the belief of the Defence team that women tend to judge men less harshly than men judge one another, especially in public, where men are often zealous on matters relating to sex, if only so they don't appear sexually suspect themselves. Women, it is felt, are less complicated about the subject – less implicated, one might say – or so the Defence team hope. They would prefer more women, but as it is, they are doing well to have three among the twelve jurors. The 'rules of engagement' actually permit Mr Gardiner to press for up to seven substitutions without the need to explain, but he cannot risk being thought to manipulate proceedings. The jury might punish the 'Prisoner' for it.

It is all so delicately judged.

While the 'sworn-in' await the last of their number, they shift self-consciously in their seats and turn their faces heavenward to ponder the great circular skylight as it streams with rain. They are, at a glance, in their mid-forties and early fifties. One woman, evidently, is quite wealthy. Another might be a schoolmistress. The men, wearing similar suits, are less distinguishable. Most, if they have hair, are greying at the temples. Several are spectacled. Two smoke as they wait.

The world's press and the tea-cups in the gallery crane forward to study the twelve. Is he/she a reader, a philistine, a liberal, a Communist, a man of the world, a spinster, a bluestocking, a wide-boy, a yes-man, a loose woman, an upstart, or a safe pair of hands? Is he/she conservative, radical, loose-lipped, tight-lipped, forward-thinking, old-fashioned, moral, sensible, bolshy, broad-minded, jolly nice, buttoned-up, or sex-mad?

The Clerk of the Court goes up and down the rows of the jurors, doling out copies of the otherwise imprisoned paperback. Then, 'Members of the Jury,' he begins, 'the Prisoner at the Bar, Penguin Books Limited, is charged that on the 16th day of August last it published an obscene article, to wit, a book entitled *Lady Chatterley's Lover* by D. H. Lawrence. To this indictment, it has pleaded not guilty, and it is your charge to say, having heard the evidence, whether it be guilty or not.'

At the word 'Prisoner', Michael Rubinstein feels the solid, pugnacious man at his side, Sir Allen Lane, flinch, as if he has just glimpsed the place he does not yet have knowledge of: the holding pen for the convicted below the dock, a pen known simply as the Cage. If found guilty as charged, the punishment is an unlimited fine – or three years' imprisonment.

Across the nation, the bookies' odds are stacked against Lady Chatterley. She might have succumbed to her gamekeeper's advances, but the country – with the exception of its literati – is not prepared to yield, or not if the early evidence is any indication. Sir Allen Lane's daily post-bag at the Penguin offices is stuffed full of vitriol.

'*You loathsome, vile hypocrite. You've known all along the book would be read for the wrong reasons … You pimp of the Harlots' Union. Bastard. What have you bribed your witnesses with?*'

'*I hope you make a lot of hay out of Lady Chatterley. I also trust that you will receive whatever judgment God may have for you.*'

'*You merit no salutation. There are three kinds of bad smell (1) a damned stink (2) a bloody stench and (3) The Penguin Press!*'

Mr Mervyn Griffith-Jones, QC opens for the Crown. He boasts clean-shaven, well-boned good looks, fitting for his role of Principal Actor of Court Number One. Indeed, in his eighteenth-century-style wig, he looks not unlike a county squire temporarily released from a portrait by, let us say, Joshua Reynolds. His gaze is one of easy assurance. His bearing suggests an attitude of restrained impatience – of knowing what needs to be done for the sake of the public good and wanting to do it, by God.

His lady-wife is not with us today, but we might imagine her at his side in the Reynolds portrait, in her middle years, well-fed and lavishly wigged. A whey-faced son, in a lace ruffle and frock-coat, stands to the other side of his father, cultivating an air of impudence. At the squire's feet, we see his docile spaniel, and in the background, perhaps a Grecian urn or two, lifted by the squire during the Grand Tour adventures of his youth. All is in order, in other words. His hand rests on his hip. His breeches reveal lean and well-proportioned 'pins'. He has the bristling appearance of someone who must be off.

He begins: 'Members of the Jury, Penguin Books Limited need no introduction. They are a well-known and, let me say at once, highly reputable firm of publishers.'

The Senior Counsel lays out the wares of the Prosecution case, educating the jurors in the salient points of the amended Obscenity Act – as he sees them. 'The evidence will be that the company proposed to publish this book, *Lady Chatterley's Lover*, at a price of three shillings and sixpence, and indeed had printed and were *in the process of* distributing to the retailers some 200,000 copies for sale for the release date, 25th August. Now then, it is not a question of whether it *has* depraved somebody, or *must* deprave, or *will* deprave. The question which you have to decide is: has this book a tendency, *may it – might it –* deprave those who are likely, in the relevant circumstances, to read it?'

A 'tendency', Michael Rubinstein privately notes, is *not* something a barrister should further define, but Griffith-Jones has no qualms, and Mr Justice Byrne does not intervene, while Lady Byrne, on her adjacent throne, stares sternly down at the jurors, as if to suggest that she is a moral compass upon which they can – and must – rely.

Mervyn Griffith-Jones continues in declamatory fashion. 'The charge is *not* that the tendency of the book is either to shock or disgust. That is not a criminal offence. The question is: *might* it deprave or corrupt? Then you say: "Well, corrupt or deprave whom?" The answer is: those whose minds are *open* to such immoral influences and into whose hands a publication of this sort *may* fall. Are we to take our literary standards as being the level of something suitable for a fourteen-year-old schoolgirl? Of course not. But when a child, be it a boy or a girl, reaches that most perilous part of life's journey which we call adolescence, and finds itself—'

*It*self? wonders Rubinstein.

'—traversing an unknown country without a map – and sometimes, I am afraid, from a bad home – it is the business of parents and/or teachers, so far as is possible, to see that that individual is wisely and naturally directed to the ultimate fulfilment of a balanced life. Members of the Jury' – the foreman of the jury gazes obsequiously up – 'the Prosecution will invite you to say that this book goes *nowhere near* assisting any young person to that fulfilment of a balanced life.' Mr Griffith-Jones's tone is cultivated but impassioned. '*Of course* there is a right to express oneself in politics or in literature. But a writer, even a genius, is a member of the community, and like *any other* member of the community, he is under the same obligation not to do harm, either mentally or physically or spiritually.

'Let me at once concede that D. H. Lawrence is a well-recognised and indeed great writer. There may indeed be some literary merit in this book – I put it no higher. But is its publication *for the public good*?

If so, is whatever element of the public good which you or we may identify significant *enough* – in objective terms, that is – to outweigh the novel's evident obscenity? Allow me to remind you.

'The story of Lady Chatterley is the story of a woman deprived of sex from her husband, a man who was wounded in the First World War, paralysed from the waist downwards and unable to have any sexual intercourse. It is the story of a *sex-starved girl* who satisfies that starvation with a particularly sensual man who happens to be' – he pauses for effect – 'her husband's gamekeeper.'

A man who does not dress for dinner? Good God, thinks Rubinstein.

'There are thirteen episodes of sexual intercourse *in but one* novel, and they are described in the greatest detail, save perhaps the first. *Nothing* is left to the imagination. The heroine, if I may so describe her, Lady Chatterley, and the hero, if I may so describe him, the gamekeeper, Oliver Mellors, are little more than bodies – bodies which continuously have sexual intercourse with one another.'

Griffith-Jones launches into a summary of each instance, his voice faintly quivering with scorn. 'We see them doing it in the undergrowth in the pouring rain, both of them stark naked and dripping with raindrops. We see them in the keeper's cottage: first in the evening on the hearth-rug; then we have to wait until dawn to see them doing it again in bed. Finally, we have it all over again in a Bloomsbury boarding house. The plot is little more than padding for thirteen bouts of sexual intercourse. The emphasis is always on the pleasure, the satisfaction and the sensuality of the episode.

'Now – and this, I put to you, is the essential point – if there is a conflict in a writer between his desire for self-expression and the sense of morality that is fundamental to the well-being of the community, then morality must prevail. It is true that freedom is the right of the minority to do what the majority disapprove of, *provided it does them no harm.*'

He produces a strip of paper. He seems to have left the house with his housekeeper's grocery list. 'These matters are not voiced normally in this court, but when it forms the whole subject matter of the Prosecution, then, Members of the Jury, we cannot *avoid* voicing them.'

The tea-cups on their shelves lean forward, straining with the acoustics, but the Senior Counsel's voice is clear to all as he flings each word into the court. 'The word "fuck",' he begins, consulting the grocery list, 'or "fucking" occurs no less than thirty times.'

There are gasps from the gallery.

Rubinstein stares fixedly at the table to prevent his face from revealing his contempt. It is as he predicted.

'I have added them up, but I do not guarantee that I have added them *all* up. "Cunt" is employed fourteen times. Yes, "cunt". I counted "balls" thirteen times; "shit" and "arse" six times apiece: "cock" four times; "piss" three times, and so on. The question you have to decide is *not* whether this book is just a *revolting* book. Clearly it is, as I have just demonstrated. You have to consider something far more serious. Does it have *a tendency*—'

Clever, Rubinstein thinks: the substitution of the usual definite article – 'the tendency' – for the indefinite 'a tendency', conveniently vague.

'—to deprave and to corrupt? That is the meaning of "obscenity" for our purposes here. Secondly, if you find there *is* a tendency to corrupt – in other words, that it *may* corrupt – the question for you is then this: is there *enough* value, enough *for the public good*, to redeem the book? Quite obviously, there are many isolated passages and chapters in it which are not obscene at all. That does not save it. You have got to judge this book *as a whole*. I should also add that you must not judge it in any priggish, high-minded, super-correct, mid-Victorian manner.'

A deceptive flourish of even-handedness. Always effective. Rubinstein has to admire the man's showmanship.

'Making all such allowances in favour of the book as you can, the Prosecution will invite you to say that it *does* tend, and certainly that it *may tend*, to induce lustful thoughts in the minds of those who read it. Indeed, it sets upon a pedestal promiscuous and adulterous intercourse. It commends sensuality as a virtue. It advocates coarseness and vulgarity of thought and language. It is the language of our so-called "hero", after all.

'You may think of *the many* who are likely to buy it at the price of 3s. 6d. You may ask yourselves: would you approve of *your* young sons, young daughters – because girls can read as well as boys! – reading this book? Is it a book you would leave lying around your *own* house? Is it a book that you would even wish your wife or your servants to read?'

In the gallery, some of the tea-cups laugh. Mr Justice Byrne glares over his spectacles. Lady Byrne frowns. Mr Griffith-Jones's strong jaw slackens with bemusement. What did he say? But his formidable assurance is quickly restored: 'Penguin Books stated in early advertisements that it had taken thirty years for it to be possible to publish the "unmutilated" version of *Lady Chatterley's Lover* in this country. You, Members of the Jury' – he pauses meaningfully – 'will have to say whether it *has* taken thirty years, or whether it will take still longer.'

The Junior Counsel for the Prosecution, a Mr Morton, calls their first witness, the Scotland Yard Detective Inspector who took collection of twelve representative copies from the office of Penguin Books. The basics are confirmed unspectacularly for the court. There is no reference to the pot of tea enjoyed by all on the occasion.

When cross-examined by Mr Gardiner, the DI agrees that, yes, this is the second case to be tried under the new Act, the other case being that of *The Ladies Directory*. 'Would you please describe to the court the nature of *that* publication, Detective Inspector Monahan?'

'It is a London guide to prostitution, sir.'

Mr Gardiner looks to the bench. 'No further questions, my Lord.'

Mr Gerald Gardiner, QC is a broad-shouldered man with a high brow and thinning hair. He is known among the judiciary both as a Quaker and a law reformer. His eyes are down-turned in shape but steady in their gaze, with a certain glint or quality of light which suggests a quick wit. His manner is unaffected; he has nothing, in other words, up his (flowing) sleeve.

He wears his silk gown – the hallmark of a Queen's Counsel – lightly, almost to the point of dishevelment, and as he takes to the floor, his gait is easy and informal, while his address to the jury is surprisingly conversational.

'You have been told that this book is full of descriptions of sexual intercourse – and so it is. That it is full of four-letter words – and so there are. You may ask yourself at once: how comes it that reputable publishers, apparently after considerable thought and quite deliberately, are publishing an appalling book of the nature that has been described to us?

'Allow me to try to furnish you with answers to at least some of your questions. Penguin Books began in 1935 under a man called Lane, who thought that people like himself, who were not very rich, should be able to buy books – for the price of ten cigarettes. Twenty-five years later they have sold 250 million books; they have published the whole of Shakespeare and most of Shaw. Many have written to Sir Allen over the years, thanking his company for allowing them an education of which they would have otherwise been deprived.

'To date, they have published fourteen books by D. H. Lawrence, and now they intend to publish the rest, including *Lady Chatterley's Lover*. There are some who feel that Lawrence is the greatest English writer since Thomas Hardy, and there is no doubt at all that he is among the five or six greatest. There is no civilised country in which this novel, as written, cannot be bought, *except* Lawrence's *own* country and the Commonwealth countries.'

Mr Griffith-Jones rises to his feet. 'My Lord, I hesitate to interrupt my learned friend, but what happens in other countries can hardly be relevant to the issue which the jury have to try here.'

Mr Justice Byrne reflects. 'I think that is right. Mr Gardiner?'

'My Lord, it is evidence of the value of the book.'

Mr Justice Byrne consults the skylight. 'I don't think it is admissible. I am against you.'

Mr Gerald Gardiner nods and resumes. 'This book has had, unfortunately, "a history". In 1928, when it was written, it was not possible to publish it, or not publicly. Since then, there have been expurgated editions, and there would have been nothing to stop Penguin years ago from publishing one of those. But' – he pauses for emphasis – 'they have always refused to publish a mutilated book. They have always refused to offer their readers a mutilated book.

'Now then: for a book to be obscene within the meaning of the law, it must obviously effect *a change* of character, a leading-on of the reader to do something wrong which he would not otherwise have done. Whole parts of the book may (and I do not doubt will) shock you; but there is nothing in the book which will in fact do anybody any *harm*. No one would suggest that the Director of

Public Prosecutions would become depraved by reading the book, nor Counsel, nor witnesses; no one would suggest that the Judge and the jury would become corrupted; it is always someone else. It is never ourselves.

'It is quite true that the book includes what are often called "four-letter words", and it is quite plain that what the author intended was to drag these words out of the rather shameful connotations they have accrued since Victorian times. Whether we feel he has succeeded or not, there is nothing in the words *themselves* which can deprave or corrupt. If there is, then ninety-five per cent of the army, navy and air force are past redemption.'

The tea-cups smile, and a few of the jurors do as well.

'When you have read the book, you will see certain things which the author was aiming at. Far from putting promiscuity on a pedestal, D. H. Lawrence's whole private and writing life was strongly in favour of marriage. You will find that the early promiscuous affairs described in this novel are, all of them, highly unsatisfactory. But Constance *does* fall in love, and the book ends with her and Mellors being about to marry.

'Mr Griffith-Jones has suggested that this is a book which contains thirteen descriptions of physical intercourse, with little but padding in between. With respect to my esteemed friend, that is a curious assertion. D. H. Lawrence, in the manner of all great writers, was preoccupied with the tragedy of the Great War. He did not believe that the ills of society that came after could be cured by political action. He believed rather that the remedy for those ills lay in the restoration of *right relations between human beings*; specifically, on unions founded on love, bodily as well as spiritual. Indeed, the book which is the subject of this trial was at one time to be entitled *Tenderness* by its author. Does that suggest a pornographer at work? Does it sound to you like a title for an obscene novel? I would suggest that you will find exactly the opposite when you read it.

'Here is a book about England of the twenties, an England that is sick, an England that is broken. I put it to you that Lawrence wrote the story of Lady Chatterley, not to titillate, and certainly not to deprave or corrupt. On the contrary, he created the character of Lady Chatterley as a symbol of hope, and her story is, above all, one of regeneration.'

The jury are soon to decide for themselves. Will they be revolted or rejuvenated?

Mr Gardiner suggests to the Judge that the usual practice is for the jury to take the book home. The Judge disagrees. Mr Gardiner points out that the jury rooms are 'jolly uncomfortable' and that the jurors would be required to read 'cheek by jowl' in one another's presence. Mr Griffith-Jones argues that the jury room is the proper way forward. Mr Gardiner counters: 'When you read anywhere, what you read is, and should be, private to the author and you.'

It occurs to the Judge that he has never been in the jury room. He consults the Clerk of the Court. The clerk does not believe that the wooden chairs are as hard as Mr Gardiner suggests, and so it is decided. The jurors *will* report to the jury room the following day to begin their reading assignment 'without the distractions of home and the opinions of spouses'. The case, Mr Justice Byrne announces, will resume in one week.

Then Lady Byrne stands and confers upon her husband the sacred book-bag, the purple fig-leaf to protect his dignity, and the principal players depart the court.

In the Great Hall outside there is relief among the supporters of Sir Allen. They gather around him, a rallying force. Well, the thing is underway at last. Best to get all the unpleasantness over and done with. The Americans have finally 'come through' in New York – Grove Press – and now it is Penguin's turn. The jurors, they all agree, look like reasonable, sound individuals, with the exception perhaps of the unctuous foreman. Mr Gardiner, they say, is exemplary. He struck precisely the right notes in his opening address.

Michael Rubinstein's 'dicky ear' misses several of these remarks in the general hubbub of the Great Hall's echoing chamber. His good ear, however, is perfectly placed to hear another, more discreet exchange just to his side – to eavesdrop on a conversation between Sir Toby Mathew, Director of Public Prosecutions, and one of his office juniors, who begins: 'If I may say, sir, it went well today, in my opinion. Mr Griffith-Jones gave a commanding performance. What is your view, sir, of our chances?'

Sir Toby makes a vague gesture of his hand, as if to indicate boredom, impatience or simply a regret that he hasn't passed the last few hours in his club, perusing the morning papers. 'I haven't *formed* a view, Mr Blewitt.'

'Yes, of course,' says Blewitt. 'One mustn't jump the gun. Apologies, sir.'

Sir Toby looks up to the dome of the Great Hall and tries, unsuccessfully, to stifle a yawn. 'I must say, Blewitt, between you and me, I don't actually *mind* whether we fail or succeed.' Then he nods 'Good-day' and makes for the door.

What, thinks Michael Rubinstein, is one to make of *that*?

Day Two, Thursday, October 27th

Mr Graham Hough, Lecturer in English at Christ's College, Cambridge, is to open for the Defence. He appears now, at the threshold of the Old Bailey, wind-blown and harried as he enters. Several puddles – incursions of rain – have blown across the marble floor of the Great Hall, and Mr Hough's spectacles are misted, which is no doubt why he slips and nearly goes 'bottoms up' under the gaze of the reigning statuary.

In the final reckoning, he does not hit the floor. He regains his balance, if not his composure, and onward he goes, checking to see, as we are all wont to do, who has noticed his near fall from grace.

Up ahead, a barrel-bodied nurse is seated on a bench, and Hough sees her eye him sharply, as if he has been flinging himself at the floor. He is about to take a seat on a distant bench outside Court Number One, when his name is barked by the usher, and up he springs, as if a starting-gun has gone off.

In the witness box, having taken the oath, Mr Hough attempts to smooth his wet hair, or what remains of it, with the palm of his hand. His tie is bedraggled, and he has to remove his spectacles to wipe them for a second time as Mr Gerald Gardiner, QC begins: 'Will you tell us something of Lawrence's place in English literature?'

Mr Hough's voice, to the surprise of the court, is far more composed than his person. It possesses a mellifluous calm, a modest timbre and a tone of resonant authority. It both persuades and mollifies as we listen. The Defence team knew exactly what they were doing when they selected Mr Hough to be their first witness.

'Lawrence,' he begins, 'is generally recognised to be one of the most important novelists of this century and one of the greatest novelists of any century. I don't think that is seriously disputed.'

'Whereabouts would you place this book amongst his works?'

'He wrote nine novels. I would place it about fifth.'

'Will you tell us what is the theme or meaning of the book?'

'It is concerned,' says Mr Hough, looking out as if to a lecture theatre, 'with the relations between men and women, with their sexual relations, with the nature of proper marriage, and this is, of course, a matter of great importance to us all.'

Mr Justice Byrne looks up from his note-taking, perplexed. 'Did you say "of *proper* marriage"?'

'I did, sir.'

Mr Hough, for all of his damp and mist, is not daunted.

'It has been claimed,' continues Mr Gardiner, 'that sex is "dragged in" at every conceivable opportunity. What is your view?'

Mr Hough reflects. 'The sexual passages cannot occupy more than thirty pages of some three hundred. No man in his senses is going to write a book of three hundred pages as mere padding for thirty pages of sexual matter.'

Mr Gardiner's voice betrays no bias. 'It has been said that the only variation in the description of the sexual intercourse is the location. Do you agree?'

Mr Hough's spectacles blink, as if his very thoughts are catching the light. 'I do not. The reason for the repetition of the sexual scenes is to show the *development* of Connie Chatterley's awareness of her own nature. They are *not* repetitive. They are different. Lawrence is making a bold experiment.'

'A *what?*' says the Judge.

'A bold experiment.'

Mr Justice Byrne makes a note.

'The author is trying to study the sexual situation more clearly and more openly than is usually done in fiction.'

'Do you spend your time teaching young people?' inquires Mr Gardiner.

'A good deal of it.'

'Have you a daughter of eighteen and a son of twelve?'

'I do.'

Mr Gardiner nods his thanks to his witness and hands over to 'the other side'.

'Mr Hough,' begins Mr Griffith-Jones, with a flourish of silk – 'I beg your pardon, Mr *Huff* – I *believe* that is the pronunciation you favour?' As if Mr Hough has somehow got his own name wrong.

The foreman of the jury chuckles obligingly.

Mr Hough nods, his expression neutral.

Mr Griffith-Jones passes him a copy of the paperback. 'Mr *Huff*, would you turn to page 140, and the paragraph starting a little down the page. "Connie went slowly home …"? I am not dealing with the so-called purple passages at the moment. "Connie went slowly home, realizing the depth of the other thing in her. Another self was alive in her, burning molten and soft in her womb and bowels, and with this self she adored him. She adored him till her knees were weak as she walked." I suppose that is good writing, or is that ludicrous?'

'Not to me.'

'"In her womb and bowels" – we have got the same two parts of her anatomy coupled together within three lines – "she was flowing and alive now …" I do not want to be unimaginative, believe me, but can one be alive in one's womb and bowels?'

'Metaphorically I think one can.'

'We have "womb" for the third time?'

'Yes.'

'Is that really good writing, to repeat again and again "womb and bowels", "womb and bowels", and "bowels and womb"?'

'That is very much Lawrence's method.'

'In a work of high literary merit that is the kind of repetition you would expect?'

'Well, knowing Lawrence, yes, I would. He always writes like that, and he brings it off.'

'Don't say "knowing Lawrence",' interposes the Judge. 'You must not suppose for the purpose of this question that Lawrence is a good writer, and therefore that anything he did is the right way to do it.'

Mr Griffith-Jones smiles and adjusts his gown: 'Would you say that was a fine piece if I had written it?'

'If I saw it in its context, I would.'

'Let us move to other contexts. Do you know of a woman called Katherine Anne Porter?' – a woman whom, as Mr Griffith-Jones inwardly laments in this moment, the FBI *failed* to locate as a witness for the Prosecution.

'I know of her as an American short-story writer. Very distinguished.'

'Allow me to read from an article by Miss Katherine Porter about the novel.' He holds a periodical aloft for all to see. 'The article was recently published in *Encounter*, which, as many here will know, is an acclaimed literary magazine edited by one of our foremost poets, Mr Stephen Spender.' Mr Griffith-Jones nods respectfully to Mr Spender, seated in the press box.

Stephen Spender does not return the nod.

Mr Griffith-Jones reads aloud several passages in which Miss Porter is nothing if not plain-speaking. She damns both author and book.

'She makes a strikingly clear case, does she not, Mr Huff? If we turn to the particulars of the character of Lady Chatterley, Miss Porter informs us that "Such a woman could use up half a dozen such men, and it is plain already that she will shortly be looking for another man; I give him" – that's to say, the gamekeeper – "two years at the rate he is going." Would you not agree?'

'I would not. Connie and Mellors really love one another.'

Mr Justice Byrne looks up. 'It took them a long time, didn't it?'

'Yes. It often does, my Lord.'

There is a tittering of tea-cups.

'Silence!' rasps the Judge.

'All the time,' continues Mr Griffith-Jones, 'it was *behind the back of* her husband. Indeed, Miss Porter merely points out what the novel itself makes clear: Lady Chatterley's behaviour is *repeatedly* licentious. Is Miss Porter wrong? You yourself just told this court that she is "very distinguished".'

'She is a distinguished short-story writer.'

'*Who* then are we to believe: Miss Katherine Anne Porter, internationally respected author, writing for one of this country's best literary journals, or' – it was a dying-fall of a phrase – '*you*, Mr Huff?'

Miss Helen Gardner, Reader in English Renaissance Literature at Oxford, is next to take the stand. She is dressed in brown tweeds, is as tidy as a sparrow, and is as light of foot in the testimony she gives.

The Senior Counsel for the Defence wastes no time. 'Miss Gardner, how far, in your view, are the descriptions of sexual intercourse relevant or necessary to the theme or meaning of the book?'

She lifts her face, rather touchingly, to address the tea-cups. 'I think that Lawrence was attempting to bring home to the imaginations of his readers certain prospects of a modern society, the failure of relations between men and women, and the degraded condition in which many people live. I think these passages *do* succeed in doing something extraordinarily difficult, which very few other writers have really attempted with such courage and devotion, and that is to put into words experiences that are really very difficult to verbalise.'

She is concise, bright-eyed, and we who watch in the court are charmed.

Mr Gardiner nods to his rival: 'Your witness.'

Mr Griffith-Jones stands, and Miss Gardner turns a challenging eye upon him. She radiates integrity, and the sun, long absent from London, suddenly streams obligingly down. Mr Griffith-Jones asks two perfunctory questions and takes to his seat again – to the visible astonishment of all.

Mrs Joan Bennett, Lecturer in English at Cambridge, is the next to enter the hallowed court. She is a woman of about sixty, although she appears to us to be a full decade older, for she is not one to indulge in such fripperies as cold cream, lipstick or a good night's sleep. She hasn't, it seems, bothered with a hairbrush. What *stuff*!

Forget the Sword of State on the wall behind the Judge – Hokum! she thinks when she sees it – her face is as long and lean as that sword, and her eyes are as fierce. In her short black jacket and a buttoned-high, starched collar, she has the appearance of a female prison warden as she mounts the stand and lays her hand upon the proffered Bible. 'Balderdash!' her face says to the holy book, but she mumbles the necessaries.

We in the court are wary. Even Mr Justice Byrne looks nervous.

Yet as soon as Mrs Joan Bennett speaks, we understand we are in safe hands. She is unflappable, unpretentious and gimlet-eyed. The tea-cups in the gallery nudge handles in approval.

Mr Gardiner begins: 'Mrs Bennett, I shall come straight to the point. Does the book set "upon a pedestal" promiscuity and adulterous intercourse? That is what the Prosecution contends.'

'The very reverse, I would have thought. It is shown as unsatisfactory, giving no fulfilment, no joy, and as really rather disgusting.'

She is a breath of fresh air.

Back and forth. Question and answer. Chapter and verse. She is excellent value, and not only for her unexpectedly down-to-earth performance. Joan Bennett delivers her views with the ease of an intelligence too acute to be undone by the sensational drama in which she finds herself.

Mr Griffith-Jones takes the floor. Who will mop the floor with whom?

'Mrs Bennett, surely you don't mean to suggest that this novel's series of adulterous intercourses depicts the author's strong support for marriage, do you?'

She pauses and looks off in the distance. She will not be rushed. 'Would you first define for me the sense in which you use the word "marriage"?'

It is not the witness who usually puts the questions.

The Judge interrupts, with no attempt to disguise his irritation. '*Lawful wedlock*, madam. You know what *that* means, do you not?'

'I do. Is that the context which I'm to address?'

Mr Griffith-Jones is losing patience with this literary scholar, and changes tactics. It is time to scandalise the jury. 'If one is talking about the *author's* views, Mrs Bennett, as you just have yourself, "adulterous intercourse" is, in fact, the very thing in which the author *himself* engaged? Am I correct? Mr Lawrence *ran off*' – he rolls his 'r' with feeling – 'with his friend's wife, did he not?'

'He did.'

Mr Griffith-Jones turns. His face seems to say to the jury and to us, the public: 'You heard it with your own ears.'

But Mrs Joan Bennett begs to differ: 'It is *also* true that it was Lawrence's *only* marriage, and that it lasted his entire life.'

She has managed – just – to get the words out, before the Judge instructs her, firmly, to step down.

As Dame Rebecca West enters the court, it is clear from the jury's sudden flurry of interest that her name is known to them all.

Observe her now. Everything about her suggests she knows the measure of things, while she herself eludes all measure and judgement. Her bearing is regal as she crosses Court Number One and takes the stand. She wears a sable fur hat over her grey coiffure, a sober but well-cut black dress, and ivory beads at her neck. Her eyes are a cool brown, her face is square, and she holds her chin aloft. If she is, as Virginia Woolf once unkindly described her, 'hard as nails, very distrustful, and no beauty', she is also, as she gazes out over the court, a force you want on your side.

She is a 'star witness' for the Defence. The Defence team can only hope that she *is* on their side. It is still something of a moot point as she looks down upon Sir Allen Lane at the solicitors' table. Her charismatic support could sway the jury in one fell swoop were she to praise the novel. By the same token, even a few equivocal statements could inflict injuries from which they would never recover.

Of course no one in Court Number One is apprised of the fact that she, in all likelihood, cooperated with the FBI to 'facilitate the Prosecution', via her old friend, Sir Toby, the Director of Public Prosecutions. Neither is anyone aware that she shares J. Edgar Hoover's zealous concern about Soviet meddling in British and American life; nor that she stopped just short of insisting that the author had never wanted his book to be read by us, the general public. *Had* she actually received such intelligence? Almost certainly not. It seems more likely that she wanted, for reasons best known to her, to undermine the Penguin case.

So why is she now in Court Number One, standing as a witness *for* the Defence? Let us examine the evidence.

1 Rebecca West has always enjoyed a good trial. Indeed, she has written extensively on legal cases – on treason and betrayal, particularly. She knows her mind. It is a formidable mind, and she likes to exercise it. Moreover, she does rather like being featured in the Sunday papers.

2 The moral high ground on the political right is, it turns out, a rather lonely summit, and Dame Rebecca has started to miss former friends – or even the prospect of friends – on the left. Their conversation is 'sparkier', she has concluded, and their parties are much more fun. She does not wish to return to that particular bosom, but it would be nice to visit. It would be nice even to be invited. This is her chance.

3 The Prosecution made a critical – or rather, another critical – error in its preparation. For reasons accidental rather than deliberate – 'a balls-up' in other words – they neglected to invite Dame Rebecca to be a witness for 'their side', even when they

were scraping the barrel to find anyone. The garlanded author could have been their coup de foudre, but no, they missed that trick. And what does Dame Rebecca tend to do when ignored – i.e. 'slighted'? She goes over to the other side.

Mr Gerald Gardiner nods to her, in a way which nearly resembles a bow from the neck – normally a mark of respect reserved for the monarch. He begins: 'It has been suggested, Dame Rebecca, that this is a book which advocates and even promotes promiscuity and adultery. May I ask? What is your view?'

Her voice has a singing quality to it, a pleasing residue of her Edinburgh childhood: '*Well*, that might *appear* to be the case after a cursory reading – if one merely *skims* the novel in a *lazy* manner, which may not, incidentally, be described as "reading". But it should be obvious to any moderately attentive reader that the book is not a *recommendation* of such intercourse. It shows, rather, a broken life, and what somebody did with it. It could not advocate either promiscuity or adultery, because D. H. Lawrence was a man who spent all his life working out *how to make a good marriage*. He thought a good marriage was perhaps the most important thing in the world. Shall I continue?'

Mr Gardiner gives a wave of his hand, as if to say, 'You have the floor.'

She raises herself to her full height. 'Lawrence believed that *culture* had become sterile and unhelpful to man's deepest needs. He wanted to have the *whole* of civilisation realise that it was not living fully enough, that it would be exploited in various ways if it did not try to get down to the springs of its being and live more fully. The impotence of the baronet character, Sir Clifford Chatterley, is a symbol of the impotent culture of Lawrence's own time. Lady Chatterley's love affair with the gamekeeper is nothing less than a *calling*, a return to the soul of—'

Mr Justice Byrne looks up, his hand cupping his ear. 'A *what*, madam?'

'A return to the *soul*, my Lord.' She is unabashed.

Mr Justice Byrne blinks, as if he has been slapped.

His lady-wife stares out over the court with an icy passion not heretofore seen on her face. As she adjusts her jewelled brooch, pinned today to her blouse, she is obviously agitated. Michael Rubinstein can only wonder if Lady Byrne is about to step down from the Judge's bench, clasping the brooch, and *stab* Dame Rebecca.

Mr Gardiner continues: 'Dame Rebecca, is Lawrence's message any less valid today than it was in the twenties?'

'No. Indeed, I believe it has more relevance. Since then we have had a war, which was due to something Lawrence had feared very much: he saw that in every country there was a *vast* urban population who had lost touch with life, with *real* life, with life honestly lived, and who could therefore be taken – *swept along* – in any direction.

'We who are alive today know that many *have* since been taken in the direction of evil by obedience to leaders such as Hitler. Lawrence was talking about something *quite* real – Fascism, Nazism – something that did of course happen in the shape of the last war, although he wasn't alive to see his fears – some might say his prophesies – realised. He was not fanciful. I would go so far as to say he was a realist, to the point of being humourless. *Lady Chatterley* is an allegory – beautiful, if full of sentences any *child* could make a fool of. Laughter and jeering, however, prove nothing in a Court of Law. Lawrence had a point. He wanted to get us back to something that would save us. As a writer and as a human being, he was *wholly* serious in whatever he set out to do.'

Mr Gardiner: 'As well as being a leading novelist and a social commentator, you are one of this country's most esteemed literary critics. Would you tell the court: what, for you, is the definition of literary merit?'

Dame Rebecca reflects, but she doesn't hesitate. Her pause is purely for dramatic effect. 'That is *quite* simple, Mr Gardiner. Literary merit is that which encourages the reader to go on living.'

'No further questions, my Lord.'

Brava! thinks Michael Rubinstein. Dame Rebecca has come up with the goods.

Only she herself appears disappointed when it becomes clear that she is *not* to be cross-examined. She had very much been looking forward to that tussle, for few got the better of her. And Mr Griffith-Jones knows it. Her reputation precedes her. What can the Prosecution do but leave well enough alone?

Only we can see Michael Rubinstein, at the solicitors' table, nod, in discreet triumph, to Sir Allen Lane and Hans Schmoller.

Then Dame Rebecca sails past their table, a stately galleon of good sense in what, her expression says, is a sea of nonsense.

J. Edgar Hoover turns to the latest scrapbook. It's been a long day in the office, but Shirley Temple is 'at his side' – kids are great company. Behind his desk, there's a whole shelf of his scrapbooks. These bulging testaments to his career go all the way back to 1924, even before the F.B.I. earned its 'Federal'.

That prefix had meant more to him than anything or anyone, except his mother and now Clyde, of course. Or it had until the Bureau got passed over for foreign intelligence work. Instead, the C.I.A. was dreamed up in '47, and those son-of-a-bitch Ivy Leaguers were handed the prize.

And to think his Bureau had been required to train *them*! It was a slap on the chops. He'd never say it wasn't. But life is full of injustice. He's known that since he was a kid. He's never had anything passed to *him* on a plate, but he doesn't give up. He has faith and stamina, and he gets what he wants in the end.

If he'd had a daughter, she would have been just like little 'Heidi' herself. It's a shame children have to grow up. If he'd been a father, he would have parceled up 'lessons for life' into little rhymes because jingles, just like slogans, stick in the brain.

The cherry in the cocktail might come a little late,
So fold your hands in your lap, be a good little girl and wait,
Because practice makes perfect, and one thing I can state,
Is that hard work pays, and you make your own fate.

He's always had a way with words, ever since grade-school. He's a stickler, too, for grammar and spelling. Someone has to keep up standards.

He's behind on his scrapbook. It's been hectic lately, and the clippings – cut out of the papers for him by Miss Gandy – have been piling up. The 'sticking in' is fiddly work for blunt fingers – those pesky corners – but if a job is worth doing, it's worth doing well. Besides, his end-of-the-day routine helps his blood pressure.

He's made history, alright – almost literally, like one of those engineers who forces rivers to flow this way or that, regardless of where it wants to go. Everything needs looking after. Everything needs managing. Life just can't run itself or there'd be no law, no order, no nation. As he sticks the articles about the Chatterley trial in *Edgar J. Hoover, 1960*, he thinks, as he often does, about how proud his mother would be. 'A trial – in *London, England*?' she'd say, agog. But it's his father who arrives, uninvited, in the inner sanctum of Hoover's skull.

Dickerson Hoover is sobbing silently again in the middle of the street outside the family home, dressed only in a pair of faded long-johns. It's the silence of those sobs, the silent movie of his father's dumb anguish, that spooks him – now, just as it did all those years ago. How is it even possible, unless you're Charlie Chaplin, to cry without making any sound at all?

Someone has to manage that particular crisis – his dear mother agrees – and manage it Hoover does. He drives his father that very day to The Laurels for a 'rest', even though his father will never rest again, or not until he's seven feet under. No one in The Laurels ever rests (on their laurels – ha! – you bet they don't). But the fact is, for a loony-bin, it's a good one, a pricey one, and it looks pleasant enough. Maybe, if you're a lunatic, it even is. Pleasant.

Hoover shudders.

If only his father had said *something* that day. Maybe then, he and his dad would have *gotten* somewhere. Maybe then, Hoover wouldn't have had to drive him away.

It's a troubling scene, there in the middle of the road outside 413 Seward Square. 'For crying out loud!' he says to his father again, as he gets him by the elbow and steers him – mute, clammy and quivering – inside the house.

The memory of the scene, all these years later, raises an unexpected trace of a smile on Hoover's face. With hindsight, it occurs to him that what he said to his father was like some kind of pun. *For crying out loud.* When his father couldn't.

Dickerson Hoover never left The Laurels.

J. Edgar Hoover sighs to sweet-faced Shirley Temple. If only his mother were alive to see the many rivers he has diverted from their misguided courses through history. He is a natural manager of men. Maybe even an engineer of the American soul. He has worked hard for his country. No one has worked harder than him.

Next to the clippings on his desk, Miss Gandy has provided, as ever, a cloth with a finger-bowl, so he can wipe the newsprint from his fingers when he's finished. He reviews the headlines.

'Day 2: "Is It a Book You Would Wish Your Wife or Servants to Read?"'

'Lady Chatterley: Could "USE UP HALF A DOZEN MEN" Says Expert'

'Cambridge Don Says: 13 Sex Scenes "NOT REPETITIVE"'

'Penguin's SIR Allen Lane Faces 3 Years LOCK-UP'

'Throw THE BOOK at Him!'

Hoover puts on his glasses, the ones he rarely reveals in public. In the small photograph which accompanies the last clipping, a woman is on her way into the Old Bailey. She's wearing a coat, unbuttoned, and a black fur hat. She's clutching a paperback, presumably the sex-maniac's.

He cannot believe his eyes.

'Dame Rebecca West: Star Witness for the Defence'.

Is it a misprint?

No. Because there she is again, in the next clipping.

He slumps back in his chair, as if his heart has given up.

He doesn't understand.

The bouquet he had Miss Gandy send her was *huge*. It cost *a bomb*. Plus, there was the American Garden, the fancy restaurant and high tea. There was his letter of congratulations on her damehood. There was all his *personal* attention.

He has to unbutton his collar and find the flask in the bottom drawer. It's no coincidence, he tells himself, that the woman wrote a book – wrote *the* book – on treason and betrayal.

Then he roars for Miss Gandy.

'Telephone the London Bureau. I don't care what time it is over there! Tell the *jerk* who works for us he's *fired*. Phone him at home if you have to, and don't let him down gently. Tell him from me it's the end of the line!'

At Whelan's Family Drugstore, Mel Harding is finished for the day. He leaves through the staff door at the back, and walks two blocks along quiet residential streets. Only then does he dip onto Main Street and double-back in the direction of his car.

One of Hoover's men falls into step behind him – again, in spite of his zig-zagging. He recognizes the beat of the man's gait, because it used to be his own. Bureau men learn, by unspoken example, how to stride in a Bureau way. He could slow down; he could force the man to pass him. But what would that achieve? It would only say that he cared enough to present a challenge. Either that, or that he was 'frit'.

He isn't followed daily or even weekly; that would be too predictable. In predictability lies comfort. *Watch – your – step, watch – your – step*. That's what the beat of the agent's shoes are telling him. The agent will be a guy from the Boston office. He'll have enjoyed the drive down to the Cape. The scenery, the sunshine.

Sure, the flashlights through the curtains in his motel room get to Harding sometimes. But this – *watch – your – step* – it's standard.

After a year and a half of controversy, he finds it odd, almost disconcerting, to walk into the bookstore on Main Street, pick a copy of the book off the shelf, the Grove Press edition, and slap $6 down on the counter.

'Would you like a paper bag, sir?' says the clerk. There's a tone to her voice which tells him most people do.

'No. That's fine,' he says. 'Thanks.'

Before his last copy was confiscated from his room by his former colleagues, he'd had about eighty pages left to read. Lady Chatterley was trying to escape Wragby Hall. Did she?

> *'And then when I come back,' she said, 'I can tell Clifford I must leave him. And you and I can go away. They never need even know it is you. We can go to another country, shall we? To Africa or Australia. Shall we?'*
> *She was quite thrilled by her plan.*
> *'You've never been to the colonies, have you?' he asked her.*
> *'No! Have you?'*

He'll get back to it tonight, for a half hour before lights-out. He wants the final chapters to last. Maybe he'll take it to work tomorrow; read a few pages over lunch. He'll be discreet. The Bureau briefcase will be more respectable than a paper bag. When he handed over his badge, revolver and manuals on the porch outside his motel room that day, he'd completely forgotten about the briefcase. He'd used it so rarely, and had had no need of it at the Kennedys'. Sometimes he heard it as he drove, knocking around in the trunk. Then he grew accustomed and stopped noticing the noise at all.

A shoeshine boy on the sidewalk outside the barber's asks if he wants a shine. 'Not today,' he says. He has a new pair of shoes. They still look okay. After the episode on the beach, his old ones were ruined beyond the talents of any shoeshine, and he'd needed a decent pair for his job interview. Old Mr. Whelan had showed him into the processing room and, from there, into the cubicle of the darkroom, waving an arm at the enlarger, the trays and the shelf of chemicals. 'My print-boy just left me. Got a job as a stringer on the local paper. A good job. He's saving up for college next year. I don't know what in the blazes to do with all this … I was going to open a soda-counter in this part of the store instead. But if you think you have an idea about how to work it all, I'll give you a three-week trial.'

Harding arrives at his car. The agent has disappeared. The nights are drawing in early now. November will soon be upon them. November 1st. All Souls'. All the ghosts. Sometimes he thinks of his mother – her unhappiness, her abandonment. He never could put it right. He never could track down his father for her. For himself. For his seven-year-old self. What would he have said if he had? He has no idea.

Maybe Howard Johnson, the Washington S.A.C., was right. Maybe that was why he'd applied to the Bureau. Not just for the investigative skills, but for a father figure – one who was always going to be there, whether you wanted him or not; an older man who was never going to leave you alone.

Now he's in a dead-end job, and living out of a crappy motel room with Hunter, Killbuck, Racer and Snap foaming at the mouth next door. He's surviving. He no longer expects anything more.

At his car, in the darkness, he opens the trunk and grabs the brief-case. It's a nice one. He turns it over and hits the light in the trunk. Good leather. No distinguishing marks or Bureau insignias – of course. And it comes to him, now that his mind is clear. He last used the thing in Butte, going to and from his one-man office. He never had anything to put in it, but it was the only mark of respectability he could cling to in that desert of a year, May '58 to May '59.

Harding eyes up the case. He's wondering if he should take it back to the shoeshine – when he hears a funny rattle inside. He turns the key that dangles on the key-chain tied to the strap, then hits the latches. They don't pop.

Which is when he remembers: the case has no compartment, only a false bottom. The button-release is on the bottom of the case. His finger locates it but the case is empty, and the rattle persists.

For a moment, there in the gathering gloom of late October, on a street that's empty except for gusts of leaves, he's back there: May of '58. Springtime in D.C. A new job and a new rank at the Washington Field Office, the office that's closest, in every sense, to HQ, and to the Director himself.

He's been tasked with the delivery of Howard Johnson's classified report to Hoover at the Mayflower. The drop-off is required by Mr. Hoover. He places the Manila envelope in the false bottom of the case and snaps it shut. It's a nice-looking briefcase, new from the Lab, and real leather, not imitation. Everyone says presentation matters. Before he leaves, he checks his teeth in the men's room.

At the Mayflower, he's shown to where Mr. Hoover and the Associate Director are having lunch, at the table always reserved for them in the dimly-lit dining room. As he approaches, Harding can smell the steam coming off the cream of mushroom soup.

Tolson isn't sitting in the chair across from Hoover, as Harding would have expected, but next to him, on the red banquette. Harding registers the fact, but he only wants to make a good impression as he approaches the Director. This has been a long time coming; twelve years in the heat and stink of the New York Field Office. Plenty of top agents. It was hard to stand out. He got his promotion a lot later than most.

When he saw the two men sitting close, he should have gotten the hell out – before he saw Hoover's hand on Tolson's. Before Hoover *saw* him see.

Instead, Harding found himself hitting the punch-latches, fiddling with the strap and turning the damned key, until his brain lurched, and he remembered the hidden compartment. Nerves. He blamed his nerves. He hit the release-button. He was never this ham-fisted, he wanted to say. Not that he could say anything. Don't speak until spoken to.

Standing by the trunk of his car, he listens to the rattle again. Then he digs for his tools, stored with the spare and the jack, and finds his Swiss Army knife.

He slices through the casing and reaches up into the internal side compartment to pull out ... a de-commissioned Robot Star II camera. He'd almost forgotten he'd ever given it a try – what? three? maybe four? years ago. A great little camera, heavy but neat. Three inches long. The only problem had been the angled viewfinder, built into the case like a bad periscope. Almost impossible for covert work. The Bureau replaced it, a year or two after, with the F-21 camera. Six ounces. Easy to fit in umbrella handles and things you could actually point. It was the F-21, not the Robot Star, which had given him his 'money-shot': Mrs. Kennedy in the G.P.O.

When he was shipped off to Butte, no one had come calling for the briefcase or its camera, and when his Bureau items were recovered at his motel door, almost two months ago already, the agent's checklist didn't mention either.

He gets in the car, and lays the camera and book on the passenger seat. Life has taught him, little by little, how *not* to hold on; how to keep expectations low. Yet here was the gift of a good camera. A bit of luck. Finally.

For twelve years, he'd been made aware on a daily basis that he wasn't the standard cut of agent. He was the butt of jokes even before the transfer to Butte. Yet something in him had always known, since the day his father had abandoned him and his mother: for someone to make you feel inferior, you had to give your permission.

He was through with giving permission.

Outside her house that day, she could have made him feel like something on the bottom of her shoe. Instead, she'd shaken his hand. She'd offered him her name. 'Jacqueline,' she said in that soft voice of hers. It wasn't forgiveness. It was something more.

She spoke to him like he existed.

Now, he had a camera, a book, and a car. And he had the freedom of the twenty-two inches inside his own head.

Outside Court Number One, the great domed hall of the Old Bailey has the look of a left-luggage office in a train station. Witnesses arrive at their appointed time and wait to be re-claimed by the Defence team. Matron keeps vigil with each on a hard bench, sometimes for hours. She keeps a careful eye on her charge's colour and composure. She makes small talk or holds her tongue, as the situation requires. She reaches into her pocket for boiled sweets. In a few instances, she pulls out a thermometer and checks a pulse. Then, at last, the heavy door opens and the bull-necked usher appears at the threshold to boom out a name. One by one, over three days, thirty-five stray souls are re-claimed.

'I once was lost but now am found,' murmurs Dr John Robinson, with a nervous smile, as his name is called. He and Matron have enjoyed their chat. She takes the liberty of passing him a comb, then watches as the 41-year-old Bishop of Woolwich, in his violet Bishop's vest and pectoral cross, disappears, as if for the Final Judgement.

At the solicitors' table, Michael Rubinstein has taken to smoking his pipe to steady his nerves. He cannot forget that each witness mounts the witness box at his behest. He has done his best to rehearse them, as has the ever-affable Mr Hutchinson, but now, like children released into the world, they have to see off Mr Griffith-Jones on their own.

Beside Michael Rubinstein, publisher Allen Lane maintains an upright, concentrated posture. Pragmatic though he is, he cannot shake entirely from his mind his official designation: 'the Prisoner'. Next to him, Hans Schmoller, Lane's right-hand man, doodles surreptitiously on the Old Bailey notepaper, and is arguably more accomplished than the artists sent by the papers to sketch the better-known faces.

The days of late autumn darken early over the Old Bailey. Indeed, the sun has hardly emerged from London's murk this week, and it tends to disappear altogether by four. After lunch, one or two of the male jurors sometimes nod off, as points of law are tested by the barristers or expanded on by the Judge.

Then: 'Dr John Robinson! The Bishop of Woolwich!'
Heads jolt.

Enter Mr Gardiner from stage-right, straightening his wig, as if he's just retrieved it from the gents. 'Bishop Robinson, I will not waste your time. What would you say are the ethical merits of the book, specifically with regards to its sexual content?'

The Bishop of Woolwich: My answer cannot be entirely straight-forward. It is obvious that Mr Lawrence did not have in mind a *Christian* valuation of sex as he wrote this novel, and the kind of sexual relationship depicted in the book is not one I would *necessarily* regard as ideal. But what I think *is* clear is that what Lawrence was trying to do was to portray the sex relationship as something essentially sacred—

Mr Justice Byrne (reddening): He was trying to – *what*?

The Bishop of Woolwich (gripping the stand): Lawrence tries to portray this relation, in a real sense, as something sacred; indeed, as a form of holy communion. For him, you see, flesh was completely sacramental of spirit.

On the Judge's bench, Mr Justice Byrne does not see. He scribbles furiously.

Mr Gardiner: Is this a book which, in your view, Christians ought to read?

The Bishop of Woolwich (looking heavenward, as if for revelation): Yes. I believe it is.

The press section, already in a lather at the 'holy communion' of the gamekeeper and the lady – they haven't heard it called *that* before – erupts. Reporters dash outside for telephone boxes. The proceedings are disrupted. 'A Book All Christians Should Read!' The headline is on its way.

'Silence!' demands the usher of those of us who remain.

Mr Gardiner: No further questions, my Lord.

Mr Griffith-Jones (taking to the floor): You have spoken of the sexual relation, Bishop Robinson. *Marriage* is another aspect of ethics, is it not?

The Bishop: It is, although it is perhaps germane to note that Lawrence revealed an astonishing sensitivity to the beauty and value of *all* organic relationships, of which he saw sex as the culmination, and in no sense sordid. Naturally the book is not a *treatise* on marriage. He is concerned with establishing a permanent, genuine, spiritual—

Mr Griffith-Jones: Bishop, I don't wish to be offensive to you, but you are not here to make speeches. Answer plainly, if you would. *Are* you suggesting this book is of *instructional value* upon the subject of ethics? Yes or no?

The Bishop: No.

Mr Justice Byrne (rapping his desk): But *does* it portray an immoral woman?!

Mr Griffith-Jones pauses in the cross-examination, either with surprise or so that the Judge's words might linger in the air. Lady Byrne reaches across to her husband. Does she steady the shifting paperwork on his desk or pat his hand? We shall, quite simply, never know.

'Professor Vivian de Sola Pinto!'

Vivian Pinto is Professor of English at the University of Nottingham and an internationally respected Lawrence expert from the author's native region. The Professor's white hair is oiled and neatly parted. He wears a dapper three-piece suit and walks with his head bowed, as if already concentrating on his testimony as he crosses the court. He is a man who must be close to retirement. There is nothing at all in or on his person to evoke his distinguished service as an infantry officer, alongside his friend the poet Siegfried Sassoon, at the Western Front during the Great War. Such is the deceit of the ageing body.

Mr Gardiner (holding the Penguin paperback high, so that even we can see it, at the back where we hover): Professor, I am aware that all standards and measures must, to a degree, be relative. But, for the benefit of the court, what do you say to the literary merits of this book?

Professor Pinto: I would give it a high place; not the highest place. I think it is a deeply moving story. There are weak passages, but it is an important and valuable work.

Mr Gardiner: Am I right in thinking it was the last novel Lawrence wrote?

Professor Pinto: Yes. The last long prose work.

Mr Gardiner: Would you kindly give the court your expert assessment of the following passages, which I shall now read aloud to you, passages identified by the Prosecution as 'obscene'. Page 27 …

Mr Gardiner reads two paragraphs in a clear, strong voice.

Professor: Competently written.

Mr Gardiner: Page 30 …

Professor: Beautifully written.

Mr Gardiner: Page 120 …

Professor: A beautiful passage, full of tenderness and insight.

Mr Gardiner: And now, the gamekeeper's letter at the very end of the novel …

Professor: A highly poetical passage, an affirmation of life.

Mr Gardiner: In your view, are the four-letter words necessary?

Professor: Perhaps what he tried to do with those words was impossible. But yes, certainly. I think, for his purpose, it was necessary to use them.

Mr Gardiner: No further questions.

Mr Griffith-Jones rises from his chair, and one eyebrow rises elaborately with him: Professor Pinto, is D. H. Lawrence, as it were, a *hobby-horse* of yours?

Professor: As Professor at Nottingham, it is very natural that I should be interested. Lawrence himself was from a small mining village in Nottinghamshire.

Mr Griffith-Jones: You tell us that you would give this novel 'a high place' in your ratings.

Professor: Yes.

Mr Griffith-Jones: Yet Miss Esther Forbes, the respected American critic, has said that *Lady Chatterley's Lover* is 'the worst of all Lawrence's books – stiff and unnatural'.

Professor: I'm afraid I don't think Esther Forbes is a person of any particular standing as a literary critic.

Mr Griffith-Jones: Allow me then to read to you from John Middleton Murry's fulsome criticism of the novel in his literary-critical work, *Son of Woman*. (He does so at length.)

Professor: I know it. It's a very unsatisfactory book.

Mr Griffith-Jones: Because he, like Esther Forbes, doesn't agree with you?

Professor: No.

The acoustics are not good at the best of times, and Professor Pinto's voice has lost some of its power.

Mr Griffith-Jones: Very well. You will, I assume, permit me to quote from the novel itself, from page 185.

Mr Griffith-Jones's reading is deliberately tone-deaf: 'Th'art good cunt, though, aren't ter? Best bit o' cunt left on earth. When ter likes! When th'art willin'!', and so on and so on. We get 'cunt', 'cunt', and 'fuck', 'fuck'. Does this novel really merit your 'high place'?

Professor (colouring): I think it should be read in Nottingham dialect—

Laughter explodes.

'Silence!' bellows the usher.

Mr Justice Byrne: If people cannot refrain from such outbursts, the court will be cleared.

Mr Griffith-Jones: That may well be so, the point you make about the accent in which it is read, but not *all* the people who would read this book, if sold by Penguins at 3s. 6d., *would* have a knowledge of Nottinghamshire dialect, would they?

He smiles, as if the very notion is amusing.

His witness does not reply.

Mr Griffith-Jones: Professor Pinto, yes or no?

Professor: No.

Mr Griffith-Jones: No further questions, my Lord.

Yet the Judge bristles still. The witness is not released.

Mr Justice Byrne: Professor, what do *you* believe is meant by the words 'literary *merit*'?

Professor Pinto: Many things.

Mr Justice Byrne: Such as?

Professor Pinto: I look for the quality of the writing, the freshness of the subject matter, the meaning of the book; whether the artistry is adequate; whether it succeeds in conveying the author's experience, and whether that experience is significant experience; whether one can come back to it and get fresh pleasure from it. I did that. I came back and read *Lady Chatterley's Lover* before this trial, after a number of years, and I found it was an even better book than I thought originally.

Mr Justice Byrne makes a sound in his throat, one that is not easily described.

Enter the Editor of the *London Churchman*, 'The Reverend Prebendary Stephan Hopkinson!'

From our perch at the threshold of Court Number One, we watch a man in his fifties – short, bald, spectacled and wearing a vicar's collar – cross the floor. We see, as he passes us, that he suffers from chilblains on his nose. For all of his reverend sensibility, Prebendary Hopkinson curses the English climate.

Mr Gardiner (checking his notes): Reverend Hopkinson, I will cut to what is perhaps the heart of the matter. Is it a proper assumption that sex can be treated in accordance with the Christian faith?

Reverend Hopkinson (radiating unexpected charm): Yes. I think it is one of the great basic emotions. All life comes through sex itself, and sex is of course essential to life as we know it. I would believe therefore that God himself created these functions, and we ought therefore to learn to regard them with respect and reverence, which does *not* mean with timidity.

Mr Gardiner: Thank you, Reverend Hopkinson. Your witness, Mr Griffith-Jones.

Mr Griffith-Jones (nodding to his rival): Do you, Reverend Hopkinson, find anywhere in the book *a single word* suggesting criticism of Lady Chatterley's adultery?

Reverend Hopkinson: Not a word, but that is because I take it that the book is intended to depict—

Mr Griffith-Jones (looking up to the public gallery): It is very difficult, you know. No expert in this case appears to be able to answer a question 'Yes' or 'No'. I will try again (returning to Reverend Hopkinson). *Do* you find one word of criticism of Lady Chatterley's adultery in this novel?

Reverend Hopkinson: No.

Mr Griffith-Jones emotes a satisfied weariness.

Reverend Hopkinson: I must add, however, that I find no criticism of *any* moral conduct in the book.

Mr Justice Byrne: Reverend Hopkinson, the question might also be thus put: would you not have *any* objection to your own children reading this book?

Reverend Hopkinson: Provided they discussed it with me – no. None.

Under the lofty dome of the Old Bailey, Reverend Stephan Hopkinson, at five feet four inches, holds his ground.

The last witness of Day Two is Senior Lecturer in English Literature at Leicester University, 'Mr Richard Hoggart!'

Mr Jeremy Hutchinson, QC, Junior Counsel for the Defence, now takes to the stage. He is a tall, broad man of forty-five, with a generous brow, a receding hairline, a pronounced nose and a modest chin. Behind his spectacles, his eyes are sharp, but characteristically merry too, as if he is determined to enjoy himself.

We make ourselves comfortable.

The witness, Mr Hoggart, is in his early forties. He runs a hand over his dark widow's peak and nods to the barrister that he is ready to begin.

Mr Jeremy Hutchinson: It has been said, Mr Hoggart, that the two main characters in the book are little more than bodies which continuously have sexual intercourse together. What say you to that?

Mr Hoggart: I should think it was grossly unfair. I should think it was based on a misreading of the book.

Mr Hutchinson: The book has also been described as little more than 'vicious indulgence in sex and sensuality'. In your view, is that a valid description?

Mr Hoggart: I think it is invalid on all three counts. It is not in any sense vicious; it is highly virtuous, and if anything, it is puritanical.

Mr Justice Byrne (craning forward): Did you say 'virtuous' and 'puritanical'?

Mr Hoggart (unperturbed): I did say that. Taken as a whole, it is a moral book. The overwhelming impression which comes out to me as a careful reader of it is of the enormous reverence which must be paid by one human being to another with whom he is in love and, in particular, the reverence towards one's physical relationship.

In this sense, it seems to me that it is highly moral and not degrading of sex. The book advocates marriage, not adultery. It takes a difficult and distressing human situation which we know exists, a marriage which has gone wrong, which never started right. D. H. Lawrence wanted us to say, 'Yes, this is what one does. In a simple, ordinary way, one fucks,' with no sniggering or dirt. He is therefore properly viewed as a British nonconformist Puritan.

Mr Hutchinson (smiling genially to the Prosecution): Your witness.

Mr Griffith-Jones is nine years Mr Hoggart's senior, an Old Etonian and an Oxbridge alumnus. Mr Hoggart grew up orphaned and poor, but, by dint of a scholarship, studied English and gained a degree from the University of Leeds.

Mr Griffith-Jones's sneer is faint but observable as he begins: I have *apparently* lived my life, Mr Hoggart, under a misapprehension as to the meaning of the word 'puritanical'. Perhaps you would be so kind as to enlighten me?

Mr Hoggart (friendly): Of course. You're not alone, Mr Griffith-Jones. Many people do misunderstand it. It's the way in which language decays. The proper meaning of the word 'puritan' is somebody who belongs to the tradition of British puritanism generally. The distinguishing feature of *that* is an intense sense of responsibility for one's conscience. Lawrence, I would argue, felt little else. His work is, for him, a profound expression, not only of his artistic sense but of his conscience too. In this sense, this book is puritanical.

(Reporters dash out, racing for the nearest phone-box. 'Lady C. "puritanical" says Potty Prof!')

Mr Griffith-Jones: I am obliged to you, Mr Hoggart, for the fullness of your lecture. This, however, is the Old Bailey and not (checking his notes) *Leicester* University. I must ask you to turn your attention to the particulars of the novel under discussion. I refer you now, in the copy you have been handed, to page 30, and to the description of Lady Chatterley's second sexual bout, with the man Michaelis, a character she has sex with and dismisses early on. Is this a passage which you would say is 'puritanical'?

Mr Hoggart (his eyes large and expressive): Yes, puritanical and poignant, and sad, about two people who have no proper relationship. It is, in that sense, an immoral relationship, as Lawrence shows us. Michaelis shows no understanding of her. Indeed, he casually humiliates her, and she is wounded.

Mr Griffith-Jones: *She* is wounded? May I remind the court that she is a married woman? Her relationship with Michaelis was conducted behind her husband's back for the satisfaction of her sexual lust. That is the position, is it not?

Mr Hoggart (in a good-natured tone): It is not.

Mr Griffith-Jones: What else is it?

Mr Hoggart: Lady Chatterley hopes that, through this act with Michaelis, which comes early in the novel, she will feel less lonely and lost. She did not judge him well, unfortunately.

Mr Griffith-Jones (with restrained indignation): On the contrary, it is done, is it not, because her husband was wounded in the War and has been incapable ever since of satisfying her sexual demands?

Mr Hoggart: It is not.

Mr Griffith-Jones: Very well. *That* is your view.

Mr Hoggart: I can substantiate that view.

Mr Griffith-Jones: Never mind about substantiating it.

Mr Justice Byrne: What you are being *asked* is this, Mr Hoggart, as I understand it. This was an *immoral* relationship between this woman and that man, was it not?

Mr Hoggart: Yes, Lawrence makes that perfectly clear. There was affection, or so she thought, but Lady Chatterley realises belatedly that Michaelis neither loves nor respects her as he should.

Mr Justice Byrne's face reddens with questions even he dares not put: Respect *her*? *That* harlot?

The Prosecution hammers at Mr Hoggart for over an hour, with a peculiar ferocity reserved for this 'jumped-up' expert from Leicester University. Shortly after the trial, the eminent author Mr E. M. Forster will write to Richard Hoggart to commiserate: 'It was for you to bear the full insolence of the prosecuting counsel, whom it is difficult to believe is not a cad, privily as well as publicly.'

Mr Griffith-Jones (with the bone between his teeth): Allow me to quote: 'Sharp soft waves of unspeakable pleasure washed over her as he entered her, and started the curious molten thrilling that spread and spread till she was carried away with the last blind flush of extremity.' Is that puritanical, Mr Hoggart?

Mr Hoggart: It is.

Mr Griffith-Jones (turning a page): 'A woman's a lovely thing when 'er's deep ter fuck, and cunt's good.' Is *that* puritanical?

Mr Hoggart: Yes. It is the gamekeeper Mellors beginning to express, in honest, realist dialogue, the reverence he feels for the female form, for what he calls 'womanness'.

Mr Griffith-Jones: *Is* it realistic, though? *Would* a gamekeeper speak in such a way to a *land-owner's* wife? Moreover, would not an *actual* woman, such as Lady Chatterley, object to the relentless vulgarity of his speech? (He pauses to give a faint smile of conde-scension.) Are you adequately acquainted, Mr Hoggart, with social spheres such as that to which Lady Chatterley belongs? Can you actually *judge* the realism of Mellors's vulgarity in this context, and are you *able* to assess the authenticity of Lady Chatterley's response?

Mr Hoggart (heedless of the slight): She does not object to Mellors's speech because she believes it to be neither vulgar nor aggressive, in the way profanity can often be. The author is evoking, quite radically, an *entire register* within that variety of speech we often term 'profane'. Lady Chatterley is able to hear beauty in it. The speech is both realistic and credible within the terms set by the novel itself. The reaction of any actual woman of a similar station in this period is, I'm afraid, irrelevant. Good novels have no use for generalisations or class 'demographics'.

Mr Griffith-Jones (looking to the jury as if for sympathy): In Chapter Ten, following another bout, we learn that 'Connie would not take her bath this evening. The sense of his flesh touching her, *the very stickiness upon her*, was dear to her, and in a sense, holy.' Is the 'very stickiness' puritanical, Mr Hoggart?

Mr Hoggart: Never more.

Mr Griffith-Jones: Our gamekeeper-hero tells Lady Chatterley that the root of sanity, no less, 'is in the balls'. Does *that* notion have literary merit and, if so, is it – and I remind you that this is a most serious question, Mr Hoggart – is it *for the public good*?

Mr Hoggart: When considered within the context of the whole story, yes, undoubtedly, and yes.

Mr Griffith-Jones: And what of this passage from Chapter Twelve: 'Her hands came timorously down his back, to the soft, smallish globes of the buttocks. Beauty! what beauty! a sudden little flame of new awareness went through her. How was it possible, this beauty here, where she had previously only been repelled? The unspeakable beauty to the touch, of the warm, living buttocks! The life within life, the sheer warm, potent loveliness. And the strange weight of the balls between his legs! What a mystery!' Is *this*, too, an expression of 'reverence', as you see it, Mr Hoggart?

Mr Hoggart (sanguine): Oh yes, quite clearly so.

Mr Griffith-Jones (expostulating): *Reverence*, Mr Hoggart? Reverence for the weight of a man's *balls*?

Mr Hoggart: Indeed.

xiii

Day Three, Friday, October 28th

At four in the morning of the third day, members of the public begin to queue in the street in perfect darkness. Each hopes for a coveted place in the gallery of Court Number One.

Five hours later, in the Great Hall, amid the marble monarchs and the muscular figures of allegorical murals, Thomas Stearns Eliot, poet and senior cultural statesman, seventy-two years of age, sits slightly stooped, as if a martyr to his digestion. He knows that, when called, it will mean one thing only: the Prosecution will bring forth, in evidence, his criticism of *Chatterley* from almost thirty years before. His moral and public duty will be to eat his words.

In the Great Hall, he looks faintly green.

This is the way the world ends
Not with a bang but a whimper.

Young Mrs Eliot sits on the bench between her husband and 'Matron'. The younger woman's hands rest in her lap; her back is straight. For her husband's sake, she endeavours to radiate the composure neither feels. Matron, in the meantime, has sugary tea at the ready.

Inside Court Number One, the tea-cups are returned to their shelves, and the parade of Defence witnesses continues.

Headmaster, 'Mr Francis Cammerts!'

'I would say it is the only book I know that treats the sexual relationship between human beings in a really serious way.'

Classics Mistress, 'Miss Sarah Beryl Jones!'

'I have inquired from a number of girls after they have left school on this matter, and most of them have been acquainted with these words by the time they were ten.'

Historian, 'Miss C.V. Wedgwood, CBE!'

'Love and tenderness was what he was trying to praise – and also, of course, Lady Chatterley's natural desire to have a child.'

Former newspaper editor, political adviser to the PM, and social commentator, 'Mr Francis Williams!'

'The first meeting with Mellors is when Lady Chatterley is going to visit one of the oldest pieces of woodland in England. Lawrence believed that the upper classes were no longer able to preserve that which was absolutely great in the old tradition of England. People and the land were being exploited as part of a crippling system.'

'Mr Edward Morgan Forster!'

His name, produced in its entirety, does not ring bells. Only a few of the twelve jurors turn to watch the diminutive Mr Forster – buttoned up to the neck in a long, loose mackintosh – walk, with difficulty, to the witness box. The day, again, is wet and cold, and, in spite of the crowning skylight of Court Number One, the room is drear.

Until moments ago, Mr Forster was stationed in the Great Hall – another stray valise – with Mr and Mrs Eliot, and Matron. Together they waited most of the morning. The Eliots wait still.

The man who is, in 1960, arguably the greatest living novelist in the English language, enters the drama of Court Number One in a manner more humble than seen so far. He nods to us as he crosses the threshold of the court, the only person yet to take note. He is a novelist of rank, and he senses the eyes of posterity.

Onward he goes.

Mr Jeremy Hutchinson, rather than Mr Gardiner, stands to take this witness, for Mr Forster and Mr Hutchinson's parents were once acquainted, and the aim of the Defence team is to make Mr Forster, given his eighty-one years, as comfortable as possible. When he arrives, at last, at the witness box, he gives a deep bow to the Judge.

The Judge nods to him.

Mr Hutchinson: Your Lordship, would you give permission for a chair to be placed for Mr Forster?

E. M. Forster (calmly): Thank you, no, I prefer to stand.

The new Defence witness is formally introduced to the court. A few jurors yawn as Mr Hutchinson reads out a very long list of honorary doctorates.

Mr Hutchinson (singling out the salient detail): Mr Forster, I believe *A Passage to India* has been made into a play and at the moment is running in London?

E. M. Forster: Yes.

Heads turn. It is the hit play of the West End. Mr Hutchinson may now begin.

Mr Hutchinson: I believe you knew D. H. Lawrence quite well?

E. M. Forster: Yes, I saw a good deal of him, in 1915 ... That was (clearing his throat) the time when I saw him most, but we ... we kept in touch.

Mr Hutchinson: When he died, I think you described him as the greatest imaginative novelist of your generation?

E. M. Forster: Yes. I would still hold to it.

Mr Hutchinson: What would you say as to the literary merit of *Lady Chatterley's Lover*?

E. M. Forster: I should say that it has very high literary merit. It is not the novel of Lawrence which I most admire. That would be *Sons and Lovers*, I think.

Mr Hutchinson: Lawrence has been described as forming part of the great Puritan stream of writers in this country. Have you any comment to make on that?

E. M. Forster: I understand that at first people might think that paradoxical. If I may speak of antecedents, of great names – Bunyan on the one hand and Blake on the other – Lawrence too had this passionate opinion of the world, and what it ought to be, but is not.

Mr Hutchinson: Is your view founded not only on what he wrote but on what you knew of him as well?

E. M. Forster: Yes. (Then, quietly) Well ...

Mr Hutchinson: Thank you very much, Mr Forster. Your wit—

Mr Justice Byrne: Did you wish to add something, Mr Forster, or qualify your remarks perhaps?

E. M. Forster: I was only qualifying my reply a little, my Lord, because I did not discuss these questions with Lawrence *personally*. But there is nothing in what I knew of him which would contradict what I said.

Mr Justice Byrne (sitting back wearily): Mr Griffith-Jones?

Mr Griffith-Jones: No questions, my Lord.

He does not dare. An elderly, frail – and celebrated – authority.

At the solicitors' table, next to a relieved Allen Lane, Michael Rubinstein gives an inward *Hip-Hip!*

Cathleen was 'Cathleen' with a 'C', she told Mel Harding, because there was no 'K' in Irish. Her family were new Boston Irish, from the South side – her parents had come over after the war – and she'd managed to talk her way past the sign in the Pilgrims Motor Inn front-office window, the one that had said, 'Irish Need Not Apply'.

She'd applied for the front-desk job and had got it against the odds. Harding could see why. She could talk to anyone. Plus, she had an easy smile, glossy black hair to her shoulders, and skin so pale, the blue veins on her forehead showed through.

'It's fine to stare,' she said, sarcastically. 'Don't mind me.'

'You have nice eyes,' he dared, as he wrote out his check for the week. Glinting, back-lit eyes. They flickered with something her customer-service smile belied.

Her laugh had a hard edge to it. 'You mean the one blue one and the one brown one. Don't pretend you weren't looking.'

He concentrated on signing his check. The office smelled of mildew, the countertop was tacky, and his checkbook stuck to it.

'I tried out for Marilyn's part in *The Misfits*, don't you know, but they only went and turned me down.'

He looked up. 'Really?' She wasn't beautiful, but she was striking, and she had the sort of luminous skin a camera would love.

'*No*, not really' – she tilted her head to read his check upside-down – '"Mel". So what's up with your hands, Mel?'

He shrugged. It was none of her business.

She pulled a postcard off the turnstile and turned it to him. 'I really want to go here.' Provincetown, at the north tip of the Cape. 'The Pilgrims actually landed there, didn't they, not at this goddamn motel, excuse my language. Radicals, even if they *did* wear big, silly, old hats. I like that. I hear it's a radical place – writers, artists, homosexuals. Avant-garde types. Geniuses. No-hopers. Escapees from life. Fishermen. Not like Boston *at all*. God, Boston is so straight-laced. So old-fashioned. Plus there's the Playhouse. In Provincetown. That's why I'm here. I'm going to audition. First, I need to go in, introduce myself – that sort of malarkey. How about you drive, and I bring lunch?'

It was strange – the sensation of dialogue. His voice was a rusty bucket coming up from the well of himself. 'Not the best time of year for sight-seeing,' he said.

'Are you turning me down, Mel?' She planted her hand on her hip, but she was smiling – or maybe laughing – at him.

He was only waiting for his receipt.

She held it without passing it across the counter to him. 'And I wonder – would you happen to have a camera?'

He glanced at the time, as if he had somewhere to be. 'Ah … yes.'

It so happened he did. F.B.I. property, complete with a 35mm black-and-white film still in it.

'I do.'

Now that he could take pictures of anything he liked, he had no idea where to start. Labor Day, on the beach, in the water – Mrs. Kennedy – he still had flashbacks that left him in a sweat.

'Marilyn had her pictures done on a beach. If it's good enough for Marilyn, it's good enough for me. I need a portfolio, you see. For my audition. When I get one, that is. Tomorrow, Saturday. You working?'

'No, I was go—'

'I can't twiddle my thumbs forever. I turn thirty next week.' Then she smiled and touched his arm. 'Nice to meet you, "Mel Harding". And thank you. I promise I'm not this bossy all the time.' For a moment, she went shy. 'Tuna, corned beef or egg salad?'

He blinked.

'Sandwiches. What's your favorite?'

He agreed to drive on one condition: they had to leave by 6 a.m., to catch the pearly light. With women, you wanted either the 'sweet light' at the end of the day or the pearly light of early morning.

She slid onto the passenger seat and slammed the door. 'I'll have circles under my eyes all the way to next year.'

It was mild for late October, calm and dry. They headed toward Barnstable, following the Old King's Highway, once a trail for the Wampanoag, then a cart-road for the early settlers. It was nice, scenic. He wondered what it would be like, to know a place from the ground up. To know every twist, turn and shortcut. He'd never lived anywhere long enough.

A soft flame of light caught hold of sea and sky, and the air was cut by the tang of salt. Lighthouses on the old shore road called to the lonely, and his Chevrolet wound its way through coastal villages, past gray-shingled houses, empty beaches and pitch-pine scrub. The dunes glowed with the rising sun, and the cranberry bogs gleamed in sheets of crimson, waiting to be raked.

She turned to him. 'I don't think I've ever seen anywhere so beautiful.'

He nodded, discomfited by her directness, by the scent of her hair, by the fullness of her thighs on the seat; by the flickering lure of happiness, the danger of it. A bright flashing thing dangled on a line before him. Should he bite? Did he even know how?

His eczema started to prickle, but he managed to settle deeper into his seat. Some people's company made you feel lonelier; the gusts of them found your gaps and holes and whistled right through. But her company was like a breeze clearing his head; he felt more awake. It had been so long since he'd felt awake, and not just restive with caffeine and nerves.

The road criss-crossed oak forests to which a few leaves still clung, gold and red. She fiddled with the radio dial, trying to get the latest campaign news, but they'd lost the signal at the last bend.

'He *has* to win,' she said. 'Do you like him?'

'Kennedy? Sure,' he said. 'I like him enough.'

'I keep *hoping* I'll see him or Mrs. Kennedy, young Mrs. Kennedy that is, in Hyannis sometime. But I imagine they have people to run their errands and all that.'

What could he say? 'The little girl's nanny comes into the drug-store sometimes, to pick up a prescription or drop off a film for Mrs. Kennedy.'

'*Caroline's* nanny? No! Get *away.*'

They didn't speak for another half hour, and it was okay, there in the space of the front seat.

Then, 'Here!' she said, slapping her door. 'Here, here, here.' He swerved to a stop on the sandy edge of the road. 'This is it,' she said, reading the sign. 'Mayflower Beach. Perfect. This is my stop. I can feel it.' She rolled down her window. 'Would you just *look* at that?'

They got out and stretched. He removed the lens cap from his camera, and held the viewfinder to his eye to check the scene. The beach was a seemingly endless stretch of wind-rippled sand. It wasn't yet seven. The bay was still milky white.

'Listen, Mel,' she said, her voice suddenly altered. 'I should have said something.'

And in his mind, he prepared, instantly, to turn back; for the day to go wrong. How had he got things wrong already? She was going to tell him she was married, or had a boyfriend, and she liked him but she didn't want him getting the wrong idea. She was reeling in the bright lure of the day.

'I *do* want to see Provincetown,' she began, 'and the Playhouse, and hopefully I'll even get an audition before long. But it's closed. Closed for the season,' she said. 'I knew that yesterday when I asked you to drive. It wasn't actually a *lie*, but—'

He leaned against his dusty car. 'So you don't want the pictures, after all.'

'I want the pictures, alright. But' – she toed a patch of dune-grass – 'mostly I just wanted' – she turned away, her eyes straining – 'you to notice me, I suppose.' She sucked in her lips. 'A bit.'

He lifted his camera and adjusted the focus. 'Look this way,' he said.

Her face was vulnerable in the viewfinder, with the strong chin that stopped her from being beautiful.

'I forgot to ask. Is that film black-and-white? I don't want my mismatched eyes to be obvious.'

He nodded, hardly listening.

'I've never seen such a little camera,' she said. 'Are you sure it's not a toy?'

'Stop talking,' he said. He clicked off the first shot. The spring-motor hummed. It worked like a dream.

She looked ahead to the dunes, to their wild fringe of grass; to their clefts and secrets. 'I have a child,' she said.

He paused, but he didn't lower the camera.

'I thought I had better say. There's no father. Not that it was the Holy Spirit either.' Her voice was throaty. 'Fallen woman, me. Thank Jesus I didn't grow up in Ireland, or the nuns would have had me down the laundries faster than a flea to a dog. I'm telling you now only because I don't want you to think I'm after anything. I might be fallen but I'm not cracked.'

He took another shot.

'The truth is, I'll probably never be any sort of actress. Maybe a character actress, if I'm lucky. Not that I've given up. I'm good – my teachers always said I was. My family thought I was going to be the next Maureen O'Hara. Last year, my mother even entered me to be a "Rose", back in Tralee – in Kerry – where she's from. There's a new pageant over there. She fibbed about my age on the form, sent an old snap, and had me lined up for the New York heat. I bought a dress and everything. Mind you, my ma said it was so tight you could see my religion, but' – she shrugged – 'it was a dress, and I was on my way. My folks were going to have my little boy so I could go. *Talk* about an acting job. But the dress was all wrong, I was all wrong, and I just couldn't do it. I'm not pageant material. So I came to the Cape.' She forced a smile. 'I am *pilgrim* material. A Misfit with a capital "M". I cannot *wait* for that movie to come out, by the way. I've been reading all about it in my movie magazines. You can be a Misfit too, if you like. Which one? Clark Gable or Montgomery Clift?'

With his free hand, he checked his light-meter. 'Not sure …'

'I think you're more Clark Gable – he's getting on a bit. They say Marilyn drove him round the twist on the set. They're filming with genu-ine wild mustangs, you know. I say we use those *big dogs* that belong to the people in the room next to yours – the Dagenharts – as stand-ins. I ask you, will those people *ever* leave? It's a motel, for God's sake. A *motor*-inn. Motor *on*, Mr. and Mrs. Dagenhart. Who goes to a motel and *stays*?' She stopped, cringed, and put her hand over her mouth. 'Sorry, Mel.'

He'd been there since June. It was almost November.

He carried on, testing the focus. 'The dogs aren't so bad. I even get to feeling sorry for them sometimes, in that car all night. No wonder they go crazy.'

'I don't think you're old. I mean, you're not as old as Clark Gable.' She closed her eyes, wincing. 'Anyway, I'm glad you *haven't* motored on. Sometimes I wonder if maybe you have when your car's gone from the lot, and – confession! – I go and check your balance in the accounts ledger, just to be sure. What I'm trying to say is, it's not why I asked you to take me out – because I have a child, I mean. Or because I wanted to wrangle you into taking pictures of me, even though I did – wrangle you. I know I did. I watch you drive out of the motel most mornings, and I—'

'Stop talking, would you?' and she blushed. 'You didn't wrangle me. Try rolling out your shoulders a little. These are just test-shots. Try to relax your face.' He couldn't stop looking at her.

Her jaw softened. He could see her now through the viewfinder – the voluptuous light of her, moonlight on dark water. He hit the shutter-release.

She gave him a crooked, skeptical smile. 'You've done this before, haven't you, Mel Harding? What's with the little camera? You some sort of peeping Tom? Do you take dirty pictures?'

It was like a sock in the jaw. He lowered his camera and stared at the ground. He felt the heat rise up his throat.

The moon of her disappeared behind a cloud. 'It was a *joke*, Mel.' Her eyes hardened. 'Try relaxing your *brain*, why don't you?'

She'd guessed right. Even if she'd never know it. Because what else remained of his whole career at the Bureau *except* dirty pictures? Stolen pictures of one sort or another. Stolen bits of other people's lives.

He reached into the open window on the passenger side, grabbed his jacket, camera case and extra lens, then headed for the path that ran between the dunes. 'Coming?' he called over his shoulder, as if he no longer cared.

What was he doing out here anyway? She was a complete stranger, for Christ's sake. Failed-actress types couldn't be trusted. That's what the profiling would have told him back at the Bureau.

'Well, there had better be some Pilgrims on this here Mayflower Beach!' she called out from behind, 'or I'll be writing to the signage authorities!'

They wouldn't stay long.

He slipped and slid as he descended the steep dune. When he turned to look back, she was barefoot – at the end of October. Barefoot. Dangling her shoes from one hand. Jesus. Why did she have to put on a show?

'I bet *they'll* vote for Kennedy,' she called.

'Who?'

'The *Pilgrims*, Mel.' As if to say, *Pay attention, will you?* 'Nixon was raised a Quaker, apparently,' she called, 'but Catholics make better company than Protestants. Protestants make more money – well, that's not nothing – but do you *think* they can tell a joke? Nope. No siree, you couldn't *pay* me to live with that crowd of WASPs in Boston, up there on the *fine* south slope of Beacon Hill. Not on your life. Not with all those stiffs.' She came up behind him. 'I bet Mr. Kennedy can tell a good joke. He's got that look about him.' Then she clapped her hand to her mouth again. 'Oh my *God*, Mel, you're a WASP yourself, aren't you?'

He turned to her, his voice still flat. 'I'm not much of anything.'

They had reached the beach. Cape Cod Bay unfolded, blue, endless and fizzing with puritan light.

His heart crashed at his ribs.

At Whelan's on Monday, he took a late lunch, so he could rely on the store being quiet. He didn't need to eat. He'd do her pictures instead.

He lifted the film out of the drying-cupboard and switched on the light-table, for the first look with the loupe. With any luck, he'd have time to cut the negatives.

He could hardly believe what he was seeing.

One look through the loupe, and he was back there. Not on Mayflower Beach with Cathleen on Saturday, but in the dim dining-room of the Mayflower Hotel in Washington in May of '58. More than two years ago already, but he could still feel the briefcase, sweaty in hands; the key not turning, the damned strap getting in his way, the punch-latches, dead; his whole being all-fingers-and-thumbs as he tried to find the release-button, but hit instead – he realised only now – the camera's concealed shutter-release.

In the first shot, the angle was about twenty-five degrees off-kilter, but it was clear, the sharpest of the three on the uncut film.

The whole scene was there, alive again on his light-table: the bright bulk of Hoover, his dark irises white and empty; beside him, the irradiated phantom of Clyde Tolson, tall and languid on the pale banquette; and on the table, next to the basket of black Saltines, their hands tenderly clasped.

Hoover assessed the latest reports in the American press. You get what you pay for, he thought, with a satisfying click of his dentures. It was like biting into gold.

'The View from London: "Lady C.: Filthy and Unprintable"'

'In International News: Lady Chatterley on Trial Today!'

'Most Controversial Book of the Century'

'Latest from LADY C. Trial – Prosecution: "Heroine is over-sexed"'

He leaned back in his chair and popped a breath mint in his mouth. Until the 'Guilty' verdict came through, the photo was safe in Miss Gandy's foot-stool, at the very top of his classified collection. As for the private collection, he kept that at home.

Through his window, Hoover watched the smoke from the Bureau's incinerator go up. Jonah was at work, far below in the basement. Every day, confidential documents were committed to the memory of his most senior agents, and then to the flames of the incinerator.

Photos, when they were sent to the basement, were delivered to Jonah double-sealed, so as to arouse neither his curiosity nor his shock. No one needed to seal the confidential memos. Good old Jonah. He'd been with the Bureau since the age of fourteen and was still, at the age of fifty-something, good-natured and illiterate. The Bureau's secrets were safe.

Meanwhile, pollsters were saying the vote was still too close to call, the closest since 1916. But Hoover trusted America. Patience and determination would win the day, not flashy celebrity songs, good looks and inexperience.

What's more, the incumbent, President Eisenhower himself – the man who had introduced Hoover to the art of Paint-by-Numbers – had just launched a late speaking-tour, to push the Nixon campaign over the line. Ike grumbled about having to do it – he didn't have a lot of time for Nixon – but, one way or the other, Kennedy would be knocked out of the race.

Clyde was away on Bureau business at the New York Field Office. The New York S.A.C. had some bee in his bonnet. He wanted more of the Bureau's budget to be spent on the Mob and less on Communists. Clyde would make him see sense. He'd tell Hoover all about it later on. They always spoke, even if long-distance, before bed.

Sometimes, when they were separated like this, it felt to Hoover as if he'd arrived back to his own address before nightfall only to find a vacant lot. As if there never *had* been a home.

It was terrible.

Each day Clyde's love restored him. It was as simple and as magnificent as that.

Clyde's love was the porch with the light left on.

Back in the Left Luggage Office of the Great Hall, Mr T. S. Eliot paces. *I said to my soul, be still, and wait without hope.* By late afternoon, he has walked, by measure of footfall, at least halfway across London. He has paused only for tea from Matron's flask, shared with his wife, and to watch another stray witness – not him – re-claimed.

'Mr Roy Jenkins, MP!'

Mr Jenkins, the son of a Welsh coal-miner, enters, wearing thick spectacles, a baggy suit and a shirt collar too big for him. It is as if, at the age of forty, he has somehow been caught wearing his father's clothes. As he crosses the court, his bald crown gleams and his eyes are avid.

As many in the assembly are aware, Mr Jenkins has recently resigned from his front-bench role in the Labour Party, in the aftermath of Labour's election defeat. He considers himself a 'progressive' and is now determined to fight. He is working to abolish the death penalty and theatre censorship. ('Good Lord!') He wants to see suicide, abortion and homosexuality decriminalised. ('Who is this little man?') He wants all remaining British colonial powers to be relinquished, and for his country to accept a reduced place in the world. ('He wants *what?*' shout the Elderlies.) He wants to live, he says, on the side of 'experiment and brightness'.

If Mr Jenkins is somewhat lost in his attire, he is not dwarfed by the edifice of the Old Bailey.

Mr Hutchinson smiles to the jury and then to the gallery, clearly in good spirits. He approaches the stand, clutching the edges of his gown at his chest as a farmer might thumb his braces.

Mr Hutchinson: May I confirm, Mr Jenkins? Were you the chief sponsor in Parliament of the recently amended Obscene Publications Bill?

Mr Jenkins: I was.

Mr Hutchinson: For the benefit of the court, I present in evidence a copy of the *Spectator* magazine, dated the 26th of August of this year. Would you be so kind, Mr Jenkins, as to read out the highlighted passages from the 'Letters' page?

Mr Jenkins: Of course. (He takes the magazine and pushes his specs up his nose.) 'Sir, as the sponsor of the Obscene Publications Act of 1959, I am surprised and distressed to learn of the recent policy of Sir Theobald Mathew, Director of Public Prosecutions ... The Act was designed to give the police the stronger powers, for which they had asked, in dealing with the trade in pornography, while affording a greater security to works with any claim to literary merit ... The powers which the police asked for, they have now received. Why, therefore, cannot the Director of Public Prosecutions show a little good sense' – he turns to Sir Toby on the floor of the court, where the DPP neither blinks nor blanches – 'and respect the compromise? Could not our prosecuting authorities learn a little from the illiterate mistakes of their predecessors? Yours faithfully, Roy Jenkins.'

Mr Hutchinson: Thank you, Mr Jenkins. Does the Act explicitly state that it is 'To provide for the protection of literature'?

Mr Jenkins: It does.

Mr Hutchinson: In your view, is this book *Lady Chatterley's Lover* (he holds aloft the Penguin paperback) literature?

Mr Jenkins: It most certainly is. Indeed, if I may add, it never *occurred* to me, in the five years I worked on the Bill, that—

Mr Justice Byrne: I really don't think we want to go into that.

Mr Jenkins: I am so sorry, my Lord (appearing not remotely sorry).

Mr Hutchinson: No further questions, my Lord.

Mr Griffith-Jones: No questions, my Lord.

Because the damage was done.

'Miss Anne Scott-James!'

The novelist, broadcaster, newspaper and magazine editor enters, statuesque at six feet tall, and in her forties. She is the most elegant of the witnesses to date and, as she takes the stand, she looks less like a person about to testify than a marvellous carved figurehead at the bow of a ship.

Mr Gardiner: Miss Scott-James, our aim today is to determine the merits of this novel, in both degree and quality. For that reason,

I should like to ask: has it, in your view, any sociological or educational merits?

Miss Scott-James (coming to life): Oh yes, *immense* merits. Lawrence was an iconoclast. He thought the times were both stiff and stuffy; that sex was treated hypocritically; and that money was the false guard around love and human relationships.

Mr Gardiner: Do you believe this novel to be relevant still?

Miss Scott-James: Even more so.

Mr Gardiner: Why is that?

Miss Scott-James (passionately yet thoughtfully): Because one might say that *we* have been in that stuffy room for even longer – for three further decades since Lawrence completed it, still with the windows shut.

Mr Gardiner: Would *you* say that?

Miss Scott-James: Absolutely.

Mr Gardiner (looking to his rival): Your witness.

Mr Griffith-Jones (who lately has been rising only for the low-hanging fruit): Please don't think that I am being rude about this, Miss Scott-James. You run, do you not, the Ladies' page in some newspaper?

Miss Scott-James (coolly): No.

Mr Griffith-Jones (apparently perplexed): No?

Miss Scott-James: No. That term has not been used since 1927.

Mr Griffith-Jones (smiling indulgently): Ah. Yes. I see … The 'Fashion' page then?

Miss Scott-James: I used to run the Women's page. I am a freelance writer now.

Mr Griffith-Jones: Thank you for the clarification. As I say, please don't think I am intending to be rude, but evidence as to the literary merit of this book is confined to *experts*. Apart from your (he scans his notes) … *Women's* page and your own literary efforts – a novel from 1952 entitled (pronouncing the title slowly) *In – the – Mink* – ha-ha, yes, very good – apart from *one* slim novel, you don't claim any special qualifications as a literary *expert*?

Miss Scott-James: I was a classical scholar at Somerville College, Oxford.

Mr Griffith-Jones: But *not* a literary expert?

Miss Scott-James: No … but it isn't a negligible qualification.

Mr Griffith-Jones: I quite agree. Even so, the job of editing the (he waves his hand as if trying to jog his own memory) Women's page is not the same as that of a literary reviewer, is it?

Miss Scott-James: It is not the same job, no.

Mr Griffith-Jones: No further questions, my Lord.

In the Great Hall, Mr Eliot stops in his revolutions. The court is at last adjourned for the day, and the elderly poet is released, a man free again to join the greater gloom of London. He has been spared, he learns: spared interrogation by Mr Griffith-Jones, spared the harassment of the press, and spared a public humiliation.

He is not confident, however, that he will be spared by the new decade. He feels short of breath and queasy as they go. Poor Lawrence, he thinks, snuffed out so young. Only three years separated them. They might well have disliked each other, had they been introduced, but even so, it was all terribly sad.

The dark afternoon is brightened by the whoosh of red buses and the blinking of traffic lights at Ludgate Circus. The eminent poet is steered along the foggy road, up kerbs and down, by his capable young wife. Only the sooty splendour of St Paul's dome oversees their progress, until the couple disappear at last, on Ludgate Hill, into a hackney cab. Only then, does Thomas Stearns Eliot allow himself, finally and belatedly, to collapse on the back seat, while Mrs Eliot administers the smelling-salts provided, with prescience, by Matron.

Day Four, Monday, October 31st
Once again, the Judge enters, more gown than man, and Lady Byrne awaits him, more Chief Justice than wife. They are of one mind as concerns the novel, and that mind is Lady Byrne's. In life, there are certain matters of morality over which the 'gentle sex' must hold sway.

As the Judge takes his seat and glides into place, an editor in the press section notes that Lady Byrne wears tweed today with a Liberty scarf. She is 'most distinguished'. And so the readers of the *Lady* are both up-to-date, and safe in the knowledge that all is right with the world.

Enter the next witness: a barrister, a tutor at Oxford in jurisprudence, a former student of moral theology, and the author of *Obscenity and the Law*. 'Mr Norman St John-Stevas!'

Mr Hutchinson: Mr Stevas, please tell us. How, in your *expert* view, do you judge, one, the literary merit and, two, the morality of this paperback edition?

Mr Stevas: The literary merit is high indeed. It is a uniquely powerful response both to the dilemmas of human sexuality, and to the Great War which scarred a generation. In response to your second question, the moral question ... it does seem to me that this is undoubtedly a moral book. It is not, of course, a book that puts forward an orthodox Christian view, or an orthodox Roman Catholic view – and this is not surprising because Lawrence was not a Christian or a Catholic. Yet Lawrence, for all that he would challenge my assertion, is essentially a writer 'within the Catholic tradition', by which I mean the tradition which regards the sexual instinct as good in itself. This tradition has been opposed since the Reformation era when sex came to be regarded as something essentially evil or at the very least base. I would have no hesitation in saying that every Catholic priest and every Catholic would profit by reading this book. I have certainly read a great many books of a pornographic and obscene nature, in connection with my study of them, and *Lady Chatterley's Lover* has nothing—

Mr Griffith-Jones: Objection!

Sunday Times reviewer, 'Miss Dilys Powell!'

Mr Gardiner: Does this book, in your view, implicitly or explicitly advocate sexual promiscuity?

Miss Powell: Certainly not. In Lawrence's book, which has great elements of sacredness, sex is something to be taken seriously, and as a basis for a holy life.

Mr Griffith-Jones (from Counsel's Row, cupping his hand to his ear): Did I hear you aright, Miss Powell, that sex is treated on – *a* – *holy* – *basis*?

Miss Powell (as if bored by his performance):You did.

Director of Religious Education in the Diocese of Birmingham, 'the Reverend Donald Tytler!'

'No, I do not think there is any advocating of adultery at all.'

Mr Justice Byrne (exasperated): But does it really deal with anything *other* than adultery?

The day goes on, the air is close, and the barristerial scalps begin to itch under their wigs.

Professor of Poetry at Oxford, 'Mr Cecil Day-Lewis!'

Mr Hutchinson:Would you, Professor, give us your frank view on a critical point of literary judgement? Does the fact that the heroine of a book or a novel is an adulteress mean that the author is extolling adultery?

Professor Day-Lewis: Lawrence is most certainly *not* extolling adultery. Lady Chatterley is an adulteress, in that she has committed adultery. Yet I would not call her an immoral woman.

Mr Hutchinson: No further questions, my Lord.

Mr Griffith-Jones (adopting a weary face): Let me be sure I understand your view, Professor. Is it possible that any two people *can* really love one another in the way you describe when they have said practically not *a word* to one another about any subject except copulation?

Professor Day-Lewis (as if addressing a dim schoolboy): Yes, because we cannot assume the dialogue in the novel is the *only* conversation between the two characters. I should not wish to complicate matters for you unduly, Mr Griffith-Jones, but, you see, characters *do* have lives which exceed the lines of print.They have conversations *other* than those which we overhear. *They* do not know that they live in a book.

Novelist, poet and critic, 'Mr Kingsley Amis!'

Mr Amis, one of Michael Rubinstein's A-list witnesses – and sure to be loved by the jury – is slow to appear.

Does he wish to make a noteworthy entrance? Is he in the lavatory? The usher calls again. The tea-cups lean forward to see the famous author of *Lucky Jim*. Several have seen the film. But there is no author in sight. Mr Amis fails to materialise, and the court is thrown into disarray.

The press start scribbling. The Defence exchange notes. The jurors don't hide their disappointment and, in the commotion, Lady Chatterley stumbles.

Mr Amis will write belatedly to Michael Rubinstein, weeks later: he feels 'rather humiliated' and must apologise for not being in court when called. He was away when the date of his appearance arrived in the post, and only discovered it six hours after his scheduled time on the stand. He hopes his no-show didn't 'derange' things too much.

Dear Mr Amis,

Thank you for your letter. I must say that I was puzzled to know what had happened to you since it was rumoured – evidently without foundation – that you <u>had</u> in fact come up to London on the day. When you did not answer the call, Mr Gerald Gardiner called the next witness. This said, even in absentia (or the Garrick Club Bar, Rubinstein thinks) you – that is, your name – may very well have (if one is inclined to optimism) served a useful purpose!

Your sincerely,
Michael Rubinstein

One witness who dearly wishes in this moment that he might join Kingsley Amis in the bar is Sir Allen Lane, founder of Penguin Books.

In the eyes of the public, Sir Allen is both the man of the hour *and* the 'Prisoner'. If the case has been brought against the *entity* of Penguin Books, an entity cannot be sent to prison. Such a sentence, as all are aware, would take the man himself – for up to three years.

Mr Hutchinson calls his witness, and the usher refrains, on this one occasion, from barking out his summons, as Sir Allen is seated only at the solicitors' table, and doesn't need a ringing ear.

With a discreet nod to his solicitor, Michael Rubinstein, and Hans Schmoller, Board Director, Sir Allen rises, fastens the top button of his jacket, and walks the few yards to the witness box, where he takes the oath. From the stand, his eyes search out those of his wife and eldest daughter. Then he turns to face the jury.

Mr Hutchinson: When you first founded Penguins, Sir Allen, what was the idea you had in mind?

Sir Allen: My idea was to produce a book which would sell at the price of ten cigarettes, which would give no excuse for anybody not being able to buy it. For people like myself, who had left school and started work when they were sixteen, it would be another form of education.

Mr Hutchinson: I think you have used the phrase that you wanted to make Penguin a 'University Press in paperbacks'.

Sir Allen: Yes, I have used the phrase.

Mr Hutchinson: Now, I think in 1952 you were knighted for your services to literature?

Sir Allen: Yes.

Mr Hutchinson: The court has heard that you have been, over a number of years, publishing all the major works by D. H. Lawrence; that you and your Board believed *Lady Chatterley* to be essential to that aim. Is that correct?

Sir Allen: Yes.

Mr Hutchinson: In your view, does it have high literary merit?

Sir Allen: Yes, certainly.

Mr Hutchinson: Why did you take the view that you should not publish an expurgated edition?

Sir Allen: Because it is against our principle. When we publish, we only publish a book as written by the author. We would not offer less to our readers. We would not publish a book in an emasculated form.

Mr Hutchinson: No further questions, my Lord.

Mr Griffith-Jones (crossing the floor): Sir Allen, you say you believe the novel has *high* literary merit? Would you qualify that at all?

Sir Allen: No. It's straightforward. It's why we decided to publish.

Mr Griffith-Jones: I have here a cutting from the *Manchester Guardian* dated the 7th of March of this year, 1960. I believe it is a newspaper you respect?

Sir Allen: It is.

Mr Griffith-Jones: In this article, you appear to be expanding on something you said to the press the previous day, the 6th of March. As you elaborate, you say, as reported here, and I quote: '*Lady Chatterley's Lover* is no great novel.' (He looks up and fixes Sir Allen with his gaze.) Did you say that?

Mr Gardiner (getting to his feet): Might the witness see the full article?

Mr Griffith-Jones: Certainly. (He hands it up.) You know as well as I, Sir Allen, how inaccurate reports sometimes are. Hence my first question: *Did* you say, '*Lady Chatterley's Lover* is no great novel'?

Sir Allen (pondering, unsettled): I will take that as being correct, but I cannot remember the remark or the context.

Mr Griffith-Jones: Was that your *view* as you proceeded towards publication? '*No great novel*'.

Sir Allen: No, no.

Mr Griffith-Jones: Had you been talking about it?

Sir Allen (flashing irritation): I have been talking about very little else since the beginning of the year.

Mr Griffith-Jones: Please do look again at the article. Does it not bring back to your mind *any* occasion to which the article's author might be referring?

Sir Allen: I can't recall any.

Mr Griffith-Jones: Are there any words ascribed to you in it which you *do* recognise? Any at all?

Sir Allen: Yes ... I think I might well have said something of that which is quoted near the start of the piece.

Mr Griffith-Jones: Would you read that, please, for the benefit of the court, the words you believe you remember saying?

Sir Allen (hesitating): 'Either I'll go to prison or not.'

Mr Griffith-Jones: No further questions, my Lord.

A message is sent by the foreman of the jury to the Clerk of the Court, who, in turn, passes it to the Judge. Mr Justice Byrne raises a hand to 'pray, silence'.

'Some members of the jury have asked whether they could have an indication as to the probable length of this trial. It is a reasonable inquiry. Mr Gardiner?'

'I have another thirty-six witnesses of the same character, but in view of the decrease in the amount of cross-examination, I propose to call only one further witness.'

'One.' The Judge nods, makes a note and turns to the Prosecution. 'Mr Griffith-Jones?'

He scarcely looks up. 'No further witnesses, my Lord.'

The acoustics are poor. Did the court hear right? An astonished buzz rises up. *No* further witnesses? To date, the Prosecution have called but one witness, and a dull one at that, the Detective Inspector who made the seizure of the books – by appointment – in the office of Penguins. *Where* are the mystery witnesses, the experts, the guardians of Queen and Country as promised by the press?

The buzz of surprise grows louder and angrier until Mr Justice Byrne, in a reedy, ageing voice – and with the bellowing assistance of the usher – screws down the lid on the jar of the Old Bailey.

'Good news,' Cathleen tells Mel Harding, looking up. She's on his bed, on her stomach, with her head propped up by her elbows. 'The place is dead. I've had only three people in the front office all day, and the owner's in Florida for the winter, from tomorrow.' She has read his copy of the novel almost straight through, leaning over the countertop in the office, next to the bell that says 'Ring for Service'.

She fascinates and frightens him. But Harding carries on, changing the fly-strip by the overhead light and opening the bathroom window to let out her cigarette smoke.

'You really don't smoke?' she says. 'You know, it used to be I wouldn't go out with a man who didn't smoke.' She grins at him, over a bare shoulder. 'But I've become a more tolerant person with age.'

He climbs back into bed beside her, but she doesn't pause in her monologue: 'About this novel, okay ... When Mellors is standing outside Wragby Hall on that grand drive in the darkness, *yearning* for Lady Chatterley – with Mrs Bolton, that paid companion or nurse woman, all the while, getting suspicious inside – I was so gripped I didn't even hear the mailman come into the office until he rang the bell. *That's* a good story.'

And besides, he felt cruelly his own unfinished nature. He felt his own unfinished condition of aloneness cruelly. He wanted her, to touch her, to hold her fast against him in one moment of completeness and sleep.

He got up again and went out, towards the park gates this time: then slowly along the path towards the house. It was nearly four o'clock, still clear, and cold, but no sign of dawn. He was so used to the dark, he could see well.

Slowly, slowly the great house drew him, as a magnet.

In the parking lot outside, something sets off the Dagenharts' dogs. Cathleen looks up, startled.

'It's Halloween,' he says. 'Just teenagers.' He hopes it is.

She shifts on the pillow and strokes his neck, rubbing the bristles of his day-old shave. Her touch is light, delicate, like something he last felt as a child.

'Where's your little boy?' he says.

'He spends half the week in Boston with my parents, so I can work and save up. Did you see the pumpkin I carved for the office steps?'

'The self-portrait?'

She sits up, pulls out her pillow and smacks him. Her breasts rise over the bedspread, white, heavy blooms, rosy-nippled. One is slightly larger than the other. Her veins run blue. He has never lain next to such softness.

She doesn't ask why he never married, why he isn't from anywhere, why he's working in his forties in someone else's family business as the Cape battens down for winter. He considered telling her about the Bureau. But why burden her with all that ... darkness, just to sound like someone who matters – like someone who used to matter?

He still doesn't know what, if anything, he'll do with the black-and-white shot of Hoover and Tolson. Their relationship is none of his business. He tries to be objective when he thinks about it; tries to forget who is involved – to remove from the question his fear and loathing of Hoover.

Love is love. That's what he thinks. Who is he to tell people who to be with? Not everyone can be a round peg in a round hole. He understands that better than most. If people *could* fit in, they would, wouldn't they – if only for an easy life? Who wants to risk jail? Besides, you only had to be a trainee agent steaming open mail in the G.P.O. post-room to know that very few lives were straight out of the American Dream.

All he wants is to be rid of the Bureau – and yet, that picture plays on his mind. Because, no matter how clear-thinking he tries to be, he can't erase from his thoughts the knowledge – the fact – that it's the Director in the picture. No one has persecuted more so-called 'sexual deviants' than Hoover himself. Thousands of people have lost their jobs, thanks to his reign of terror, and the net is widening still. All because the Director loves Clyde Tolson and wants to purge himself of the shame he doesn't know how not to carry.

As for him and his past, it isn't that Cathleen isn't curious about the man beside her in bed. Everything about her is curious, awake, vibrant, alert. Yet she seems happy to simply be in the moment; happy, too, to volunteer her own history to fill in the gaps and uneasy silences of his.

At first, he thought it was some sort of desperation in her to please – or just desperation. He'd been looking at people suspiciously for so long, with his own narrowing lens on the world, that at first, he couldn't see it for what it was: generosity, a reckless abundance of it. She had a way of pretending she was the damaged one – the 'fallen woman', the Misfit, the 'fall guy' of her own jokes – to keep him, Mel Harding, from feeling as broken as they both knew he was.

Beside him now, she touches the eczema-damaged skin of his arm, the stripped patches of white scarring that run the length of it. On his chest, there is a new flare-up, red with dozens of tiny sores. 'Is it sensitive?' she says.

The sensation of nakedness with someone – of being out of his long sleeves, out from under cover – is hard. It took him a while just to take off his shirt. 'It's darned ugly, I know. Forget about it, okay?'

She yawns. 'Forget about what?' Then she turns to the night-table, reaches for the hardback, and opens to the bookmarked page.

'What are you doing?'

'We're on the same page now. I told you: I caught up. Clever old me.' She starts reading, from Mellors's letter to Connie at the end of the novel, as the two lovers wait, separated – him on a farm and her pregnant at her sister's – until they can leave for Canada.

'*I like farming all right. It's not inspiring, but then I don't ask to be inspired.*' Her voice is husky as she reads in the voice of Mellors. She makes it go stark somehow, hard but vulnerable. He wonders how she does it.

'*I'm used to horses, and cows, though they are very female, have a soothing effect on me. When I sit with my head in her side, milking, I feel solaced. They have six rather fine Herefords. Oat-harvest is just over – and I enjoyed it, in spite of sore hands—*'

Outside, in the motel parking lot, the four dogs start up again, louder and more frantic.

'Keep reading,' he says, as he climbs out of bed. 'I'm listening.'

At the side of the window, he draws back the edge of the curtain to look. 'Only a skunk,' he tells her. 'Keep going. You're a great reader.' She is, but there is no skunk. At the sink on the wall, he fills a Dixie cup and gulps. He drums his fingers on the hot-plate. He doesn't return to bed, but stands, apart from her, wanting to be apart, to stop the need of her, to teach his brain to remember that people leave and don't come back.

She is still reading Mellors's letter, resting on her stomach, her legs bent at the knees, her feet in the air. Her voice is resonant as she reads, magnetic. It draws him to her like a spell, although he makes himself stay put, watching by the window.

Mellors, still, to Connie. *'That's why I don't like to start thinking of you actually. It only tortures me, and does you no good. I don't want you to be away from me. But if I start fretting, it wastes something. Patience, always patience. This is my fortieth winter. And I can't help all the winters that have been. But this winter I'll stick to my little pentecost flame, and have some peace. And I won't let the breath of people blow it out. I believe in a higher mystery, that doesn't even let the crocus be blown out.*

'God, I love that line,' she says, rolling onto her back. Then she turns to him, her waist twisting, her ribs lifting, her hand pulling her dark hair away from her face, and her mismatched eyes glinting in the light of the bedside lamp. 'It's not like it usually is in books, is it? No one ever says it, but he – this D. H. Lawrence – he does.'

'Says what?'

'That love's a lonely thing – not just the missing or the waiting for someone, or not only that, but love itself. It's beautiful but windshot, like that trembling crocus flower.'

The tap drips in the bathroom. The sheet slides from the rise of her hip.

When he explodes within her, he gives it up, the shame: the shame of his thin skin and red, raw body; the shame of the secret things he knows about good people, and the dark things he's hidden for the rest; the shame of being someone his own father didn't want; some-one who felt, not touched by his aging mother's love, but nauseated by her aging, clinging loneliness, a loneliness that reminded him too much of his own.

Longing gives way within him, reverberating through his body like a slingshot, and he gives up, too, the shame of being the man who betrayed nice, shy Mrs. Kennedy for a ticket out of Butte and its dead-end emptiness.

He gives up the fear of never having been enough, of existing and not living; of not living like other men. He lets go of the failures of having looked for love through peepholes; of having looked for life through lenses, always at a remove from life itself. Of having hidden whenever possible behind the orders of other men; of having hemmed his life into the narrow space of a cheap motel room in a backwater of a place.

In these incandescent moments, by the light of a mean lamp, with the all of Cathleen pressed to him, soft, alive and wanting, he simply *is he is he is he is*, and there is peace at last.

But – *what?* – she's rising from his chest and shaking his shoulder, her voice low and urgent. 'Mel, wake up. Mel, there's someone outside.' Lights through the thin curtains catch her across her face and she raises her arm to her eyes.

He opens his eyes; sits up, rigid. She's reaching for her dress and pulling it over her head, as if someone is about to break down the door. 'You in some kind of trouble with the police.' She says it flatly, as a statement, not a question. But it's not an accusation either. She's frightened.

The strobing brightness comes again and again, like searchlights slashing the dark.

Harding stumbles into his trousers, gets to the window, and looks, his hands pressed to the pane.

Gone. They're gone. 'It's not the police,' he says.

'Are you sure?'

He opens the curtains to show her and steps back. 'Not the police.'

He unlocks the door and the storm-door, and steps outside onto the low porch that borders the parking lot. In the Dagenharts' station wagon, the dogs are going wild.

Whoever it is will still be watching him, from some vantage point, before they drive back to their own accommodation, or maybe back to Boston while the roads are still quiet.

Cathleen is at the door, on the threshold, just behind him. 'Who then?'

'It's cold out here,' he says. 'It's nothing. Some Halloween prank.' He can see his breath on the air, fast and shallow. What if they've seen her?

There's no 'what if' about it. The bastards. They'll know who she is and where her family lives by the time they file their end-of-day reports tomorrow.

She hugs herself against the night. 'It's two in the morning, for God's sake, Mel. That was no prank.'

They go back inside. She crawls into bed in her dress, her skin goose-pimpled under the covers as he holds her. The dogs don't settle. They bark for hours: banging up against the car windows, smelling something through the cracks, baying for blood.

On Irving Avenue, Jacqueline Kennedy is seated at her desk which, in her final trimester, has become increasingly difficult to reach. Although she has been assured that all is well, she remains fretful. She doesn't know why. It's a boy, she senses — just a feeling, but it's strong.

She hasn't told Jack. Best not raise his hopes. One of each. Caroline and a son. It's all he's ever wanted.

Well, not all.

Never all.

She shakes herself and concentrates on her letter to Lionel.

October 31st, 1960
Hyannis Port

Dear Professor Jack,

It does still make me smile to call you that. Jacks and I seem naturally to go together.

Bad news out of London, I'm afraid. The reports I managed to get off the wire this evening said it didn't go well for Allen Lane on the witness stand today. Also, Kingsley Amis failed to turn up. That must have been a blow. Perhaps I'm merely feeling gloomy — the time of year — but now I wonder whether Lady Chatterley will walk free. The Defense have one more witness to call. I so hope poor Allen Lane doesn't land in prison.

Yours, in hope,
Jacqueline

She addresses the envelope, Maud appears at the door, and she looks up: 'Ah, yes! Bath-time!'

'I'm afraid she's still covered in green paint, Mrs. Kennedy. I don't mind bathing her if it's—'

She stands, smiles, and rubs the small of her back. 'Thank you, Maud. I'll manage.'

Caroline is growing fast — she'll be three next month. She was a happy wicked witch for the children's party. Jackie had *suggested* she dress up as 'Madeline', the little Parisian schoolgirl from her favorite storybook, but Caroline insisted on a witch's hat and cape. She wanted a magic wand. Who didn't? Mrs. Clyde ran up her cape on her Singer, and Jackie made the pointy hat and wand.

It is a moment before Jackie realizes that Maud has something in her hand, something that, judging by her face, looks like bad news. 'I picked these up today from Whelan's, Mrs. Kennedy.' She hesitates. 'A young girl served me. But I *did* glimpse Mr. Harding through the service window in the processing room. He's still in Hyannis, I'm afraid. He saw me too. He handed out the pictures to the clerk. He even nodded to me.'

'Thank you, Maud. That's very helpful,' and she takes the envelope of photos and stuffs them in her desk. She doesn't know why she doesn't want to see. Perhaps it's the thought of Mel Harding's finger-prints all over her life. Again.

Jack arrives home late that evening from another 'Kitchen Cabinet' meeting across the lawn at the Big House. She is reading – it's only ten – but he goes straight to bed. He hasn't touched her for most of the year. Her body is either sacred or taboo when she's pregnant. She forgets which. Either way, she's off-limits. Plus, her father-in-law reminds him often enough: she's fragile.

She takes deep baths and rubs rich emollients into her touch-starved skin.

Mrs. Clyde has packed her husband's bags, as she has ever since his boyhood. Tomorrow, with just a week to Election Day, Jack will begin a seventeen-state tour.

Only later, as Jackie climbs into bed beside his softly rumbling bulk, does she switch on the low bedside lamp and break the seal of the Whelan's photo envelope. She'll glance through the Labor Day pictures before sleep, for the happy little faces – for the semblance of warm company – then she'll put out the light.

But the image on top, she can see right away, is black-and-white, and much larger than an ordinary snap. She eases out the print and stares.

It's not the Labor Day children's party in the sun-room of the Big House.

There's no note of explanation with it.

Nor does she need one.

It's a protective amulet.

From Mel Harding.

She glances at Jack, sleeping soundly, and she stares again at the glossy print, mesmerized by the two clasped hands on the tabletop; by the way the fingers – on the one hand, short and blunt; on the other, long and refined with a ring – close round each other like a completed circuit. Like two chambers of a heart.

She holds the shot closer to the lamp-light.

Whatever else is rushing through her mind – triumph at last over Hoover – envy of him – gratitude to Mel Harding – there's no mistaking what it is: love doesn't lie.

In the alleyway opposite the Old Bailey, the Magpie & Stump is packed at the lunchtime adjournment. Here, during any trial, the Old Bailey's lawyers and functionaries share the saloon bar with the whizzers, jigglers and firecrackers of the East End – the pickpockets, lock-picks and safecrackers to you and me – individuals they might well, on some future occasion, either defend or put away.

Today, the Queen's English and Cockney jostle for position at the bar. Journalists dash off court reports in the lavatory stalls, while those who can pay for the privilege congregate at private tables upstairs. In a bygone era, these were the diners who wanted a clear view of the executions across the road at Newgate Prison. These days, with the old gaol demolished, they are 'gov'nors' and 'geezers' in search of low lighting, rolls of snout, and a gander at the latest 'April fool', wrapped in chamois leather, with the safety in place.

The entire pub is carpeted in a mucky-brown weave which masks spillages and the ubiquitous soot that comes in on shoes. The carpet, if rancid, is an improvement on the sawdust from the days before the last war. It's a proud establishment. The old panelling is dark, the windows are leaded, and the winged benches are famously uncomfortable. The atmosphere is one of cheerful resignation in the face of life's trials.

A spirit of goodwill pervades the fug of smoke, ale and cheap perfume. Traditionally, the publican always sent a final pint over the road on Execution Day. A forgiving outlook – or blind eye turned – remains the tradition on which the clientele still rely.

On the afternoon of the 31st of October, Day Four of the trial, and the final day of the witness parade, Dina and Nick have managed to get a corner table, with a good view of all the comings-and-goings. Last week, Mr Rubinstein asked her to make sure she was in the Great Hall by two o'clock sharp. He wasn't able to say exactly what time she would be called – it might be a long wait – but she was not to worry on any account. She only had to tell the court what she had told him. Mr Hutchinson – who was jolly nice, he assured her – would help her to say what she wanted to say when she took the stand.

Now, at the table, her walk-on part is finally becoming real. What if she makes a hash of it? Every other witness has been a true expert.

She is only a graduate. She hopes what she is wearing is all right: a long grey jumper and a red-and-black woollen skirt. Nick tells her she looks both 'bookish and lovely', and she relaxes a little. 'Perhaps,' he says, squeezing her hand, 'you'll be spotted by a literary agent who will snap up your novel!'

'I've not written even half of it yet,' she says, 'and it might all be nonsense.'

'*That's* nonsense. Now,' he says, springing to his feet, 'a shandy? Rations?'

'Just a soda and lemon. I have to keep my wits about me. But I am hungry: sausage-and-mash for me, please.'

She is relieved he's come up from Cambridge, to offer moral support, although she said he really didn't have to. He's missing his Monday lectures for her, and there wasn't even one spare ticket for him for the afternoon session in court. 'Don't fret,' he said to her on the Tube. 'I'm Nobody, and Grossmiths' *The Diary of* has come with me.' He taps his paperback. 'I'll stay in the pub and read. I'll be there whenever you emerge. I'm not going anywhere.'

At the bar, he competes with many others for the barmaid's attention. He's rather out of his depth, Dina can see, a country boy from somewhere on the Norfolk fens, which seemed to her, when they visited his parents, marshy and less comforting than the solid green Downs of her childhood.

A copy of *LIFE* magazine lies on the bench beside her. It's a couple of weeks old and marked with glass rings. But she leafs through it, to distract herself from thoughts of the witness box, and arrives at the centre spread: 'New York to Washington: On the Campaign Trail with John F. Kennedy'. John and Jackie Kennedy are perched aloft an open-top car in New York City. They're riding on the top of the back seat.

Yonder come the train, she coming down the line ... Blowing every station—

A blizzard of ticker-tape drifts down on them from offices which go up, up and up, out of the frame of the shot. They look like they're having the best time ever. When she was a child living with her Granny Madeline in Greatham, her Aunt Mary (actually her mother's older cousin) taught her some foot-tapping old song, an American ballad about a president whose name Dina couldn't remember. She has never been much good at remembering songs or jokes, but she *does* have a good memory for learning poetry by heart.

Surely Mr Kennedy has to win. He and Mrs Kennedy look so dreamy as a pair, and doesn't the world deserve youth and freshness at last, to blow out all the grey old cobwebs and brokenness of the war? Mrs Kennedy is only thirty or so. In the picture, she's wearing an ivory maternity coat with big buttons, a matching hat against her pretty dark hair, and three-quarter-length white gloves.   *It's hard times, it's hard times*   She looks *effortless*.

Look-it here, you rascal, you see what you've done
You shot my hus—

Nick returns with the drinks, and toasts both her and their day's adventure 'in the Smoke'. He's wearing a green tweed jacket, a tie and a pair of brown polished brogues. She lowers her voice and says he really must stop calling London the 'Smoke', especially here, in the Magpie, or he might get taken out back and dusted up. She reminds him that he doesn't get out of Cambridge or his box-room at the library *that* often. She, on the other hand, has grown up in London. She knows it intimately, and if it is foggy and besmirched, it is also thrillingly real.

'Does Bayswater really equip you for the East End?' he asks, his brow quizzical. Under the table, he runs a hand over her left leg and leans towards her ear: 'Fuck, you're sexy.' She presses his hand between her skirted thighs, and he surreptitiously reaches up under her jumper and strokes her warm flank. It's a year since they first met, and electricity still fizzes.

'You might get your picture in the paper,' he says.

'Don't be silly. I'm the *least* starry of the witnesses. I only hope that that Mr Griffith-Jones doesn't make mince of me.'

'When they see you, the photographers won't be able to help themselves. I expect your granny will cut out your picture, frame it, and hang it on the wall at Winborn's for ever.'

'She's old, Nick. Not daft.' But she smiles. She'll be fine, she tells herself, once it's all in motion. The waiting is the worst bit.

She reaches into her skirt pocket and produces a curled-up hand, magic-trick style.

'What is it?' he says.

She opens her fingers. 'My lucky charm. I found it in Shed Hall. My grandmother said it's an eye-stone. It's ancient.' She places it over her eye and peers through.

'I spy ...' he begins.

'With my third eye ...' she says.

'Something beginning with ...'

'H! Look, there's Mr Hutchinson at the bar. I recognise him from the papers. And how sweet! He's forgotten to take off his wig!'

'Who's that he's speaking to?'

The woman is in her seventies, and tall, with her hair loose across her shoulders. It's mostly silver, but it might have once been chestnut, Dina thinks – it still glints with hints of copper under the lamps at either side of the bar.

She has soft features, good cheekbones still, and deep-set, intelligent eyes. She's wearing a grey cashmere cardigan over a matching cashmere dress; understated, elegant garments, but sensuous. One almost wants to reach out and touch her. At her breast is a delicate gold chain with a small crucifix pendant. A handbag and an old Burberry coat hang over one arm. An ivory-coloured headscarf trails from the sleeve. She's upright, with a still-womanly form, though she leans on a cane.

'Do you recognise her?' Nick says.

'Not at all.'

'She's *Someone*,' he says, 'because *that* was just an admission ticket Mr Hutchinson passed her.'

From a bench along the rear wall, a solicitous, middle-aged woman stands and waves to catch the attention of Mr Hutchinson's interlocutor. 'Rosalind! Ros, I found a seat! Over here.'

Dina peers again through her stone monocle. 'She looks ... warm.'

'Takes one to know one.' Nick kisses the top of her head and goes off in search of the gents.

Rosalind, Ros, she thinks. Rosalind, Ros ...

He feels a rush to the head, a wind knocking at his soul.

'Mr Meynell, may I present,' says Joan, 'my sister, Mrs Rosalind Baynes.'

'How do you do?' says Mrs Baynes to the crowd of Meynells and friends.

Rosalind. Ros. Rose ... Thorn ... Rose ... and, as if in reverse, through the eye-stone, the sight of a Lawrence poem loops back through time to her, from the English Tripos exam question of the previous year.

She did quite well on it, apparently. She read the poem twice before composing her essay. Lawrence had written the poem – she remembered in the exam room – in 1920, during a short stay in a village called San Gervasio, a village on a hillside which over-looked Florence. That would have been about five years after he left the Colony and Sussex, escaping England when borders opened again after the First World War. It was about five years, too, after he published the story about Granny Madeline and Grandfather Percy.

The location, 'San Gervasio', she recalls, was noted by Lawrence at the bottom of each poem in the series. She can see it now, in her memory of the layout of the page. He'd lived alone there for a time – in a borrowed house, without windowpanes, although she couldn't remember why.

His letters of that year show he was writing to his wife, Frieda, and resisting her appeals to join her and her family in Baden-Baden. This was, Dina noted in her exam essay – to identify a sense of context – six years before he would begin to write *Lady Chatterley's Lover*, in '26, on another hill on the *opposite* side of Florence, and less than ten years before he died in France.

In her essay's introduction, she enthusiastically highlighted the erotically-charged fruit and 'rose' imagery of his lush San Gervasio sequence. In his deployment of the rose motif, the poet had, she argued, not merely drawn upon the traditional conceit in which the beloved woman is compared to a rose; he had reinvented it.

Lawrence's 'universe of the unfolded rose' was not merely a mechanical nod to a poetic tradition; nor was it purely an engage-ment with the mystic tradition of the rose, such as we find in the Song of Solomon in the Bible, or in the rose windows of the great Catholic cathedrals of the Gothic period. It was a vital dynamic – she had underlined 'dynamic' on her ruled exam paper – an active, 'on-the-pulse' expression of the narrator's longing – the narrator's, or perhaps *even* the poet's himself.

The summoning of the rose to the page was an invocation of a living, 'unfolding' beloved, not one fixed or pinned in memory.

'Here's to the thorn in the flower! Here is to Utterance!'

But why the thorn? she asked. Might it be phallic? One could be forgiven for thinking so, given this was D. H. Lawrence, and the phallus was central to his principles of 'the life-force' and 'blood-consciousness'. But the thorn, she pointed out, belonged to and was intrinsic *to the rose* − to the beloved − *not* to the admiring narrator.

Because her tutor had warned her: avoid claiming everything in Lawrence is 'phallic'. It was a line almost every undergraduate trotted out, and it flattened textual analyses into low grades.

In the exam hall, she carried on writing, as if in a dream. Was the 'Utterance' − with which that thorn was elided − the gift of expression itself; namely, the life-giving power of breath, the word, the Word, and the Naming of Creation − all in one? Was the power of that Utterance necessarily bound up in risk, in the *wound* − holy and corporeal − of the thorn, and the intrinsic *vulnerability* of the experience of love?

In reality, she had *no idea* why Lawrence had given the thorn such significance, but in a close reading, she could not afford to skip past such a detail. She had done her best. *'Here's to the thorn in the flower! Here is to Utterance! /* The brave, adventurous rosaceae. / Folded upon itself, and secret unutterable ...'

Having tried her best to make the case for the centrality of the rose imagery in Lawrence's 'San Gervasio' poetry sequence, and having related the intense sensuality of the fruit and the flower motifs (not to mention the mating tortoises!) to Lawrence's evocation of sacred-sexual mystery, she went on to write fulsomely on the poem itself.

Now, in the Magpie & Stump, she can see the poem again, line upon line, as if she is reading it off the exam page once more:

So many fruits come from roses
From the rose of all roses
From the unfolded rose
Rose of all the world.

Admit that apples and strawberries and peaches and pears
*   and blackberries*
Are all Rosaceae,

Issue of the explicit rose,
The open-countenanced, skyward-smiling rose.

What then of the vine?
Oh, what of the tendrilled vine?

Ours is the universe of the unfolded rose,
The explicit,
The candid revelation.

Nick returns and drops cutlery on the table. Dina blinks, loses the remaining stanzas and looks up. He grips a cigarette between his lips and smiles down. She realises only now that she is still holding the eye-stone to her face.

She feels dumbfounded somehow, as if the answer to a question she never knew has just slipped back, like a jumping fish, into the invisible well of the stone.

Her sausage-and-mash arrives, and Nick tells the barmaid who serves them that he is very much enjoying his day out in 'the Smoke', and that his girlfriend is going to be a literary sensation 'from today hence'.

The barmaid assesses them with a cool eye, shifting her head back on her shoulders. 'Right-o, ducks.'

Dina and Nick stare as they eat. Mr Hutchinson is escorting the elderly woman – Rosalind – across the pub floor to the bench claimed for her by her intrepid friend, or daughter perhaps. Rosalind's sight seems limited. A narrow path clears as she makes her slow progress, and some indefinable quality in her presence makes drinkers at the bar turn to watch.

Perhaps the aura of a beautiful woman outlasts her beauty, or perhaps she inspires something more than passing admiration, for she seems to carry an ageless, untouchable quality; the glow of an inner life undimmed by time. As she walks, her right hand grips her cane, and the left is closed around the pink admission ticket, like a bloom over nectar.

At her bench, she reaches up to kiss Mr Hutchinson goodbye, a peck on each cheek. He bends low to receive each, for although she is still of a good height, he is a very tall, broad-shouldered man, and he seems, there on the pub floor, to be a mighty oak sheltering her. Together, they radiate affection, the sort which gives not a jot for the differences of form, sex, height, or the gaps of generations.

Finally, the erstwhile Rosalind Thornycroft smiles and reaches up to straighten Jeremy Hutchinson's wig, and all at the bar and beyond it who watch are briefly … beguiled.

The sun blazes briefly as Ros is escorted to her seat on the floor of the court. She takes her chair and glances skyward to the dome of the Old Bailey, and for a moment, it makes her long to see the duomo again. Will she?

She never tired of it in Florence. She used to love drawing or painting it, in all weather from her hillside. She only hopes she *will* see it again; that the sight in her other eye won't go as well. She fears that, to not see the world – to no longer be able to draw it – would be an exile from which she is not sure she would recover. Every day, the smallest of details still fill her with the same joy they gave her as a child, when she used to want to *eat* the world, and her elder sister, Joan, had to chide her for always putting things in her mouth.

How kind it was of Jeremy to ensure she had a ticket. She couldn't have faced the queue for the public gallery. Not with her hip. She and his mother, Mary, had been friendly in London before the Great War and perhaps, through the filaments of those old connections, Mary's son had understood or intuited something of the reason for her unexpected request. If he had, he had been too discreet to say.

Mary Hutchinson wrote stories and essays in her youth, and, together with her husband – Jeremy's barrister father, Jack – they threw some of the most sparkling parties, both in London and at their house in the South Downs, before the War. Ros had met her through their mutual friend David Garnett, and had warmed to her immediately. They lost touch with one another only after the War, when she herself had escaped to Italy, at the time of her divorce, at Lawrence's suggestion.

She and Mary had once shared a great love of lace, needlework, fabrics, cushions and interior design, something generally thought, in both their circles, to be undeserving of genuine conversation. Indeed, some people had claimed Mary's great love of fashion and surfaces made her frivolous, but Ros had understood. It was a love of the beauty of the fleeting – of colour, line, texture and light – a deep appreciation for the surfaces of life and all their ephemeral joys. Mary had even posed twice for Matisse, a man who had loved surfaces, designs and fabrics as much as Mary herself.

Seated in her row, Rosalind reaches into her handbag for her specs – not that they actually correct her bad eye, but they make the other a little better. The ophthalmologist was honest with her, as she had asked him to be. Painting and drawing are already difficult, and sewing, or the fine work at least, is almost impossible. As the barristers, including Jeremy, take up their positions, she tests the strength of her good left eye, holding a hand over her right to see if she can make out individual faces in the public gallery above. She can, if indistinctly. When she reverses the exercise, she sees only blancmange – until, that is, she turns to the great vessel of the dock and a voltage surges through her.

He is pale and gaunt in his old corduroy jacket.

It seems to wear him, rather than the reverse, and he looks older than his forty-four years.

But he stands upright. His red beard flickers. He wears a sprig of a wildflower in his button-hole, and his blue eyes flare when they meet hers.

How is it possible? She feels again the strength, the pull, the light of him.

So many fruits come from roses
From the rose of all roses
From the unfolded rose
Rose of all the world.

She hasn't been so close to him in forty years, not since the morning he walked back down the hill, away from her.

Then Mr Justice Byrne enters the court, and Ros struggles to her feet, grappling for her cane.

'My Lord,' begins Jeremy Hutchinson, 'the Defence calls its final witness.'

'Miss Bernardine Wall!' shouts the usher.

Rosalind can make out the figure of a girl crossing the floor of the court. Tallish – graceful and athletic in form – with dark hair cut in what was once called a Joan of Arc style.

Jeremy Hutchinson (merrily): Miss Wall, would you please introduce yourself to the court?

Dina (gripping the eye-stone in her pocket): My name is Bernardine Anna-Livia Wall. I can confirm for the court that I live in London and am twenty-one years old. I am a Roman Catholic by birth, my family being all Roman Catholics, and also by conviction. I was educated at the Convent of Our Lady of Sion, Bayswater, and my Catholic outlook was strengthened by the education and surroundings there. I continued my education at Newnham College, Cambridge, and graduated with an Honours degree in English in June 1960.

She was well rehearsed by Michael Rubinstein, but only now does she wonder if she was supposed to say so much all at once.

Under the lens of the court, Dina seems to present an intriguing fusion of the exotic and the chaste.

She is a surprising choice of witness, Ros remarks to herself, not only for her youth but in that she is a practising Catholic. A coup, clearly, for the Defence. It is assumed, in the stereotyping of the times, that Catholics can only disapprove of *Lady Chatterley*. Yet, her own belief in the goodness of the body and the power of images were the principal reasons she converted to Catholicism. It was the influence of Florence. Plus, she had always loved her childhood copy of Raphael's *Alba Madonna*.

And Lawrence. He had opened windows within her.

Jeremy Hutchinson: Miss Wall, since you came down from Cambridge, have you started to write your first novel?

Dina: Yes.

Jeremy Hutchinson: Have you also assisted in editing the November issue of *The Twentieth Century*, which is devoted, is it not, to the writings of those under twenty-five?

Dina: Yes, that is right.

Jeremy Hutchinson: Have you contributed an article to that issue?

Dina: I have.

Jeremy Hutchinson (smiling his thanks): Now then, in your studies at Cambridge, did you have to read the works of D. H. Lawrence?

Dina: I did. I started reading Lawrence's works when I went up to Cambridge and studied him for Part I of the Tripos. I also selected his novels and poetry for my specialism in my final year. I can confirm for the court I was then twenty years old. I am now twenty-one.

Her brain clings to her script as she rehearsed it, but – how stupid she feels! – she has already given her age.

Jeremy Hutchinson: Did your reading include *Lady Chatterley's Lover*?

Dina: Yes. I read all his novels.

Jeremy Hutchinson: And when you were (he checks his notes) seventeen, did you read an expurgated version of *Lady Chatterley's Lover*? A censored edition, that is.

Dina: I did.

Jeremy Hutchinson: You now have an Honours degree in English. Will you tell us, what in your view is the literary merit of the *expurgated* version?

Dina: I think it has very little literary merit because— well, it is not the book Lawrence wrote, and it is therefore very difficult to assess it in a critical way at all.

Jeremy Hutchinson: In the expurgated version, does there appear to be any difference in the relationship between Connie and Mellors the gamekeeper, and the earlier unsuccessful relationships described or experienced by either of them?

Dina: No. *All* the relationships seem to be merely trivial and promiscuous.

Jeremy Hutchinson: About a year ago, did you read the full, unexpurgated version, as Lawrence wrote it?

Dina: I did. A friend lent me a copy – obtained in America – and I have read it once since. (In truth, she also read the uncensored novel *before* the American copy, thanks to Nick and the Arc Collection. But the chronology is not what matters here, she assures herself.)

Jeremy Hutchinson: What was your opinion of the literary merit of the unexpurgated novel, compared with the expurgated?

Dina: The unexpurgated version gave the balance of all the elements, because it showed there was, in the love affair of Lady Chatterley and Oliver Mellors, the contrast with the deadness of industrial civilisation. Lawrence was presenting a new hope that there was some way out of what he saw as the drab, numbed daily existence forced upon his generation. I believe that is why the novel opens with the sentence, 'Ours is essentially a tragic age, so we refuse to take it tragically.' He says to the reader, 'we are among the ruins … there is now no smooth road into the future'. The novel as he wrote it held out hope that this state of affairs wasn't all; that there was some way out of the drab and dead existence he describes.

Jeremy Hutchinson: It has been suggested that it encourages promiscuity. What is your view of that?

Dina: I think it is completely untrue.

On the Judge's bench, Lady Byrne tuts conspicuously into her bosom.

Dina: It does precisely the opposite. Connie and Michaelis's affair, early on in the novel, is most unsatisfactory, but her affair with Mellors is a serious, responsible affair, even if it is not within wedlock. The influence of the book, in unexpurgated form, on me, and on my many friends with whom I discussed it at the time, was to turn our thought entirely against experimental sexual relations and in favour of a settled and lifelong one …

Jeremy Hutchinson: As far as the four-letter words are concerned, had you known them when you read the book?

Dina: Yes, I knew them all by that time. I heard them all, I should say, between the ages of five and fourteen.

Mr Griffith-Jones (standing): With respect to my learned friend, does this go to the *literary* merit of the book, my Lord?

Mr Justice Byrne: I am not quite sure …

Mr Griffith-Jones: While I am on my feet, may I say that this witness is tendered as an *expert* on literary merit. She has a First Class Honours degree, and that appears to be her only qualification.

Dina (smiling shyly): Not a First, I'm afraid.

The court is charmed.

Mr Griffith-Jones: Does that mean that anybody with an Honours degree is qualified to speak as an expert?

Mr Justice Byrne (smiling benignly for the first time): She *has* started to write a novel.

Even Lady Byrne's features soften.

Mr Griffith-Jones (reading the mood of the room): Well, I suppose we *have* all got to start.

Ros leans forward to peer. Ah-ha! Here is the man she teased.

14 Melbury Road
London W14
8th September, 1960

Dear Sir,

I understand that you might be requiring witnesses in the forthcoming case Crown v. Penguin Books Ltd. I place myself at your disposal.

Yours faithfully,
Constance Chatterley

The address is a bomb-site: a once lovely gabled house in Kensington, down the road from her father's former studio in the house which was still in her family. She had needed only a non-address to use. Even at her advanced age, she enjoyed the little prank at the expense of the Prosecution Counsel. It had amused her no end.

Jeremy Hutchinson (resuming): From the point of view of literary merit, Miss Wall, how does this book compare with any other books you have read or studied in its handling of human relations, including sexual relations?

In this moment, everyone privately contemplates questions of greater interest: is Miss Wall still a virgin? Does she have any experience with which to judge the sexual relations? Does she have a lover?

She intrigues the assembly, with her wide, bright eyes, her generously sculpted face and her full bottom lip.

Tabloid reporters start digging. Once again, a few dash for the nearest phone-box.

She lingers over the last question, her face pensive, her mind a blank. She cannot think what else she has read, or how to make a comparison. Mr Hutchinson's patient examination suddenly seems like an oral exam, a *viva voce* she must not fail, but will. She feels herself go rigid. In her pocket, her fingers turn her touchstone. She wishes she could look out past all the heads and see Nick's face.

Dina (eyes straining): Well … *Lady Chatterley's Lover*, the unexpurgated version, treated the human relationship with … great dignity. The relationship between Lady Chatterley and Oliver Mellors was, I believe, a … very, very serious, important and valuable one, which I think I have rarely read in any other novel. The story of Lady Chatterley gave hope of a less cramped and sordid mode of existence, from a full, and fully developed, description of a human relationship. This I found (she blushes) … deeply moving.

Mr Hutchinson nods kindly to her. 'Thank you, Miss Wall.' Does that mean she has said enough or that he thinks it best to stop her from saying more? She spoke much more intelligently when she gave her statement to Mr Rubinstein.

Only after she stops speaking does she realise that she failed to answer Mr Hutchinson's final question. He asked her to compare the unexpurgated story with other books she has read or studied. She didn't mention any. Not one.

Will the Prosecution have a go at her? They confer in their chairs. It's said Mr Griffith-Jones can be frightening. He humiliates people.

She looks over the well of the court, past the heads of Sir Allen Lane and Mr Rubinstein, her father's friend, and past the rows of wigs. Everyone is staring. It's rather terrifying. Among them, she spots the woman – Rosalind – from the pub. She has her ivory head-scarf and seems to be dabbing her face. She is either hot or tearful. But which and why?

There is no time to wonder because there are no further questions, says Mr Griffith-Jones – *thank God!* – the Judge is telling her she may now step down – and though she doesn't know it, though the minutes she's spent on the stand have felt like hours, time does not hold – it splits, frays and unravels until—

.0291, htoı eht rebmetpeS
September the 10th, 1920.
,sehcrot sa thgirb, smuinareg eht gnomA
Among the geraniums, bright as torches,
,edis yb edis tis yeht
they sit side by side,
hcuoc eekrooR s'ynoclab eht no
on the balcony's Roorkee couch
.eredevleB onilliV eht ta
at the Villino Belvedere.
,thgin eht otni erats yehT
They stare into the night,
,sdlofnu ehs dna
and she unfolds,
the rose of herself,
leaf by leaf,
Sepal by sepal. Petal by petal.
Pistil. Stigma. Stamen.

xxi

The unfolding.

She tells him that ... when she was small, her father called her 'Rosebud'.

In the hour she was born, new and furled, he measured her length and breadth. He recorded the circumference of her head, and the position of her ears in relation to her crown. He was a sculptor, and these truths carried more meaning in his heart than the weight recorded by the midwife on the kitchen scales.

She tells him that, when she was a child, they lived in Surrey on a half-acre estate by a sandy heath, a murky green canal and a little wood which formed the geography of her dreams for years and years.

The heath seemed to stretch away into infinity, and was populated with firs, oak and white birch coppices. In the autumn, the purple of the heather was like a sea as she ran and rolled. Its purple made her want to draw and paint, and she did endlessly, because she and her sister Joan had a governess, whom they always outran.

Unlike other girls they knew, they wore Liberty smocks and Natureform shoes. They used to run from poor Miss Henderson into the wood or up to the heath, where they'd hide in the heather or climb a tree.

Sometimes, during hot summers, fires swept the heath. Then she and Joan and her brother Oliver would watch from the nursery as their father and neighbours went out to beat back the flames before they could reach the houses. Entire trees would burst into sheets of fire, just like Harriet the little girl in the Penny Dreadful who plays with matches and goes up in flames until she is only a pile of smoking ashes next to a singed tree.

She used to adore the pictures in that story.

Slowly, the lights go out over Florence, but his arms, his chest, are warm.

As girls, she tells him, they weren't allowed fashionable dresses and hair-styles – 'how I wanted ringlets!' Their hair hung loose and natural. 'But Mother did used to make us the most wonderful costumes for special occasions. I envied Joan her Lady Jane Grey gown terribly.'

She tells him her parents had many lovely parties and, as children, on still summer nights, they'd fall asleep to the clacking of croquet balls on the lawn and the sounds of adult voices and laughter. A neighbour on the heath, a female composer, would always be the last to arrive, in dinner-dress on her bicycle, and Ros would strain to stay awake to listen to her sing Brahms and Schubert on the terrace below the nursery window.

'My mother would be beautiful in a silk dress, with her hair held up with such mystery I couldn't fathom it. She wore a touch of boracic powder on her nose and cheeks, and had lovely straight white teeth. On special occasions, her ear-rings and pendants emerged, glittering, from velvet boxes, an expensive cook was hired, and we were not allowed anywhere near the kitchen.

'But my mother was entirely without airs. I remember watching her, in her best Henrietta Maria dress, as she taught Thomas Hardy – who was then nearly sixty! – to ride our neighbour's bicycle in the road outside our house, while all our other guests launched into charades in the garden. The game was specifically organised by Father as a form of cover for Mr Hardy's lesson. And Mother did teach him too! Mr Hardy wobbled along our road while I clapped and shouted encouragement.

'My first real glimpse of my father as a person in his own right was when we all went down with a bug and he, feverish himself, went about in his nightshirt and smoking-jacket, looking after us with hot drinks, cold face-flannels and steam kettles. To teach us astronomy, he set up a miniature solar system of balls, of various colours and sizes, spinning in their orbits on the breeze. He suspended hammocks among the trees where we could daydream and read. It seems to me that my father, his sculpture aside, had more talents than any one man had a right to. He could fell a tree, lay a hedge, puddle a pond, make a haystack, remove a wasps' nest, handle a scythe and skin a rabbit.

'Although I didn't follow him into sculpture – none of us did and that was a sadness for him – he did teach me a great deal about drawing: the seven-and-a-half heads of human proportion; how to "lose and find" a line; the convex versus the concave; how to capture an action before or after it, rather than during, and why that at times is the more powerful choice.

'He was a natty dresser, my father, even when only on his way to his studio, although once there, he'd change into his linen smock. Typically, he wore a pink silk tie run through a ring, and in the evenings, a green velvet jacket, which was splendid with his headful of auburn hair. On his train journey into the studio in the warmer months, he always filled his pockets with wildflower seeds, and would scatter them from the carriage window along the more dismal stretches of the line into London, through Kensal Rise and Willesden. To this day, I can hardly think of a lovelier thing to do for strangers.

'When I was sixteen, I was sent to a grand Surrey boarding-school – to rid me of my bumpkin ways, I expect. Mrs Burton Brown was second in command, and she was also the art mistress. She encouraged me a great deal. My best friend, Bridget Tallents, was very pretty and winsome. Although of course it was against the rules, she agreed when I asked if she would model for me. At the appointed hour, I went to her cubicle in the dormitory where, with only a little hesitation, she stripped to the waist and reclined on the bed.

'We had always had nude models, half-robed, walking about our house as we grew up, both men and women – often Italians who came especially for the work – and we thought little of it. But alas, the episode somehow reached the ears of the "very disappointed" Mrs Burton Brown, who summoned me for a walk in the woods – an unexpected break from lessons – where she told me that Bridget and I had done something "very, very dangerous indeed". She spoke at great length about two girls behaving in such a way, and I had no idea what she meant. But my drawing of Bridget was marvellous, and I hid it under my mattress till the summer hols when I smuggled it out.

'As young men and women, we attended the Fabian Nursery. H. G. Wells himself used to address us. My husband, Godwin, joined our gang after my uncle introduced him during one of our musical evenings in Hampstead. We were, all of us then, seized by the possibilities of a free and natural life, and we spent almost every weekend together, walking over the Sussex Downs. We even started taking tents and a Primus cooking stove.

'But the first time we camped out, at the top of Ashdown Forest, everything was very rugged. So Godwin and I made ourselves a bed of moss with a roof of evergreen boughs, then lay down in the darkness and listened to the yearning of the wind in the fir trees.

It was weird and magical. I can still feel the charge that hummed in the space between our bodies, and yet it wouldn't have occurred to either of us to act on it, and perhaps it would have spoiled things if we had. We were all curiously idealistic.

'Then, as I said, we had a great snowy winter, the toboggans came out, Godwin walked me home and, when faced with four feet of snow blocking the road, he simply scooped me up and carried me the half a mile to my parents' door.

'That was more or less it, I suppose, although my father never warmed to him, and I couldn't understand why. Godwin was a medical student, a talented singer, hale, hearty and admired by all. But my dear pa saw Godwin's weaknesses long before I could, although he refused to enlighten me in any detail. So I dismissed his concerns, imagining he would one day see what a good husband Godwin was. I believe it broke my dear father's heart to give me away, and I regret that now. Yet I cannot regret the marriage itself, for I have my darling girls.'

He nods. 'The three Young Graces! What's more, you are free to shape your life, to live it.'

She rests in his arms, and although he is so different in form from Godwin, she is drawn to the lithe energy of him.

No one, she thinks, has ever spoken to her so directly, so honestly. All the pretences of the world drop away as he speaks, there in the quietude of the night, on her small balcony, a ledge in the darkness.

For nearly a year, he has been offering her guidance by letter and stalwart directives from a distance. Such communication has been possible because they share a connection: Bertie Farjeon, playwright-friend to Lawrence since his Greatham days, and husband to Rosalind's sister.

By letter, Lawrence first recommended Italy to her, as a place of escape after the War and in the aftermath of her separation from her husband. He wrote to say, indeed, he might opt for Italy too; then, that he would travel ahead, and send guidance for her solo journey with Ivy the nurse and three little ones.

'If you think of starting very soon,' he wrote, 'wire me tomorrow, and I could look after you at Turin or Rome: otherwise I should write you immediately I have an address. Your luggage you can send direct. Will you take Ivy? Watch the Italian exchange and buy before it goes down. A good bank should give you 51 Lira – but ask them first. Your father or Godwin might do that for you. It is perfectly easy getting the visas at the Italian Consulate, but go pretty early in the morning. Push forward, ask the clerk if you can go inside the barrier to fill up the inquiry form. Don't forget – you want an extra photograph for each visa. D.H.L.'

Then: 'The journey to Italy is all perfectly easy – only slow slow – slow. No bother at frontiers – only rather a crush. Change a little French money on Dieppe boat in 1st Class saloon – get ready to disembark as boat draws near, and move to the passport gangway on boat – near the lower deck (1st class) cabins, in front. Seize the first porter the moment you get anywhere & make him do everything for you. They are very trustworthy & sensible. The Customs is a very slight business – so is passports – only the crowd – which is not so bad on the trains. Take three or four bags in the train with you – porters will cope with them. Also take some nice food. Any English Tommy will tell you everything you might need to know. Italy is nice – very nice indeed – lovely lovely sun & sea. I'll tell you when I have an address, in Florence, I expect. Au revoir, D.H.L.'

He himself had originally planned on America as his place of escape – and Frieda was off to family in Germany – but he changed his mind and decided on Italy again. Rosalind had been offered a house in Picinisco for her and the children. Should she take it? 'Primitive,' he said after he'd travelled to survey it on her behalf. 'Staggeringly' so.

Had he privately determined that Florence would be the setting for their encounter?

'I think you might like Florence for a couple of months – there is an English Institute, everything English you need for a start. I feel one must coast around before settling on any permanent place. Florence is a good town, the cheapest in Italy probably. I would really advise you to try it. There are a good many English people around, but one needn't know them.

'Frieda will come here, in Florence, next Wednesday. You might possibly arrive before we leave – fun it would be. You change at Pisa for Florence. At Pisa, you must wait unfortunately, till 8.30 p.m., arrive Florence 11.50 p.m. If you like, I will meet you in Pisa, if we are still in Florence. We could have a meal, look at the Cathedral, & so to Florence. If you wire, say if you will bring nurse—& for how long here. No doubt you could come at once.'

Frieda had taken to the notion of Sicily for the two of them. In any event, they couldn't afford Florence. It was not as cheap as he'd suggested to Ros, but then, she was not as penniless as he.

Rosalind arrived in San Gervasio, a village overlooking Florence, at the start of a new year and new decade, 1920.

'Frieda,' he wrote to her, 'loves it here in Taormina. Etna is a beautiful mountain, far lovelier than Vesuvius, which is a heap. We've got the house for a year. The summer here will be very hot. Will you still be in San Gervasio? Shall we plan to come and see you in the hot summer weather? We <u>must</u> meet in Italy, now we are here. I expect the babies will hold you faster here even than in England. Do you think you could manage to get to Taormina? There is room if ever you could. How is Godwin's divorce proceeding? It all seems far away and unreal doesn't it – a weariness of the flesh.'

In May of 1920: 'Cara Rosalind, are you over your flue? Was it bad? Did Joan and Bertie enjoy their Italian interlude? Joan sent word from Siena to say you might all dash south to us. Then – not a word. Why not? What are your summer plans? Where are the three Graces to frolic? We have a large garden shaded by almond trees. It will be harvest time and we can whack the branches to our heart's content. I assure you, it won't be a furnace here. The house is cool and spacious. We are high up on a steep slope – we catch the breeze off the sea. Why not come? Or shall we meet in July? Where will you spend the winter? How long is your lease on La Canovaia? We must rendezvous somewhere. Send your plans by return. *In attesa di una sua pronta risposta*, D.H.L.'

June: 'Where do you want to go for little Bridget for the sea for winter? Why not come here? I can find you a house, and Taormina is simply perfect in the winter. How much does it cost you to live in San Gervasio? It will be far less here. Are the three Young Graces well?'

July: 'Dear R., Your letter this morning – sorry you won't come here – could have found you a house, very nice. F. thinks of going to Germany second week in August or thereabouts. Where will you be? I might come & see you – I shall come north, I think, but shan't go out of Italy. Perhaps to Florence, perhaps to Venice. Give me your La Canovaia address at once – & I might meet you about end of August or September. I feel all unstuck, as if I might drift off anywhere. It isn't at all unbearably hot here, in the house. How are the unstoppable sugarplums? Write at once with your plans, post is slow. D.H.L.'

And now, the geraniums burn, Florence sleeps, she hears his voice in the darkness, and feels it resonate from his chest as she reclines in his arms: 'What's more, you are free to shape your life, to live it,' he is telling her.

'I hope so,' she says. 'Yes, that is my hope, certainly.' And yet, inwardly, how frightened she feels in that moment, as if she were poised, not on a beautiful Italian balcony, but in the grip of a hungry, roaring wind.

Her feet rest in his lap. His hands cup her ankles and are warm. They stare out at the night, both close and solitary. They listen to the melancholy pulsing of the crickets. A pair of tawny owls, male and female, call to each other – tu-whit! tu-whoo! – and he speaks again: 'I imagine you must feel something of a paradox to yourself these days.'

She turns to him, her eyes wide and wondering.

'Living as a demi-vierge,' he adds.

'A demi-vierge!' replied Connie vaguely.

'Without sex, I mean.'

Oddly, she does not mind his curiosity. It surprises her that she does not. She laughs. 'Well, I should like to have it again, naturally.'

'What's stopping you?'

'I'm not sure anything is.' She lifts the weight of her hair from her neck. 'Only one has to be discriminating.'

'Of course. One can hardly bear to share a bus seat with most people, let alone a bed.'

'Precisely. And at a certain age, one wants more than dew-drops of flattery and off-to-bed-we-go.'

'I agree: that's tawdry. Love is a force. Impersonal, to some extent; something sprung from the elemental world. What are we to it?' He pauses. 'It's up to you.'

She turns to him, and can make out only the white of his brow and the gleam of his eyes. Their lantern smokes.

Now, in the court, as the former Rosalind Thornycroft Baynes watches the girl – Miss Wall – step down from the stand and cross to the door, she sees, too, with her cloudy eye, the vision of Lawrence, still in the dock. He has taken off his jacket and stands, in his shirt-sleeves, like a working man. His eyes still burn.

The scene returns to her, not with the force of a memory, but with the direct sense of *feeling* moving through her: the sense, from that long-ago night, of life being given back after the grief and humiliation of her marriage; after what had felt like the theft of her future, when she had resigned herself to lovelessness – except as a mother – and sexlessness.

She hears him again, his words in her ear.

He is married. She still is married herself. It is said that Frieda has liaisons, often, and that Lawrence does not forbid it. Even so, it would be – it is – wrong to be with him. His wife's dalliances have nothing to do with her own conscience, and can be no excuse. She has already scandalised society with the affair she had with Kenneth, her childhood friend, at the Savoy that night, 13 October, 1917, when her husband, a medical officer, was en route to the East with the troops.

'Another man's! What other man's?'

'Perhaps Duncan Forbes. He has been our friend all his life...'

She was jubilant when she found herself so quickly pregnant. Delighted at the prospect of a third child. And relieved because not even Godwin could overlook the fact of an illegitimate child on the way. Or so she assumed.

'So don't you think you'd better divorce me and have done with me?' she said.

'No! You can go where you like, but I shan't divorce you,' he said idiotically.

He was silent, in the silence of imbecile obstinacy.

'Would you even let the child be legally yours, and your heir?' she said.

'I care nothing about the child.'

'But if it's a boy, it will be legally your son, and it will inherit your title, and have Wragby.'

'I care nothing about that.'

'But you must!— I shall prevent the child from being legally yours, if I can. I'd so much rather it were illegitimate, and mine: if it can't be Mellors'.'

'Do as you like about that.'

He was immovable.
'And you won't divorce me?' she said.

When she explained that she would not allow her husband to give her child his name, she thought he must then give in to her pleas for a divorce. His practice would fail when people learned it was led by a doctor with a scandalous wife and an illegitimate child. His own affairs scandalised few, except her dear family, but at last she had made it impossible for him *not* to initiate a divorce, not if he still wanted his living. Kenneth Hooper, she told her husband, had agreed to be named as co-respondent. She herself would prepare the evidence required for his petition to succeed in court.

All of that had seemed sensible and necessary. But could she now add another illicit love to her life?

She would never deny her history, not to anyone. Nor will she lie. She refuses to feel ashamed.

Whatever the rights and wrongs of it, there on the little balcony, joy quietly re-arranges her.

She presses a heel lightly into his thigh, and feels him harden. His hand moves blindly under her dress. His thumb is calloused, and his palm is wide. His hand climbs; he reads her with light fingertips.

Sepal, petal, pistil, stigma, stamen.

the rose of all roses from the unfolded rose.

As he presses her close, she feels his heart echo hers.

How simple everything is.

She is close, close to her crisis, to that profound giving-way, when 'I love thee,' he murmurs, his breath on her neck. It's his old voice, his native voice. 'I love thee an' th' touch on thee.'

The flashbulbs go off as Dina steps from the Old Bailey into the pall of late afternoon.

She dashes past the reporters as quickly as she can, fearing humiliation in the morning papers. She didn't sound anything like an expert. Mr Griffith-Jones was right to cast doubt on her credentials. She didn't make the case for the novel any better than any other competent reader might have, and yet *she'd* been the final witness.

Why didn't she remember to say everything she'd practised? Why, at the end, did she sound so simple-minded?

She'd let everyone down: not only the wonderful Misters Rubinstein and Hutchinson, but also poor Sir Allen Lane, who might actually go to *prison* now. Then there was the author and his novel – the novel which had half-*killed* him to write. Somehow she felt she'd even let down Lady Chatterley.

She often came undone on oral examinations. She got too keyed-up by all she *wanted* to say – and then said not enough! Or too many things that were irrelevant. No wonder she didn't get a First.

Her mother will not say so, but she will suggest that she was right to have had reservations about Dina appearing in court. Such an 'unpleasant business', and for what? To champion an author who had betrayed the family. Her father, Bernard, will feel embarrassed that she, Dina, had let down his friend Mr Rubinstein, and he will not beat about the bush in saying so.

She will escape to Greatham, she decides, where she'll hide away until the papers have done their worst. Granny Madeline will remind Dina that she tried her best. She will say it was brave of her to speak up for a good book, and for Lawrence too, whatever had happened in the past.

Weeks before, when her grandmother had overheard that Mr Rubinstein had requested Dina's support, she'd taken her granddaughter to one side and told her that she and 'Mr Lawrence' had actually got on 'rather well' during his stay in Greatham, and that, in spite of all that followed, she bore neither him, nor his memory, any ill will. Indeed, she'd said, with characteristic brightness, she continued to admire his work and to feel a fondness for him. It was the future that mattered, she said, and if Dina wanted to take part in the trial, then she must, and that was an end to it. To all of it, down the decades!

How generous her grandmother was. In fact, it had been Granny Madeline's example that had inspired her to say yes. Together, they'd hatched the plan to turn up at Mr Rubinstein's office in Gray's Inn. What an adventure it would be! Barbara had insisted on accompanying them only at the last minute, to ensure they didn't get themselves into hot water.

Dina imagines hot buttered crumpets in front of the fire at Winborn's. Perhaps they'll make jam or a fruitcake for Christmas. Her grandmother will give her a bolthole for as long as she needs it.

She darts through the fog and traffic, making a run for the Magpie & Stump. She will find Nick and confess her poor showing. He will buy her a drink and tell her he doesn't believe her and, for now, she thinks, that will be more solace than she deserves.

Across the Atlantic, the *Boston Globe* has picked up the story. 'CONVENT GIRL LIKES LADY C'. Even the *Cape Cod Times* has 'Girl, 21, Speaks Up for Lady C', another story picked up from the wire.

Jackie studies the girl in the article's photo: a full heart of a face; an ivory complexion; wide, intelligent eyes, and a shiny dark bob. She wears a touch of lipstick and a little eye make-up; a V-neck sweater and a hooded raincoat. She is both striking and unaware that she is. Her eyes glance knowingly to the photographer to her left, and yet she is wary. She withholds something. Good girl, thinks Jackie. You do that.

She glances down the column inches. 'The defense of Lady Chatterley and her gamekeeper lover finished yesterday.' Isn't it odd how often it seems that Connie and Mellors are on trial, rather than the novel? 'The final witness to defend Lawrence's controversial story was 21-year-old Bernardine Wall. Miss Wall, a Roman Catholic, convent-educated, and a Cambridge graduate, said: "The novel as Lawrence wrote it holds out hope that this is not all … That there is some way out of this drab and dead existence." Miss Wall is writing her first novel.'

How remarkable she seems, Jackie thinks, and for a moment, seven months pregnant, and with the overwhelming prospect of the White House before her, she envies this girl her freedom and forthrightness. How did she come to have the confidence to speak with such assurance – and honesty – to the most important court in the land?

Did Miss Wall win the hearts of the jury? There's no denying it: some will wonder what a 21-year-old Cambridge graduate can know of this 'drab and dead existence'.

Mel Harding tells old Mr Whelan that he has an appointment 'out of town'. He tells Cathleen he'll see her in a couple of days. 'Don't give my room away!' Behind the front desk, she smirks. As he pulls out of Pilgrims Motor Inn onto Route 6A, he checks to make sure he isn't being followed.

He has people to think about, not only himself. Lots of people suddenly: Cathleen, who stood on the motel porch, behind him, on Halloween. The lamp was on in the room, and they couldn't have missed her. The Bureau will know all about her, her parents and even her little boy by now. Nor does he forget Mrs. Kennedy and Caroline, not to mention the baby on the way.

Then there are all those government employees living in daily fear of humiliation and joblessness. There's the country itself. As highfalutin as it sounds, even to him, the country can't afford for Nixon to win the election, not with Hoover at his ear it can't.

The election polls say Kennedy and Nixon are still neck-and-neck. His own picture of Mrs. Kennedy at the hearing will be out of Miss Gandy's foot-stool by now. Multiple copies of the print will be 'primed and ready', waiting in envelopes addressed to 'cooperative' newspaper editors around the country. The Director will only be hanging on for the 'Guilty' verdict out of London. All the witnesses have been called.

Maybe Hoover is betting all wrong. Maybe he can't read the public like he thinks he can. But in his gut, Harding is sure he's right, and it was he who gave Hoover the idea in the first place. Harding knows exactly what the Director plans to do with the picture. It doesn't take a mastermind.

No trail will ever lead back to the Bureau. And poor Jack Kennedy won't be able to stop the leak, not even if he's tipped off. Because Hoover has *thousands* of pages, plus all the sex-audio, on Kennedy, and Kennedy knows it. The challenger for the White House, for the Oval Office itself, is as good as gagged.

With that 'Guilty' verdict, the shot of Mrs. Kennedy will need no more than a headline from the sensational trial. Every major paper around the world is watching events in London, plus thousands of smaller ones. He can easily imagine it: 'Lady Kennedy Caught Red-Handed'. 'Our Next First Lady – Chatterley?'

Hoover will get on the blower to MI5 too. He'll bribe some lackey to find out exactly what she got up to during that spell in England, when everyone in the know said the Kennedy marriage was on the rocks. Hoover will dig up any pictures he can find of her in London society that autumn – '56, was it? – with good-looking or wealthy men. By the time Hoover finishes with her, she won't be looking like First Lady material. It's the old stand-by plot from detective stories: *Cherchez la femme*. The public will eat it up.

If the scandal doesn't topple the Democrats outright, it will inflict a serious wound, right before Election Day. Mrs. Kennedy herself *lustrous eyes, widely spaced lips parted* will be collateral damage. Hoover won't bat an eye.

And he, Harding, had made it possible. Which means he has to be the one to stop it.

Earlier that morning, he sealed a typed note in a Manila envelope: 'Hoover: see "Insurance Policy" of interest. As you will appreciate, this now makes, not one, but <u>two</u> photographic documents to be "cleared", in accordance with classified protocols. Negative for enclosure has been retained. P.S. Call off the hounds.'

There was no need to sign it. Hoover would know who it was from, alright.

At Washington HQ, in the Justice Department building, Mel Harding will hand the envelope to the security agent in the foyer. He will draw the man's attention to its code. He has addressed it: c/o Secretary to the Director, Miss Helen Gandy, Attn: JEH, Code: JUNE.

It will go straight into the internal mail. The Manila envelope will arrive on Miss Gandy's desk within an hour of Harding's exit from the building. Before the end of the day, she will be in the elevator, traveling all the way down to the windowless basement where Jonah works. 'Clearance Officer' is not so much Jonah's job title, as code for a 'destruction order'.

Staring from his window on the twelfth floor of the Justice Department, Hoover, in a reflective frame of mind, will watch the smoke from the incinerator rise up. In its fading gusts will be the carbon remains of the two photos.

A loss, granted, Hoover will conclude. A setback. It's rare that anyone gets the better of him.

But he will not risk Clyde. He cannot risk Clyde.

Patience, he will counsel himself. Patience.

Nixon will take the presidency still. Hoover knows it in his bones.

Day Five, Tuesday, November 1st
November rolls into London with another heavy mist, as if the damp of the day is the exhalation of a weary River Thames. The weather brings with it, too, a claustrophobia; a faint sense of panic, as when it's impossible to see clear of something, or to get one's bearings. Distances are deceptive. On street corners, the braziers of the chestnut-sellers flicker and glow. Even in respectable parts of the city, the old bomb-sites are still hazards, and never more illusory than on days like today; one stumbles in and out of them, blinking and dusting oneself off.

Bowler hats progress down streets as if independent of their owners. Headlamps on cars make slotted yellow eyes. Sounds reverberate cunningly: the hiss of bus brakes, the click of heels, and newspaper vendors calling out the headlines: 'No Further Witnesses! Will Lady C. Walk Free?'

At half past ten, under the great glass skylight of Court Number One, Mr Gerald Gardiner, Lead Counsel for the Defence, stands to make his closing address.

She who was once Rosalind Thornycroft swivels in her chair. Jeremy Hutchinson promised to keep her in admission tickets until the verdict was delivered, and he has been as good as his word.

'Members of the Jury, this case has lasted some days, and if you will permit me to say so, nobody, whether concerned with the Prosecution or with the Defence, can have failed to observe the patience with which you have borne your duties and the close attention which you have paid to the evidence. You may perhaps console yourselves with the reflection that, if you had been here for three weeks on some complicated financial fraud, it might well have been a case of rather less human interest than this.

'I should point out to you that if either my learned friend, Mr Griffith-Jones, or I say anything which is not accurate on the law, then my Lord will direct you to what the law is. On the other hand, the facts are entirely for you, *and are not for my Lord at all.* Just as you have no responsibility at all for any decisions of law, so my Lord has *no responsibility at all* for decisions of fact.

'This is a prosecution of Penguin Books, whose directors thought, as they still think, that there is nothing in this book, as written by its author, which in truth and in fact would deprave or corrupt anyone. They were of course conscious that, owing to its history, they might risk a prosecution. They were not concerned with the financial aspect of it. They could have published an expurgated edition in this country and the unexpurgated edition abroad. They are concerned with the question of principle.

'You will be aware that there is a vast amount of pornography about today – "dirt for dirt's sake", one might say. In amending the law last year, Parliament was, as we heard from Mr Jenkins, providing for the protection of *literature*, while also strengthening the law concerning pornography. You will still, I know, have your copies of the book. Two passages, to my mind, are the best expressions of what Lawrence was really after with this novel.

'On page 292, near the end of the novel, Mellors says: "I stand for the touch of bodily awareness between human beings, and the touch of tenderness. And she is my mate. And it is a battle against the money, and the machine, and the insentient ideal monkeyishness of the world. And she will stand behind me there." On page 317, Mellors writes to Constance, because they cannot yet be together. He writes: "Well, so many words, because I can't touch you. If I could sleep with my arms round you, the ink could stay in the bottle. We could be chaste together just as we can fuck together. But we have to be separate for a while …"

'From certain questions asked by the Prosecution – or perhaps they would be not unfairly described as insults rather than questions – observations such as "You are not giving a lecture now" – it sounds as if it might today be suggested to you that you should *ignore* the evidence which has been called, on the ground that these are "professors" of literature and people who are living rarefied lives; people who would not know what the effect of a book like this, whether conscious or unconscious, would be on ordinary people who read it. Yet you will know for yourselves that the expert witnesses I called included professors of English Literature, yes – naturally – but also school-teachers of public schools, grammar schools and ordinary schools. They included veterans, many parents, as well as students of literature. We heard from authors, churchmen and critics; from a

Member of Parliament who is the son of a coal-miner; from newspaper editors and broadcasters, who are required by their profession to be keenly in touch with public attitudes. I would suggest that no higher class of experts could have been called in any similar case. You may have seen how, when the first few witnesses were called, they were attacked by the Prosecution, and properly so, in their pursuit of a prosecution. Then, gradually, the Prosecution – plainly – was overwhelmed by the evidence.

'There was also a suggestion to you from the Prosecution to the effect of "Don't let us pay any attention to these eminent people because you and I are ordinary people, and we understand 'what's what' as they cannot. They don't really know what goes on in the *actual* world as lived by most people." Well, of course, Lawrence *himself* was precisely that, was he not, a man of the people. How far the *Prosecution lawyers* are in touch with real life we do not know.

'When their turn came to call evidence, *they called no expert evidence at all.* Not one single witness was found to come into the witness box and say anything against Lawrence or this book. No one could point to *any* passage in the book which seems to condone or advocate promiscuous relations.

'The Prosecution will again draw your attention, no doubt, to the fact that this book, published at three shillings and sixpence, will be available to the general public. Indeed, the Lead Counsel for the Prosecution invited you to consider this question after you had read it: "Is it a book that you would even wish your wife or your servants to read?" I do not wish to upset the Prosecution by suggesting that there are a certain number of people nowadays who as a matter of fact don't *have* servants. But of course, that whole attitude is one which Penguin Books was formed to fight against – in other words, the attitude that it is all right to publish a special edition at five or ten guineas so that people who are less well off cannot read what other people read.

'Isn't everybody, whether earning £10 a week or £20 a week, *equally* interested in the society in which we live, in the problems of human relationships, including sexual relationships? Regarding the reference made, in the same statement, to wives, aren't *women* equally interested in human relations, including sexual relationships? If it is right that this book should be read, it should be available to the man or woman who is working in the factory, or to the teacher who is working in the school. It is rather extraordinary on the face of it, is it not, that, when a visiting professor goes from this country to another country, he is not supposed, really, to know anything about this book at all.

'Nor has a single opportunity been missed by the Prosecution to attack D. H. Lawrence as a person. It has been noted that he himself "ran off" with someone else's wife. That is true, but Lawrence was only married once in his life and that marriage lasted until his death. Lawrence lived and died suffering from a public opinion – caused by the banning of this book – that he had written a piece of pornography called *Lady Chatterley's Lover*. The slur was never justified.

'Is it not time that we rescued Lawrence's name from the quite unjust reputation which, because of this book, it has always had, and allowed our people, his people, to judge for themselves its high purpose? We are a country known throughout the world for two things in particular, our literature and our democratic institutions: Parliament, trial by jury, and so forth. Strange indeed if this were the only country where this man's work, an Englishman's work, could not be read.

'As for the book itself, you may agree with some of the expert witnesses who were of the view that this book is not his best book. Since it is his last novel, however, we might say it is the crux of his work. It is, we might also say, uneven, and not always easy to read. The conversation between Constance's father and Mellors, for instance, reads most unconvincingly, because Lawrence's own England, of course, was not the England of the elite schools of this country and its well-appointed West End clubs; he just didn't know how a member of the aristocracy would speak in such a situation. Or perhaps he *did*, and he "over-egged" what was in effect a caricature of Sir Malcolm. Yet the Obscenity Act makes clear that the book must be judged *as a whole*.

'I respectfully protest at the sort of statements made about the character of Constance. There is this love affair in Germany. *Then* she marries. There she is all through the War, and at the end of the War; then her husband comes back, unable to take further part in the physical side of marriage. When the man Michaelis suggests to Constance that she should go off with him, her regard for marriage is perfectly clear; she says she can't possibly do that. There is no further inconstancy on her part until *her husband* suggests she should have a child by another man so that there can be an heir to inherit Wragby Hall.

'No one would suggest, on a specifically Christian standard, that her adultery was right, but the *subject* of the book is her human dilemma. Lawrence didn't *have* to put her husband in a wheelchair; he might have simply created a Sir Clifford Chatterley who was bored with his spouse, and our sympathies would have been more easily turned in Constance's favour. But it was a sense of a *true* and testing human dilemma Lawrence wished to evoke. Even if we agree that her actions were not "right", it is not really right, is it, to convict Constance as if she were some kind of nymphomaniac?

'In the case of particular passages relating to the lovemaking, you will recall that they were read out by my learned friend in such a manner as to make fun of the dialect and so on. Yet you may have thought the ultimate effect, *even though so read*, was only to underline the sensitiveness and beauty of it. Because there is, is there not, a high breathlessness about beauty which cancels lust?'

Yes, thinks Rosalind, as she leans forward, hands on cane. *Yes. There is. Was. A beauty.*

Still, she feels the presence of the exile in the dock. She does not need to turn to see. 'Do not forget,' he wrote.

As Mr Gardiner continues, she is walking once more with Lawrence to the top of Fiesole. Time is a welter.

Yes, her lover nods, grinning as they walk from her little villa to the market square, with the children in tow. The baby is in a farmer's cart, with straw and the bolsters from her bed. At the top of the hill, on the walls of the square, they stop to stare at posters depicting huge bottles of castor oil and a warning that all anti-fascists will be dosed with it, to purge them. The decade's new hatreds blow like dark spores.

At the edge of the market, white oxen stand hitched to carts. They brood in the midday heat, as still and heavy as marble. Every ox wears a collar of silver bells, and their horns and tails are adorned with red tassels. In rare moments, when their primordial inertia gives way – as their tails swat at flies or as they bend to drink at their trough – the bells on their collars tinkle, and their tassels twitch and flick, to the delight of the children who stare.

Nearby, old men and women sit selling all manner of things under big bright umbrellas, and in the hilltop square, the English visitors discover curious little shops. They treat themselves to cool drinks and almond cakes – the climb has made them all hungry.

She watches her lover buy a bottle of golden oil, a queer head of cheese and a string of sausages; they laugh as he wraps the string around his neck like a jazz-girl's beads. She buys beautiful coloured paper for herself, and dolls' crockery for Bridget and Chloë. She and Lawrence choose red wine in bottles with long necks and great, round bodies.

The most popular shop seems to be a cave-like place, full of deep wooden drawers of pasta of every shape and size, and a range of colours. Lawrence buys a heavy sack of brown *penne*. They have agreed that he will carry Nan back down the hill, and they will use the cart for their shopping. She buys a dozen types of pasta so that the girls can thread them into beads and bracelets.

When they return at last to Villino Belvedere, he stops only for water and to deposit Nan, whom he never fails to charm. He continues down the hill, through the olive groves to the Canovaia, where he is working, he tells her, on his 'Tortoise' poems. As he removes his hat to fan his face, she sees the stubby pencil he keeps on his person, tucked behind his ear. She tells him, with mischief in her smile, that she is glad the tortoises are so obliging. How wonderful that Mr and Mrs Tortoise have served as muses.

'I don't wish to shock you,' he says, 'but I suspect they are not Mr and Mrs.' His smile twitches.

A rain shower begins, and they turn their faces to it, to cool themselves. It won't last. Before he sets off down the hill to her former home, he draws her close, under the cover of the grapevine at her door. His lips are hard and salty. He will return that evening if she will have him.

'You must come to me each evening,' she says.

'We will have outings, too. Adventures.'

She watches him go through the rain, knowing he won't turn around to raise his arm or tip his old straw hat. She knows that a part of him will grieve, or even resent his discovery of his need of her;

he will regret that his writer's defences have been breached. *A kiss, and a vivid spasm of farewell, a moment's orgasm of rupture, / Then along the damp road alone, till the next turning. / And there, a new partner, a new parting, a new unfusing into twain, / A new gasp of further isolation ...*

She, for her part, feels only sustained. Her chest still buzzes with the joy of the night before. Joy — when she had resigned herself to stoicism, to the mere endurance of the heart.

She goes inside where, during the children's nap, she re-arranges and tidies her room; to make it nice for him when he returns to her. When she emerges from it, she looks up to discover Mr Griffith-Jones of the Prosecution addressing the court, in a sombre manner, heavy with deliberation.

'Members of the Jury, you can have no doubt left in your minds that this case, both from the point of view of Penguins, and you may think of the literary profession and of the public too, is one of immense importance, the effect of which will go far beyond the actual question which you have to decide. On an issue in a matter of such gravity, I am not going to occupy and indeed waste your time by answering the debating points which have been made against me. It is easy enough, particularly in a case of this kind, to poke fun at the Prosecution, to draw laughs as to the conduct and the observations which have passed. That can easily be done on both sides.'

Ros's eyes narrow. She very much doubts it.

'It has been emphasised to you in my friend's closing address again, again and again that you heard no witnesses called by the Prosecution to answer the witnesses called by the Defence. Members of the Jury, the Act is *perfectly* clear: expert witnesses are confined in their evidence to the *literary, artistic, or other merit* of the book.

'As to the merit of this book as literature, from the very first I have conceded, as you will recall, that Lawrence is a great writer. I never challenged his honesty of purpose. I never challenged that this book was a book of *some* merit. These were matters upon which the Prosecution never sought to argue. They were matters, therefore, upon which it would have been wholly irrelevant and redundant to call evidence for the Prosecution. Goodness alone knows, you have had *enough* of your time occupied with a sufficient number of witnesses already in this case, without hearing me ask leave to call further witnesses to say only what I made clear from the start.

'Upon the question of whether this book is obscene, Members of the Jury, I am barred from calling any evidence relating to that issue because the Act restricts me to calling evidence *only as to the literary and other merits of the book.*'

He dissembles well, Ros decides.

'There are essentially only two questions for you to consider. The first is: is this obscene? The second – arising only if you should answer the first question in the affirmative – is: is its publication justified as being *for the public good* because it is in the interests of literature? Perhaps it is not entirely easy to divorce the one from the other.

'My friend Mr Gardiner has suggested to you that to "deprave and corrupt", as with obscenity, the effect of such abuse must entail a *change* of character in the person corrupted or left depraved. Surely that cannot be right. One can deprave and corrupt, can one not, without pointing to someone – the reader – who immediately goes off and has sexual intercourse after reading the book.

'Members of the Jury, there must be *standards*, must there not, which we are to maintain; some standards of *morality*, some standards of language and *conversation*, some standards of *conduct* which are essential to the well-being of our society? There must be standards of respect, respect for the conventions of society, for the kind of conduct of which society approves, respect for other people's feelings; respect, you may think too, for the intimacy, the *privacy*, of relations between people. There must be standards of *restraint*. And when one sees what is happening today and has been happening, perhaps all the more since the war, restraint becomes all the more essential, does it not, in the education of the youth of our country.

'And I do say to you – as my learned friend anticipated I would – I do say to you, are these views that you have heard from these most eminent and academic ladies and gentlemen, are they really of *such* value as the views which *you* hold and can see from the ordinary life in which you live? Allow me to help you review a little of the "evidence" given. The sample may speak for the whole, without imposing too greatly, again, on your patience.

'It was put forward by the Bishop of Woolwich that this was a book of ethical value. The Bishop himself, however, knocked that argument upon the head when he subsequently said, "I would not say it was of instructional value upon the subject of ethics." Members of the Jury, I do not suppose that there will be any of you who will disagree with him upon that point!

'The unexpurgated edition of the novel, opined Miss Dilys Powell, offers its readers a "treatment of sex on a holy basis". Miss Powell is otherwise known as Mrs Leonard Russell, wife of the Literary Editor of the *Sunday Times*, who is a well-known devotee of the book. But is *that* how tens of thousands of young men and boys are going to read this book – as a "treatment of sex on a holy basis"? Can *that* be a realistic view? The Bishop actually went one better than Mrs Russell, referring to the author's depiction of "something sacred, in a real sense as an act of holy communion". Do you think *that* is how the girls working in the factory are going to read this book, or does it show us that the Bishop, with great respect to him, is wholly out of touch?

'Miss Rebecca West, for whom, I am quite sure, we *all* have the highest respect and regard, was asked about this book and gave, you will remember, a number of rather long answers to the questions put to her. I have no doubt that, with the learning and reading that lies behind Miss West, *she* is capable of reading so very much into this book, but I ask you, is that typical of the effect this book will have upon the *average* reader, and all the more, the *average young* reader? Again, I am asking you to look at it, not from the Olympian heights, but as the ordinary man in the street. Did you not think, as you read that book, that, generally speaking, its emphasis is upon the thrill and the sensation of these two persons having sexual intercourse together? Is there really anything other of any weight that this book contains? Is there any moral teaching at all?

'Would you please look at page 258? It is a passage which I have not – and I do not think anybody has – referred to during the course of cross-examination, or indeed at any time during this trial. I find that rather curious. Allow me to read some of that page aloud for you.' He takes out his spectacles, rather slowly, and finds his chosen page, with an air of having something grave to impart. Then he begins to read, clearly and audibly to all, notwithstanding the acoustics.

'"It was a night of sensual passion, in which she was a little startled and almost unwilling: yet pierced again with piercing thrills of sensuality, different, sharper, more terrible than the thrills of tenderness, but, at the moment, more desirable. Though a little frightened, she let him have his way ..."

Mr Griffith-Jones pauses dramatically to look up. 'Not very easy, sometimes, not very easy, you know, to know *what* the author is driving at in that passage.'

Ros straightens in her chair to search the faces of the jury. Some are clearly shocked. At the solicitors' table, Sir Allen Lane and his solicitor – a Mr Rubinstein – stare at their hands on the tabletop. The colour seems to have drained from their faces at this, Mr Griffith-Jones's surprise delivery of such powerful innuendo. 'Sodomy' is of course illegal, and, in the minds of most, that which is illegal is highly likely to deprave or corrupt.

Mr Griffith-Jones has held back his trump card until now, the final moments of the trial.

Penguins and Sir Allen Lane may have just lost the case.

Nor is the Lead Counsel for the Prosecution finished. On he reads ...

"'Though a little frightened, she let him have his way, and the reckless, shameless sensuality shook her to the foundations, stripped her to the very last, and made a different woman of her.'"

Yes, Ros thinks – a woman who was unafraid; unafraid of her body, unafraid of his.

She finds it hard to bear Mr Griffith-Jones's reading from her lover's account of their night, no matter how confused it might have been at the time.

But he does not relent. He has the attention of all: "'It was not really love. It was not voluptuousness. It was sensuality sharp and searing as fire, burning the soul to the tinder.'"

He looks up again over his half-moon specs. 'I don't know: is this stuff having a *good* influence on the young reader? Clearly it *will* influence, but the question is *how*.' He resumes. "'Burning out the shames, the deepest, oldest shames, in the most secret places. It cost her an effort to let him have his way and his will of her. She had to be a passive, consenting thing, like a slave, a physical slave. Yet the passion licked round her, consuming, and when the sensual flame of it passed through her'" – he paused for emphasis – "'*bowels* and breast, she really thought she was dying: yet a poignant, marvellous death.'"

Seated where she is, Ros can see, even with her one bad eye, the stricken and confounded faces of many of the jurors. The Prosecutor speaks directly to them. 'You must decide for yourselves of course, but *that* is not my understanding of poignancy.' He turns again to the open book in his hand: '"In the short summer night she learnt so much. She would have thought a woman would have died of shame ... She felt, now, she had come to the real bed-rock of her nature, and was essentially shameless. She was her sensual self, naked and unashamed."' Mr Griffith-Jones pauses. His expression is strained and lofty. '*I* do not know what that means precisely; you will have to think.

'"She felt a triumph, almost a vainglory. So! That was how it was! That was life! That was how oneself really was! There was nothing left to disguise or be ashamed of. She shared her ultimate nakedness with a man, another being.

'"And what a reckless devil the man was! Really like a devil! One had to be strong to bear him. But it took some getting at, the core of the physical jungle, the last *and the deepest recess of organic shame*."' Mr Griffith-Jones surfaces from the paperback with an expression of distaste. 'What *does* it mean, ladies and gentlemen of the jury? Well, that is for you to say.

'And what of all this tenderness we keep hearing of? Is that a theme which is in the public good to read, as expressed in this book? Allow me to remind you of this ostensible "tenderness", in the words of the book itself: "Fuck warm-heartedly and everything will come all right." Is *that* the message you wish to impart to the young of this country? Or this, perhaps? "Ay! It's tenderness, really; it's cunt-awareness. Sex is really only the touch, the closest of all touch." *That*, Members of the Jury, is the tenderness this book is advocating: in a phrase, "cunt tenderness".'

'The end cracks open with the beginning: / Rosy, tender, glittering within the fissure.'

On the tram back from their day in Florence, Ros peers over her lover's shoulder as he scribbles. Earlier, at the Uffizi, they treated themselves to Botticelli, Fra Angelico and Filippino Lippi, their mutual favourites. After, in a piazza café, they fattened themselves on *panna montata*, cream turrets rising from bowls lined in crisp, sweet biscuit.

Ivy has the children for the day. In the café, he told her that Frieda, his wife of six years, has long encouraged him to make love to other women, as she has with other men. Frieda has actually said, he told her, that she would find it a relief. Sometimes, he nearly believes her.

Ros pretended to be a little shocked. In fact, she already knew this to be the state of his marriage from their mutual friend, Eleanor Farjeon. She did not realise, however, that until herself, until now, for him, there *had* been no other woman.

Nor can Ros know, as their tram rumbles along, that, for him, there never will be another lover; that before long he and Frieda will agree on separate beds.

In the window seat, he is jotting in his notebook, and she sees, out of the side of her eyes, a poem called 'Pomegranate'. 'The end cracks open with the beginning: / Rosy, tender, glittering within the fissure.'

On the tram, their bag of pomegranates, sorb-apples and medlars jiggles in her lap, almost as satisfying a weight as a sleeping toddler. *I love you, rotten, / Delicious rottenness. / I love to suck you out from your skins / So brown and soft and coming suave.* The tram bounces, smoking as it goes, up the steep hill to San Gervasio. Then a man at the front tells the driver his feet are hot and the tram is on fire. The driver shrugs, pulls over and, in no rush, steps out to investigate. Eventually, watering-cans topped full are carried from nearby houses, the fire is put out, and onward they go. Everyone seems accustomed.

His free hand discreetly strokes her thigh. The day has cooled a little, at last, and through the tram windows, the locals are emerging to stroll and chat. The journey takes them past girls in vibrant head-scarves and aprons, and men in fields, who seem even to harvest the golden light of late afternoon.

Their scythes flash.

How beautiful the world is, she thinks.

He disembarks in San Gervasio, and she remains on the tram as it struggles up the hill to Fiesole. He returns to them after seven, bearing a duck for her girls to adopt and mother. The duck, he assures her, will be fine. It will outrun them and take to the wing soon enough.

After the children and the duck are tucked up for the night, in bed and coop respectively, they cook together, then eat on the balcony, where the geraniums glow. 'How rare our time has been,' he says, his voice low. 'Beyond measure. I shall not forget it: this balcony, our hillside, our words – you.'

They are loving words, and she is moved. They are also the words which tell her he will not be hers; that he will leave. The knowledge comes like a punch to her lungs.

She smiles faintly.

No one has known her as he has known her. Through him, she has come to know herself. Her children are happy and at ease in his company – they have been a little family these three weeks. What of *them*, her fatherless little ones? No one save her has offered them more sincere, unaffected attention, not even Godwin.

She cannot force back the grief that wells in her breast – nor her rising anger.

For nearly a year, his words and letters pursued her across borders and boundaries, overcoming her reservations. Now, he has satisfied his curiosity. He has satisfied his desire. How foolish she was to imagine it might be more. Her children will sob after he leaves them. She will sob.

She looks out into the Florentine night. Every new grief plunges one back into another. She is still healing from the end of her marriage, from the death of its future. Why did he not know it?

I only want one thing of men, and that is, that they should leave me alone.

Perhaps this is what he *does*. Perhaps he makes women feel that he alone can 'see' them. Was he pursuing another even now? Was that woman already in Venice, his next destination? Was she awaiting a tryst, before Frieda's return?

She doesn't believe it. Yet it was cruel of him to use her so; to make her feel the need of him. Why, she wonders, are women so often 'bit parts' in the lives of men? Why had he not known that she was real and human and vulnerable?

Perhaps he had.

That was the worst of it.

She'd been foolish to give him her trust.

And yet she'd been *hungry*.

That final night, she slept fitfully in his arms, with his legs wrapped around her as if he would never let them be parted.

Day Six, Wednesday, November 2nd
The verdict is one of the most anticipated in the Old Bailey's history. As the curtain goes up for the final act of *Regina v. Penguin Books Limited*, the ancient heating system bangs into life. Cleaners, from the British West Indies, mop up dirty puddles in the Great Hall and on the floor of the court. Their backs are proud and their eyes smoulder. Jurors and reporters duly lift boots and galoshes. Noses blow like signal horns, pipes emerge from pockets, and the air gives way to a thin, yellow miasma. Even the oak panelling of the court seems, on this, the sixth day, to exhale more than its usual quantity of Edwardian dust.

Mr Jeremy Hutchinson, in his barrister's seat, adjusts his wig. A nuisance. He has never grown to appreciate the thing in the way that some of his balding colleagues have.

Rosalind is seated, this time in the dignitaries' section. The faces of the Defence team look grave this morning, she decides. Not a good sign. Mr Griffith-Jones, it is generally agreed, ended the previous day with a bang. Penguin Books took a serious hit. Whether it would prove fatal, who could say? The jury was to begin its deliberations after the Judge's summing-up.

She turns to the dock, and the vision of Lawrence turns in that moment to her. Her cloudy eye sees him clearly. He has donned his corduroy jacket – for the final reckoning, as if, again, he isn't long for this world. He is good at departures.

High above Ros's head, in the public cupboard, Dina and Nick have managed to get seats together. 'Watch out for nosebleeds!' Nick calls to her, as they scramble for a pair of empty places. They started queuing with the crowd at four in the morning. A woman in the row behind them taps Dina's shoulder and asks for her autograph. The woman says she saw her picture in the paper. Dina blushes and declines, still tense with worry about her failure in the witness box the day before. Nick gets hold of her hand.

On the floor below, in the dignitaries' section, Dina spots Rebecca West in a black fur hat and large pearl, clip-on earrings. The woman called Rosalind is there too, and Dina's mind dallies again, for reasons she can't quite assemble, over fragments of Lawrence's 'San Gervasio poems'. *Rose, ros, thorn.*

E. M. Forster, she remarks to Nick, has not made the journey from Cambridge into London again – at least, she cannot see him in the press of people below. She points out the poet Sylvia Plath, who is seated next to Stephen Spender in the press section. Mr Spender, she tells Nick, must have got Plath the admission ticket. He's a starry poet, and the Editor of *Encounter*. Plath was in the year ahead of her at Newnham.

She used to live in the overseas student house, Whitstead, off Barton Road, and Dina would notice her sometimes, as they passed each other on the college grounds. Plath stood out, with her long, blonde American hair, like Veronica Lake's. Sometimes, she wore it in a high pony-tail, and you could tell immediately that she was American, just from its optimistic swing.

She must have felt lonely sometimes. 'Rather out of her depth. She wouldn't have had the faintest idea of the snobberies she was up against.'

'Why do you think she's stayed?' asks Nick.

'Ambition. She started writing almost straightaway for some of the Cambridge papers.' Why hadn't she, Dina wonders, thought of that herself? 'She published her first poetry collection with Fabers, just a couple of weeks ago, to good reviews. *The Colossus.*' Lucky thing. 'And now she's married to the poet Ted Hughes. They must be quite the pair.'

Then, everyone is upstanding, and Dina grips the stone in her pocket as Nick takes her other hand in his.

The Judge, his wife and his retinue enter. Mr Justice Byrne is, as ever, hierophantical in scarlet and ermine. The Lord Mayor clinks. The Aldermen swish. The Sheriff grips his cocked hat so tightly under his arm, one might expect the thing to crow.

'God Save the Queen' is sung vigorously but, even so, one never can quite overcome the mechanical dreariness of the tune, thinks Rosalind. She watches Sir Allen Lane stand, stalwart but sombre, beside the Instructing Solicitor, Michael Rubinstein. They appear to sing, but with something of the look of the condemned.

She knows that Sir Allen's wife and elder daughter are, again, close to hand, or as close as the seating arrangements permit. How wretched for them. Might their dear husband and father be escorted *down* the steps? Everyone has heard tales.

There is no doubt, thinks Michael Rubinstein, in his solicitor's capacity: Mervyn Griffith-Jones dealt their case a potentially mortal blow yesterday by lingering over the alleged 'anal intercourse' material. If found guilty, the punishment is an unlimited fine or three years' imprisonment. It is still unclear what, or who, might be found guilty: Penguin Books or publisher Allen Lane himself. The ambiguity is grim. There is too much room for interpretation. The Judge, as he himself has repeatedly demonstrated, is not on the publisher's side.

Mr Justice Byrne bows three times to the barristers; they bow to him. Behind the Judge, the Sword of State gleams. Lady Byrne bears the totemic paperback in its damask cushion cover and confers it upon her husband. Then everyone takes their seats, and the final performance gets underway.

'Members of the Jury,' his Lordship begins, 'you have listened with the greatest care and attention to this case, and you have read this book. Now the time is rapidly approaching when you will have to return a verdict. As Mr Gardiner told you, quite rightly, questions of law are my province. You are the sole judges of the facts. They are nothing to do with me. Furthermore, I must point out that *our criminal law in this country is based upon the view that a jury takes of the facts, and not upon the view that "experts" may have.*'

Michael Rubinstein turns in his chair. Yes, the Defence barristers in Counsel's Row are indeed exchanging looks. Can a judge *properly* tell a jury to ignore expert evidence and to form their own views? It is surely a misdirection, and yet Mr Gardiner, as Lead Counsel for the Defence, is, in this moment, powerless. It would take a conviction, followed by an appeal, to undo that particular act of damage – or sabotage.

Mr Justice Byrne carries on, heedless. 'This is, naturally, an important case from the point of view of the defendant company, Penguin Books, but it is an equally important case from the point of view of the public, which *you* represent. Because – is it right or is it wrong to say? – in these days our moral standards have reached a low ebb.'

Michael Rubinstein dares not signal his frustration. Nor does anyone. The situation is perilous.

'You must decide whether it has been proved beyond reasonable doubt that this book is obscene. That is the first question. And you will observe that no *intent* to deprave or corrupt needs to be proved *in order that this offence shall be committed*. It is an objective test. Having read the book, the question is, does it *tend to* deprave or corrupt?

'Now, what are the relevant circumstances for you to bear in mind? Well, what we know is this. According to the verdict you give, it was to be put, or is to be put, upon the market at three shillings and sixpence a copy, which is by no means an excessive price for the book. In these days when there are not only high wages but, shall I say, high pocket-money for younger members of the community, this book could soon be within the grasp of a vast mass of the population. I must also say that a good deal of the evidence given by the witnesses was not relevant to *this issue of obscenity*. You must decide that upon the evidence of *the book itself*.

'As Mr Gardiner correctly explained, you must consider the book as a whole. You must not select a passage here and a passage there. Nor is it a question of taste. There is a considerable difference between that which shocks or even disgusts, and that which depraves and corrupts. If you hate the sight of the book when you read it, that does not satisfy beyond reasonable doubt the obscenity question.

'I should like to draw your attention to observations once made by Mr Justice Devlin, when he was trying a case similar to this. He said: "Then there is obscene libel; and just as loyalty is one of the things which is essential to the well-being of a nation, so some sense of morality is something that is essential to the healthy life of the community; and, accordingly, anyone who seeks by his writing to corrupt that fundamental sense of morality is guilty of obscene libel."

'*Now*, where he says, "… anyone who *seeks* by his writing to corrupt", *I* would prefer to say, "anyone who by his writing *tends* to corrupt that fundamental sense of morality is guilty of an obscene libel." In this respect, I cannot agree with Mr Gardiner, who seems to take exception to the quite proper widening of the net of possible harms to include a "tendency" to corrupt. To corrupt is first to foster an attitude, a disposition or, indeed, an openness to a *tendency*, evident in a work, which is obscene.'

Dina and Nick turn to each other, dumbfounded. The Judge is, again, doing the job of the Prosecution!

'You must ask yourselves, as men and women of this world, not with prudish minds but with liberal minds, this question: is the *tendency* of this book to deprave and corrupt those who are likely to read it? Because, you know, once the book goes into circulation, it does not spend time in the rarefied atmosphere of some academic institution, where a young mind will perhaps be shown *how* to read it, as in an institution such as Cambridge University' – the tea-cups glance at Dina. 'It finds its way into the bookshops, on to bookstalls, and into libraries for all and sundry to read.

'Now, what is the story? Let us remind ourselves. Is it right to say it is the story of a woman who first of all, *before* she is married, has sexual intercourse, and then, after marriage, when her husband has met with disaster in the War and has become confined to a wheel-chair – as so *very* many men tragically were in the Great War – after he is paralysed from the waist downwards, after marriage, she, living with her husband in this dreary place called Wragby – I think it is called that – she commits adultery on *two* occasions with somebody called Michaelis, while her husband is downstairs in the *same* house, and *then* proceeds to have an adulterous affair with her husband's gamekeeper? And that is described – please feel free to disagree with me – in the *most* lurid way, and the whole sensuality and passion of the various pieces of sexual intercourse is fully and completely related.

'Section 4 of the new, amended Act provides that a person' – Michael Rubinstein notes, with a pang, the Judge's choice of the word 'person' rather than 'company' or 'organisation' – 'shall not be convicted *if* it is proved that publication of the article in question is justified as being for the public good, in this case as a work of liter-ature, art, learning or other object of general concern. Sub-section 2 allows for the calling of expert witnesses.

'As I understand Section 4, it was *not* the intention of Parliament to provide *immunity* to an author or publisher simply because the work in question had literary or other merits. The law states that more is required. Any literary merit proven *must be sufficient* to be "for the public good". The burden of proof is, in this Section, upon the defendants. Regarding the question of obscenity, the burden of proof is on the Prosecution.

'Your questions are therefore as follows. One. Is the book obscene? Will it *tend* to deprave and corrupt those who are likely to read it? If not, there's an end to it. Two. If it is obscene, does it possess any literary merit? The Prosecution has conceded it has some. All the witnesses subscribed to the view that it is a book of some literary merit. Again, you are not governed by the opinions which they have possessed. *You* are the judges of the matter. Three. *If* the book does, in your view, possess literary merit, have the defendants established the probability that the merits of the book as a novel are *so* high that they outbalance the obscenity; *so* high that its publication is *for the public good?*'

He left her at the end of September, walking down the track through the olive grove, until she and the girls could no longer see anything of his white shirt and old straw hat. He left before he had needed to leave, for Mrs Lawrence wasn't due to arrive at their meeting point in Venice for several days. He felt 'blasted' by their love, he'd told her the night before.

He said that the years had made a married man of him. 'When a man is married, he is not in love. A husband is not a lover. Well, I am a husband, you see, and I shall never be a lover again, not while I live … You were – you remain – the beloved, and you have been most generous, generous in every way it is possible to be.'

'You love your wife,' she conceded, tears rising. She was trying her best to be gracious, as 'nice' women were expected to be in such situations. 'That is as it should be.'

Was it, though?

'Not quite love …' he replied. 'But when one has been married for six years and intimate for longer – because I did love Frieda once – then, some sort of bond grows. Some sort of connection. And it isn't natural, quite, to break it.'

Later, Ros found almost the exact words in *Aaron's Rod*, which he had been writing at the time of their affair, alongside his 'San Gervasio poems'. In the novel, Aaron says these things to the Marchesa as he leaves her.

She kept his letters and cards. Indeed, the first was dated September 29th, the very date he would eventually choose for Mellors's letter to Constance, the letter the gamekeeper writes when he is labouring on a farm, seeking his divorce and aching for her. That letter pierced her through when she read it for the first time in '28.

'I believe in a higher mystery, that doesn't let even the crocus be blown out. And if you're in Scotland and I'm in the Midlands, and I can't put my arms round you, and wrap my legs round you, yet I've got something of you …

I love this chastity, which is the pause and the peace of our fucking, between us now like a snowdrop of forked white fire … Well, so many words because I can't touch you.'

Today, on the day of the verdict, she had slipped Lawrence's old cards and notes into her handbag. Bits of him. Fragments of his voice.

29th September, 1920

Darling R.,

The pan'forte was delicious. Sustained me throughout. A shrouded sky on arrival, then a thundering downpour. My painter chum and I have hired a gondola. The Grand Canal is quavery: long lozenges of light yielding to the shadows of autumn. The year dies but Venice ignores it extravagantly. Frieda to arrive in a week. She pesters from Baden-Baden. How are the Young Graces? When will you reinstate yourselves in Canovaia? How are our tortoises? Send word via Cooks, Piazza Leoncini. Do not forget. Forget nothing. D.H.L.

7th October, 1920

My dear Rosalind,

Frieda arrives this evening, if her passport is finally in order. I am weary of hanging about Venice feeling queasy-green. We're out each day in the gondola, and I have written little that isn't watery and adrift.

Today the Lido is abandoned. Not so much as a single exuberant American in earshot. I'm at the southern end. The dunes are thirty feet high, and the brigs and sloops lie to in the Lagoon, imperturbable, with sails ablaze in the grate of the day.

After the commotion of Venice, the open sea feels quite free. I had a bathe earlier and am now perched aloft, with pencil and foolscap pressed to knees. The Evening Star has just appeared. The clouds advance. They put me in mind of the tumult over the sea in Titian's Bacchus and Ariadne. An elemental pair if ever there was.

This morning we felt the first bite of autumn: chill but golden light. Wonder when we'll meet again.

D. H. L.

They would not meet again. He who had once been so determined to know her would never propose another meeting. Convention prevented her from doing so. His subsequent letters took on an amiable tone, the tone of a married friend.

She stayed in Italy for five years, and in 1926, the year he began *Lady Chatterley's Lover* on a remote hilltop, on the opposite side of Florence, she re-married.

He sent her a copy, in '28, of the first edition of *Lady Chatterley's Lover*, fresh from the press of a Florentine publisher, with his own drawing of a phoenix rising from the cover-boards. He posted it to her London home. He'd obtained her new address from Bertie Farjeon.

Naturally, she saw her life, their secrets, and her own likeness on its pages. Perhaps she should have minded, as so many of his friends and former friends had minded when Lawrence borrowed, stole or cannibalised their lives and histories. At the sight of the volume, however, she felt only the warmth of their old, ragged joy.

On the title page, he had written:

For dear Ros,

For my part, I prefer my heart to be broken.
It is so lovely, dawn-kaleidoscopic within the crack.

Yours,
D.H.L.

They were the last lines from 'Pomegranate', the poem he had been scribbling beside her the day the tram caught fire, on their way back from Florence. Now, it was the first poem in his collection, *Birds, Beasts and Flowers*, a volume which opened with his 'San Gervasio' sequence.

When she learned of his death in March of 1930, she opened her *Chatterley* again, and found, without even looking, one of his descriptions of their lovemaking. She found, too, in its pages, the trimmings of his red-brown hair, which, unknown to him, she'd saved, sentimentally – that first night on her terrace. She'd forgotten she'd hidden it there, in a small envelope between the pages. The hair was still soft to the touch.

In her mind, she closes the book and raises her eyes. Mr Justice Byrne is concluding his address, and Lawrence, her vision, is gone for good.

'Members of the Jury,' says the Judge, 'you must ask yourselves whether you can agree with all the things the expert witnesses said Lawrence was saying, or was trying to say, the things that they indicate were the messages that he was trying to give his readers. You must ask yourselves whether you agree with these expressions of opinion, or whether you disagree; because although these witnesses are called to assist you, you, of course, are not bound by the evidence. *You* are the judges. *You* make up your minds. The verdict must be the verdict of *each* one of you. And now, will you be kind enough to retire, consider your verdict, and tell me how you find?'

At three minutes before midday, the jury files out.

The court is adjourned, and the great marble-floored hall outside Court Number One fills, as if for a mis-timed drinks reception. A loud tumult of voices goes up, but the mood around Sir Allen Lane – his Defence team, his Board of Directors, his friends – is gloomy. The publisher gently suggests to his wife that she should step outside and put their daughter in a cab on Ludgate Hill. The verdict and the Judge's sentencing may well be serious, and he wants to spare his eighteen-year-old daughter that – although the girl quickly protests.

Michael Rubinstein is, as ever, at Sir Allen's side. As he lights his pipe, he suggests, in a jocular fashion, that he should escort their daughter, Clare, to a cab. He understands that Sir Allen must have a few moments alone with his wife. It is true, there is no telling what might unfold once the jury returns, although he blithely tells Lane's daughter as they walk that he learned, in 'tight spots' during the war, that one must never give in to defeatism. If one does, then one fails to 'look smart' – and one misses the escape routes, the opportunities, and the bits of random good luck. They are often there, if one keeps one's eyes peeled.

He wonders if those are tears welling in hers.

He tells her about his beloved retriever, Fetch, and how much he misses him when he is away from home. Fetch has been much neglected during the trial, he says, and she laughs as he narrates Fetch's misadventures with badgers and hedgehogs. 'They always get the better of him, poor, dear Fetch – even the rabbits!'

Across the hall from the defendants' gathering, the Attorney General, Sir Reginald Manningham-Buller – 'Bull' – is congratulating the Director of Public Prosecutions, Sir Theobald Mathew, on the 'lacerating' performance of his Lead Counsel, Griffith-Jones, in his closing address the day before. They both expect the speedy return of the jury, as do the public who mill about, marvelling that statues of the Kings and Queens of England can be so very dreary.

In time, when the jury fails to make a swift return, many cross over the road and traipse down the alley to the Magpie & Stump for lunch and something to chase it down. By one o'clock, the old floorboards in the pub creak and heave. Finally, at seven minutes to three, a whisper sweeps through the Old Bailey's Great Hall, and a thoughtful soul runs with it as far as the pub, by which point the whisper has grown into a shout: 'They're coming back!'

Court Number One quickly fills and, when no more seats are to be had, people cram into any available nook and corner, on the floor of the court itself and upstairs, in the already packed gallery. Onlookers grip door frames and crouch between rows. They obscure our view a little, but who can blame them? Even Matron, stationed in the hall, where she has faithfully attended her charges, allows herself to draw near enough to listen. We make room.

The twelve men and women emerge from a door in an oak-panelled wall and file across the court. Each clutches his or her orange-and-white copy of the paperback. They are led by the usher and the Clerk of the Court, and after they are again seated in their two rows, they have their names checked, to ensure they are who they were before they departed the jury box. Collectively, they seem to wear an attitude of assurance but, in itself, that reveals nothing.

The prisoner, Sir Allen Lane, is asked to stand.

Then the Clerk of the Court asks the foreman if they have reached a unanimous decision.

'We have,' he replies.

'Guilty or not guilty?'

Upstairs, Nick puts his arm tightly around Dina.

She grips her eye-stone.

Ros clutches her cane.

Sir Allen Lane, aged fifty-eight, stands straight-backed at the solicitors' table. He stares impassively ahead, but there is sweat on his balding head and, behind his back, his hands are clasped and his knuckles are white.

'Not guilty,' says the foreman.

There is a gasp, then an outburst of loud clapping from the back of the court.

'Silence!' bellows the usher.

'And that is the verdict of you all?' confirms the clerk.

'It is.'

Sir Allen Lane bows his head with unspeakable relief.

Mr Gerald Gardiner promptly begs leave to address Mr Justice Byrne regarding the extensive costs of the trial to his client, Penguin

Books. It is a huge sum, £13,000, and he proposes that the Office of Public Prosecutions, having brought the case, is asked to make a very substantial contribution.

Lady Byrne looks as if Mr Gardiner has just demanded the family silver.

The Judge smiles cryptically and shuffles his papers. 'I will say no more than this. I will make *no* order as to costs.'

It is customary for the Judge to express thanks to the jury, but Mr Justice Byrne wordlessly declines to do so, delegating the task instead to the Clerk of the Court. As the clerk begins, the Judge passes his wife the paperback, for suffocation under her cushion cover. She pulls the drawstring tight. Then all are upstanding for the departure of the Judge.

Which is when it goes off.

First, there is the white, purifying flash – a dread light which reveals the features of each shocked and vulnerable face in Court Number One that day. The electric lights fizzle and die. A curious sound is heard overhead. It is a member of the public, in the upstairs gallery, who is the first to understand. She stammers and points, as if the sky is falling, then stumbles from her chair.

The great skylight of Court Number One is cracking open.

London's rain turns to shards of glass.

People cover their heads with their arms. Several put up umbrellas, although these quickly blow out in the mass movement of air which follows the blast. The oak-panelled walls of the court contract by several inches. The blast-wind catches hold of hats and wigs. Only Jeremy Hutchinson is happy to see his go.

The stone in Dina's hand is seized by the gust, as is Lady Byrne's cushion cover and Ros's letters as well.

Michael Rubinstein's pipe is lost to him. Rebecca West's fur hat spins past our feet.

Court Number One is under siege from itself. Shock waves travel through, shaking the witness box, the Judge's bench and the empty dock. Wooden nails pop from walls, and panels fall free. The Sword of Justice clatters to the floor, which, even as we watch, is splitting asunder and rising like a mighty wave of timber. The gallery groans, and the hull of the dock is rent in two.

See if I don't bring you down, and all your high opinion
And all your ponderous roofed-in erection of right and wrong
Your particular heavens,
With a smash.

The faces of the jurors – the well-to-do lady, the chastened fore-man, the schoolmistress-like woman, the bespectacled, middle-aged men – are caught in the explosion of thunder and light, as if in a storm at sea. They seem to grow larger with the violence of the flash – larger than life as the future is hauled free from the edifice of the past. What forces have they unleashed?

The jurors' copies of the liberated book are not spared the blast. Pages from burst bindings rise in their hundreds in the gale-force wind. They ascend in flocks through the cracked-open day, flying into the late November afternoon of the nation, where the exile's step-daughter, Mrs Barbara Barr – Barby – stands on the front step of her home in Streatham, London, taking questions from reporters. She is asked her opinion of the jury's verdict. Her stepfather is thirty years dead. Her mother, Frieda, died four years ago. She stares into the darkness of south London, watching bright gulls soar between the mean rooftops.

'I feel,' she says, 'as if a window has been opened and fresh air has been blown right through England.'

xxvi

Within an hour of the verdict, advance-copies of the novel are rushed to Leicester Square Bookshop, where a queue of excited book-buyers has already formed. By five o'clock, the queue lines the entirety of Leicester Square itself, and the same phenomenon is repeated outside Hatchards Bookshop, Piccadilly. The race is on to get the books out of the warehouse into the hands of the nation.

3rd November, 1960

Dear Dina,

You were magnificent – in what can only have been a terrific ordeal for you. Very many thanks indeed from us all, and please also thank your mother and father for introducing you to me.

Please let me know the amount of your expenses incurred in connection with this matter so that I can let you have a cheque for them.

I hope that we shall meet again soon.

Yours sincerely,
Michael Rubinstein

November 3rd: 'It's a sell-out for "Innocent" Lady C!'
A MONSTROUS pile of 200,000 slim books in a bleak warehouse near London Airport will start thinning out today: *Lady Chatterley's Lover*, four-letter words and all, is off to the shops. A jury of three women and nine men gave a verdict yesterday that the late D. H. Lawrence's novel is fit to be published as a work of literary art.

3rd November, 1960

Dear Matron,

Here, as we promised you, is your copy of <u>Lady Chatterley's Lover</u> with many thanks again for having entertained so many of our patiently – and impatiently – waiting witnesses.

Yours sincerely,
Michael Rubinstein

5th November, 1960

My dear Allen,

Thank you very much for the wonderful present of champagne which awaited me on my return home last night.

The last three months have been the most exhilarating of my life, and I have been tremendously grateful for the experience.

Yours ever,
Michael

7th November, 1960

To Her Majesty the Queen

Madam,

It is with temerity born of deep concern and alarm that I venture to approach Your Majesty on this matter.

I must surely speak for thousands of mothers of adolescent children when I beg of Your Majesty to use your influence to reverse the decision to allow <u>Lady Chatterley's Lover</u> to be retailed to the public at a price within the allowance of youths and girls still at school.

The depravity of this book is unspeakable, and, with your sheltered upbringing in a Christian home, Your Majesty cannot conceive the immoral situations which will be put before innocent minds.

Many a girl, who, reading out of a desire to be up-to-date, will have her approach to marriage warped, and boys of the age of your son, the Prince of Wales, and mine a year older, may learn such things from school fellows that will refute the sanctity of the body, and turn healthy inquisitive minds to furtive, lewd and immoral pursuits.

I do beg of Your Majesty and Prince Philip to make your wishes on the subject public, and so shame those who are responsible for this outrage of Christian principles, that a change of legislation will be brought about before it is too late.

I remain,
Your Majesty's faithful and
dutiful servant,
Kathleen Everett

Across the Atlantic, in what Mrs Everett might view as the break-away republic of the United States, the mood in the Big House is as nervous as it is electric on this, the night of November 8th.

Each Kennedy has arrived. The neighbors have sent a ten-foot-high, good-luck rose horseshoe, which no one knows where to put. The rented television is switched on to CBS, with Walter Cronkite leading the election-night special.

Jack and Jackie voted, a little before nine, in Boston's West End Library polling station. In the early morning, they were hardly recognized as they walked the short distance from their car: he in a sober, well-cut suit; she in a bright purple coat and black beret. Jackie is heavily pregnant, and has been fighting a cold for a month.

Jack took her arm, and held his arm in front of her as they went, to ensure nothing and no one might disturb her on their way. Each showed their identification. She cast her vote first in the black-curtained polling booth; he followed and exited, a smile playing at his lips, as if he wanted to chuckle at the oddity of voting for oneself as President. An official photo was snapped, and, within the hour, they boarded the *Caroline* for Hyannis, where a crowd of two hundred greeted them as they stepped from the plane. Well-wishers waved an optimistic banner: 'Welcome home, President Jack'.

The day had a chill on it. They breakfasted at home with Caroline. Secret Service agents surrounded the Kennedy compound. Breakfast was followed by a game of touch-football with Bobby and whoever the brothers could round up. Joe Sr. looked on. He'd spent $10 million on this day.

At half past three, Jack napped. It was going to be a long night.

It's still too close to call but, by five thirty, the networks are predicting a Kennedy win. The *New York Times* goes to press with headlines announcing victory. Someone starts singing 'When Irish Eyes Are Smiling'.

By seven thirty, the tide has turned: a huge IBM computer at CBS predicts Nixon will be the victor. The *Times* stops its presses. Hopes of a landslide are dead.

Ted Kennedy looks sick. They're losing every state he has over-seen, and in a rare, unguarded moment, he kicks the ten-foot floral horseshoe. He calms himself only when he catches his mother's eye and her silent reproach. They have reporters in their midst, her eyes tell him. At eight fifteen, the big computer has changed its mind and is predicting that Jack Kennedy will take fifty-one percent of the popular vote.

In other words, no one knows.

Jackie slips outside to walk a stretch of the Nantucket Sound. The night is moonless, starless. She hears a fish jump somewhere, her baby kicks, and something scurries out of her way across the dunes. A dog off its leash perhaps.

The thought of losing is grim; the thought of winning is terrifying. 'First Lady'. How can she give away her anonymity, her privacy and her independence at the age of thirty-one? If Jack wins, they will both belong to the nation.

'I myself was a figure somebody had read about.'

Lady Chatterley's words flicker through her.

Professor Trilling's note is still in her pocket. It arrived in the morning mail as she and Jack came through the door from Boston. 'Lady C. and Mellors are free! The world is on a winning streak. Keep going! Yours ever, Lionel (Jack).'

By midnight, the mood in the Big House is one of bleak exhaustion. Jackie can't face it, and her mother-in-law advises her, reproachfully, to go home to bed.

By two thirty, the tide has seemingly turned again, and, from across the lawn, through the crack in the window she left open, Jackie hears the raucous cheers go up. Then, unexpectedly, Jack climbs into bed beside her, and fumbles for her hand.

'Am I sleeping with the Leader of the Free World?' she murmurs groggily.

'Still too close to say.' He sounds tense, tired, and she shifts towards him, taking him in her arms. Between their bodies, their baby turns.

The following morning at ten to nine, Jack Kennedy receives the news in the bath. Pierre Salinger, his press secretary, bursts in. It's official, he says. It's broken over the wire, and Associated Press is on the phone wanting a statement.

The President-Elect isn't quick to move. Jackie hovers at the open door. She can see it on his face: her husband is shaken by the infinitesimally narrow margin of his victory.

Pierre throws him a towel.

Jackie goes to her study, dashes off a note, adds an enclosure, and calls for Maud Shaw. Would she deliver something for her, by hand, please?

Far beyond the Nantucket Sound, across the Atlantic, the Channel and the River Arun, tea stands in the pot on the trolley at Winborn's, and newspaper cuttings of Dina in London cover her grandmother's desk.

Madeline has been busy with the family scrapbook, and her husband, the late Percy Lucas, for ever handsome in his cricket flannels, overlooks her work. She, Dina and Nick are watching a brand-new telly and the picture comes buzzing through. Mr and Mrs Kennedy stand on a vast lawn outside a big white house with dark shutters. 'Isn't she lovely?' says Dina.

'She is,' says her grandmother, 'and yet she looks a little shy ...' She peers at the screen. 'I like her all the more for it. I daresay she has grit in her soul.'

Kennedy, Nick notes, is the first president to be born in this century.

'And the first Catholic president,' adds Madeline, although of course everyone knows that.

They all feel a bit daft with the happiness of the day. They watch Mr Kennedy bounce their little girl, Caroline, in his arms. He gives her a piggy-back ride, jogging to and fro on the lawn. The camera is jerky as it follows, revealing the crowd of reporters, photographers and camera-men jostling for position.

In the road behind, a huge white Lincoln waits, ready – according to the broadcasting voice – to drive Mr and Mrs Kennedy and his parents to a place called the Armoury, a few miles away, where the President-Elect will make his victory speech.

Cathleen couldn't get the time off to join the jubilant crowd lining Irving Avenue in Hyannis Port, or she would have been down there like a shot. Mel called her earlier from the drugstore. He had a surprise for her, he said. She was to switch on the television at 11 a.m. sharp. So she puts the 'Back in 15 minutes' sign on the door, locks it and draws the blinds against the strong morning sun.

What the ...?

Her hand flies to her mouth when he comes into view – *there* in the press section on the lawn, standing slightly apart.

She cannot move.

She can hardly breathe.

The sound in the broadcast is halting, as the wind catches at the questions from the reporters and Mr. Kennedy's replies. Then the camera pans again, and she sees Mel gripping his camera, the same one he used to take pictures of her. He has a press badge pinned to his jacket, just like the other men. Where in God's name did he get that?

She sits down, clutching herself.

She watched him leave for work in a crumpled shirt and trousers, with his white lab coat slung over the passenger seat. Did he go straight out onto Main Street and buy himself a new suit? None of that matters.

Maybe it's the angle or something, but from what she can see, it looks as if Mrs. Kennedy is turning *to* him. *Turning to* Mel.

Mary, Queen of Heaven.

Cathleen hops up only to change channels, to watch the footage on another.

Over and over.

It's something, how humble Mr. and Mrs. Kennedy look standing there together. Mrs. Kennedy's face is relaxed, a little tired maybe, and her smile is soft.

She and Mrs. Kennedy are about the same age.

Even on television her eyes are dark and bright in a way that makes you look twice. She's intuitive maybe. Smart. And it occurs to Cathleen as she peers that Mrs. Kennedy has known trouble, or sorrow at least. Her eyes have depths.

Then the First-Lady-to-be raises her hand to shield her face, and the moment's gone. The sun out there *is* strong, Cathleen recalls, and it's breezy.

Ding-ding!

The desk-bell rings out under her hand. The cameras roll on in black-and-white, and the silvery expanse of the Sound flashes and flickers, as if the scene, its players – and the year itself at its close – have been rinsed in a wide, New World light.

Epilogue: Tenderness

'But it is a tender and sensitive work, and, I think, proper and necessary, and I have it, so to speak, in my arms.'

D. H. Lawrence

Everything came tenderly out of the old hardness.

That first day, primroses and violets had splashed the forest floor. Bluebells were rearing up on their thin pale stalks, and leaf-buds were bursting green. In her mind's eye, she saw it again – beyond the hazel copse and down the narrow track: the *dark, brown-stone cottage*, protected by the old oaks, *silent and alone*. She would have turned back and carried on her way were it not for the five coops. A quick look, she told herself, could do no harm.

Inside the first coop, she found two brown hens sitting on pheasants' eggs. Among the others, a further five nested and clucked: three brown, a grey and a black. Oh!

She fed them from the corn-bin and brought them water in a tin cup. At the edge of the clearing, she spotted a bucket and shower contraption of sorts, plus what she imagined must be a privy. Then she knocked on the door, and when the man did not appear, she pushed gently, surprising herself, and entered.

The room was empty, but swept and clean. The fireplace spanned the rear wall, and there was a high stack of logs in a basket. Across from it stood a bare table and a single chair. She peered up the steep staircase to the loft, where the man must have slept. In a corner downstairs, by the wood basket, a tool chest squatted.

The first time she stayed, he took his old soldier's blanket from that chest and spread it before the fire for her.

'Think about it! Think how lowered: you'll feel – one of your husband's servants!'

'Is it— is it that you don't want me?'

'Think what if folks find out—'

'Are you sorry?' she asked him, as he walked her through the darkness to the gates of Wragby Hall.

'In a way!' he replied, and how broken she'd felt. *'I thought I'd done with it all. Now I've begun again.'*

'Begun what?' she said.

'Life,' he replied.

Yet he sounded so mournful withal.

'You're not normal,' her husband told her coldly.

She told him of the child on its way. Still he would not free her.

So she spoke to her sister. Connie would join her in Scotland and wait – till her lover's divorce was granted, till their child was safely delivered, till he'd raised money of his own, labouring on a farm. It would be six months at least.

'*We can go to another country, shall we?*' she had said. '*To Africa or Australia. Shall we?*' She'd felt inspired by her plan.

'*You've never been to the colonies, have you?*'

'*No! Have you?*'

'*I've been in India, and South Africa, and Egypt.*'

'*Why shouldn't we go to South Africa?*'

'*We might,*' he said slowly.

'*Or don't you want to?*'

'*I've no business,*' he said, '*to take a woman into my life, unless my life does something and gets somewhere, inwardly at least, to keep us both fresh. A man must offer a woman meaning in his life, if it's going to be an isolated life, and if she's a genuine woman.*'

'*Yes, he must,*' she said, '*and so must she.*'

Connie raises her blouse and presses her infant son to her breast. They christened him Oliver Reid Mellors. Oliver, for his father. Reid, her maiden-name. At home, they call him Oli. He is healthy with dark, wondering blue eyes like hers, and the milky-white colouring of his father.

One day before too long, Oli will meet his older half-sister, and life will heal over. She will make sure of it.

It was an early summer's morning the year before when Flossie started up her yapping. Oliver set down his plate, climbed into his shirt, and went down the path. A bicycle bell tinkled. It was a registered letter.

'*Canada,*' said the postman, passing him the large envelope.

'*Ay! That's a mate o' mine out there in British Columbia.*'

'*Registered? Did he send you a fortune?*'

Oliver's grin flickered as he showed her: '*Only some photographs and papers about a place out there, a farm he knows that's for sale. It's a second England, 'e says. A paradise – if you can overlook all th' English folk. Fertile for farming. Hot dry summers, wet warm winters. Some snow, plenty o' rain. Mountains, pure air, and forests* with trees, some near three hundred feet high, and forty foot in girth.'

'Heavens! *Would you go there?*'

'*I thought perhaps we might …*'

They bought the small-holding on Vancouver Island, far enough away from the capital, Victoria, with its simulacrum of an already lost, pre-war England: bowls clubs, cricket pavilions, croquet matches, Shakespeare clubs, petty snobberies, and high tea at four o'clock.

How extraordinary the island is. Whales explode from the depths, just off the coast. Sometimes, Oliver arranges for a local man to take them by canoe to see the totems of the Haida. The great eyes stare out from the shore, and she feels gripped in their presence. The raven carvings, in particular, are majestic, and one day, she will take photographs and send them to her sculptor-father.

The mountains are verdant, mist-veiled, and evocative of every mood. The climate is both mild and cold. Last December, she had Christmas roses for their table from their garden.

As for the forests, they are of the lushest, darkest green. Sometimes, it's true, the trees of this place frighten her, especially if she has stayed out too late with her sketchbook. But to stand alongside the colossi of the Douglas firs and red cedars is to be returned to one's proper proportions. That humbling is a steadying force, a profound reassurance and, if the place is still new to her, the earth always remembers her.

Locally, the wood they most often explore is known as Cathedral Grove, where the very boughs breathe; in it, she has started to sketch and paint again.

At home, she picks, cans and bottles the fruit from their orchard, and she is digging out a kitchen garden. Her husband – for he is that in all but law – tends to their six cows and ten horses. His old brooding anxiety is gone. He complains, as he must, about the ravages of the European loggers, and the smoke from the pulp mill in the Alberni Valley. But he is well in himself.

With the help of Niis K'aalas, the local Haida man who has befriended them, they are producing pamphlets which protest against the failures of the local government. A Royal Commission was set up to preserve the ancient woodland, so that it is not squandered for trifles of development, but the recommendations go unheeded.

Niis said she and Oliver could call him 'Harvey', but she said, no, they would like to use his actual name, if that was not a liberty, and he'd laughed at her formality.

Oliver and Niis write the pamphlets, and she illustrates them. Niis often claps Oliver on the back: 'Our next Chief Forester!' he announces, laughing wickedly.

'Why not?' her husband rejoins. 'Indeed, why not?'

'Because people will need to understand you first!'

Niis finds nothing so amusing as Oliver's Midlands dialect. He is the better pamphleteer of the pair – Oliver tends too much towards poetry – but Oliver has the better understanding of what is afoot in the lumber industry and the pulp mill. It's all too familiar from the villages of Tevershall and Uthwaite, near Wragby.

'You *wait*,' Oliver retorts, and back to work they go, arguing.

A few weeks ago, a woman painter in her fifties, a Miss Carr, came to see them, looking to buy a sturdy horse for her travels around the island's coast. Connie was most taken with her.

She is the daughter of an English couple, though she herself was born in Victoria. She was educated in Paris, and in London at the Westminster School of Art, but her work – Connie realises when she sees it in an out-of-the-way gallery in Victoria – possesses a strangeness and spirit that is unlike anything she has known. It is European in its sensibility and something other all at once. It is hauntingly good.

As Oliver led another horse from the stable for Miss Carr to consider, the woman – Emily, they are to call her – told Connie, 'I confess, I cling to the earth and her dear shapes.'

She said they must arrange a painting expedition together, and Connie was delighted by the idea. Then their visitor produced salmon sandwiches from her pack and offered her and Oliver a half each. It was the best salmon Connie has tasted.

She too wants to paint mass, weight and earthen forms. The landscapes of the island are like nothing she has experienced in either Britain or Italy. The forest which surrounds their farm is a darkness, as a womb is a darkness. Its shafts of light and shadows reveal and obscure, obscure and reveal. There are mysteries in this place which speak only in green soaring silences and in the forking tongues of ancient root systems.

Oli stares rapt at the pine-cone his father brought for him in his pocket the other day. He tries to hold it, although it is bigger than both his hands together. When they walk into the woods, he lights up when she presses his fingers gently to pine-needles – 'Ouch!' she laughs, and he laughs too at the surprise. Sometimes, she presses his nose to a drop of sap on tree-bark. 'Mmmm!' she says, and his face is as happy as when he latches on to her breast.

In her arms, he sleeps now, a smear of milk on his lips. When her husband enters, she raises a warning finger. *Hush.*

He's still in his boots and gaiters, and his breeches are half-covered in muck. He bends over the sink to splash his face, and crosses the room to peer at their son. Then he lifts her hair and kisses her neck, before turning to stoke the fire.

Perhaps they will return to England one day. To Sussex if anywhere, to downland.

For now, they have what they need.

In one's essence, one knows the eternal things, and is glad.

Author's Note

Perhaps every novel begins life as an ineffable spark of a story: an atom of the imagination, a flash in a synapse, an electric 'hit' to the heart – the moment one knows a story wants to be written.

The pulse of *Tenderness* has been with me through six years of research, long periods of literary 'detective work' and the midnight labour of writing itself. It is a work of fiction, although clearly some of its characters were inspired by real people who are used in my novel, to varying degrees, fictitiously. Some scenes and circumstances have been changed, invented or imagined for artistic purposes, and to offer a wider window of understanding on particular historical events: to evoke, in other words, the 'human moments' that might have occurred between the date-points on the timelines of official history. I have included letters and documents that have been faithfully reproduced; other such items have been invented, condensed, added to or modified for clarity. Readers who are interested in specific correspondence or documents should refer to the appropriate biographies, archives or editions of collected letters.

While *Tenderness* is a 'dialogue' across time with *Lady Chatterley*, it is not a substitute for it. I hope some readers of my novel might return to D. H. Lawrence's novel, or go on to discover it for the first time.

Although a work of fiction, *Tenderness* grew out of extensive research – archival, travel-based and textual. Above all, it is a celebration of Lawrence's daring and vision, and the courage of the publishers, lawyers and witnesses who put their heads above the parapet to defend one novel. It's a testament to the power of readers and the human imagination. It's a story about life itself – life lived against the odds, amid the flux of its failures and everyday beauty.

Alison MacLeod
10 May 2021

Acknowledgements

This novel has long been in the making, and there are many people who have been vital in helping it come into being as it is now, in your hands or on your screen.

I would like to thank my agent, David Godwin. After almost twenty years at DGA, I continue to find his passion for good writing inspirational. I'm grateful, too, to Philippa Sitters and Heather Godwin, for their thoughtful efforts on behalf of my work.

I am grateful, above all, to Alexandra Pringle, Executive Publisher of Bloomsbury Publishing. Her innate understanding of this novel, from its earliest promise to publication, has been a gift of trust, patience and insight. At each stage, I have benefitted from her legendary editorial talent and verve, as well as her intelligence and kindness.

I am privileged to have the support and expertise of Anton Mueller, Executive Editor of Bloomsbury USA, an unfailingly generous champion of *Tenderness*. His passion for it helped to sustain me through the long 'lockdown' of writing. I continue to be touched by and grateful for his commitment to my work.

At Bloomsbury, I would like also to offer my sincere thanks to the following people who have helped to publish my books so brilliantly: Paul Baggaley, Ros Ellis, Sarah Ruddick, Greg Heinimann, Patti Ratchford, Kathleen Farrar, Marie Coolman, Allegra Le Fanu, Morgan Jones, Rachel Wilkie, Philippa Cotton, Laura Meyer, Angelique Tran Van Sang, Katie Aitken-Quack, Tara Kennedy, Ellen Whitaker, Nicole Jarvis, Amber Mears-Brown,

Grace McNamee, Francesca Sturiale, Natasha Qureshi, Georgina Slater, Amy Wong, Jude Crozier, Carrie Hsieh, Suzanne Keller, Callie Garnett, Madeleine Feeny, Rachel Mannheimer, Jo Forshaw and Tom Skipp. I'm indebted to Sarah-Jane Forder for her excellent eye and her generous company at the copy-edit stage; also to Ellis Levine for his care and guidance on questions related to copyright.

I am grateful to Nigel Newton, Founder and Publisher of Bloomsbury, for providing an impeccable publishing home for writers. As the story of *Tenderness* hopefully illustrates, the efforts of great literary publishers can be far-reaching and profound.

At Penguin Canada, I am fortunate to have another extraordinary publisher, Nicole Winstanley, who has created a place for my work in my native country for more than fifteen years, and who has been a source of intelligent, warm and generous support. I must also thank Stephen Myers, Manager of Marketing & Publicity at Penguin CA, for his kindness and calm professionalism.

I am indebted to my family for their good spirits throughout: my mother, Freda, and Kate, Ellen, Ian and Liz; also to Theresa Burgess, a steadfast friend and supporter of my writing.

Karen Stevens and Hugh Dunkerley have been generous writer-friends, and I am, again, thankful. I would like to convey, too, my gratitude to Glynis Ross, David Craig, Vicki Feaver and Linda Anderson for the inspiration of their words over time.

My thanks must also go to:

Penguin Books UK for the trove of the Penguin Archive in the University of Bristol's Special Collections; in particular to Joanna Prior, Managing Director of Penguin Books, for kindly granting me access;

Hannah Lowery, Archivist and Special Collections Manager, and her 2016 team – Jamie Carstairs, Ian Coates, Pawel Radek, David Trigg, Mike Hunkin – for their time, generosity and helpful facilitation of my (often dogged) research in the Penguin and Rubinstein Archives; Hannah, wondrously, never begrudged my request for yet another box, or still more photocopying back-up; to Michael Richardson,

Special Collections Librarian, for his assistance; to Philip Kent, former Director of Library Services, for his kind interest; to Ed Fay, Director of Library Services, for the library's ongoing support and goodwill;

the children of Instructing Solicitor Michael Rubinstein – Imogen, Polly, Adam and Zac – for their kind permission for me to quote from their father's notes and letters; the material was a privilege to explore;

Helen Atkinson, literary executor and great-niece of Rebecca West, for permission, generously granted, for my use of West's letters and words;

Charlotte Du Cann for her kind permission to use, for the endpapers of the UK hardback edition of *Tenderness*, the notes of her father Richard Du Cann, QC from the 1960 courtroom notebooks of the Old Bailey trial of Penguin Books.

the Provost and Scholars of King's College, Cambridge and The Society of Authors as the E. M. Forster Estate: for their kind permission to quote the words of E. M. Forster;

the British Library's 2016 Eccles Centre Team – Professor Philip Davies, Dr Cara Rodway and Bibliographical Editor, Jean Petrovic – for their friendship and their expert support of this novel, as well as their kind hospitality in a range of events;

John Eccles, 2nd Viscount Eccles, Diana Catherine Eccles, Viscountess Eccles and Catherine Eccles for their family's magnanimous support of the Eccles Centre & Hay Festival Writer's Award, which I was fortunate to receive in 2016 in support of *Tenderness*;

Professor Philip Davies, also, for putting me in touch with Rhodri Jeffreys-Jones, Emeritus Professor, History, University of Edinburgh, and to Professor Jeffreys-Jones for his recommendations regarding FBI resources;

the Authors' Foundation, Arts Council England, and the Society of Authors for awards over the years in support of my writing. In the wake of the Covid-19 pandemic, their efforts on behalf of writers and books are more precious than ever;

Rebecca and Mark Ford for their enthusiasm and support, and for leading me to D. H. Lawrence's 1915 home;

Oliver Hawkins, great-grandson of Wilfrid and Alice Meynell, who, in the spirit of his great-grandparents' openness and generous support of the arts, enabled my research for the Sussex sections of *Tenderness*;

Laura Mulvey, great-granddaughter of Wilfrid and Alice Meynell, and granddaughter of Perceval and Madeline Lucas, for her kind interest in this novel;

Miriam Moss, for making it possible – with her great goodwill – to find the balcony on which Rosalind Baynes and Lawrence shared their Marsala in September 1920. Also, our taxi driver, Tommaso Crocetti, of Radio Taxi Firenze Società Cooperativa, who did not give up;

Richard Alford, former British Council Director (Italy) and Secretary of the Charles Wallace India Trust, for his friendship and very kind support of my writing, and particularly for his gift of a source which arrived by surprise in the early stages of my research into Lawrence's time in Italy;

Thomas Grant, QC for his thoughtful sharing of certain Hutchinson–Eliot documents, and for his observations relating to Court Number One;

Virginia Nicholson, for her early enthusiasm regarding my exploration of the personal story of her step-grandmother, Rosalind Thornycroft Baynes Popham;

The Pari Center, Tuscany its Co-founder, Maureen Doolan, and joint Co-founder, late F. David Peat, for their ongoing support of writers, artists and scientists;

the people of the village of Pari for their welcome and hospitality while I wrote, read and meandered;

Anne Lloyd Davey, a champion of literature, for leading me towards the Arc Collection at Cambridge;

and to all readers, 'subversive', dedicated, entertained or passionate – and quietly present on the other side of these traversable boundary-lines of print.

Alison MacLeod

Sources

Page numbers refer to *Tenderness*. Where multiple quotations from one source appear on one page, a single citation for that page applies to each.

Title Abbreviations:

BBF	*Birds, Beasts and Flowers*
LCL	*Lady Chatterley's Lover*
'EME'	'England, My England' (version 1)
EME	*England, My England and Other Stories* (version 2)
TSP	*The Savage Pilgrimage: A Narrative of D. H. Lawrence*
N&A	*Nation and the Athenaeum*
LI	*The Liberal Imagination: Essays on Literature and Society*

Preliminary Matter

endpapers (hardback only UK edition) Richard Du Cann, QC, notes, Court Notebook, trial of 'Regina *v.* Penguin Books'; '*Lady Chatterley* Trial Papers', Rubinstein Archive, DM 1679/10, Special Collections, University of Bristol Library; with the kind permission of Charlotte Du Cann

p. vii D. H. Lawrence, 'Grapes', *Birds, Beasts and Flowers* (Secker, 1923)

p. ix Gwyn Thomas, extract from letter to M. Rubinstein (1960), '*Lady Chatterley* Trial Papers', Rubinstein Archive, DM 1679, Special Collections, University of Bristol Library

p. 3 Frieda Lawrence, *Not I, But the Wind ...* (Heinemann, 1935)

p. 11 D. H. Lawrence to W. E. Hopkins (1915); D. H. Lawrence to O. Morrell (1915); composited extracts from two letters; *The Letters of D.H. Lawrence,* Aldous Huxley, ed. (Heinemann, 1935)

p. 13 D. H. Lawrence, *Lady Chatterley's Lover* (Knopf, 1932)

p. 15 ibid.

p. 18 D. H. Lawrence to M. Secker, extract from letter (1928), *The Letters of D. H. Lawrence,* Aldous Huxley, ed. (Heinemann, 1935)

p. 18 Lawrence, *LCL*

p. 21 D. H. Lawrence to C. Asquith, extract from letter (1928), *The Letters of D. H. Lawrence,* Aldous Huxley, ed. (Heinemann, 1935)

p. 21 Lawrence, *LCL*

p. 24 ibid.

p. 25 D. H. Lawrence, review, 'Eric Gill's "Art Nonsense"', *The Book-collector's Quarterly,* Vol. 3 (Cassell and Company Limited, 1933)

p. 26 George Eliot, *The Mill on the Floss* (William Blackwood, 1860)

p. 26 Anon., traditional song, variously titled; sung by D. H. Lawrence, 1915; usage of assorted extracts throughout text

p. 26 Lawrence, *LCL*

p. 26 Lawrence, 'Grapes', *BBF*

p. 28 E. M. Forster, letter, *Nation and the Athenaeum* (1930); with the kind permission of The Provost and Scholars of King's College, Cambridge and The Society of Authors as the E. M. Forster Estate

p. 31 D. H. Lawrence, 'Man and Bat', *Birds, Beasts and Flowers* (Secker, 1923)

p. 32 D. H. Lawrence, 'Peach', *Birds, Beasts and Flowers* (Secker, 1923)

p. 32 D. H. Lawrence, 'Tortoise Shout', *Birds, Beasts and Flowers* (Secker, 1923)

p. 32 D. H. Lawrence, 'Tortoise Gallantry', *Birds, Beasts and Flowers* (Secker, 1923)

p. 33 Lawrence, 'Grapes', *BBF*

p. 33 D. H. Lawrence, 'Lui et Elle', *Birds, Beasts and Flowers* (Secker, 1923)

pp. 34–43 Lawrence, *LCL*

pp. 37, 309 D. H. Lawrence to B. Jennings, extract from letter (1910), *Letters,* I, Moore, ed.

pp. 39–40, 539–42, 545–7, 557–9, 571 principal sources of biographical data: *Time Which Spaces Us Apart,* Rosalind Thornycroft;

completed by Chloë Baynes (Batcombe, Somerset, 1991); privately published memoir; British Library: General Reference Collection YD.2005.b.1622; *Jung's Apprentice: A Biography of Helton Godwin Baynes*, Diana Baynes Jansen (Daimon Verlag, 2003); *Lady Chatterley's Villa: D. H. Lawrence on the Italian Riviera*, Richard Owen (The Armchair Traveller, 2014); narration/commentary and dialogue by Alison MacLeod

p. 43 Lawrence, 'Grapes', *BBF*

p. 43 Lawrence, *LCL*

pp. 53–4 ibid.

pp. 56–9 ibid.

pp. 71, 73 ibid.

pp. 74–8 composited extracts (with added headings) from transcript of 14 May, 1959 hearing of United States Post Office Dept. and Grove Press; 'Lady Chatterley Trial Papers', Rubinstein Archive, DM 1679/10, Special Collections, University of Bristol Library

p. 79 Lionel Trilling, *The Liberal Imagination: Essays on Literature and Society* (Viking Press, 1950)

p. 81 Dwight D. Eisenhower, Remarks at the Ground-Breaking Ceremonies for the Lincoln Center for the Performing Arts, New York City; 14 May, 1959

p. 86 Frieda Lawrence, extract from letter to B. Rosset (1954), 'Lady Chatterley Trial Papers', Rubinstein Archive, DM 1679, Special Collections, University of Bristol Library

p. 87 FBI telegram (1959), released in response to Freedom of Information Request by Robert Delaware, reported in 'The FBI's decades-long war on D. H. Lawrence', MuckRock, 31 October, 2012

p. 90 Rebecca West, letter to J. E. Hoover (1959), 'Rebecca West' FBI file, Freedom of Information release to Carl Rollyson (1997); *Rebecca West and the God that Failed: Essays*, Carl Rollyson (iUniverse, 2005); with the kind permission of Helen Atkinson, Executor, the Rebecca West Estate

p. 102 D. H. Lawrence, *Studies in Classic American Literature* (Thomas Seltzer, 1923)

p. 102 D. H. Lawrence, 'The Evening Land', *Birds, Beasts and Flowers* (Martin Secker, 1923)

p. 102 D. H. Lawrence, extract from letter to B. Russell (1915); *The Collected Letters of D. H. Lawrence*, Vol. 1, Harry T. Moore, ed. (Heinemann, 1962)

p. 102 D. H. Lawrence, 'Things', *Bookman* (1928)

p. 103 Lawrence, *LCL*

p. 113 ibid.

p. 115 ibid.

pp. 117, 248 WWI government recruitment poster

p. 118 D. H. Lawrence, 'England, my England', *England, My England and Other Stories* (Seltzer, 1922)

p. 125 ibid.

p. 126 ibid.

p. 126 D. H. Lawrence, composited extracts from letters to S. Koteliansky (1915); *The Quest for Rananim, D. H. Lawrence's Letters to S. S. Koteliansky 1914–1930*; George J. Zyraruk, ed. (McGill-Queen's University Press, 1970)

p. 129 Lawrence, *EME*

p. 131 D. H. Lawrence, extract from letter to C. Carswell (1916); *The Savage Pilgrimage: A Narrative of D. H. Lawrence*, Catherine Carswell (Martin Secker, 1932)

p. 131 D. H. Lawrence, 'England, my England', *The English Review* (1915)

p. 137 Lawrence, *EME*

pp. 139, 323 dialogue and narration inspired by paraphrase of D. H. Lawrence remarks; Francis Meynell, *My Lives* (Bodley Head, 1971)

p. 141 Lawrence, *EME*

p. 143 Anon., traditional blessing

p. 144 Lawrence to C. Carswell, extract, *TSP*

p. 144 Lawrence, *EME*

p. 145 Lawrence, *LCL*

pp. 147–8 ibid.

p. 149 Lawrence to C. Carswell, extract, *TSP*

p. 150 John Middleton Murry report of K. Mansfield remark; *D. H. Lawrence: A Composite Biography*, Vol. I, Edward Nehls, ed. (University of Wisconsin Press, 1957)

p. 152 Ottoline Morrell remark, *Ottoline: the Early Memoirs of Lady Ottoline Morrell*, Robert Gathorne-Hardy, ed. (Faber, 1963)

p. 154 Lawrence to S. Koteliansky (1915); one extract from letter and one extract with minor modification; *Letters,* I, Moore, ed.

p. 154 E. M. Forster, extract from letter to F. Barger (1915), *Selected Letters of E. M. Forster: 1879–1920*, Mary Lago and P. N. Furbank, eds. (Arrow Books, 1983), with the kind permission of The Provost and Scholars of King's College, Cambridge and The Society of Authors as the E. M. Forster Estate

pp. 155, 347 account of Lawrence remarks to Forster derived from extracts, Lawrence to B. Russell, letter (1915); *Letters,* I, Moore, ed.

p. 157 Frieda Lawrence, extract from letter to O. Morrell (1915); 'I Will Send Address: Unpublished Letters of D. H. Lawrence', Mark Schorer, *London Magazine,* iii., Feb. 1956

p. 157 D. H. Lawrence, *Aaron's Rod* (Thomas Seltzer, 1922)

p. 162 D. H. Lawrence, 'Jack Murry is a bad boy' (with modification); *D. H. Lawrence: A Composite Biography,* Vol. I, Edward Nehls, ed. (University of Wisconsin Press, 1957)

p. 164 Lawrence, *EME*

p. 165 Lawrence, *LCL*

p. 167 Lawrence, *EME*

pp. 168, 169 Lawrence, *EME*; Lawrence, 'EME'; Lawrence, *EME*

pp. 169–70 Anon., traditional Sussex folk song, 'The Cuckoo'

pp. 170–1 Lawrence, *EME*; Lawrence, 'EME'

p. 174 Lawrence to B. Russell extract (1915); *Letters,* I, Moore, ed.

p. 175 Lawrence, *LCL*

pp. 175–6 Katherine Mansfield, letter (with minor modifications) to J. Middleton Murry (1915); *Katherine Mansfield's Letters to John Middleton Murry,* John Middleton Murry, ed. (Constable, 1951)

pp. 176, 179 Lawrence to S. Koteliansky extract (1915); *Quest,* Zyraruk, ed.

p. 178 Lawrence, *EME*

p. 178 Lawrence, 'EME'

p. 182 derived from remarks, Lawrence to S. Koteliansky letter (1915); *Quest,* Zyraruk, ed., and Lawrence to Ottoline Morrell letter (1915); *Letters,* Huxley, ed.

p. 184 S. Koteliansky and F. Lawrence dialogue recounted by S. Koteliansky to L. Woolf; obituary, 'Kot.', Leonard Woolf, *New Statesman,* 5 Feb. 1955

p. 186 John Drinkwater, 'On Greatham', *Georgian Poetry: 1913–1915,* Sir Edward Howard Marsh, ed. (The Poetry Bookshop, London, 1915)

p. 188 fictional composition inspired by Mary Saleeby Fisher, 'Rackham Cottage' (1915); *D. H. Lawrence: A Composite Biography,* Vol. I, Edward Nehls, ed. (University of Wisconsin Press, 1957)

p. 190 Lawrence, *EME*

p. 191 fictional composition inspired by Mary Saleeby Fisher, untitled account (1915), *Biography*, I, Nehls, ed.

p. 193 Lawrence, *EME*

pp. 195–6 Lawrence, *EME*; Lawrence, 'EME'

p. 227 Lawrence, *LCL*

p. 231 John Middleton Murry, review 'Matthew Arnold Today', *Times Literary Supplement*, March 1939

p. 232 Lionel Trilling, 'Introduction', *The Portable Matthew Arnold* (Viking Press, 1949)

p. 233 D.H. Lawrence, 'The Odour of Chrysanthemums', *The Prussian Officer and Other Stories* (Duckworth, 1914)

p. 234 Lionel Trilling, 'Introduction' and 'Reality in America', *LI*

p. 235 Lionel Trilling, 'Introduction', *The Partisan Reader: Ten Years of Partisan Review* (Dial Press, 1946)

pp. 239–40 Forster, *N&A*

pp. 240–3 Lawrence, *LCL*

p. 248 D. H. Lawrence to D. Radford, letter (1915), *Biography*, I, Nehls, ed.

p. 248 Lawrence, *EME*

pp. 248–9 Lawrence, 'EME'

p. 250 D. H. Lawrence to agent J. B. Pinker (May and April 1915), extract from letter, *Letters*, Huxley, ed.

p. 251 Lawrence, *EME*

p. 252 Lawrence, 'EME'

p. 256 Cynthia Asquith, extract from diary entry (1915), *Lady Cynthia Asquith: Diaries 1915–18* (Hutchinson, 1968)

pp. 257, 258 Lawrence, *LCL*

p. 260 Lawrence, 'EME'

p. 260 D. H. Lawrence to V. Meynell, extract from letter (1915); *Letters*, I, Moore, ed.

p. 263 H. Muskett speaking for Police Commissioner; court hearing of charge of 'obscenity', 13 Nov., 1915; reported in "The Rainbow", *The Times*, 15 Nov. 1915

p. 264 derived from Lawrence, *LCL*

pp. 266–9 Lawrence, *LCL*

p. 269 Lawrence, *EME*

p. 269 Lawrence, 'EME'

pp. 269–70 Franz Schubert *Lied* composition (1814), with words (trans.) from Johann Wolfgang von Goethe, *Faust*, Part One, Scene 15

p. 271 Lawrence, *EME*

pp. 271, 272 Lawrence, 'EME'

p. 274 ibid.

pp. 276–9 Lawrence, 'EME'

p. 280 Lawrence to C. Carswell, extract, *TSP*

p. 281 D. H. Lawrence to Cynthia Asquith, extract from letter (1915); minor modification; *The Collected Letters of D. H. Lawrence*, Vol. 1, Harry T. Moore, ed. (Heinemann, 1962)

pp. 281, 282 Lawrence, 'EME'

p. 285 Lawrence, *EME*

p. 290 *English Review* header (1915)

pp. 292, 294–5 Lawrence, 'EME'

p. 295 Lawrence, *EME*

p. 296 Thomas Arne, 'Where the Bee Sucks, There Lurk I', *The Second Volume of Lyric Harmony* (London, 1746); based on 'Ariel's Song', *The Tempest*, William Shakespeare, 1623

pp. 298, 299 Perceval Lucas to E. V. Lucas, letter (July 1916); with added salutation and signature line; *Post-Bag Diversions*, E.V. Lucas, ed. (Methuen, 1934)

p. 298 Lawrence, 'EME'

pp. 300–1 Lawrence, *EME*

p. 303 Lawrence to C. Carswell, extract, *TSP*

p. 304 Lawrence, *EME*

pp. 307, 308 Lawrence, *LCL*

pp. 308, 309 Lawrence, *EME*

p. 310 D. H. Lawrence to V. Meynell, extract from letter (1915); *Biography*, I, Nehls, ed.

p. 334 Bernardine Wall, extract from witness statement (1960) given to M. Rubinstein, Instructing Solicitor for the Defence, Regina *v.* Penguin Books; with minor modification; 'Lady Chatterley Trial Papers', Rubinstein Archive, DM 1679, Special Collections, University of Bristol Library

pp. 337, 339 Lawrence, *LCL*

p. 347 D.H.Lawrence, 'Why the Novel Matters', *Phoenix: the Posthumous Papers of D.H. Lawrence*, Edward D. McDonald, ed. (Viking, 1936)

p. 348 D. H. Lawrence to G. Campbell, extract from letter (1914), *The Intelligent Heart: the Story of D. H. Lawrence*, Harry T. Moore, ed. (Heinemann, 1965)

Part Two: *Fly Little Boat*

Special Collections, University of Bristol Library; with the kind permission of the children of Michael Rubinstein

p. 390 Hallen Viney to A. Lane, composited extracts from letter (1960); Penguin Archive, Special Collections, University of Bristol Library

p. 392 Rebecca West, 'What a Stupid Thing to Do!', extracts; *Evening Standard*, 13 Oct. 1947; with the kind permission of Helen Atkinson, Executor, the Rebecca West Estate

p. 396 Hans Schmoller to A. Lane, extract (modified) from letter (1960); Penguin Archive, Special Collections, University of Bristol Library

p. 397 Mervyn Griffith-Jones to Director of Public Prosecutions, 'Opinion' (1960); Director of Public Prosecutions: Case Papers, New Series, Regina *v* Penguin Books Ltd.: *Lady Chatterley's Lover* by D. H. Lawrence; prosecution under Obscene Publications Act, 1959; DPP 2/3077, The National Archives, Kew

p. 401 William Emrys Williams and Hans Schmoller to A. Lane, telegram (1960); Penguin Archive, Special Collections, University of Bristol Library

p. 401 Court Summons (1960) of Allen Lane, Publisher, Penguin Books; Penguin Archive, Special Collections, University of Bristol Library

p. 402 Douglas Eric Hacking to T. Mathew, extract from letter (1961); Director of Public Prosecutions: Case Papers, DPP 2/3077, The National Archives

p. 402 Reginald Manningham-Buller, Attorney General, to T. Mathew, Director of Public Prosecutions, extract from letter (1960); Director of Public Prosecutions: Case Papers, DPP 2/3077, The National Archives

p. 403 Dorothy Byrne, extract from notes (1960) accompanying 'Judge's copy of *Lady Chatterley's Lover* Penguin paperback'; '*Lady Chatterley* Trial' collection, DM 2936, Special Collections, University of Bristol Library

pp. 404–5 F. R. Leavis to unnamed recipient, extract (verb tense modified) from letter (1962); DM662/12/13, Special Collections, University of Bristol Library; addendum: F. R. Leavis declined M. Rubinstein's request to give evidence; see M. Rubinstein, 'Letter', *The Times*, 14 Jan. 1978

p. 405 Evelyn Waugh to M. Rubinstein, extract from letter (1960); 'Lady Chatterley Trial Papers', Rubinstein Archive, DM 1679, Special Collections, University of Bristol Library

p. 405 Robert Graves to M. Rubinstein, extract from letter (1960); 'Lady Chatterley Trial Papers', Rubinstein Archive, DM 1679, Special Collections, University of Bristol Library

p. 405 L. P. Hartley to M. Rubinstein, extract from letter (1960); 'Lady Chatterley Trial Papers', Rubinstein Archive, DM 1679, Special Collections, University of Bristol Library

p. 405 Alec Guinness to M. Rubinstein, extract from letter (1960); 'Lady Chatterley Trial Papers', Rubinstein Archive, DM 1679, Special Collections, University of Bristol Library

p. 405 Enid Blyton to M. Rubinstein, extract from letter (1960); 'Lady Chatterley Trial Papers', Rubinstein Archive, DM 1679, Special Collections, University of Bristol Library

p. 405 Graham Greene to M. Rubinstein, extract from letter (1960); 'Lady Chatterley Trial Papers', Rubinstein Archive, DM 1679, Special Collections, University of Bristol Library

p. 405 Huw Wheldon to M. Rubinstein, extract from letter (1960); 'Lady Chatterley Trial Papers', Rubinstein Archive, DM 1679, Special Collections, University of Bristol Library

p. 406 F. Spencer of Students' Bookshop Ltd. to M. Rubinstein, extract from letter (1960); 'Lady Chatterley Trial Papers', Rubinstein Archive, DM 1679, Special Collections, University of Bristol Library

p. 406 John Hoare of Hatchards to M. Rubinstein, extract from letter (1960); 'Lady Chatterley Trial Papers', Rubinstein Archive, DM 1679, Special Collections, University of Bristol Library

p. 406 Basil Blackwell, submitted/unpublished Letter to the Editor of The Times (1960), extract; reported by S. Unwin to M. Rubinstein 26 Aug. 1960

p. 406 Leslie D. Weatherhead to M. Rubinstein, extract from letter (1960); 'Lady Chatterley Trial Papers', Rubinstein Archive, DM 1679, Special Collections, University of Bristol Library

p. 406 T. S. Eliot, extract from witness statement (1960) given to M. Rubinstein; Regina v. Penguin Books; 'Lady Chatterley Trial Papers', Rubinstein Archive, DM 1679, Special Collections, University of Bristol Library pp. 406–7 John Braine to W. E. Williams of Penguin Books, extract from letter (1960); 'Lady Chatterley Trial Papers', Rubinstein Archive, DM 1679, Special Collections, University of Bristol Library

p. 407 Doris Lessing to M. Rubinstein, extract from letter (1960); 'Lady Chatterley Trial Papers', Rubinstein Archive, DM 1679, Special Collections, University of Bristol Library

p. 407 Iris Murdoch, extract from witness statement (1960) given to M. Rubinstein; 'Lady Chatterley Trial Papers', Rubinstein Archive, DM 1679, Special Collections, University of Bristol Library

p. 407 Kingsley Amis, extract from witness statement given to M. Rubinstein (1960); 'Lady Chatterley Trial Papers', Rubinstein Archive, DM 1679, Special Collections, University of Bristol Library

p. 407 Mary Middleton Murry, extract from witness statement (1960) given to M. Rubinstein; 'Lady Chatterley Trial Papers', Rubinstein Archive, DM 1679, Special Collections, University of Bristol Library

p. 408 Leonard Woolf to M. Rubinstein, extract from letter (1960); 'Lady Chatterley Trial Papers', Rubinstein Archive, DM 1679, Special Collections, University of Bristol Library

p. 408 John Lehmann to M. Rubinstein, extract from letter (1960); 'Lady Chatterley Trial Papers', Rubinstein Archive, DM 1679, Special Collections, University of Bristol Library

p. 408 Christina Foyle, extract from witness statement (1960) given to M. Rubinstein; 'Lady Chatterley Trial Papers', Rubinstein Archive, DM 1679, Special Collections, University of Bristol Library

p. 409 Stephen Spender to M. Rubinstein, extract from letter (1960); 'Lady Chatterley Trial Papers', Rubinstein Archive, DM 1679, Special Collections, University of Bristol Library

p. 417 Lawrence, EME

pp. 420–1 ibid.

p. 422 Rebecca West, extract from D. H. Lawrence (Secker, 1930); with the kind permission of Helen Atkinson, Executor, the Rebecca West Estate

p. 423 D. H. Lawrence to W. Bynner, extracts from letter (1928); The Selected Letters of D. H. Lawrence, Diana Trilling, ed. (Farrar, Strauss and Cudahay, 1958)

p. 423–4 Michael Rubinstein to R. West, letter (1960) with added contextual clarification; 'Lady Chatterley Trial Papers', Rubinstein Archive, DM 1679, Special Collections, University of Bristol Library; with the kind permission of the children of Michael Rubinstein

p. 432 Katherine Anne Porter, 'A Wreath for the Gamekeeper', Encounter, Feb. 1960

p. 433 John Middleton Murry, Son of Woman: the Story of D. H. Lawrence (Jonathan Cape, 1931)

p. 434 David Cecil, 'D. H. Lawrence in his Letters', the Spectator, 1 Oct. 1932

p. 435 Helen Gardner to T. Mathew, Director of Public Prosecutions, extract from letter; Director of Public Prosecutions: Case Papers, DPP 2/3077, The National Archives

pp. 435–6 John Holroyd-Reece to A. Lane, extract of letter (1960), with paraphrased selection of remainder of letter; Penguin Archive, Special Collections, University of Bristol Library

p. 437 Porter, 'Wreath', Encounter

pp. 438, 536–7 Anon., letter (1960), with sender's address modified; sent to M. Griffith-Jones; Director of Public Prosecutions: Case Papers, DPP 2/3077, The National Archives

p. 440 D. H. Lawrence to R. Gardiner, extract from letter (1928), The Letters of D.H. Lawrence, Aldous Huxley, ed.

p. 440 Lawrence to M. Secker, extract from letter (1928), Letters, Huxley, ed.

p. 442 John F. Kennedy, CBS Nixon-Kennedy debate, 29 Sept. 1960

pp. 448–9 Author(s) unidentified, misc. Defence team preparatory notes and communications; 'Lady Chatterley Trial Papers', Rubinstein Archive, DM 1679, Special Collections, University of Bristol

p. 449 Lawrence, LCL

p. 449 Author unidentified, Defence team preparatory notes, Rubinstein Archive

p. 450 Michael Rubinstein, preparatory notes (1960); 'Lady Chatterley Trial Papers', Rubinstein Archive, DM 1679, Special Collections, University of Bristol; with the kind permission of the children of Michael Rubinstein

p. 458 Trial transcript, 'the Charge', extract, *The Trial of Lady Chatterley: Regina v. Penguin Books Limited,* C. H. Rolph, ed.; 'Penguin Special' (Penguin, 1961); trial narration/commentary for courtroom scenes in *Tenderness* by Alison MacLeod

p. 459 [full signature illegible] G. Watkins; D. Horrocks; 'Vox Populi'; selection of complaints or extracts of complaints (1960) to Penguin Books; Penguin Archive, Special Collections, University of Bristol Library

pp. 459–65 'Penguin Books *v* Regina' trial transcript, 'The First Day', selections with minor modifications; Rolph, ed.

pp. 468–76 'Penguin Books *v* Regina' trial transcript, 'The Second Day', selections with minor modifications; Rolph, ed.; with additions to R. West testimony, including statement by R. West; with the kind permission of Helen Atkinson, Executor, the Rebecca West Estate

p. 480 Lawrence, *LCL*

pp. 485–93 'Penguin Books *v* Regina' trial transcript, 'The Second Day'; selections with minor modifications; Rolph, ed.

p. 492 E. M. Forster to R. Hoggart, extract from letter (1960), *Richard Hoggart: Virtue and Reward,* Fred Inglis (Wiley, 2014); with the kind permission of The Provost and Scholars of King's College, Cambridge and The Society of Authors as the E. M. Forster Estate

p. 494 T. S. Eliot, extract from 'The Hollow Men', *Poems 1909–1925* (Faber and Gwyer, 1925)

pp. 494–6, 505–8 'Penguin Books *v* Regina' trial transcript, 'The Third Day'; selections with minor modifications; Rolph, ed.

p. 505 T. S. Eliot, extract from 'East Coker', 'Easter Number' 1940, *New English Weekly*

pp. 509–14, 534–8 'Penguin Books *v* Regina' trial transcript, 'The Fourth Day'; selections with minor modifications; Rolph, ed.

p. 511 Kingsley Amis to M. Rubinstein, extracts from letter (1960), 'Lady Chatterley Trial Papers', Rubinstein Archive, DM 1679, Special Collections, University of Bristol

p. 511 Michael Rubinstein to K. Amis, letter (1960); with minor modification; 'Lady Chatterley Trial Papers', Rubinstein Archive, DM 1679, Special Collections, University of Bristol; with the kind permission of the children of Michael Rubinstein

p. 515 Lawrence, *LCL*

pp. 517, 518 ibid.

pp. 528–30 Lawrence, 'Grapes', *BBF*

p. 533 ibid.

pp. 533–7 B. Wall, testimony (transcript, Rolph, ed. 1960), with extracts from witness statement and modifications

pp. 542–3 D. H. Lawrence to R. Baynes, composited extracts from letter; minor modification (1919); *D. H. Lawrence: A Composite Biography*, Vol. II, Edward Nehls, ed. (University of Wisconsin Press, 1958)

p. 543 D. H. Lawrence to R. Baynes, composited extracts from letter (1919); minor modifications; *Biography* II, Nehls, ed.

pp. 543–4 D. H. Lawrence to R. Baynes, composited extracts from letter (1919); minor modifications, with extracted observation from D. H. Lawrence to F. Cacoprado letter (1920); *Biography* II, Nehls, ed.

p. 544 D. H. Lawrence to R. Baynes, extract from letter (1920); minor modification; *The Letters of D.H. Lawrence*, Aldous Huxley, ed. (Heinemann, 1935)

p. 544 D. H. Lawrence to R. Baynes, composited extracts from letter; minor modifications (1920); *D. H. Lawrence: A Composite Biography*, Vol. II, Edward Nehls, ed. (University of Wisconsin Press, 1958)

pp. 544–5 D. H. Lawrence to R. Baynes, composited extracts from two letters (1920); modification; *D. H. Lawrence: A Composite Biography*, Vol. II, Edward Nehls, ed. (University of Wisconsin Press, 1958)

p. 545 Lawrence, *LCL*

pp. 553–7, 559–63 'Penguin Books *v* Regina' trial transcript, 'The Fifth Day'; selections with minor modifications; Rolph, ed.

p. 559 D. H. Lawrence, 'Medlars and Sorb-Apples', *Birds, Beasts and Flowers* (Secker, 1923)

pp. 563, 564 D. H. Lawrence, 'Pomegranate', *Birds, Beasts and Flowers* (Secker, 1923)

p. 564 Lawrence, 'Medlars and Sorb-Apples', *BBF*

p. 565 Lawrence, *LCL*

pp. 566–71, 574, 576–7 'Penguin Books *v* Regina' trial transcript, 'The Sixth Day'; selections with minor modifications; Rolph, ed.

pp. 571–2 Lawrence, *LCL*

p. 573 Lawrence, 'Pomegranate', *BBF*

p. 578 D. H. Lawrence, 'The Revolutionary', *Birds, Beasts and Flowers* (Secker, 1923)

p. 578 Barbara Barr, comment following trial, widely cited without orig. source; e.g. *Lady Chatterley's Villa: D. H. Lawrence on the Italian Riveria*, Richard Owen (Armchair Traveller at the bookHaus, 2014)

p. 579 Michael Rubinstein to B. Wall, letter (1960); minor modification; 'Lady Chatterley Trial Papers', Rubinstein Archive, DM 1679, Special Collections, University of Bristol Library; with the kind permission of the children of Michael Rubinstein

p. 579 'It's a sell-out for "Innocent" Lady C!', extract from article, *Express*, 3 Nov. 1960

pp. 579–80 Michael Rubinstein to 'Matron', letter (1960); 'Lady Chatterley Trial Papers', Rubinstein Archive, DM 1679, Special Collections, University of Bristol Library with the kind permission of the children of Michael Rubinstein;

p. 580 Michael Rubinstein to A. Lane, extract from letter (1960); Penguin Archive, Special Collections, University of Bristol Library; with the kind permission of the children of Michael Rubinstein

p. 580 Kathleen Everett to Her Majesty the Queen, letter (1960); Home Office: Indecent Publications Files – Complaints: 'Lady Chatterley's Lover' (1960–1); HO 302/11, National Archives, Kew

p. 582 Lawrence, *LCL*

Epilogue: *Tenderness*

p. 587 D. H. Lawrence to C. Brown, extract from letter (1927); *D. H. Lawrence: a Composite Biography,* Vol. III, Edward Nehls, ed. (University of Wisconsin Press, 1959)

pp. 589–91 Lawrence, *LCL*

p. 592 Emily Carr, extract with minor modification, *Growing Pains: The Autobiography of Emily Carr* (O.U.P., 1946)

A Note on the Author

Alison MacLeod is the author of three novels – *The Changeling*, *The Wave Theory of Angels* and *Unexploded*, which was longlisted for the Man Booker Prize 2013 – and two story collections. She is the joint winner of the Eccles British Library Writer's Award 2016 and was a finalist for the 2017 Governor General's Award. She was Professor of Contemporary Fiction at the University of Chichester until 2018, when she became Visiting Professor to write full-time. She lives in Brighton.

alison-macleod.com

A Note on the Type

The text of this book is set in Bembo, which was first used in 1495 by the Venetian printer Aldus Manutius for Cardinal Bembo's *De Aetna*. The original types were cut for Manutius by Francesco Griffo. Bembo was one of the types used by Claude Garamond (1480–1561) as a model for his Romain de l'Université, and so it was a forerunner of what became the standard European type for the following two centuries. Its modern form follows the original types and was designed for Monotype in 1929.